The Editors

HERSHEL PARKER, H. Fletcher Brown Professor Emeritus of the University of Delaware, is the author of *Herman Melville: A Biography, 1819–1851* (1996) and *Herman Melville: A Biography, 1851–1891* (2002). He is co-editor of the Norton Critical Edition of *Moby-Dick* and Associate General Editor of the Northwestern-Newberry *The Writings of Herman Melville*. He lives in Morro Bay, California.

MARK NIEMEYER is a Maître de Conférences at the Sorbonne (University of Paris IV), where he has taught since 1998. He is an Associate Editor of the French "Pléiade" edition of the works of Herman Melville and co-editor of *Literature on the Move: Comparing Diasporic Ethnicities in Europe and the Americas* (2002).

A NORTON CRITICAL EDITION

Herman Melville
THE CONFIDENCE-MAN: HIS MASQUERADE

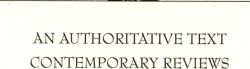

AN AUTHORITATIVE TEXT
CONTEMPORARY REVIEWS
BIOGRAPHICAL OVERVIEWS
SOURCES, BACKGROUNDS, AND CRITICISM

SECOND EDITION

Edited by

HERSHEL PARKER
EMERITUS, UNIVERSITY OF DELAWARE

MARK NIEMEYER
THE SORBONNE, PARIS

W. W. NORTON & COMPANY
New York • London

W. W. Norton & Company has been independent since its founding in 1923, when William Warder Norton and Mary D. Herter Norton first published lectures delivered at the People's Institute, the adult education division of New York City's Cooper Union. The Nortons soon expanded their program beyond the Institute, publishing books by celebrated academics from America and abroad. By mid-century, the two major pillars of Norton's publishing program—trade books and college texts—were firmly established. In the 1950s, the Norton family transferred control of the company to its employees, and today—with a staff of four hundred and a comparable number of trade, college, and professional titles published each year—W. W. Norton & Company stands as the largest and oldest publishing house owned wholly by its employees.

Every effort has been made to contact the copyright holders for each of the selections. Rights holders of any selections not credited should contact W. W. Norton & Company, Inc., 500 Fifth Avenue, New York, N.Y. 10110, for a correction to be made in the next printing of our work.

The text of this book is composed in Fairfield Medium
with the display set in Bernhard Modern.
Composition by PennSet, Inc.
Manufacturing by the Courier Companies—Westford Division.
Production manager: Benjamin Reynolds.

Library of Congress Cataloging-in-Publication Data
Melville, Herman, 1819–1891.
The confidence-man : his masquerade : an authoritative text, contemporary reviews, biographical overviews, sources, backgrounds, and criticism / edited by Hershel Parker, Mark Niemeyer.— 2nd ed.
p. cm.— (A Norton critical edition)

ISBN 0–393–97927–X (pbk.)

1. Swindlers and swindling—Fiction. 2. Melville, Herman, 1819–1891. Confidence-man. 3. Swindlers and swindling in literature. 4. Mississippi River—Fiction. 5. Steamboats—Fiction. I. Parker, Hershel. II. Niemeyer, Mark. III. Title. IV. Series.

PS2384.C6 2005
813′.3—dc22

2005052326

W. W. Norton & Company, Inc., 500 Fifth Avenue, New York, N.Y. 10110-0017
www.wwnorton.com

W. W. Norton & Company Ltd., Castle House,
75/76 Wells Street, London W1T 3QT

1 2 3 4 5 6 7 8 9 0

Contents

Biographical Overviews

Backgrounds, Sources, and Criticism

Preface

A sentence from the preface to the 2001 Norton Critical Edition (NCE) of *Moby-Dick* applies to this volume, with only a change of book title and date: "This Second Norton Critical Edition of *The Confidence-Man* embodies the transformation of knowledge about Melville that has occurred since the original 1971 edition, particularly about his life." The Northwestern-Newberry (NN) Edition of *The Confidence-Man* (1984) reported some new biographical discoveries, but in the next decades scholars, amateurs, and book dealers made many more discoveries, the most startling of which revealed for the first time Melville's extreme poverty in the years after *Moby-Dick*. His disastrous indebtedness underlies all of *The Confidence-Man*, most painfully Chapter 40, "The Story of China Aster." This grim new story is told in Hershel Parker's second volume of his *Herman Melville: A Biography*. The gist of the new evidence is in his "Damned by Dollars," the final article in the 2001 NCE of *Moby-Dick*. Here, in a new section called "Biographical Overviews," that essay is condensed, but also augmented by new paragraphs on 1856, the year *The Confidence-Man* was finished. In that section we print a wide-ranging new introductory article by Parker, "The Confidence Man's Masquerade," and part of Johannes Dietrich Bergmann's discussion of his 1969 discovery that the term *confidence man* was an American invention coined in 1849 to identify a particular crook whose inventive ploy was to demand that his victims entrust to him a watch or other token of their confidence in him. Among the several new articles in the section, an essay by Dennis Marnon shows how very wealthy Melville's Boston family had been before his profligate father threw away his part of the family fortune. Another article by Stephen D. Hoy places the financial struggles of Melville's youth in the context of the national economy. The section also includes a salutary reminder by Jonathan A. Cook of how profoundly Melville steeped himself in the Greek and Roman writers during a decade of personal and national disaster.

Beginning in 1954 with Elizabeth S. Foster, in the first scholarly edition of *The Confidence-Man*, all editors have acknowledged that in this book Melville was commenting mordantly on many contem-

porary movements—religious, political, social, physical, psychological, and medical. We deal with these diverse themes in "Backgrounds, Sources, and Criticism," which begins with a section
titled "Utopias, Sects, Cults, and Cure-Alls." Throughout this edition, new headnotes and new articles (some freshly commissioned)
help establish specific contexts for social experiments and augment
the articles carried forward from 1971. Using brief passages from
Melville's early works and Melville's own testimony that he was
sought out by Fourierites for advice, we demonstrate that Melville
was more than just another commentator on social experiments:
some of his contemporaries took *Typee* as a textbook on the superiority of "savagery" to "civilization." (Thomas Low Nichols, who read
Typee in manuscript, became one of the most conspicuous social
and sexual reformers of the 1850s.) This NCE for the first time
links tightly the motley array of what Melville called "new-fangled"
social experiments by their one common feature—rejection of the
harsh account of God's curse in Genesis, rejection, that is, of the
theological concept of Original Sin.

Almost as startling as the new evidence about Melville's poverty
are the recent discoveries detailed in both volumes of Parker's biography about the concerted attacks on Melville by, especially, Presbyterian, Congregationalist, and Methodist reviewers, and (in the
second volume) about Melville's horror at the implications of Unitarian attitudes toward poverty in America. Melville agreed to expurgate his criticisms of missionaries in Polynesia from his first
book, *Typee* (1846), but the "low church" Protestants (those who
rejected more of the Roman Catholic beliefs and practices than the
"high church" Episcopalians) were not appeased. (See the section
"Before *Moby-Dick*: International Controversy over Melville" in the
2001 NCE of *Moby-Dick*.) They renewed their onslaughts on his
next book, *Omoo* (1847), and continued to attack him for what
they called blasphemy in later books, particularly *Moby-Dick*. As he
was finishing *Moby-Dick* Melville was so financially and emotionally damaged by the reviews that he identified with victims of European witch hunts in the seventeenth century. (We know this from
Geoffrey Sanborn's 1992 discovery that words Melville jotted down
in the last volume of his set of Shakespeare—puzzling to earlier
scholars—were simply his reading notes on an article about the
persecution of witches, "Superstition and Knowledge," in the July
1823 issue of the London *Quarterly Review*.) After having suffered
through the reviews of *Moby-Dick* and *Pierre* (1852) and having
seen his next book, *The Isle of the Cross* (which he finished in late
May 1853) fail to reach print at all, in 1856 Melville thought of
dedicating *The Confidence-Man* to victims of auto da fe, those tortured and burned alive by the Spanish inquisition.

Although Presbyterians and other low church reviewers had condemned him since 1846, Melville was at home with their Calvinist theology rather than currently fashionable alternatives, particularly Unitarianism. He read with a critical eye an abridgment of *The Light of Nature Revealed* by Abraham Tucker, a philosophical father of English Unitarianism. We include a section of Tucker's "Benevolence" as well as part of Melville's oblique commentary on Tucker and other Utilitarians and Unitarians, the Plinlimmon pamphlet in *Pierre*. Melville knew the history of the double revolt in the 1770s and 1780s in which Bostonians, among them his grandfather Thomas Melvill, first freed the city of British secular rule then seized the principal Anglican church, King's Chapel, not for an old Protestant sect that believed in the Trinity but for the new American Unitarians. (This Melvill grandfather himself owned a pew at the Brattle Street Unitarian Church, known as the "Manifesto Church.") *The Confidence-Man*, and some of Melville's stories, notably "Bartleby, the Scrivener," embody Melville's critique of contemporary American Unitarianism, especially as promulgated by Orville Dewey, who baptized three of Melville's children and preached his father-in-law's funeral sermon.

In "Utopias, Sects, Cults, and Cure-Alls," background pieces by Melville himself as well as pieces by Orville Dewey suggest just what Melville thought of the coolness with which leading Unitarians responded to Jesus's saying "The poor ye have always with you." In New York, Unitarians contrasted their views on begging with those of the reforming newspaper editor Horace Greeley, who, as Scott Norsworthy shows, was determined to use his New York *Tribune* to help the poor of the city. In a major new historical and critical essay Susan M. Ryan examines "the ambiguities of benevolence" in the context of antebellum debates over race, slavery, and citizenship. The chronology of Melville's knowledge of Emerson and Thoreau printed in the 1971 NCE is revised as "The Latest Heresy: Melville and the Transcendentalists." Printed immediately following the items on Unitarianism, this section now makes fuller sense, for Melville, like many others, understood some of Ralph Waldo Emerson's extreme opinions as those to be expected from a former Unitarian minister.

A newspaper writer in 1855 identified the re-arrested rogue (who had been briefly notorious in 1849) as the "Original Confidence Man." For Melville, the Original Confidence Man was the snake in the Garden of Eden, Satan, the source of Original Sin. In 1857 the reviewer in the London *Critic* sensed what Elizabeth S. Foster first traced out in detail: a pattern of devil imagery associated with the Confidence Man. In 1971 Parker, perhaps too confidently, delineated a "standard interpretation" of *The Confidence-Man* according to which Melville puts the Devil on a Mississippi steamboat in a series of disguises designed to test the quality of contemporary Christianity. We approached this new edition prepared to place less emphasis on the devil allegory, but we found that Melville's use of the Devil in *The Confidence-Man* was thicker and more complicated than previously noticed. Among the newly annotated devil allusions is the one to Robert Burns's "Tam o'Shanter," where Satan takes the shape of a big rough-coated black dog—perhaps a way of tying the last avatar of the Confidence Man to one of the earliest, the Black Guinea, who is compared to a (presumably black) Newfoundland dog. In "Melville and the Devil in the Bible and Popular Literature" we retain Nathaniel Hawthorne's "The Celestial Railroad" and a shorter piece to identify the current conventions of devil allegory within which Melville was working. In new items we quote the notes Melville made for a story in which the Devil as a gentleman moves confidently in Manhattan's high society and we use part of Stubb's devil allegory in *Moby-Dick*. Concluding this section is Thomas McHaney's essay on the way Melville built into *The Confidence-Man* some of Satan's disguises in John Milton's *Paradise Lost*. Here we provide new editorial footnotes identifying passages cited by McHaney that Melville marked and annotated in his recently discovered copy of Milton's poems.

Elaborating the footnotes to biblical references required us to call attention to Melville's repeated allusions to biblical shape-changing and cosmos-traversing passages, where Satan walks on earth and in heaven and where angels and demons appear on earth in human form and are dangerously mistaken for men. Many new annotations document Melville's complex use of the shape changing in the Roman poet Ovid's *Metamorphoses* as well as his thickly strewn allusions to other historical and literary shape changers. There is room for controversy, for instance on the role of the mute at the start of the book (the first disguise of the Confidence Man or not?), but Melville's highly conscious and sophisticated use of devil allegory as well as other shape-changing or subhuman and extra-human sources runs throughout *The Confidence-Man*.

Ever since Foster's edition appeared, the most fervent and diverse interpretations (except perhaps those centering on the identity of the Confidence Man) have involved Melville's recasting of the Ohio writer James Hall's account of "Indian hating." Because the topic of allegorizing Indian hating is, by its nature, politically sensitive and emotionally charged, Parker, a party to the history of criticism on this section, contributes a fresh personal account of his ambivalence, as an American with close Choctaw and Cherokee ancestors, toward responses to his "The Metaphysics of Indian-hating" in 1961 (when it was delivered as a talk) and afterward. We have divided the treatment of Indian hating into two parts. The first, "Historical Background" includes Hall's chapter and new pieces that document the long-lived and disturbing reality of Indian hating, sometimes as expressed from within the circle of Melville's relations and acquaintances. We also make clear Melville's own stance on racism as unambiguously expressed outside of *The Confidence-Man*. A disturbing piece from the *New York Times* in 1972 is followed by the novelist Margaret Coel's devastating updating of the topic, a personal testimonial written especially for this edition. In "Political Background" we print Foster's pioneering analysis of Melville's use of Indian hating as religious allegory and follow it with the elaborations and clarifications made shortly afterward by John W. Shroeder and Parker.

The biographical portions of the NN "Historical Note" to *The Confidence-Man* are superseded by discoveries Parker made during his expansion of Jay Leyda's *The Melville Log* (1951 and 1969) in the process of writing his two-volume biography of Melville (1996 and 2002). The NN section on contemporary reviews stands up well, but more reviews have been discovered, mainly by Parker and by Richard E. Winslow III, and many of these are available in full in a collection edited by Brian Higgins and Parker, *Herman Melville: The Contemporary Reviews* (1995). A sample of both English and American reviews is offered in this volume, enough to show that it was the English who paid, at best, scrupulous attention and who came very close to penetrating Melville's theological allegory.

The Confidence-Man waited long for fit readers. The first was a distant cousin of Melville's, Carl Van Vechten, whose 1922 comments on the book as a satire of Transcendentalism are infused with joyous discovery. In the 1940s a handful of academic critics exhibited comparable excitement as college teaching of American literature spread and professors began to publish readings of the book for the first time. Until the end of the 1940s the only texts were the 1857 American and English editions and the 1923 volume in the Constable set (published in London). In 1948 a new edition was published in England by John Lehmann and the next year Grove Press published one in the United States. Thereafter, no critic had to reenact Richard Chase's writing on the basis of one hasty devouring of a library copy that could not be checked out, although for a carefully introduced and annotated text critics had to wait until 1954, when Elizabeth S. Foster published her edition.

We dare to hope that a sense of joyous discovery informs that most humble of genres, the footnotes to the text, for in writing them we experienced many hours worth marking with a Melvillean white stone (to use a phrase from Chapter 25). Some identifications of Melville's allusions, it developed, could hardly have been made before the age of the Internet, when, if one catches a browser on a good day, one can find, using only key words from the last chapter, that a reference to Napoleon is to a particular 1830 engraving of the ghost of Napoleon standing at his tomb in St. Helena. This was a then-famous example of "hidden art," appreciated (the Internet may also reveal, on a good day) by the Danish philosopher Soren Kierkegaard as well as by Melville. In *The Confidence-Man* Melville refers to Heraclitus, who knew that all things were a-changing; in that spirit we confidently advise that on a good day a student may immediately summon up a reproduction of the Napoleonic engraving or an inferior copy of it produced in 1831. Melville's allusion to a popular example of hidden art is a happy one, for *The Confidence-Man* itself may be perceived as a great work of hidden art, one in which the reader at first glance may fail to perceive the central figure (or theme, or implication) in one scene or another, then may experience, repeatedly, the shock of joyous perception and appreciation.

Hershel Parker
Mark Niemeyer

Acknowledgments

Our deepest debts are to Dennis Marnon of Harvard College Library, forensic librarian, and Scott Norsworthy, who proved himself equally at home in newspaper microfilms and on the Internet. We are particularly grateful to Margaret Coel, Patricia Cline Cohen, Jonathan A. Cook, and Stephen D. Hoy, all of whom, like Marnon and Norsworthy, wrote pieces specially for this edition. We are grateful to Ruth Degenhardt, formerly of the Berkshire Athenaeum. We are indebted also to Mary K. Bercaw, Watson G. Branch, Cook (for advice on matters biblical as well as classical), Donald F. Crosby, S.J., Jane Donahue Eberwein (for help with Joel Barlow and Manco Capac), Robin Grey, Brian Higgins, Philippe Jaworski, Frederick Kennedy, Joyce Deveau Kennedy, Alma MacDougall, Robert D. Madison, Dominique Marçais, Lion G. Miles (the great Berkshire County researcher), Deborah M. Norsworthy, Lois Potter, Steven Olsen-Smith, Nathaniel Philbrick, Tom Quirk, Todd Richardson, Douglas Robillard, Susan M. Ryan, Adam Tuchinsky, Michael Williams, S.J., Richard E. Winslow III, and Mark Wojnar. Four scholars deserve special mention, foremost the late Elizabeth S. Foster. As recently as 1969 Hans Bergmann pioneered research on the confidence man of 1849. In 1977 Patricia Barber published the May 1856 letters from Melville to his father-in-law, which are now incorporated into the 1993 Northwestern-Newberry *Correspondence* volume (see Selected Bibliography) and into Parker's biography of Melville. Harrison Hayford's work has been incorporated into many parts of this volume, as well as into all serious Melville scholarship.

Heddy-Ann Richter, who proofread the 2001 Norton *Moby Dick* with Hershel Parker, punctuation and all, kindly performed the same feat for this edition of *The Confidence-Man*. Jim Kosvanec generously digitized the cover picture by Robert Shore. At W. W. Norton Candace Levy copyedited expertly and thoughtfully. Managing Editor Marian Johnson, Production Manager Ben Reynolds, and Assistant Editor Brian Baker expedited the stages of production during which the proofreader, Ann J. Kirschner, the cover designer, Joan Greenfield, and Gina Webster of the art department all made their admirable contributions. Our greatest debt at Norton is to Carol Bemis, the editor of the Norton Critical Editions.

The Text of
THE CONFIDENCE-MAN

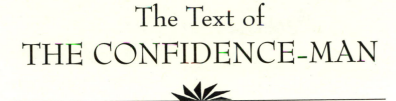

(Dedicated to victims of Auto da Fe)

Contents.

---

1. The formula "in which" signals to the reader that this is to be a highly bookish book, for it plays with a way of constructing titles much favored by Henry Fielding in *Tom Jones* (1749) and *Amelia* (1752), and by other eighteenth-century British writers, then more recently imitated, very much as Melville does, by William Makepeace Thackeray in *Vanity Fair* (1847–1848).

The Confidence-Man:
His Masquerade.

Chapter 1.

A MUTE GOES ABOARD A BOAT ON THE MISSISSIPPI.

At sunrise on a first of April,[1] there appeared, suddenly as Manco Capac[2] at the lake Titicaca, a man in cream-colors, at the water-side in the city of St. Louis.

His cheek was fair, his chin downy, his hair flaxen, his hat a white fur one, with a long fleecy nap. He had neither trunk, valise, carpet-bag, nor parcel. No porter followed him. He was unaccompanied by friends. From the shrugged shoulders, titters, whispers, wonderings of the crowd, it was plain that he was, in the extremest sense of the word, a stranger.

In the same moment with his advent, he stepped aboard the favorite steamer Fidèle,[3] on the point of starting for New Orleans. Stared at, but unsaluted, with the air of one neither courting nor shunning regard, but evenly pursuing the path of duty, lead it through solitudes or cities, he held on his way along the lower deck until he chanced to come to a placard nigh the captain's office, offering a reward for the capture of a mysterious impostor, supposed to have recently arrived from the East;[4] quite an original genius in his vocation, as would appear, though wherein his originality con-

---

1. Then, as now, "April Fool Day" (later "April Fools' Day"), appropriate for a probing of confidence in national practices and policies and in the benevolence of the universe.
2. The founder of the Incan Empire, sent to earth by his father, the sun. In *The Vision of Columbus* (1787) or *The Columbiad* (1807), by Joel Barlow (1754–1812), American diplomat and poet, Manco Capac is treated as a man only pretending to be a descendant of the sun. Members of Melville's family were well acquainted with Barlow. See Jane Donahue Eberwein, in the Selected Bibliography. This supernatural "advent" initiates a pattern in which Melville superimposes geography and theology from other times and places onto the United States of the 1850s. In *Mardi* (1849), chapter 113, Melville in an obvious allegory treats "Manko" as an earlier avatar of Jesus.
3. Faithful, from the Latin for "faith."
4. The eastern United States, or the Near East of the Holy Land, an example of Melville's ambiguously blurring the contemporary United States with biblical times. In 1850 an impostor had traveled in Georgia and North Carolina as "Herman Melville." On December 8, 1854, the Pittsfield paper, the *Berkshire County Eagle*, reported on an impostor who had told hard-luck stories to local clergymen. According to the paper, he "assumed

sisted was not clearly given; but what purported to be a careful description of his person followed.

As if it had been a theatre-bill, crowds were gathered about the announcement, and among them certain chevaliers,[5] whose eyes, it was plain, were on the capitals, or, at least, earnestly seeking sight of them from behind intervening coats; but as for their fingers, they were enveloped in some myth; though, during a chance interval, one of these chevaliers somewhat showed his hand in purchasing from another chevalier, ex-officio[6] a peddler of money-belts, one of his popular safe-guards, while another peddler, who was still another versatile chevalier, hawked, in the thick of the throng, the lives of Measan, the bandit of Ohio, Murrel,[7] the pirate of the Mississippi, and the brothers Harpe,[8] the Thugs of the Green River country, in Kentucky—creatures, with others of the sort, one and all exterminated at the time, and for the most part, like the hunted generations of wolves in the same regions, leaving comparatively few successors; which would seem cause for unalloyed gratulation, and is such to all except those who think that in new countries, where the wolves are killed off, the foxes increase.[9]

Pausing at this spot, the stranger so far succeeded in threading his way, as at last to plant himself just beside the placard, when,

a different name in each case." Melville was fascinated by the first criminal, Satan, and his guises during his travels on earth (see his "Devil as a Quaker" and notes on p. 445 herein).

5. Swindlers, here engaged in picking pockets.
6. By virtue of his office, used humorously of the "chevalier." "Myth": this peculiar use may be what Melville wrote, but Watson G. Branch suggests "night" and Jonathan A. Cook "mystery."
7. Born in Tennessee, John A. Murrel or Murrall (1804–1844) was a robber on the Natchez Trace, the land route from Mississippi through Tennessee, and a river pirate, often posing as an itinerant preacher. He specialized in stealing Negro slaves and reselling them. Grave robbers decapitated his corpse. Born in Virginia, Samuel Meason or Mason (1739–1803) robbed boats on the Ohio River in the 1790s, lurking, toward the end, in Cave-in-Rock, a limestone formation a hundred miles above the mouth of the Ohio River. His own gang beheaded him for a five-hundred-dollar reward offered by the governor of Mississippi. James Hall told his story in *Sketches of History, Life, and Manners in the West* (1835), 2.88–89. Melville was fascinated by criminals and methods of punishment, particularly public executions (see Parker, p. 343 herein). See "Who Is Happier?" (p. 367 herein) for his knowledge of gibbeting and of the last man to be drawn and quartered in England; see also n. 3, p. 151 herein.
8. Micajah (or William) and Wiley (or Joshua) Harpe, brothers or cousins, were American "Thugs." (In northern India Thugs were worshipers of Kali who strangled their victims and plundered the corpses; they were in the news in Melville's youth as the British suppressed them.) The Harpes slaughtered people from the Cumberland Gap in Virginia to Cave-in-Rock in southeastern Illinois, mainly in Tennessee and Kentucky. Sexual predators, killers of children, masters of disguise (they passed as itinerant ministers), opportunistic murderers of some four dozen people in all, they were memorialized by James Hall, in *The Harpe's Head; a Legend of Kentucky* (1833), who described them as displaying a "savage thirst for blood—a deep rooted malignity against human nature." It was "Little Harpe" (Wiley) who beheaded Mason or Measan for evidence in his attempt to collect a reward. Both the Harpe brothers were beheaded, like Mason and Murrall (heads being good for identification and comparatively lightweight to transport).
9. I.e., sly, crafty, more "civilized" predators (including human predators) multiply even as ferocious wild beasts are exterminated from a region.

producing a small slate and tracing some words upon it, he held it up before him on a level with the placard, so that they who read the one might read the other. The words[1] were these:—

"Charity thinketh no evil."

As, in gaining his place, some little perseverance, not to say persistence, of a mildly inoffensive sort, had been unavoidable, it was not with the best relish that the crowd regarded his apparent intrusion; and upon a more attentive survey, perceiving no badge of authority about him,[2] but rather something quite the contrary—he being of an aspect so singularly innocent; an aspect, too, which they took to be somehow inappropriate to the time and place, and inclining to the notion that his writing was of much the same sort: in short, taking him for some strange kind of simpleton, harmless enough, would he keep to himself, but not wholly unobnoxious as an intruder—they made no scruple to jostle him aside; while one, less kind than the rest, or more of a wag, by an unobserved stroke, dexterously flattened down his fleecy hat upon his head. Without readjusting it, the stranger quietly turned, and writing anew upon the slate, again held it up:—

"Charity suffereth long, and is kind."

Illy pleased with his pertinacity, as they thought it, the crowd a second time thrust him aside, and not without epithets and some buffets, all of which were unresented. But, as if at last despairing of so difficult an adventure, wherein one, apparently a non-resistant, sought to impose his presence upon fighting characters, the stranger now moved slowly away, yet not before altering his writing to this:—

"Charity endureth all things."

Shield-like bearing his slate before him,[3] amid stares and jeers he moved slowly up and down, at his turning points again changing his inscription to—

1. The words on the slate (here and below) are from 1 Corinthians 13. Melville blurs the New Testament sense of *charity* (love) into something like the common sense of benevolence or generosity toward the poor.
2. Whether or not the mute "is" the Devil in a most cynical disguise, he behaves in ways that recall Jesus directly or indirectly, particularly Jesus' meekness under arrest. In the Books of Matthew, Mark, and Luke the question is repeatedly raised as to the "authority" by which Jesus speaks and acts, and in Matthew 7.29 Jesus is said to have taught "as one having authority, and not as the scribes." The crushing of the hat later in the paragraph serves as a reminder of the crown of thorns crushed onto Jesus's head by Roman soldiers (John 19.2).
3. In this book laced with bits of the letters of the Apostle Paul to the new Christian groups in Asia Minor, Greece, and as far away as Rome, a reminder of Ephesians 6.16: "Above all, taking the shield of faith, wherewith ye shall be able to quench all the fiery darts of the wicked." See also Ephesians 6.13–14: "Wherefore take unto you the whole armour of God, that ye may be able to withstand in the evil day, and having done all, to stand. Stand therefore, having your loins girt about with truth, and having on the breastplate of righteousness."

"Charity believeth all things."

and then—

"Charity never faileth."

The word charity, as originally traced, remained throughout un-effaced, not unlike the left-hand numeral of a printed date, other-wise left for convenience in blank.

To some observers, the singularity, if not lunacy, of the stranger was heightened by his muteness, and, perhaps also, by the contrast to his proceedings afforded in the actions—quite in the wonted and sensible order of things—of the barber of the boat, whose quarters, under a smoking-saloon, and over against a bar-room, was next door but two to the captain's office. As if the long, wide, covered deck, hereabouts built up on both sides with shop-like windowed spaces, were some Constantinople arcade or bazaar, where more than one trade is plied, this river barber, aproned and slippered, but rather crusty-looking for the moment, it may be from being newly out of bed, was throwing open his premises for the day, and suitably arranging the exterior. With business-like dispatch, having rattled down his shutters, and at a palm-tree angle set out in the iron fixture his little ornamental pole, and this without overmuch tenderness for the elbows and toes of the crowd, he concluded his operations by bidding people stand still more aside, when, jumping on a stool, he hung over his door, on the cus-tomary nail, a gaudy sort of illuminated pasteboard sign, skillfully exe-cuted by himself, gilt with the likeness of a razor elbowed in readiness to shave, and also, for the public benefit, with two words not unfre-quently seen ashore gracing other shops besides barbers':—

"NO TRUST."[4]

An inscription which, though in a sense not less intrusive than the contrasted ones of the stranger, did not, as it seemed, provoke any corresponding derision or surprise, much less indignation; and still less, to all appearances, did it gain for the inscriber the repute of being a simpleton.

Meanwhile, he with the slate continued moving slowly up and down, not without causing some stares to change into jeers, and some jeers into pushes, and some pushes into punches; when sud-denly, in one of his turns, he was hailed from behind by two porters carrying a large trunk; but as the summons, though loud, was with-out effect, they accidentally or otherwise swung their burden against him, nearly overthrowing him; when, by a quick start, a peculiar inarticulate moan, and a pathetic telegraphing of his fingers, he in-voluntarily betrayed that he was not alone dumb,[5] but also deaf.

4. Cash only.
5. Isaiah 53.7: "He was oppressed, and he was afflicted, yet he opened not his mouth: he is brought as a lamb to the slaughter, and as a sheep before her shearers is dumb, so he

Presently, as if not wholly unaffected by his reception thus far, he went forward, seating himself in a retired spot on the forecastle, nigh the foot of a ladder[6] there leading to a deck above, up and down which ladder some of the boatmen, in discharge of their duties, were occasionally going.

From his betaking himself to this humble quarter, it was evident that, as a deck-passenger, the stranger, simple though he seemed, was not entirely ignorant of his place, though his taking a deck-passage might have been partly for convenience; as, from his having no luggage,[7] it was probable that his destination was one of the small wayside landings within a few hours' sail. But, though he might not have a long way to go, yet he seemed already to have come from a very long distance.

Though neither soiled nor slovenly, his cream-colored suit had a tossed look, almost linty, as if, traveling night and day from some far country beyond the prairies, he had long been without the solace of a bed. His aspect was at once gentle and jaded, and, from the moment of seating himself, increasing in tired abstraction and dreaminess. Gradually overtaken by slumber, his flaxen head drooped, his whole lamb-like figure relaxed, and, half reclining against the ladder's foot, lay motionless, as some sugar-snow[8] in March, which, softly stealing down over night, with its white placidity startles the brown farmer peering out from his threshold at daybreak.

Chapter 2.

SHOWING THAT MANY MEN HAVE MANY MINDS.

"Odd fish!"
"Poor fellow!"
"Who can he be?"
"Casper Hauser."[9]

---

openeth not his mouth." (Widely interpreted by Christians as a prophecy of Jesus's behavior under arrest.) Cf. the depiction by John of the glorified Christ in Revelation 1.14: "His head and his hairs were white like wool, as white as snow."

6. The ladder is suggestive—possibly literal, possibly symbolic (see n. 4, p. 14). By this point any reader who knows the Bible will already have sensed that events are being described so as to evoke biblical precedents and parallels.

7. The typical modern Christian tries to take too much worldly luggage along as he attempts to get to heaven, according to Hawthorne in "The Celestial Railroad" (see p. 429 herein), who puns on literal and psychological "burdens" as he shows the futility of thinking that someone else can carry yours for you.

8. Snow consisting of faceted crystals that crunch underfoot (sugar then not being finely granulated but sold by cone or cube); thought to provide a late slow saturation that encourages sap production in maples for the next season.

9. A "wild boy" (1812?–1833) who was found in the marketplace of Nuremberg in 1828. By his accounts, he had been kept in a dark place until finally taught to stand and walk by a man who abandoned him and who, five years later, gave him a mortal wound. For more in the pattern of subhuman or extra-human beings, see the references to Peter the Wild Boy in chapter 21 and to Hairy Orson in chapter 26.

"Bless my soul!"

"Uncommon countenance."

"Green prophet from Utah."[1]

"Humbug!"

"Singular innocence."

"Means something."

"Spirit-rapper."

"Moon-calf."[2]

"Piteous."

"Trying to enlist interest."

"Beware of him."

"Fast asleep here, and, doubtless, pick-pockets on board."

"Kind of daylight Endymion."[3]

"Escaped convict, worn out with dodging."

"Jacob dreaming at Luz."[4]

Such the epitaphic comments, conflictingly spoken or thought, of a miscellaneous company, who, assembled on the overlooking, cross-wise balcony at the forward end of the upper deck near by, had not witnessed preceding occurrences.

Meantime, like some enchanted man in his grave, happily oblivious of all gossip, whether chiseled or chatted, the deaf and dumb stranger still tranquilly slept, while now the boat started on her voyage.

The great ship-canal of Ving-King-Ching,[5] in the Flowery Kingdom, seems the Mississippi in parts, where, amply flowing between low, vine-tangled banks, flat as tow-paths, it bears the huge toppling steamers, bedizened and lacquered within like imperial junks.

Pierced along its great white bulk with two tiers of small embrasure-like windows, well above the waterline, the Fidèle,

---

1. A Mormon. "Green" because still inexperienced.
2. A simpleton. "Spirit-rapper": One who practices spiritualism, with mediums channeling the dead during séances. Two sisters, Margaretta and Kate Fox of Lily Dale, near Rochester, New York, in 1848 claimed to have induced the spirit of a dead man to knock on their table. Spirit-rapping became an international movement, lasting for decades in Great Britain. By the mid-1850s Christian churches were condemning it as a heathenish new pseudo-religion.
3. The contrast is with the nocturnal dreaming of the shepherd who falls in love with the moon in "Endymion" (1818), by the English poet John Keats (1795–1821).
4. In his flight toward Padanaram, fearing his wronged older brother, Esau, Jacob paused without a shelter in an area called Luz, and slept, using stones for pillows. He dreamed that he beheld "a ladder set up on the earth, and the top of it reached to heaven," and beheld "the angels of God ascending and descending on it" (Genesis 28.12). The Lord stood at the top of the ladder and blessed him, confirming his precedence over Esau. At daybreak, recognizing the location as the gate to heaven, Jacob made a pillar of one of the stones and renamed the place Bethel, the house of God.
5. Melville is equally cavalier in *Moby-Dick*, chapter 64, "Stubb's Supper": "upon the great canal of Hang-Ho, or whatever they call it, in China, four or five laborers on the foot-path will draw a bulky freighted junk at the rate of a mile an hour." "Hang-Ho" or "Huang-ho" is the Yellow River, whose old bed the canal partly followed.

though, might at distance have been taken by strangers for some whitewashed fort on a floating isle.

Merchants on 'change seem the passengers that buzz on her decks, while, from quarters unseen, comes a murmur as of bees in the comb. Fine promenades, domed saloons, long galleries, sunny balconies, confidential passages, bridal chambers, state-rooms plenty as pigeonholes, and out-of-the-way retreats like secret drawers in an escritoire, present like facilities for publicity or privacy. Auctioneer or coiner,[6] with equal ease, might somewhere here drive his trade.

Though her voyage of twelve hundred miles extends from apple to orange, from clime to clime, yet, like any small ferry-boat, to right and left, at every landing, the huge Fidèle still receives additional passengers in exchange for those that disembark; so that, though always full of strangers, she continually, in some degree, adds to, or replaces them with strangers still more strange; like Rio Janeiro fountain, fed from the Corcovado mountains, which is ever overflowing with strange waters,[7] but never with the same strange particles in every part.

Though hitherto, as has been seen, the man in cream-colors had by no means passed unobserved, yet by stealing into retirement, and there going asleep and continuing so, he seemed to have courted oblivion, a boon not often withheld from so humble an applicant as he. Those staring crowds on the shore were now left far behind, seen dimly clustering like swallows on eaves; while the passengers' attention was soon drawn away to the rapidly shooting high bluffs and shot-towers on the Missouri shore, or the bluff-looking Missourians and towering Kentuckians[8] among the throngs on the decks.

By-and-by—two or three random stoppages having been made, and the last transient memory of the slumberer vanished, and he himself, not unlikely, waked up and landed ere now—the crowd, as is usual, began in all parts to break up from a concourse into various clusters or squads, which in some cases disintegrated again

6. Counterfeiter.
7. Aqueducts from the Corcovado Mountains brought water to Rio de Janeiro. In August 1844 the *United States* anchored in the bay at Rio de Janeiro with Melville aboard; he could have seen the high aqueducts even though not allowed to go ashore.
8. Melville attributed great height and physical prowess to Virginians (pleasantly aware that many of them were Scottish, like the Melvilles) and to former Virginians who crossed the Alleghenies to Kentucky and Tennessee. "Shot-towers": where lead shot was made. Americans had learned from the English to make lead spheres for gunshot by running molten lead through a sieve and letting the pieces fall into a water tank far below. Lead was available (the name of the town Galena, on the Illinois side of the Mississippi and upriver from St. Louis, which Melville visited in 1840, is from the Latin for "lead ore"), and there was a successful shot-tower twenty-five miles south of St. Louis at Herculaneum, Missouri.

into quartettes, trios, and couples, or even solitaires; involuntarily submitting to that natural law which ordains dissolution equally to the mass, as in time to the member.

As among Chaucer's Canterbury pilgrims, or those oriental ones crossing the Red Sea towards Mecca in the festival month, there was no lack of variety.[9] Natives of all sorts, and foreigners; men of business and men of pleasure; parlor men and backwoodsmen; farm-hunters and fame-hunters; heiress-hunters, gold-hunters, buffalo-hunters, bee-hunters, happiness-hunters, truth-hunters, and still keener hunters after all these hunters. Fine ladies in slippers, and moccasined squaws; Northern speculators and Eastern philosophers; English, Irish, German, Scotch, Danes; Santa Fé traders in striped blankets, and Broadway bucks in cravats of cloth of gold; fine-looking Kentucky boatmen, and Japanese-looking[1] Mississippi cotton-planters; Quakers in full drab, and United States soldiers in full regimentals; slaves, black, mulatto, quadroon; modish young Spanish Creoles, and old-fashioned French Jews; Mormons and Papists; Dives and Lazarus; jesters and mourners, teetotalers and convivialists, deacons and blacklegs; hard-shell Baptists and clay-eaters;[2] grinning negroes, and Sioux chiefs solemn as high-priests. In short, a piebald parliament, an Anachar-

---

9. Among the pilgrims in the *Canterbury Tales* (c. 1387) by the English poet Geoffrey Chaucer (c. 1343–1400) are the host, knight, miller, reeve, cook, man of law, wife of Bath, friar, summoner, clerk, and merchant, all of whom, and many others, tell stories. T. B. Thorpe's very popular story "The Big Bear of Arkansas" (1841) had helped create the convention of listing the motley array of passengers one might encounter on a Mississippi steamboat. Melville in his review "Mr Parkman's Tour" (1849) commented on the mix of passengers described in *The California and Oregon Trail*: "In a steamer, crammed with all sorts of adventurers, Spaniards and Indians, Santa-Fe traders and trappers, gamblers and Mormons, the party ascend the Mississippi and Missouri, and at last debark on the banks of the latter stream at a point on the verge of the wilderness."
1. I.e., yellow skinned from malaria, transmitted by mosquitoes.
2. In the South "geophagy" was a not uncommon practice, mainly among the poorest classes. Iron and other minerals were available in a clay favored by these people, white kaolin (long used as the absorbent element in antidiarrheal medicine). "Dives and Lazarus": Rich man and beggar, from Jesus' parable in Luke 16.19–31 about the rich man who "was clothed in purple and fine linen, and fared sumptuously every day," and the "beggar named Lazarus, which was laid at his gate, full of sores, And desiring to be fed with the crumbs which fell from the rich man's table: moreover the dogs came and licked his sores." Lazarus dies and is carried by the angels into Abraham's bosom, then the rich man dies; from hell he begs Abraham: "send Lazarus, that he may dip the tip of his finger in water, and cool my tongue; for I am tormented in this flame." Abraham is implacable: between heaven and hell "there is a great gulf fixed." Furthermore, Abraham refuses to send Lazarus to warn the rich man's brothers that he is in hell: like anyone else, they already have the opportunity of heeding Moses and the prophets. Dives is sometimes mistaken as the name of the rich man because *dives* was the word for "rich man" in St. Jerome's translation, known as the "Vulgate" Bible because it was in the common spoken language, Latin. "Hard-shell Baptists": "primitive" Baptists who opposed societies advocating the temperance movement, missionary work, distribution of religious tracts, abolitionism—anything not specifically biblical, according to their reading of the scriptures. Presbyterians, Congregationalists, and members of other "low" churches carried on missionary work as far away as the Pacific islands, and became Melville's severest critics when he exposed missionary abuses of natives in *Typee* (1846) and *Omoo* (1847).

sis Cloots[3] congress of all kinds of that multiform pilgrim species, man.

As pine, beech, birch, ash, hackmatack, hemlock, spruce, basswood, maple, interweave their foliage in the natural wood, so these varieties of mortals blended their varieties of visage and garb. A Tartar-like picturesqueness;[4] a sort of pagan abandonment and assurance. Here reigned the dashing and all-fusing spirit of the West, whose type is the Mississippi itself, which, uniting the streams of the most distant and opposite zones, pours them along, helter-skelter, in one cosmopolitan and confident tide.

Chapter 3.

IN WHICH A VARIETY OF CHARACTERS APPEAR.

In the forward part of the boat,[5] not the least attractive object, for a time, was a grotesque negro cripple, in tow-cloth attire and an old coal-sifter of a tamborine in his hand, who, owing to something wrong about his legs, was, in effect, cut down to the stature of a Newfoundland dog;[6] his knotted black fleece and good-natured, honest black face rubbing against the upper part of people's thighs as he made shift to shuffle about, making music, such as it was, and raising a smile even from the gravest.[7] It was curious to see him, out of his very deformity, indigence, and houselessness, so cheerily endured, raising mirth in some of that crowd, whose own purses, hearths, hearts, all their possessions, sound limbs included, could not make gay.

3. Anacharsis Cloots (1755–1794), the Prussian-born, Paris-reared Baron Jean Baptiste de Cloots, self-styled "orator of the human race," led a multiracial and multinational deputation into the French National Assembly in 1790 to symbolize the support of the French Revolution by all mankind. He chose the sobriquet Anacharsis in allusion to the ancient "barbaric" Scythian (son of a Greek mother) who visited King Croesus in Athens to learn civilized values. In Cloots's analogy, Prussia is Scythia, and Paris is the new capital of civilization. Ironically, Cloots was executed, in Paris, during the Reign of Terror.
4. Melville thought of the Tartar warriors, rulers of the great plains to the east of the Danube, as recklessly daring horsemen and as archers so powerful they could pull their formidable bows into a semicircle, the shape of an unborn whale (*Moby-Dick*, chapter 87). "Tartar air" (*Moby-Dick*, chapter 13) is a liberating, exalting invitation to wild adventure. Tartary is the present Turkmenistan or Kazakhstan.
5. Where the mute was last seen.
6. For Satan in the shape of a large shaggy black dog see n. 6, p. 224.
7. Contrast Thorpe's straightforward, unironic depiction in his 1855 "Reminiscences of the Mississippi," 37 (see Selected Bibliography): "The negroes of the Mississippi are happy specimens of God's image done up in ebony, and in many lighter colors, and they have frequently a deserved reputation as 'deck-hands.' It is astonishing what an amount of hard work they will perform, and yet retain their vivacity and spirits. If they have the good fortune to be employed on a 'bully boat,' they take a lively personal interest in its success, and become as much a part of the propelling machinery as the engines. Their custom of singing at all important landings, has a pleasing and novel effect, and if stimulated by an appreciative audience, they will roll forth a volume of vocal sounds that, for harmony and pathos, sink into obscurity the best performances of 'imitative Ethiopians' [whites in blackface]."

"What is your name, old boy?" said a purple-faced drover, putting his large purple hand on the cripple's bushy wool, as if it were the curled forehead of a black steer.

"Der Black Guinea dey calls me, sar."

"And who is your master, Guinea?"

"Oh sar, I am der dog widout massa."

"A free dog, eh? Well, on your account, I'm sorry for that, Guinea. Dogs without masters fare hard."

"So dey do, sar; so dey do. But you see, sar, dese here legs? What ge'mman want to own dese here legs?"

"But where do you live?"

"All 'long shore, sar; dough now I'se going to see brodder at der landing; but chiefly I libs in der city."

"St. Louis, ah? Where do you sleep there of nights?"

"On der floor of der good baker's oven, sar."[8]

"In an oven? whose, pray? What baker, I should like to know, bakes such black bread in his oven, alongside of his nice white rolls, too. Who is that too charitable baker, pray?"

"Dar he be," with a broad grin lifting his tambourine high over his head.

"The sun is the baker, eh?"

"Yes sar, in der city dat good baker warms der stones for dis ole darkie when he sleeps out on der pabements o'nights."

"But that must be in the summer only, old boy. How about winter, when the cold Cossacks[9] come clattering and jingling? How about winter, old boy?"

"Den dis poor old darkie shakes werry bad, I tell you, sar. Oh sar, oh! don't speak ob der winter," he added, with a reminiscent shiver, shuffling off into the thickest of the crowd, like a half-frozen black sheep nudging itself a cozy berth in the heart of the white flock.

Thus far not very many pennies had been given him, and, used at last to his strange looks, the less polite passengers of those in that part of the boat began to get their fill of him as a curious object; when suddenly the negro more than revived their first interest by an expedient which, whether by chance or design, was a singular temptation at once to *diversion* and charity, though, even more than his crippled limbs, it put him on a canine footing. In short, as in appearance he seemed a dog, so now, in a merry way, like a dog he began to be treated. Still shuffling among the crowd, now and then

---

8. Another hint of the diabolic nature of the Black Guinea. James Hall in *Notes on the Western States* mentions a Mississippi bluff called the Devil's Bake-oven. See the reference to a bluff called Devil's Joke, at the end of chapter 22.

9. Here, bitterly cold winds or sleet, driving as hard as troops of Cossacks (feared as ferocious cavalrymen) when they rode out on forays from the river Don in the steppes of Russia.

he would pause, throwing back his head and opening his mouth like an elephant for tossed apples at a menagerie; when, making a space before him, people would have a bout at a strange sort of pitch-penny game, the cripple's mouth being at once target and purse, and he hailing each expertly-caught copper with a cracked bravura from his tambourine. To be the subject of alms-giving is trying, and to feel in duty bound to appear cheerfully grateful under the trial, must be still more so; but whatever his secret emotions, he swallowed them, while still retaining each copper this side the œsophagus. And nearly always he grinned, and only once or twice did he wince, which was when certain coins, tossed by more playful almoners, came inconveniently nigh to his teeth, an accident whose unwelcomeness was not unedged by the circumstance that the pennies thus thrown proved buttons.

While this game of charity was yet at its height, a limping, gimlet-eyed, sour-faced person—it may be some discharged custom-house officer,[1] who, suddenly stripped of convenient means of support, had concluded to be avenged on government and humanity by making himself miserable for life, either by hating or suspecting everything and everybody—this shallow unfortunate, after sundry sorry observations of the negro, began to croak out something about his deformity being a sham, got up for financial purposes, which immediately threw a damp upon the frolic benignities of the pitch-penny players.

But that these suspicions came from one who himself on a wooden leg went halt, this did not appear to strike anybody present. That cripples, above all men, should be companionable, or, at least, refrain from picking a fellow-limper to pieces, in short, should have a little sympathy in common misfortune, seemed not to occur to the company.

Meantime, the negro's countenance, before marked with even more than patient good-nature, drooped into a heavy-hearted expression, full of the most painful distress. So far abased beneath its proper physical level, that Newfoundland-dog face turned in passively hopeless appeal, as if instinct told it that the right or the wrong might not have overmuch to do with whatever wayward mood superior intelligences might yield to.

---

1. This reference involves some complicated private joke or jokes, perhaps pertaining to Melville's paternal grandfather, whom Andrew Jackson in 1829 removed from his high post as naval officer in Boston, or Hawthorne, whose removal as the surveyor at the Salem Custom House led to his temporary residence in the Berkshires, or to Melville's own attempts to gain a job in the New York Custom House (beginning in 1847, long before he held the job of customs inspector for nineteen years, from December 1866 through the whole of 1885). Also involved may be Melville's perhaps odd habit of projecting future roles for himself. "Gimlet-eyed": squinted tight, seeming to pierce. "Gimlet": a tool for boring, consisting of a cross-handle at the top—like that on a corkscrew—and a grooved shaft.

But instinct, though knowing, is yet a teacher set below reason, which itself says, in the grave words of Lysander in the comedy, after Puck has made a sage of him with his spell:—[2]

"The will of man is by his reason swayed."

So that, suddenly change as people may, in their dispositions, it is not always waywardness, but improved judgment, which, as in Lysander's case, or the present, operates with them.

Yes, they began to scrutinize the negro curiously enough; when, emboldened by this evidence of the efficacy of his words, the wooden-legged man hobbled up to the negro, and, with the air of a beadle, would, to prove his alleged imposture on the spot, have stripped him and then driven him away, but was prevented by the crowd's clamor, now taking part with the poor fellow, against one who had just before turned nearly all minds the other way. So he with the wooden leg was forced to retire; when the rest, finding themselves left sole judges in the case, could not resist the opportunity of acting the part: not because it is a human weakness to take pleasure in sitting in judgment upon one in a box, as surely this unfortunate negro now was, but that it strangely sharpens human perceptions, when, instead of standing by and having their fellow-feelings touched by the sight of an alleged culprit severely handled by some one justiciary, a crowd suddenly come to be all justiciaries in the same case themselves; as in Arkansas once, a man proved guilty, by law, of murder, but whose condemnation was deemed unjust by the people, so that they rescued him to try him themselves; whereupon, they, as it turned out, found him even guiltier than the court had done, and forthwith proceeded to execution; so that the gallows presented the truly warning spectacle of a man hanged by his friends.

But not to such extremities, or anything like them, did the present crowd come; they, for the time, being content with putting the

---

2. Shakespeare's A Midsummer Night's Dream 2.2.115. Lysander's courtship of Helena (and rejection of Hermia) while under the power of Puck's magical flower juice: "The will of man is by his reason swayed; / And reason says you are the worthier maid." (Quotations from Shakespeare in the footnotes are from Melville's 1837 Hilliard, Gray seven-volume edition.) What Lysander calls "reason" is drug-induced and only temporary. Melville's reading of this passage reappears in his first lecture "Statues in Rome," where the Boston Evening Traveller (December 3, 1857) quoted him as asserting that "science is beneath art, just as the instinct is beneath reason," an echo of Lysander's words. "The problem is not so much to establish what Melville said but what he thought he meant by it, for the context in The Confidence-Man is suffused with ironies—the Black Guinea's face is turned in passively hopeless appeal, 'as if' instinct told it something; and Lysander's words rejecting one lover for another are described as 'grave' words, 'after Puck has made a sage of him with his spell' " (Parker 2:362). The allusion to A Midsummer Night's Dream, set in Athens and woods nearby, may remind the reader that in that play Nick Bottom, the weaver, is given the head of an ass—a partial and temporary metamorphosis, unlike the complete shape changing that occurs elsewhere in The Confidence-Man.

negro fairly and discreetly to the question; among other things, asking him, had he any documentary proof, any plain paper about him, attesting that his case was not a spurious one.

"No, no, dis poor ole darkie haint none o' dem waloable papers," he wailed.

"But is there not some one who can speak a good word for you?" here said a person newly arrived from another part of the boat, a young Episcopal clergyman, in a long, straight-bodied black coat; small in stature, but manly; with a clear face and blue eye; innocence, tenderness, and good sense triumvirate in his air.

"Oh yes, oh yes, ge'mmen," he eagerly answered, as if his memory, before suddenly frozen up by cold charity, as suddenly thawed back into fluidity at the first kindly word.[3] "Oh yes, oh yes, dar is aboard here a werry nice, good ge'mman wid a weed,[4] and a ge'mman in a gray coat and white tie, what knows all about me; and a ge'mman wid a big book, too; and a yarb-doctor; and a ge'mman in a yaller west; and a ge'mman wid a brass plate; and a ge'mman in a wiolet robe; and a ge'mman as is a sodjer; and ever so many good, kind, honest ge'mmen more aboard what knows me and will speak for me, God bress 'em; yes, and what knows me as well as dis poor old darkie knows hisself,[5] God bress him! Oh, find 'em, find 'em," he earnestly added, "and let 'em come quick, and show you all, ge'mmen, dat dis poor ole darkie is werry well wordy of all you kind ge'mmen's kind confidence."

"But how are we to find all these people in this great crowd?" was the question of a bystander, umbrella in hand; a middle-aged person, a country merchant apparently, whose natural good-feeling had been made at least cautious by the unnatural ill-feeling of the discharged custom-house officer.

"Where are we to find them?" half-rebukefully echoed the young Episcopal clergyman. "I will go find one to begin with," he quickly added, and, with kind haste suiting the action to the word, away he went.

"Wild goose chase!" croaked he with the wooden leg, now again drawing nigh. "Don't believe there's a soul of them aboard. Did ever beggar have such heaps of fine friends? He can walk fast enough when he tries, a good deal faster than I; but he can lie yet faster. He's some white operator, betwisted and painted up for a decoy. He and his friends are all humbugs."

---

3. What follows seems intended as a complete list of the successive disguises of the Confidence Man, but it does not quite jibe with the text as it stands. Melville may later have altered his plan without changing this list.
4. A band of mourning crape, here worn on a man's hat.
5. Not the last time the Confidence Man taunts his listeners with double entendres like "know me as well as dis poor old darkie knows hisself."

"Have you no charity, friend?" here in self-subdued tones, singularly contrasted with his unsubdued person, said a Methodist
minister, advancing; a tall, muscular, martial-looking man, a Ten-
nessean by birth, who in the Mexican war had been volunteer
chaplain to a volunteer rifle-regiment.[6]

"Charity is one thing, and truth is another," rejoined he with the
wooden leg: "he's a rascal, I say."

"But why not, friend, put as charitable a construction as one can
upon the poor fellow?" said the soldier-like Methodist, with increased difficulty maintaining a pacific demeanor towards one
whose own asperity seemed so little to entitle him to it: "he looks
honest, don't he?"

"Looks are one thing, and facts are another," snapped out the
other perversely; "and as to your constructions, what construction
can you put upon a rascal, but that a rascal he is?"

"Be not such a Canada thistle,"[7] urged the Methodist, with
something less of patience than before. "Charity, man, charity."

"To where it belongs with your charity! to heaven with it!" again
snapped out the other, diabolically; "here on earth, true charity
dotes, and false charity plots. Who betrays a fool with a kiss,[8] the
charitable fool has the charity to believe is in love with him, and
the charitable knave on the stand gives charitable testimony for his
comrade in the box."

"Surely, friend," returned the noble Methodist, with much ado
restraining his still waxing indignation—"surely, to say the least,
you forget yourself. Apply it home," he continued, with exterior
calmness tremulous with inkept emotion. "Suppose, now, I should
exercise no charity in judging your own character by the words
which have fallen from you; what sort of vile, pitiless man do you
think I would take you for?"

"No doubt"—with a grin—"some such pitiless man as has lost his
piety in much the same way that the jockey loses his honesty."

"And how is that, friend?" still conscientiously holding back

---

6. Here high church Episcopalians are depicted as more effete, Methodists as more muscular. In Boston after the Revolution, Unitarians took over what had been the chief Anglican (Church of England) house of worship, and Northern Episcopalians for many
   years were suspected of being not quite American in their religion or even as being
   quasi-Catholics. (In 1849 at the christening of Melville's niece in an Episcopalian
   church in Manhattan, one of the Dutch Church Van Rensselaer cousins saw worshipers
   making the sign of the Cross and fled in horror, unwilling to attend the party held afterward in the Melville house.)

7. An aggressive creeping perennial weed capable of taking over whole pastures and tilled
   fields.

8. Knowing that the chief priests in Jerusalem were plotting how to "take Jesus by subtilty,
   and kill him," Judas, one of Jesus' twelve disciples, went to them after the Passover supper and in the dark led "a multitude with swords and staves" to Gethsemane, on the
   Mount of Olives, where Jesus had gone to pray. See Matthew 26.48–49: "Now he that
   betrayed him gave them a sign, saying, Whomsoever I shall kiss, that same is he: hold
   him fast. And forthwith he came to Jesus, and said, Hail, master; and kissed him."

the old Adam[9] in him, as if it were a mastiff he had by the neck.

"Never you mind how it is"—with a sneer; "but all horses aint virtuous, no more than all men kind; and come close to, and much dealt with, some things are catching. When you find me a virtuous jockey, I will find you a benevolent wise man."

"Some insinuation there."

"More fool you that are puzzled by it."

"Reprobate!" cried the other, his indignation now at last almost boiling over; "godless reprobate! if charity did not restrain me, I could call you by names you deserve."

"Could you, indeed?" with an insolent sneer.

"Yea, and teach you charity on the spot," cried the goaded Methodist, suddenly catching this exasperating opponent by his shabby coat-collar, and shaking him till his timber-toe clattered on the deck like a nine-pin.[1] "You took me for a non-combatant did you?—thought, seedy coward that you are, that you could abuse a Christian with impunity. You find your mistake"—with another hearty shake.

"Well said and better done, church militant!" cried a voice.

"The white cravat against the world!" cried another.

"Bravo, bravo!" chorused many voices, with like enthusiasm taking sides with the resolute champion.

"You fools!" cried he with the wooden leg, writhing himself loose and inflamedly turning upon the throng; "you flock of fools, under this captain of fools, in this ship of fools!"[2]

With which exclamations, followed by idle threats against his admonisher, this condign victim to justice hobbled away, as disdaining to hold further argument with such a rabble. But his scorn was more than repaid by the hisses that chased him, in which the brave Methodist, satisfied with the rebuke already administered, was, to omit still better reasons, too magnanimous to join. All he said was, pointing towards the departing recusant, "There he shambles off on his one lone leg, emblematic of his one-sided view of humanity."

"But trust your painted decoy," retorted the other from a distance, pointing back to the black cripple, "and I have my revenge."

"But we aint agoing to trust him!" shouted back a voice.

9. Not simply a reference to the biblical first man but also a theological term for Original Sin, as in "Bartleby."

1. However admirable by secular standards, this representative of muscular Christianity is, by Melville's biblical standards, weighed and found wanting. See Melville's *Pierre* (1852), Book XIV, "The Journey and the Pamphlet," where Melville holds up the worldliness of "professed Christian nations" in contrast to the ideal, other-worldly behavior enjoined in Jesus' words in his Sermon on the Mount (Matthew 5.39): "I say unto you, That ye resist not evil: but whosoever shall smite thee on thy right cheek, turn to him the other also." See pp. 381–85 herein.

2. If only in the form of popular woodcuts, including one by Albrecht Durer, Melville may have known something about the German poet Sebastian Brant's 1494 "Narrenschiff" and the Scottish poet Alexander Barclay's 1509 translation (as "Ship of Fools").

"So much the better," he jeered back. "Look you," he added, coming to a dead halt where he was; "look you, I have been called a Canada thistle. Very good. And a seedy one: still better. And the seedy Canada thistle has been pretty well shaken among ye: best of all. Dare say some seed has been shaken out; and won't it spring though? And when it does spring, do you cut down the young thistles, and won't they spring the more? It's encouraging and coaxing 'em. Now, when with my thistles your farms shall be well stocked, why then—you may abandon 'em!"

"What does all that mean, now?" asked the country merchant, staring.

"Nothing; the foiled wolf's parting howl," said the Methodist. "Spleen, much spleen, which is the rickety child of his evil heart of unbelief: it has made him mad. I suspect him for one naturally reprobate. Oh, friends," raising his arms as in the pulpit, "oh beloved, how are we admonished by the melancholy spectacle of this raver. Let us profit by the lesson; and is it not this: that if, next to mistrusting Providence, there be aught that man should pray against, it is against mistrusting his fellow-man. I have been in mad-houses full of tragic mopers, and seen there the end of suspicion: the cynic, in the moody madness muttering in the corner; for years a barren fixture there; head lopped over, gnawing his own lip, vulture of himself; while, by fits and starts, from the corner opposite came the grimace of the idiot at him."

"What an example," whispered one.

"Might deter Timon,"[3] was the response.

"Oh, oh, good ge'mmen, have you no confidence in dis poor ole darkie?" now wailed the returning negro, who, during the late scene, had stumped apart in alarm.

"Confidence in you?" echoed he who had whispered, with abruptly changed air turning short round; "that remains to be seen."

"I tell you what it is, Ebony," in similarly changed tones said he who had responded to the whisperer, "yonder churl," pointing toward the wooden leg in the distance, "is, no doubt, a churlish fellow enough, and I would not wish to be like him; but that is no reason why you may not be some sort of black Jeremy Diddler."[4]

"No confidence in dis poor ole darkie, den?"

---

3. The bounteous host turned misanthrope in Shakespeare's *Timon of Athens*, called by Melville in his essay on Nathaniel Hawthorne's *Mosses from an Old Manse* one of the "dark characters" (Hamlet, Timon, Lear, and Iago) through whom Shakespeare "craftily says, or sometimes insinuates the things, which we feel to be so terrifically true, that it were all but madness for any good man, in his own proper character, to utter, or even hint of them" (2001 NCE of *Moby-Dick*, 522).

4. Swindler, from the name of the penniless borrower in *Raising the Wind* (1803), by the English playwright James Kenney.

"Before giving you our confidence," said a third, "we will wait the report of the kind gentleman who went in search of one of your friends who was to speak for you."

"Very likely, in that case," said a fourth, "we shall wait here till Christmas. Shouldn't wonder, did we not see that kind gentleman again. After seeking awhile in vain, he will conclude he has been made a fool of, and so not return to us for pure shame. Fact is, I begin to feel a little qualmish about the darkie myself. Something queer about this darkie, depend upon it."

Once more the negro wailed, and turning in despair from the last speaker, imploringly caught the Methodist by the skirt of his coat. But a change had come over that before impassioned intercessor. With an irresolute and troubled air, he mutely eyed the suppliant; against whom, somehow, by what seemed instinctive influences, the distrusts first set on foot were now generally reviving, and, if anything, with added severity.

"No confidence in dis poor ole darkie," yet again wailed the negro, letting go the coat-skirts and turning appealingly all round him.

"Yes, my poor fellow, *I* have confidence in you," now exclaimed the country merchant before named, whom the negro's appeal, coming so piteously on the heel of pitilessness, seemed at last humanely to have decided in his favor. "And here, here is some proof of my trust," with which, tucking his umbrella under his arm, and diving down his hand into his pocket, he fished forth a purse, and, accidentally, along with it, his business card, which, unobserved, dropped to the deck. "Here, here, my poor fellow," he continued, extending a half dollar.

Not more grateful for the coin than the kindness, the cripple's face glowed like a polished copper saucepan, and shuffling a pace nigher, with one upstretched hand he received the alms, while, as unconsciously, his one advanced leather stump covered the card.

Done in despite of the general sentiment, the good deed of the merchant was not, perhaps, without its unwelcome return from the crowd, since that good deed seemed somehow to convey to them a sort of reproach. Still again, and more pertinaciously than ever, the cry arose against the negro, and still again he wailed forth his lament and appeal; among other things, repeating that the friends, of whom already he had partially run off the list, would freely speak for him, would anybody go find them.

"Why don't you go find 'em yourself?" demanded a gruff boatman.

"How can I go find 'em myself? Dis poor ole game-legged darkie's friends must come to him. Oh, whar, whar is dat good friend of dis darkie's, dat good man wid de weed?"

At this point, a steward ringing a bell came along, summoning all persons who had not got their tickets to step to the captain's office; an announcement which speedily thinned the throng about the black cripple, who himself soon forlornly stumped out of sight, probably on much the same errand as the rest.

Chapter 4.

RENEWAL OF OLD ACQUAINTANCE.[5]

"How do you do, Mr. Roberts?"

"Eh?"

"Don't you know me?"

"No, certainly."

The crowd about the captain's office, having in good time melted away, the above encounter took place in one of the side balconies astern, between a man in mourning clean and respectable, but none of the glossiest, a long weed on his hat, and the country-merchant before-mentioned, whom, with the familiarity of an old acquaintance, the former had accosted.

"Is it possible, my dear sir," resumed he with the weed, "that you do not recall my countenance? why yours I recall distinctly as if but half an hour, instead of half an age, had passed since I saw you. Don't you recall me, now? Look harder."

"In my conscience—truly—I protest," honestly bewildered, "bless my soul, sir, I don't know you—really, really. But stay, stay," he hurriedly added, not without gratification, glancing up at the crape on the stranger's hat, "stay—yes—seems to me, though I have not the pleasure of personally knowing you, yet I am pretty sure I have at least *heard* of you, and recently too, quite recently. A poor negro aboard here referred to you, among others, for a character, I think."

"Oh, the cripple. Poor fellow, I know him well. They found me. I have said all I could for him. I think I abated their distrust. Would I could have been of more substantial service. And apropos, sir," he added, "now that it strikes me, allow me to ask, whether the circumstance of one man, however humble, referring for a character to another man, however afflicted, does not argue more or less of moral worth in the latter?"

The good merchant looked puzzled.

"Still you don't recall my countenance?"

"Still does truth compel me to say that I cannot, despite my best efforts," was the reluctantly-candid reply.

"Can I be so changed? Look at me. Or is it I who am mis-

5. The title is loaded, since Roberts has just met the Confidence Man in the guise of the Black Guinea. Double entendres follow, such as "Poor fellow, I know him well."

taken?—Are you not, sir, Henry Roberts, forwarding merchant, of Wheeling, Virginia?[6] Pray, now, if you use the advertisement of business cards, and happen to have one with you, just look at it, and see whether you are not the man I take you for."

"Why," a bit chafed, perhaps, "I hope I know myself."

"And yet self-knowledge is thought by some not so easy. Who knows, my dear sir, but for a time you may have taken yourself for somebody else? Stranger things have happened."

The good merchant stared.

"To come to particulars, my dear sir, I met you, now some six years back, at Brade Brothers & Co.'s office, I think. I was traveling for a Philadelphia house. The senior Brade introduced us, you remember; some business-chat followed, then you forced me home with you to a family tea, and a family time we had. Have you forgotten about the urn, and what I said about Werter's Charlotte,[7] and the bread and butter, and that capital story you told of the large loaf. A hundred times since, I have laughed over it. At least you must recall my name—Ringman, John Ringman."

"Large loaf? Invited you to tea? Ringman? Ringman? Ring? Ring?"

"Ah sir," sadly smiling, "don't ring the changes that way. I see you have a faithless memory, Mr. Roberts. But trust in the faithfulness of mine."

"Well, to tell the truth, in some things my memory aint of the very best," was the honest rejoinder. "But still," he perplexedly added, "still I—"

"Oh sir, suffice it that it is as I say. Doubt not that we are all well acquainted."

"But—but I don't like this going dead against my own memory; I—"

"But didn't you admit, my dear sir, that in some things this memory of yours is a little faithless? Now, those who have faithless memories, should they not have some little confidence in the less faithless memories of others?"

6. In the first edition, "Pennsylvania" was an error for "Virginia," probably from a misreading of Melville's abbreviation (*Va.* and *Pa.* were both currently acceptable). Founded by Virginians in 1769–70, the city became part of the newly formed West Virginia only later, when western counties that had voted against secession at the beginning of the Civil War created their own government and were admitted to the Union as a separate state in 1863.

7. In Goethe's epistolary novel of romantic tragedy *The Sorrows of Young Werther* (1774, final version 1787), Werther falls in love with Charlotte. William Makepeace Thackeray's parody, "The Sorrows of Werther," targets for satire sudden extravagant romantic posturing: "Werther had a love for Charlotte / Such as words could never utter; / Would you know how first he met her? / She was cutting bread and butter." She "was married," and he "was moral," so (after various extreme reactions) Werther "blew his silly brains out." Charlotte sees his body borne before her on a shutter, but "Like a well-conducted person" she goes on "cutting bread and butter."

"But, of this friendly chat and tea, I have not the slightest—"

"I see, I see; quite erased from the tablet. Pray, sir," with a sudden illumination, "about six years back, did it happen to you to receive any injury on the head? Surprising effects have arisen from such a cause. Not alone unconsciousness as to events for a greater or less time immediately subsequent to the injury, but likewise—strange to add—oblivion, entire and incurable, as to events embracing a longer or shorter period immediately preceding it; that is, when the mind at the time was perfectly sensible of them, and fully competent also to register them in the memory, and did in fact so do; but all in vain, for all was afterwards bruised out by the injury."

After the first start, the merchant listened with what appeared more than ordinary interest. The other proceeded:

"In my boyhood I was kicked by a horse, and lay insensible for a long time. Upon recovering, what a blank! No faintest trace in regard to how I had come near the horse, or what horse it was, or where it was, or that it was a horse at all that had brought me to that pass. For the knowledge of those particulars I am indebted solely to my friends, in whose statements, I need not say, I place implicit reliance, since particulars of some sort there must have been, and why should they deceive me? You see, sir, the mind is ductile, very much so: but images, ductilely received into it, need a certain time to harden and bake in their impressions, otherwise such a casualty as I speak of will in an instant obliterate them, as though they had never been. We are but clay, sir, potter's clay, as the good book says, clay, feeble, and too-yielding clay.[8] But I will not philosophize. Tell me, was it your misfortune to receive any concussion upon the brain about the period I speak of? If so, I will with pleasure supply the void in your memory by more minutely rehearsing the circumstances of our acquaintance."

The growing interest betrayed by the merchant had not relaxed as the other proceeded. After some hesitation, indeed, something more than hesitation, he confessed that, though he had never received any injury of the sort named, yet, about the time in question, he had in fact been taken with a brain fever, losing his mind completely for a considerable interval. He was continuing, when the stranger with much animation exclaimed:

---

8. Isaiah 64.8: "But now, O Lord, thou art our father; we are the clay, and thou our potter; and we all are the work of thy hand." On the *Fidèle*, as in much satanic lore, the Devil quotes Scripture for his purposes, as in Matthew 4.6 when he takes Jesus up to the pinnacle of the temple and quotes Psalm 91.12 to him, tempting him to test God: "If thou be the Son of God, cast thyself down: for it is written, He shall give his angels charge concerning thee: and in their hands they shall bear thee up, lest at any time thou dash thy foot against a stone." In Shakespeare's *Merchant of Venice* 1.3.98 Antonio tells Bassanio "The devil can cite Scripture for his purpose."

"There now, you see, I was not wholly mistaken. That brain fever accounts for it all."

"Nay; but—"

"Pardon me, Mr. Roberts," respectfully interrupting him, "but time is short, and I have something private and particular to say to you. Allow me."

Mr. Roberts, good man, could but acquiesce, and the two having silently walked to a less public spot, the manner of the man with the weed suddenly assumed a seriousness almost painful. What might be called a writhing expression stole over him. He seemed struggling with some disastrous necessity inkept. He made one or two attempts to speak, but words seemed to choke him. His companion stood in humane surprise, wondering what was to come. At length, with an effort mastering his feelings, in a tolerably composed tone he spoke:

"If I remember, you are a mason,[9] Mr. Roberts?"

"Yes, yes."

Averting himself a moment, as to recover from a return of agitation, the stranger grasped the other's hand; "and would you not loan a brother a shilling if he needed it?"

The merchant started, apparently, almost as if to retreat.

"Ah, Mr. Roberts, I trust you are not one of those business men, who make a business of never having to do with unfortunates. For God's sake don't leave me. I have something on my heart— on my heart. Under deplorable circumstances thrown among strangers, utter strangers, I want a friend in whom I may confide. Yours, Mr. Roberts, is almost the first known face I've seen for many weeks."

It was so sudden an outburst; the interview offered such a contrast to the scene around, that the merchant, though not used to be very indiscreet, yet, being not entirely inhumane, remained not entirely unmoved.

The other, still tremulous, resumed:

"I need not say, sir, how it cuts me to the soul, to follow up a social salutation with such words as have just been mine. I know that I jeopardize your good opinion. But I can't help it: necessity knows no law, and heeds no risk. Sir, we are masons, one more step aside; I will tell you my story."

In a low, half-suppressed tone, he began it. Judging from his auditor's expression, it seemed to be a tale of singular interest, involv-

9. One ploy of the "Original Confidence Man" in 1849 was to win the confidence of a victim by identifying himself as a fellow Mason. Melville's paternal grandfather was a prominent Mason; the anti-Masonic Party was a contentious part of the political background of his youth; and ritualistic secrecy involving what purported to be ancient Egyptian symbols appealed to Melville's sense of the abiding mysteries of the universe.

ing calamities against which no integrity, no forethought, no energy, no genius, no piety, could guard.

At every disclosure, the hearer's commiseration increased. No sentimental pity. As the story went on, he drew from his wallet a bank note, but after a while, at some still more unhappy revelation, changed it for another, probably of a somewhat larger amount;[1] which, when the story was concluded, with an air studiously disclamatory of almsgiving, he put into the stranger's hands; who, on his side, with an air studiously disclamatory of alms-taking, put it into his pocket.

Assistance being received, the stranger's manner assumed a kind and degree of decorum which, under the circumstances, seemed almost coldness. After some words, not over ardent, and yet not exactly inappropriate, he took leave, making a bow which had one knows not what of a certain chastened independence about it; as if misery, however burdensome, could not break down self-respect, nor gratitude, however deep, humiliate a gentleman.

He was hardly yet out of sight, when he paused as if thinking; then with hastened steps returning to the merchant, "I am just reminded that the president, who is also transfer-agent, of the Black Rapids Coal Company, happens to be on board here, and, having been subpœnaed as witness in a stock case on the docket in Kentucky, has his transfer-book with him. A month since, in a panic contrived by artful alarmists, some credulous stock-holders sold out; but, to frustrate the aim of the alarmists, the Company, previously advised of their scheme, so managed it as to get into its own hands those sacrificed shares, resolved that, since a spurious panic must be, the panic-makers should be no gainers by it. The Company, I hear, is now ready, but not anxious, to redispose of those shares; and having obtained them at their depressed value, will now sell them at par, though, prior to the panic, they were held at a handsome figure above. That the readiness of the Company to do this is not generally known, is shown by the fact that the stock still stands on the transfer-book in the Company's name, offering to one in funds a rare chance for investment. For, the panic subsiding more and more every day, it will daily be seen how it originated; confidence will be more than restored; there will be a reaction; from the stock's descent its rise will be higher than from no fall, the holders trusting themselves to fear no second fate."[2]

---

1. Possibly a recollection of the scene in Franklin's autobiography in which Whitefield's sermon progressively enlarges the amount Franklin decides that he will donate to a Georgia orphanage. Franklin was much in Melville's mind in the mid-1850s, as *Israel Potter* (serialized 1854–55) shows.
2. As Henry F. Pommer pointed out in *Milton and Melville* (1950), this is an echo of *Paradise Lost* (2.14–17): "From this descent / Celestial virtues rising, will appear / More glorious and more dread than from no fall, / And trust themselves to fear no second fate." Stock in Hell is so good that holders should weather out any temporary panics, such as those during religious revivals. Pommer's acute ear caught many of Melville's echoes of Milton, as verified by Melville's copy of Milton's poetry, which was discovered in the

Having listened at first with curiosity, at last with interest, the merchant replied to the effect, that some time since, through friends concerned with it, he had heard of the company, and heard well of it, but was ignorant that there had latterly been fluctuations. He added that he was no speculator; that hitherto he had avoided having to do with stocks of any sort, but in the present case he really felt something like being tempted. "Pray," in conclusion, "do you think that upon a pinch anything could be transacted on board here with the transfer-agent? Are you acquainted with him?"

"Not personally. I but happened to hear that he was a passenger. For the rest, though it might be somewhat informal, the gentleman might not object to doing a little business on board. Along the Mississippi, you know, business is not so ceremonious as at the East."

"True," returned the merchant, and looked down a moment in thought, then, raising his head quickly, said, in a tone not so benign as his wonted one, "This would seem a rare chance, indeed; why, upon first hearing it, did you not snatch at it? I mean for yourself!"

"I?—would it had been possible!"

Not without some emotion was this said, and not without some embarrassment was the reply. "Ah, yes, I had forgotten."

Upon this, the stranger regarded him with mild gravity, not a little disconcerting; the more so, as there was in it what seemed the aspect not alone of the superior, but, as it were, the rebuker; which sort of bearing, in a beneficiary towards his benefactor, looked strangely enough; none the less, that, somehow, it sat not altogether unbecomingly upon the beneficiary, being free from anything like the appearance of assumption, and mixed with a kind of painful conscientiousness, as though nothing but a proper sense of what he owed to himself swayed him. At length he spoke:

"To reproach a penniless man with remissness in not availing himself of an opportunity for pecuniary investment—but, no, no; it was forgetfulness; and this, charity will impute to some lingering effect of that unfortunate brain-fever, which, as to occurrences dating yet further back, disturbed Mr. Roberts's memory still more seriously."

"As to that," said the merchant, rallying, "I am not—"

"Pardon me, but you must admit, that just now, an unpleasant distrust, however vague, was yours. Ah, shallow as it is, yet, how subtle a thing is suspicion, which at times can invade the human-

---

1980s and is now at Princeton University. Melville in fact underlined the last two lines in this passage, "More glorious" through "second fate." See Robin Grey and Douglas Robillard, in consultation with Hershel Parker, "Melville's Milton: A Transcription of Melville's Marginalia in His Copy of The Poetical Works of John Milton," Leviathan 4 (March/October 2002), 128.

est[3] of hearts and wisest of heads. But, enough. My object, sir, in calling your attention to this stock, is by way of acknowledgment of your goodness. I but seek to be grateful; if my information leads to nothing, you must remember the motive."

He bowed, and finally retired, leaving Mr. Roberts not wholly without self-reproach, for having momentarily indulged injurious thoughts against one who, it was evident, was possessed of a self-respect which forbade his indulging them himself.

Chapter 5.

THE MAN WITH THE WEED MAKES IT AN EVEN QUESTION WHETHER HE BE A GREAT SAGE OR A GREAT SIMPLETON.

"Well, there is sorrow in the world, but goodness too; and goodness that is not greenness, either, no more than sorrow is. Dear good man. Poor beating heart!"

It was the man with the weed, not very long after quitting the merchant, murmuring to himself with his hand to his side like one with the heart-disease.

Meditation over kindness received seemed to have softened him something, too, it may be, beyond what might, perhaps, have been looked for from one whose unwonted self-respect in the hour of need, and in the act of being aided, might have appeared to some not wholly unlike pride out of place; and pride, in any place, is seldom very feeling. But the truth, perhaps, is, that those who are least touched with that vice, besides being not unsusceptible to goodness, are sometimes the ones whom a ruling sense of propriety makes appear cold, if not thankless, under a favor. For, at such a time, to be full of warm, earnest words, and heart-felt protestations, is to create a scene; and well-bred people dislike few things more than that; which would seem to look as if the world did not relish earnestness; but, not so; because the world, being earnest itself, likes an earnest scene, and an earnest man, very well, but only in their place—the stage. See what sad work they make of it, who, ignorant of this, flame out in Irish enthusiasm[4] and with Irish sincerity, to a benefactor, who, if a man of sense and respectability, as well as kindliness, can but be more or less annoyed by it; and, if of a nervously fastidious nature, as some are, may be led to think almost as much less favorably of the beneficiary paining him by his gratitude, as if he had been guilty of its contrary, instead only of an indiscretion. But, beneficiaries who know better, though they may feel as much, if not

3. Here, most humane, most kindly (but perhaps with a reminder that the human form is subject to shape changes).
4. In the stereotype, overly extravagant enthusiasm.

more, neither inflict such pain, nor are inclined to run any risk of so doing. And these, being wise, are the majority. By which one sees how inconsiderate those persons are, who, from the absence of its officious manifestations in the world, complain that there is not much gratitude extant; when the truth is, that there is as much of it as there is of modesty; but, both being for the most part votarists of the shade,[5] for the most part keep out of sight.

What started this was, to account, if necessary, for the changed air of the man with the weed, who, throwing off in private the cold garb of decorum, and so giving warmly loose to his genuine heart, seemed almost transformed into another being.[6] This subdued air of softness, too, was toned with melancholy, melancholy unreserved; a thing which, however at variance with propriety, still the more attested his earnestness; for one knows not how it is, but it sometimes happens that, where earnestness is, there, also, is melancholy.

At the time, he was leaning over the rail at the boat's side, in his pensiveness, unmindful of another pensive figure near—a young gentleman with a swan-neck, wearing a lady-like open shirt collar, thrown back, and tied with a black ribbon. From a square, tableted broach, curiously engraved with Greek characters, he seemed a collegian—not improbably, a sophomore—on his travels; possibly, his first. A small book bound in Roman vellum was in his hand.

Overhearing his murmuring neighbor, the youth regarded him with some surprise, not to say interest. But, singularly for a collegian, being apparently of a retiring nature, he did not speak; when the other still more increased his diffidence by changing from soliloquy to colloquy, in a manner strangely mixed of familiarity and pathos.

"Ah, who is this? You did not hear me, my young friend, did you? Why, you, too, look sad. My melancholy is not catching!"

"Sir, sir," stammered the other.

"Pray, now," with a sort of sociable sorrowfulness, slowly sliding along the rail,[7] "Pray, now, my young friend, what volume have you there? Give me leave," gently drawing it from him. "Tacitus"[8] Then opening it at random, read: "In general a black and shameful period

5. *1 Henry the Fourth* 1.2.26, where Prince Hal's companion Falstaff (punning on "booty") asks the prince not to call robbers (like Falstaff) by their proper name when he becomes king: "let us not us that are squires of the night's body be called thieves of the day's beauty: let us be Diana's foresters, gentlemen of the shade, minions of the moon."
6. Another suggestion that supernatural transformations may be at work.
7. This sliding imagery is an early link between the Confidence Man and the serpent, which was "more subtil than any beast of the field" (Genesis 3.1). See the allusion to Genesis 3.14 at the end of chapter 23.
8. Cornelius Tacitus (55?–120?), historian of imperial Rome. His view of Roman society, which suggests how men must react when faced with tyranny, is pessimistic and can be contrasted with the more positive picture offered by his contemporary, Pliny the Younger.

lies before me."[9] "Dear young sir," touching his arm alarmedly, "don't read this book. It is poison, moral poison. Even were there truth in Tacitus, such truth would have the operation of falsity, and so still be poison, moral poison. Too well I know this Tacitus. In my college-days he came near souring me into cynicism. Yes, I began to turn down my collar, and go about with a disdainfully joyless expression."

"Sir, sir, I—I—"

"Trust me. Now, young friend, perhaps you think that Tacitus, like me, is only melancholy; but he's more—he's ugly. A vast difference, young sir, between the melancholy view and the ugly. The one may show the world still beautiful, not so the other. The one may be compatible with benevolence, the other not. The one may deepen insight, the other shallows it. Drop Tacitus. Phrenologically, my young friend, you would seem to have a well-developed head, and large; but cribbed within the ugly view, the Tacitus view, your large brain, like your large ox in the contracted field, will but starve the more. And don't dream, as some of you students may, that, by taking this same ugly view, the deeper meanings of the deeper books will so alone become revealed to you. Drop Tacitus. His subtlety is falsity. To him, in his double-refined anatomy of human nature, is well applied the Scripture saying—'There is a subtle man, and the same is deceived.'[1] Drop Tacitus. Come, now, let me throw the book overboard."

"Sir, I—I—"

"Not a word; I know just what is in your mind, and that is just what I am speaking to. Yes, learn from me that, though the sorrows of the world are great, its wickedness—that is, its ugliness—is small. Much cause to pity man, little to distrust him. I myself have

9. Helen P. Trimpi first located this passage at the end of book 3, section 65, in the *Annals*, in *The Works of Cornelius Tacitus with an Essay on His Life and Genius*, trans. Arthur Murphy (reprinted 1822), 1.327; also n. 5, p. 349 herein. The passage in the *Annals* reads: "In general, a black and shameful period lies before me. The age was sunk to the lowest depth of sordid adulation; insomuch that not only the most illustrious citizens, in order to secure their preeminence, were obliged to crouch and bend the knee; but men of consular and praetorian rank, and the whole body of the senate, tried with emulation which should be the most obsequious slave. We are informed by tradition that Tiberius, as often as he went from the senate house, was used to say in Greek, 'Devoted men! how they rush headlong into bondage!' Even he, the enemy of civil liberty, was disgusted with adulation: he played the tyrant, and despised the voluntary slave." *Devoted* carries the meaning of "doomed."

1. As Foster says, "not an exact quotation but apparently a way of referring the reader to a passage in Ecclesiasticus 19 that suits the colloquy between the man in mourning and the sophomore." Melville possessed a Bible that included the Old Testament and New Testament and "the books called Apocrypha," as the King James translators called the books that were not considered fully canonical. In the Apocrypha see Ecclesiasticus 19.25–27: "There is an exquisite subtilty, and the same is unjust; and there is one that turneth aside to make judgment appear; and there is a wise man that justifieth in judgment. There is a wicked man that hangeth down his head sadly; but inwardly he is full of deceit. Casting down his countenance, and making as if he heard not: where he is not known, he will do thee a mischief before thou be aware."

known adversity, and know it still. But for that, do I turn cynic? No, no: it is small beer that sours. To my fellow-creatures I owe alleviations. So, whatever I may have undergone, it but deepens my confidence in my kind. Now, then" (winningly), "this book—will you let me drown it for you?"

"Really, sir—I—"

"I see, I see. But of course you read Tacitus in order to aid you in understanding human nature—as if truth was ever got at by libel. My young friend, if to know human nature is your object, drop Tacitus and go north to the cemeteries of Auburn and Greenwood."[2]

"Upon my word, I—I—"

"Nay, I foresee all that. But you carry Tacitus, that shallow Tacitus. What do *I* carry? See"—producing a pocket-volume—"Akenside—his 'Pleasures of Imagination.'[3] One of these days you will know it. Whatever our lot, we should read serene and cheery books, fitted to inspire love and trust. But Tacitus! I have long been of opinion that these classics are the bane of colleges; for—not to hint of the immorality of Ovid, Horace, Anacreon,[4] and the rest, and the dangerous theology of Eschylus[5] and others—where will one find views so injurious to human nature as in Thucydides, Juvenal, Lucian,[6] but more particularly Tacitus? When I consider

2. In Brooklyn, New York, a notable example of a beautiful recreational cemetery designed with elegant vistas and charming paths for families to walk in and drive through in carriages, recreating themselves while honoring the dead. Mount Auburn in Cambridge, Massachusetts, near Harvard, was a rural cemetery and arboretum. During the planning of Central Park in the 1850s a belief was articulated that such landscapes would lead to physical and moral improvement as the public seized its new opportunities to listen to the voice of nature (as enhanced by the new urban planners).

3. Melville knew the English poet and physician Mark Akenside (1721–1770) from childhood. Akenside's *The Pleasures of Imagination* (1744) "presents a benevolent universe in which whatever is is right" (Foster, 304). Sorrows are "heart-ennobling," not devastating, rending, lacerating. The "man of feeling, the graveyard sentimentalist, appropriately extols the sentimental optimism of the eighteenth century," Foster says. She also cites *Characteristics of Men, Manners, Opinions, and Times* (1711) by Anthony Ashley Cooper, third earl of Shaftsbury (1671–1713), English philosopher, for arguments to the effect that "morality, like art, is a matter of Taste," that evil is the ugly.

4. The man with the weed sweepingly lumps together three dissimilar ancients. Ovid, or Publius Ovidius Naso (43 B.C.E.–17 C.E.), Roman writer whose works include love poetry and elegies of nostalgic complaint and who was considered immoral by the early Christian Church. Horace, or Quintus Horatius Flaccus (65–8 B.C.E.), Roman author of odes, letters, and satires as well as a treatise, *The Art of Poetry*. Anacreon (582?–485? B.C.E.), native of Asia Minor, who wrote poems about love and wine in a form later given his name, *anacreonics*, and who was said to have choked to death on a grape seed. Ovid is important throughout *The Confidence-Man* for his *Metamorphoses*, poetic narratives of transformations, as from woman to bird. See the start of chapter 32 for a reference to "such a change as one reads of in fairy-books," a category to which belong the books *A Wonder Book* (1851) and *Tanglewood Tales* (1853) by Melville's friend Nathaniel Hawthorne.

5. The great Greek tragic dramatist (525–456? B.C.E.), whose *Prometheus Bound* was especially influential on the English poets of Melville's time; his plays were "dangerous" in the sense that they provoked questioning of the justness of the gods toward mankind.

6. Again, the man in the weed lumps together ancient writers. The least condemnatory of human behavior is Thucydides (c. 460–400 B.C.E.), the Greek who wrote a military history of the Peloponnesian War (between Athens and Sparta), in which he had been a

that, ever since the revival of learning, these classics have been the favorites of successive generations of students and studious men, I tremble to think of that mass of unsuspected heresy on every vital topic which for centuries must have simmered unsurmised in the heart of Christendom. But Tacitus—he is the most extraordinary example of a heretic; not one iota of confidence in his kind. What a mockery that such an one should be reputed wise, and Thucydides be esteemed the statesman's manual![7] But Tacitus—I hate Tacitus; not, though, I trust, with the·hate that sins, but a righteous hate. Without confidence himself, Tacitus destroys it in all his readers. Destroys confidence, fraternal confidence, of which God knows that there is in this world none to spare. For, comparatively inexperienced as you are, my dear young friend, did you never observe how little, very little, confidence, there is? I mean between man and man—more particularly between stranger and stranger. In a sad world it is the saddest fact. Confidence! I have sometimes almost thought that confidence is fled; that confidence is the New Astrea[8]—emigrated—vanished—gone." Then softly sliding nearer, with the softest air, quivering down and looking up, "could you now, my dear young sir, under such circumstances, by way of experiment, simply have confidence in *me?*"

From the outset, the sophomore, as has been seen, had struggled with an ever-increasing embarrassment, arising, perhaps, from such strange remarks coming from a stranger—such persistent and prolonged remarks, too. In vain had he more than once sought to break the spell by venturing a deprecatory or leave-taking word. In vain. Somehow, the stranger fascinated him.[9] Little wonder, then,

---

general on the Athenian side. Unlike the earlier historian Herodotus, who recorded any information without challenging it, Thucydides gathered and sifted evidence into what he presented as the truth of the war. Decimus Junius Juvenalis, Roman satirical poet, early in the 2nd century C.E. wrote realistic exposes of the excesses of his society. Lucian (c. 120–180), a Syrian who traveled widely in the Roman Empire as a rhetorician or public speaker of declamations and wrote dialogues satiric of Greco-Roman religion, philosophy, mythology, and culture. Athens is evoked frequently in *The Confidence-Man*—by characters from Greek myth; by names of real people of classical times, ranging from historians to philosophers; and by the settings of two of Shakespeare's plays, *A Midsummer Night's Dream* and *Timon of Athens*. In April 1859 two students from Williams College visited Melville at Arrowhead wanting to hear about his Polynesian adventures. Instead, he talked about the ancient Greeks so as to suggest that in his seclusion he was living imaginatively in the Greek and Roman world (and as always in the world of the Bible). See Jonathan A. Cook herein and Parker 2.397-400.

7. This would make the judicious Thucydides as dangerous as the Renaissance Italian Niccolo Machiavelli (1469–1527), whose *The Prince* (1532) is often considered a cynical, ruthless "statesman's manual" (see n. 6, p. 135).
8. Greek goddess of justice who fled to the heavens to escape the impiety of mortals. She was placed among the stars under the name Virgo.
9. On the power of snakes to fascinate see the tenth letter in *Letters of an American Farmer* (1782) by J. Hector St. Jean de Crevecoeur (1735–1813): "When they have fixed their eyes on an animal [a bird or squirrel], they become immovable; only turning their head sometimes to the right and sometimes to the left, but still with their sight invariably directed to the object. The distracted victim, instead of flying its enemy, seems to be ar-

that, when the appeal came, he could hardly speak, but, as before intimated, being apparently of a retiring nature, abruptly retired from the spot, leaving the chagrined stranger to wander away in the opposite direction.

Chapter 6.

AT THE OUTSET OF WHICH CERTAIN PASSENGERS PROVE DEAF TO THE CALL OF CHARITY.

—"You—pish! Why will the captain suffer these begging fellows on board?"

These pettish words were breathed by a well-to-do gentleman in a ruby-colored velvet vest, and with a ruby-colored cheek, a ruby-headed cane in his hand, to a man in a gray coat and white tie, who, shortly after the interview last described, had accosted him for contributions to a Widow and Orphan Asylum recently founded among the Seminoles.[1] Upon a cursory view, this last person might have seemed, like the man with the weed, one of the less unrefined children of misfortune; but, on a closer observation, his countenance revealed little of sorrow, though much of sanctity.

With added words of touchy disgust, the well-to-do gentleman hurried away. But, though repulsed, and rudely, the man in gray did not reproach, for a time patiently remaining in the chilly loneliness to which he had been left, his countenance, however, not without token of latent though chastened reliance.

At length an old gentleman, somewhat bulky, drew nigh, and from him also a contribution was sought.

"Look, you," coming to a dead halt, and scowling upon him. "Look, you," swelling his bulk out before him like a swaying balloon, "look, you, you on others' behalf ask for money; you, a fellow with a face as long as my arm. Hark ye, now: there is such a thing as grav-

---

rooted by some invincible power; it screams; now approaches, and then recedes; and after skipping about with unaccountable agitation, finally rushes into the jaws of the snake, and is swallowed, as soon as it is covered with a slime or glue to make it slide easily down the throat of the devourer."

1. Indians who had been much in the news since the time of Melville's birth, when the hero of the Battle of New Orleans, Andrew Jackson, subdued the tribe in Florida, then newly acquired by the United States. Under the provisions of the Indian Removal Act, passed in 1830 during Jackson's first term as president, the United States (in the years 1835–42) determined to move the tribe from Florida to what is now Oklahoma. The Seminoles fought a successful guerrilla war even after the army treacherously captured their leader, Osceola, while he was negotiating under a flag of truce. Later an officer brought a new weapon into play against the Seminoles, land mines. Many of the Seminoles were removed from Florida but the tribe never surrendered. Here, the heroic virtues of historical Seminoles are irrelevant; in Melville's joke, which depends on the common identification of Indians with devils, as in Cotton Mather's *Magnalia Christi Americana*, the Devil canvasses Christians for the support of widows and orphans of devils.

ity, and in condemned felons it may be genuine; but of long faces there are three sorts; that of grief's drudge, that of the lantern-jawed man, and that of the impostor. You know best which yours is."

"Heaven give you more charity, sir."

"And you less hypocrisy, sir."

With which words, the hard-hearted old gentleman marched off.

While the other still stood forlorn, the young clergyman, before introduced, passing that way, catching a chance sight of him, seemed suddenly struck by some recollection; and, after a moment's pause, hurried up with: "Your pardon, but shortly since I was all over looking for you."

"For me?" as marveling that one of so little account should be sought for.

"Yes, for you; do you know anything about the negro, apparently a cripple, aboard here? Is he, or is he not, what he seems to be?"

"Ah, poor Guinea! have you, too, been distrusted? you, upon whom nature has placarded the evidence of your claims?"

"Then you do really know him, and he is quite worthy? It relieves me to hear it—much relieves me. Come, let us go find him, and see what can be done."

"Another instance that confidence may come too late. I am sorry to say that at the last landing I myself—just happening to catch sight of him on the gangway-plank—assisted the cripple ashore. No time to talk, only to help. He may not have told you, but he has a brother in that vicinity."

"Really, I regret his going without my seeing him again; regret it, more, perhaps, than you can readily think. You see, shortly after leaving St. Louis, he was on the forecastle, and there, with many others, I saw him, and put trust in him;[2] so much so, that, to convince those who did not, I, at his entreaty, went in search of you, you being one of several individuals he mentioned, and whose personal appearance he more or less described, individuals who he said would willingly speak for him. But, after diligent search, not finding you, and catching no glimpse of any of the others he had enumerated, doubts were at last suggested; but doubts indirectly originating, as I can but think, from prior distrust unfeelingly proclaimed by another. Still, certain it is, I began to suspect."

"Ha, ha, ha!"

A sort of laugh more like a groan than a laugh; and yet, somehow, it seemed intended for a laugh.

Both turned, and the young clergyman started at seeing the

---

2. Possibly an oblique allusion to the disciple Thomas's skepticism about Jesus' resurrection after his crucifixion (John 20.29): "Jesus saith unto him, Thomas, because thou hast seen me, though hast believed: blessed are they that have not seen, and yet have believed."

wooden-legged man close behind him, morosely grave as a criminal judge with a mustard-plaster on his back. In the present case the mustard-plaster might have been the memory of certain recent biting rebuffs and mortifications.

"Wouldn't think it was I who laughed, would you?"

"But who was it you laughed at? or rather, tried to laugh at?" demanded the young clergyman, flushing, "me?"

"Neither you nor any one within a thousand miles of you. But perhaps you don't believe it."

"If he were of a suspicious temper, he might not," interposed the man in gray calmly, "it is one of the imbecilities of the suspicious person to fancy that every stranger, however absent-minded, he sees so much as smiling or gesturing to himself in any odd sort of way, is secretly making him his butt. In some moods, the movements of an entire street, as the suspicious man walks down it, will seem an express pantomimic jeer at him. In short, the suspicious man kicks himself with his own foot."

"Whoever can do that, ten to one he saves other folks' sole-leather," said the wooden-legged man with a crusty attempt at humor. But with augmented grin and squirm, turning directly upon the young clergyman, "you still think it was *you* I was laughing at, just now. To prove your mistake, I will tell you what I *was* laughing at; a story I happened to call to mind just then."

Whereupon, in his porcupine way, and with sarcastic details, unpleasant to repeat, he related a story, which might, perhaps, in a good-natured version, be rendered as follows:

A certain Frenchman of New Orleans, an old man, less slender in purse than limb, happening to attend the theatre one evening, was so charmed with the character of a faithful wife, as there represented to the life, that nothing would do but he must marry upon it. So, marry he did, a beautiful girl from Tennessee, who had first attracted his attention by her liberal mould, and was subsequently recommended to him through her kin, for her equally liberal education and disposition. Though large, the praise proved not too much. For, ere long, rumor more than corroborated it, by whispering that the lady was liberal to a fault. But though various circumstances, which by most Benedicts[3] would have been deemed all but conclusive, were duly recited to the old Frenchman by his friends, yet such was his confidence that not a syllable would he credit, till, chancing one night to return unexpectedly from a journey, upon entering his apartment, a stranger burst from the alcove: "Begar!" cried he, "now I *begin* to suspec."

---

3. Newly married men, especially those who have vociferously defended their bachelor status, like Benedict in Shakespeare's *Much Ado about Nothing*.

His story told, the wooden-legged man threw back his head, and gave vent to a long, gasping, rasping sort of taunting cry, intolerable as that of a high-pressure engine jeering off steam;[4] and that done, with apparent satisfaction hobbled away.

"Who is that scoffer?" said the man in gray, not without warmth. "Who is he, who even were truth on his tongue, his way of speaking it would make truth almost offensive as falsehood? Who is he?"

"He who I mentioned to you as having boasted his suspicion of the negro," replied the young clergyman, recovering from disturbance, "in short, the person to whom I ascribe the origin of my own distrust; he maintained that Guinea was some white scoundrel, betwisted and painted up for a decoy. Yes, these were his very words, I think."

"Impossible! he could not be so wrong-headed. Pray, will you call him back, and let me ask him if he were really in earnest?"

The other complied; and, at length, after no few surly objections, prevailed upon the one-legged individual to return for a moment. Upon which, the man in gray thus addressed him: "This reverend gentleman tells me, sir, that a certain cripple, a poor negro, is by you considered an ingenious impostor. Now, I am not unaware that there are some persons in this world, who, unable to give better proof of being wise, take a strange delight in showing what they think they have sagaciously read in mankind by uncharitable suspicions of them. I hope you are not one of these. In short, would you tell me now, whether you were not merely joking in the notion you threw out about the negro? Would you be so kind?"

"No, I won't be so kind, I'll be so cruel."

"As you please about that."

"Well, he's just what I said he was."

"A white masquerading as a black?"

"Exactly."

The man in gray glanced at the young clergyman a moment, then quietly whispered to him, "I thought you represented your friend here as a very distrustful sort of person, but he appears endued with a singular credulity.—Tell me, sir, do you really think that a white could look the negro so? For one, I should call it pretty good acting."

"Not much better than any other man acts."

"How? Does all the world act? Am *I*, for instance, an actor? Is my reverend friend here, too, a performer?"

"Yes, don't you both perform acts? To do, is to act; so all doers are actors."

---

4. An echo of Hawthorne's description of the diabolical Apollyon in "The Celestial Railroad" (see p. 433 herein).

"You trifle.—I ask again, if a white, how could he look the negro so?"

"Never saw the negro-minstrels, I suppose?"

"Yes, but they are apt to overdo the ebony; exemplifying the old saying, not more just than charitable, that 'the devil is never so black as he is painted.'[5] But his limbs, if not a cripple, how could he twist his limbs so?"

"How do other hypocritical beggars twist theirs? Easy enough to see how they are hoisted up."

"The sham is evident, then?"

"To the discerning eye," with a horrible screw of his gimlet one.

"Well, where is Guinea?" said the man in gray; "where is he? Let us at once find him, and refute beyond cavil this injurious hypothesis."

"Do so," cried the one-legged man, "I'm just in the humor now for having him found, and leaving the streaks of these fingers on his paint, as the lion leaves the streaks of his nails on a Caffre.[6] They wouldn't let me touch him before. Yes, find him, I'll make wool fly, and him after."

"You forget," here said the young clergyman to the man in gray, "that yourself helped poor Guinea ashore."

"So I did, so I did; how unfortunate. But look now," to the other, "I think that without personal proof I can convince you of your mistake. For I put it to you, is it reasonable to suppose that a man with brains, sufficient to act such a part as you say, would take all that trouble, and run all that hazard, for the mere sake of those few paltry coppers, which, I hear, was all he got for his pains, if pains they were?"

"That puts the case irrefutably," said the young clergyman, with a challenging glance towards the one-legged man.

"You two green-horns! Money, you think, is the sole motive to pains and hazard, deception and deviltry, in this world. How much money did the devil make by gulling Eve?"[7]

Whereupon he hobbled off again with a repetition of his intolerable jeer.

The man in gray stood silently eying his retreat a while, and then, turning to his companion, said: "A bad man, a dangerous man; a man to be put down in any Christian community.—And this

---

5. German proverb. Many popular stories play on the tendency of people to converse with the Devil without recognizing him and sometimes to strain for ways of excusing his behavior. See Hawthorne's "The Celestial Railroad" (p. 429 herein), where the modern, liberal, nominally Christian narrator is unfailingly courteous to the Devil.

6. Or Kafir, Arabic for infidel (non-Mohammedans); here, probably a member of the Bantu people of South Africa.

7. In Genesis 3.4–6 the serpent ("more subtil than any beast of the field"), knowing Adam and Eve will live forever if they obey God, tricks Eve into eating of the only tree in the Garden of Eden whose fruit is forbidden to them.

was he who was the means of begetting your distrust? Ah, we should shut our ears to distrust, and keep them open only for its opposite."

"You advance a principle, which, if I had acted upon it this morning, I should have spared myself what I now feel.—That but one man, and he with one leg, should have such ill power given him; his one sour word leavening into congenial sourness (as, to my knowledge, it did) the dispositions, before sweet enough, of a numerous company. But, as I hinted, with me at the time his ill words went for nothing; the same as now; only afterwards they had effect; and I confess, this puzzles me."

"It should not. With humane minds, the spirit of distrust works something as certain potions do; it is a spirit which may enter such minds, and yet, for a time, longer or shorter, lie in them quiescent; but only the more deplorable its ultimate activity."

"An uncomfortable solution; for, since that baneful man did but just now anew drop on me his bane, how shall I be sure that my present exemption from its effects will be lasting?"

"You cannot be sure, but you can strive against it."

"How?"

"By strangling the least symptom of distrust, of any sort, which hereafter, upon whatever provocation, may arise in you."

"I will do so." Then added as in soliloquy, "Indeed, indeed, I was to blame in standing passive under such influences as that one-legged man's. My conscience upbraids me.—The poor negro: You see him occasionally, perhaps?"

"No, not often; though in a few days, as it happens, my engagements will call me to the neighborhood of his present retreat; and, no doubt, honest Guinea, who is a grateful soul, will come to see me there."

"Then you have been his benefactor?"

"His benefactor? I did not say that. I have known him."

"Take this mite. Hand it to Guinea when you see him; say it comes from one who has full belief in his honesty, and is sincerely sorry for having indulged, however transiently, in a contrary thought."

"I accept the trust. And, by-the-way, since you are of this truly charitable nature, you will not turn away an appeal in behalf of the Seminole Widow and Orphan Asylum?"

"I have not heard of that charity."

"But recently founded."

After a pause, the clergyman was irresolutely putting his hand in his pocket, when, caught by something in his companion's expression, he eyed him inquisitively, almost uneasily.

"Ah, well," smiled the other wanly, "if that subtle bane, we were speaking of but just now, is so soon beginning to work, in vain my appeal to you. Good-by."

"Nay," not untouched, "you do me injustice; instead of indulging present suspicions, I had rather make amends for previous ones. Here is something for your asylum. Not much; but every drop helps. Of course you have papers?"

"Of course," producing a memorandum book and pencil. "Let me take down name and amount. We publish these names. And now let me give you a little history of our asylum, and the providential way in which it was started."[8]

Chapter 7.

A GENTLEMAN WITH GOLD SLEEVE-BUTTONS.

At an interesting point of the narration, and at the moment when, with much curiosity, indeed, urgency, the narrator was being particularly questioned upon that point, he was, as it happened, altogether diverted both from it and his story, by just then catching sight of a gentleman who had been standing in sight from the beginning, but, until now, as it seemed, without being observed by him.

"Pardon me," said he, rising, "but yonder is one who I know will contribute, and largely. Don't take it amiss if I quit you."

"Go: duty before all things," was the conscientious reply.

The stranger was a man of more than winsome aspect. There he stood apart and in repose, and yet, by his mere look, lured the man in gray from his story, much as, by its graciousness of bearing, some full-leaved elm, alone in a meadow, lures the noon sickleman to throw down his sheaves, and come and apply for the alms of its shade.

But, considering that goodness is no such rare thing among men—the world familiarly know the noun; a common one in every language—it was curious that what so signalized the stranger, and made him look like a kind of foreigner, among the crowd (as to some it make him appear more or less unreal in this portraiture), was but the expression of so prevalent[9] a quality. Such goodness seemed his, allied with such fortune, that, so far as his own personal experience could have gone, scarcely could he have known ill, physical or moral; and as for knowing or suspecting the latter in any serious degree (supposing such degree of it to be), by observation or philosophy; for that, probably, his nature, by its opposition,

---

8. "Providential" wryly points to the founding of Hell (allowed by divine providence) as described in *Paradise Lost*, book 1.
9. The spelling *prevalent* was already standard, but Melville may have intended the different emphasis gained by "prevailent."

imperfectly qualified, or from it wholly exempted him. For the rest, he might have been five and fifty, perhaps sixty, but tall, rosy, between plump and portly, with a primy, palmy air, and for the time and place, not to hint of his years, dressed with a strangely festive finish and elegance. The inner-side of his coat-skirts was of white satin, which might have looked especially inappropriate, had it not seemed less a bit of mere tailoring than something of an emblem, as it were; an involuntary emblem, let us say, that what seemed so good about him was not all outside; no, the fine covering had a still finer lining. Upon one hand he wore a white kid glove, but the other hand, which was ungloved, looked hardly less white. Now, as the Fidèle, like most steamboats, was upon deck a little soot-streaked here and there, especially about the railings, it was a marvel how, under such circumstances, these hands retained their spotlessness. But, if you watched them a while, you noticed that they avoided touching anything; you noticed, in short, that a certain negro body-servant, whose hands nature had dyed black, perhaps with the same purpose that millers wear white, this negro servant's hands did most of his master's handling for him; having to do with dirt on his account, but not to his prejudice. But if, with the same undefiledness of consequences to himself, a gentleman could also sin by deputy, how shocking would that be! But it is not permitted to be; and even if it were, no judicious moralist would make proclamation of it.

This gentleman, therefore, there is reason to affirm, was one who, like the Hebrew governor,[1] knew how to keep his hands clean, and who never in his life happened to be run suddenly against by hurrying house-painter, or sweep; in a word, one whose very good luck it was to be a very good man.

Not that he looked as if he were a kind of Wilberforce[2] at all; that superior merit, probably, was not his; nothing in his manner bespoke him righteous, but only good, and though to be good is much below being righteous, and though there is a difference between the two, yet not, it is to be hoped, so incompatible as that a righteous man can not be a good man; though, conversely, in the pulpit it has been with much cogency urged, that a merely good man, that is, one good merely by his nature, is so far from thereby being righ-

---

1. While he was the Roman procurator of Judea (26–36 C.E.), Pontius Pilate (goaded by the chief priests and elders) turned Jesus over to the mob and then symbolically washed his hands in public to disclaim responsibility for the fate of the captive (Matthew 27.24). This allusion complicates the problem of just how Melville meant the gentleman to be judged, because Pilate is most commonly perceived as lacking the courage of his conviction that Jesus was innocent.
2. The English philanthropist William Wilberforce (1759–1833) led the agitation against the British slave trade until its abolition in 1807. In his later years he was looked on as the conscience of the nation.

teous,[3] that nothing short of a total change and conversion can make him so; which is something which no honest mind, well read in the history of righteousness, will care to deny; nevertheless, since St. Paul himself, agreeing in a sense with the pulpit distinction, though not altogether in the pulpit deduction, and also pretty plainly intimating which of the two qualities in question enjoys his apostolic preference; I say, since St. Paul has so meaningly said, that, "scarcely for a righteous man will one die, yet peradventure for a good man some would even dare to die;" therefore, when we repeat of this gentleman, that he was only a good man, whatever else by severe censors may be objected to him, it is still to be hoped that his goodness will not at least be considered criminal in him. At all events, no man, not even a righteous man, would think it quite right to commit this gentleman to prison for the crime, extraordinary as he might deem it; more especially, as, until everything could be known, there would be some chance that the gentleman might after all be quite as innocent of it as he himself.

It was pleasant to mark the good man's reception of the salute of the righteous man, that is, the man in gray; his inferior, apparently, not more in the social scale than in stature. Like the benign elm again, the good man seemed to wave the canopy of his goodness over that suitor, not in conceited condescension, but with that even amenity of true majesty, which can be kind to any one without stooping to it.

To the plea in behalf of the Seminole widows and orphans, the gentleman, after a question or two duly answered, responded by producing an ample pocketbook in the good old capacious style, of fine green French morocco and workmanship, bound with silk of the same color, not to omit bills crisp with newness, fresh from the bank, no muckworms' grime upon them. Lucre those bills might be, but as yet having been kept unspotted from the world, not of the filthy sort. Placing now three of those virgin bills in the applicant's hands, he hoped that the smallness of the contribution would be pardoned; to tell the truth, and this at last accounted for his toilet, he was bound but a short run down the river, to attend, in a festive grove, the afternoon wedding of his niece: so did not carry much money with him.

The other was about expressing his thanks when the gentleman in his pleasant way checked him: the gratitude was on the other

3. Paul, in Romans 5.6–8: "For when we were yet without strength, in due time Christ died for the ungodly. For scarcely for a righteous man will one die: yet peradventure for a good man some would even dare to die. But God commendeth his love toward us, in that, while we were yet sinners, Christ died for us." The full title of this book in the King James Version, "The Epistle of Paul the Apostle to the Romans," makes clear what the text soon specifies, that Paul is writing a letter of encouragement and counsel to all members of the new Christian group in Rome.

side. To him, he said, charity was in one sense not an effort, but a luxury; against too great indulgence in which his steward, a humorist, had sometimes admonished him.

In some general talk which followed, relative to organized modes of doing good, the gentleman expressed his regrets that so many benevolent societies as there were, here and there isolated in the land, should not act in concert by coming together, in the way that already in each society the individuals composing it had done, which would result, he thought, in like advantages upon a larger scale. Indeed, such a confederation might, perhaps, be attended with as happy results as politically attended that of the states.[4]

Upon his hitherto moderate enough companion, this suggestion had an effect illustrative in a sort of that notion of Socrates, that the soul is a harmony;[5] for as the sound of a flute, in any particular key, will, it is said, audibly affect the corresponding chord of any harp in good tune, within hearing, just so now did some string in him respond, and with animation.

Which animation, by the way, might seem more or less out of character in the man in gray, considering his unsprightly manner when first introduced, had he not already, in certain after colloquies, given proof, in some degree, of the fact, that, with certain natures, a soberly continent air at times, so far from arguing emptiness of stuff, is good proof it is there, and plenty of it, because unwasted, and may be used the more effectively, too, when opportunity offers. What now follows on the part of the man in gray will still further exemplify, perhaps somewhat strikingly, the truth, or what appears to be such, of this remark.

"Sir," said he eagerly, "I am before you. A project, not dissimilar to yours, was by me thrown out at the World's Fair in London."[6]

"World's Fair? You there? Pray how was that?"

---

4. Written during inflamed debate over the enforcement of the Fugitive Slave Law and the attempts to extend slavery into Kansas and other lands west of the Mississippi, this sentence (Melville knew) would strike a great many American readers in 1857 as ironic.

5. In *Phaedo*, which relates the conversation between Socrates and his friends on the day of the philosopher's death, Plato describes Socrates as rejecting Simmias' analogy that the soul is to the body as harmony is to the lyre. For Socrates, harmony comes into existence only after the lyre itself and thus the analogy would contradict one of the central tenets of his thinking, that knowledge is recollection and that the soul must therefore have existed before becoming imprisoned in the body. Socrates further argues that the soul exercises a control over the body that harmony cannot exercise on the lyre and that the soul, by the nature of its role in maintaining discipline, is characterized by conflict, the very opposite of harmony.

6. The Exposition of the Industry of All Nations (1851), housed in the famous Crystal Palace (so called because of the innovative use of glass panes on an iron framework) that covered almost nineteen acres. Among the inventions displayed was the Connecticut-manufactured Colt repeating pistol, referred to in chapter 29. In 1854 Phineas T. Barnum, the great showman, briefly accepted the presidency of New York's imitation of the London fair, which also included a crystal palace, near the site of the present main New York Public Library. The publisher G. P. Putnam invited Melville to attend a "Complimentary Fruit & Flower Festival" there on September 27, 1855 (*Log*, 507).

"First, let me—"

"Nay, but first tell me what took you to the Fair?"

"I went to exhibit an invalid's easy-chair I had invented."

"Then you have not always been in the charity business?"

"Is it not charity to ease human suffering? I am, and always have been, as I always will be, I trust, in the charity business, as you call it; but charity is not like a pin, one to make the head, and the other the point; charity is a work to which a good workman may be competent in all its branches. I invented my Protean easy-chair in odd intervals stolen from meals and sleep."

"You call it the Protean easy-chair;[7] pray describe it."

"My Protean easy-chair is a chair so all over bejointed, behinged, and bepadded, everyway so elastic, springy, and docile to the airiest touch, that in some one of its endlessly-changeable accommodations of back, seat, footboard, and arms, the most restless body, the body most racked, nay, I had almost added the most tormented conscience must, somehow and somewhere, find rest. Believing that I owed it to suffering humanity to make known such a chair to the utmost, I scraped together my little means and off to the World's Fair with it."

"You did right. But your scheme; how did you come to hit upon that?"

"I was going to tell you. After seeing my invention duly catalogued and placed, I gave myself up to pondering the scene about me. As I dwelt upon that shining pageant of arts, and moving concourse of nations, and reflected that here was the pride of the world glorying in a glass house, a sense of the fragility of worldly grandeur profoundly impressed me. And I said to myself, I will see if this occasion of vanity cannot supply a hint toward a better profit than was designed. Let some world-wide good to the world-wide cause be now done. In short, inspired by the scene, on the fourth day I issued at the World's Fair my prospectus of the World's Charity."

"Quite a thought. But, pray explain it."

"The World's Charity is to be a society whose members shall comprise deputies from every charity and mission extant; the one object of the society to be the methodization of the world's benevolence; to which end, the present system of voluntary and promiscu-

---

7. Proteus, the Greek god of the sea, was hard to catch because he could change shape instantly (as the Confidence Man does?). In this book Melville mentions shape changers from the Bible; from ancient myths; from retellings of myths as "fairy-books" (chapter 32), such as Ovid's or Hawthorne's children's books; and from many modern writers, including Shakespeare, Milton, and Burns. Foster showed that at the 1851 London World's Fair a Philadelphia manufacturer exhibited reclining chairs for invalids "so constructed that the degree of inclination is regulated with facility by the weight of the body." A "Protean easy-chair" would be as lulling to the conscience and intelligence as a celestial railroad, a fast and easy way to heaven, and is the ideological opposite of Procrustes' bed (see n. 5, p. 78).

ous contribution to be done away, and the Society to be empowered by the various governments to levy, annually, one grand benevolence tax upon all mankind; as in Augustus Cæsar's time, the whole world to come up to be taxed;[8] a tax which, for the scheme of it, should be something like the income-tax in England, a tax, also, as before hinted, to be a consolidation-tax of all possible benevolence taxes; as in America here, the state-tax, and the county-tax, and the town-tax, and the poll-tax, are by the assessors rolled into one. This tax, according to my tables, calculated with care, would result in the yearly raising of a fund little short of eight hundred millions; this fund to be annually applied to such objects, and in such modes, as the various charities and missions, in general congress represented, might decree; whereby, in fourteen years, as I estimate, there would have been devoted to good works the sum of eleven thousand two hundred millions; which would warrant the dissolution of the society, as that fund judiciously expended, not a pauper or heathen could remain the round world over."[9]

"Eleven thousand two hundred millions! And all by passing round a *hat*, as it were."

"Yes, I am no Fourier,[1] the projector of an impossible scheme, but a philanthropist and a financier setting forth a philanthropy and a finance which are practicable."

"Practicable?"

"Yes. Eleven thousand two hundred millions; it will frighten none but a retail philanthropist. What is it but eight hundred millions for

---

8. Luke 2.1: "And it came to pass in those days, that there went out a decree from Caesar Augustus, that all the world should be taxed." Although living in Nazareth, Joseph was obliged to go to Bethlehem ("his own city") to be taxed. He went, accompanied by "Mary his espoused wife, being great with child" (verse 5). On this trip she gives birth to Jesus in a stable in Bethlehem, "because there was no room for them in the inn" (verse 7).

9. A variety of grandiose social schemes had been common in the United States in the years before the mid-1850s, when slavery became the dominant issue among reformers. Horace Greeley in the New York *Tribune* on February 9, 1844, under the heading "The Prevention of Pauperism" reported on Walter Channing's 1843 address in Boston on his plans to form a "Society for the Prevention of Pauperism." In the first week of October 1845 the *Tribune* reported on the raucous "World's Convention," a forum for socialists, abolitionists, evangelicals, champions of women's rights, free-soilers, anti-renters, and other groups. The free-soilers made up an extreme offshoot of the Democratic Party that demanded any new states admitted to the Union be free, not slave. The anti-renters were upstate Hudson River area tenants demanding to be allowed to own their land rather than to continue under the semifeudal barony of the Van Rensselaer patroons. (These patroons were close relatives of Melville's mother, so all the Melvilles would have paid attention to comments at the convention such as this: "Mr. Bovay again insisted that no man had a right to 24 miles square of land, like Van Rensselaer in this State—for if he had, it was evident that many other men could get no land at all.") The convention, hosted by Robert Owen (1771–1858), British social visionary who was called "the eminent Communist" (September 24, 1845), was devoted to the "improvement of the condition of society, irrespective of any exciting injurious divisions, which PREVENT UNION AND DESTROY THE GERMS OF CHARITY" (September 27, 1845, advertisement). (Scott Norsworthy provided these *Tribune* items.)

1. Charles Fourier (1772–1837), French advocate of communal living. See Melville's "New-Fangled Notions of the Social State" (p. 397 herein).

each of fourteen years? Now eight hundred millions—what is that, to average it, but one little dollar a head for the population of the planet? And who will refuse, what Turk or Dyak[2] even, his own little dollar for sweet charity's sake? Eight hundred millions! More than that sum is yearly expended by mankind, not only in vanities, but miseries. Consider that bloody spendthrift, War. And are mankind so stupid, so wicked, that, upon the demonstration of these things they will not, amending their ways, devote their superfluities to blessing the world instead of cursing it? Eight hundred millions! They have not to make it, it is theirs already; they have but to direct it from ill to good. And to this, scarce a self-denial is demanded. Actually, they would not in the mass be one farthing the poorer for it; as certainly would they be all the better and happier. Don't you see? But admit, as you must, that mankind is not mad, and my project is practicable. For, what creature but a madman would not rather do good than ill, when it is plain that, good or ill, it must return upon himself?"

"Your sort of reasoning," said the good gentleman adjusting his gold sleeve-buttons, "seems all reasonable enough, but with mankind it wont do."

"Then mankind are not reasoning beings, if reason wont do with them."

"That is not to the purpose. By-the-way, from the manner in which you alluded to the world's census, it would appear that, according to your world-wide scheme, the pauper not less than the nabob is to contribute to the relief of pauperism, and the heathen not less than the Christian to the conversion of heathenism. How is that?"

"Why, that—pardon me—is quibbling. Now, no philanthropist likes to be opposed with quibbling."

"Well, I won't quibble any more. But, after all, if I understand your project, there is little specially new in it, further than the magnifying of means now in operation."

"Magnifying and energizing. For one thing, missions I would thoroughly reform. Missions I would quicken with the Wall street spirit."

"The Wall street spirit?"

"Yes; for if, confessedly, certain spiritual ends are to be gained but through the auxiliary agency of worldly means, then, to the surer gaining of such spiritual ends, the example of worldly policy in worldly projects should not by spiritual projectors be slighted. In brief, the conversion of the heathen, so far, at least, as depending

2. In Melville's mind Turkish men were associated with gorgeous costumes, beards, swords, and powerful sexuality; Dyaks were associated with bloodthirstiness.

on human effort, would, by the World's Charity, be let out on contract.[3] So much by bid for converting India, so much for Borneo, so
much for Africa. Competition allowed, stimulus would be given.
There would be no lethargy of monopoly. We should have no
mission-house or tract-house of which slanderers could, with any
plausibility, say that it had degenerated in its clerkships into a sort
of custom-house. But the main point is the Archimedean money-
power[4] that would be brought to bear."

"You mean the eight hundred million power?"

"Yes. You see, this doing good to the world by driblets amounts to
just nothing. I am for doing good to the world with a will. I am for
doing good to the world once for all and having done with it. Do but
think, my dear sir, of the eddies and maëlstroms of pagans in China.
People here have no conception of it. Of a frosty morning in Hong
Kong, pauper pagans are found dead in the streets like so many
nipped peas in a bin of peas. To be an immortal being in China is no
more distinction than to be a snow-flake in a snow-squall. What are
a score or two of missionaries to such a people? A pinch of snuff to
the kraken. I am for sending ten thousand missionaries in a body
and converting the Chinese *en masse* within six months of the de-
barkation. The thing is then done, and turn to something else."

"I fear you are too enthusiastic."

"A philanthropist is necessarily an enthusiast; for without enthusiasm what was ever achieved but commonplace? But again: consider the poor in London. To that mob of misery, what is a joint
here and a loaf there? I am for voting to them twenty thousand bul-
locks and one hundred thousand barrels of flour to begin with.
They are then comforted, and no more hunger for one while among
the poor of London. And so all round."

"Sharing the character of your general project, these things, I
take it, are rather examples of wonders that were to be wished, than
wonders that will happen."

"And is the age of wonders passed? Is the world too old? Is it barren? Think of Sarah."

"Then I am Abraham reviling the angel (with a smile).[5] But still,
as to your design at large, there seems a certain audacity."

3. A close parallel in grandiosity is in the October 6, 1845, *Tribune* report "The World's
Convention." Robert Owen announced a plan to "so educate the world that there should
never be a single bad man, woman or child in the world again. This is as much a manufacture as the manufacture of your shirt. . . . Men and women are as easily made what
we wish, under proper arrangements, as can be imagined." (Scott Norsworthy provided
this item.) This speech by Owen was outright blasphemy, almost any Christian reader
would have said, particularly any Calvinist or Calvinist sympathizer who would feel that
a realistic view of human nature had to allow for Original Sin.
4. Power from the leverage money gives in personal and public relations, from the claim of
the ancient Sicilian mathematician Archimedes (287–212 B.C.E.) that given a lever long
enough and a place to stand he could move the world.
5. In Genesis 17.17 Abraham cannot believe the good news delivered by an angel: "Then

"But if to the audacity of the design there be brought a commensurate circumspectness of execution, how then?"

"Why, do you really believe that your World's Charity will ever go into operation?"

"I have confidence that it will."

"But may you not be over-confident?"

"For a Christian to talk so!"

"But think of the obstacles!"

"Obstacles? I have confidence to remove obstacles, though mountains.[6] Yes, confidence in the World's Charity to that degree, that, as no better person offers to supply the place, I have nominated myself provisional treasurer, and will be happy to receive subscriptions, for the present to be devoted to striking off a million more of my prospectuses."

The talk went on; the man in gray revealed a spirit of benevolence which, mindful of the millennial promise,[7] had gone abroad over all the countries of the globe, much as the diligent spirit of the husbandman, stirred by forethought of the coming seed-time, leads him, in March reveries at his fireside, over every field of his farm. The master chord of the man in gray had been touched, and it seemed as if it would never cease vibrating. A not unsilvery tongue, too, was his, with gestures that were a Pentecost[8] of added ones, and persuasiveness before which granite hearts might crumble into gravel.

Strange, therefore, how his auditor, so singularly good-hearted as he seemed, remained proof to such eloquence; though not, as it turned out, to such pleadings. For, after listening a while longer with pleasant incredulity, presently, as the boat touched his place of destination, the gentleman, with a look half humor, half pity, put another bank-note into his hands; charitable to the last, if only to the dreams of enthusiasm.

Abraham fell upon his face, and laughed, and said in his heart, Shall a child be born unto him that is an hundred years old? and shall Sarah, that is ninety years old, bear?" The comparison to Abraham and the angel is a hint that the man in gray may be something other than human.

6. 1 Corinthians 13.2: "though I have all faith, so that I could remove mountains, and have not charity, I am nothing."

7. For Jesus' millennial (thousand-year) reign, see Revelation 20.1–2: "And I saw an angel come down from heaven, having the key of the bottomless pit and a great chain in his hand. And he laid hold on the dragon, that old serpent, which is the Devil, and Satan, and bound him a thousand years." Later, John, the author of Revelation, sees thrones on which sat the souls of those who "were beheaded for the witness of Jesus, and for the word of God, . . . and they lived and reigned with Christ a thousand years" (verse 4).

8. On the day of Pentecost (described in the Book of the Acts of the Apostles chapter 2) the twelve disciples (including Matthias, chosen to replace Judas, who had betrayed Jesus and then fallen headlong and died; Acts 1.18) were gathered together when "cloven tongues like as of fire" "sat upon each of them" (Acts 2.3) and "they were all filled with the Holy Ghost, and began to speak with other tongues" (verse 4), so that these Galileans could speak in their own languages with Parthians, Medes, Elamites, and others, down to the last named, Cretes and Arabians, and thus could spread the news of Jesus' teachings, death, resurrection, and ascension to heaven (described in Acts 1.9–11).

Chapter 8.

A CHARITABLE LADY.

If a drunkard in a sober fit is the dullest of mortals, an enthusiast in a reason-fit is not the most lively. And this, without prejudice to his greatly improved understanding; for, if his elation was the height of his madness, his despondency is but the extreme of his sanity. Something thus now, to all appearance, with the man in gray. Society his stimulus, loneliness was his lethargy. Loneliness, like the sea-breeze, blowing off from a thousand leagues of blankness, he did not find, as veteran solitaires do, if anything, too bracing. In short, left to himself, with none to charm forth his latent lymphatic, he insensibly resumes his original air, a quiescent one, blended of sad humility and demureness.

Ere long he goes laggingly into the ladies' saloon, as in spiritless quest of somebody; but, after some disappointed glances about him, seats himself upon a sofa with an air of melancholy exhaustion and depression.

At the sofa's further end sits a plump and pleasant person, whose aspect seems to hint that, if she have any weak point, it must be anything rather than her excellent heart. From her twilight dress, neither dawn nor dark, apparently she is a widow just breaking the chrysalis of her mourning. A small gilt testament is in her hand, which she has just been reading. Half-relinquished, she holds the book in reverie, her finger inserted at the xiii. of 1st Corinthians, to which chapter possibly her attention might have recently been turned, by witnessing the scene of the monitory mute and his slate.

The sacred page no longer meets her eye; but, as at evening, when for a time the western hills shine on though the sun be set, her thoughtful face retains its tenderness though the teacher is forgotten.

Meantime, the expression of the stranger is such as ere long to attract her glance. But no responsive one. Presently, in her somewhat inquisitive survey, her volume drops. It is restored. No encroaching politeness in the act, but kindness, unadorned. The eyes of the lady sparkle. Evidently, she is not now unprepossessed. Soon, bending over, in a low, sad tone, full of deference, the stranger breathes, "Madam, pardon my freedom, but there is something in that face which strangely draws me. May I ask, are you a sister of the Church?"

"Why—really—you—"

In concern for her embarrassment, he hastens to relieve it, but, without seeming so to do. "It is very solitary for a brother here," eying the showy ladies brocaded in the background, "I find none to mingle souls with. It may be wrong—I *know* it is—but I cannot force myself to be easy with the people of the world. I prefer the company, however silent, of a brother or sister in good standing. By the way, madam, may I ask if you have confidence?"

"Really, sir—why, sir—really—I—"

"Could you put confidence in *me* for instance?"

"Really, sir—as much—I mean, as one may wisely put in a—a—stranger, an entire stranger, I had almost said," rejoined the lady, hardly yet at ease in her affability, drawing aside a little in body, while at the same time her heart might have been drawn as far the other way. A natural struggle between charity and prudence.

"Entire stranger!" with a sigh. "Ah, who would be a stranger? In vain, I wander; no one will have confidence in me."

"You interest me," said the good lady, in mild surprise. "Can I any way befriend you?"

"No one can befriend me, who has not confidence."

"But I—I have—at least to that degree—I mean that—"

"Nay, nay, you have none—none at all. Pardon, I see it. No confidence. Fool, fond fool that I am to seek it!"

"You are unjust, sir," rejoins the good lady with heightened interest; "but it may be that something untoward in your experiences has unduly biased you. Not that I would cast reflections. Believe me, I—yes, yes—I may say—that—that—"

"That you have confidence? Prove it. Let me have twenty dollars."

"Twenty dollars!"

"There, I told you, madam, you had no confidence."

The lady was, in an extraordinary way, touched. She sat in a sort of restless torment, knowing not which way to turn. She began twenty different sentences, and left off at the first syllable of each. At last, in desperation, she hurried out, "Tell me, sir, for what you want the twenty dollars?"

"And did I not—" then glancing at her half-mourning, "for the widow and the fatherless. I am traveling agent of the Widow and Orphan Asylum, recently founded among the Seminoles."

"And why did you not tell me your object before?" As not a little relieved. "Poor souls—Indians, too—those cruelly-used Indians. Here, here; how could I hesitate? I am so sorry it is no more."

"Grieve not for that, madam," rising and folding up the bank-notes. "This is an inconsiderable sum, I admit, but," taking out his pencil and book, "though I here but register the amount, there is another register, where is set down the motive. Good-bye; you have confidence. Yea, you can say to me as the apostle said to the Corinthians, 'I rejoice that I have confidence in you in all things.' "[9]

Chapter 9.

TWO BUSINESS MEN TRANSACT A LITTLE BUSINESS.

—"Pray, sir, have you seen a gentleman with a weed hereabouts, rather a saddish gentleman? Strange where he can have gone to. I was talking with him not twenty minutes since."

By a brisk, ruddy-cheeked man in a tasseled traveling-cap, carrying under his arm a ledger-like volume, the above words were addressed to the collegian before introduced, suddenly accosted by the rail to which not long after his retreat, as in a previous chapter recounted, he had returned, and there remained.

"Have you seen him, sir?"

Rallied from his apparent diffidence by the genial jauntiness of the stranger, the youth answered with unwonted promptitude: "Yes, a person with a weed was here not very long ago."

"Saddish?"

"Yes, and a little cracked, too, I should say."

"It was he. Misfortune, I fear, has disturbed his brain. Now quick, which way did he go?"

"Why just in the direction from which you came, the gangway yonder."

"Did he? Then the man in the gray coat, whom I just met, said right:[1] he must have gone ashore. How unlucky!"

He stood vexedly twitching at his cap-tassel, which fell over by his whisker, and continued: "Well, I am very sorry. In fact, I had something for him here."—Then drawing nearer, "you see, he applied to me for relief, no, I do him injustice, not that, but he began to intimate, you understand. Well, being very busy just then, I declined; quite rudely, too, in a cold, morose, unfeeling way, I fear. At all events, not three minutes afterwards I felt self-reproach, with a kind of prompting, very peremptory, to deliver over into that unfortunate man's hands a ten-dollar bill. You smile. Yes, it may be superstition, but I can't help it; I have my weak side, thank God. Then again," he rapidly went on, "we have been so very prosperous lately in our affairs—by we, I mean the Black Rapids Coal Company— that, really, out of my abundance, associative and individual, it is

9. 2 Corinthians 7.16, Paul addressing the Christians of Corinth. The register the man in gray refers to would seem to be the one kept, according to Christian lore, by the Recording Angel. That angel has some biblical authority (see Revelation 5) but is colored by depictions in popular art and in folk religion.
1. In this intricate comic byplay, the man with a traveling cap accepts the word of the Confidence Man in his fifth disguise as to the word of the Confidence Man in his fourth disguise about the whereabouts of himself in his third disguise.

but fair that a charitable investment or two should be made, don't you think so?"

"Sir," said the collegian without the least embarrassment, "do I understand that you are officially connected with the Black Rapids Coal Company?"

"Yes, I happen to be president and transfer-agent."

"You are?"

"Yes, but what is it to you? You don't want to invest?"

"Why, do you sell the stock?"

"Some might be bought, perhaps; but why do you ask? you don't want to invest?"

"But supposing I did," with cool self-collectedness, "could you do up the thing for me, and here?"

"Bless my soul," gazing at him in amaze, "really, you are quite a business man. Positively, I feel afraid of you."

"Oh, no need of that.—You could sell me some of that stock, then?"

"I don't know, I don't know. To be sure, there are a few shares under peculiar circumstances bought in by the Company; but it would hardly be the thing to convert this boat into the Company's office.[2] I think you had better defer investing. So," with an indifferent air, "you have seen the unfortunate man I spoke of?"

"Let the unfortunate man go his ways.—What is that large book you have with you?"

"My transfer-book. I am subpœnaed with it to court."[3]

"Black Rapids Coal Company," obliquely reading the gilt inscription on the back; "I have heard much of it. Pray do you happen to have with you any statement of the condition of your company?"

"A statement has lately been printed."

"Pardon me, but I am naturally inquisitive. Have you a copy with you?"

"I tell you again, I do not think that it would be suitable to convert this boat into the Company's office.—That unfortunate man, did you relieve him at all?"

"Let the unfortunate man relieve himself.—Hand me the statement."

"Well, you are such a business-man, I can hardly deny you. Here," handing a small, printed pamphlet.

2. I.e., to convert Earth into an office for transferring souls to hell, as the Devil is dedicated to doing.
3. The court is God's, although the occasion is not necessarily so high a court as the Last Judgment or (the variant in *Billy Budd*) the "Last Assizes." See Job 1.6–7 and 2.1–2 on Satan's walking up and down in the earth and then presenting himself before God. In 1850, in *A Summary View of the Millenial Church* (on the Shakers), Melville read a passage on false testimony inspired by Satan and checked this reference to Job 2.1: "Again there was a day when the sons of God came to present themselves before the Lord, and Satan came also among them to present himself before the Lord."

The youth turned it over sagely.

"I hate a suspicious man," said the other, observing him; "but I must say I like to see a cautious one."

"I can gratify you there," languidly returning the pamphlet; "for, as I said before, I am naturally inquisitive; I am also circumspect. No appearances can deceive me. Your statement," he added, "tells a very fine story; but pray, was not your stock a little heavy a while ago? downward tendency? Sort of low spirits among holders on the subject of that stock?"

"Yes, there was a depression. But how came it? who devised it? The 'bears,' sir. The depression of our stock was solely owing to the growling, the hypocritical growling, of the bears."[4]

"How, hypocritical?"

"Why, the most monstrous of all hypocrites are these bears: hypocrites by inversion; hypocrites in the simulation of things dark instead of bright; souls that thrive, less upon depression, than the fiction of depression; professors of the wicked art of manufacturing depressions; spurious Jeremiahs; sham Heraclituses, who, the lugubrious day done, return, like sham Lazaruses[5] among the beggars, to make merry over the gains got by their pretended sore heads—scoundrelly bears!"

"You are warm against these bears?"

"If I am, it is less from the remembrance of their stratagems as to our stock, than from the persuasion that these same destroyers of confidence, and gloomy philosophers of the stock-market, though false in themselves, are yet true types of most destroyers of confidence and gloomy philosophers, the world over. Fellows who, whether in stocks, politics, bread-stuffs, morals, metaphysics, religion—be it what it may—trump up their black panics in the naturally-quiet brightness, solely with a view to some sort of covert advantage. That corpse of calamity which the gloomy philosopher parades, is but his Good-Enough-Morgan."[6]

4. For-profit pessimists, Wall Street investors who speculate on downturns in the market.
5. Phony beggars, not honest beggars like the Lazarus in Jesus' parable about the rich man and the beggar (see n. 2, p. 16). In the Bible the Book of Jeremiah is devoted to God's use of Jeremiah to deliver stern messages to Israel foretelling desolation to come—the ravaging of Jerusalem and ultimately the scattering of the Jews and their captivity in Babylon. In Israel false prophets who opposed Jeremiah assured the people that all was well, that there would be neither sword nor famine but "peace in this place" (Jeremiah 14.13). These false prophets (ancient confidence men) were doomed, God told Jeremiah, to be consumed by "sword and famine" (verse 15). In writing *The Confidence-Man* Melville takes on the role of a true prophet, albeit an ironic and skeptical one. Heraclitus (c. 540–475 B.C.E.), Greek philosopher from Ephesus on the Ionian (Greek-controlled) coast of Asia Minor (now Turkey), believed that all things were in a state of flux and that fire and "strife" ruled the universe. He was accordingly dubbed the "weeping Philosopher" during the Renaissance. A sham Heraclitus might, for instance, reassuringly prophesy that the stock market was in no danger of a sudden panic.
6. Any "device, scheme, etc., which can be used temporarily to influence voters" (*Dictionary of Americanisms*). William Morgan (1774?–1825?) disappeared from Canandaigua, New York, while under arrest for petty theft. "It was freely charged that Masons had

"I rather like that," knowingly drawled the youth. "I fancy these gloomy souls as little as the next one. Sitting on my sofa after a champagne dinner, smoking my plantation cigar, if a gloomy fellow come to me—what a bore!"

"You tell him it's all stuff, don't you?"

"I tell him it ain't natural. I say to him, you are happy enough, and you know it; and everybody else is as happy as you, and you know that, too; and we shall all be happy after we are no more, and you know that, too; but no, still you must have your sulk."

"And do you know whence this sort of fellow gets his sulk? not from life; for he's often too much of a recluse, or else too young to have seen anything of it. No, he gets it from some of those old plays he sees on the stage, or some of those old books he finds up in garrets. Ten to one, he has lugged home from auction a musty old Seneca,[7] and sets about stuffing himself with that stale old hay; and, thereupon, thinks it looks wise and antique to be a croaker, thinks it's taking a stand 'way above his kind."

"Just so," assented the youth. "I've lived some, and seen a good many such ravens at second hand. By the way, strange how that man with the weed, you were inquiring for, seemed to take me for some soft sentimentalist, only because I kept quiet, and thought, because I had a copy of Tacitus with me, that I was reading him for his gloom, instead of his gossip. But I let him talk. And, indeed, by my manner humored him."

"You shouldn't have done that, now. Unfortunate man, you must have made quite a fool of him."

"His own fault if I did. But I like prosperous fellows, comfortable fellows; fellows that talk comfortably and prosperously, like you.[8] Such fellows are generally honest. And, I say now, I happen to have a superfluity in my pocket, and I'll just—"

"—Act the part of a brother to that unfortunate man?"

"Let the unfortunate man be his own brother. What are you dragging him in for all the time? One would think you didn't care to register any transfers, or dispose of any stock—mind running on something else. I say I will invest."

murdered him in order to prevent the publication of the book he was believed to be writing on Masonic secrets" (*Dictionary of American Biography*). A body found in the Niagara River was inconclusively identified as Morgan's, but there was a rival identification. In 1827 the anti-Masonic Thurlow Weed (1797–1882) answered a jest of an attorney for the Masons by calling the body "a good-enough Morgan for us until you bring back the one you carried off." The press quickly improved this into the boast that the body was a "good-enough Morgan until after the election." See Weed's *Autobiography* (1883), 1.319. The phrase *good-enough Morgan* died out, but the political phenomenon it defined still flourishes—the cynical strategy of making a false accusation in full confidence that it will not be disproved until after the upcoming election.

7. Lucius Annaeus Seneca (c. 5 B.C.E.–65 C.E.), Roman stoic philosopher and tragic poet.

8. The sophomore has borrowed his dislike of gloomy souls from the Confidence Man himself, in his disguise as the man with the weed.

"Stay, stay, here come some uproarious fellows—this way, this way."

And with off-handed politeness the man with the book escorted his companion into a private little haven removed from the brawling swells without.

Business transacted, the two came forth, and walked the deck.

"Now tell me, sir," said he with the book, "how comes it that a young gentleman like you, a sedate student at the first appearance, should dabble in stocks and that sort of thing?"

"There are certain sophomorean errors in the world," drawled the sophomore, deliberately adjusting his shirt-collar, "not the least of which is the popular notion touching the nature of the modern scholar, and the nature of the modern scholastic sedateness."

"So it seems, so it seems. Really, this is quite a new leaf in my experience."

"Experience, sir," originally observed the sophomore, "is the only teacher."

"Hence am I your pupil; for it's only when experience speaks, that I can endure to listen to speculation."

"My speculations, sir," dryly drawing himself up, "have been chiefly governed by the maxim of Lord Bacon;[9] I speculate in those philosophies which come home to my business and bosom—pray, do you know of any other good stocks?"

"You wouldn't like to be concerned in the New Jerusalem,[1] would you?"

"New Jerusalem?"

"Yes, the new and thriving city, so called, in northern Minnesota. It was originally founded by certain fugitive Mormons. Hence the name. It stands on the Mississippi.[2] Here, here is the map," producing a roll. "There—there, you see are the public buildings— here the landing—there the park—yonder the botanic gardens— and this, this little dot here, is a perpetual fountain, you

---

9. Francis Bacon, Lord Verulam (1561–1626), English statesman and moralist, who in the 1612 edition of his *Essays* says that what he wrote would "come home to men's business and bosoms."

1. See Revelation 21.1–2, for John's vision of "a new heaven and a new earth," in which there is "the holy city, new Jerusalem, coming down from God out of heaven, prepared as a bride adorned for her husband."

2. Charles Dickens in *Martin Chuzzlewit* (1843–44) describes an American swindle in which lots are sold in a swamp (around Cairo, Illinois, at the confluence of the Ohio and Mississippi rivers), renamed Eden by the developer. Young Martin is shown a "great plan which occupied one whole side" of an office, depicting Eden: "A flourishing city too! An architectural city! There were banks, churches, cathedrals, market-places, factories, hotels, stores, mansions; wharfs; an exchange, a theatre; public buildings of all kinds, down to the office of the Eden Stinger, a daily journal; all faithfully depicted in the view before them." Martin learns to his horror that none of this exists but is reassured by his American companion (in disregard for proper grammar) that "The soil being very fruitful, public buildings grows spontaneous, perhaps."

understand. You observe there are twenty asterisks. Those are for the lyceums. They have lignum-vitæ rostrums."[3]

"And are all these buildings now standing?"

"All standing—bona fide."[4]

"These marginal squares here, are they the water-lots?"

"Water-lots in the city of New Jerusalem? All terra firma—you don't seem to care about investing, though?"

"Hardly think I should read my title clear,[5] as the law students say," yawned the collegian.

"Prudent—you are prudent. Don't know that you are wholly out, either. At any rate, I would rather have one of your shares of coal stock than two of this other. Still, considering that the first settlement was by two fugitives,[6] who had swum over naked from the opposite shore—it's a surprising place. It is, *bona fide.*—But dear me, I must go. Oh, if by possibility you should come across that unfortunate man—"

"—In that case," with drawling impatience, "I will send for the steward, and have him and his misfortunes consigned overboard."

"Ha ha!—now were some gloomy philosopher here, some theological bear, forever taking occasion to growl down the stock of human nature (with ulterior views, d'ye see, to a fat benefice in the gift of the worshipers of Arimanius),[7] he would pronounce that the sign of a hardening heart and a softening brain. Yes, that would be his sinister construction. But it's nothing more than the oddity of a genial humor—genial but dry. Confess it. Good-bye."

3. Asinine American lectures given from behind lecterns made of "lignum-vitae" (wood of life), from a West Indian tree, would remind Christian readers by contrast of the "tree of life" depicted in the heavenly New Jerusalem of Revelation 22.2. "Lyceums": public halls available to local and visiting lecturers. In Hawthorne's "The Celestial Railroad" (see p. 439 herein) just one lyceum is enough to allow the citizens of a town to "acquire an omnigenous erudition without the trouble of even learning to read." For Hawthorne, as for Melville, there was no fast, easy way to moral, spiritual, intellectual, or aesthetic perfection.
4. Latin for "in good faith."
5. The sophomore is unwittingly alluding not only to the words of law students but also to a hymn by the Dissenting (rigorously Calvinistic) English hymn writer Isaac Watts (1674–1748): "When I can read my title clear / To Mansions in the skies, / I'll bid farewell to ev'ry fear, / And wipe my weeping eyes." See *Moby-Dick,* chapter 22, for another reference to Watts.
6. Perhaps Christian and Faithful, in John Bunyan's *Pilgrim's Progress.*
7. *Ariamius,* in the first American edition, seems to be an error for Arimanius, the death dealer in the ancient Persian religion of Zoroastrianism, identified with the unnamed "prince of the kingdom of Persia" in Daniel 10.20 who was so powerful that he held an angel away from Daniel for twenty-one days, until the archangel Michael came to help him resist the "prince." "Theological bear": a Calvinist, one who believes in innate depravity; that human beings are born sinful.

Chapter 10.

IN THE CABIN.

Stools, settees, sofas, divans, ottomans; occupying them are clusters of men, old and young, wise and simple; in their hands are cards spotted with diamonds, spades, clubs, hearts; the favorite games are whist, cribbage, and brag. Lounging in arm-chairs or sauntering among the marble-topped tables, amused with the scene, are the comparatively few, who, instead of having hands in the games, for the most part keep their hands in their pockets. These may be the philosophes. But here and there, with a curious expression, one is reading a small sort of handbill of anonymous poetry, rather wordily entitled:—

"ODE

ON THE INTIMATIONS

OF

DISTRUST IN MAN,

UNWILLINGLY INFERRED FROM REPEATED REPULSES,

IN DISINTERESTED ENDEAVORS

TO PROCURE HIS

CONFIDENCE."[8]

On the floor are many copies, looking as if fluttered down from a balloon. The way they came there was this: A somewhat elderly person, in the quaker dress, had quietly passed through the cabin, and, much in the manner of those railway book-peddlers who precede their proffers of sale by a distribution of puffs, direct or indirect, of the volumes to follow, had, without speaking, handed about the odes, which, for the most part, after a cursory glance, had been disrespectfully tossed aside, as no doubt, the moonstruck production of some wandering rhapsodist.

In due time, book under arm, in trips the ruddy man with the traveling-cap, who, lightly moving to and fro, looks animatedly about him, with a yearning sort of gratulatory affinity and longing, expressive of the very soul of sociality; as much as to say, "Oh, boys, would that I were personally acquainted with each mother's son of you, since what a sweet world, to make sweet acquaintance in, is ours, my brothers; yea, and what dear, happy dogs are we all!"

And just as if he had really warbled it forth, he makes fraternally up to one lounging stranger or another, exchanging with him some pleasant remark.

8. A play on the title of Wordsworth's "Immortality" ode. In Melville's roughly chronological survey of several varieties of eighteenth- and nineteenth-century optimistic philosophies, the English Romantics are lightly skipped over. The markings in Melville's own copy of Wordsworth reveal how carefully he studied the late poet laureate in the 1850s.

"Pray, what have you there?" he asked of one newly accosted, a little, dried-up man, who looked as if he never dined.

"A little ode, rather queer, too," was the reply, "of the same sort you see strewn on the floor here."

"I did not observe them. Let me see;" picking one up and looking it over. "Well now, this is pretty; plaintive, especially the opening:—

> 'Alas for man, he hath small sense
> Of genial trust and confidence.'[9]

—If it be so, alas for him, indeed. Runs off very smoothly, sir. Beautiful pathos. But do you think the sentiment just?"

"As to that," said the little dried-up man, "I think it a kind of queer thing altogether, and yet I am almost ashamed to add, it really has set me to thinking; yes and to feeling. Just now, somehow, I feel as it were trustful and genial. I don't know that ever I felt so much so before. I am naturally numb in my sensibilities; but this ode, in its way, works on my numbness not unlike a sermon, which, by lamenting over my lying dead in trespasses and sins, thereby stirs me up to be all alive in well-doing."

"Glad to hear it, and hope you will do well, as the doctors say. But who snowed the odes about here?"

"I cannot say; I have not been here long."

"Wasn't an angel, was it? Come, you say you feel genial, let us do as the rest, and have cards."

"Thank you, I never play cards."

"A bottle of wine?"

"Thank you, I never drink wine."

"Cigars?"

"Thank you, I never smoke cigars."

"Tell stories?"

"To speak truly, I hardly think I know one worth telling."

"Seems to me, then, this geniality you say you feel waked in you, is as water-power in a land without mills. Come, you had better take a genial hand at the cards. To begin, we will play for as small a sum as you please; just enough to make it interesting."

"Indeed, you must excuse me. Somehow I distrust cards."

"What, distrust cards? Genial cards? Then for once I join with our sad Philomel[1] here:—

9. The English poet, aesthetician, and art historian John Ruskin (1819–1900), in "Mount Blanc Revisited.—June 9th, 1845": "Alas, for man! who hath no sense / Of gratefulness nor confidence, / But still rejects and raves: / That all God's love can hardly win / One soul from taking pride in sin, / And pleasure over graves." (The phrase *That all God's love* means "So that, or to the point that, all God's love").

1. The Greek girl Philomela is "sad" because of her rape and mutilation; after she avenges herself (with her sister's help) she is transformed into a swallow (or, according to the Roman poet Ovid, a nightingale). Ovid's *Metamorphoses* is used in this book to play Greek myth off against biblical parallels, as when Melville alludes to Satan's appearance in the form of a snake and (in one of Ovid's stories) Cadmus' transformation into a snake.

'Alas for man, he hath small sense
Of genial trust and confidence.'

Good-bye!"

Sauntering and chatting here and there, again, he with the book
at length seems fatigued, looks round for a seat, and spying a
partly-vacant settee drawn up against the side, drops down there;
soon, like his chance neighbor, who happens to be the good merchant, becoming not a little interested in the scene more immediately before him; a party at whist; two cream-faced, giddy,
unpolished youths, the one in a red cravat, the other in a green, opposed to two bland, grave, handsome, self-possessed men of middle
age, decorously dressed in a sort of professional black, and apparently doctors of some eminence in the civil law.

By-and-by, after a preliminary scanning of the new comer next
him the good merchant, sideways leaning over, whispers behind a
crumpled copy of the Ode which he holds: "Sir, I don't like the
looks of those two, do you?"[2]

"Hardly," was the whispered reply; "those colored cravats are not
in the best taste, at least not to mine; but my taste is no rule for
all."

"You mistake; I mean the other two, and I don't refer to dress,
but countenance. I confess I am not familiar with such gentry any
further than reading about them in the papers—but those two
are—are sharpers, aint they?"

"Far be from us the captious and fault-finding spirit, my dear sir."

"Indeed, sir, I would not find fault; I am little given that way; but
certainly, to say the least, these two youths can hardly be adepts,
while the opposed couple may be even more."

"You would not hint that the colored cravats would be so
bungling as to lose, and the dark cravats so dextrous as to cheat?—
Sour imaginations, my dear sir. Dismiss them. To little purpose
have you read the Ode you have there. Years and experience, I
trust, have not sophisticated you. A fresh and liberal construction
would teach us to regard those four players—indeed, this whole
cabin-full of players—as playing at games in which every player
plays fair, and not a player but shall win."

"Now, you hardly mean that; because games in which all may
win, such games remain as yet in this world uninvented, I think."

"Come, come," luxuriously laying himself back, and casting a
free glance upon the players, "fares all paid; digestion sound; care,
toil, penury, grief, unknown; lounging on this sofa, with waistband

---

2. Like Mark Winsome in chapter 36, the good merchant recognizes lesser evil but not the
   original Confidence Man. The merchant is oblivious to any possible cosmic implications
   in a "transfer-book" in which the Devil might record his traffic in human souls.

relaxed, why not be cheerfully resigned to one's fate, nor peevishly pick holes in the blessed fate of the world?"

Upon this, the good merchant, after staring long and hard, and then rubbing his forehead, fell into meditation, at first uneasy, but at last composed, and in the end, once more addressed his companion: "Well, I see it's good to out with one's private thoughts now and then. Somehow, I don't know why, a certain misty suspiciousness seems inseparable from most of one's private notions about some men and some things; but once out with these misty notions, and their mere contact with other men's soon dissipates, or, at least, modifies them."

"You think I have done you good, then? may be, I have. But don't thank me, don't thank me. If by words, casually delivered in the social hour, I do any good to right or left, it is but involuntary influence—locust-tree sweetening the herbage under it; no merit at all; mere wholesome accident, of a wholesome nature.—Don't you see?"

Another stare from the good merchant, and both were silent again.

Finding his book, hitherto resting on his lap, rather irksome there, the owner now places it edgewise on the settee, between himself and neighbor; in so doing, chancing to expose the lettering on the back—"*Black Rapids Coal Company*"—which the good merchant, scrupulously honorable, had much ado to avoid reading, so directly would it have fallen under his eye, had he not conscientiously averted it. On a sudden, as if just reminded of something, the stranger starts up, and moves away, in his haste leaving his book; which the merchant observing, without delay takes it up, and, hurrying after, civilly returns it; in which act he could not avoid catching sight by an involuntary glance of part of the lettering.

"Thank you, thank you, my good sir," said the other, receiving the volume, and was resuming his retreat, when the merchant spoke: "Excuse me, but are you not in some way connected with the—the Coal Company I have heard of?"

"There is more than one Coal Company that may be heard of, my good sir," smiled the other, pausing with an expression of painful impatience, disinterestedly mastered.

"But you are connected with one in particular.—The 'Black Rapids,' are you not?"

"How did you find that out?"

"Well, sir, I have heard rather tempting information of your Company."

"Who is your informant, pray?" somewhat coldly.

"A—a person by the name of Ringman."

"Don't know him. But, doubtless, there are plenty who know our

Company, whom our Company does not know; in the same way that one may know an individual, yet be unknown to him.—Known this Ringman long? Old friend, I suppose.—But pardon, I must leave you."

"Stay, sir, that—that stock."

"Stock?"

"Yes, it's a little irregular, perhaps, but—"

"Dear me, you don't think of doing any business with me, do you? In my official capacity I have not been authenticated to you. This transfer-book, now," holding it up so as to bring the lettering in sight, "how do you know that it may not be a bogus one? And I, being personally a stranger to you, how can you have confidence in me?"

"Because," knowingly smiled the good merchant, "if you were other than I have confidence that you are, hardly would you challenge distrust that way."

"But you have not examined my book."

"What need to, if already I believe that it is what it is lettered to be?"

"But you had better. It might suggest doubts."

"Doubts, may be, it might suggest, but not knowledge; for how, by examining the book, should I think I knew any more than I now think I do; since, if it be the true book, I think it so already; and since if it be otherwise, then I have never seen the true one, and don't know what that ought to look like."

"Your logic I will not criticize, but your confidence I admire, and earnestly, too, jocose as was the method I took to draw it out. Enough, we will go to yonder table, and if there be any business which, either in my private or official capacity, I can help you do, pray command me."

Chapter 11.

ONLY A PAGE OR SO.

The transaction concluded, the two still remained seated, falling into familiar conversation, by degrees verging into that confidential sort of sympathetic silence, the last refinement and luxury of unaffected good feeling. A kind of social superstition, to suppose that to be truly friendly one must be saying friendly words all the time, any more than be doing friendly deeds continually. True friendliness, like true religion, being in a sort independent of works.[3]

---

3. In Melville's time neither Calvinist nor Unitarian would argue that religion is wholly "independent" of works, but Melville is riskily stepping over a hot theological controversy. At issue for Unitarians and "orthodox" Calvinists is the apparent contradiction between Paul and James. In Ephesians 2.8–9 Paul says: "For by grace are ye saved through faith;

At length, the good merchant, whose eyes were pensively resting upon the gay tables in the distance, broke the spell by saying that, from the spectacle before them, one would little divine what other quarters of the boat might reveal. He cited the case, accidentally encountered but an hour or two previous, of a shrunken old miser, clad in shrunken old moleskin, stretched out, an invalid, on a bare plank in the emigrants' quarters, eagerly clinging to life and lucre, though the one was gasping for outlet, and about the other he was in torment lest death, or some other unprincipled cut-purse, should be the means of his losing it; by like feeble tenure holding lungs and pouch, and yet knowing and desiring nothing beyond them; for his mind, never raised above mould, was now all but mouldered away. To such a degree, indeed, that he had no trust in anything, not even in his parchment bonds, which, the better to preserve from the tooth of time, he had packed down and sealed up, like brandy peaches, in a tin case of spirits.

The worthy man proceeded at some length with these dispiriting particulars. Nor would his cheery companion wholly deny that there might be a point of view from which such a case of extreme want of confidence might, to the humane mind, present features not altogether welcome as wine and olives after dinner. Still, he was not without compensatory considerations, and, upon the whole, took his companion to task for evincing what, in a good-natured, round-about way, he hinted to be a somewhat jaundiced sentimentality. Nature, he added, in Shakespeare's words, had meal and bran;[4] and, rightly regarded, the bran in its way was not to be condemned.

The other was not disposed to question the justice of Shakespeare's thought, but would hardly admit the propriety of the application in this instance, much less of the comment. So, after some further temperate discussion of the pitiable miser, finding that they could not entirely harmonize, the merchant cited another case, that of the negro cripple. But his companion suggested whether the alleged hardships of that alleged unfortunate might not exist more in

and that not of yourselves: it is the gift of God. Not of works, lest any man should boast." James 2.14–26 insists that faith without works is dead. Jesus declares that the way to know his followers is by their works ("by their fruits ye shall know them", Matthew 7.20). The debate raged on in American churches. On June 22, 1873, Melville's cousin Kate Gansevoort, raised like him in the Calvinist Dutch Church, accompanied Elizabeth Shaw Melville to All Souls and the next day wrote: "I went to hear Dr. Bellows preach—he had a pure Unitarian sermon putting forth the idea, that 'works was better than faith'—& that creeds were useless for man or woman, seldom lived up, to them & the living a good, honest pure & true life was better than all else." She commented: "Such a contradiction to an orthodox belief—but very beautiful & very moving—but oh Abe—how much better in Faith & hope that our Risen Saviour stands ready to receive [sic] & forgive all who come to him in humility & trust."

4. Shakespeare's *Cymbeline* 4.2.26–27: "Cowards father cowards, and base things sire base: Nature hath meal, and bran; contempt and grace." *Cymbeline* may have supplied the name of Melville's steamboat, since Imogen in her disguise calls herself Fidele.

the pity of the observer than the experience of the observed. He knew nothing about the cripple, nor had seen him, but ventured to surmise that, could one but get at the real state of his heart, he would be found about as happy as most men, if not, in fact, full as happy as the speaker himself.[5] He added that negroes were by nature a singularly cheerful race; no one ever heard of a native-born African Zimmermann or Torquemada;[6] that even from religion they dismissed all gloom; in their hilarious rituals they danced, so to speak, and, as it were, cut pigeon-wings. It was improbable, therefore, that a negro, however reduced to his stumps by fortune, could be ever thrown off the legs of a laughing philosophy.[7]

Foiled again, the good merchant would not desist, but ventured still a third case, that of the man with the weed, whose story, as narrated by himself, and confirmed and filled out by the testimony of a certain man in a gray coat, whom the merchant had afterwards met, he now proceeded to give; and that, without holding back those particulars disclosed by the second informant, but which delicacy had prevented the unfortunate man himself from touching upon.

But as the good merchant could, perhaps, do better justice to the man than the story, we shall venture to tell it in other words than his, though not to any other effect.

Chapter 12.

STORY OF THE UNFORTUNATE MAN, FROM WHICH MAY BE GATHERED WHETHER OR NO HE HAS BEEN JUSTLY SO ENTITLED.

It appeared that the unfortunate man had had for a wife one of those natures, anomalously vicious, which would almost tempt a metaphysical lover of our species to doubt whether the human form be, in all cases, conclusive evidence of humanity, whether, sometimes, it may not be a kind of unpledged and indifferent tabernacle, and whether, once for all to crush the saying of Thrasea,[8] (an unaccountable one, considering that he himself was so good a man) that "he who hates vice, hates humanity," it should not, in

---

5. Another double entendre. See n. 7, p. 17 herein for an unironic example of the racial stereotype set forth by the man with the traveling cap.
6. Johann Georg Zimmermann (1728–1795) wrote *Uber die Einsamkeit* (Solitude considered with respect to its influence upon the mind and heart; 1756, enlarged 1784–85), a discussion of the edifying effects of time spent alone. Here, the assumption is that a writer about solitude must be a miserable person, as must be Tomas de Torquemada (1420–1498), the Spanish inquisitor general who tortured those he regarded as heretics (see Melville's *White-Jacket*, chapter 70).
7. A reminder of Democritus of Abdera (460?–370? B.C.E.), known as the "laughing Philosopher" (for Heraclitus, known as the "weeping Philosopher," see n. 5, p. 56).
8. Publius Clodius Thrasea Paetus, Roman senator and Stoic, slain about 66 C.E. on Nero's orders. The Roman historian Pliny in *Epistle* 22.8.3 quoted Thrasea as saying, "He who hates vice hates mankind."

self-defense, be held for a reasonable maxim, that none but the good are human.

Goneril was young, in person lithe and straight, too straight, indeed, for a woman, a complexion naturally rosy, and which would have been charmingly so, but for a certain hardness and bakedness, like that of the glazed colors on stone-ware. Her hair was of a deep, rich chestnut, but worn in close, short curls all round her head. Her Indian figure was not without its impairing effect on her bust, while her mouth would have been pretty but for a trace of moustache. Upon the whole, aided by the resources of the toilet, her appearance at distance was such, that some might have thought her, if anything, rather beautiful, though of a style of beauty rather peculiar and cactus-like.

It was happy for Goneril that her more striking peculiarities were less of the person than of temper and taste. One hardly knows how to reveal, that, while having a natural antipathy to such things as the breast of chicken, or custard, or peach, or grape, Goneril could yet in private make a satisfactory lunch on hard crackers and brawn of ham. She liked lemons, and the only kind of candy she loved were little dried sticks of blue clay, secretly carried in her pocket. Withal she had hard, steady health like a squaw's, with as firm a spirit and resolution. Some other points about her were likewise such as pertain to the women of savage life. Lithe though she was, she loved supineness, but upon occasion could endure like a stoic. She was taciturn, too. From early morning till about three o'clock in the afternoon she would seldom speak—it taking that time to thaw her, by all accounts, into but talking terms with humanity. During the interval she did little but look, and keep looking out of her large, metallic eyes, which her enemies called cold as a cuttle-fish's,[9] but which by her were esteemed gazelle-like; for Goneril was not without vanity. Those who thought they best knew her, often wondered what happiness such a being could take in life, not considering the happiness which is to be had by some natures in the very easy way of simply causing pain to those around them. Those who suffered from Goneril's strange nature, might, with one of those hyperboles to which the resentful incline, have pronounced her some kind of toad; but her worst slanderers could never, with any show of justice, have accused her of being a toady. In a large sense she possessed the virtue of independence of mind. Goneril held it flattery to hint praise even of the absent, and even if merited; but honesty, to fling people's imputed faults into their faces. This was thought malice, but it certainly was not passion.

---

9. A formidable-looking ten-armed marine mollusk with a calcified internal shell. Its weapon, like a writer's, is ink.

Passion is human. Like an icicle-dagger, Goneril at once stabbed and froze; so at least they said; and when she saw frankness and innocence tyrannized into sad nervousness under her spell, according to the same authority, inly she chewed her blue clay, and you could mark that she chuckled. These peculiarities were strange and unpleasing; but another was alleged, one really incomprehensible. In company she had a strange way of touching, as by accident, the arm or hand of comely young men, and seemed to reap a secret delight from it, but whether from the humane satisfaction of having given the evil-touch, as it is called, or whether it was something else in her, not equally wonderful, but quite as deplorable, remained an enigma.

Needless to say what distress was the unfortunate man's, when, engaged in conversation with company, he would suddenly perceive his Goneril bestowing her mysterious touches, especially in such cases where the strangeness of the thing seemed to strike upon the touched person, notwithstanding good-breeding forbade his proposing the mystery, on the spot, as a subject of discussion for the company. In these cases, too, the unfortunate man could never endure so much as to look upon the touched young gentleman afterwards, fearful of the mortification of meeting in his countenance some kind of more or less quizzingly-knowing expression. He would shudderingly shun the young gentleman. So that here, to the husband, Goneril's touch had the dread operation of the heathen taboo. Now Goneril brooked no chiding. So, at favorable times, he, in a wary manner, and not indelicately, would venture in private interviews gently to make distant allusions to this questionable propensity. She divined him. But, in her cold loveless way, said it was witless to be telling one's dreams, especially foolish ones; but if the unfortunate man liked connubially to rejoice his soul with such chimeras, much connubial joy might they give him. All this was sad—a touching case—but all might, perhaps, have been borne by the unfortunate man—conscientiously mindful of his vow—for better or for worse—to love and cherish his dear Goneril so long as kind heaven might spare her to him—but when, after all that had happened, the devil of jealousy entered her, a calm, clayey, cakey devil, for none other could possess her, and the object of that deranged jealousy, her own child, a little girl of seven, her father's consolation and pet; when he saw Goneril artfully torment the little innocent, and then play the maternal hypocrite with it, the unfortunate man's patient long-suffering gave way. Knowing that she would neither confess nor amend, and might, possibly, become even worse than she was, he thought it but duty as a father, to withdraw the child from her; but, loving it as he did, he could not do so without accompanying it into domestic exile himself. Which, hard though it was, he did. Whereupon the whole female neighborhood, who till now had little enough admired dame Goneril, broke out in indignation against a husband, who, without assigning a cause, could deliberately abandon the wife of his bosom, and sharpen the sting to her, too, by depriving her of the solace of retaining her off-spring. To all this, self-respect, with Christian charity towards Goneril, long kept the unfortunate man dumb. And well had it been had he continued so; for when, driven to desperation, he hinted something of the truth of the case, not a soul would credit it; while for Goneril, she pronounced all he said to be a malicious invention. Ere long, at the suggestion of some woman's-rights women, the injured wife began a suit, and, thanks to able counsel and accommodating testimony, succeeded in such a way, as not only to recover custody of the child, but to get such a settlement awarded upon a separation, as to make penniless the unfortunate man (so he averred), besides, through the legal sympathy she en-listed, effecting a judicial blasting of his private reputation. What made it yet more lamentable was, that the unfortunate man, think-ing that, before the court, his wisest plan, as well as the most Christian besides, being, as he deemed, not at variance with the truth of the matter, would be to put forth the plea of the mental de-rangement of Goneril, which done, he could, with less of mortifica-tion to himself, and odium to her, reveal in self-defense those eccentricities which had led to his retirement from the joys of wed-lock, had much ado in the end to prevent this charge of derange-ment from fatally recoiling upon himself—especially, when, among other things, he alleged her mysterious touchings. In vain did his counsel, striving to make out the derangement to be where, in fact, if anywhere, it was, urge that, to hold otherwise, to hold that such a being as Goneril was sane, this was constructively a libel upon womankind. Libel be it. And all ended by the unfortunate man's subsequently getting wind of Goneril's intention to procure him to be permanently committed for a lunatic. Upon which he fled, and was now an innocent outcast, wandering forlorn in the great valley of the Mississippi, with a weed on his hat for the loss of his Goneril; for he had lately seen by the papers that she was dead, and thought it but proper to comply with the prescribed form of mourn-ing in such cases. For some days past he had been trying to get money enough to return to his child, and was but now started with inadequate funds.

Now all of this, from the beginning, the good merchant could not but consider rather hard for the unfortunate man.

Chapter 13.

THE MAN WITH THE TRAVELING-CAP EVINCES MUCH HUMANITY, AND IN
A WAY WHICH WOULD SEEM TO SHOW HIM TO BE ONE OF THE MOST
LOGICAL OF OPTIMISTS.

Years ago, a grave American savan, being in London, observed at
an evening party there, a certain coxcombical fellow, as he thought,
an absurd ribbon in his lapel, and full of smart persiflage, whisking
about to the admiration of as many as were disposed to admire.
Great was the savan's disdain; but, chancing ere long to find himself in a corner with the jackanapes, got into conversation with
him, when he was somewhat ill-prepared for the good sense of the
jackanapes, but was altogether thrown aback, upon subsequently
being whispered by a friend that the jackanapes was almost as great
a savan as himself, being no less a personage than Sir Humphrey
Davy.[1]

The above anecdote is given just here by way of an anticipative
reminder to such readers as, from the kind of jaunty levity, or what
may have passed for such, hitherto for the most part appearing in
the man with the traveling-cap, may have been tempted into a more
or less hasty estimate of him; that such readers, when they find the
same person, as they presently will, capable of philosophic and humanitarian discourse—no mere casual sentence or two as heretofore at times, but solidly sustained throughout an almost entire
sitting; that they may not, like the American savan, be thereupon
betrayed into any surprise incompatible with their own good opinion of their previous penetration.

The merchant's narration being ended, the other would not deny
but that it did in some degree affect him. He hoped he was not
without proper feeling for the unfortunate man. But he begged to
know in what spirit he bore his alleged calamities. Did he despond
or have confidence?

The merchant did not, perhaps, take the exact import of the last
member of the question; but answered, that, if whether the unfortunate man was becomingly resigned under his affliction or no, was
the point, he could say for him that resigned he was, and to an ex-
emplary degree: for not only, so far as known, did he refrain from
any one-sided reflections upon human goodness and human jus-

---

1. English chemist (1778–1829), inventor of a miner's safety lamp. Melville had access in
   Boston and New York to men who had met Davy, notably his friend Dr. John W. Francis,
   about whose student life Henry T. Tuckerman wrote in an 1866 biographical essay in a
   new edition of Francis's *Old New York*: "Sir Humphrey Davy in chemistry, Erskine and
   Romilly in legal reform, and Byron in poetry, had awakened a spirit of reaction and vi-
   tality which marked a progressive epoch; and to one constituted like Dr. Francis, the
   sight of these men, whose American reputation had been aptly compared to the verdict
   of a 'kind of living posterity,' was fraught with the deepest interest."

tice, but there was observable in him an air of chastened reliance, and at times tempered cheerfulness.

Upon which the other observed, that since the unfortunate man's alleged experience could not be deemed very conciliatory towards a view of human nature better than human nature was, it largely redounded to his fair-mindedness, as well as piety, that under the alleged dissuasives, apparently so, from philanthropy, he had not, in a moment of excitement, been warped over to the ranks of the misanthropes. He doubted not, also, that with such a man his experience would, in the end, act by a complete and beneficent inversion, and so far from shaking his confidence in his kind, confirm it, and rivet it. Which would the more surely be the case, did he (the unfortunate man) at last become satisfied (as sooner or later he probably would be) that in the distraction of his mind his Goneril had not in all respects had fair play. At all events, the description of the lady, charity could not but regard as more or less exaggerated, and so far unjust. The truth probably was that she was a wife with some blemishes mixed with some beauties. But when the blemishes were displayed, her husband, no adept in the female nature, had tried to use reason with her, instead of something far more persuasive. Hence his failure to convince and convert. The act of withdrawing from her, seemed, under the circumstances, abrupt. In brief, there were probably small faults on both sides, more than balanced by large virtues; and one should not be hasty in judging.

When the merchant, strange to say, opposed views so calm and impartial, and again, with some warmth, deplored the case of the unfortunate man, his companion, not without seriousness, checked him, saying, that this would never do; that, though but in the most exceptional case, to admit the existence of unmerited misery, more particularly if alleged to have been brought about by unhindered arts of the wicked, such an admission was, to say the least, not prudent; since, with some, it might unfavorably bias their most important persuasions.[2] Not that those persuasions were legitimately servile to such influences. Because, since the common occurrences of life could never, in the nature of things, steadily look one way and tell one story, as flags in the trade-wind; hence, if the conviction of a Providence, for instance, were in any way made dependent

2. The story about the man with the weed and Goneril (made up by the man with the weed and substantiated and elaborated by the man in gray) is told (though not in the words used in chapter 12) by Mr. Roberts to the man with the book (Truman) to convince him of the occasional existence of hardship in the world. The joke is capped when the man with the book—who originated the story in an earlier disguise—mildly doubts that the "alleged experience" happened, at least as recounted by Mr. Roberts. The humor of the chapter depends on the reader's knowledge that the Confidence Man reappears in several forms. Among "important persuasions" that might be shaken if one believed the story of the man with the weed is the confidence that one never suffers unjustly and that evil is always punished.

upon such variabilities as everyday events, the degree of that conviction would, in thinking minds, be subject to fluctuations akin to
those of the stock-exchange during a long and uncertain war. Here
he glanced aside at his transfer-book, and after a moment's pause
continued. It was of the essence of a right conviction of the divine
nature, as with a right conviction of the human, that, based less on
experience than intuition, it rose above the zones of weather.

When now the merchant, with all his heart, coincided with this
(as being a sensible, as well as religious person, he could not but
do), his companion expressed satisfaction, that, in an age of some
distrust on such subjects, he could yet meet with one who shared
with him, almost to the full, so sound and sublime a confidence.

Still, he was far from the illiberality of denying that philosophy
duly bounded was permissible. Only he deemed it at least desirable
that, when such a case as that alleged of the unfortunate man was
made the subject of philosophic discussion, it should be so philoso-
phized upon, as not to afford handles to those unblessed with the
true light. For, but to grant that there was so much as a mystery
about such a case, might by those persons be held for a tacit surrender of the question. And as for the apparent license temporarily
permitted sometimes, to the bad over the good (as was by implication alleged with regard to Goneril and the unfortunate man), it
might be injudicious there to lay too much polemic stress upon the
doctrine of future retribution as the vindication of present impunity. For though, indeed, to the right-minded that doctrine was
true, and of sufficient solace, yet with the perverse the polemic
mention of it might but provoke the shallow, though mischievous
conceit, that such a doctrine was but tantamount to the one which
should affirm that Providence was not now, but was going to be. In
short, with all sorts of cavilers, it was best, both for them and everybody, that whoever had the true light should stick behind the secure Malakoff[3] of confidence, nor be tempted forth to hazardous
skirmishes on the open ground of reason. Therefore, he deemed it
unadvisable in the good man, even in the privacy of his own mind,
or in communion with a congenial one, to indulge in too much lat-
itude of philosophizing, or, indeed, of compassionating, since this
might beget an indiscreet habit of thinking and feeling which might
unexpectedly betray him upon unsuitable occasions. Indeed,
whether in private or public, there was nothing which a good man
was more bound to guard himself against than, on some topics, the

---

3. A Russian fortification in southeast Sebastopol, thought impregnable when the French
besieged it in 1855 during the Crimean War, fell on September 8, 1855. Foster points
out that Melville's hometown paper, the *Berkshire County Eagle*, carried news of the
siege through the summer before announcing its fall on October 5, 1855 (news from
Europe still traveling by ship).

emotional unreserve of his natural heart; for, that the natural heart, in certain points, was not what it might be, men had been authoritatively admonished.

But he thought he might be getting dry.

The merchant, in his good-nature, thought otherwise, and said that he would be glad to refresh himself with such fruit all day. It was sitting under a ripe pulpit, and better such a seat than under a ripe peach-tree.

The other was pleased to find that he had not, as he feared, been prosing; but would rather not be considered in the formal light of a preacher; he preferred being still received in that of the equal and genial companion. To which end, throwing still more of sociability into his manner, he again reverted to the unfortunate man. Take the very worst view of that case; admit that his Goneril was, indeed, a Goneril; how fortunate to be at last rid of this Goneril, both by nature and by law! If he were acquainted with the unfortunate man, instead of condoling with him, he would congratulate him. Great good fortune had this unfortunate man. Lucky dog, he dared say, after all.

To which the merchant replied, that he earnestly hoped it might be so, and at any rate he tried his best to comfort himself with the persuasion that, if the unfortunate man was not happy in this world, he would, at least, be so in another.

His companion made no question of the unfortunate man's happiness in both worlds; and, presently calling for some champagne,[4] invited the merchant to partake, upon the playful plea that, whatever notions other than felicitous ones he might associate with the unfortunate man, a little champagne would readily bubble away.

At intervals they slowly quaffed several glasses in silence and thoughtfulness. At last the merchant's expressive face flushed, his eye moistly beamed, his lips trembled with an imaginative and feminine sensibility. Without sending a single fume to his head, the wine seemed to shoot to his heart, and begin soothsaying there. "Ah," he cried, pushing his glass from him, "Ah, wine is good, and confidence is good; but can wine or confidence percolate down through all the stony strata of hard considerations, and drop warmly and ruddily into the cold cave of truth? Truth will *not* be comforted. Led by dear charity, lured by sweet hope, fond fancy essays this feat; but in vain; mere dreams and ideals, they explode in your hand, leaving naught but the scorching behind!"

4. This is still early morning, ante meridian drinking being a custom among American travelers even in the nineteenth century. See T. B. Thorpe, "Reminiscences of the Mississippi," 34: "The 'social hall' of a Western steamer is the lounging-place, and 'the bar' the centre of attraction. However much we may be opposed to the abuse of alcoholic beverages, the opposition is, in intellectual minds, here often neutralized by the professional manner displayed in their indulgence, and is charmed by the entire ignorance that many evince of any possible moral or physical wrong in their use."

"Why, why, why!" in amaze, at the burst; "bless me, if *In vino veritas* be a true saying, then, for all the fine confidence you professed with me, just now, distrust, deep distrust, underlies it; and ten thousand strong, like the Irish Rebellion,[5] breaks out in you now. That wine, good wine, should do it! Upon my soul," half seriously, half humorously, securing the bottle, "you shall drink no more of it. Wine was meant to gladden the heart, not grieve it; to heighten confidence, not depress it."

Sobered, shamed, all but confounded, by this raillery, the most telling rebuke under such circumstances, the merchant stared about him, and then, with altered mien, stammeringly confessed, that he was almost as much surprised as his companion, at what had escaped him. He did not understand it; was quite at a loss to account for such a rhapsody popping out of him unbidden. It could hardly be the champagne; he felt his brain unaffected; in fact, if anything, the wine had acted upon it something like white of egg in coffee, clarifying and brightening.

"Brightening?[6] brightening it may be, but less like the white of egg in coffee, than like stove-lustre on a stove—black, brightening. Seriously, I repent calling for the champagne. To a temperament like yours, champagne is not to be recommended. Pray, my dear sir, do you feel quite yourself again? Confidence restored?"

"I hope so; I think I may say it is so. But we have had a long talk, and I think I must retire now."

So saying, the merchant rose, and making his adieus, left the table with the air of one, mortified at having been tempted by his own honest goodness, accidentally stimulated into making mad disclosures—to himself as to another—of the queer, unaccountable caprices of his natural heart.

Chapter 14.

WORTH THE CONSIDERATION OF THOSE TO WHOM IT MAY PROVE WORTH CONSIDERING.

As the last chapter was begun with a reminder looking forwards, so the present must consist of one glancing backwards.

To some, it may raise a degree of surprise that one so full of confidence, as the merchant has throughout shown himself, up to the

---

5. Probably the rebellion of 1798, which was strongly influenced by the American and the French revolutions.
6. The narrator merely summarizes the merchant's comments, which must have included the word *brightening*; in a resumption of dialogue the man with the traveling cap echoes the word, showing he had heard it. The copyist or compositor seems to have found this shift confusing, for in the first edition a double quotation mark after "clarifying and brightening," at the end of the previous paragraph concluded the summarizing passages as if had been direct speech. That double quotation mark is deleted in this Norton edition.

moment of his late sudden impulsiveness, should, in that instance, have betrayed such a depth of discontent. He may be thought inconsistent, and even so he is. But for this, is the author to be blamed? True, it may be urged that there is nothing a writer of fiction should more carefully see to, as there is nothing a sensible reader will more carefully look for, than that, in the depiction of any character, its consistency should be preserved. But this, though at first blush, seeming reasonable enough, may, upon a closer view, prove not so much so. For how does it couple with another requirement—equally insisted upon, perhaps—that, while to all fiction is allowed some play of invention, yet, fiction based on fact should never be contradictory to it; and is it not a fact, that, in real life, a consistent character is a *rara avis?*[7] Which being so, the distaste of readers to the contrary sort in books, can hardly arise from any sense of their untrueness. It may rather be from perplexity as to understanding them. But if the acutest sage be often at his wits' ends to understand living character, shall those who are not sages expect to run and read character in those mere phantoms which flit along a page, like shadows along a wall?[8] That fiction, where every character can, by reason of its consistency, be comprehended at a glance, either exhibits but sections of character, making them appear for wholes, or else is very untrue to reality; while, on the other hand, that author who draws a character, even though to common view incongruous in its parts, as the flying-squirrel, and, at different periods, as much at variance with itself as the caterpillar is with the butterfly into which it changes, may yet, in so doing, be not false but faithful to facts.[9]

If reason be judge, no writer has produced such inconsistent characters as nature herself has. It must call for no small sagacity in a reader unerringly to discriminate in a novel between the inconsistencies of conception and those of life. As elsewhere, experience is the only guide here; but as no one man can be coextensive with *what is*, it may be unwise in every case to rest upon it. When the duck-billed beaver[1] of Australia was first brought stuffed to En-

---

7. See Tom Quirk (p. 263 herein) for demonstration that this chapter is built from a passage from "Of the Inconsistency of Our Actions" in an essay by Michel de Montaigne (1533–1592).

8. Eye-catching signs and handbills had been part of the American urban scene all Melville's life. In reaction to the simplification of information and ideas, Melville had arrived at a theory that private, "eagle-eyed" reading was the proper response to great literature. See his essay on Hawthorne's *Mosses from an Old Manse* in the 2001 NCE of *Moby-Dick*, p. 530. Reading while on the run is from Habakkuk 2.2: "And the Lord answered me, and said, Write the vision, and make it plain upon tables, that he may run that readeth it."

9. The difficulty of copying this passage probably led to the error in the first edition, which has the butterfly changing into a caterpillar.

1. The platypus, an egg-laying mammal with a bill like a duck and tail like a beaver, found in Australia and on the island of Tasmania.

gland, the naturalists, appealing to their classifications, maintained that there was, in reality, no such creature; the bill in the specimen must needs be, in some way, artificially stuck on.

But let nature, to the perplexity of the naturalists, produce her duck-billed beavers as she may, lesser authors, some may hold, have no business to be perplexing readers with duck-billed characters. Always, they should represent human nature not in obscurity, but transparency, which, indeed, is the practice with most novelists, and is, perhaps, in certain cases, someway felt to be a kind of honor rendered by them to their kind. But whether it involve honor or otherwise might be mooted, considering that, if these waters of human nature can be so readily seen through, it may be either that they are very pure or very shallow. Upon the whole, it might rather be thought, that he, who, in view of its inconsistencies, says of human nature the same that, in view of its contrasts, is said of the divine nature, that it is past finding out, thereby evinces a better appreciation of it than he who, by always representing it in a clear light, leaves it to be inferred that he clearly knows all about it.

But though there is a prejudice against inconsistent characters in books, yet the prejudice bears the other way, when what seemed at first their inconsistency, afterwards, by the skill of the writer, turns out to be their good keeping. The great masters excel in nothing so much as in this very particular. They challenge astonishment at the tangled web of some character, and then raise admiration still greater at their satisfactory unraveling of it; in this way throwing open, sometimes to the understanding even of school misses, the last complications of that spirit which is affirmed by its Creator to be fearfully and wonderfully made.[2]

At least, something like this is claimed for certain psychological novelists; nor will the claim be here disputed. Yet, as touching this point, it may prove suggestive, that all those sallies of ingenuity, having for their end the revelation of human nature on fixed principles, have, by the best judges, been excluded with contempt from the ranks of the sciences—palmistry, physiognomy, phrenology, psychology. Likewise, the fact, that in all ages such conflicting views have, by the most eminent minds, been taken of mankind, would, as with other topics, seem some presumption of a pretty general and pretty thorough ignorance of it. Which may appear the less improbable if it be considered that, after poring over the best novels professing to portray human nature, the studious youth will still run risk of being too often at fault upon actually entering the

---

2. Part of a song of rejoicing (Psalm 139.14): "I will praise thee; for I am fearfully and wonderfully made."

world; whereas, had he been furnished with a true delineation, it
ought to fare with him something as with a stranger entering, map
in hand, Boston town;[3] the streets may be very crooked, he may often pause; but, thanks to his true map, he does not hopelessly lose
his way. Nor, to this comparison, can it be an adequate objection,
that the twistings of the town are always the same, and those of human nature subject to variation. The grand points of human nature
are the same to-day they were a thousand years ago. The only vari-
ability in them is in expression, not in feature.

But as, in spite of seeming discouragement, some mathemati-
cians are yet in hopes of hitting upon an exact method of determining the longitude, the more earnest psychologists may, in the face
of previous failures, still cherish expectations with regard to some
mode of infallibly discovering the heart of man.

But enough has been said by way of apology for whatever may
have seemed amiss or obscure in the character of the merchant; so
nothing remains but to turn to our comedy, or, rather, to pass from
the comedy of thought to that of action.

Chapter 15.

AN OLD MISER, UPON SUITABLE REPRESENTATIONS, IS PREVAILED UPON TO VENTURE AN INVESTMENT.

The merchant having withdrawn, the other remained seated
alone for a time, with the air of one who, after having conversed
with some excellent man, carefully ponders what fell from him,
however intellectually inferior it may be, that none of the profit
may be lost; happy if from any honest word he has heard he can derive some hint, which, besides confirming him in the theory of
virtue, may, likewise, serve for a finger-post to virtuous action.

Ere long his eye brightened, as if some such hint was now
caught. He rises, book in hand, quits the cabin, and enters upon a
sort of corridor, narrow and dim, a by-way to a retreat less ornate
and cheery than the former; in short, the emigrants' quarters; but
which, owing to the present trip being a down-river one, will doubtless be found comparatively tenantless. Owing to obstructions
against the side windows, the whole place is dim and dusky; very
much so, for the most part; yet, by starts, haggardly lit here and
there by narrow, capricious sky-lights in the cornices. But there
would seem no special need for light, the place being designed
more to pass the night in, than the day; in brief, a pine barrens dor-
mitory, of knotty pine bunks, without bedding. As with the nests in

3. The streets of Boston, which Melville knew from his childhood visits, were notoriously
   crooked, worse even than those in lower Manhattan (see n. 4, p. 78).

the geometrical towns of the associate penguin and pelican, these
bunks were disposed with Philadelphian regularity,[4] but, like the
cradle of the oriole, they were pendulous, and, moreover, were, so
to speak, three-story cradles; the description of one of which will
suffice for all.

Four ropes, secured to the ceiling, passed downwards through
auger-holes bored in the corners of three rough planks, which at
equal distances rested on knots vertically tied in the ropes, the low-
ermost plank but an inch or two from the floor, the whole affair resembling, on a large scale, rope book-shelves; only, instead of
hanging firmly against a wall, they swayed to and fro at the least
suggestion of motion, but were more especially lively upon the
provocation of a green emigrant sprawling into one, and trying to
lay himself out there, when the cradling would be such as almost to
toss him back whence he came. In consequence, one less inexperienced, essaying repose on the uppermost shelf, was liable to serious
disturbance, should a raw beginner select a shelf beneath. Sometimes a throng of poor emigrants, coming at night in a sudden rain
to occupy these oriole nests, would—through ignorance of their peculiarity—bring about such a rocking uproar of carpentry, joining to
it such an uproar of exclamations, that it seemed as if some luck-
less ship, with all its crew, was being dashed to pieces among the
rocks. They were beds devised by some sardonic foe of poor travelers, to deprive them of that tranquillity which should precede, as
well as accompany, slumber.—Procrustean beds,[5] on whose hard
grain humble worth and honesty writhed, still invoking repose,
while but torment responded. Ah, did any one make such a bunk
for himself, instead of having it made for him, it might be just, but
how cruel, to say, You must lie on it!

But, purgatory as the place would appear, the stranger advances
into it; and, like Orpheus[6] in his gay descent to Tartarus, lightly
hums to himself an opera snatch.

Suddenly there is a rustling, then a creaking, one of the cradles
swings out from a murky nook, a sort of wasted penguin-flipper is

4. The streets of colonial Philadelphia, on the west bank of the Delaware River, were laid
   out in a grid pattern—unlike less systematic lower Manhattan and particularly unlike
   the "cow trail" streets of Boston.
5. Legendary Greek robber who made all his victims fit his bed either by stretching their
   legs or by cutting off the parts that stuck over. (The root of the name means "to
   stretch.") Cf. "protean easy-chair," n. 7, p. 47.
6. In Greek mythology, one of the sons of the muse Calliope, who was a famed musician.
   In order to see his wife, Eurydice, who had been killed, he descended into Hades
   (though Melville here uses the term "Tartarus," which designates a section of Hades reserved for the wicked). His playing of the lyre so enchanted the ruler of the underworld
   that Orpheus was permitted to return with Eurydice, provided that he did not look back
   at her before they reached the land of the living. Concerned because he was unsure
   whether or not Eurydice was indeed following him, Orpheus looked back at her just before they reached the upper world and thus lost his love, who was forced to return to
   Hades.

supplicatingly put forth, while a wail like that of Dives[7] is heard:—
"Water, water!"

It was the miser of whom the merchant had spoken.

Swift as a sister-of-charity, the stranger hovers over him:—

"My poor, poor sir, what can I do for you?"

"Ugh, ugh—water!"

Darting out, he procures a glass, returns, and, holding it to the sufferer's lips, supports his head while he drinks: "And did they let you lie here, my poor sir, racked with this parching thirst?"[8]

The miser, a lean old man, whose flesh seemed salted cod-fish, dry as combustibles; head, like one whittled by an idiot out of a knot; flat, bony mouth, nipped between buzzard nose and chin; expression, flitting between hunks and imbecile—now one, now the other—he made no response. His eyes were closed, his cheek lay upon an old white moleskin coat, rolled under his head like a wizened apple upon a grimy snow-bank.

Revived at last, he inclined towards his ministrant, and, in a voice disastrous with a cough, said:—"I am old and miserable, a poor beggar, not worth a shoe-string—how can I repay you?"

"By giving me your confidence."

"Confidence!" he squeaked, with changed manner, while the pallet swung, "little left at my age, but take the stale remains, and welcome."

"Such as it is, though, you give it. Very good. Now give me a hundred dollars."

Upon this the miser was all panic. His hands groped towards his waist, then suddenly flew upward beneath his moleskin pillow, and there lay clutching something out of sight. Meantime, to himself he incoherently mumbled:—"Confidence? Cant, gammon! Confidence? hum, bubble!—Confidence? fetch, gouge![9]—Hundred dollars?—hundred devils!"

Half spent, he lay mute awhile, then feebly raising himself, in a voice for the moment made strong by the sarcasm, said, "A hundred dollars? rather high price to put upon confidence. But don't you see I am a poor, old rat here, dying in the wainscot? You have served me; but, wretch that I am, I can but cough you my thanks,—ugh, ugh, ugh!"

This time his cough was so violent that its convulsions were im-

---

7. See n. 2, p. 16.
8. As Jonathan A. Cook points out, the biblical reference moves from Luke 16 to Mark 9.41, where Jesus promises: "For whosoever shall give you a cup of water to drink in my name, because ye belong to Christ, verily I say unto you, he shall not lose his reward." Below, "hunks": surly old cuss.
9. The old miser is speaking the secret language of the underworld. "Cant": the secret language or jargon of gypsies, thieves, and professional beggars. "Gammon": the accomplice of a pickpocket. "Bubble": a dupe, a person cheated (*A Dictionary of the Underworld*). "Fetch": steal (*Oxford English Dictionary*). "Gouge": swindle.

parted to the plank, which swung him about like a stone in a sling preparatory to its being hurled.

"Ugh, ugh, ugh!"

"What a shocking cough. I wish my friend, the herb-doctor, was here now; a box of his Omni-Balsamic Reinvigorator would do you good."

"Ugh, ugh, ugh!"

"I've a good mind to go find him. He's aboard somewhere. I saw his long, snuff-colored surtout. Trust me, his medicines are the best in the world."

"Ugh, ugh, ugh!"

"Oh, how sorry I am."

"No doubt of it," squeaked the other again, "but go, get your charity out on deck. There parade the pursy peacocks; they don't cough down here in desertion and darkness, like poor old me. Look how scaly a pauper I am, clove with this churchyard cough. Ugh, ugh, ugh!"

"Again, how sorry I feel, not only for your cough, but your poverty. Such a rare chance made unavailable. Did you have but the sum named, how I could invest it for you. Treble profits. But confidence—I fear that, even had you the precious cash, you would not have the more precious confidence I speak of."

"Ugh, ugh, ugh!" flightily raising himself. "What's that? How, how? Then you don't want the money for yourself?"

"My dear, *dear* sir, how could you impute to me such preposterous self-seeking? To solicit out of hand, for my private behoof, an hundred dollars from a perfect stranger? I am not mad, my dear sir."[1]

"How, how?" still more bewildered, "do you, then, go about the world, gratis, seeking to invest people's money for them?"

"My humble profession, sir. I live not for myself; but the world will not have confidence in me, and yet confidence in me were great gain."[2]

"But, but," in a kind of vertigo, "what do—do you do—do with people's money? Ugh, ugh! How is the gain made?"

"To tell that would ruin me. That known, every one would be going into the business, and it would be overdone. A secret, a mys-

---

1. Held captive in Caesarea, Paul was allowed to tell King Agrippa and Porcius Festus the story of how, having persecuted the new followers of Jesus, he was converted on the road to Damascus. Because this story sounds implausible (Jesus speaks from heaven in Hebrew and asks why Paul is persecuting him), Festus loudly calls out, "Paul, thou art beside thyself; much learning doth make thee mad" (Acts 26.24). In verse 25, Paul replies, "I am not mad, most noble Festus; but speak forth the words of truth and soberness." Moved, Agrippa says to Paul, "Almost thou persuadest me to be a Christian" (verse 28). See 96.18 below.
2. A blasphemous conglomeration of phrases. One close parallel is 1 Timothy 6.6: "But godliness with contentment is great gain."

tery—all I have to do with you is to receive your confidence, and all you have to do with me is, in due time, to receive it back, thrice paid in trebling profits."

"What, what?" imbecility in the ascendant once more; "but the vouchers, the vouchers," suddenly hunkish again.

"Honesty's best voucher is honesty's face."

"Can't see yours, though," peering through the obscurity.

From this last alternating flicker of rationality, the miser fell back, sputtering, into his previous gibberish, but it took now an arithmetical turn. Eyes closed, he lay muttering to himself—

"One hundred, one hundred—two hundred, two hundred—three hundred, three hundred."

He opened his eyes, feebly stared, and still more feebly said—

"It's a little dim here, ain't it? Ugh, ugh! But, as well as my poor old eyes can see, you look honest."

"I am glad to hear that."

"If—if, now, I should put"—trying to raise himself, but vainly, excitement having all but exhausted him—"if, if now, I should put, put—"

"No ifs. Downright confidence, or none. So help me heaven, I will have no half-confidences."

He said it with an indifferent and superior air, and seemed moving to go.

"Don't, don't leave me, friend; bear with me; age can't help some distrust; it can't, friend, it can't. Ugh, ugh, ugh! Oh, I am so old and miserable. I ought to have a guard*ee*an. Tell me, if—"

"If? No more!"

"Stay! how soon—ugh, ugh!—would my money be trebled? How soon, friend?"

"You won't confide. Good-bye!"

"Stay, stay," falling back now like an infant, "I confide, I confide; help, friend, my distrust!"[3]

From an old buckskin pouch, tremulously dragged forth, ten hoarded eagles,[4] tarnished into the appearance of ten old horn-buttons, were taken, and half-eagerly, half-reluctantly, offered.

"I know not whether I should accept this slack confidence," said the other coldly, receiving the gold, "but an eleventh-hour confidence, a sick-bed confidence, a distempered, death-bed confidence, after all. Give me the healthy confidence of healthy men, with their healthy wits about them. But let that pass. All right. Good-bye!"

"Nay, back, back—receipt, my receipt! Ugh, ugh, ugh! Who are

---

3. A parody of Mark 9.24: "And straightway the father of the child cried out, and said with tears, Lord, I believe; help thou mine unbelief." "Confide": here, to trust, not to tell secrets.
4. An eagle was an American gold coin worth ten dollars.

you? What have I done? Where go you? My gold, my gold! Ugh, ugh, ugh!"

But, unluckily for this final flicker of reason, the stranger was now beyond ear-shot, nor was any one else within hearing of so feeble a call.

Chapter 16.

A SICK MAN, AFTER SOME IMPATIENCE, IS INDUCED TO BECOME A PATIENT.

The sky slides into blue, the bluffs into bloom; the rapid Mississippi expands; runs sparkling and gurgling, all over in eddies; one magnified wake of a seventy-four.[5] The sun comes out, a golden huzzar, from his tent, flashing his helm on the world. All things, warmed in the landscape, leap. Speeds the dædal[6] boat as a dream.

But, withdrawn in a corner, wrapped about in a shawl, sits an unparticipating man, visited, but not warmed, by the sun—a plant whose hour seems over, while buds are blowing and seeds are astir. On a stool at his left sits a stranger in a snuff-colored surtout, the collar thrown back; his hand waving in persuasive gesture, his eye beaming with hope. But not easily may hope be awakened in one long tranced into hopelessness by a chronic complaint.

To some remark the sick man, by word or look, seemed to have just made an impatiently querulous answer, when, with a deprecatory air, the other resumed:

"Nay, think not I seek to cry up my treatment by crying down that of others. And yet, when one is confident he has truth on his side, and that it is not on the other, it is no very easy thing to be charitable; not that temper is the bar, but conscience; for charity would beget toleration, you know, which is a kind of implied permitting, and in effect a kind of countenancing; and that which is countenanced is so far furthered. But should untruth be furthered? Still, while for the world's good I refuse to further the cause of these mineral doctors, I would fain regard them, not as willful wrongdoers, but good Samaritans erring.[7] And is this—I put it to you, sir—is this the view of an arrogant rival and pretender?"

5. A warship mounting seventy-four cannons. This is still the early morning of the first of April, at the arrival of full daylight.
6. Cunningly fashioned, ingenious, like the flying apparatus Daedelus constructed and with which his son, Icarus, made a disastrous test flight.
7. Would-be rescuers, not true rescuers like the Samaritan in Jesus' parable (Luke 10.30–37). The biblical story is of the man who was going from Jerusalem to Jericho when he fell among thieves who "stripped him of his raiment, and wounded him, and departed, leaving him half dead." The next people to see him, fellow citizens, first a priest and then a Levite, cross the road so as not to go near him. Then a Samaritan (traditionally hostile to the Jews) sees him and not only carries him to an inn but arranges for his care while he recuperates. The "Good Samaritan," as the proverbial but nonbibli-

His physical power all dribbled and gone, the sick man replied not by voice or by gesture; but, with feeble dumb-show of his face, seemed to be saying, "Pray leave me; who was ever cured by talk?"

But the other, as if not unused to make allowances for such despondency, proceeded; and kindly, yet firmly:

"You tell me, that by advice of an eminent physiologist in Louisville, you took tincture of iron. For what? To restore your lost energy. And how? Why, in healthy subjects iron is naturally found in the blood, and iron in the bar is strong; ergo, iron is the source of animal invigoration. But you being deficient in vigor, it follows that the cause is deficiency of iron. Iron, then, must be put into you; and so your tincture. Now as to the theory here, I am mute. But in modesty assuming its truth, and then, as a plain man viewing that theory in practice, I would respectfully question your eminent physiologist: 'Sir,' I would say, 'though by natural processes, lifeless natures taken as nutriment become vitalized, yet is a lifeless nature, under any circumstances, capable of a living transmission, with all its qualities as a lifeless nature unchanged? If, sir, nothing can be incorporated with the living body but by assimilation, and if that implies the conversion of one thing to a different thing (as, in a lamp, oil is assimilated into flame), is it, in this view, likely, that by banqueting on fat, Calvin Edson[8] will fatten? That is, will what is fat on the board prove fat on the bones? If it will, then, sir, what is iron in the vial will prove iron in the vein.' Seems that conclusion too confident?"

But the sick man again turned his dumb-show look, as much as to say, "Pray leave me. Why, with painful words, hint the vanity of that which the pains of this body have too painfully proved?"

But the other, as if unobservant of that querulous look, went on:

---

cal phrase identifies him, is good *because* he was a Samaritan, on whom the injured man had no claim beyond that of simple humanity. A year or so before beginning this book, Melville was examined by his friend and then-neighbor Dr. Oliver Wendell Holmes (who summered at Holmesdale, across what is now Holmes Road, where Arrowhead is located). What if any medication Holmes prescribed is unknown, but it is possible that Melville regarded him as well-intentioned but useless, a good Samaritan erring. The causes of Melville's illnesses in the mid-1850s were complex, and he was in no position to confide in a doctor. At the simplest level, Melville was living and laboring with the knowledge that ignorant and vicious critics by jeering at his greatest works had all but destroyed his career. He carried the burden of secret guilt over incurring a huge debt on which he was defaulting on interest payments every six months. Melville's interest in *Merchant of Venice* as he wrote *The Confidence-Man* owes something to his identification with Antonio, who feels forced to accept a loan from Shylock at life-threatening terms, much as Melville had felt forced to take a loan from his friend T. D. Stewart to make *Moby-Dick* as good as he could. By 1855, before Melville began work on *The Confidence-Man*, Stewart was demanding his pound of Melville's flesh.

8. A "living skeleton" displayed by P. T. Barnum at his American Museum in New York City. By references to feral children, children raised by beasts, deformed bodies, conjoined bodies, human beings becoming animals or animals turning into human shapes, angels appearing as human beings, Satan appearing in human or animal guise, and other anomalous creatures, Melville raises questions about what is really human and what if anything is unnatural or freakish.

"But this notion, that science can play farmer to the flesh, making there what living soil it pleases, seems not so strange as that other conceit—that science is now-a-days so expert that, in consumptive cases, as yours, it can, by prescription of the inhalation of certain vapors, achieve the sublimest act of omnipotence, breathing into all but lifeless dust the breath of life. For did you not tell me, my poor sir, that by order of the great chemist in Baltimore, for three weeks you were never driven out without a respirator, and for a given time of every day sat bolstered up in a sort of gasometer, inspiring vapors generated by the burning of drugs? as if this concocted atmosphere of man were an antidote to the poison of God's natural air. Oh, who can wonder at that old reproach against science, that it is atheistical? And here is my prime reason for opposing these chemical practitioners, who have sought out so many inventions. For what do their inventions indicate, unless it be that kind and degree of pride in human skill, which seems scarce compatible with reverential dependence upon the power above? Try to rid my mind of it as I may, yet still these chemical practitioners with their tinctures, and fumes, and braziers, and occult incantations, seem to me like Pharaoh's vain sorcerers,[9] trying to beat down the will of heaven. Day and night, in all charity, I intercede for them, that heaven may not, in its own language, be provoked to anger with their inventions; may not take vengeance of their inventions.[1] A thousand pities that you should ever have been in the hands of these Egyptians."

But again came nothing but the dumb-show look, as much as to say, "Pray leave me; quacks, and indignation against quacks, both are vain."

But, once more, the other went on: "How different we herb-doctors! who claim nothing, invent nothing; but staff in hand, in glades, and upon hillsides, go about in nature, humbly seeking her cures.[2] True Indian doctors, though not learned in names, we are not unfamiliar with essences—successors of Solomon the Wise,

9. The magic practiced by Pharaoh's wise men and sorcerers proves ineffectual against Moses and Aaron in Exodus 7–8; at last, in Exodus 9, the magicians are stricken with boils breaking forth with blains (blisters).
1. In Psalm 106.29, forgetting the great things God had done in Egypt, the Israelites provoked God "to anger with their inventions: and the plague brake in upon them."
2. Herb doctors in Melville's time purveyed compounds not unlike some of those available in modern natural-food stores. Scott Norsworthy discovered a striking connection between herb doctors and world's charity proponents (see n. 9, p. 48). At the World's Convention in New York in October 1845 a speaker recommended the British social planner Robert Owen (1771–1858) as the man to treat "the present diseased condition of society": "Brother Owen has come opportunely to feel the pulse of our great mother [i.e., society]! (Cheers.) And he had [i.e., has] herbs and minerals in his mortar that would doubtless check the disease if not effect a cure. (Applause.) Disease is in our midst but health is on its heels. (Cheers.)" (The New York *Tribune*, October 2, 1845.)

who knew all vegetables, from the cedar of Lebanon, to the hyssop on the wall.[3] Yes, Solomon was the first of herb-doctors. Nor were the virtues of herbs unhonored by yet older ages. Is it not writ, that on a moonlight night,

> 'Medea gathered the enchanted herbs
> That did renew old Æson?'[4]

Ah, would you but have confidence, you should be the new Æson, and I your Medea. A few vials of my Omni-Balsamic Reinvigorator would, I am certain, give you some strength."

Upon this, indignation and abhorrence seemed to work by their excess the effect promised of the balsam. Roused from that long apathy of impotence, the cadaverous man started, and, in a voice that was as the sound of obstructed air gurgling through a maze of broken honey-combs, cried: "Begone! You are all alike. The name of doctor, the dream of helper, condemns you. For years I have been but a gallipot for you experimentizers to rinse your experiments into, and now, in this livid skin, partake of the nature of my contents. Begone! I hate ye."

"I were inhuman, could I take affront at a want of confidence, born of too bitter an experience of betrayers. Yet, permit one who is not without feeling—"

"Begone! Just in that voice talked to me, not six months ago, the German doctor at the water cure, from which I now return, six months and sixty pangs nigher my grave."

"The water-cure? Oh, fatal delusion of the well-meaning Preisnitz![5]—Sir, trust me—"

"Begone!"

"Nay, an invalid should not always have his own way. Ah, sir, reflect how untimely this distrust in one like you. How weak you are; and weakness, is it not the time for confidence? Yes, when through

3. In 1 Kings 4.33 the mighty "cedar tree that is in Lebanon" and the small "hyssop" (a caper, or a sort of mint) "that springeth out of the wall" are two of the many things of which Solomon speaks wisely. "Indian doctors": including white people.
4. Shakespeare's *The Merchant of Venice* 5.1.12–14: "In such a night. / Medea gathered the enchanted herbs / That did renew old Æson." In this love scene between Lorenzo and Jessica (Shylock's daughter) old stories, including this from Virgil's *The Aeneid*, are recalled as happening "in such a night" as the lovers now experience.
5. Vincenz Preissnitz, the usual spelling (1799–1851), born in what is now the Czech Republic, author of *The Manual of the Water-Cure* (c. 1835), and operator of a pioneering hydrotherapeutic establishment, may be regarded as a father of holistic medicine. Hydropathy was a great fad in the 1840s and 1850s, popularized in the United States by R. T. Trall in his *The Water-Cure Journal* and a book published in the early 1850s in New York by Fowler and Wells (remembered as the publishers in 1855 of Walt Whitman's *Leaves of Grass*). An acquaintance of Melville's, Dr. Thomas Low Nichols, edited a water-cure journal in the 1850s. Bigelow (see n. 7, p. 87) described Preissnitz as dying "in the midst of his own water-cure," deluded to the end about the efficacy of his treatment. For another major figure in the pattern of deluded optimists in *The Confidence-Man*, see Anacharsis Cloots, executed by those he had inspired to revolt (see n. 3, p. 17).

weakness everything bids despair, then is the time to get strength by confidence."[6]

Relenting in his air, the sick man cast upon him a long glance of beseeching, as if saying, "With confidence must come hope; and how can hope be?"

The herb-doctor took a sealed paper box from his surtout pocket, and holding it towards him, said solemnly, "Turn not away. This may be the last time of health's asking. Work upon yourself; invoke confidence, though from ashes; rouse it; for your life, rouse it, and invoke it, I say."

The other trembled, was silent; and then, a little commanding himself, asked the ingredients of the medicine.

"Herbs."

"What herbs? And the nature of them? And the reason for giving them?"

"It cannot be made known."

"Then I will none of you."

Sedately observant of the juiceless, joyless form before him, the herb-doctor was mute a moment, then said:—"I give up."

"How?"

"You are sick, and a philosopher."

"No, no;—not the last."

"But, to demand the ingredient, with the reason for giving, is the mark of a philosopher; just as the consequence is the penalty of a fool. A sick philosopher is incurable."

"Why?"

"Because he has no confidence."

"How does that make him incurable?"

"Because either he spurns his powder, or, if he take it, it proves a blank cartridge, though the same given to a rustic in like extremity, would act like a charm. I am no materialist; but the mind so acts upon the body, that if the one have no confidence, neither has the other."

Again, the sick man appeared not unmoved. He seemed to be thinking what in candid truth could be said to all this. At length, "You talk of confidence. How comes it that when brought low himself, the herb-doctor, who was most confident to prescribe in other cases, proves least confident to prescribe in his own; having small confidence in himself for himself?"

"But he has confidence in the brother he calls in. And that he does so, is no reproach to him, since he knows that when the body

---

6. In Isaiah 30.15–16 God tells the Israelites how they *should* have behaved, but did not: "In returning and rest shall ye be saved; in quietness and in confidence shall be your strength: and ye would not. But ye said, No; for we will flee upon horses; therefore shall ye flee: and, We will ride upon the swift; therefore shall they that pursue you be swift."

is prostrated, the mind is not erect. Yes, in this hour the herb-doctor does distrust himself, but not his art."

The sick man's knowledge did not warrant him to gainsay this. But he seemed not grieved at it; glad to be confuted in a way tending towards his wish.

"Then you give me hope?" his sunken eye turned up.

"Hope is proportioned to confidence. How much confidence you give me, so much hope do I give you. For this," lifting the box, "if all depended upon this, I should rest. It is nature's own."

"Nature!"

"Why do you start?"

"I know not," with a sort of shudder, "but I have heard of a book entitled 'Nature in Disease.' "[7]

"A title I cannot approve; it is suspiciously scientific. 'Nature in Disease?' As if nature, divine nature, were aught but health; as if through nature disease is decreed! But did I not before hint of the tendency of science, that forbidden tree?[8] Sir, if despondency is yours from recalling that title, dismiss it. Trust me, nature is health;[9] for health is good, and nature cannot work ill. As little can she work error. Get nature, and you get well. Now, I repeat, this medicine is nature's own."

Again the sick man could not, according to his light, conscientiously disprove what was said. Neither, as before, did he seem

---

7. The author of *Nature in Disease* (1854), Dr. Jacob Bigelow (1786 or 1787–1879) was the husband of Mary Scollay, Melville's father's first cousin. Bigelow was also a neighbor and intimate friend of Melville's father-in-law, Lemuel Shaw, the chief justice of the Supreme Court of Massachusetts. *Nature in Disease* is a collection of essays on various diseases and medical subjects, including quackery, homeopathy, and the history of medicine. Melville would have seen the review of Bigelow's book in the January 1855 *Harper's New Monthly Magazine*, which said it contained "papers devoted to subjects of more general interest, like those on the Burial of the Dead, on Coffee and Tea, on the History and Use of Tobacco, and so forth," then commented that Bigelow "belongs to that branch of the old school of medical practice which trusts less, in the curative treatment of disease, to the active interferences of art than to the observance of the salutary indications of nature." On the same page as the review of Melville's *Pierre* in *Littell's Living Age* (September 4, 1852), was a notice of an American edition of *God in Disease; or the Manifestations of Design in Morbid Phenomena*, by James F. Duncan, M.D. (1852). Duncan wrote, "Most persons are in the habit of admitting that the visitation of sickness is the result of the direct appointment of God; but scarcely any one appears to think that such an admission implies the existence of features stamped upon the dispensation, similar to what are to be found in other parts of the Divine proceedings and that are eminently deserving of being studied carefully."

8. The herb doctor, having earlier denounced scientific medical researchers as being like Pharaoh's vain sorcerers (see n. 9, p. 84), reinforces his argument by charging them with seeking what God forbade mankind to know, the knowledge of good and evil (Genesis 2:17).

9. This plausible statement of a pre-Romantic and Romantic assumption was not yet a common phrase. In Melville's "Poor Man's Pudding" (published June 1854 in *Harper's*) the ameliorist poet and country gentleman Blandmour proclaims: "the blessed almoner, Nature, is in all things beneficent; and not only so, but considerate in her charities, as any discreet human philanthropist might be." "Almoner": one who dispenses alms, charitable gifts. Melville's narrator decides otherwise in "Why the Poor in the United States Suffer More than the Poor Elsewhere" (p. 391 herein).

over-anxious to do so; the less, as in his sensitiveness it seemed to him, that hardly could he offer so to do without something like the appearance of a kind of implied irreligion; nor in his heart was he ungrateful, that since a spirit opposite to that pervaded all the herb-doctor's hopeful words, therefore, for hopefulness, he (the sick man) had not alone medical warrant, but also doctrinal.

"Then you do really think," hectically, "that if I take this medicine," mechanically reaching out for it, "I shall regain my health?"

"I will not encourage false hopes," relinquishing to him the box, "I will be frank with you. Though frankness is not always the weakness of the mineral practitioner, yet the herb doctor must be frank, or nothing. Now then, sir, in your case, a radical cure—such a cure, understand, as should make you robust—such a cure, sir, I do not and cannot promise."

"Oh, you need not! only restore me the power of being something else to others than a burdensome care, and to myself a droning grief. Only cure me of this misery of weakness; only make me so that I can walk about in the sun and not draw the flies to me, as lured by the coming of decay. Only do that—but that."

"You ask not much; you are wise; not in vain have you suffered. That little you ask, I think, can be granted. But remember, not in a day, nor a week, nor perhaps a month, but sooner or later; I say not exactly when, for I am neither prophet nor charlatan. Still, if, according to the directions in your box there, you take my medicine steadily, without assigning an especial day, near or remote, to discontinue it, then may you calmly look for some eventual result of good. But again I say, you must have confidence."

Feverishly he replied that he now trusted he had, and hourly should pray for its increase. When suddenly relapsing into one of those strange caprices peculiar to some invalids, he added: "But to one like me, it is so hard, so hard. The most confident hopes so often have failed me, and as often have I vowed never, no, never, to trust them again. Oh," feebly wringing his hands, "you do not know, you do not know."

"I know this, that never did a right confidence come to naught. But time is short; you hold your cure, to retain or reject."

"I retain," with a clinch, "and now how much?"

"As much as you can evoke from your heart and heaven."

"How?—the price of this medicine?"

"I thought it was confidence you meant; how much confidence you should have. The medicine,—that is half a dollar a vial. Your box holds six."

The money was paid.

"Now, sir," said the herb-doctor, "my business calls me away, and it may so be that I shall never see you again; if then—"

He paused, for the sick man's countenance fell blank.

"Forgive me," cried the other, "forgive that imprudent phrase 'never see you again.' Though I solely intended it with reference to myself, yet I had forgotten what your sensitiveness might be. I repeat, then, that it may be that we shall not soon have a second interview, so that hereafter, should another of my boxes be needed, you may not be able to replace it except by purchase at the shops; and, in so doing, you may run more or less risk of taking some not salutary mixture. For such is the popularity of the Omni-Balsamic Reinvigorator—thriving not by the credulity of the simple, but the trust of the wise—that certain contrivers have not been idle, though I would not, indeed, hastily affirm of them that they are aware of the sad consequences to the public. Homicides and murderers, some call those contrivers; but I do not; for murder (if such a crime be possible) comes from the heart, and these men's motives come from the purse. Were they not in poverty, I think they would hardly do what they do. Still, the public interests forbid that I should let their needy device for a living succeed. In short, I have adopted precautions. Take the wrapper from any of my vials and hold it to the light, you will see water-marked in capitals the word '*confidence*,' which is the countersign of the medicine, as I wish it was of the world. The wrapper bears that mark or else the medicine is counterfeit. But if still any lurking doubt should remain, pray enclose the wrapper to this address," handing a card, "and by return mail I will answer."

At first the sick man listened, with the air of vivid interest, but gradually, while the other was still talking, another strange caprice came over him, and he presented the aspect of the most calamitous dejection.

"How now?" said the herb-doctor.

"You told me to have confidence, said that confidence was indispensable, and here you preach to me distrust. Ah, truth will out!"[1]

"I told you, you must have confidence, unquestioning confidence, I meant confidence in the genuine medicine, and the genuine *me*."

"But in your absence, buying vials purporting to be yours, it seems I cannot have unquestioning confidence."

"Prove all the vials; trust those which are true."[2]

"But to doubt, to suspect, to prove—to have all this wearing work to be doing continually—how opposed to confidence. It is evil!"

"From evil comes good. Distrust is a stage to confidence. How has it proved in our interview? But your voice is husky; I have let

---

1. Launcelot speaks this conventional phrase in Shakespeare's *Merchant of Venice* 2.2.73.
2. Cf. "Prove all things; hold fast that which is good" (1 Thessalonians 5.21). As in "the exception proves the rule," the word *prove* means "test."

you talk too much. You hold your cure; I leave you. But stay—when I hear that health is yours, I will not, like some I know, vainly make boasts; but, giving glory where all glory is due, say, with the devout herb-doctor, Iapis in Virgil, when, in the unseen but efficacious presence of Venus, he with simples healed the wound of Æneas:—

> 'This is no mortal work, no cure of mine,
> Nor art's effect, but done by power[3] divine.' "

Chapter 17.

TOWARDS THE END OF WHICH THE HERB-DOCTOR PROVES HIMSELF A FORGIVER OF INJURIES.

In a kind of ante-cabin, a number of respectable looking people, male and female, way-passengers, recently come on board, are listlessly sitting in a mutually shy sort of silence.

Holding up a small, square bottle, ovally labeled with the engraving of a countenance full of soft pity as that of the Romish-painted Madonna,[4] the herb-doctor passes slowly among them, benignly urbane, turning this way and that, saying:—

"Ladies and gentlemen, I hold in my hand here the Samaritan Pain Dissuader, thrice-blessed discovery of that disinterested friend of humanity whose portrait you see. Pure vegetable extract. Warranted to remove the acutest pain within less than ten minutes. Five hundred dollars to be forfeited on failure. Especially efficacious in heart disease and tic-douloureux. Observe the expression of this pledged friend of humanity.—Price only fifty cents."

In vain. After the first idle stare, his auditors—in pretty good health, it seemed—instead of encouraging his politeness, appeared, if anything, impatient of it; and, perhaps, only diffidence, or some small regard for his feelings, prevented them from telling him so. But, insensible to their coldness, or charitably overlooking it, he more wooingly than ever resumed: "May I venture upon a small supposition? Have I your kind leave, ladies and gentlemen?"

To which modest appeal, no one had the kindness to answer a syllable.

"Well," said he, resignedly, "silence is at least not denial, and may be consent. My supposition is this: possibly some lady, here present, has a dear friend at home, a bed-ridden sufferer from spinal complaint. If so, what gift more appropriate to that sufferer than this tasteful little bottle of Pain Dissuader?"

---

3. In Dryden's translation of Virgil's *Aeneid* 12.632–33, which Melville owned, the word is *hands*, not "power." Thus the hands of Venus, Aeneas' mother, who has helped Iapis heal the wounded hero. "Simples": common medicinal herbs.

4. Mary, the mother of Jesus, as portrayed by popular sentimental Roman Catholic painters.

Again he glanced about him, but met much the same reception as before. Those faces, alien alike to sympathy or surprise, seemed patiently to say, "We are travelers; and, as such, must expect to meet, and quietly put up with, many antic fools, and more antic quacks."

"Ladies and gentlemen," (deferentially fixing his eyes upon their now self-complacent faces) "ladies and gentlemen, might I, by your kind leave, venture upon one other small supposition? It is this: that there is scarce a sufferer, this noonday, writhing on his bed, but in his hour he sat satisfactorily healthy and happy; that the Samaritan Pain Dissuader is the one only balm for that to which each living creature—who knows?—may be a draughted victim, present or prospective. In short:—Oh, Happiness on my right hand, and oh, Security on my left, can ye wisely adore a Providence, and not think it wisdom to provide?—Provide!" (Uplifting the bottle.)

What immediate effect, if any, this appeal might have had, is uncertain. For just then the boat touched at a houseless landing, scooped, as by a land-slide, out of sombre forests; back through which led a road, the sole one, which, from its narrowness, and its being walled up with story on story of dusk, matted foliage, presented the vista of some cavernous old gorge in a city, like haunted Cock Lane in London.[5] Issuing from that road, and crossing that landing, there stooped his shaggy form in the door-way, and entered the ante-cabin, with a step so burdensome that shot seemed in his pockets, a kind of invalid Titan[6] in homespun; his beard blackly pendant, like the Carolina-moss, and dank with cypress dew; his countenance tawny and shadowy as an iron-ore country in a clouded day. In one hand he carried a heavy walking-stick of swamp-oak; with the other, led a puny girl, walking in moccasins, not improbably his child, but evidently of alien maternity, perhaps Creole,[7] or even Camanche. Her eye would have been large for a woman, and was inky as the pools of falls among mountain-pines. An Indian blanket, orange-hued, and fringed with bead tassel-work, appeared that morning to have shielded the child from heavy showers. Her limbs were tremulous; she seemed a little Cassandra,[8] in nervousness.

5. Dr. Samuel Johnson in 1762 exposed the "ghost" in London's Cock-Lane as faked. Here Melville omits the exposure of the fakery; in *Moby-Dick*, chapter 69, "The Funeral," he had mistakenly made Johnson gullible about the ghost rather than skeptical.
6. In Greek mythology the Titans, giant children of heaven and earth, were the old gods, ruling before the Olympian gods. The Titans were injured when they were deposed and hurled into Tartarus, or hell. For Melville's powerful vision of the Mount of the Titans, see *Pierre*, book 25, chapter 4.
7. A Caribbean or, specifically, New Orleans French-speaking caste, primarily of Spanish and French descent and sometimes racially mixed.
8. Daughter of Priam, king of Troy, whose fate was to foretell the future and not be believed.

No sooner was the pair spied by the herb-doctor, than with a cheerful air, both arms extended like a host's, he advanced, and taking the child's reluctant hand, said, trippingly: "On your travels, ah, my little May Queen?[9] Glad to see you. What pretty moccasins. Nice to dance in." Then with a half caper sang—

> " 'Hey diddle,[1] diddle, the cat and the fiddle;
> The cow jumped over the moon.'

Come, chirrup, chirrup, my little robin!"

Which playful welcome drew no responsive playfulness from the child, nor appeared to gladden or conciliate the father; but rather, if anything, to dash the dead weight of his heavy-hearted expression with a smile hypochondriacally scornful.

Sobering down now, the herb-doctor addressed the stranger in a manly, business-like way—a transition which, though it might seem a little abrupt, did not appear constrained, and, indeed, served to show that his recent levity was less the habit of a frivolous nature, than the frolic condescension of a kindly heart.

"Excuse me," said he, "but, if I err not, I was speaking to you the other day;—on a Kentucky boat, wasn't it?"

"Never to me," was the reply; the voice deep and lonesome enough to have come from the bottom of an abandoned coal-shaft.

"Ah!—But am I again mistaken, (his eye falling on the swamp-oak stick,) or don't you go a little lame, sir?"

"Never was lame in my life."

"Indeed? I fancied I had perceived not a limp, but a hitch, a slight hitch;—some experience in these things—divined some hidden cause of the hitch—buried bullet, may be—some dragoons in the Mexican war discharged with such, you know.—Hard fate!" he sighed, "little pity for it, for who sees it?—have you dropped anything?"

Why, there is no telling, but the stranger was bowed over, and might have seemed bowing for the purpose of picking up something, were it not that, as arrested in the imperfect posture, he for the moment so remained; slanting his tall stature like a mainmast yielding to the gale, or Adam to the thunder.[2]

The little child pulled him. With a kind of a surge he righted himself, for an instant looked toward the herb-doctor; but, either from emotion or aversion, or both together, withdrew his eyes, say-

---

9. Character in the medieval English Morris (Moorish) dance celebrating the coming of spring.
1. To cheat or trick; here colors the effect of the nonsense words "diddle diddle" in the familiar nursery rhyme.
2. Elsewhere in the Bible God speaks with a voice like thunder (e.g., Job 40.9: "Hast thou an arm like God? or canst thou thunder with a voice like him?"), but not when he expels Adam and Eve from the Garden of Eden in Genesis 3. Melville may have been visualizing some popular image of the expulsion from the garden.

ing nothing. Presently, still stooping, he seated himself, drawing his child between his knees, his massy hands tremulous, and still averting his face, while up into the compassionate one of the herb-doctor the child turned a fixed, melancholy glance of repugnance.

The herb-doctor stood observant a moment, then said:

"Surely you have pain, strong pain, somewhere; in strong frames pain is strongest. Try, now, my specific," (holding it up). "Do but look at the expression of this friend of humanity. Trust me, certain cure for any pain in the world. Won't you look?"

"No," choked the other.

"Very good. Merry time to you, little May Queen."

And so, as if he would intrude his cure upon no one, moved pleasantly off, again crying his wares, nor now at last without result. A new-comer, not from the shore, but another part of the boat, a sickly young man, after some questions, purchased a bottle. Upon this, others of the company began a little to wake up as it were; the scales of indifference or prejudice fell from their eyes;[3] now, at last, they seemed to have an inkling that here was something not undesirable which might be had for the buying.

But while, ten times more briskly bland than ever, the herb-doctor was driving his benevolent trade, accompanying each sale with added praises of the thing traded, all at once the dusk giant, seated at some distance, unexpectedly raised his voice with—

"What was that you last said?"

The question was put distinctly, yet resonantly, as when a great clock-bell—stunning admonisher—strikes one; and the stroke, though single, comes bedded in the belfry clamor.

All proceedings were suspended. Hands held forth for the specific were withdrawn, while every eye turned towards the direction whence the question came. But, no way abashed, the herb-doctor, elevating his voice with even more than wonted self-possession, replied—

"I was saying what, since you wish it, I cheerfully repeat, that the Samaritan Pain Dissuader, which I here hold in my hand, will either cure or ease any pain you please, within ten minutes after its application."

"Does it produce insensibility?"

"By no means. Not the least of its merits is, that it is not an opiate. It kills pain without killing feeling."

"You lie! Some pains cannot be eased but by producing insensibility, and cannot be cured but by producing death."[4]

3. Ananias, acting on a message from Jesus, finds the blinded Saul in Damascus and tells him that his sight will be restored and that he will be filled with the Holy Ghost. What next happens to Saul is told in Acts of the Apostles 9.18: "And immediately there fell from his eyes as it had been scales: and he received sight forthwith, and arose, and was baptized." Thereafter, Saul is known as Paul, the apostle to the Gentiles.

4. Melville reflects the intense innovation in medical theory and practice in recent years,

Beyond this the dusk giant said nothing; neither, for impairing the other's market, did there appear much need to. After eying the rude speaker a moment with an expression of mingled admiration and consternation, the company silently exchanged glances of mutual sympathy under unwelcome conviction. Those who had purchased looked sheepish or ashamed; and a cynical-looking little man, with a thin flaggy beard, and a countenance ever wearing the rudiments of a grin, seated alone in a corner commanding a good view of the scene, held a rusty hat before his face.

But, again, the herb-doctor, without noticing the retort, overbearing though it was, began his panegyrics anew, and in a tone more assured than before, going so far now as to say that his specific was sometimes almost as effective in cases of mental suffering as in cases of physical; or rather, to be more precise, in cases when, through sympathy, the two sorts of pain coöperated into a climax of both—in such cases, he said, the specific had done very well. He cited an example: Only three bottles, faithfully taken, cured a Louisiana widow (for three weeks sleepless in a darkened chamber) of neuralgic sorrow for the loss of husband and child, swept off in one night by the last epidemic. For the truth of this, a printed voucher was produced, duly signed.

While he was reading it aloud, a sudden side-blow all but felled him.

It was the giant, who, with a countenance lividly epileptic with hypochondriac[5] mania, exclaimed—

"Profane fiddler on heart-strings! Snake!"

More he would have added, but, convulsed, could not; so, without another word, taking up the child, who had followed him, went with a rocking pace out of the cabin.

"Regardless of decency, and lost to humanity!" exclaimed the herb-doctor, with much ado recovering himself. Then, after a pause, during which he examined his bruise, not omitting to apply externally a little of his specific, and with some success, as it would seem, plained to himself:

"No, no, I won't seek redress; innocence is my redress. But," turning upon them all, "if that man's wrathful blow provokes me to no wrath, should his evil distrust arouse you to distrust? I do de-

---

especially after the pioneering work with anesthesia (in Boston) in the mid-1840s. Among the pioneers were Charles T. Jackson, brother of Ralph Waldo Emerson's second wife; Horace Wells, a Hartford dentist; and the man who took most of the credit, William Thomas Morton, who conducted a successful demonstration of surgery under anesthesia in 1846. A Calvinist could consider these improvements in the fight against pain as signs that people were trying to escape God's punishment of Adam and Eve for disobedience.

5. Morbidly depressive (without implying that the sickness is desired or imagined). Below, "plained": grumbled (archaic for bemoaned).

voutly hope," proudly raising voice and arm, "for the honor of humanity—hope that, despite this coward assault, the Samaritan Pain
Dissuader stands unshaken in the confidence of all who hear me!"

But, injured as he was, and patient under it, too, somehow his
case excited as little compassion as his oratory now did enthusiasm.
Still, pathetic to the last, he continued his appeals, notwithstanding
the frigid regard of the company, till, suddenly interrupting himself,
as if in reply to a quick summons from without, he said hurriedly, "I
come, I come," and so, with every token of precipitate dispatch, out
of the cabin the herb-doctor went.

Chapter 18.

INQUEST INTO THE TRUE CHARACTER OF THE HERB-DOCTOR.

"Sha'n't see that fellow again in a hurry," remarked an auburn-
haired gentleman, to his neighbor with a hook-nose. "Never knew
an operator so completely unmasked."

"But do you think it the fair thing to unmask an operator that way?"

"Fair? It is right."

"Supposing that at high 'change on the Paris Bourse, Asmodeus[6]
should lounge in, distributing hand-bills, revealing the true
thoughts and designs of all the operators present—would that be
the fair thing in Asmodeus? Or, as Hamlet says, were it 'to consider
the thing too curiously?' "[7]

"We won't go into that. But since you admit the fellow to be a
knave—"

"I don't admit it. Or, if I did, I take it back. Shouldn't wonder if,
after all, he is no knave at all, or, but little of one. What can you
prove against him?"

---

6. The demon in *Le Diable Boiteux* (1707) by Alain René Lesage (1668–1747). The title (a
reference to the Devil's being portrayed as cloven footed), was sometimes translated as
The Lame Devil and sometimes as *The Devil on Two Sticks*. ("Two sticks": two crutches.)
A translation by Joseph Thomas, *Asmodeus: The Devil on Two Sticks; or, The Force of
Friendship*" (1841), was made into a play. In Lesage, Asmodeus, the demon of lust,
emerges from imprisonment in a flask and shows a young student what goes on inside
houses of Madrid, accompanying their voyeurism with a series of anecdotes. For *White-
Jacket* (1850), Melville had plundered Nathaniel Ames's *A Mariner's Sketches, Originally
Published in the Manufacturers and Farmers Journal* (1830). He knew the passage where
Ames says, "I should suppose that when a man is hermetically sealed up, like Asmodeus,
in the 'Devil on two sticks,' his prospects in this world must be gloomy and circum-
scribed." In the Apocrypha, Tobit 3, the evil spirit Asmodeus kills Sara's seven husbands,
one by one, before "they had lain with her." The archangel Raphael came down "to bind
Asmodeus the evil spirit," so that Tobit's son, Tobias, was free to marry Sara and live
with her. "high 'change": the stock exchange at the height of activity, like Wall Street at
midday.

7. *Hamlet* 5.1.205. In the graveyard, inspired by the skull of the jester Yorick, Hamlet (in
the Hilliard, Gray text Melville used) philosophizes about death and says to Horatio, "To
what base uses we may return, Horatio! Why may not imagination trace the noble dust
of Alexander, till he find it stopping a bunghole?" (5.1.202–4). Horatio responds,
" 'Twere to consider too curiously, to consider so" (5.1.205–6).

"I can prove that he makes dupes."

"Many held in honor do the same; and many, not wholly knaves, do it too."

"How about that last?"

"He is not wholly at heart a knave, I fancy, among whose dupes is himself. Did you not see our quack friend apply to himself his own quackery? A fanatic quack; essentially a fool, though effectively a knave."

Bending over, and looking down between his knees on the floor, the auburn-haired gentleman meditatively scribbled there awhile with his cane, then, glancing up, said:

"I can't conceive how you, in any way, can hold him a fool. How he talked—so glib, so pat, so well."

"A smart fool always talks well; takes a smart fool to be tonguey."

In much the same strain the discussion continued—the hook-nosed gentleman talking at large and excellently, with a view of demonstrating that a smart fool always talks just so. Ere long he talked to such purpose as almost to convince.

Presently, back came the person of whom the auburn-haired gentleman had predicted that he would not return. Conspicuous in the door-way he stood, saying, in a clear voice, "Is the agent of the Seminole Widow and Orphan Asylum within here?"

No one replied.

"Is there within here any agent or any member of any charitable institution whatever?"

No one seemed competent to answer, or, no one thought it worth while to.

"If there be within here any such person, I have in my hand two dollars for him."

Some interest was manifested.

"I was called away so hurriedly, I forgot this part of my duty. With the proprietor of the Samaritan Pain Dissuader it is a rule, to devote, on the spot, to some benevolent purpose, the half of the proceeds of sales. Eight bottles were disposed of among this company. Hence, four half-dollars remain to charity. Who, as steward, takes the money?"

One or two pair of feet moved upon the floor, as with a sort of itching; but nobody rose.

"Does diffidence prevail over duty? If, I say, there be any gentleman, or any lady, either, here present, who is in any connection with any charitable institution whatever, let him or her come forward. He or she happening to have at hand no certificate of such connection, makes no difference. Not of a suspicious temper, thank God, I shall have confidence in whoever offers to take the money."

A demure-looking woman, in a dress rather tawdry and rumpled, here drew her veil well down and rose; but, marking every eye upon her, thought it advisable, upon the whole, to sit down again.

"Is it to be believed that, in this Christian company, there is no one charitable person? I mean, no one connected with any charity? Well, then, is there no object of charity here?"

Upon this, an unhappy-looking woman, in a sort of mourning, neat, but sadly worn, hid her face behind a meagre bundle, and was heard to sob. Meantime, as not seeing or hearing her, the herb-doctor again spoke, and this time not unpathetically:

"Are there none here who feel in need of help, and who, in accepting such help, would feel that they, in their time, have given or done more than may ever be given or done to them? Man or woman, is there none such here?"

The sobs of the woman were more audible, though she strove to repress them. While nearly every one's attention was bent upon her, a man of the appearance of a day-laborer, with a white bandage across his face, concealing the side of the nose, and who, for cool-ness' sake, had been sitting in his red-flannel shirt-sleeves, his coat thrown across one shoulder, the darned cuffs drooping behind—this man shufflingly rose, and, with a pace that seemed the linger-ing memento of the lock-step of convicts, went up for a duly-qualified claimant.

"Poor wounded huzzar!" sighed the herb-doctor, and dropping the money into the man's clam-shell of a hand turned and de-parted.

The recipient of the alms was about moving after, when the auburn-haired gentleman staid him: "Don't be frightened, you; but I want to see those coins. Yes, yes; good silver, good silver. There, take them again, and while you are about it, go bandage the rest of yourself behind something. D'ye hear? Consider yourself, wholly, the scar of a nose, and be off with yourself."

Being of a forgiving nature, or else from emotion not daring to trust his voice, the man silently, but not without some precipitancy, withdrew.

"Strange," said the auburn-haired gentleman, returning to his friend, "the money was good money."

"Aye, and where your fine knavery now? Knavery to devote the half of one's receipts to charity? He's a fool I say again."

"Others might call him an original genius."

"Yes, being original in his folly. Genius? His genius is a cracked pate, and, as this age goes, not much originality about that."

"May he not be knave, fool, and genius all together?"

"I beg pardon," here said a third person with a gossiping expres-sion who had been listening, "but you are somewhat puzzled by this man, and well you may be."

"Do you know anything about him?" asked the hooked-nosed gentleman.

"No, but I suspect him for something."

"Suspicion. We want knowledge."

"Well, suspect first and know next. True knowledge comes but by suspicion or revelation. That's my maxim."

"And yet," said the auburn-haired gentleman, "since a wise man will keep even some certainties to himself, much more some suspicions, at least he will at all events so do till they ripen into knowledge."

"Do you hear that about the wise man?" said the hook-nosed gentleman, turning upon the new comer. "Now what is it you suspect of this fellow?"

"I shrewdly suspect him," was the eager response, "for one of those Jesuit emissaries prowling all over our country.[8] The better to accomplish their secret designs, they assume, at times, I am told, the most singular masques; sometimes, in appearance, the absurdest."

This, though indeed for some reason causing a droll smile upon the face of the hook-nosed gentleman, added a third angle to the discussion, which now became a sort of triangular duel, and ended, at last, with but a triangular result.

Chapter 19.

A SOLDIER OF FORTUNE.[9]

"Mexico? Molino del Rey? Resaca de la Palma?"

"Resaca de la *Tombs!*"[1]

Leaving his reputation to take care of itself, since, as is not seldom the case, he knew nothing of its being in debate, the herb-doctor, wandering towards the forward part of the boat, had there

---

8. "It is an ascertained fact, that Jesuits are prowling about all parts of the United States in every possible disguise, expressly to ascertain the most advantageous situations and modes to disseminate popery. A minister of the gospel from Ohio, has informed us, that he discovered one carrying on his devices in his congregation; and he says, that the western country swarms with them under the names of puppet show-men, dancing masters, music teachers, pedlars of images and ornaments, barrel organ players, and similar practitioners. . . . Beware of Jesuits!" (*American Protestant Vindicator*, December 24, 1834). ("Western country": roughly, the area between the original states and the Mississippi River.) Melville is satirizing the current paranoia of the ultra-American Know-Nothings. One of the Harper brothers, Melville's second American publishers, was elected mayor of New York after an anti-Catholic campaign. Below, "triangular duel" was famous as the title of a farcical episode in Captain Frederick Marryat's *Mr. Midshipman Easy* (1836).

9. A dashing fellow who follows a military career wherever there is promise of profit, adventure, or pleasure.

1. The speaker is brusquely crediting his condition not to one glorious Mexican battlefield or another (Molino del Rey, 1847; Resaca de la Palma, 1846) but to the jail cells in the Halls of Justice in lower Manhattan. The architecture of the Halls of Justice reminded readers of an Egyptian tomb in John Lloyd Stephens's *Travels in Egypt, Arabia Petraea, and the Holy Land* (1837), so the building became known as "the Tombs." Like many

espied a singular character in a grimy old regimental coat, a countenance at once grim and wizened, interwoven paralyzed legs, stiff
as icicles, suspended between rude crutches, while the whole rigid
body, like a ship's long barometer on gimbals, swung to and fro, mechanically faithful to the motion of the boat. Looking downward
while he swung, the cripple seemed in a brown study.[2]

As moved by the sight, and conjecturing that here was some battered hero from the Mexican battle-fields, the herb-doctor had sym-
pathetically accosted him as above, and received the above rather
dubious reply. As, with a half moody, half surly sort of air that reply
was given, the cripple, by a voluntary jerk, nervously increased his
swing (his custom when seized by emotion), so that one would have
thought some squall had suddenly rolled the boat and with it the
barometer.

"Tombs? my friend," exclaimed the herb-doctor in mild surprise.
"You have not descended to the dead, have you? I had imagined you
a scarred campaigner, one of the noble children of war, for your
dear country a glorious sufferer. But you are Lazarus,[3] it seems."

"Yes, he who had sores."

"Ah, the *other* Lazarus. But I never knew that either of them was
in the army," glancing at the dilapidated regimentals.

"That will do now. Jokes enough."

"Friend," said the other reproachfully, "you think amiss. On principle, I greet unfortunates with some pleasant remark, the better to
call off their thoughts from their troubles. The physician who is at
once wise and humane seldom unreservedly sympathizes with his
patient. But come, I am a herb-doctor, and also a natural bone-
setter. I may be sanguine, but I think I can do something for you.
You look up now. Give me your story. Ere I undertake a cure, I require a full account of the case."

"You can't help me," returned the cripple gruffly. "Go away."

"You seem sadly destitute of—"

"No I ain't destitute; to-day, at least, I can pay my way."

"The Natural Bone-setter is happy, indeed, to hear that. But you

---

other New Yorkers, Melville retained a strong interest in tales coming out of the jail long
after the novelty of its design wore off, as in his references to Colt's murder of Adams in
"Bartleby" and Tom Hyer's escapades in *Israel Potter* (see "Melville's Fascination with
Criminals," p. 343 herein). Melville's attitude toward the Mexican War was complex (especially after it became clear that a Whig general, Zachary Taylor, would win the presidency after a war started by an expansionist Democrat, James K. Polk, toward whose
election Melville's brother Gansevoort had made notable contributions as a speech-
maker). Melville's satires of General Taylor, the "Authentic Anecdotes of 'Old Zack,' " are
available in the Northwestern-Newberry edition of *The Piazza Tales and Other Prose
Pieces, 1839–1860* (1987), pp. 212–29.

2. This now almost obsolete term means a deep meditative state in which one is oblivious
   to one's surroundings.
3. The Lazarus whom Jesus raised from the dead (John 11–12). For the Lazarus who had
   sores, see Luke 16.19–31 and n. 2, p. 16 herein.

were premature. I was deploring your destitution, not of cash, but of confidence. You think the Natural Bone-setter can't help you. Well, suppose he can't, have you any objection to telling him your story? You, my friend, have, in a signal way, experienced adversity. Tell me, then, for my private good, how, without aid from the noble cripple, Epictetus,[4] you have arrived at his heroic sang-froid in misfortune."

At these words the cripple fixed upon the speaker the hard ironic eye of one toughened and defiant in misery, and, in the end, grinned upon him with his unshaven face like an ogre.

"Come, come, be sociable—be human, my friend. Don't make that face; it distresses me."

"I suppose," with a sneer, "you are the man I've long heard of—The Happy Man."

"Happy? my friend. Yes, at least I ought to be. My conscience is peaceful. I have confidence in everybody. I have confidence that, in my humble profession, I do some little good to the world. Yes, I think that, without presumption, I may venture to assent to the proposition that I am the Happy Man—the Happy Bone-setter."

"Then you shall hear my story. Many a month I have longed to get hold of the Happy Man, drill him, drop the powder, and leave him to explode at his leisure."

"What a demoniac unfortunate," exclaimed the herb-doctor retreating. "Regular infernal machine!"

"Look ye," cried the other, stumping after him, and with his horny hand catching him by a horn button, "my name is Thomas Fry. Until my—"

—"Any relation of Mrs. Fry?"[5] interrupted the other. "I still correspond with that excellent lady on the subject of prisons. Tell me, are you anyway connected with *my* Mrs. Fry?"

"Blister Mrs. Fry! What do them sentimental souls know of prisons or any other black fact? I'll tell ye a story of prisons. Ha, ha!"

The herb-doctor shrank, and with reason, the laugh being strangely startling.

"Positively, my friend," said he, "you must stop that; I can't stand that; no more of that. I hope I have the milk of kindness, but your thunder will soon turn it."

"Hold, I haven't come to the milk-turning part yet. My name is Thomas Fry. Until my twenty-third year I went by the nickname of Happy Tom—happy—ha, ha! They called me Happy Tom, d'ye see?

4. Epictetus of Hieropolis (50?–135?), Stoic philosopher, born a slave, then lamed, "gave as a formula for the good life, 'Endure and renounce' " (Foster).
5. Elizabeth Gurney Fry (1780–1845), English Quaker and philanthropist, best known for her reform of conditions in London's notorious Newgate and other prisons. In 1827 she published *Observations, on the Visiting, Superintendence, and Government of Female Prisoners*.

because I was so good-natured and laughing all the time, just as I am now—ha, ha!"

Upon this the herb-doctor would, perhaps, have run, but once more the hyæna clawed him. Presently, sobering down, he continued:

"Well, I was born in New York, and there I lived a steady, hardworking man, a cooper[6] by trade. One evening I went to a political meeting in the Park[7]—for you must know, I was in those days a great patriot. As bad luck would have it, there was trouble near, between a gentleman who had been drinking wine, and a pavior[8] who was sober. The pavior chewed tobacco, and the gentleman said it was beastly in him, and pushed him, wanting to have his place. The pavior chewed on and pushed back. Well, the gentleman carried a sword-cane, and presently the pavior was down—skewered."

"How was that?"

"Why you see the pavior undertook something above his strength."

"The other must have been a Samson[9] then. 'Strong as a pavior,' is a proverb."

"So it is, and the gentleman was in body a rather weakly man, but, for all that, I say again, the pavior undertook something above his strength."

"What are you talking about? He tried to maintain his rights, didn't he?"

"Yes; but, for all that, I say again, he undertook something above his strength."

"I don't understand you. But go on."

"Along with the gentleman, I, with other witnesses, was taken to the Tombs. There was an examination, and, to appear at the trial, the gentleman and witnesses all gave bail—I mean all but me."

"And why didn't you?"

"Couldn't get it."

"Steady, hard-working cooper like you; what was the reason you couldn't get bail?"

"Steady, hard-working cooper hadn't no friends. Well, souse I went into a wet cell, like a canal-boat splashing into the lock; locked up in pickle, d'ye see? against the time of the trial."

"But what had you done?"

6. One who makes and repairs wooden barrels, casks, and tubs.
7. City Hall Park, the downtown triangular park where Melville's brother Gansevoort in 1844 roused his listeners to fight the Whig Henry Clay and to elect James K. Polk, crying "Up, Democrats, and at them!" Central Park was under construction when Melville wrote *The Confidence-Man*.
8. Or paver, one who laid cobblestones for streets.
9. In Judges 15.15 Samson demonstrates his strength by killing a thousand Philistines with a single weapon, a "new jawbone of an ass."

"Why, I hadn't got any friends, I tell ye. A worse crime than murder, as ye'll see afore long."

"Murder? Did the wounded man die?"

"Died the third night."

"Then the gentleman's bail didn't help him. Imprisoned now, wasn't he?"

"Had too many friends. No, it was *I* that was imprisoned.—But I was going on: They let me walk about the corridor by day; but at night I must into lock. There the wet and the damp struck into my bones. They doctored me, but no use. When the trial came, I was boosted up and said my say."

"And what was that?"

"My say was that I saw the steel go in, and saw it sticking in."

"And that hung the gentleman."

"Hung him with a gold chain! His friends called a meeting in the Park, and presented him with a gold watch and chain upon his acquittal."

"Acquittal?"

"Didn't I say he had friends?"

There was a pause, broken at last by the herb-doctor's saying: "Well, there is a bright side to everything. If this speak prosaically for justice, it speaks romantically for friendship! But go on, my fine fellow."

"My say being said, they told me I might go. I said I could not without help. So the constables helped me, asking *where* would I go? I told them back to the 'Tombs.' I knew no other place. 'But where are your friends?' said they. 'I have none.' So they put me into a hand-barrow with an awning to it, and wheeled me down to the dock and on board a boat, and away to Blackwell's Island[1] to the Corporation Hospital. There I got worse—got pretty much as you see me now. Couldn't cure me. After three years, I grew sick of lying in a grated iron bed alongside of groaning thieves and mouldering burglars. They gave me five silver dollars, and these crutches, and I hobbled off. I had an only brother who went to Indiana, years ago. I begged about, to make up a sum to go to him; got to Indiana at last, and they directed me to his grave. It was on a great plain, in a log-church yard with a stump fence, the old gray roots sticking all ways like moose-antlers. The bier, set over the grave, it being the last dug, was of green hickory; bark on, and green twigs sprouting from it. Some one had planted a bunch of violets on the mound, but it was a poor soil (always choose the

---

1. Named for the English-born medical doctor and educator, Elizabeth Blackwell (1821–1910), the island lies in the East River between Manhattan and Queens. Now Roosevelt Island, it was the site of several charitable or correctional facilities, including Blackwell's Penitentiary (1832) and Blackwell's Workhouse (1852).

poorest soils for grave-yards), and they were all dried to tinder. I was going to sit and rest myself on the bier and think about my brother in heaven, but the bier broke down, the legs being only tacked. So, after driving some hogs out of the yard that were rooting there, I came away, and, not to make too long a story of it, here I am, drifting down stream like any other bit of wreck."

The herb-doctor was silent for a time, buried in thought. At last, raising his head, he said: "I have considered your whole story, my friend, and strove to consider it in the light of a commentary on what I believe to be the system of things; but it so jars with all, is so incompatible with all, that you must pardon me, if I honestly tell you, I cannot believe it."

"That don't surprise me."

"How?"

"Hardly anybody believes my story, and so to most I tell a different one."

"How, again?"

"Wait here a bit and I'll show ye."

With that, taking off his rag of a cap, and arranging his tattered regimentals the best he could, off he went stumping among the passengers in an adjoining part of the deck, saying with a jovial kind of air: "Sir, a shilling for Happy Tom, who fought at Buena Vista. Lady, something for General Scott's soldier, crippled in both pins at glorious Contreras."[2]

Now, it so chanced that, unbeknown to the cripple, a prim-looking stranger had overheard part of his story. Beholding him, then, on his present begging adventure, this person, turning to the herb-doctor, indignantly said: "Is is not too bad, sir, that yonder rascal should lie so?"

"Charity never faileth,[3] my good sir," was the reply. "The vice of this unfortunate is pardonable. Consider, he lies not out of wantonness."

"Not out of wantonness. I never heard more wanton lies. In one breath to tell you what would appear to be his true story, and, in the next, away and falsify it."

"For all that, I repeat he lies not out of wantonness. A ripe philosopher, turned out of the great Sorbonne[4] of hard times, he thinks that woes, when told to strangers for money, are best su-

---

2. During the Mexican War General Winfield Scott led the victorious American troops at the Battle of Contreras (August 1847). General Zachary Taylor defeated Santa Anna's soldiers at the Battle of Buena Vista (February 1847).

3. Paul in 1 Corinthians 13.8.

4. Founded in 1257 in Paris, a leading center of theological study and an ecclesiastical tribunal, making it the highest religious authority in the Catholic Church after the pope. Suppressed during the French Revolution, its buildings were given to the University of Paris in 1808.

gared. Though the inglorious lock-jaw of his knee-pans in a wet dungeon is a far more pitiable ill than to have been crippled at glorious Contreras, yet he is of opinion that this lighter and false ill shall attract, while the heavier and real one might repel."

"Nonsense; he belongs to the Devil's regiment; and I have a great mind to expose him."[5]

"Shame upon you. Dare to expose that poor unfortunate, and by heaven—don't you do it, sir."

Noting something in his manner, the other thought it more prudent to retire than retort. By-and-by, the cripple came back, and with glee, having reaped a pretty good harvest.

"There," he laughed, "you know now what sort of soldier I am."

"Aye, one that fights not the stupid Mexican, but a foe worthy your tactics—Fortune!"

"Hi, hi!" clamored the cripple, like a fellow in the pit of a sixpenny theatre, then said, "don't know much what you meant, but it went off well."

This over, his countenance capriciously put on a morose ogreness. To kindly questions he gave no kindly answers. Unhandsome notions were thrown out about "free Ameriky," as he sarcastically called his country. These seemed to disturb and pain the herbdoctor, who, after an interval of thoughtfulness, gravely addressed him in these words:

"You, my worthy friend, to my concern, have reflected upon the government under which you live and suffer. Where is your patriotism? Where your gratitude? True, the charitable may find something in your case, as you put it, partly to account for such reflections as coming from you. Still, be the facts how they may, your reflections are none the less unwarrantable. Grant, for the moment, that your experiences are as you give them; in which case I would admit that government might be thought to have more or less to do with what seems undesirable in them. But it is never to be forgotten that human government, being subordinate to the divine, must needs, therefore, in its degree, partake of the characteristics of the divine. That is, while in general efficacious to happiness, the world's law may yet, in some cases, have, to the eye of reason, an unequal operation, just as, in the same imperfect view, some inequalities may appear in the operations of heaven's law; nevertheless, to one who has a right confidence, final benignity is, in every instance, as sure with the one law as the other. I expound the point at some length, because these are the considerations, my poor fellow, which, weighed as they merit, will enable you to sus-

---

5. The prim stranger identifies a run-of-the-mill confidence man as a member of the Devil's regiment, never suspecting that he might be conversing with the Devil himself.

tain with unimpaired trust the apparent calamities which are yours."

"What do you talk your hog-latin to me for?" cried the cripple, who, throughout the address, betrayed the most illiterate obduracy; and, with an incensed look, anew he swung himself.

Glancing another way till the spasm passed, the other continued:

"Charity marvels not that you should be somewhat hard of conviction, my friend, since you, doubtless, believe yourself hardly dealt by; but forget not that those who are loved are chastened."[6]

"Mustn't chasten them too much, though, and too long, because their skin and heart get hard, and feel neither pain nor tickle."

"To mere reason, your case looks something piteous, I grant. But never despond; many things—the choicest—yet remain. You breathe this bounteous air, are warmed by this gracious sun, and, though poor and friendless, indeed, nor so agile as in your youth, yet, how sweet to roam, day by day, through the groves, plucking the bright mosses and flowers, till forlornness itself becomes a hilarity, and, in your innocent independence, you skip for joy."[7]

"Fine skipping with these 'ere hoist-posts[8]—ha ha!"

"Pardon; I forgot the crutches. My mind, figuring you after receiving the benefit of my art, overlooked you as you stand before me."

"Your art? You call yourself a bone-setter—a natural bone-setter, do ye? Go, bone-set the crooked world, and then come bone-set crooked me."

"Truly, my honest friend, I thank you for again recalling me to my original object. Let me examine you," bending down; "ah, I see, I see; much such a case as the negro's. Did you see him? Oh no, you came aboard since. Well, his case was a little something like yours. I prescribed for him, and I shouldn't wonder at all if, in a very short time, he were able to walk almost as well as myself. Now, have you no confidence in my art?"

6. The closest biblical text is "For whom the Lord loveth he chasteneth, and scourgeth every son whom he receiveth" (Hebrews 12.6).

7. The satiric target is Romantic optimism, which could be inane, even more often in U.S. poets than English poets. A ready example is "To the Dandelion" (1848) by Melville's contemporary James Russell Lowell: "How like a prodigal doth nature seem, / When thou, for all thy gold, so common art! / Thou teachest me to deem / More sacredly of every human heart, / Since each reflects in joy its scanty gleam / Of heaven, and could some wondrous secret show, / Did we but pay the love we owe, / And with a child's undoubting wisdom look / On all these living pages of God's book." When he wrote *The Confidence-Man* Melville knew very well William Wordsworth's more complex nature poems, including several written to flowers (such as "To the Daisy," "To the Small Celadine," "To the Daisy" (again), and "To the Same Flower" (again the daisy) and collected as "Poems of the Fancy" in Melville's edition of *Wordsworth's Poetical Works*. Melville also knew some of Orville Dewey's sermons and essays such as the passage from "Inequality of Lot" reprinted herein (p. 389–90; particularly the paragraph about "the natural gifts of Providence").

8. This emendation by Parker for the 1857 "horse-posts" is new in this second Norton Critical Edition. See 41.9.

"Ha, ha!"

The herb-doctor averted himself; but, the wild laugh dying away, resumed:

"I will not force confidence on you. Still, I would fain do the friendly thing by you. Here, take this box; just rub that liniment on the joints night and morning. Take it. Nothing to pay. God bless you. Good-bye."

"Stay," pausing in his swing, not untouched by so unexpected an act; "stay—thank'ee—but will this really do me good? Honor bright, now; will it? Don't deceive a poor fellow," with changed mien and glistening eye.

"Try it. Good-bye."

"Stay, stay! *Sure* it will do me good?"

"Possibly, possibly; no harm in trying. Good-bye."

"Stay, stay; give me three more boxes, and here's the money."

"My friend," returning towards him with a sadly pleased sort of air, "I rejoice in the birth of your confidence and hopefulness. Believe me that, like your crutches, confidence and hopefulness will long support a man when his own legs will not. Stick to confidence and hopefulness, then, since how mad for the cripple to throw his crutches away. You ask for three more boxes of my liniment. Luckily, I have just that number remaining. Here they are. I sell them at half-a-dollar apiece. But I shall take nothing from you. There; God bless you again; good-bye."

"Stay," in a convulsed voice, and rocking himself, "stay, stay! You have made a better man of me. You have borne with me like a good Christian, and talked to me like one, and all that is enough without making me a present of these boxes. Here is the money. I won't take nay. There, there; and may Almighty goodness go with you."

As the herb-doctor withdrew, the cripple gradually subsided from his hard rocking into a gentle oscillation. It expressed, perhaps, the soothed mood of his reverie.

Chapter 20.

REAPPEARANCE OF ONE WHO MAY BE REMEMBERED.

The herb-doctor had not moved far away, when, in advance of him, this spectacle met his eye. A dried-up old man, with the stature of a boy of twelve, was tottering about like one out of his mind, in rumpled clothes of old moleskin, showing recent contact with bedding, his ferret eyes, blinking in the sunlight of the snowy boat, as imbecilely eager, and, at intervals, coughing, he peered hither and thither as if in alarmed search for his nurse. He pre-

sented the aspect of one who, bed-rid, has, through overruling excitement, like that of a fire, been stimulated to his feet.

"You seek some one," said the herb-doctor, accosting him. "Can I
assist you?"

"Do do; I am so old and miserable," coughed the old man.
"Where is he? This long time I've been trying to get up and find
him. But I haven't any friends, and couldn't get up till now. Where
is he?"

"Who do you mean?" drawing closer, to stay the further wanderings of one so weakly.

"Why, why, why," now marking the other's dress, "why you, yes
you—you, you—ugh, ugh, ugh!"

"I?"

"Ugh, ugh, ugh!—you are the man he spoke of. Who is he?"

"Faith, that is just what I want to know."

"Mercy, mercy!" coughed the old man, bewildered, "ever since
seeing him, my head spins round so. I ought to have a guard*ee*an. Is
this a snuff-colored surtout of yours, or ain't it? Somehow, can't
trust my senses any more, since trusting him—ugh, ugh, ugh!"

"Oh, you have trusted somebody? Glad to hear it. Glad to hear of
any instance of that sort. Reflects well upon all men. But you inquire whether this is a snuff-colored surtout. I answer it is; and will
add that a herb-doctor wears it."

Upon this the old man, in his broken way, replied that then he
(the herb-doctor) was the person he sought—the person spoken of
by the other person as yet unknown. He then, with flighty eager-
ness, wanted to know who this last person was, and where he was,
and whether he could be trusted with money to treble it.

"Aye, now, I begin to understand; ten to one you mean my worthy
friend, who, in pure goodness of heart, makes people's fortunes
for them—their everlasting fortunes, as the phrase goes—only
charging his one small commission of confidence. Aye, aye; before intrusting funds with my friend, you want to know about him.
Very proper—and, I am glad to assure you, you need have no
hesitation, none, none, just none in the world; bona fide, none,
Turned me in a trice a hundred dollars the other day into as many
eagles."

"Did he? did he? But where is he? Take me to him."

"Pray, take my arm! The boat is large! We may have something of
a hunt! Come on! Ah, is that he?"

"Where? where?"

"O, no; I took yonder coat-skirts for his. But no, my honest friend
would never turn tail that way. Ah!—"

"Where? where?"

"Another mistake. Surprising resemblance. I took yonder clergy-man for him. Come on!"

Having searched that part of the boat without success, they went to another part, and, while exploring that, the boat sided up to a landing, when, as the two were passing by the open guard, the herb-doctor suddenly rushed towards the disembarking throng, cry-ing out: "Mr. Truman, Mr. Truman! There he goes—that's he. Mr. Truman, Mr. Truman!—Confound that steam-pipe. Mr. Truman! for God's sake, Mr. Truman!—No, no.—There, the plank's in—too late—we're off."

With that, the huge boat, with a mighty, walrus wallow, rolled away from the shore, resuming her course.

"How vexatious!" exclaimed the herb-doctor, returning. "Had we been but one single moment sooner.—There he goes, now, towards yon hotel, his portmanteau following. You see him, don't you?"

"Where? where?"

"Can't see him any more. Wheel-house shot between. I am very sorry. I should have so liked you to have let him have a hundred or so of your money. You would have been pleased with the invest-ment, believe me."

"Oh, I *have* let him have some of my money," groaned the old man.

"You have? My dear sir," seizing both the miser's hands in both his own and heartily shaking them. "My dear sir, how I congratu-late you. You don't know."

"Ugh, ugh! I fear I don't," with another groan. "His name is Tru-man, is it?"

"John Truman."

"Where does he live?"

"In St. Louis."

"Where's his office?"

"Let me see. Jones street, number one hundred and—no, no—anyway, it's somewhere or other up-stairs in Jones street."

"Can't you remember the number? Try, now."

"One hundred—two hundred—three hundred—"

"Oh, my hundred dollars! I wonder whether it will be one hun-dred, two hundred, three hundred, with them! Ugh, ugh! Can't re-member the number?"

"Positively, though I once knew, I have forgotten, quite forgotten it. Strange. But never mind. You will easily learn in St. Louis. He is well known there."

"But I have no receipt—ugh, ugh! Nothing to show—don't know where I stand—ought to have a guardeean—ugh, ugh! Don't know anything. Ugh, ugh!"

"Why, you know that you gave him your confidence, don't you?"

"Oh, yes."

"Well, then?"

"But what, what—how, how—ugh, ugh!"

"Why, didn't he tell you?"

"No."

"What! Didn't he tell you that it was a secret, a mystery?"

"Oh—yes."

"Well, then?"

"But I have no bond."

"Don't need any with Mr. Truman. Mr. Truman's word is his bond."

"But how am I to get my profits—ugh, ugh!—and my money back? Don't know anything. Ugh, ugh!"

"Oh, you must have confidence."

"Don't say that word again. Makes my head spin so. Oh, I'm so old and miserable, nobody caring for me, everybody fleecing me, and my head spins so—ugh, ugh!—and this cough racks me so. I say again, I ought to have a guardeean."

"So you ought; and Mr. Truman is your guardian to the extent you invested with him. Sorry we missed him just now. But you'll hear from him, all right. It's imprudent, though, to expose yourself this way. Let me take you to your berth."

Forlornly enough the old miser moved slowly away with him. But, while descending a stairway, he was seized with such coughing that he was fain to pause.

"That is a very bad cough."

"Church-yard—ugh, ugh!—church-yard cough.—Ugh!"

"Have you tried anything for it?"

"Tired of trying. Nothing does me any good—ugh! ugh! Not even the Mammoth Cave.[9] Ugh! ugh! Denned there six months, but coughed so bad the rest of the coughers—ugh! ugh!—black-balled me out. Ugh, ugh! Nothing does me good."

"But have you tried the Omni-Balsamic Reinvigorator, sir?"

"That's what that Truman—ugh, ugh!—said I ought to take. Yarb-medicine; you are that yarb-doctor, too?"

"The same. Suppose you try one of my boxes now. Trust me, from what I know of Mr. Truman, he is not the gentleman to recommend, even in behalf of a friend, anything of whose excellence he is not conscientiously satisfied."

"Ugh!—how much?"

"Only two dollars a box."

---

9. The famous Kentucky cave had in fact been occupied by consumptives who thought its uniform temperature might be curative. In 1852 Melville's friend Nathaniel Parker Willis had written that men venturing into the cave might wear a mustard colored stuffed skull cap and a short garment called a devil-may-care.

"Two dollars? Why don't you say two millions? ugh, ugh! Two dollars, that's two hundred cents; that's eight hundred farthings; that's two thousand mills; and all for one little box of yarb-medicine. My head, my head!—oh, I ought to have a guard*ee*an for my head. Ugh, ugh, ugh, ugh!"

"Well, if two dollars a box seems too much, take a dozen boxes at twenty dollars; and that will be getting four boxes for nothing, and you need use none but those four, the rest you can retail out at a premium, and so cure your cough, and make money by it.[1] Come, you had better do it. Cash down. Can fill an order in a day or two. Here now," producing a box; "pure herbs."

At that moment, seized with another spasm, the miser snatched each interval to fix his half distrustful, half hopeful eye upon the medicine, held alluringly up. "Sure—ugh! Sure it's all nat'ral? Nothing but yarbs? If I only thought it was a purely nat'ral medicine now—all yarbs—ugh, ugh!—oh this cough, this cough—ugh, ugh!—shatters my whole body. Ugh, ugh, ugh!"

"For heaven's sake try my medicine, if but a single box. That it is pure nature you may be confident. Refer you to Mr. Truman."

"Don't know his number—ugh, ugh, ugh, ugh! Oh this cough. He did speak well of this medicine though; said solemnly it would cure me—ugh, ugh, ugh, ugh!—take off a dollar and I'll have a box."

"Can't sir, can't."

"Say a dollar-and-half. Ugh!"

"Can't. Am pledged to the one-price system, only honorable one."

"Take off a shilling—ugh, ugh!"

"Can't."

"Ugh, ugh, ugh—I'll take it.—There."

Grudgingly he handed eight silver coins, but while still in his hand, his cough took him, and they were shaken upon the deck.

One by one, the herb-doctor picked them up, and, examining them, said: "These are not quarters, these are pistareens; and clipped, and sweated,[2] at that."

"Oh don't be so miserly—ugh, ugh!—better a beast than a miser—ugh, ugh!"

"Well, let it go. Anything rather than the idea of your not being cured of such a cough. And I hope, for the credit of humanity, you

---

1. The herb doctor's arithmetic may be deliberately shaky, but several such errors appear in Melville's books; and after 1856 his brother Allan and later his wife kept track of his own financial matters.
2. Techniques for removing small amounts of either silver or gold from coins before passing them on, the first through cutting or shaving off small portions and the second through abrasion. Coins made of precious metals came to be minted with ridges on the edges so that any such tampering would be obvious. "Pistareens": old Spanish silver coins that circulated in America and the West Indies at a debased rate.

have not made it appear worse than it is, merely with a view to working upon the weak point of my pity, and so getting my medicine the cheaper. Now, mind, don't take it till night. Just before retiring is the time. There, you can get along now, can't you? I would attend you further, but I land presently, and must go hunt up my luggage."

Chapter 21.

A HARD CASE.

"Yarbs, yarbs; natur, natur; you foolish old file you! He diddled you with that hocus-pocus, did he? Yarbs and natur will cure your incurable cough, you think."

It was a rather eccentric-looking person who spoke; somewhat ursine in aspect; sporting a shaggy spencer of the cloth called bear's-skin;[3] a high-peaked cap of raccoon-skin, the long bushy tail switching over behind; raw-hide leggings; grim stubble chin; and to end, a double-barreled gun in hand—a Missouri bachelor, a Hoosier gentleman, of Spartan leisure and fortune, and equally Spartan manners and sentiments; and, as the sequel may show, not less acquainted, in a Spartan way of his own, with philosophy and books, than with woodcraft and rifles.

He must have overheard some of the talk between the miser and the herb-doctor; for, just after the withdrawal of the one, he made up to the other—now at the foot of the stairs leaning against the baluster there—with the greeting above.

"Think it will cure me?" coughed the miser in echo; "why shouldn't it? The medicine is nat'ral yarbs, pure yarbs; yarbs must cure me."

"Because a thing is nat'ral, as you call it, you think it must be good. But who gave you that cough? Was it, or was it not, nature?"

"Sure, you don't think that natur, Dame Natur, will hurt a body, do you?"

"Natur is good Queen Bess;[4] but who's responsible for the cholera?"

"But yarbs, yarbs; yarbs are good?"

"What's deadly-nightshade? Yarb, ain't it?"

"Oh, that a Christian man should speak agin natur and yarbs—ugh, ugh, ugh!—ain't sick men sent out into the country; sent out to natur and grass?"

"Aye, and poets send out the sick spirit to green pastures, like lame horses turned out unshod to the turf to renew their hoofs. A

---

3. A shaggy, coarse woolen cloth used for overcoats. In the 1850s, however, a "buffalo" robe was just what it said, a robe made from the skin of a buffalo. "Spencer": a waist-length jacket.

4. English Queen Elizabeth I (1533–1603), who reigned 1558–1603.

sort of yarb-doctors in their way, poets have it that for sore hearts, as for sore lungs, nature is the grand cure. But who froze to death my teamster on the prairie? And who made an idiot of Peter the Wild Boy?"[5]

"Then you don't believe in these 'ere yarb-doctors?"

"Yarb-doctors? I remember the lank yarb-doctor I saw once on a hospital-cot in Mobile. One of the faculty passing round and seeing who lay there, said with professional triumph, 'Ah, Dr. Green, your yarbs don't help ye now, Dr. Green. Have to come to us and the mercury now, Dr. Green.'—Natur! Y-a-r-b-s!"

"Did I hear something about herbs and herb-doctors?" here said a flute-like voice, advancing.

It was the herb-doctor in person. Carpet-bag in hand, he happened to be strolling back that way.

"Pardon me," addressing the Missourian, "but if I caught your words aright, you would seem to have little confidence in nature; which, really, in my way of thinking, looks like carrying the spirit of distrust pretty far."

"And who of my sublime species may you be?" turning short round upon him, clicking his rifle-lock, with an air which would have seemed half cynic, half wild-cat, were it not for the grotesque excess of the expression, which made its sincerity appear more or less dubious.

"One who has confidence in nature, and confidence in man, with some little modest confidence in himself."

"That's your Confession of Faith, is it? Confidence in man, eh? Pray, which do you think are most, knaves or fools?"

"Having met with few or none of either, I hardly think I am competent to answer."

"I will answer for you. Fools are most."

"Why do you think so?"

"For the same reason that I think oats are numerically more than horses. Don't knaves munch up fools just as horses do oats?"

"A droll, sir; you are a droll. I can appreciate drollery—ha, ha, ha!"

"But I'm in earnest."

"That's the drollery, to deliver droll extravagance with an earnest air—knaves munching up fools as horses oats.—Faith, very droll, indeed, ha, ha, ha! Yes, I think I understand you now, sir. How silly I was

---

5. Peter (1712–1785) was found in 1725 in the woods near Hamelin, Germany, walking on his hands and feet, climbing trees like an animal, and eating grass and moss. His Hanoverian ruler, who also reigned as George I of England, brought him to London in 1726 and put him under the care of Dr. John Arbuthnot, amid speculation on what wild creature might have suckled him. Jonathan Swift and Daniel Defoe were among the many who wrote about him. Foster points out that he became a center for the controversy about the existence of innate ideas.

to have taken you seriously, in your droll conceits, too, about having no confidence in nature. In reality you have just as much as I have."

"*I* have confidence in nature? *I*? I say again there is nothing I am more suspicious of. I once lost ten thousand dollars by nature. Nature embezzled that amount from me; absconded with ten thousand dollars' worth of my property; a plantation on this stream, swept clean away by one of those sudden shiftings of the banks in a freshet; ten thousand dollars' worth of alluvion thrown broad off upon the waters."

"But have you no confidence that by a reverse shifting that soil will come back after many days?[6]—ah, here is my venerable friend," observing the old miser, "not in your berth yet? Pray, if you *will* keep afoot, don't lean against that baluster; take my arm."

It was taken; and the two stood together; the old miser leaning against the herb-doctor with something of that air of trustful fraternity with which, when standing, the less strong of the Siamese twins habitually leans against the other.[7]

The Missourian eyed them in silence, which was broken by the herb-doctor.

"You look surprised, sir. Is it because I publicly take under my protection a figure like this? But I am never ashamed of honesty, whatever his coat."

"Look you," said the Missourian, after a scrutinizing pause, "you are a queer sort of chap. Don't know exactly what to make of you. Upon the whole though, you somewhat remind me of the last boy I had on my place."

"Good, trustworthy boy, I hope?"

"Oh, very! I am now started to get me made some kind of machine to do the sort of work which boys are supposed to be fitted for."

"Then you have passed a veto upon boys?"

"And men, too."

"But, my dear sir, does not that again imply more or less lack of confidence?—(Stand up a little, just a very little, my venerable friend; you lean rather hard.)—No confidence in boys, no confidence in men, no confidence in nature. Pray, sir, who or what may you have confidence in?"

"I have confidence in distrust; more particularly as applied to you and your herbs."

---

6. In using the expression "thrown broad off upon the waters" followed by "will come back after many days" Melville seems to be echoing (in a secular context) Ecclesiastes 11.1: "Cast thy bread upon the waters: for thou shalt find it after many days."

7. The famous Chang and Eng (1811–1874), conjoined at the chest area, were displayed at Barnum's American Museum and taken on various tours. Chang seemed weaker than Eng. Part Chinese, they were born in Siam, present-day Thailand. Their marriage to North Carolina sisters in 1843 and subsequent fathering of twenty-one children was the subject of keen private and even public interest in the United States and abroad throughout the Victorian era.

"Well," with a forbearing smile, "that is frank. But pray, don't forget that when you suspect my herbs you suspect nature."

"Didn't I say that before?"

"Very good. For the argument's sake I will suppose you are in earnest. Now, can you, who suspect nature, deny, that this same nature not only kindly brought you into being, but has faithfully nursed you to your present vigorous and independent condition? Is it not to nature that you are indebted for that robustness of mind which you so unhandsomely use to her scandal? Pray, is it not to nature that you owe the very eyes by which you criticise her?"

"No! for the privilege of vision I am indebted to an oculist, who in my tenth year operated upon me in Philadelphia. Nature made me blind and would have kept me so. My oculist counterplotted her."

"And yet, sir, by your complexion, I judge you live an out-of-door life; without knowing it, you are partial to nature; you fly to nature, the universal mother."

"Very motherly! Sir, in the passion-fits of nature, I've known birds fly from nature to me, rough as I look; yes, sir, in a tempest, refuge here," smiting the folds of his bearskin. "Fact, sir, fact. Come, come, Mr. Palaverer,[8] for all your palavering, did you yourself never shut out nature of a cold, wet night? Bar her out? Bolt her out? Lint her out?"[9]

"As to that," said the herb-doctor calmly, "much may be said."

"Say it, then," ruffling all his hairs. "You can't, sir, can't." Then, as in apostrophe: "Look you, nature! I don't deny but your clover is sweet, and your dandelions don't roar; but whose hailstones smashed my windows?"

"Sir," with unimpaired affability, producing one of his boxes, "I am pained to meet with one who holds nature a dangerous character. Though your manner is refined your voice is rough; in short, you seem to have a sore throat. In the calumniated name of nature, I present you with this box; my venerable friend here has a similar one; but to you, a free gift, sir. Through her regularly-authorized agents, of whom I happen to be one, Nature delights in benefiting those who most abuse her. Pray, take it."

"Away with it! Don't hold it so near. Ten to one there is a torpedo[1] in it. Such things have been. Editors been killed that way. Take it further off, I say."

"Good heavens! my dear sir—"

---

8. Slick talker (cf. *palabra*, Spanish for "word").
9. I.e., keep nature out by stuffing cracks in the walls with lint, particles of cloth scraped off, usually to cover wounds the way we would use gauze. (Elizabeth Shaw Melville, Herman Melville's wife, joined other Pittsfield women in scraping lint during the Civil War.)
1. A land mine or other explosive device used in war, not yet restricted to mean an underwater weapon.

"I tell you I want none of your boxes," snapping his rifle.

"Oh, take it—ugh, ugh! do take it," chimed in the old miser; "I wish he would give me one for nothing."

"You find it lonely, eh," turning short round; "gulled yourself, you would have a companion."

"How can he find it lonely," returned the herb-doctor, "or how desire a companion, when here I stand by him; I, even I, in whom he has trust? For the gulling, tell me, is it humane to talk so to this poor old man? Granting that his dependence on my medicine is vain, is it kind to deprive him of what, in mere imagination, if nothing more, may help eke out, with hope, his disease? For you, if you have no confidence, and, thanks to your native health, can get along without it, so far, at least, as trusting in my medicine goes; yet, how cruel an argument to use, with this afflicted one here. Is it not for all the world as if some brawny pugilist, aglow in December, should rush in and put out a hospital-fire, because, forsooth, he feeling no need of artificial heat, the shivering patients shall have none? Put it to your conscience, sir, and you will admit, that, whatever be the nature of this afflicted one's trust, you, in opposing it, evince either an erring head or a heart amiss. Come, own, are you not pitiless?"

"Yes, poor soul," said the Missourian, gravely eying the old man—"yes, it *is* pitiless in one like me to speak too honestly to one like you. You are a late sitter-up in this life; past man's usual bed-time; and truth, though with some it makes a wholesome breakfast, proves to all a supper too hearty. Hearty food, taken late, gives bad dreams."

"What, in wonder's name—ugh, ugh!—is he talking about?" asked the old miser, looking up to the herb-doctor.

"Heaven be praised for that!" cried the Missourian.

"Out of his mind, ain't he?" again appealed the old miser.

"Pray, sir," said the herb-doctor to the Missourian, "for what were you giving thanks just now?"

"For this: that, with some minds, truth is, in effect, not so cruel a thing after all, seeing that, like a loaded pistol found by poor devils of savages, it raises more wonder than terror—its peculiar virtue being unguessed, unless, indeed, by indiscreet handling, it should happen to go off of itself."

"I pretend not to divine your meaning there," said the herb-doctor, after a pause, during which he eyed the Missourian with a kind of pinched expression, mixed of pain and curiosity, as if he grieved at his state of mind, and, at the same time, wondered what had brought him to it, "but this much I know," he added, "that the general cast of your thoughts is, to say the least, unfortunate. There is strength in them, but a strength, whose source, being physical, must wither. You will yet recant."

"Recant?"

"Yes, when, as with this old man, your evil days of decay come on, when a hoary captive in your chamber, then will you, something like the dungeoned Italian[2] we read of, gladly seek the breast of that confidence begot in the tender time of your youth, blessed beyond telling if it return to you in age."

"Go back to nurse again, eh? Second childhood, indeed. You are soft."

"Mercy, mercy!" cried the old miser, "what is all this!—ugh, ugh! Do talk sense, my good friends. Ain't you," to the Missourian, "going to buy some of that medicine?"

"Pray, my venerable friend," said the herb-doctor, now trying to straighten himself, "don't lean *quite* so hard; my arm grows numb; abate a little, just a very little."

"Go," said the Missourian, "go lay down in your grave, old man, if you can't stand of yourself. It's a hard world for a leaner."

"As to his grave," said the herb-doctor, "that is far enough off, so he but faithfully take my medicine."

"Ugh, ugh, ugh!—He says true. No, I ain't—ugh! a going to die yet—ugh, ugh, ugh! Many years to live yet, ugh, ugh, ugh!"

"I approve your confidence," said the herb-doctor; "but your coughing distresses me, besides being injurious to you. Pray, let me conduct you to your berth. You are best there. Our friend here will wait till my return, I know."

With which he led the old miser away, and then, coming back, the talk with the Missourian was resumed.

"Sir," said the herb-doctor, with some dignity and more feeling, "now that our infirm friend is withdrawn, allow me, to the full, to express my concern at the words you allowed to escape you in his hearing. Some of those words, if I err not, besides being calculated to beget deplorable distrust in the patient, seemed fitted to convey unpleasant imputations against me, his physician."

"Suppose they did?" with a menacing air.

"Why, then—then, indeed," respectfully retreating, "I fall back upon my previous theory of your general facetiousness. I have the fortune to be in company with a humorist—a wag."

"Fall back you had better, and wag it is," cried the Missourian, following him up, and wagging his raccoon tail almost into the herb-doctor's face, "look you!"

"At what?"

"At this coon. Can you, the fox, catch him?"

---

2. Probably the Italian patriot Silvio Pellico (1789–1854), author of *My Prisons* (1833) about whom Melville later (1859?) wrote the poem "Pausilippo (In the time of Bomba)." The Austrian rulers imprisoned Pellico at hard labor for eight years then released him, broken in health, in 1830.

"If you mean," returned the other, not unselfpossessed, "whether I flatter myself that I can in any way dupe you, or impose upon you, or pass myself off upon you for what I am not, I, as an honest man, answer that I have neither the inclination nor the power to do aught of the kind."

"Honest man? Seems to me you talk more like a craven."

"You in vain seek to pick a quarrel with me, or put any affront upon me. The innocence in me heals me."

"A healing like your own nostrums. But you are a queer man—a very queer and dubious man; upon the whole, about the most so I ever met."

The scrutiny accompanying this seemed unwelcome to the diffidence of the herb-doctor. As if at once to attest the absence of resentment, as well as to change the subject, he threw a kind of familiar cordiality into his air, and said: "So you are going to get some machine made to do your work? Philanthropic scruples, doubtless, forbid your going as far as New Orleans for slaves?"

"Slaves?" morose again in a twinkling, "won't have 'em! Bad enough to see whites ducking and grinning round for a favor, without having those poor devils of niggers congeeing[3] round for their corn. Though, to me, the niggers are the freer of the two. You are an abolitionist, ain't you?" he added, squaring himself with both hands on his rifle, used for a staff, and gazing in the herb-doctor's face with no more reverence than if it were a target. "You are an abolitionist, ain't you?"

"As to that, I cannot so readily answer. If by abolitionist you mean a zealot, I am none; but if you mean a man, who, being a man, feels for all men, slaves included, and by any lawful act, opposed to nobody's interest, and therefore, rousing nobody's enmity, would willingly abolish suffering (supposing it, in its degree, to exist) from among mankind, irrespective of color, then am I what you say."[4]

"Picked and prudent sentiments. You are the moderate man, the invaluable understrapper of the wicked man. You, the moderate man, may be used for wrong, but are useless for right."

"From all this," said the herb-doctor, still forgivingly, "I infer, that you, a Missourian, though living in a slave-state, are without slave sentiments."

"Aye, but are you? Is not that air of yours, so spiritlessly enduring

---

3. A congé is a ceremonious bow, normally offered upon taking leave. Here "congeeing" suggests a stereotypical image of excessive and obsequious gestures shrewdly used by slaves.

4. Ironically, this fatuous shilly-shallying has been taken as Melville's own considered opinion on abolitionism. The judgment of Jesus is relevant: "So then because thou art lukewarm, and neither cold nor hot, I will spue thee out of my mouth" (Revelation 3.16). Melville may be remembering how the Unitarian minister Orville Dewey protested that his similarly ambivalent remarks on slavery in a speech in Pittsfield in December 1850 had been misinterpreted (see Parker 2.66–67).

and yielding, the very air of a slave? Who is your master, pray; or are you owned by a company?"

"*My* master?"

"Aye, for come from Maine or Georgia, you come from a slave-state, and a slave-pen, where the best breeds are to be bought up at any price from a livelihood to the Presidency. Abolitionism, ye gods, but expresses the fellow-feeling of slave for slave."

"The back-woods would seem to have given you rather eccentric notions," now with polite superiority smiled the herb-doctor, still with manly intrepidity forbearing each unmanly thrust, "but to return; since, for your purpose, you will have neither man nor boy, bond nor free, truly, then some sort of machine for you is all there is left. My desires for your success attend you, sir.—Ah!" glancing shoreward, "here is Cape Girardeau;[5] I must leave you."

Chapter 22.

IN THE POLITE SPIRIT OF THE TUSCULAN[6] DISPUTATIONS.

—" 'PHILOSOPHICAL INTELLIGENCE OFFICE'—novel idea! But how did you come to dream that I wanted anything in your absurd line, eh?"

About twenty minutes after leaving Cape Girardeau, the above was growled out over his shoulder by the Missourian to a chance stranger who had just accosted him; a round-backed, baker-kneed[7] man, in a mean five-dollar suit, wearing, collar-wise by a chain, a small brass plate, inscribed P.I.O., and who, with a sort of canine deprecation, slunk obliquely behind.

"How did you come to dream that I wanted anything in your line, eh?"

"Oh, respected sir," whined the other, crouching a pace nearer, and, in his obsequiousness, seeming to wag his very coat-tails behind him, shabby though they were, "oh, sir, from long experience, one glance tells me the gentleman who is in need of our humble services."

"But suppose I did want a boy—what they jocosely call a good boy—how could your absurd office help me?—Philosophical Intelligence Office?"[8]

5. In southeast Missouri, on the Mississippi River.
6. On a mountain about fifteen miles southeast of Rome, the site of villas of several wealthy Romans, including the writer Marcus Tullius Cicero (106–43 B.C.E.), who used the quiet retreat as the appropriate setting for his "disputations," which were more like genteel philosophical conversations than debates.
7. The *Oxford English Dictionary* quotes from *Figure Training* (1871) on this occupational hazard: "An inclining inwards of the right knee-joint until it closely resembles the right side of a letter K, is the almost certain penalty of habitually bearing any burden of bulk in the right hand."
8. Employment agency (as in Hawthorne's story "The Intelligence Office"). "Philosophical" is Melville's flourish.

"Yes, respected sir, an office founded on strictly philosophical and physio—"

"Look you—come up here—how, by philosophy or physiology either, make good boys to order? Come up here. Don't give me a crick in the neck. Come up here, come, sir, come," calling as if to his pointer. "Tell me, how put the requisite assortment of good qualities into a boy, as the assorted mince into the pie?"

"Respected sir, our office—"

"You talk much of that office. Where is it? On board this boat?"

"Oh no, sir, I just came aboard. Our office—"

"Came aboard at that last landing, eh? Pray, do you know a herb-doctor there? Smooth scamp in a snuff-colored surtout?"[9]

"Oh, sir, I was but a sojourner at Cape Girardeau. Though, now that you mention a snuff-colored surtout, I think I met such a man as you speak of stepping ashore as I stepped aboard, and 'pears to me I have seen him somewhere before. Looks like a very mild Christian sort of person, I should say. Do you know him, respected sir?"

"Not much, but better than you seem to. Proceed with your business."

With a low, shabby bow, as grateful for the permission, the other began: "Our office—"

"Look you," broke in the bachelor with ire, "have you the spinal complaint? What are you ducking and groveling about? Keep still. Where's your office?"

"The branch one which I represent, is at Alton, sir, in the free state we now pass," (pointing somewhat proudly ashore).

"Free, eh? You a freeman, you flatter yourself? With those coat-tails and that spinal complaint of servility? Free? Just cast up in your private mind who is your master, will you?"

"Oh, oh, oh! I don't understand—indeed—indeed. But, respected sir, as before said, our office, founded on principles wholly new—"

"To the devil with your principles! Bad sign when a man begins to talk of his principles. Hold, come back, sir; back here, back, sir, back! I tell you no more boys for me. Nay, I'm a Mede and Persian.[1] In my old home in the woods I'm pestered enough with squirrels,

---

9. Brownish yellow overcoat, the color of snuff (finely ground tobacco to be sniffed into the nostrils or "dipped" between jaw and cheek like chewing tobacco). Melville's gross Captain Riga in *Redburn* wears an old-fashioned snuff-colored coat at sea. Melville's fondness for the derogatory term may come from "London Antiques" in Washington Irving's *The Sketch-Book* (1819–20), where the narrator describes an odd-looking old gentleman in a small brown wig and "a snuff-colored coat." In his "The Paradise of Bachelors and Tartarus of Maids" (*Harper's New Monthly Magazine*, April 1855) Melville had lovingly plundered "London Antiques."

1. In Daniel 6 the presidents and princes of Babylon trick King Belshazzar into making a decree aimed specifically at Daniel, whom they knew prayed only to Jehovah. By the new decree, (unchangeable, "according to the law of the Medes and Persians, which altereth not"; verse 8), anyone who prayed to a God or man other than Belshazzar would be cast

weasels, chipmunks, skunks. I want no more wild vermin to spoil my temper and waste my substance. Don't talk of boys; enough of your boys; a plague of your boys; chilblains on your boys! As for Intelligence Offices, I've lived in the East, and know 'em. Swindling concerns kept by low-born cynics, under a fawning exterior wreaking their cynic malice upon mankind. You are a fair specimen of 'em."

"Oh dear, dear, dear!"

"Dear? Yes, a thrice dear purchase one of your boys would be to me. A rot on your boys!"

"But, respected sir, if you will not have boys, might we not, in our small way, accommodate you with a man?"

"Accommodate? Pray, no doubt you could accommodate me with a bosom-friend too, couldn't you? Accommodate! Obliging word accommodate:[2] there's accommodation notes now, where one accommodates another with a loan, and if he don't pay it pretty quickly, accommodates him with a chain to his foot. Accommodate! God forbid that I should ever be accommodated. No, no. Look you, as I told that cousin-german of yours, the herb-doctor, I'm now on the road to get me made some sort of machine to do my work. Machines for me. My cider-mill—does that ever steal my cider? My mowing-machine—does that ever lay a-bed mornings? My corn-husker—does that ever give me insolence? No: cider-mill, mowing-machine, corn-husker—all faithfully attend to their business. Disinterested, too; no board, no wages; yet doing good all their lives long; shining examples that virtue is its own reward—the only practical Christians I know."

"Oh dear, dear, dear, dear!"

"Yes, sir:—boys? Start my soul-bolts, what a difference, in a moral point of view, between a corn-husker and a boy! Sir, a corn-husker, for its patient continuance in well-doing, might not unfitly go to heaven.[3] Do you suppose a boy will?"

"A corn-husker in heaven! (turning up the whites of his eyes). Respected sir, this way of talking as if heaven were a kind of Washington patent-office museum—oh, oh, oh!—as if mere machine-work and puppet-work went to heaven—oh, oh, oh! Things incapable of free agency, to receive the eternal reward of well-doing—oh, oh, oh!"

---

into the den of lions. Daniel is so punished, but survives unharmed because God sends an angel to shut the lions' mouths. Earlier in Daniel Nebuchadnezzar sees "four men loose" in the fiery furnace, not the three who had been thrown into it; "the form of the fourth" is different—"like the Son of God" (3.25). See also n. 7, p. 225.

2. Bardolph and Shallow mouth back and forth the "good phrase" "accommodated" in Shakespeare's 2 Henry IV 3.2.

3. In Romans 2.7 Paul promises that God will give eternal life to those "who by patient continuance in well doing seek for glory and honour and immortality."

"You Praise-God-Barebones[4] you, what are you groaning about? Did I say anything of that sort? Seems to me, though you talk so good, you are mighty quick at a hint the other way, or else you want to pick a polemic quarrel with me."

"It may be so or not, respected sir," was now the demure reply; "but if it be, it is only because as a soldier out of honor is quick in taking affront, so a Christian out of religion is quick, sometimes perhaps a little too much so, in spying heresy."

"Well," after an astonished pause, "for an unaccountable pair, you and the herb-doctor ought to yoke together."

So saying, the bachelor was eying him rather sharply, when he with the brass plate recalled him to the discussion by a hint, not unflattering, that he (the man with the brass plate) was all anxiety to hear him further on the subject of servants.

"About that matter," exclaimed the impulsive bachelor, going off at the hint like a rocket, "all thinking minds are, now-a-days, coming to the conclusion—one derived from an immense hereditary experience—see what Horace[5] and others of the ancients say of servants—coming to the conclusion, I say, that boy or man, the human animal is, for most work-purposes, a losing animal. Can't be trusted; less trustworthy than oxen; for conscientiousness a turnspit dog excels him. Hence these thousand new inventions—carding machines, horseshoe machines, tunnel-boring machines, reaping machines, apple-paring machines, boot-blacking machines, sewing machines, shaving machines, run-of-errand machines, dumb-waiter machines, and the Lord-only-knows-what machines; all of which announce the era when that refractory animal, the working or serving man, shall be a buried by-gone, a superseded fossil. Shortly prior to which glorious time, I doubt not that a price will be put upon their peltries as upon the knavish 'possums, especially the boys. Yes, sir (ringing his rifle down on the deck), I rejoice to think that the day is at hand, when, prompted to it by law, I shall shoulder this gun and go out a boy-shooting."

"Oh, now! Lord, Lord, Lord!—But our office, respected sir, conducted as I ventured to observe—"

---

4. Praisegod Barbon or Barebones (1596?–1679), a London Anabaptist leather dealer, under Oliver Cromwell in 1653 was a member of Parliament, called by its enemies "Barebone's Parliament" or the "Little Parliament." He was a fervid opponent of the restoration of Charles II. An Anabaptist was a member of a sect that opposed infant baptism and advocated separation of church and state.

5. Quintus Horatius Flaccus (65–8 B.C.E.) in his *Epistles* and *Satires* comments frequently on rascality and inefficiency of slaves. The *Epistle* 1.2, to Julius Florus, begins with a hypothetical attempt to sell Florus a slave who the seller asserts would be malleable to Florus's wishes; the seller also admits the faults the slave has committed, such as running away. In *Satire* 2.7, in which master and slave change roles during Saturnalia, the slave Davus dares to suggest that his master in his own way is slave to those outranking him—an argument not unrelated to Ishmael's question in chapter 1 of *Moby-Dick*: "Who aint a slave? Tell me that."

"No, sir," bristlingly settling his stubble chin in his coon-skins. "Don't try to oil me; the herb-doctor tried that. My experience, carried now through a course—worse than salivation[6]—a course of five and thirty boys, proves to me that boyhood is a natural state of rascality."

"Save us, save us!"

"Yes, sir, yes. My name is Pitch; I stick to what I say. I speak from fifteen years' experience; five and thirty boys; American, Irish, English, German, African, Mulatto; not to speak of that China boy sent me by one who well knew my perplexities, from California; and that Lascar boy[7] from Bombay. Thug! I found him sucking the embryo life from my spring eggs. All rascals, sir, every soul of them; Caucasian or Mongol. Amazing the endless variety of rascality in human nature of the juvenile sort. I remember that, having discharged, one after another, twenty-nine boys—each, too, for some wholly unforeseen species of viciousness peculiar to that one peculiar boy—I remember saying to myself: Now, then, surely, I have got to the end of the list, wholly exhausted it; I have only now to get me a boy, any boy different from those twenty-nine preceding boys, and he infallibly shall be that virtuous boy I have so long been seeking. But, bless me! this thirtieth boy—by the way, having at the time long forsworn your intelligence offices, I had him sent to me from the Commissioners of Emigration, all the way from New York, culled out carefully, in fine, at my particular request, from a standing army of eight hundred boys, the flowers of all nations, so they wrote me, temporarily in barracks on an East River island—I say, this thirtieth boy was in person not ungraceful; his deceased mother a lady's maid, or something of that sort; and in manner, why, in a plebeian way, a perfect Chesterfield;[8] very intelligent, too—quick as a flash. But, such suavity! 'Please sir! please sir!' always bowing and saying, 'Please sir.' In the strangest way, too, combining a filial affection with a menial respect. Took such warm, singular interest in my affairs. Wanted to be considered one of the family—sort of adopted son of mine, I suppose. Of a morning, when I would go out to my stable, with what childlike good nature he would trot out my nag, 'Please sir, I think he's getting fatter and fatter.' 'But, he don't look very clean, does he?'

6. Inducing excessive saliva was a treatment for a disordered liver.
7. A menial East Indian boy.
8. In Melville's absolute scales, Philip Dormer Stanhope, fourth earl of Chesterfield (1694–1773), on the basis of his posthumous *Letters to His Son* (1774), is a symbol of the worldly gentleman, which in Melville's theology means someone at the other extreme from Jesus—Chesterfield embodying terrestrial rather than celestial values. In the Melville house was a book owned by his father as a boy, Chesterfield's *Principles of Politeness, and of Knowing the World* (1786) (see n. 6, p. 175). In Melville's view, the phrase *Christian gentleman* is an oxymoron because no gentleman could obey Jesus' words to and about the rich (and honorable) young man who would have been His disciple if he could have kept all his possessions (Matthew 19.16–26).

unwilling to be downright harsh with so affectionate a lad; 'and he seems a little hollow inside the haunch there, don't he? or no, perhaps I don't see plain this morning.' 'Oh, please sir, it's just there I think he's gaining so, please.' Polite scamp! I soon found he never gave that wretched nag his oats of nights; didn't bed him either. Was above that sort of chambermaid work. No end to his willful neglects. But the more he abused my service, the more polite he grew."

"Oh, sir, some way you mistook him."

"Not a bit of it. Besides, sir, he was a boy who under a Chesterfieldian exterior hid strong destructive propensities. He cut up my horse-blanket for the bits of leather, for hinges to his chest. Denied it point-blank. After he was gone, found the shreds under his mattress. Would slyly break his hoe-handle, too, on purpose to get rid of hoeing. Then be so gracefully penitent for his fatal excess of industrious strength. Offer to mend all by taking a nice stroll to the nighest settlement—cherry-trees in full bearing all the way—to get the broken thing cobbled. Very politely stole my pears, odd pennies, shillings, dollars, and nuts; regular squirrel at it. But I could prove nothing. Expressed to him my suspicions. Said I, moderately enough, 'A little less politeness, and a little more honesty would suit me better.' He fired up; threatened to sue for libel. I won't say anything about his afterwards, in Ohio, being found in the act of gracefully putting a bar across a rail-road track, for the reason that a stoker called him the rogue that he was. But enough: polite boys or saucy boys, white boys or black boys, smart boys or lazy boys, Caucasian boys or Mongol boys—all are rascals."

"Shocking, shocking!" nervously tucking his frayed cravat-end out of sight. "Surely, respected sir, you labor under a deplorable hallucination. Why, pardon again, you seem to have not the slightest confidence in boys. I admit, indeed, that boys, some of them at least, are but too prone to one little foolish foible or other. But, what then, respected sir, when, by natural laws, they finally outgrow such things, and wholly?"

Having until now vented himself mostly in plaintive dissent of canine whines and groans, the man with the brass-plate seemed beginning to summon courage to a less timid encounter. But, upon his maiden essay, was not very encouragingly handled, since the dialogue immediately continued as follows:

"Boys outgrow what is amiss in them? From bad boys spring good men? Sir, 'the child is father of the man;'[9] hence, as all boys are rascals, so are all men. But, God bless me, you must know these things better than I; keeping an intelligence office as you do; a business

---

9. From William Wordsworth's poem beginning "My heart leaps up when I behold" (1802), not marked by Melville in his copy of Wordsworth's *Complete Poetical Works* (1837), p. 27.

which must furnish peculiar facilities for studying mankind. Come, come up here, sir; confess you know these things pretty well, after all. Do you not know that all men are rascals, and all boys, too?"

"Sir," replied the other, spite of his shocked feelings seeming to pluck up some spirit, but not to an indiscreet degree, "Sir, heaven be praised, I am far, very far from knowing what you say. True," he thoughtfully continued, "with my associates, I keep an intelligence office, and for ten years, come October, have, one way or other, been concerned in that line; for no small period in the great city of Cincinnati, too; and though, as you hint, within that long interval, I must have had more or less favorable opportunity for studying mankind—in a business way, scanning not only the faces, but ransacking the lives of several thousands of human beings, male and female, of various nations, both employers and employed, genteel and ungenteel, educated and uneducated; yet—of course, I candidly admit, with some random exceptions, I have, so far as my small observation goes, found that mankind thus domestically viewed, confidentially viewed, I may say; they, upon the whole—making some reasonable allowances for human imperfection—present as pure a moral spectacle as the purest angel could wish. I say it, respected sir, with confidence."

"Gammon! You don't mean what you say. Else you are like a landsman at sea: don't know the ropes, the very things everlastingly pulled before your eyes. Serpent-like, they glide about, traveling blocks[1] too subtle for you. In short, the entire ship is a riddle. Why, you green ones wouldn't know if she were unseaworthy; but still, with thumbs stuck back into your arm-holes, pace the rotten planks, singing, like a fool, words put into your green mouth by the cunning owner, the man who, heavily insuring it, sends his ship to be wrecked—

'A wet sheet and a flowing sea!'—

and, sir, now that it occurs to me, your talk, the whole of it, is but a wet sheet and a flowing sea, and an idle wind that follows fast, offering a striking contrast to my own discourse."

"Sir," exclaimed the man with the brass-plate, his patience now more or less tasked, "permit me with deference to hint that some of your remarks are injudiciously worded. And thus we say to our patrons, when they enter our office full of abuse of us because of some worthy boy we may have sent them—some boy wholly misjudged for the time. Yes, sir, permit me to remark that you do not sufficiently consider that, though a small man, I may have my small share of feelings."

1. Pulleys. Below: a line from *The Songs of Scotland, Ancient and Modern* (1825), by Allan Cunningham (1784–1842).

"Well, well, I didn't mean to wound your feelings at all. And that
they are small, very small, I take your word for it. Sorry, sorry. But
truth is like a thrashing-machine; tender sensibilities must keep out
of the way. Hope you understand me. Don't want to hurt you. All I
say is, what I said in the first place, only now I swear it, that all
boys are rascals."

"Sir," lowly replied the other, still forbearing like an old lawyer
badgered in court, or else like a good-hearted simpleton, the butt of
mischievous wags, "Sir, since you come back to the point, will you
allow me, in my small, quiet way, to submit to you certain small,
quiet views of the subject in hand?"

"Oh, yes!" with insulting indifference, rubbing his chin and looking the other way. "Oh, yes; go on."

"Well, then, respected sir," continued the other, now assuming as
genteel an attitude as the irritating set of his pinched five-dollar
suit would permit; "well, then, sir, the peculiar principles, the
strictly philosophical principles, I may say," guardedly rising in dignity, as he guardedly rose on his toes, "upon which our office is
founded, have led me and my associates, in our small, quiet way, to
a careful analytical study of man, conducted, too, on a quiet theory,
and with an unobtrusive aim wholly our own. That theory I will not
now at large set forth. But some of the discoveries resulting from it,
I will, by your permission, very briefly mention; such of them, I
mean, as refer to the state of boyhood scientifically viewed."

"Then you have studied the thing? expressly studied boys, eh?
Why didn't you out with that before?"

"Sir, in my small business way, I have not conversed with so
many masters, gentlemen masters, for nothing. I have been taught
that in this world there is a precedence of opinions as well as of
persons. You have kindly given me your views, I am now, with modesty, about to give you mine."

"Stop flunkying—go on."

"In the first place, sir, our theory teaches us to proceed by analogy from the physical to the moral. Are we right there, sir? Now, sir,
take a young boy, a young male infant rather, a man-child in
short—what sir, I respectfully ask, do you in the first place remark?"

"A rascal, sir! present and prospective, a rascal!"

"Sir, if passion is to invade, surely science must evacuate. May I
proceed? Well, then, what, in the first place, in a general view, do
you remark, respected sir, in that male baby or man-child?"

The bachelor privily growled, but this time, upon the whole, better governed himself than before, though not, indeed, to the degree
of thinking it prudent to risk an articulate response.

"What do you remark? I respectfully repeat." But, as no answer came, only the low, half-suppressed growl, as of Bruin in a hollow trunk,[2] the questioner continued: "Well, sir, if you will permit me, in my small way, to speak for you, you remark, respected sir, an incipient creation; loose sort of sketchy thing; a little preliminary rag-paper study, or careless cartoon, so to speak, of a man. The idea, you see, respected sir, is there; but, as yet, wants filling out. In a word, respected sir, the man-child is at present but little, every way; I don't pretend to deny it; but, then, he *promises* well, does he not? Yes, promises very well indeed, I may say. (So, too, we say to our patrons in reference to some noble little youngster objected to for being a *dwarf*.) But, to advance one step further," extending his thread-bare leg, as he drew a pace nearer, "we must now drop the figure of the rag-paper cartoon, and borrow one—to use presently, when wanted—from the horticultural kingdom. Some bud, lily-bud, if you please. Now, such points as the new-born man-child has—as yet not all that could be desired, I am free to confess—still, such as they are, there they are, and palpable as those of an adult. But we stop not here," taking another step. "The man-child not only possesses these present points, small though they are, but, likewise—now our horticultural image comes into play—like the bud of the lily, he contains concealed rudiments of others; that is, points at present invisible, with beauties at present dormant."

"Come, come, this talk is getting too horticultural and beautiful altogether. Cut it short, cut it short!"

"Respected sir," with a rustily martial sort of gesture, like a decayed corporal's, "when deploying into the field of discourse the vanguard of an important argument, much more in evolving the grand central forces of a new philosophy of boys, as I may say, surely you will kindly allow scope adequate to the movement in hand, small and humble in its way as that movement may be. Is it worth my while to go on, respected sir?"

"Yes, stop flunkying and go on."

Thus encouraged, again the philosopher with the brass-plate proceeded:

"Supposing, sir, that worthy gentleman (in such terms, to an applicant for service, we allude to some patron we chance to have in our eye), supposing, respected sir, that worthy gentleman, Adam, to have been dropped overnight in Eden, as a calf in the pasture; supposing that, sir—then how could even the learned serpent himself have foreknown that such a downy-chinned little innocent would eventually rival the goat in a beard? Sir, wise as the serpent was, that eventuality would have been entirely hidden from his wisdom."

"I don't know about that. The devil is very sagacious. To judge by

---

2. I.e., a bear hibernating in a hollow tree trunk.

the event, he appears to have understood man better even than the Being who made him."

"For God's sake, don't say that, sir! To the point. Can it now with fairness be denied that, in his beard, the man-child prospectively possesses an appendix, not less imposing than patriarchal; and for this goodly beard, should we not by generous anticipation give the man-child, even in his cradle, credit? Should we not now, sir? respectfully I put it."

"Yes, if like pig-weed he mows it down soon as it shoots," porcinely rubbing his stubble-chin against his coon-skins.

"I have hinted at the analogy," continued the other, calmly disregardful of the digression; "now to apply it. Suppose a boy evince no noble quality. Then generously give him credit for his prospective one. Don't you see? So we say to our patrons when they would fain return a boy upon us as unworthy: 'Madam, or sir,' (as the case may be) 'has this boy a beard?' 'No.' 'Has he, we respectfully ask, as yet, evinced any noble quality?' 'No, indeed.' 'Then, madam, or sir, take him back, we humbly beseech; and keep him till that same noble quality sprouts; for, have confidence, it, like the beard, is in him.' "

"Very fine theory," scornfully exclaimed the bachelor, yet in secret, perhaps, not entirely undisturbed by these strange new views of the matter; "but what trust is to be placed in it?"

"The trust of perfect confidence, sir. To proceed. Once more, if you please, regard the man-child."

"Hold!" paw-like thrusting out his bearskin arm, "don't intrude that man-child upon me too often. He who loves not bread, dotes not on dough. As little of your man-child as your logical arrangements will admit."

"Anew regard the man-child," with inspired intrepidity repeated he with the brass-plate, "in the perspective of his developments, I mean. At first the man-child has no teeth, but about the sixth month—am I right, sir?"

"Don't know anything about it."

"To proceed then, though at first deficient in teeth, about the sixth month the man-child begins to put forth in that particular. And sweet those tender little puttings-forth are."

"Very, but blown out of his mouth directly, worthless enough."

"Admitted. And, therefore, we say to our patrons returning with a boy alleged not only to be deficient in goodness, but redundant in ill: 'The lad, madam or sir, evinces very corrupt qualities, does he?' 'No end to them.' 'But, have confidence, there will be; for pray, madam, in this lad's early childhood, were not those frail first teeth, then his, followed by his present sound, even, beautiful and permanent set? And the more objectionable those first teeth became, was not that, madam, we respectfully submit, so much the more reason to look for their speedy substitution by the present sound, even, beautiful and permanent ones?' 'True, true, can't deny that.' 'Then, madam, take him back, we respectfully beg, and wait till, in the now swift course of nature, dropping those transient moral blemishes you complain of, he replacingly buds forth in the sound, even, beautiful and permanent virtues.' '

"Very philosophical again," was the contemptuous reply—the outward contempt, perhaps, proportioned to the inward misgiving. "Vastly philosophical, indeed, but tell me—to continue your analogy—since the second teeth followed—in fact, came from—the first, is there no chance the blemish may be transmitted?"

"Not at all." Abating in humility as he gained in the argument. "The second teeth follow, but do not come from, the first; successors, not sons. The first teeth are not like the germ blossom of the apple, at once the father of, and incorporated into, the growth it foreruns; but they are thrust from their place by the independent undergrowth of the succeeding set—an illustration, by the way, which shows more for me than I meant, though not more than I wish."

"What does it show?" Surly-looking as a thunder-cloud with the inkept unrest of unacknowledged conviction.

"It shows this, respected sir, that in the case of any boy, especially an ill one, to apply unconditionally the saying, that the 'child is father of the man', is, besides implying an uncharitable aspersion of the race, affirming a thing very wide of—"

"—Your analogy," like a snapping turtle.

"Yes, respected sir."

"But is analogy argument? You are a punster."

"Punster, respected sir?" with a look of being aggrieved.

"Yes, you pun with ideas as another man may with words."

"Oh well, sir, whoever talks in that strain, whoever has no confidence in human reason, whoever despises human reason, in vain to reason with him. Still, respected sir," altering his air, "permit me to hint that, had not the force of analogy moved you somewhat, you would hardly have offered to contemn it."

"Talk away," disdainfully; "but pray tell me what has that last analogy of yours to do with your intelligence office business?"

"Everything to do with it, respected sir. From that analogy we derive the reply made to such a patron as, shortly after being supplied by us with an adult servant, proposes to return him upon our hands; not that, while with the patron, said adult has given any cause of dissatisfaction, but the patron has just chanced to hear something unfavorable concerning him from some gentleman who employed said adult long before, while a boy. To which too fastidious patron, we, taking said adult by the hand, and graciously reintroducing him to the patron, say: 'Far be it from you, madam, or sir, to proceed in your censure against this adult, in anything of the spirit of an ex-post-facto law.[3] Madam, or sir, would you visit upon the butterfly the sins of the caterpillar? In the natural advance of all creatures, do they not bury themselves over and over again in the endless resurrection of better and better? Madam, or sir, take back this adult; he may have been a caterpillar, but is now a butterfly.' "

"Pun away; but even accepting your analogical pun, what does it amount to? Was the caterpillar one creature, and is the butterfly another? The butterfly is the caterpillar in a gaudy cloak; stripped of which, there lies the impostor's long spindle of a body, pretty much worm-shaped as before."

"You reject the analogy. To the facts then. You deny that a youth of one character can be transformed into a man of an opposite character. Now then—yes, I have it. There's the founder of La Trappe, and Ignatius Loyola;[4] in boyhood, and someway into manhood, both devil-may-care bloods, and yet, in the end, the wonders of the world for anchoritish self-command. These two examples, by-the-way, we cite to such patrons as would hastily return rakish young waiters upon us. 'Madam, or sir—patience; patience,' we say; 'good madam, or sir, would you discharge forth your cask of good wine, because, while working, it riles more or less? Then discharge not forth this young waiter; the good in him is working.' 'But he is a sad rake.' 'Therein is his promise; the rake being crude material for the saint.' "

"Ah, you are a talking man—what I call a wordy man. You talk, talk."

"And with submission, sir, what is the greatest judge, bishop or prophet, but a talking man? He talks, talks. It is the peculiar vocation of a teacher to talk. What's wisdom itself but table-talk?[5] The best wisdom in this world, and the last spoken by its teacher, did it not literally and truly come in the form of table-talk?"

"You, you, you!" rattling down his rifle.

---

3. A law with retroactive effects, such as a law (unconstitutional in the United States) that retroactively alters the prescribed punishment to the disadvantage of someone accused or convicted of a crime.

4. Two men who led worldly lives before turning to the church. Jean-Armand de Bouthillier de Rancé (1626–1700), French nobleman who reformed the Cistercian abbey of La Trappe, in the department of Orne, which was rebuilt in Melville's youth. Ignatius of Loyola (1491?–1556), Spanish founder of the Jesuits.

5. A familiar literary genre of Melville's time, with volumes of celebrity conversation available from Samuel Johnson, William Cowper, Richard Brinsley Sheridan, Samuel Taylor Coleridge, Samuel Rogers, and many others. Classical precedents were in the *Moralia* (moral essays) by the Greek writer Plutarch (46–120 C.E.). Melville heavily marked his late brother Gansevoort's copy of William Hazlitt's *Table Talk: Opinions on Books, Men, and Things* (1821–1822). Here, an ironic way of recalling Jesus at the Last Supper (John 13–14). For Melville table-talk books, especially during the years of his isolation and neglect, were a way of recapturing the joy of participating in spirited conversations with literary and artistic people in London in 1849 and in New York beginning in 1846 and never quite ending.

"To shift the subject, since we cannot agree. Pray, what is your opinion, respected sir, of St. Augustine?"[6]

"St. Augustine? What should I, or you either, know of him? Seems to me, for one in such a business, to say nothing of such a coat, that though you don't know a great deal, indeed, yet you know a good deal more than you ought to know, or than you have a right to know, or than it is safe or expedient for you to know, or than, in the fair course of life, you could have honestly come to know. I am of opinion you should be served like a Jew in the middle ages with his gold; this knowledge of yours, which you haven't enough knowledge to know how to make a right use of, it should be taken from you. And so I have been thinking all along."

"You are merry, sir. But you have a little looked into St. Augustine I suppose?"

"St. Augustine on Original Sin is my text book. But you, I ask again, where do you find time or inclination for these out-of-the-way speculations? In fact, your whole talk, the more I think of it, is altogether unexampled and extraordinary."

"Respected sir, have I not already informed you that the quite new method, the strictly philosophical one, on which our office is founded, has led me and my associates to an enlarged study of mankind. It was my fault, if I did not, likewise, hint, that these studies directed always to the scientific procuring of good servants of all sorts, boys included, for the kind gentlemen, our patrons— that these studies, I say, have been conducted equally among all books of all libraries, as among all men of all nations. Then, you rather like St. Augustine, sir?"

"Excellent genius!"

"In some points he was; yet, how comes it that under his own hand, St. Augustine confesses that, until his thirtieth year, he was a very sad dog?"

"A saint a sad dog?"

"Not the saint, but the saint's irresponsible little forerunner—the boy."

"All boys are rascals, and so are all men," again flying off at his tangent; "my name is Pitch; I stick to what I say."

6. Author of *Confessions* who profoundly influenced Melville's concept of Original Sin as derived from the influence of Augustine (354–430) on the Renaissance theologian and Protestant reformer John Calvin (1509–1564) and subsequently on the Dutch Reformed Church of Melville's Albany family. See "Hawthorne and His Mosses" in the 2001 NCE of *Moby-Dick*, p. 521: "Certain it is, however, that this great power of blackness in him [Hawthorne] derives its force from its appeals to that Calvinistic sense of innate Depravity and Original Sin, from whose visitations, in some shape or other, no deeply thinking mind is always and wholly free. For, in certain moods, no man can weigh this world, without throwing in something, somehow like Original Sin, to strike the uneven balance." For Calvinists, "total depravity" (p. 152 herein) is the natural condition of all human beings.

"Ah, sir, permit me—when I behold you on this mild summer's eve, thus eccentrically clothed in the skins of wild beasts, I cannot but conclude that the equally grim and unsuitable habit of your mind is likewise but an eccentric assumption, having no basis in your genuine soul, no more than in nature herself."

"Well, really, now—really," fidgeted the bachelor, not unaffected in his conscience by these benign personalities, "really, really, now, I don't know but that I may have been a little bit too hard upon those five and thirty boys of mine."

"Glad to find you a little softening, sir. Who knows now, but that flexile gracefulness, however questionable at the time of that thirtieth boy of yours, might have been the silky husk of the most solid qualities of maturity. It might have been with him as with the ear of the Indian corn."

"Yes, yes, yes," excitedly cried the bachelor, as the light of this new illustration broke in, "yes, yes; and now that I think of it, how often I've sadly watched my Indian corn in May, wondering whether such sickly, half-eaten sprouts, could ever thrive up into the stiff, stately spear of August."

"A most admirable reflection, sir, and you have only, according to the analogical theory first started by our office, to apply it to that thirtieth boy in question, and see the result. Had you but kept that thirtieth boy—been patient with his sickly virtues, cultivated them, hoed round them, why what a glorious guerdon would have been yours, when at last you should have had a St. Augustine for an ostler."[7]

"Really, really—well, I am glad I didn't send him to jail, as at first I intended."

"Oh that would have been too bad. Grant he was vicious. The petty vices of boys are like the innocent kicks of colts, as yet imperfectly broken. Some boys know not virtue only for the same reason they know not French; it was never taught them. Established upon the basis of parental charity, juvenile asylums exist by law for the benefit of lads convicted of acts which, in adults, would have received other requital. Why? Because, do what they will, society, like our office, at bottom has a Christian confidence in boys. And all this we say to our patrons."

"Your patrons, sir, seem your marines to whom you may say anything,"[8] said the other, relapsing. "Why do knowing employers shun youths from asylums, though offered them at the smallest wages? I'll none of your reformado boys."

7. Or hostler, someone who takes care of horses at an inn or stable.
8. As landlubbers, the marines—soldiers stationed on warships, in part to keep the sailors in order—were resented, and scoffed at as believing any tall tale they were told about the ocean and its inhabitants.

"Such a boy, respected sir, I would not get for you, but a boy that never needed reform. Do not smile, for as whooping-cough and measles are juvenile diseases, and yet some juveniles never have them, so are there boys equally free from juvenile vices. True, for the best of boys, measles may be contagious, and evil communications corrupt good manners; but a boy with a sound mind in a sound body—such is the boy I would get you. If hitherto, sir, you have struck upon a peculiarly bad vein of boys, so much the more hope now of your hitting a good one."

"That sounds a kind of reasonable, as it were—a little so, really. In fact, though you have said a great many foolish things, very foolish and absurd things, yet, upon the whole, your conversation has been such as might almost lead one less distrustful than I to repose a certain conditional confidence in you, I had almost added in your office, also. Now, for the humor of it, supposing that even I, I myself, really had this sort of conditional confidence, though but a grain, what sort of a boy, in sober fact, could you send me? And what would be your fee?"[9]

"Conducted," replied the other somewhat loftily, rising now in eloquence as his proselyte, for all his pretenses, sunk in conviction, "conducted upon principles involving care, learning, and labor, exceeding what is usual in kindred institutions, the Philosophical Intelligence Office is forced to charges somewhat higher than customary. Briefly, our fee is three dollars in advance. As for the boy, by a lucky chance, I have a very promising little fellow now in my eye—a very likely little fellow, indeed."

"Honest?"

"As the day is long. Might trust him with untold millions. Such, at least, were the marginal observations on the phrenological chart of his head, submitted to me by the mother."

"How old?"

"Just fifteen."

"Tall? Stout?"

"Uncommonly so, for his age, his mother remarked."

"Industrious?"

"The busy bee."

The bachelor fell into a troubled reverie. At last, with much hesitancy, he spoke:

9. Because 19th-century ways of living are hard to comprehend today, the Melvilles' servant problem forms a subplot throughout Parker's biography, especially the second volume. Melville's first "boy" at Arrowhead was a man, an Irishman named David. At Arrowhead, no matter how poor they were, the Melvilles always had a cook or were looking for a replacement and may always have had a "boy" or been looking for one. In the early 1850s Melville's mother at least once met ships in Manhattan and selected a likely worker from the newly arrived Irish. After the Civil War slowed immigration, good help was harder than ever to find and keep.

"Do you think now, candidly, that—I say candidly—candidly—could I have some small, limited—some faint, conditional degree of confidence in that boy? Candidly, now?"

"Candidly, you could."

"A sound boy? A good boy?"

"Never knew one more so."

The bachelor fell into another irresolute reverie; then said: "Well, now, you have suggested some rather new views of boys, and men, too. Upon those views in the concrete I at present decline to determine. Nevertheless, for the sake purely of a scientific experiment, I will try that boy. I don't think him an angel, mind. No, no. But I'll try him. There are my three dollars, and here is my address. Send him along this day two weeks. Hold, you will be wanting the money for his passage. There," handing it somewhat reluctantly.

"Ah, thank you. I had forgotten his passage;" then, altering in manner, and gravely holding the bills, continued: "Respected sir, never willingly do I handle money not with perfect willingness, nay, with a certain alacrity, paid. Either tell me that you have a perfect and unquestioning confidence in me (never mind the boy now) or permit me respectfully to return these bills."

"Put 'em up, put 'em up!"

"Thank you. Confidence is the indispensable basis of all sorts of business transactions. Without it, commerce between man and man, as between country and country, would, like a watch, run down and stop. And now, supposing that against present expectation the lad should, after all, evince some little undesirable trait, do not, respected sir, rashly dismiss him. Have but patience, have but confidence. Those transient vices will, ere long, fall out, and be replaced by the sound, firm, even and permanent virtues. Ah," glancing shoreward, towards a grotesquely-shaped bluff, "there's the Devil's Joke,[1] as they call it; the bell for landing will shortly ring. I must go look up the cook I brought for the inn-keeper at Cairo."

---

1. James Hall in *Notes on the Western States* mentions a Mississippi bluff called the Devil's Bake-oven. Melville knew places named for the Devil, among them Spuyten Duyvil (commonly translated as "Spitting Devil"), the strait at the north end of Manhattan connecting the East River and the Hudson, and the Devil's Pulpit on Monument Mountain in the Berkshires.

Chapter 23.

IN WHICH THE POWERFUL EFFECT OF NATURAL SCENERY IS EVINCED IN THE CASE OF THE MISSOURIAN, WHO, IN VIEW OF THE REGION ROUND-ABOUT CAIRO, HAS A RETURN OF HIS CHILLY FIT.

At Cairo, the old established firm of Fever & Ague is still settling up its unfinished business; that Creole grave-digger, Yellow Jack—his hand at the mattock and spade has not lost its cunning; while Don Saturninus Typhus taking his constitutional with Death, Calvin Edson[2] and three undertakers, in the morass, snuffs up the mephitic breeze with zest.

In the dank twilight, fanned with mosquitoes, and sparkling with fire-flies, the boat now lies before Cairo. She has landed certain passengers, and tarries for the coming of expected ones. Leaning over the rail on the inshore side, the Missourian eyes through the dubious medium that swampy and squalid domain; and over it au-ᶜ dibly mumbles his cynical mind to himself, as Apemantus'[3] dog may have mumbled his bone. He bethinks him that the man with the brass-plate was to land on this villainous bank, and for that cause, if no other, begins to suspect him. Like one beginning to rouse himself from a dose of chloroform treacherously given, he half divines, too, that he, the philosopher, had unwittingly been betrayed into being an unphilosophical dupe. To what vicissitudes of light and shade is man subject! He ponders the mystery of human subjectivity in general. He thinks he perceives with Crossbones,[4] his favorite author, that, as one may wake up well in the morning, very well, indeed, and brisk as a buck, I thank you, but ere bed-time get under the weather, there is no telling how—so one may wake up wise, and slow of assent, very wise and very slow, I assure you, and for all that, before night, by like trick in the atmosphere, be left in the lurch a ninny. Health and wisdom equally precious, and equally little as unfluctuating possessions to be relied on.

But where was slipped in the entering wedge? Philosophy, knowledge, experience—were those trusty knights of the castle recreant?[5]

---

2. See n. 8, p. 83. "Yellow Jack": malaria; identified as a "Creole" because malaria was a chief cause of death in New Orleans. "Cunning": cf. "If I forget thee, O Jerusalem, let my right hand forget her cunning" (Psalm 137.5). "Don Saturninus Thyphus": the Spanish-Latin-sounding form of address, drawing on the stereotype of the melancholy Spaniard, pays ironic honor to the ferocity of typhus, a horrific, prolonged rickettsial febrile disease caused by body lice and marked by delirium and red skin eruptions. Saturn was the source of melancholy, according to medieval astrology.
3. The churlish philosopher of Shakespeare's *Timon of Athens*. Melville is punning on the Latin sense of cynic ("doglike").
4. Any wise, old, out-of-fashion, classical author who tells the morbid or deadly (hence "Crossbones") truth about human nature and experience.
5. Disloyal or betrayed. The passage echoes *Paradise Lost*, marked by Melville in his copy, where Satan, "the false dissembler unperceiv'd" tricks Uriel, although he is considered the "sharpest sighted spirit of all in heaven." Milton explains (3.682–89): "For neither

No, but unbeknown to them, the enemy stole on the castle's south side, its genial one, where Suspicion, the warder, parleyed. In fine, his too indulgent, too artless and companionable nature betrayed him. Admonished by which, he thinks he must be a little splenetic in his intercourse henceforth.

He revolves the crafty process of sociable chat, by which, as he fancies, the man with the brass-plate wormed into him, and made such a fool of him as insensibly to persuade him to waive, in his exceptional case, that general law of distrust systematically applied to the race. He revolves, but cannot comprehend, the operation, still less the operator. Was the man a trickster, it must be more for the love than the lucre. Two or three dirty dollars the motive to so many nice wiles? And yet how full of mean needs his seeming. Before his mental vision the person of that threadbare Talleyrand, that impoverished Machiavelli, that seedy Rosicrucian[6]—for something of all these he vaguely deems him—passes now in puzzled review. Fain, in his disfavor, would he make out a logical case. The doctrine of analogies recurs. Fallacious enough doctrine when wielded against one's prejudices, but in corroboration of cherished suspicions not without likelihood. Analogically, he couples the slanting cut of the equivocator's coat-tails with the sinister cast in his eye; he weighs slyboot's sleek speech in the light imparted by the oblique import of the smooth slope of his worn boot-heels; the insinuator's undulating flunkyisms dovetail into those of the flunky beast that windeth his way on his belly.[7]

From these uncordial reveries he is roused by a cordial slap on the shoulder, accompanied by a spicy volume of tobacco-smoke, out of which came a voice, sweet as a seraph's:

"A penny for your thoughts, my fine fellow."

---

man nor angel can discern / Hypocrisy, the only evil that walks / Invisible, except to GOD alone, / By his permissive will, through heaven and earth: / And oft, though wisdom wake, suspicion sleeps / At wisdom's gate, and to simplicity / Resigns her charge, while goodness thinks no ill / Where no ill seems."

6. A member of an esoteric and mystical religious movement, which first appeared in Germany in the early 17th century. Its supposed founder, Christian Rosenkreutz, whose actual existence is uncertain, claimed to possess occult powers, which are incorporated into the teachings of Rosicrucianism. His name, like the name of the order, is a combination of the words meaning "rose" and "cross," the two elements of the movement's symbol. Charles Maurice de Talleyrand-Périgord (1754–1838), French statesman, known directly to Melville's uncle Thomas Melvill as an extortionist. Niccolo Machiavelli (1469–1527), Italian statesman, author of the posthumous *The Prince* (1532), a practical guide to how to acquire and retain power.

7. In Genesis 3.14 God punishes the serpent for having tempted Eve: "Because thou hast done this, thou art cursed above all cattle, and above every beast of the field; upon thy belly shalt thou go, and dust shalt thou eat all the days of thy life." Pitch is the loser by three dollars plus passage money for the "boy," but among the passengers of the *Fidèle* he is the most admirable opponent of the Confidence Man's false, delusive optimism; and at this moment he becomes the only one—except perhaps the invalid Titan—to penetrate the masquerade.

Chapter 24.

A PHILANTHROPIST UNDERTAKES TO CONVERT A MISANTHROPE, BUT
DOES NOT GET BEYOND CONFUTING HIM.

"Hands off!" cried the bachelor, involuntarily covering dejection with moroseness.

"Hands off? that sort of label won't do in our Fair.[8] Whoever in our Fair has fine feelings loves to feel the nap of fine cloth, especially when a fine fellow wears it."

"And who of my fine-fellow species may you be? From the Brazils, ain't you? Toucan fowl. Fine feathers on foul meat."

This ungentle mention of the toucan was not improbably suggested by the parti-hued, and rather plumagy aspect of the stranger, no bigot it would seem, but a liberalist, in dress, and whose wardrobe, almost anywhere than on the liberal Mississippi, used to all sorts of fantastic informalities, might, even to observers less critical than the bachelor, have looked, if anything, a little out of the common; but not more so perhaps, than, considering the bear and raccoon costume, the bachelor's own appearance. In short, the stranger sported a vesture barred with various hues, that of the cochineal predominating, in style participating of a Highland plaid, Emir's robe, and French blouse; from its plaited sort of front peeped glimpses of a flowered regatta-shirt, while, for the rest, white trowsers of ample duck flowed over maroon-colored slippers, and a jaunty smoking-cap of regal purple crowned him off at top; king of traveled good-fellows, evidently. Grotesque as all was, nothing looked stiff or unused; all showed signs of easy service, the least wonted thing setting like a wonted glove. That genial hand, which had just been laid on the ungenial shoulder, was now carelessly thrust down before him, sailor-fashion, into a sort of Indian belt, confining the redundant vesture; the other held, by its long bright cherry-stem, a Nuremburgh pipe in blast, its great porcelain bowl painted in miniature with linked crests and arms of interlinked nations—a florid show. As by subtle saturations of its mellowing essence the tobacco had ripened the bowl, so it looked as if something similar of the interior spirit came rosily out on the cheek. But rosy pipe-bowl, or rosy countenance, all was lost on that unrosy man, the bachelor, who, waiting a moment till the commotion, caused by the boat's renewed progress, had a little abated, thus continued:

8. An allusion to Vanity Fair, in John Bunyan's *Pilgrim's Progress* (1678, 1684), a favorite book of Melville's friend Hawthorne, whose "Celestial Railroad" (see p. 429 herein) constitutes a memorable updating of the fair. Bunyan had been in Melville's mind when he wrote *Moby-Dick* (chapter 36) and *Pierre* (book 25, chapter 4).

"Hark ye," jeeringly eying the cap and belt, "did you ever see Signor Marzetti in the African pantomime?"[9]

"No;—good performer?"

"Excellent; plays the intelligent ape till he seems it. With such naturalness can a being endowed with an immortal spirit enter into that of a monkey. But where's your tail? In the pantomime, Marzetti, no hypocrite in his monkery, prides himself on that."

The stranger, now at rest, sideways and genially, on one hip, his right leg cavalierly crossed before the other, the toe of his vertical slipper pointed easily down on the deck, whiffed out a long, leisurely sort of indifferent and charitable puff, betokening him more or less of the mature man of the world, a character which, like its opposite, the sincere Christian's, is not always swift to take offense; and then, drawing near, still smoking, again laid his hand, this time with mild impressiveness, on the ursine shoulder, and not unamiably said: "That in your address there is a sufficiency of the *fortiter in re* few unbiased observers will question; but that this is duly attempered with the *suaviter in modo*[1] may admit, I think, of an honest doubt. My dear fellow," beaming his eyes full upon him, "what injury have I done you, that you should receive my greeting with a curtailed civility?"

"Off hands;" once more shaking the friendly member from him. "Who in the name of the great chimpanzee, in whose likeness, you, Marzetti, and the other chatterers are made, who in thunder are you?"

"A cosmopolitan,[2] a catholic man; who, being such, ties himself to no narrow tailor or teacher, but federates, in heart as in costume, something of the various gallantries of men under various suns. Oh, one roams not over the gallant globe in vain. Bred by it, is a

---

9. Joseph Marzetti pantomimed the role of an ape in more than one New York theater, acting in *The Brazilian Ape* at Burton's in Chambers Street in 1848 and in *Jocko* at Niblo's Garden at Broadway and Prince in 1849. These productions may have been almost identical, for they were both based on a Paris Ballet called *Jocko or the Brazilian Ape*.
1. Gently in manner. *"Fortiter in re"*: strongly in deed. The proverbial usage has the Latin phrases in the other order: *"fortiter in re, suaviter in modo."*
2. A shadowy English trickster, John Dix, alias John Ross, ingratiated himself with Bostonians by claiming acquaintance with English celebrities; he published *Pen and Ink Sketches / by a Cosmopolitan; to which is added Chatterton, A Romance of Literary Life* (1845). Melville may have known of this man, and he knew a great deal about a later English arrival, the forger Thomas Powell, who had indeed been intimate with English literary people. Powell is compared to Dix–Ross in the review of Powell's *Living Authors of England* in the New York *Evening Mirror* for November 2, 1849. Hans-Joachim Lang and Benjamin Lease (see "Selected Bibliography") have argued that the Cosmopolitan is based on the travel writer Bayard Taylor (1825–1878), who had been in the public eye through his lectures and writings ever since his triumphal return from world travels in December 1853. In 1855 he was painted by Thomas Hicks in Egyptian garb not unlike the clothing Melville gives the Cosmopolitan. Taylor may have contributed to the costume of the Cosmopolitan, but hardly to his characterization. Melville could have picked up pointers from "The History of a Cosmopolite" in the September 1854 *Putnam's Monthly*, pp. 325–26.

fraternal and fusing feeling. No man is a stranger. You accost any-body. Warm and confiding, you wait not for measured advances. And though, indeed, mine, in this instance, have met with no very hilarious encouragement, yet the principle of a true citizen of the world is still to return good for ill.—My dear fellow, tell me how I can serve you."

"By dispatching yourself, Mr. Popinjay-of-the-world, into the heart of the Lunar Mountains.[3] You are another of them. Out of my sight!"

"Is the sight of humanity so very disagreeable to you then? Ah, I may be foolish, but for my part, in all its aspects, I love it. Served up à la Pole, or à la Moor, à la Ladrone, or à la Yankee, that good dish, man, still delights me; or rather is man a wine I never weary of comparing and sipping; wherefore am I a pledged cosmopoli-tan, a sort of London-Dock-Vault[4] connoisseur, going about from Teheran to Natchitoches, a taster of races; in all his vintages, smacking my lips over this racy creature, man, continually. But as there are teetotal palates which have a distaste even for Amontil-lado, so I suppose there may be teetotal souls which relish not even the very best brands of humanity. Excuse me, but it just oc-curs to me that you, my dear fellow, possibly lead a solitary life."

"Solitary?" starting as at a touch of divination.

"Yes: in a solitary life one insensibly contracts oddities,—talking to one's self now."

"Been eaves-dropping, eh?"

"Why, a soliloquist in a crowd can hardly but be overheard, and without much reproach to the hearer."

"You are an eaves-dropper."

"Well. Be it so."

"Confess yourself an eaves-dropper?"

"I confess that when you were muttering here I, passing by, caught a word or two, and, by like chance, something previous of your chat with the Intelligence-office man;—a rather sensible fel-low, by the way; much of my style of thinking; would, for his own

3. The Ruwenzori mountain range in east central Africa on the present-day Uganda–Congo border, called the Mountains of the Moon, once thought to contain the source of the Nile. "Popinjay": fop or dandy. Members of Melville's family said such a man was "an ex-quisite." "Popinjay" evokes a passage in *I Henry IV* 1.3.49–52 where (in Melville's edi-tion) Hotspur excuses his not surrendering prisoners to the king: "I then, all smarting, with my wounds being cold, / To be so pestered with a popinjay, / Out of my grief and my impatience, / Answered neglectingly, I know not what." Melville used lines from this speech for an "Extract" in *Moby-Dick*, where it is slightly misquoted as "The sovereignest thing on earth is parmacetti for an inward bruise." Hotspur was on Melville's mind, for Melville in Pittsfield signed an autograph album with Hotspur's words to Glendower (*I Henry IV* 3.1.58), "Tell Truth, and shame the Devil" (which he spelled *devel* or *Devel*).
4. In 1849 Melville was struck by the fitfully lighted gloom and awesome magnitude of the wine vaults beneath the warehouses at the London Docks, the depot for the Wine Mer-chants of London.

sake, he were of my style of dress. Grief to good minds, to see a man of superior sense forced to hide his light under the bushel[5] of an inferior coat.—Well, from what little I heard, I said to myself, Here now is one with the unprofitable philosophy of disesteem for man. Which disease, in the main, I have observed—excuse me—to spring from a certain lowness, if not sourness, of spirits inseparable from sequestration. Trust me, one had better mix in, and do like others. Sad business, this holding out against having a good time. Life is a pic-nic *en costume;* one must take a part, assume a character, stand ready in a sensible way to play the fool. To come in plain clothes, with a long face, as a wiseacre, only makes one a discomfort to himself, and a blot upon the scene. Like your jug of cold water among the wine-flasks, it leaves you unelated among the elated ones. No, no. This austerity won't do. Let me tell you too—*en confiance*—that while revelry may not always merge into ebriety, soberness, in too deep potations, may become a sort of sottishness. Which sober sottishness, in my way of thinking, is only to be cured by beginning at the other end of the horn, to tipple a little."

"Pray, what society of vintners and old topers are you hired to lecture for?"

"I fear I did not give my meaning clearly. A little story may help. The story of the worthy old woman of Goshen, a very moral old woman, who wouldn't let her shoats[6] eat fattening apples in fall, for fear the fruit might ferment upon their brains, and so make them swinish. Now, during a green Christmas, inauspicious to the old, this worthy old woman fell into a moping decline, took to her bed, no appetite, and refused to see her best friends. In much concern her good man sent for the doctor, who, after seeing the patient and putting a question or two, beckoned the husband out, and said: 'Deacon, do you want her cured?' 'Indeed I do.' 'Go directly, then, and buy a jug of Santa Cruz.'[7] 'Santa Cruz? my wife drink Santa Cruz?' 'Either that or die.' 'But how much?' 'As much as she can get down.' 'But she'll get drunk!' 'That's the cure.' Wise men, like doctors, must be obeyed. Much, against the grain, the sober deacon got the unsober medicine, and, equally against her conscience, the

---

5. Jesus' injunction to his disciples in Matthew 5.14–16: "Ye are the light of the world. A city that is set on an hill cannot be hid. Neither do men light a candle, and put it under a bushel, but on a candlestick; and it giveth light unto all that are in the house. Let your light so shine before men, that they may see your good works, and glorify your Father which is in heaven." "Bushel": a container (which the King James translators would have visualized as holding about thirty-two English quarts, dry measure).

6. Pigs, usually less than one year old. In Exodus 8.22 because the Pharaoh will not let Moses guide his people back to Israel God punishes Egypt with plagues but protects the land of Goshen, where the descendants of Jacob live. There were Goshens in many of the states because whites settling a new area wanted to signify that they were a righteous people worthy of being singled out by God for special protection (particularly from the Indians newly expelled from those lands). Here as elsewhere in *The Confidence-Man*, biblical geography and occurrences overlap and blur into modern geography and events.

7. Rum from the West Indian island of that name.

poor old woman took it; but, by so doing, ere long recovered health and spirits, famous appetite, and glad again to see her friends; and having by this experience broken the ice of arid abstinence, never afterwards kept herself a cup too low."

This story had the effect of surprising the bachelor into interest, though hardly into approval.

"If I take your parable right," said he, sinking no little of his former churlishness, "the meaning is, that one cannot enjoy life with gusto unless he renounce the too-sober view of life. But since the too-sober view is, doubtless, nearer true than the too-drunken; I, who rate truth, though cold water, above untruth, though Tokay, will stick to my earthen jug."

"I see," slowly spirting upward a spiral staircase of lazy smoke, "I see; you go in for the lofty."

"How?"

"Oh, nothing! but if I wasn't afraid of prosing, I might tell another story about an old boot in a pieman's loft, contracting there between sun and oven an unseemly, dry-seasoned curl and warp. You've seen such leathery old garretteers, haven't you? Very high, sober, solitary, philosophic, grand, old boots, indeed; but I, for my part, would rather be the pieman's trodden slipper on the ground. Talking of piemen, humble-pie before proud-cake for me. This notion of being lone and lofty is a sad mistake. Men I hold in this respect to be like roosters; the one that betakes himself to a lone and lofty perch is the hen-pecked one, or the one that has the pip."

"You are abusive!" cried the bachelor, evidently touched.

"Who is abused? You, or the race? You won't stand by and see the human race abused? Oh, then, you have some respect for the human race."

"I have some respect for *myself*," with a lip not so firm as before.

"And what race may *you* belong to? now don't you see, my dear fellow, in what inconsistencies one involves himself by affecting disesteem for men? To a charm, my little stratagem succeeded. Come, come, think better of it, and, as a first step to a new mind, give up solitude. I fear, by the way, you have at some time been reading Zimmermann, that old Mr. Megrims of a Zimmermann, whose book on Solitude is as vain as Hume's on Suicide, as Bacon's[8] on Knowledge; and, like these, will betray him who seeks to steer soul and body by it, like a false religion. All they, be they what boasted ones you please, who, to the yearning of our kind after a founded rule of content, offer aught not in the spirit of fellowly

---

8. Francis Bacon, author of *Advancement of Learning* (1605). "Megrims": blues, melancholy. Johann Georg Zimmermann (see n. 6, p. 89). David Hume (1711–1776), Scottish philosopher whose *Essay on Suicide* justifies self-murder in certain circumstances.

gladness based on due confidence in what is above, away with them for poor dupes, or still poorer impostors."

His manner here was so earnest that scarcely any auditor, perhaps, but would have been more or less impressed by it, while, possibly, nervous opponents might have a little quailed under it. Thinking within himself a moment, the bachelor replied: "Had you experience, you would know that your tippling theory, take it in what sense you will, is poor as any other. And Rabelais's pro-wine Koran[9] no more trustworthy than Mahomet's anti-wine one."

"Enough," for a finality knocking the ashes from his pipe, "we talk and keep talking, and still stand where we did. What do you say for a walk? My arm, and let's a turn. They are to have dancing on the hurricane-deck to-night. I shall fling them off a Scotch jig, while, to save the pieces, you hold my loose change; and following that, I propose that you, my dear fellow, stack your gun, and throw your bearskins in a sailor's hornpipe—I holding your watch. What do you say?"

At this proposition the other was himself again, all raccoon.

"Look you," thumping down his rifle, "are you Jeremy Diddler[1] No. 3?"

"Jeremy Diddler? I have heard of Jeremy the prophet, and Jeremy Taylor the divine, but your other Jeremy is a gentleman I am unacquainted with."

"You are his confidential clerk, ain't you?"

"*Whose*, pray? Not that I think myself unworthy of being confided in, but I don't understand."

"You are another of them. Somehow I meet with the most extraordinary metaphysical scamps to-day. Sort of visitation of them. And yet that herb-doctor Diddler somehow takes off the raw edge of the Diddlers that come after him."

"Herb-doctor? who is he?"

"Like you—another of them."

"Who?" Then drawing near, as if for a good long explanatory chat, his left hand spread, and his pipe stem coming crosswise down upon it like a ferule, "You think amiss of me. Now to undeceive you, I will just enter into a little argument and—"

---

9. The sacred book of Islam, which believers accept as the word of God as revealed to Muhammad ("Mahomet"), forbids the consumption of alcohol. François Rabelais (1494?–1553), French cleric, physician, and author, best known for his *Gargantua and Pantagruel* (published in several parts, 1532–64). In his frequently boisterous style, Rabelais celebrates and satirizes both the physical and the intellectual dimensions of life; one section relates the quest for the oracle of the Holy Bottle, a sort of hymn to wine.

1. A trickster, not the biblical prophet Jeremiah nor Jeremy Taylor (1613–1667), the English theologian. Pitch numbers the disguises of the Confidence Man he has encountered, the herb doctor, the Philosophical Intelligence (PIO) man, and now the Cosmopolitan.

"No you don't. No more little arguments for me. Had too many little arguments to-day."

"But put a case. Can you deny—I dare you to deny—that the man leading a solitary life is peculiarly exposed to the sorriest misconceptions touching strangers?"

"Yes, I *do* deny it," again, in his impulsiveness, snapping at the controversial bait, "and I will confute you there in a trice. Look, you—"

"Now, now, now, my dear fellow," thrusting out both vertical palms for double shields, "you crowd me too hard. You don't give one a chance. Say what you will, to shun a social proposition like mine, to shun society in any way, evinces a churlish nature—cold, loveless; as, to embrace it, shows one warm and friendly, in fact, sunshiny."

Here the other, all agog again, in his perverse way, launched forth into the unkindest references to deaf old worldlings keeping in the deafening world; and gouty gluttons limping to their gouty gormandizings; and corseted coquets clasping their corseted cavaliers in the waltz, all for disinterested society's sake; and thousands, bankrupt through lavishness, ruining themselves out of pure love of the sweet company of man—no envies, rivalries, or other unhandsome motive to it.

"Ah, now," deprecating with his pipe, "irony is so unjust; never could abide irony; something Satanic about irony. God defend me from Irony, and Satire, his bosom friend."

"A right knave's prayer, and a right fool's, too," snapping his riflelock.

"Now be frank. Own that was a little gratuitous. But, no, no, you didn't mean it; any way, I can make allowances. Ah, did you but know it, how much pleasanter to puff at this philanthropic pipe, than still to keep fumbling at that misanthropic rifle. As for your worldling, glutton, and coquette, though, doubtless, being such, they may have their little foibles—as who has not?—yet not one of the three can be reproached with that awful sin of shunning society; awful I call it, for not seldom it presupposes a still darker thing than itself—remorse."

"Remorse drives man away from man? How came your fellow-creature, Cain, after the first murder, to go and build the first city?[2]

---

2. In Genesis 4 Cain, the first child born to Adam and Eve, jealous that God favored the animal sacrifice of his younger brother, Abel, over his own agricultural offering, kills Abel. Exiled to the land of Nod, he founds the first city. Remorse was a preoccupation of Melville's. The English literary man and forger Thomas Powell claimed that Melville once told him the plan of a work not yet published as of 1856: "It was intended to illustrate the *principle of remorse*, and to demonstrate that there is, very often, less real virtue in moral respectability than in accidental crime." Crook though he was, Powell had talked to Melville in 1849, and sometimes he told the simple truth about celebrities he had known (see Steven Olsen-Smith, in the "Selected Bibliography").

And why is it that the modern Cain dreads nothing so much as solitary confinement?"

"My dear fellow, you get excited. Say what you will, I for one must have my fellow-creatures round me. Thick, too—I must have them thick."

"The pick-pocket, too, loves to have his fellow-creatures round him. Tut, man! no one goes into the crowd but for his end; and the end of too many is the same as the pick-pocket's—a purse."

"Now, my dear fellow, how can you have the conscience to say that, when it is as much according to natural law that men are social as sheep gregarious. But grant that, in being social, each man has his end, do you, upon the strength of that, do you yourself, I say, mix with man, now, immediately, and be your end a more genial philosophy. Come, let's take a turn."

Again he offered his fraternal arm; but the bachelor once more flung it off, and, raising his rifle in energetic invocation, cried: "Now the high-constable catch and confound all knaves in towns and rats in grain-bins, and if in this boat, which is a human grain-bin for the time, any sly, smooth, philandering rat be dodging now, pin him, thou high rat-catcher, against this rail."

"A noble burst! shows you at heart a trump. And when a card's that, little matters it whether it be spade or diamond. You are good wine that, to be still better, only needs a shaking up. Come, let's agree that we'll to New Orleans, and there embark for London—I staying with my friends nigh Primrose-hill, and you putting up at the Piazza, Covent Garden—Piazza, Covent Garden;[3] for tell me— since you will not be a disciple to the full—tell me, was not that humor, of Diogenes, which led him to live, a merry-andrew, in the flower-market, better than that of the less wise Athenian, which made him a skulking scare-crow in pine-barrens? An injudicious gentleman, Lord Timon."[4]

"Your hand!" seizing it.

"Bless me, how cordial a squeeze. It is agreed we shall be brothers, then?"

---

3. Famous London locations. Primrose Hill, north of Regent's Park, known as a duelling ground. The great Covent Garden Piazza (open square) designed in the 17th century by Inigo Jones, bordered by shops, was a marketplace and theater district from the mid-1600s, declining to become an area of baths and brothels. In Melville's time it was London's main fruit, vegetable, and flower market.

4. Timon (after he turned misanthrope) is the "less wise Athenian." Diogenes (412–323 B.C.E.), Greek cynic philosopher, was said to go about with a lantern in daytime looking for an honest man. In the pervasive blurring of ancient and modern in this book, Melville may have in mind the strange behavior of Thomas Powell, who, signing himself "Diogenes Junior," wrote for a Manhattan paper called "*Diogenes hys Lantern*" (meaning "*Diogenes's lantern*," the way *The Confidence-Man his Masquerade* in the American contract meant "The confidence-man's masquerade") or simply *The Lantern*, the inveterate liar casting himself as searching Manhattan with his brave little light in search of an honest man. As "Diogenes Junior," Powell made unkind remarks about Melville in 1852.

"As much so as a brace of misanthropes can be," with another and terrific squeeze. "I had thought that the moderns had degenerated beneath the capacity of misanthropy. Rejoiced, though but in one instance, and that disguised, to be undeceived."

The other stared in blank amaze.

"Won't do. You are Diogenes, Diogenes in disguise. I say—Diogenes masquerading as a cosmopolitan."

With ruefully altered mien, the stranger still stood mute awhile. At length, in a pained tone, spoke: "How hard the lot of that pleader who, in his zeal conceding too much, is taken to belong to a side which he but labors, however ineffectually, to convert!" Then with another change of air: "To you, an Ishmael,[5] disguising in sportiveness my intent, I came ambassador from the human race, charged with the assurance that for your mislike they bore no answering grudge, but sought to conciliate accord between you and them. Yet you take me not for the honest envoy, but I know not what sort of unheard-of spy. Sir," he less lowly added, "this mistaking of your man should teach you how you may mistake all men. For God's sake," laying both hands upon him, "get you confidence. See how distrust has duped you. I, Diogenes? I he who, going a step beyond misanthropy, was less a man-hater than a man-hooter? Better were I stark and stiff!"

With which the philanthropist moved away less lightsome than he had come, leaving the discomfited misanthrope to the solitude he held so sapient.

Chapter 25.

THE COSMOPOLITAN MAKES AN ACQUAINTANCE.

In the act of retiring, the cosmopolitan was met by a passenger, who, with the bluff *abord* of the West, thus addressed him, though a stranger.

"Queer 'coon, your friend. Had a little skrimmage with him myself. Rather entertaining old 'coon, if he wasn't so deuced analytical. Reminded me somehow of what I've heard about Colonel John Moredock,[6] of Illinois, only your friend ain't quite so good a fellow at bottom, I should think."

It was in the semicircular porch of a cabin, opening a recess from the deck, lit by a zoned lamp swung overhead, and sending its light vertically down, like the sun at noon. Beneath the lamp stood

---

5. Abraham's oldest son, by Hagar, his wife's handmaid (Genesis 16). He was banished so that Isaac, Abraham's younger son by his wife, Sarah, would be the sole heir (Genesis 21). According to God's promise, Ishmael survived to become the ancestor of a nation (traditionally taken as the Arabs). Here, Pitch is the Ishmael.
6. For the real Moredock see James Hall (pp. 456–61 herein).

the speaker, affording to any one disposed to it no unfavorable chance for scrutiny; but the glance now resting on him betrayed no such rudeness.

A man neither tall nor short, neither stout nor gaunt;[7] but with a body fitted, as by measure, to the service of his mind. For the rest, one less favored perhaps in his features than his clothes; and of these the beauty may have been less in the fit than the cut; to say nothing of the fineness of the nap, seeming out of keeping with something the reverse of fine in the skin; and the unsuitableness of a violet vest, sending up sunset hues to a countenance betokening a kind of bilious habit.

But, upon the whole, it could not be fairly said that his appearance was unprepossessing; indeed, to the congenial, it would have been doubtless not uncongenial; while to others, it could not fail to be at least curiously interesting, from the warm air of florid cordiality, contrasting itself with one knows not what kind of aguish sallowness of saving discretion lurking behind it. Ungracious critics might have thought that the manner flushed the man, something in the same fictitious way that the vest flushed the cheek. And though his teeth were singularly good, those same ungracious ones might have hinted that they were too good to be true; or rather, were not so good as they might be; since the best false teeth are those made with at least two or three blemishes, the more to look like life. But fortunately for better constructions, no such critics had the stranger now in eye; only the cosmopolitan, who, after, in the first place, acknowledging his advances with a mute salute—in which acknowledgment, if there seemed less of spirit than in his way of accosting the Missourian, it was probably because of the saddening sequel of that late interview—thus now replied: "Colonel John Moredock," repeating the words abstractedly; "that surname recalls reminiscences. Pray," with enlivened air, "was he anyway connected with the Moredocks of Moredock Hall, Northamptonshire, England?"

"I know no more of the Moredocks of Moredock Hall than of the Burdocks of Burdock Hut," returned the other, with the air somehow of one whose fortunes had been of his own making; "all I know is, that the late Colonel John Moredock was a famous one in his time; eye like Lochiel's;[8] finger like a trigger; nerve like a cata-

7. Watson G. Branch pointed out that the first edition's "neither tall nor stout, neither short nor gaunt" was the kind of awkwardness that could easily result from misreading Melville's bad handwriting and coping with his elaborate revisions.
8. Sir Ewan Cameron of Lochiel (1629–1719). Foster quotes from Thomas Babington Macaulay's *History of England* (4 vols. 1849–55): "In agility and skill at his weapons he had few equals among the inhabitants of the hills. He had repeatedly been victorious in single combat. He was a hunter of great fame. He made vigorous war on the wolves." Macaulay credited him with killing the last wolf "known to have wandered at large in our island."

mount's; and with but two little oddities—seldom stirred without his rifle, and hated Indians like snakes."

"Your Moredock, then, would seem a Moredock of Misanthrope Hall—the Woods. No very sleek creature, the colonel, I fancy."

"Sleek or not, he was no uncombed one, but silky bearded and curly headed, and to all but Indians juicy as a peach. But Indians—how the late Colonel John Moredock, Indian-hater of Illinois, did hate Indians, to be sure!"

"Never heard of such a thing. Hate Indians? Why should he or anybody else hate Indians? I admire Indians. Indians I have always heard to be one of the finest of the primitive races, possessed of many heroic virtues. Some noble women, too. When I think of Pocahontas, I am ready to love Indians. Then there's Massasoit, and Philip of Mount Hope, and Tecumseh, and Red-Jacket, and Logan—all heroes; and there's the Five Nations, and Araucanians[9]—federations and communities of heroes. God bless me; hate Indians? Surely the late Colonel John Moredock must have wandered in his mind."

"Wandered in the woods considerably, but never wandered elsewhere, that I ever heard."

"Are you in earnest? Was there ever one who so made it his particular mission to hate Indians that, to designate him, a special word has been coined—Indian-hater?"

"Even so."

"Dear me, you take it very calmly.—But really, I would like to know something about this Indian-hating. I can hardly believe such a thing to be. Could you favor me with a little history of the extraordinary man you mentioned?"

"With all my heart," and immediately stepping from the porch, gestured the cosmopolitan to a settee near by, on deck. "There, sir,

9. South American Indians, some of whom offered serious resistance to Spanish and then Chilean authority for over three centuries; they were not subdued until the late 19th century. Pocahontas (1595–1617), daughter of chief Powhatan, reputed to have saved the life of Captain John Smith at Jamestown in 1607. She later married John Rolfe and accompanied him to England, where she died. Massasoit (1580?–1661), chief of the Wampanoag Indians, whose aid was instrumental in the survival of the Pilgrims at Plymouth Colony in Massachusetts. Massasoit's son and successor, Metacom, known to the English colonists as King Philip, lived at Mount Hope, near present-day Swansea, Massachusetts. He led a large-scale armed attack (known as King Philip's War, 1675–76) on the encroaching colonists. As Melville knew, Washington Irving paid tribute to him in "Philip of Pokanoket" in The Sketch Book (1819–20). Shawnee chief Tecumseh (1768–1813) led Indian resistance against white expansion in the Old Northwest. Red Jacket (1758?–1830), Seneca chief and noted orator, having sided with the British during the American Revolution, later made peace with the U.S. government and was given a medal by George Washington in 1792. John (or James) Logan (1725?–1780), Iroquois leader, was friendly with whites until members of his family were massacred by settlers. His speech delivered during efforts to calm tensions was much admired by the American public. The Five Nations that made up the Iroquois Confederacy were the Mohawk, Oneida, Onondaga, Cayuga, and Seneca. They were known for their skill in battle. The Tuscarora joined the Confederacy in 1722.

sit you there, and I will sit here beside you—you desire to hear of
Colonel John Moredock. Well, a day in my boyhood is marked with
a white stone[1]—the day I saw the colonel's rifle, powder-horn attached, hanging in a cabin on the West bank of the Wabash river. I
was going westward a long journey through the wilderness with my
father. It was nigh noon, and we had stopped at the cabin to un-
saddle and bait. The man at the cabin pointed out the rifle, and
told whose it was, adding that the colonel was that moment sleeping on wolf-skins in the corn-loft above, so we must not talk very
loud, for the colonel had been out all night hunting (Indians,
mind), and it would be cruel to disturb his sleep. Curious to see
one so famous, we waited two hours over, in hopes he would come
forth; but he did not. So, it being necessary to get to the next cabin
before nightfall, we had at last to ride off without the wished-for
satisfaction. Though, to tell the truth, I, for one, did not go away
entirely ungratified, for, while my father was watering the horses, I
slipped back into the cabin, and stepping a round or two up the ladder, pushed my head through the trap, and peered about. Not
much light in the loft; but off, in the further corner, I saw what I
took to be the wolf-skins, and on them a bundle of something, like
a drift of leaves; and at one end, what seemed a moss-ball; and over
it, deer-antlers branched; and close by, a small squirrel sprang out
from a maple-bowl of nuts, brushed the moss-ball with his tail,
through a hole, and vanished, squeaking. That bit of woodland
scene was all I saw. No Colonel Moredock there, unless that moss-
ball was his curly head, seen in the back view. I would have gone
clear up, but the man below had warned me, that though, from his
camping habits, the colonel could sleep through thunder, he was
for the same cause amazing quick to waken at the sound of footsteps, however soft, and especially if human."

"Excuse me," said the other, softly laying his hand on the narrator's wrist, "but I fear the colonel was of a distrustful nature—little
or no confidence. He was a little suspicious-minded, wasn't he?"

"Not a bit. Knew too much. Suspected nobody, but was not ignorant of Indians. Well: though, as you may gather, I never fully saw
the man, yet, have I, one way and another, heard about as much of
him as any other; in particular, have I heard his history again and
again from my father's friend, James Hall,[2] the judge, you know. In

1. The meaning is that the day was memorable, from the practice of using a white stone "as
   a memorial of a fortunate event" (*OED*), but Melville may have in mind Revelation 2.17.
2. Illinois judge (1793–1868), whose *The Wilderness and the War-Path* had been listed next
   to Melville's first book, *Typee*, in advertisements for the Wiley & Putnam "Library of
   American Books" edited by Evert A. Duyckinck. In the early 1850s Hall had corre-
   sponded with Duyckinck and his brother George about his inclusion in the Duyckincks'
   Cyclopedia of American Literature (1855). Art historians remember him as the writing
   member of the team that produced the great "McKenney and Hall" folio of portraits of
   American Indians.

every company being called upon to give this history, which none could better do, the judge at last fell into a style so methodic, you would have thought he spoke less to mere auditors than to an invisible amanuensis; seemed talking for the press; very impressive way with him indeed. And I, having an equally impressible memory, think that, upon a pinch, I can render you the judge upon the colonel almost word for word."

"Do so, by all means," said the cosmopolitan, well pleased.

"Shall I give you the judge's philosophy, and all?"

"As to that," rejoined the other gravely, pausing over the pipe-bowl he was filling, "the desirableness, to a man of a certain mind, of having another man's philosophy given, depends considerably upon what school of philosophy that other man belongs to. Of what school or system was the judge, pray?"

"Why, though he knew how to read and write, the judge never had much schooling. But, I should say he belonged, if anything, to the free-school system. Yes, a true patriot, the judge went in strong for free-schools."

"In philosophy? The man of a certain mind, then, while respecting the judge's patriotism, and not blind to the judge's capacity for narrative, such as he may prove to have, might, perhaps, with prudence, waive an opinion of the judge's probable philosophy. But I am no rigorist; proceed, I beg; his philosophy or not, as you please."

"Well, I would mostly skip that part, only, to begin, some reconnoitering of the ground in a philosophical way the judge always deemed indispensable with strangers. For you must know that Indian-hating was no monopoly of Colonel Moredock's; but a passion, in one form or other, and to a degree, greater or less, largely shared among the class to which he belonged. And Indian-hating still exists; and, no doubt, will continue to exist, so long as Indians do. Indian-hating, then, shall be my first theme, and Colonel Moredock, the Indian-hater, my next and last."

With which the stranger, settling himself in his seat, commenced—the hearer paying marked regard, slowly smoking, his glance, meanwhile, steadfastly abstracted towards the deck, but his right ear so disposed towards the speaker that each word came through as little atmospheric intervention as possible. To intensify the sense of hearing, he seemed to sink the sense of sight. No complaisance of mere speech could have been so flattering, or expressed such striking politeness as this mute eloquence of thoroughly digesting attention.

Chapter 26.

CONTAINING THE METAPHYSICS OF INDIAN-HATING, ACCORDING TO
THE VIEWS OF ONE EVIDENTLY NOT SO PREPOSSESSED AS ROUSSEAU[3]
IN FAVOR OF SAVAGES.

"The judge always began in these words: 'The backwoodsman's hatred of the Indian has been a topic for some remark. In the earlier times of the frontier the passion was thought to be readily accounted for. But Indian rapine having mostly ceased through regions where it once prevailed, the philanthropist is surprised that Indian-hating has not in like degree ceased with it. He wonders why the backwoodsman still regards the red man in much the same spirit that a jury does a murderer, or a trapper a wild cat—a creature, in whose behalf mercy were not wisdom; truce is vain; he must be executed.

" 'A curious point,' the judge would continue, 'which perhaps not everybody, even upon explanation, may fully understand; while, in order for any one to approach to an understanding, it is necessary for him to learn, or if he already know, to bear in mind, what manner of man the backwoodsman is; as for what manner of man the Indian is, many know, either from history or experience.

" 'The backwoodsman is a lonely man. He is a thoughtful man. He is a man strong and unsophisticated. Impulsive, he is what some might call unprincipled. At any rate, he is self-willed; being one who less hearkens to what others may say about things, than looks for himself, to see what are things themselves. If in straits, there are few to help; he must depend upon himself; he must continually look to himself. Hence self-reliance, to the degree of standing by his own judgment, though it stand alone. Not that he deems himself infallible; too many mistakes in following trails prove the contrary; but he thinks that nature destines such sagacity as she had given him, as she destines it to the 'possum. To these fellow-beings of the wilds their untutored sagacity is their best depen-

3. The French philosopher Jean-Jacques Rousseau (1712–1778) was understood to have regarded uncivilized peoples as "noble savages," not as sinners in need of Christianizing. In chapter 17 of *Typee* (1846) Melville described the happiness in the Typee Valley as springing "principally from that all-pervading sensation which Rousseau has told us he at one time experienced, the mere buoyant sense of a healthful physical existence." Partly because of this passage, Melville's account of life with natives in an island of the Marquesas was seen as a validation of Rousseau's theories. Melville, despite his Calvinist leanings, was thus identified throughout his lifetime with the French philosopher. "Metaphysics" is a warning that the chapter will not deal with the real phenomenon of Indian hating but instead will deal with the theological implications of Indian hating. The *Oxford English Dictionary* cites from Melville's acquaintance Oliver Wendell Holmes a newly emerging use of the word *metaphysics* to mean the "theoretical principles" or "higher philosophical rationale" of a branch of knowledge. See the discussion of Scott Norsworthy's discovery of a well-known contemporary title, "Metaphysics of Bear Hunting," on pp. 467–68 herein.

dence. If with either it prove faulty, if the 'possum's betray it to the trap, or the backwoodsman's mislead him into ambuscade, there are consequences to be undergone, but no self-blame. As with the 'possum, instincts prevail with the backwoodsman over precepts. Like the 'possum, the backwoodsman presents the spectacle of a creature dwelling exclusively among the works of God, yet these, truth must confess, breed little in him of a godly mind. Small bowing and scraping is his, further than when with bent knee he points his rifle, or picks its flint. With few companions, solitude by necessity his lengthened lot, he stands the trial—no slight one, since, next to dying, solitude, rightly borne, is perhaps of fortitude the most rigorous test. But not merely is the backwoodsman content to be alone, but in no few cases is anxious to be so. The sight of smoke ten miles off is provocation to one more remove from man, one step deeper into nature. Is it that he feels that whatever man may be, man is not the universe? that glory, beauty, kindness, are not all engrossed by him? that as the presence of man frights birds away, so, many bird-like thoughts? Be that how it will, the backwoodsman is not without some fineness to his nature. Hairy Orson[4] as he looks, it may be with him as with the Shetland seal—beneath the bristles lurks the fur.

" 'Though held in a sort a barbarian, the backwoodsman would seem to America what Alexander[5] was to Asia—captain in the vanguard of conquering civilization. Whatever the nation's growing opulence or power, does it not lackey his heels? Pathfinder, provider of security to those who come after him, for himself he asks nothing but hardship. Worthy to be compared with Moses in the Exodus, or the Emperor Julian in Gaul,[6] who on foot, and bare-browed, at the head of covered or mounted legions, marched so through the elements, day after day. The tide of emigration, let it roll as it will, never overwhelms the backwoodsman into itself; he rides upon advance, as the Polynesian upon the comb of the surf.[7]

" 'Thus, though he keep moving on through life, he maintains with respect to nature much the same unaltered relation throughout; with her creatures, too, including panthers and Indians.

4. In the fifteenth-century French romance *Valentin et Orson*, the title characters are twin brothers abandoned in the woods. Valentine is brought up in court, Orson, in a bear's den. (The word *ourson* in French means "baby bear.") The allusion is another reminder that human beings may be close to subhuman or extra-human creatures.
5. Alexander the Great (356–323 B.C.E.), king of Macedonia, who conquered much of Asia Minor and Asia, greatly expanding the influence of Greek civilization.
6. Successful in his campaign in Gaul, Julian (331?–363), declared emperor by his troops, publicly embraced paganism in 361, thus acquiring the epithet "the Apostate," one who repudiates one religion for another. Moses led the Hebrews from Egypt toward Israel, dying before reaching it.
7. See Parker (1.249–50) for white men's envious descriptions of surfing, which some young Hawaiians managed to practice while Melville was there in 1842, despite the Protestant missionaries' attempts to suppress all native sports.

Hence, it is not unlikely that, accurate as the theory of the Peace Congress[8] may be with respect to those two varieties of beings, among others, yet the backwoodsman might be qualified to throw out some practical suggestions.

" 'As the child born to a backwoodsman must in turn lead his father's life—a life which, as related to humanity, is related mainly to Indians—it is thought best not to mince matters, out of delicacy; but to tell the boy pretty plainly what an Indian is, and what he must expect from him. For however charitable it may be to view Indians as members of the Society of Friends,[9] yet to affirm them such to one ignorant of Indians, whose lonely path lies a long way through their lands, this, in the event, might prove not only injudicious but cruel. At least something of this kind would seem the maxim upon which backwoods' education is based. Accordingly, if in youth the backwoodsman incline to knowledge, as is generally the case, he hears little from his schoolmasters, the old chroniclers of the forest, but histories of Indian lying, Indian theft, Indian double-dealing, Indian fraud and perfidy, Indian want of conscience, Indian blood-thirstiness, Indian diabolism—histories which, though of wild woods, are almost as full of things unangelic as the Newgate Calendar or the Annals of Europe.[1] In these Indian narratives and traditions the lad is thoroughly grounded. "As the twig is bent the tree's inclined."[2] The instinct of antipathy against an Indian grows in the backwoodsman with the sense of good and bad, right and wrong. In one breath he learns that a brother is to be loved, and an Indian to be hated.

" 'Such are the facts,' the judge would say, 'upon which, if one seek to moralize, he must do so with an eye to them. It is terrible that one creature should so regard another, should make it conscience to abhor an entire race. It is terrible; but is it surprising? Surprising, that one should hate a race which he believes to be red from a cause akin to that which makes some tribes of garden insects green? A race whose name is upon the frontier a *memento mori*; painted to him in every evil light, now a horse-thief like those in Moyamensing;[3] now an assassin like a New York rowdy, now a

---

8. Several such Peace conferences were held between 1848 and 1851.
9. Commonly called Quakers.
1. Published from 1739 to 1744, it consisted of accounts of momentous events, year by year. "*Newgate Calendar*": first published about 1773, contained descriptions of notorious crimes. Similar works appeared over the next half century under various titles, including *The Malefactor's Register* (1779).
2. Alexander Pope's *Moral Essays* (1732), *Epistle* 1.150: " 'Tis education forms the common mind, / Just as the twig is bent, the tree's inclined."
3. The Philadelphia County Prison. Melville in *Typee* chapter 17 (the section on "Comparative Wickedness of civilized and unenlightened People") raged against a supposedly humane innovation in punishing lawbreakers, the Pennsylvania "reform" of solitary confinement—"civilized barbarity," according to Melville. See "Who Is Happier?" (p. 367 herein).

treaty-breaker like an Austrian;[4] now a Palmer with poisoned arrows; now a judicial murderer and Jeffries,[5] after a fierce farce of trial condemning his victim to bloody death; or a Jew with hospitable speeches cozening some fainting stranger into ambuscade, there to burke him, and account it a deed grateful to Manitou,[6] his god.

" 'Still, all this is less advanced as truths of the Indians than as examples of the backwoodsman's impression of them—in which the charitable may think he does them some injustice. Certain it is, the Indians themselves think so; quite unanimously, too. The Indians, indeed, protest against the backwoodsman's view of them; and some think that one cause of their returning his antipathy so sincerely as they do, is their moral indignation at being so libeled by him, as they really believe and say. But whether, on this or any point, the Indians should be permitted to testify for themselves, to the exclusion of other testimony, is a question that may be left to the Supreme Court.[7] At any rate, it has been observed that when an Indian becomes a genuine proselyte to Christianity (such cases, however, not being very many; though, indeed, entire tribes are sometimes nominally brought to the true light,) he will not in that case conceal his enlightened conviction, that his race's portion by nature is total depravity; and, in that way, as much as admits that the backwoodsman's worst idea of it is not very far from true; while, on the other hand, those red men who are the greatest sticklers for the theory of Indian virtue, and Indian loving-kindness, are sometimes the arrantest horse-thieves and tomahawkers among them. So, at least, avers the backwoodsman. And though, knowing the Indian nature, as he thinks he does, he fancies he is not ignorant that

4. Rapidly broken promises of greater autonomy and freedom for Hungary and parts of northern Italy characterized the Austrian Habsburg monarchy before and after the revolutions of 1848.

5. George Jeffreys (1648–1689), a brutal judge under Charles II and James II. He presided at the trial for treason of Algernon Sidney (1622–1683), the antimonarchist patriot (1683), and the trial in 1685 of Titus Oates (1649–1705), the fabricator of the alleged "Popish Plot" in 1678 to murder Charles II and reestablish the Roman Catholic Church. Many were executed on Oates's false evidence. The Popish Plot is a link to the 1840s and 1850s anti-Catholicism; see n. 8 p. 98. Dr. William Palmer (1824–1856), a notorious British poisoner, was arrested December 15, 1855, tried at Old Bailey on May 14, 1856, and hanged June 14, 1856, with many thousands of watchers. Besides family members, his victims included some of his creditors.

6. Powerful North American Indian nature God. "Jew": perhaps the closest biblical situation involves a Jewish woman, Jael, who treats the exhausted Sisera hospitably but as he sleeps drives a long nail through his temples and into the ground (Judges 4.15–21). William Burke (executed January 28, 1829) and his accomplice William Hare were "resurrection men," paid for freshly dug up corpses to be used in anatomy classes in Edinburgh. They resorted to murder as an easier way of acquiring bodies. Hare turned state's evidence and was released, but Burke was hanged before many thousands of witnesses. Lurid accounts of these serial killers were available all during Melville's youth.

7. See n. 5, p. 500 herein). Melville may be alluding ironically to the Supreme Court decision in *Cherokee Nation v. Georgia* (1831) in which the Court ruled that the Cherokees should be considered "domestic dependent nations." Below, the "total depravity" of all human beings was a central doctrine of Calvinism familiar to Melville from the teachings of the Dutch Reformed Church.

an Indian may in some points deceive himself almost as effectually as in bush-tactics he can another, yet his theory and his practice as above contrasted seem to involve an inconsistency so extreme, that the backwoodsman only accounts for it on the supposition that when a tomahawking red-man advances the notion of the benignity of the red race, it is but part and parcel with that subtle strategy which he finds so useful in war, in hunting, and the general conduct of life.'

"In further explanation of that deep abhorrence with which the backwoodsman regards the savage, the judge used to think it might perhaps a little help, to consider what kind of stimulus to it is furnished in those forest histories and traditions before spoken of. In which behalf, he would tell the story of the little colony of Wrights and Weavers,[8] originally seven cousins from Virginia, who, after successive removals with their families, at last established themselves near the southern frontier of the Bloody Ground, Kentucky:[9] 'They were strong, brave men; but, unlike many of the pioneers in those days, theirs was no love of conflict for conflict's sake. Step by step they had been lured to their lonely resting-place by the ever-beckoning seductions of a fertile and virgin land, with a singular exemption, during the march, from Indian molestation. But clearings made and houses built, the bright shield was soon to turn its other side. After repeated persecutions and eventual hostilities, forced on them by a dwindled tribe in their neighborhood—persecutions resulting in loss of crops and cattle; hostilities in which they lost two of their number, illy to be spared, besides others getting painful wounds—the five remaining cousins made, with some serious concessions, a kind of treaty with Mocmohoc,[1] the chief—being to this induced by the harryings of the enemy, leaving them no peace. But they were further prompted, indeed, first incited, by the suddenly changed ways of Mocmohoc, who, though hitherto deemed a savage almost perfidious as Cæsar Borgia,[2] yet now put on a seeming

8. No source for the "Wrights and Weavers" has been found. Shakespeare's artisans were on Melville's mind, possibly those from *A Midsummer Night's Dream*, where Bottom is a weaver (see n. 2, p. 20), certainly those from *Julius Caesar* (see n. 9, p. 209); he alludes to *2 Henry VI*, where one of Jack Cade's men is Smith, the weaver. The occupation names suggest that Melville may have invented them from kinds of artisans needed in newly settled lands. (Weaver is obvious, but *wright* meant "worker," specifically a carpenter unless used in compounds such as wheelwright and shipwright.)
9. Since Daniel Boone's time Kentucky had been known as a "dark and bloody ground" because of the ferocity with which Indians fought to repel white settlers.
1. Suggests to some readers a play on "Mohawk," either false (mock) Mohawk or son-of-Mohawk (McMohawk). No source for the name has been found.
2. Borgia (1476?–1507), member of an Italian family of Spanish origin, was known for his ruthlessness in achieving and wielding political power and for his false hospitality, which turned into treacherous murder. The bloody story of the avenging of the rape of Dinah (Genesis 34) is a strong biblical example of the topic of treacherous hosts that fascinated Melville at this time. (The ingratitude of guests toward their hosts was also on his mind, as in his references to Timon of Athens, who had entertained lavishly while he was wealthy; see n. 3, p. 24.)

the reverse of this, engaging to bury the hatchet, smoke the pipe, and be friends forever; not friends in the mere sense of renouncing enmity, but in the sense of kindliness, active and familiar.

" 'But what the chief now seemed, did not wholly blind them to what the chief had been; so that, though in no small degree influenced by his change of bearing, they still distrusted him enough to covenant with him, among other articles on their side, that though friendly visits should be exchanged between the wigwams and the cabins, yet the five cousins should never, on any account, be expected to enter the chief's lodge together. The intention was, though they reserved it, that if ever, under the guise of amity, the chief should mean them mischief, and effect it, it should be but partially; so that some of the five might survive, not only for their families' sake, but also for retribution's. Nevertheless, Mocmohoc did, upon a time, with such fine art and pleasing carriage win their confidence, that he brought them all together to a feast of bear's meat, and there, by stratagem, ended them. Years after, over their calcined bones and those of all their families, the chief, reproached for his treachery by a proud hunter whom he had made captive, jeered out, "Treachery? pale face! 'Twas they who broke their covenant first, in coming all together; they that broke it first, in trusting Mocmohoc." '

"At this point the judge would pause, and lifting his hand, and rolling his eyes, exclaim in a solemn enough voice, 'Circling wiles and bloody lusts. The acuteness and genius of the chief but make him the more atrocious.'

"After another pause, he would begin an imaginary kind of dialogue between a backwoodsman and a questioner:

" 'But are all Indians like Mocmohoc?—Not all have proved such; but in the least harmful may lie his germ. There is an Indian nature. "Indian blood is in me," is the half-breed's threat.—But are not some Indians kind?—Yes, but kind Indians are mostly lazy, and reputed simple—at all events, are seldom chiefs; chiefs among the red men being taken from the active, and those accounted wise. Hence, with small promotion, kind Indians have but proportionate influence. And kind Indians may be forced to do unkind biddings. So "beware the Indian, kind or unkind," said Daniel Boone,[3] who lost his sons by them.—But, have all you backwoodsmen been some way victimized by Indians?—No.—Well, and in certain cases may not at least some few of you be favored by them?—Yes, but

---

3. American trapper, hunter, and frontiersman (1734–1820), who was instrumental in the settlement of Kentucky. While Boone was leading several families into this area, his son James was killed by Indians. Three years later, in 1776, Boone's daughter Jemima was captured by a small party of Shawnee and Cherokees, but was later rescued. Another of Boone's sons, Israel, was killed in Kentucky at the Revolutionary War Battle of Blue Licks (1782) by Indians fighting on the side of the British.

scarce one among us so self-important, or so selfish-minded, as to hold his personal exemption from Indian outrage such a set-off against the contrary experience of so many others, as that he must needs, in a general way, think well of Indians; or, if he do, an arrow in his flank might suggest a pertinent doubt.

" 'In short,' according to the judge, 'if we at all credit the back-woodsman, his feeling against Indians, to be taken aright, must be considered as being not so much on his own account as on others', or jointly on both accounts. True it is, scarce a family he knows but some member of it, or connection, has been by Indians maimed or scalped. What avails, then, that some one Indian, or some two or three, treat a backwoodsman friendly-like? He fears me, he thinks. Take my rifle from me, give him motive, and what will come? Or if not so, how know I what involuntary preparations may be going on in him for things as unbeknown in present time to him as me—a sort of chemical preparation in the soul for malice, as chemical preparation in the body for malady.'

"Not that the backwoodsman ever used those words, you see, but the judge found him expression for his meaning. And this point he would conclude with saying, that, 'what is called a "friendly Indian" is a very rare sort of creature; and well it was so, for no ruthlessness exceeds that of a "friendly Indian" turned enemy. A coward friend, he makes a valiant foe.

" 'But, thus far the passion in question has been viewed in a general way as that of a community. When to his due share of this the backwoodsman adds his private passion, we have then the stock out of which is formed, if formed at all, the Indian-hater *par excellence*.'

"The Indian-hater *par excellence* the judge defined to be one 'who, having with his mother's milk drank in small love for red men, in youth or early manhood, ere the sensibilities become osseous, receives at their hand some signal outrage, or, which in effect is much the same, some of his kin have, or some friend. Now, nature all around him by her solitudes wooing or bidding him muse upon this matter, he accordingly does so, till the thought develops such attraction, that much as straggling vapors troop from all sides to a storm-cloud, so straggling thoughts of other outrages troop to the nucleus thought, assimilate with it, and swell it. At last, taking counsel with the elements, he comes to his resolution. An intenser Hannibal,[4] he makes a vow, the hate of which is a vortex from whose suction scarce the remotest chip of the guilty race may reasonably feel secure. Next, he declares himself and settles his temporal affairs. With the solemnity of a Spaniard turned monk, he

4. Hannibal, the Carthaginian (247–182? B.C.E.), was said to have vowed lifelong enmity to Rome at the age of nine. With elephants he crossed the Pyrenees and then the Alps from the north, conquering much of Italy, though not Rome itself.

takes leave of his kin; or rather, these leave-takings have something of the still more impressive finality of death-bed adieus. Last, he commits himself to the forest primeval; there, so long as life shall be his, to act upon a calm, cloistered scheme[5] of strategical, implacable, and lonesome vengeance. Ever on the noiseless trail; cool, collected, patient; less seen than felt; snuffing, smelling—a Leather-stocking Nemesis.[6] In the settlements he will not be seen again; in eyes of old companions tears may start at some chance thing that speaks of him; but they never look for him, nor call; they know he will not come. Suns and seasons fleet; the tiger-lily blows and falls; babes are born and leap in their mothers' arms; but, the Indian-hater is good as gone to his long home,[7] and "Terror" is his epitaph.'

"Here the judge, not unaffected, would pause again, but presently resume: 'How evident that in strict speech there can be no biography of an Indian-hater *par excellence*, any more than one of a sword-fish, or other deep-sea denizen; or, which is still less imaginable, one of a dead man. The career of the Indian-hater *par excellence* has the impenetrability of the fate of a lost steamer. Doubtless, events, terrible ones, have happened, must have happened; but the powers that be in nature have taken order that they shall never become news.

" 'But, luckily for the curious, there is a species of diluted Indian-hater, one whose heart proves not so steely as his brain. Soft enticements of domestic life too often draw him from the ascetic trail; a monk who apostatizes to the world at times. Like a mariner, too, though much abroad, he may have a wife and family in some green harbor which he does not forget. It is with him as with the Papist converts in Senegal;[8] fasting and mortification prove hard to bear.'

"The judge, with his usual judgment, always thought that the intense solitude to which the Indian-hater consigns himself, has, by its overawing influence, no little to do with relaxing his vow. He

---

5. Scheme slowly matured in isolation, like that of a monk in a monastery. "Forest primeval": a phrase that entered the language in 1847 from the opening of Henry W. Longfellow's *Evangeline*, set in French Acadia (now Nova Scotia): "This is the forest primeval."
6. Relentless avenger; from the Greek goddess of divine retribution and vengeance. "Leather-stocking": tales making up a series of five novels published between 1823 and 1841 by James Fenimore Cooper. Leather Stocking is the nickname of their hero, Natty Bumpo, a frontiersman, who, though on friendly terms with some Indians, is a skilled Indian fighter.
7. Ecclesiastes 12.5: "when they shall be afraid of that which is high, and fears shall be in the way, and the almond tree shall flourish, and the grasshopper shall be a burden, and desire shall fall: because man goeth to his long home, and the mourners go about the streets."
8. Blacks in West African Senegal forcibly Christianized, by Portuguese in the fifteenth century and again in the eighteenth century by Jesuits. In "Benito Cereno" Melville, elaborately exploring the consequences of living by racial stereotypes, used Senegal as the symbolic home of a kind of primitive evil.

would relate instances where, after some months' lonely scoutings, the Indian-hater is suddenly seized with a sort of calenture;[9] hurries openly towards the first smoke, though he knows it is an Indian's, announces himself as a lost hunter, gives the savage his rifle, throws himself upon his charity, embraces him with much affection, imploring the privilege of living a while in his sweet companionship. What is too often the sequel of so distempered a procedure may be best known by those who best know the Indian. Upon the whole, the judge, by two and thirty good and sufficient reasons, would maintain that there was no known vocation whose consistent following calls for such self-containings as that of the Indian-hater *par excellence*. In the highest view, he considered such a soul one peeping out but once an age.[1]

"For the diluted Indian-hater, although the vacations he permits himself impair the keeping of the character, yet, it should not be overlooked that this is the man who, by his very infirmity, enables us to form surmises, however inadequate, of what Indian-hating in its perfection is."

"One moment," gently interrupted the cosmopolitan here, "and let me refill my calumet."[2]

Which being done, the other proceeded:—

Chapter 27.

SOME ACCOUNT OF A MAN OF QUESTIONABLE MORALITY, BUT WHO, NEVERTHELESS, WOULD SEEM ENTITLED TO THE ESTEEM OF THAT EMINENT ENGLISH MORALIST[3] WHO SAID HE LIKED A GOOD HATER.

"Coming to mention the man to whose story all thus far said was but the introduction, the judge, who, like you, was a great smoker, would insist upon all the company taking cigars, and then lighting a fresh one himself, rise in his place, and, with the solemnest voice, say—'Gentlemen, let us smoke to the memory of Colonel John Moredock;' when, after several whiffs taken standing in deep silence and deeper reverie, he would resume his seat and his discourse, something in these words:

9. Feverish frenzy as if from a heat stroke (from the Latin for "heat," like calorie).
1. Cf. "Elegy to the Memory of an Unfortunate Lady" by English poet Alexander Pope: "Most souls, 'tis true, but peep out once an age." Melville knew the poem well enough that while reading Edmund Spenser's *Faerie Queene* 3.3.3.8 he wrote down lines 15–16 from memory, recognizing them as Pope's borrowings from Spenser.
2. Indian peace pipe (in an ironically timed reference) (see n. 5, p. 174).
3. Samuel Johnson (1709–1784), English lexicographer, essayist and poet, most famous for his *Dictionary of the English Language* (1755). In *Anecdotes of the Late Samuel Johnson, L. L. D.* (1786), Hester Lynch Thrale Piozzi recorded that no man was more zealous in love of his party than Johnson: "he not only loved a Tory himself, but he loved a man the better if he heard he hated a Whig. '*Dear Bathurst*,' said he to me one day, '*was a man to my very heart's content: he hated a fool, and he hated a rogue, and he hated a* Whig; *he was a very good hater.*' "

" 'Though Colonel John Moredock was not an Indian-hater *par excellence*, he yet cherished a kind of sentiment towards the red man, and in that degree, and so acted out his sentiment as sufficiently to merit the tribute just rendered to his memory.

" 'John Moredock was the son of a woman married thrice, and thrice widowed by a tomahawk. The three successive husbands of this woman had been pioneers, and with them she had wandered from wilderness to wilderness, always on the frontier. With nine children, she at last found herself at a little clearing, afterwards Vincennes. There she joined a company about to remove to the new country of Illinois. On the eastern side of Illinois there were then no settlements; but on the west side, the shore of the Mississippi, there were, near the mouth of the Kaskaskia, some old hamlets of French. To the vicinity of those hamlets, very innocent and pleasant places, a new Arcadia, Mrs. Moredock's party was destined; for thereabouts, among the vines, they meant to settle. They embarked upon the Wabash in boats, proposing descending that stream into the Ohio, and the Ohio into the Mississippi, and so, northwards, towards the point to the reached. All went well till they made the rock of the Grand Tower on the Mississippi, where they had to land and drag their boats round a point swept by a strong current. Here a party of Indians, lying in wait, rushed out and murdered nearly all of them. The widow was among the victims with her children, John excepted, who, some fifty miles distant, was following with a second party.

" 'He was just entering upon manhood, when thus left in nature sole survivor of his race. Other youngsters might have turned mourners; he turned avenger. His nerves were electric wires—sensitive, but steel. He was one who, from self-possession, could be made neither to flush nor pale. It is said that when the tidings were brought him, he was ashore sitting beneath a hemlock eating his dinner of venison—and as the tidings were told him, after the first start he kept on eating, but slowly and deliberately, chewing the wild news with the wild meat, as if both together, turned to chyle,[4] together should sinew him to his intent. From that meal he rose an Indian-hater. He rose; got his arms, prevailed upon some comrades to join him, and without delay started to discover who were the actual transgressors. They proved to belong to a band of twenty renegades from various tribes, outlaws even among Indians, and who had formed themselves into a marauding crew. No opportunity for action being at the time presented, he dismissed his friends; told them to go on, thanking them, and saying he would ask their aid at

---

4. A milky fluid made of lymph and emulsified fats; formed in the small intestine during digestion.

some future day. For upwards of a year, alone in the wilds, he watched the crew. Once, what he thought a favorable chance having occurred—it being midwinter, and the savages encamped, apparently to remain so—he anew mustered his friends, and marched against them; but, getting wind of his coming, the enemy fled, and in such panic that everything was left behind but their weapons. During the winter, much the same thing happened upon two subsequent occasions. The next year he sought them at the head of a party pledged to serve him for forty days. At last the hour came. It was on the shore of the Mississippi. From their covert, Moredock and his men dimly descried the gang of Cains[5] in the red dusk of evening, paddling over to a jungled island in mid-stream, there the more securely to lodge; for Moredock's retributive spirit in the wilderness spoke ever to their trepidations now, like the voice calling through the garden.[6] Waiting until dead of night, the whites swam the river, towing after them a raft laden with their arms. On landing, Moredock cut the fastenings of the enemy's canoes, and turned them, with his own raft, adrift; resolved that there should be neither escape for the Indians, nor safety, except in victory, for the whites. Victorious the whites were; but three of the Indians saved themselves by taking to the stream. Moredock's band lost not a man.

" 'Three of the murderers survived. He knew their names and persons. In the course of three years each successively fell by his own hand. All were now dead. But this did not suffice. He made no avowal, but to kill Indians had become his passion. As an athlete, he had few equals; as a shot, none; in single combat, not to be beaten. Master of that woodland-cunning enabling the adept to subsist where the tyro would perish, and expert in all those arts by which an enemy is pursued for weeks, perhaps months, without once suspecting it, he kept to the forest. The solitary Indian that met him, died. When a number[7] was descried, he would either secretly pursue their track for some chance to strike at least one blow; or if, while thus engaged, he himself was discovered, he would elude them by superior skill.

" 'Many years he spent thus, and though after a time he was, in a degree, restored to the ordinary life of the region and period, yet it is believed that John Moredock never let pass an opportunity of

5. Murderers, from Cain, the first murderer (Genesis 4.8).
6. Like God's voice in the Garden of Eden after Adam and Eve have sinned (Genesis 3.10).
7. Parker's 1963 emendation for "murder" in the 1857 edition. The context requires a word that means "more than one person" and can be misread as "murder." Unlike most conjectural emendations, this one is readily confirmed by the source Melville is closely following, because the corresponding word in Hall (p. 460 herein) is *party*, meaning a group.

quenching an Indian. Sins of commission in that kind may have been his, but none of omission.

" 'It were to err to suppose,' the judge would say, 'that this gentleman was naturally ferocious, or peculiarly possessed of those qualities, which, unhelped by provocation of events, tend to withdraw man from social life. On the contrary, Moredock was an example of something apparently self-contradicting, certainly curious, but, at the same time, undeniable: namely, that nearly all Indian-haters have at bottom loving hearts; at any rate, hearts, if anything, more generous than the average. Certain it is, that, to the degree in which he mingled in the life of the settlements, Moredock showed himself not without humane feelings. No cold husband or colder father, he; and, though often and long away from his household, bore its needs in mind, and provided for them. He could be very convivial; told a good story (though never of his more private exploits), and sung a capital song. Hospitable, not backward to help a neighbor; by report, benevolent, as retributive, in secret; while, in a general manner, though sometimes grave—as is not unusual with men of his complexion, a sultry and tragical brown—yet with nobody, Indians excepted, otherwise than courteous in a manly fashion; a moccasined gentleman, admired and loved. In fact, no one more popular, as an incident to follow may prove.

" 'His bravery, whether in Indian fight or any other, was unquestionable. An officer in the ranging service during the war of 1812, he acquitted himself with more than credit. Of his soldierly character, this anecdote is told: Not long after Hull's dubious surrender at Detroit,[8] Moredock with some of his rangers rode up at night to a log-house, there to rest till morning. The horses being attended to, supper over, and sleeping-places assigned the troop, the host showed the colonel his best bed, not on the ground like the rest, but a bed that stood on legs. But out of delicacy, the guest declined to monopolize it, or, indeed, to occupy it at all; when, to increase the inducement, as the host thought, he was told that a general officer had once slept in that bed. "Who, pray?" asked the colonel.

8. The Michigan Territorial governor, William Hull, was entrusted by President Madison with attacking Canada at the start of the War of 1812. Unnerved by the war cries from the Indians in league with the British under Major-General Isaac Brock and grossly overestimating the strength of the enemy, General Hull surrendered Detroit (including many cannons) on ignominious terms on August 16, 1812, shaming and outraging his country. No patriotic American accepted Hull's justification that he was saving Detroit and the whole territory from the horrors of an Indian massacre, and no American could forget stories of the triumphant ceremonies performed by Brock and the Shawnee leader Tecumseh. Born only four years after the end of the war, Melville became familiar with details of many battles on land and on sea. His systematic brother Gansevoort compiled a lengthy list of naval battles, and by the time he wrote *The Confidence-Man* Melville had been at some of the battle grounds and even in the waters of the Pacific where a major battle had occurred. Many of Melville's readers would have understood without having it pointed out that Moredock's contempt of Hull arises not from the mere fact of his abject surrender but from stories of Hull's hysterical fear of the Indian war cries.

"General Hull." "Then you must not take offense," said the colonel, buttoning up his coat, "but, really, no coward's bed, for me, however comfortable." Accordingly he took up with valor's bed—a cold one on the ground.

" 'At one time the colonel was a member of the territorial council of Illinois, and at the formation of the state government, was pressed to become candidate for governor, but begged to be excused. And, though he declined to give his reasons for declining, yet by those who best knew him the cause was not wholly unsurmised. In his official capacity he might be called upon to enter into friendly treaties with Indian tribes, a thing not to be thought of. And even did no such contingency arise, yet he felt there would be an impropriety in the Governor of Illinois stealing out now and then, during a recess of the legislative bodies, for a few days' shooting at human beings, within the limits of his paternal chief-magistracy. If the governorship offered large honors, from Moredock it demanded larger sacrifices. These were incompatibles. In short, he was not unaware that to be a consistent Indian-hater involves the renunciation of ambition, with its objects—the pomps and glories of the world; and since religion, pronouncing such things vanities, accounts it merit to renounce them, therefore, so far as this goes, Indian-hating, whatever may be thought of it in other respects, may be regarded as not wholly without the efficacy of a devout sentiment.' "

Here the narrator paused. Then, after his long and irksome sitting, started to his feet, and regulating his disordered shirt-frill, and at the same time adjustingly shaking his legs down in his rumpled pantaloons, concluded: "There, I have done; having given you, not my story, mind, or my thoughts, but another's. And now, for your friend Coonskins, I doubt not, that, if the judge were here, he would pronounce him a sort of comprehensive Colonel Moredock, who, too much spreading his passion, shallows it."

Chapter 28.

MOOT POINTS TOUCHING THE LATE COLONEL JOHN MOREDOCK.

"Charity, charity!" exclaimed the cosmopolitan, "never a sound judgment without charity. When man judges man, charity is less a bounty from our mercy than just allowance for the insensible leeway of human fallibility. God forbid that my eccentric friend should be what you hint. You do not know him, or but imperfectly. His outside deceived you; at first it came near deceiving even me. But I seized a chance, when, owing to indignation against some wrong, he laid himself a little open; I seized that lucky chance, I say, to inspect his heart, and found it an inviting oyster in a forbidding shell. His outside is but put on. Ashamed of his own goodness, he treats mankind as those strange old uncles in romances do their nephews—snapping at them all the time and yet loving them as the apple of their eye."

"Well, my words with him were few. Perhaps he is not what I took him for. Yes, for aught I know, you may be right."

"Glad to hear it. Charity, like poetry, should be cultivated, if only for its being graceful. And now, since you have renounced your notion, I should be happy would you, so to speak, renounce your story, too. That story strikes me with even more incredulity than wonder. To me some parts don't hang together. If the man of hate, how could John Moredock be also the man of love? Either his lone campaigns are fabulous as Hercules';[9] or else, those being true, what was thrown in about his geniality is but garnish. In short, if ever there was such a man as Moredock, he, in my way of thinking, was either misanthrope or nothing; and his misanthropy the more intense from being focused on one race of men. Though, like suicide, man-hatred would seem peculiarly a Roman and a Grecian passion—that is, Pagan; yet, the annals of neither Rome nor Greece can produce the equal in man-hatred of Colonel Moredock, as the judge and you have painted him. As for this Indian-hating in general, I can only say of it what Dr. Johnson said of the alleged Lisbon earthquake: 'Sir, I don't believe it.' "[1]

"Didn't believe it? Why not? Clashed with any little prejudice of his?"

"Doctor Johnson had no prejudice; but, like a certain other person," with an ingenuous smile, "he had sensibilities, and those were pained."

"Dr. Johnson was a good Christian, wasn't he?"

"He was."

"Suppose he had been something else."

"Then small incredulity as to the alleged earthquake."

"Suppose he had been also a misanthrope?"

"Then small incredulity as to the robberies and murders alleged to have been perpetrated under the pall of smoke and ashes. The

9. Or Heracles, a mythological figure of extraordinary strength. He gained immortality by completing the "fabulous" (fabled) Labors, which included killing the Nemean lion, slaying the Hydra of Lerna, capturing the boar of Mount Erymanthus, capturing the hind of Artemis, killing the man-eating Stymphalian birds, cleaning the Augean stables, capturing the Cretan bull, capturing the horses of Diomedes, taking the girdle of Hippolyta, killing the monster Geryon, capturing Cerberus, and stealing the apples of Hesperides.
1. Melville is echoing Piozzi (see n. 3, p. 157) on Dr. Johnson's refusal to believe reports of the cataclysmic earthquake that occurred in Lisbon, Portugal, on November 1, 1755, resulting in heavy damage and a death toll as high as sixty thousand. Curiously, in view of the setting of this book, Melville may not have known of the 1811–12 series of violent earthquakes that changed the course of the Mississippi.

infidels of the time were quick to credit those reports and worse. So true is it that, while religion, contrary to the common notion, implies, in certain cases, a spirit of slow reserve as to assent, infidelity, which claims to despise credulity, is sometimes swift to it."

"You rather jumble together misanthropy and infidelity."

"I do not jumble them; they are coördinates. For misanthropy, springing from the same root with disbelief of religion, is twin with that. It springs from the same root, I say; for, set aside materialism, and what is an atheist, but one who does not, or will not, see in the universe a ruling principle of love; and what a misanthrope, but one who does not, or will not, see in man a ruling principle of kindness? Don't you see? In either case the vice consists in a want of confidence."

"What sort of a sensation is misanthropy?"

"Might as well ask me what sort of sensation is hydrophobia. Don't know; never had it. But I have often wondered what it can be like. Can a misanthrope feel warm, I ask myself; take ease? be companionable with himself? Can a misanthrope smoke a cigar and muse? How fares he in solitude? Has the misanthrope such a thing as an appetite? Shall a peach refresh him? The effervescence of champagne, with what eye does he behold it? Is summer good to him? Of long winters how much can he sleep? What are his dreams? How feels he, and what does he, when suddenly awakened, alone, at dead of night, by fusilades of thunder?"

"Like you," said the stranger, "I can't understand the misanthrope. So far as my experience goes, either mankind is worthy one's best love, or else I have been lucky. Never has it been my lot to have been wronged, though but in the smallest degree. Cheating, backbiting, superciliousness, disdain, hard-heartedness, and all that brood, I know but by report. Cold regards tossed over the sinister shoulder of a former friend, ingratitude in a beneficiary, treachery in a confidant—such things may be; but I must take somebody's word for it.[2] Now the bridge that has carried me so well over, shall I not praise it?"

"Ingratitude to the worthy bridge not to do so. Man is a noble fellow, and in an age of satirists, I am not displeased to find one who has confidence in him, and bravely stands up for him."

2. Melville may be wryly reversing some words in his source for "Benito Cereno," Amasa Delano's *Voyages* (1817): "After our arrival at Conception, I was mortified and very much hurt at the treatment which I received from Don Bonito Sereno [*sic*]; but had this been the only time that I ever was treated with ingratitude, injustice, or want of compassion, I would not complain" (329). And later: "When I take a retrospective view of my life, I cannot find in my soul, that I ever have done any thing to deserve such misery and ingratitude as I have suffered at different periods, and in general, from the very persons to whom I have rendered the greatest services" (331). The source chapter from Delano is reprinted in facsimile in the Northwestern-Newberry Edition of *The Piazza Tales and Other Prose Pieces, 1839–1860* (1987), 809–47 (see Selected Bibliography).

"Yes, I always speak a good word for man; and what is more, am always ready to do a good deed for him."

"You are a man after my own heart," responded the cosmopolitan, with a candor which lost nothing by its calmness. "Indeed," he added, "our sentiments agree so, that were they written in a book, whose was whose, few but the nicest critics might determine."

"Since we are thus joined in mind," said the stranger, "why not be joined in hand?"

"My hand is always at the service of virtue," frankly extending it to him as to virtue personified.

"And now," said the stranger, cordially retaining his hand, "you know our fashion here at the West. It may be a little low, but it is kind. Briefly, we being newly-made friends must drink together. What say you?"

"Thank you; but indeed, you must excuse me."

"Why?"

"Because, to tell the truth, I have to-day met so many old friends, all free-hearted, convivial gentlemen, that really, really, though for the present I succeed in mastering it, I am at bottom almost in the condition of a sailor who, stepping ashore after a long voyage, ere night reels with loving welcomes, his head of less capacity than his heart."

At the allusion to old friends, the stranger's countenance a little fell, as a jealous lover's might at hearing from his sweetheart of former ones. But rallying, he said: "No doubt they treated you to something strong; but wine—surely, that gentle creature, wine; come, let us have a little gentle wine at one of these little tables here. Come, come." Then essaying to roll about like a full pipe in the sea, sang in a voice which had had more of good-fellowship, had there been less of a latent squeak to it:

> "Let us drink of the wine of the vine benign,
> That sparkles warm in Zansovine."[3]

The cosmopolitan, with longing eye upon him, stood as sorely tempted and wavering a moment; then, abruptly stepping towards him, with a look of dissolved surrender, said: "When mermaid songs move figure-heads, then may glory, gold, and women try their blandishments on me. But a good fellow, singing a good song, he woos forth my every spike, so that my whole hull, like a ship's, sailing by a magnetic rock, caves in with acquiescence. Enough: when one has a heart of a certain sort, it is in vain trying to be resolute."

---

3. Slightly misquoted from *Bacchus in Tuscany* by the English Romantic poet Leigh Hunt (1784–1859).

Chapter 29.

THE BOON COMPANIONS.

The wine, port, being called for, and the two seated at the little table, a natural pause of convivial expectancy ensued; the stranger's eye turned towards the bar near by, watching the red-cheeked, white-aproned man there, blithely dusting the bottle, and invitingly arranging the salver and glasses; when, with a sudden impulse turning round his head towards his companion, he said, "Ours is friendship at first sight, ain't it?"

"It is," was the placidly pleased reply: "and the same may be said of friendship at first sight as of love at first sight: it is the only true one, the only noble one. It bespeaks confidence. Who would go sounding his way into love or friendship, like a strange ship by night, into an enemy's harbor?"

"Right. Boldly in before the wind. Agreeable, how we always agree. By-the-way, though but a formality, friends should know each other's names. What is yours, pray?"

"Francis Goodman. But those who love me, call me Frank. And yours?"

"Charles Arnold Noble.[4] But do you call me Charlie."

"I will, Charlie; nothing like preserving in manhood the fraternal familiarities of youth. It proves the heart a rosy boy to the last."

"My sentiments again. Ah!"

It was a smiling waiter, with the smiling bottle, the cork drawn; a common quart bottle, but for the occasion fitted at bottom into a little bark basket, braided with porcupine quills, gayly tinted in the Indian fashion. This being set before the entertainer, he regarded it with affectionate interest, but seemed not to understand, or else to pretend not to, a handsome red label pasted on the bottle, bearing the capital letters, P. W.

"P. W.," said he at last, perplexedly eying the pleasing poser, "now what does P. W. mean?"

"Shouldn't wonder," said the cosmopolitan gravely, "if it stood for port wine. You called for port wine, didn't you?"

"Why so it is, so it is!"

"I find some little mysteries not very hard to clear up," said the other, quietly crossing his legs.

This commonplace seemed to escape the stranger's hearing, for,

---

4. A Charley Noble was a brass smokestack in the galley; later it meant any busywork, because sailors could be put to polishing brass that already gleamed (Horace Beck, *Folklore of the Sea*, 1973). A related expression, "to shoot Charlie Noble" (in which Charlie Noble also means "a galley stovepipe") means "to clear the pipe of soot by firing a blank shot inside it," according to the *Random House Historical Dictionary of American Slang*, 1994).

full of his bottle, he now rubbed his somewhat sallow hands over it, and with a strange kind of cackle, meant to be a chirrup, cried: "Good wine, good wine; is it not the peculiar bond of good feeling?" Then brimming both glasses, pushed one over, saying, with what seemed intended for an air of fine disdain: "Ill betide those gloomy skeptics who maintain that now-a-days pure wine is unpurchasable; that almost every variety on sale is less the vintage of vineyards than laboratories; that most bar-keepers are but a set of male Brinvillierses,[5] with complaisant arts practicing against the lives of their best friends, their customers."

A shade passed over the cosmopolitan. After a few minutes' down-cast musing, he lifted his eyes and said: "I have long thought, my dear Charlie, that the spirit in which wine is regarded by too many in these days is one of the most painful examples of want of confidence. Look at these glasses. He who could mistrust poison in this wine would mistrust consumption in Hebe's[6] cheek. While, as for suspicions against the dealers in wine and sellers of it, those who cherish such suspicions can have but limited trust in the human heart. Each human heart they must think to be much like each bottle of port, not such port as this, but such port as they hold to. Strange traducers, who see good faith in nothing, however sacred. Not medicines, not the wine in sacraments, has escaped them. The doctor with his phial, and the priest with his chalice, they deem equally the unconscious dispensers of bogus cordials to the dying."

"Dreadful!"

"Dreadful indeed," said the cosmopolitan solemnly. "These distrusters stab at the very soul of confidence. If this wine," impressively holding up his full glass, "if this wine with its bright promise be not true, how shall man be, whose promise can be no brighter? But if wine be false, while men are true, whither shall fly convivial geniality? To think of sincerely-genial souls drinking each other's health at unawares in perfidious and murderous drugs!"

"Horrible!"

"Much too much so to be true, Charlie. Let us forget it. Come, you are my entertainer on this occasion, and yet you don't pledge me. I have been waiting for it."

"Pardon, pardon," half confusedly and half ostentatiously lifting his glass. "I pledge you, Frank, with my whole heart, believe me," taking a draught too decorous to be large, but which, small though it was, was followed by a slight involuntary wryness to the mouth.

---

5. I.e., treacherous poisoners, from the notorious Marquise de Brinvilliers (1630–1676) who murdered her father and two brothers, and perhaps others.
6. Daughter of Zeus, Greek goddess of youth, and a cupbearer to the gods. She married Heracles when he was received into heaven.

"And I return you the pledge, Charlie, heart-warm as it came to me, and honest as this wine I drink it in," reciprocated the cosmopolitan with princely kindliness in his gesture, taking a generous swallow, concluding in a smack, which, though audible, was not so much so as to be unpleasing.

"Talking of alleged spuriousness of wines," said he, tranquilly setting down his glass, and then sloping back his head and with friendly fixedness eying the wine, "perhaps the strangest part of those allegings is, that there is, as claimed, a kind of man who, while convinced that on this continent most wines are shams, yet still drinks away at them; accounting wine so fine a thing, that even the sham article is better than none at all. And if the temperance people urge that, by this course, he will sooner or later be undermined in health, he answers, 'And do you think I don't know that? But health without cheer I hold a bore; and cheer, even of the spurious sort, has its price, which I am willing to pay.' "

"Such a man, Frank, must have a disposition ungovernably bacchanalian."

"Yes, if such a man there be, which I don't credit. It is a fable, but a fable from which I once heard a person of less genius than grotesqueness draw a moral even more extravagant than the fable itself. He said that it illustrated, as in a parable, how that a man of a disposition ungovernably good-natured might still familiarly associate with men, though, at the same time, he believed the greater part of men false-hearted—accounting society so sweet a thing that even the spurious sort was better than none at all. And if the Rochefoucaultites[7] urge that, by this course, he will sooner or later be undermined in security, he answers, 'And do you think I don't know that? But security without society I hold a bore; and society, even of the spurious sort, has its price, which I am willing to pay.' "

"A most singular theory," said the stranger with a slight fidget, eying his companion with some inquisitiveness, "indeed, Frank, a most slanderous thought," he exclaimed in sudden heat and with an involuntary look almost of being personally aggrieved.

"In one sense it merits all you say, and more," rejoined the other with wonted mildness, "but, for a kind of drollery in it, charity might, perhaps, overlook something of the wickedness. Humor is, in fact, so blessed a thing, that even in the least virtuous product of the human mind, if there can be found but nine good jokes, some philosophers are clement enough to affirm that those nine good jokes should redeem all the wicked thoughts, though plenty as the

---

7. Followers of François, duc de La Rochefoucauld (1613–1680), French nobleman best known for *Maxims*, first published in 1665, many of which express a pessimistic and cynical view of human nature as motivated by self-interest and social ambition. Virtue and disinterested behavior are presented in the *Maxims* as either delusions or conscious lies.

populace of Sodom.[8] At any rate, this same humor has something, there is no telling what, of beneficence in it, it is such a catholicon and charm—nearly all men agreeing in relishing it, though they may agree in little else—and in its way it undeniably does such a deal of familiar good in the world, that no wonder it is almost a proverb, that a man of humor, a man capable of a good loud laugh—seem how he may in other things—can hardly be a heartless scamp."

"Ha, ha, ha!" laughed the other, pointing to the figure of a pale pauper-boy on the deck below, whose pitiableness was touched, as it were, with ludicrousness by a pair of monstrous boots, apparently some mason's discarded ones, cracked with drouth, half eaten by lime, and curled up about the toe like a bassoon. "Look—ha, ha, ha!"

"I see," said the other, with what seemed quiet appreciation, but of a kind expressing an eye to the grotesque, without blindness to what in this case accompanied it, "I see; and the way in which it moves you, Charlie, comes in very apropos to point the proverb I was speaking of. Indeed, had you intended this effect, it could not have been more so. For who that heard that laugh, but would as naturally argue from it a sound heart as sound lungs? True, it is said that a man may smile, and smile, and smile, and be a villain;[9] but it is not said that a man may laugh, and laugh, and laugh, and be one, is it, Charlie?"

"Ha, ha, ha!—no no, no no."

"Why Charlie, your explosions illustrate my remarks almost as aptly as the chemist's imitation volcano did his lectures. But even if experience did not sanction the proverb, that a good laugher cannot be a bad man, I should yet feel bound in confidence to believe it, since it is a saying current among the people, and I doubt not originated among them, and hence *must* be true; for the voice of the people is the voice of truth. Don't you think so?"

"Of course I do. If Truth don't speak through the people, it never speaks at all; so I heard one say."

"A true saying. But we stray. The popular notion of humor, considered as index to the heart, would seem curiously confirmed by Aristotle—I think, in his 'Politics,' (a work, by-the-by, which, however it may be viewed upon the whole, yet, from the tenor of certain

8. Genesis 18 recounts Abraham's intercession on behalf of the city of Sodom, which God plans to destroy because of the wickedness of its inhabitants. Abraham convinces the Lord to spare the city if fifty righteous people can be found there. He then gets God to lower the number to forty-five, then forty, then thirty, then twenty, and finally ten. In Genesis 19, Sodom is destroyed. Based on a literal interpretation of Abraham's bargain with the Lord, at the time it was destroyed Sodom could have contained up to nine righteous inhabitants.

9. *Hamlet* 1.5.108, where Hamlet takes from his father's ghost this lesson about his uncle: "That one may smile, and smile, and be a villain."

sections, should not, without precaution, be placed in the hands of youth)—who remarks that the least lovable men in history seem to have had for humor not only a disrelish, but a hatred; and this, in some cases, along with an extraordinary dry taste for practical punning. I remember it is related of Phalaris,[1] the capricious tyrant of Sicily, that he once caused a poor fellow to be beheaded on a horseblock, for no other cause than having a horse-laugh."

"Funny Phalaris!"

"Cruel Phalaris!"

As after fire-crackers, there was a pause, both looking downward on the table as if mutually struck by the contrast of exclamations, and pondering upon its significance, if any. So, at least, it seemed; but on one side it might have been otherwise: for presently glancing up, the cosmopolitan said: "In the instance of the moral, drolly cynic, drawn from the queer bacchanalian fellow we were speaking of, who had his reasons for still drinking spurious wine, though knowing it to be such—there, I say, we have an example of what is certainly a wicked thought, but conceived in humor. I will now give you one of a wicked thought conceived in wickedness. You shall compare the two, and answer, whether in the one case the sting is not neutralized by the humor, and whether in the other the absence of humor does not leave the sting free play. I once heard a wit, a mere wit, mind, an irreligious Parisian wit, say, with regard to the temperance movement, that none, to their personal benefit, joined it sooner than niggards and knaves; because, as he affirmed, the one by it saved money and the other made money, as in shipowners cutting off the spirit ration without giving its equivalent,[2] and gamblers and all sorts of subtle tricksters sticking to cold water, the better to keep a cool head for business."

"A wicked thought, indeed!" cried the stranger, feelingly.

"Yes," leaning over the table on his elbow and genially gesturing at him with his forefinger: "yes, and, as I said, you don't remark the sting of it?"

"I do, indeed. Most calumnious thought, Frank!"

"No humor in it?"

"Not a bit!"

"Well now, Charlie," eying him with moist regard, "let us drink. It appears to me you don't drink freely."

"Oh, oh—indeed, indeed—I am not backward there. I protest, a freer drinker than friend Charlie you will find nowhere," with fever-

1. Notoriously cruel Sicilian tyrant (d. 544? B.C.E.), who was said to have roasted some of his victims in a bronze bull. "Practical punning": Aristotle on punning is unlocated. Melville may be making some private joke (see n. 5, p. 170).
2. Melville knew from experience and from Richard Henry Dana in *Two Years before the Mast* the miserliness of ship owners. For Melville's comments on the harshness of ship owners, see his "Etchings of a Whaling Cruise" (1847) in the 2001 NCE of *Moby-Dick*.

ish zeal snatching his glass, but only in the sequel to dally with it. "By-the-way, Frank," said he, perhaps, or perhaps not, to draw attention from himself, "by-the-way, I saw a good thing the other day; capital thing; a panegyric on the press. It pleased me so, I got it by heart at two readings. It is a kind of poetry, but in a form which stands in something the same relation to blank verse which that does to rhyme. A sort of free-and-easy chant with refrains to it. Shall I recite it?"

"Anything in praise of the press I shall be happy to hear," rejoined the cosmopolitan, "the more so," he gravely proceeded, "as of late I have observed in some quarters a disposition to disparage the press."

"Disparage the press?"

"Even so; some gloomy souls affirming that it is proving with that great invention as with brandy or eau-de-vie, which, upon its first discovery, was believed by the doctors to be, as its French name implies, a panacea—a notion which experience, it may be thought, has not fully verified."

"You surprise me, Frank. Are there really those who so decry the press? Tell me more. Their reasons."

"Reasons they have none, but affirmations they have many; among other things affirming that, while under dynastic despotisms, the press is to the people little but an improvisatore, under popular ones it is too apt to be their Jack Cade.[3] In fine, these sour sages regard the press in the light of a Colt's revolver,[4] pledged to no cause but his in whose chance hands it may be; deeming the one invention an improvement upon the pen, much akin to what the other is upon the pistol; involving, along with the multiplication of the barrel, no consecration of the aim. The term 'freedom of the press' they consider on a par with *freedom of Colt's revolver*. Hence, for truth and the right, they hold, to indulge hopes from the one is little more sensible than for Kossuth and Mazzini[5] to indulge hopes

3. The Kentish leader of a 1450 rebellion; remembered as a cynical and arbitrary exploiter of mob fury, an archetypal manipulative rebel, because Shakespeare put him in a history play and gave his cohort Dick the butcher this response: "The first thing we do, let's kill all the lawyers" (2 *Henry VI* 4.2.77). "Improvisatore": someone who composes, sings, or recites poems or songs extemporaneously.
4. Samuel Colt patented his famous revolving-breech pistol in 1836. It was later adopted for use by the U.S. Army and became a popular firearm on the frontier. This passage distills Melville's well-justified hostility to the newspapers of his era.
5. Hungarian Lajos Kossuth (1802–1894) and Italian Giuseppe Mazzini (1805–1872) were both leaders in the failed popular revolutions of 1848. Melville is assuming that Mazzini raised money for his cause in London during his long exile there before and after the revolution of 1848–49. Kossuth (pronounced, roughly, *KO-shoot*, the final *h* silent) also lived several years in London in the early 1850s and conducted a fund-raising tour of the United States late in 1851 (just after the publication of *Moby-Dick*), which became a prolonged media sensation. Melville did his best to ignore the publicity as he worked on *Pierre* in December 1851, saying to a friend who had heard Kossuth speak at Tripler Hall in New York that if he "left home to look after Hungary" his family

from the other. Heart-breaking views enough, you think; but their refutation is in every true reformer's contempt. Is it not so?"

"Without doubt. But go on, go on. I like to hear you," flatteringly brimming up his glass for him.

"For one," continued the cosmopolitan, grandly swelling his chest, "I hold the press to be neither the people's improvisatore, nor Jack Cade; neither their paid fool, nor conceited drudge. I think interest never prevails with it over duty. The press still speaks for truth though impaled, in the teeth of lies though intrenched. Disdaining for it the poor name of cheap diffuser of news, I claim for it the independent apostleship of Advancer of Knowledge:—the iron Paul![6] Paul, I say; for not only does the press advance knowledge, but righteousness. In the press, as in the sun, resides, my dear Charlie, a dedicated principle of beneficent force and light. For the Satanic press, by its coappearance with the apostolic, it is no more an aspersion to that, than to the true sun is the coappearance of the mock one. For all the baleful-looking parhelion,[7] god Apollo dispenses the day. In a word, Charlie, what the sovereign of England is titularly, I hold the press to be actually—Defender of the Faith![8]—defender of the faith in the final triumph of truth over error, metaphysics over superstition, theory over falsehood, machinery over nature, and the good man over the bad. Such are my views, which, if stated at some length, you, Charlie, must pardon, for it is a theme upon which I cannot speak with cold brevity. And now I am impatient for your panegyric, which, I doubt not, will put mine to the blush."

"It is rather in the blush-giving vein," smiled the other; "but such as it is, Frank, you shall have it."

"in hunger would suffer" (Parker 2.4). That month Melville's lawyer brother Allan, known in the family circle as an inveterate punster but not as a particularly humorous man, complained of having "a shocking bad cold—a regular Kossuth." Funds collected by European revolutionaries in England or in the United States, Melville assumes, would be used to buy guns for use in Hungary and Italy. The great excitement in the United States over Kossuth was an exercise in northern feel-good emotionality, like the 1820s sympathy for Greeks suffering under Turkish rule. Congress was not prepared to help the Hungarians.

6. I.e., the metal printing press. Saul, a devout Jew and a ferocious persecutor of the early followers of Jesus, stood by approvingly as Stephen (the first Christian martyr) was stoned to death and thereafter made havoc on the Christians, "entering into every house, and haling men and women" out to commit them to prison (Acts 8.3). On his way to Damascus to capture Christians, a light from heaven blinds him and Jesus says to him, "Saul, Saul, why persecutest thou me?" (Acts 9.5). Converted, he takes the name Paul and becomes a fervent Christian. Several books of the New Testament are letters Paul wrote to newly established Christian churches, thereby spreading the Gospel (good news) the way newspapers are here said (quite ironically) to advance knowledge.

7. Commonly called a sundog or mock sun; a bright patch appearing twenty-two degrees or more on either side of the sun at morning or evening, but not seen after the sun is higher than sixty-one degrees. Apollo, the sun god in Greek mythology, when high in the sky would banish a parhelion.

8. The title conferred upon Henry VIII of England by the pope for his opposition to Protestantism. Though revoked by Rome when Henry broke with Catholicism, it was restored by Parliament and is still used by British monarchs.

"Tell me when you are about to begin," said the cosmopolitan, "for, when at public dinners the press is toasted, I always drink the toast standing, and shall stand while you pronounce the panegyric."

"Very good, Frank; you may stand up now."

He accordingly did so, when the stranger likewise rose, and uplifting the ruby wine-flask, began.

Chapter 30.

OPENING WITH A POETICAL EULOGY OF THE PRESS AND CONTINUING WITH TALK INSPIRED BY THE SAME.

" 'Praise be unto the press, not Faust's, but Noah's;[9] let us extol and magnify the press, the true press of Noah, from which breaketh the true morning. Praise be unto the press, not the black press but the red; let us extol and magnify the press, the red press of Noah, from which cometh inspiration. Ye pressmen of the Rhineland and the Rhine, join in with all ye who tread out the glad tidings on isle Madeira or Mitylene.[1]—Who giveth redness of eyes by making men long to tarry at the fine print?—Praise be unto the press, the rosy press of Noah, which giveth rosiness of hearts, by making men long to tarry at the rosy wine.—Who hath babblings and contentions? Who, without cause, inflicteth wounds?[2] Praise be unto the press, the kindly press of Noah, which knitteth friends, which fuseth foes.—Who may be bribed?—Who may be bound?—Praise be unto the press, the free press of Noah, which will not lie for tyrants, but make tyrants speak the truth.—Then praise be unto the press, the frank old press of Noah; then let us extol and magnify the press, the brave old press of Noah; then let us with roses garland and enwreath the press, the grand old press of Noah, from which flow streams of knowledge which give man a bliss no more unreal than his pain.' "

9. As the first vintner mentioned in the Bible (Genesis 9), Noah is associated with the wine press. Johann Fust (1400?–1466), German financial backer of Johannes Gutenberg (before 1400–1468), generally considered the inventor of movable type. Fust won the Gutenberg press in a suit for recovery of funds and then published the Bible (1456) and the Psalms (1457). Melville's spelling recalls the legendary figure of Faust, a German necromancer who sold his soul to the Devil in exchange for special knowledge and powers.

1. In his hotel at Cologne in 1849 every man in the dining saloon "had his bottle of Rhenish and his cigar," Melville noted. He knew of Madeira and Mitilene as grape-growing islands in the west and east Mediterranean Sea, respectively.

2. As Nathalia Wright (1949) pointed out, this is an imitation of biblical formulas. See Proverbs 23.29–32: "Who hath woe? who hath sorrow? who hath contentions? who hath babbling? who hath wounds without cause? who hath redness of eyes? They that tarry long at the wine; they that go to seek mixed wine. Look not thou upon the wine when it is red, when it giveth his colour in the cup, when it moveth itself aright. At the last it biteth like a serpent, and stingeth like an adder."

"You deceived me," smiled the cosmopolitan, as both now re-sumed their seats; "you roguishly took advantage of my simplicity; you archly played upon my enthusiasm. But never mind; the of-fense, if any, was so charming, I almost wish you would offend again. As for certain poetic left-handers in your panegyric, those I cheerfully concede to the indefinite privileges of the poet. Upon the whole, it was quite in the lyric style—a style I always admire on ac-count of that spirit of Sibyllic[3] confidence and assurance which is, perhaps, its prime ingredient. But come," glancing at his compan-ion's glass, "for a lyrist, you let the bottle stay with you too long."

"The lyre and the vine forever!" cried the other in his rapture, or what seemed such, heedless of the hint, "the vine, the vine! is it not the most graceful and bounteous of all growths? And, by its being such, is not something meant—divinely meant? As I live, a vine, a Catawba[4] vine, shall be planted on my grave!"

"A genial thought; but your glass there."

"Oh, oh," taking a moderate sip, "but you, why don't you drink?"

"You have forgotten, my dear Charlie, what I told you of my pre-vious convivialities to-day."

"Oh," cried the other, now in manner quite abandoned to the lyric mood, not without contrast to the easy sociability of his com-panion. "Oh, one can't drink too much of good old wine—the gen-uine, mellow old port. Pooh, pooh! drink away."

"Then keep me company."

"Of course," with a flourish, taking another sip—"suppose we have cigars. Never mind your pipe there; a pipe is best when alone. I say, waiter, bring some cigars—your best."

They were brought in a pretty little bit of western pottery, repre-senting some kind of Indian utensil, mummy-colored, set down in a mass of tobacco leaves, whose long, green fans, fancifully grouped, formed with peeps of red the sides of the receptacle.

Accompanying it were two accessories, also bits of pottery, but smaller, both globes; one in guise of an apple flushed with red and gold to the life, and, through a cleft at top, you saw it was hollow. This was for the ashes. The other, gray, with wrinkled surface, in the likeness of a wasp's nest, was the match-box.

"There," said the stranger, pushing over the cigarstand, "help yourself, and I will touch you off," taking a match. "Nothing like to-bacco," he added, when the fumes of the cigar began to wreathe,

3. Sibyl was the name given to any of several prophetesses in Greek and Roman legend. In 1817 Samuel Taylor Coleridge published the first edition of his collected poems under the title *Sibylline Leaves*.

4. A grape, native to North America, celebrated in Henry Wadsworth Longfellow's humor-ously enthusiastic 1854 tribute to the "Catawba Wine" produced in Cincinnati, the "Queen City of the West" by the "Beautiful River," the Ohio.

glancing from the smoker to the pottery, "I will have a Virginia tobacco-plant set over my grave beside the Catawba vine."[5]

"Improvement upon your first idea, which by itself was good—but you don't smoke."

"Presently, presently—let me fill your glass again. You don't drink."

"Thank you; but no more just now. Fill *your* glass."

"Presently, presently; do you drink on. Never mind me. Now that it strikes me, let me say, that he who, out of superfine gentility or fanatic morality, denies himself tobacco, suffers a more serious abatement in the cheap pleasures of life than the dandy in his iron boot, or the celibate on his iron cot. While for him who would fain revel in tobacco, but cannot, it is a thing at which philanthropists must weep, to see such an one, again and again, madly returning to the cigar, which, for his incompetent stomach, he cannot enjoy, while still, after each shameful repulse, the sweet dream of the impossible good goads him on to his fierce misery once more—poor eunuch!"

"I agree with you," said the cosmopolitan, still gravely social, "but you don't smoke."

"Presently, presently, do you smoke on. As I was saying about—"

"But *why* don't you smoke—come. You don't think that tobacco, when in league with wine, too much enhances the latter's vinous quality—in short, with certain constitutions tends to impair self-possession, do you?"

"To think that, were treason to good fellowship," was the warm disclaimer. "No, no. But the fact is, there is an unpropitious flavor in my mouth just now. Ate of a diabolical ragout at dinner, so I shan't smoke till I have washed away the lingering memento of it with wine. But smoke away, you, and pray, don't forget to drink. By-the-way, while we sit here so companionably, giving loose to any companionable nothing, your uncompanionable friend, Coonskins, is, by pure contrast, brought to recollection. If he were but here now, he would see how much of real heart-joy he denies himself by not hob-a-nobbing with his kind."

"Why," with loitering emphasis, slowly withdrawing his cigar, "I thought I had undeceived you there. I thought you had come to a better understanding of my eccentric friend."

"Well, I thought so, too; but first impressions will return, you know. In truth, now that I think of it, I am led to conjecture from chance things which dropped from Coonskins, during the little in-

---

5. "Now a bunch of cigars, all banded together, is a type and a symbol of the brotherly love between smokers. Likewise, for the time, in a community of pipes is a community of hearts. Nor was it an ill thing for the Indian Sachems to circulate their calumet tobacco-bowl—even as our fore-fathers circulated their punch-bowl—in token of peace, charity, and good-will, friendly feelings, and sympathizing souls" (*White-Jacket*, chapter 91).

terview I had with him, that he is not a Missourian by birth, but years ago came West here, a young misanthrope from the other side of the Alleghanies, less to make his fortune, than to flee man. Now, since they say trifles sometimes effect great results, I shouldn't wonder, if his history were probed, it would be found that what first indirectly gave his sad bias to Coonskins was his disgust at reading in boyhood the advice of Polonius to Laertes[6]—advice which, in the selfishness it inculcates, is almost on a par with a sort of ballad upon the economies of money-making, to be occasionally seen pasted against the desk of small retail traders in New England."

"I do hope now, my dear fellow," said the cosmopolitan with an air of bland protest, "that, in my presence at least, you will throw out nothing to the prejudice of the sons of the Puritans."

"Hey-day and high times indeed," exclaimed the other, nettled, "sons of the Puritans[7] forsooth! And who be Puritans, that I, an Alabamaian, must do them reverence? A set of sourly conceited old Malvolios,[8] whom Shakespeare laughs his fill at in his comedies."

"Pray, what were you about to suggest with regard to Polonius," observed the cosmopolitan with quiet forbearance, expressive of the patience of a superior mind at the petulance of an inferior one; "how do you characterize his advice to Laertes?"

"As false, fatal, and calumnious," exclaimed the other, with a degree of ardor befitting one resenting a stigma upon the family escutcheon, "and for a father to give his son—monstrous. The case you see is this: The son is going abroad, and for the first. What does the father? Invoke God's blessing upon him? Put the blessed Bible in his trunk? No. Crams him with maxims smacking of my Lord Chesterfield, with maxims of France, with maxims of Italy."[9]

6. For Melville, the courtier Polonius in Shakespeare's *Hamlet* is a type of expedient, worldly morality to be judged by the absolute, heavenly standards of Jesus. His son Laertes is the reluctant recipient of Polonius's advice. Kindred figures in Melville's mind are historical figures like Francis Bacon (1561–1626) and Lord Chesterfield (1694–1773) and some of his own characters, notably the Reverend Mr. Falsgrave and Plotinus Plinlimmon in *Pierre* (1852). At the time Melville was writing *The Confidence-Man*, Polonius had an especially sour significance for him because of his sententious warning to Laertes not to be either a borrower or a lender. Melville had read this advice but had not heeded it, especially not in May 1851, when he went into debt so he could finish *Moby Dick* and could pay to have it stereotyped so he might sell the plates to the highest bidder (although in fact he settled for the Harpers).
7. I.e., New Englanders. Melville is playing with regional prejudices. Like Washington Irving, James Fenimore Cooper, and other New Yorkers, Melville (his own Boston family being mainly recent arrivals, and Scottish, not descendants of the colonial Puritans) enjoyed the stereotype of the Yankee as materialistic, rigid, lacking a sense of the beautiful and genial, and physically awkward and unpleasant looking. Closely related to the lords of Leven and Melvill, he identified with Virginians, whom he tended to think of as broad minded, broad shouldered, and aristocratic.
8. Charlie takes Malvolio in Shakespeare's *Twelfth Night* as the embodiment of the Puritan kill-joy; another character in the "set" would be Jaques, in *As You Like It*.
9. The French maxims would be like those of the duc de la Rochefaucauld (n. 7, p. 167); any Italian maxims, in this climactic construction, would be the most cynical of all. For Lord Chesterfield, see n. 8, p. 122.

"No, no, be charitable, not that. Why, does he not among other things say:—

> 'The friends thou hast, and their adoption tried,
> Grapple them to thy soul with hooks of steel'?[1]

Is that compatible with maxims of Italy?"

"Yes it is, Frank. Don't you see? Laertes is to take the best of care of his friends—his proved friends, on the same principle that a wine-corker takes the best of care of his proved bottles. When a bottle gets a sharp knock and don't break, he says, 'Ah, I'll keep that bottle.' Why? Because he loves it? No, he has particular use for it."

"Dear, dear!" appealingly turning in distress, "that—that kind of criticism is—is—in fact—it won't do."

"Won't truth do, Frank? You are so charitable with everybody, do but consider the tone of the speech. Now I put it to you, Frank; is there anything in it hortatory to high, heroic, disinterested effort? Anything like 'sell all thou hast and give to the poor?'[2] And, in other points, what desire seems most in the father's mind, that his son should cherish nobleness for himself, or be on his guard against the contrary thing in others? An irreligious warner, Frank—no devout counselor, is Polonius. I hate him. Nor can I bear to hear your veterans of the world affirm, that he who steers through life by the advice of old Polonius will not steer among the breakers."

"No, no—I hope nobody affirms that," rejoined the cosmopolitan, with tranquil abandonment; sideways reposing his arm at full length upon the table. "I hope nobody affirms that; because, if Polonius' advice be taken in your sense, then the recommendation of it by men of experience would appear to involve more or less of

---

1. From Polonius's set speech of paternal advice to Laertes (*Hamlet* 1.3.62–63). "Hooks of steel" is not an error of Melville's for the usual "hoops of steel" but his accurate reproduction of a dubious emendation made in his Hilliard, Gray edition.
2. The words of Jesus to the rich young man, who wanted to be his follower: "If thou wilt be perfect, go and sell that thou hast, and give to the poor, and thou shalt have treasure in heaven: and come and follow me" (Matthew 19.21). The rich young man goes away sorrowful, "for he had great possessions." In *Pierre*, as in this book, this passage in Matthew is the key to Melville's religious absolutism, the standard against which nominal Christians are to be tested. It has proved hard for modern readers of Melville to apply this standard in evaluating behavior in his *Pierre* and *The Confidence-Man*, because if it were taken seriously a group of Christians could hardly organize and sustain a local church and no male or female Christian could be a good family man or responsible mother. Yet Jesus says that to follow him one must abandon not only possessions but also family. In Melville's time, all American Protestants knew John Bunyan's *The Pilgrim's Progress* in which the wife and children of the aptly named "Christian" implore him not to continue toward the Celestial City but instead to return with them to the City of Destruction. He resists their appeals. The hard lesson is that to save his soul Christian has to leave them behind, unprotected. Later Bunyan wrote a continuation of the book in which the wife (given a name, Christiana) and children set out on the same journey, so there is a happy ending for them, too. However, it is understood that whatever the ultimate fate of his family, Christian had been right to flee to save his own soul. This passage in Matthew suggests how to judge Melville's depiction of John Moredock (chapters 26–28).

an unhandsome sort of reflection upon human nature. And yet," with a perplexed air, "your suggestions have put things in such a strange light to me as in fact a little to disturb my previous notions of Polonius and what he says. To be frank, by your ingenuity you have unsettled me there, to that degree that were it not for our co-incidence of opinion in general, I should almost think I was now at length beginning to feel the ill effect of an immature mind, too much consorting with a mature one, except on the ground of first principles in common."

"Really and truly," cried the other with a kind of tickled modesty and pleased concern, "mine is an understanding too weak to throw out grapnels and hug another to it. I have indeed heard of some great scholars in these days, whose boast is less that they have made disciples than victims. But for me, had I the power to do such things, I have not the heart to desire."

"I believe you, my dear Charlie. And yet, I repeat, by your com-mentaries on Polonius you have, I know not how, unsettled me; so that now I don't exactly see how Shakespeare meant the words he puts in Polonius' mouth."

"Some say that he meant them to open people's eyes; but I don't think so."

"Open their eyes?" echoed the cosmopolitan, slowly expanding his; "what is there in this world for one to open his eyes to? I mean in the sort of invidious sense you cite?"

"Well, others say he meant to corrupt people's morals; and still others, that he had no express intention at all, but in effect opens their eyes and corrupts their morals in one operation. All of which I reject."

"Of course you reject so crude an hypothesis; and yet, to confess, in reading Shakespeare in my closet,[3] struck by some passage, I have laid down the volume, and said: 'This Shakespeare is a queer man.' At times seeming irresponsible, he does not always seem reli-able.[4] There appears to be a certain—what shall I call it?—hidden sun, say, about him, at once enlightening and mystifying. Now, I should be afraid to say what I have sometimes thought that hidden sun might be."

"Do you think it was the true light?" with clandestine geniality again filling the other's glass.

---

3. I.e., a private reading nook, a small study.
4. For the notion of Shakespeare as a "queer man" or "irresponsible" man, see Melville's theory in "Hawthorne and His Mosses" (2001 NCE of *Moby-Dick*, 517–32). The real Shakespeare is not "the all-popular" dramatist but the Shakespeare who has "deep far-away things in him; those occasional flashings-forth of the intuitive Truth in him; those short, quick probings at the very axis of reality"; through "the mouths of the dark char-acters of Hamlet, Timon, Lear, and Iago, he craftily says, or sometimes insinuates the things, which we feel to be so terrifically true, that it were all but madness for any good man, in his own proper character, to utter, or even hint of them" (522).

"I would prefer to decline answering a categorical question there. Shakespeare has got to be a kind of deity.[5] Prudent minds, having certain latent thoughts concerning him, will reserve them in a condition of lasting probation. Still, as touching avowable speculations, we are permitted a tether. Shakespeare himself is to be adored, not arraigned; but, so we do it with humility, we may a little canvass his characters. There's his Autolycus now, a fellow that always puzzled me. How is one to take Autolycus?[6] A rogue so happy, so lucky, so triumphant, of so almost captivatingly vicious a career that a virtuous man reduced to the poor-house (were such a contingency conceivable), might almost long to change sides with him. And yet, see the words put into his mouth: 'Oh,' cries Autolycus, as he comes galloping, gay as a buck, upon the stage, 'oh,' he laughs, 'oh what a fool is Honesty, and Trust, his sworn brother, a very simple gentleman.' Think of that. Trust, that is, confidence—that is, the thing in this universe the sacredest—is rattlingly pronounced just the simplest. And the scenes in which the rogue figures seem purposely devised for verification of his principles. Mind, Charlie, I do not say it *is* so, far from it; but I *do* say it seems so. Yes, Autolycus would seem a needy varlet acting upon the persuasion that less is to be got by invoking pockets than picking them, more to be made by an expert knave than a bungling beggar; and for this reason, as he thinks, that the soft heads outnumber the soft hearts. The devil's drilled recruit, Autolycus is joyous as if he wore the livery of heaven. When disturbed by the character and career of one thus wicked and thus happy, my sole consolation is in the fact that no such creature ever existed, except in the powerful imagination which evoked him. And yet, a creature, a living creature, he is, though only a poet was his maker. It may be, that in that paper-and-ink investiture of his, Autolycus acts more effectively upon mankind than he would in a flesh-and-blood one. Can his influence be salutary? True, in Autolycus there is humor; but though, according to my principle, humor is in general to be held a saving quality, yet the case of Autolycus is an exception; because it is his humor which, so to speak, oils his mischievousness. The bravadoing mischievousness of Autolycus is slid into the world on humor, as a pirate schooner, with colors flying, is launched into the sea on greased ways."

"I approve of Autolycus as little as you," said the stranger, who,

5. In "Hawthorne and His Mosses" (523–24), written halfway through the composition of *Moby-Dick*, Melville denounces the common assertion that Shakespeare is unapproachable, so great that he will never be equaled in the English language.
6. After Autolycus the robber in Greek myth, Shakespeare's Autolycus is a cunning, cynical, heartless trickster, a peddler of trashy goods, his eye on the main chance and the big haul. A consummate confidence man, he laughs, "what a fool Honesty is! And Trust, his sworn brother, a very simple gentleman!" (*The Winter's Tale* 4.4.595–96).

during his companion's commonplaces, had seemed less attentive to them than to maturing within his own mind the original conceptions destined to eclipse them. "But I cannot believe that Autolycus, mischievous as he must prove upon the stage, can be near so much so as such a character as Polonius."

"I don't know about that," bluntly, and yet not impolitely, returned the cosmopolitan; "to be sure, accepting your view of the old courtier, then if between him and Autolycus you raise the question of unprepossessingness, I grant you the latter comes off best. For a moist rogue may tickle the midriff, while a dry worldling may but wrinkle the spleen."

"But Polonius is not dry," said the other excitedly; "he drules. One sees the fly-blown old fop drule and look wise. His vile wisdom is made the viler by his vile rheuminess. The bowing and cringing, time-serving old sinner—is such an one to give manly precepts to youth? The discreet, decorous, old dotard-of-state; senile prudence; fatuous soullessness! The ribanded old dog is paralytic all down one side, and that the side of nobleness. His soul is gone out. Only nature's automatonism keeps him on his legs. As with some old trees, the bark survives the pith, and will still stand stiffly up, though but to rim round punk, so the body of old Polonius has outlived his soul."

"Come, come," said the cosmopolitan with serious air, almost displeased; "though I yield to none in admiration of earnestness, yet, I think, even earnestness may have limits. To humane minds, strong language is always more or less distressing. Besides, Polonius is an old man—as I remember him upon the stage—with snowy locks. Now charity requires that such a figure—think of it how you will—should at least be treated with civility. Moreover, old age is ripeness, and I once heard say, 'Better ripe than raw.' "

"But not better rotten than raw!" bringing down his hand with energy on the table.

"Why, bless me," in mild surprise contemplating his heated comrade, "how you fly out against this unfortunate Polonius—a being that never was, nor will be. And yet, viewed in a Christian light," he added pensively, "I don't know that anger against this man of straw is a whit less wise than anger against a man of flesh. Madness, to be mad with anything."

"That may be, or may not be," returned the other, a little testily, perhaps; "but I stick to what I said, that it is better to be raw than rotten. And what is to be feared on that head, may be known from this: that it is with the best of hearts as with the best of pears—a dangerous experiment to linger too long upon the scene. This did Polonius. Thank fortune, Frank, I am young, every tooth sound in my head, and if good wine can keep me where I am, long shall I remain so."

"True," with a smile. "But wine, to do good, must be drunk. You have talked much and well, Charlie; but drunk little and indifferently—fill up."

"Presently, presently," with a hasty and preoccupied air. "If I remember right, Polonius hints as much as that one should, under no circumstances, commit the indiscretion of aiding in a pecuniary way an unfortunate friend. He drules out some stale stuff about 'loan losing both itself and friend,' don't he? But our bottle; is it glued fast? Keep it moving, my dear Frank. Good wine, and upon my soul I begin to feel it, and through me old Polonius—yes, this wine, I fear, is what excites me so against that detestable old dog without a tooth."

Upon this, the cosmopolitan, cigar in mouth, slowly raised the bottle, and brought it slowly to the light, looking at it steadfastly, as one might at a thermometer in August, to see not how low it was, but how high. Then whiffing out a puff, set it down, and said: "Well, Charlie, if what wine you have drunk came out of this bottle, in that case I should say that if—supposing a case—that if one fellow had an object in getting another fellow fuddled, and this fellow to be fuddled was of your capacity, the operation would be comparatively inexpensive. What do you think, Charlie?"

"Why, I think I don't much admire the supposition," said Charlie, with a look of resentment; "it ain't safe, depend upon it, Frank, to venture upon too jocose suppositions with one's friends."

"Why, bless you, Charlie,[7] my supposition wasn't personal, but general. You mustn't be so touchy."

"If I am touchy it is the wine. Sometimes, when I freely drink it, it has a touchy effect on me, I have observed."

"Freely drink? you haven't drunk the perfect measure of one glass, yet. While for me, this must be my fourth or fifth, thanks to your importunity; not to speak of all I drank this morning, for old acquaintance' sake. Drink, drink; you must drink."

"Oh, I drink while you are talking," laughed the other; "you have not noticed it, but I have drunk my share. Have a queer way I learned from a sedate old uncle, who used to tip off his glass unperceived. Do you fill up, and my glass, too. There! Now away with that stump, and have a new cigar. Good fellowship forever!" again in the lyric mood. "Say, Frank, are we not men? I say are we not human? Tell me, were they not human who engendered us, as before heaven I believe they shall be whom we shall engender? Fill up, up, up, my friend. Let the ruby tide aspire, and all ruby aspirations with it! Up, fill up! Be we convivial. And conviviality, what is it? The

---

7. Leon Howard, in *Herman Melville: A Biography* (1951), pointed out the error in the 1857 text, where the name is "Frank."

word, I mean; what expresses it? A living together. But bats live together, and did you ever hear of convivial bats?"

"If I ever did," observed the cosmopolitan, "it has quite slipped
my recollection."

"But *why* did you never hear of convivial bats, nor anybody else?
Because bats, though they live together, live not together genially.
Bats are not genial souls. But men are; and how delightful to think
that the word which among men signifies the highest pitch of geniality, implies, as indispensable auxiliary, the cheery benediction of
the bottle. Yes, Frank, to live together in the finest sense, we must
drink together. And so, what wonder that he who loves not wine,
that sober wretch has a lean heart—a heart like a wrung-out old
bluing-bag, and loves not his kind? Out upon him, to the rag-house
with him, hang him—the ungenial soul!"

"Oh, now, now, can't you be convivial without being censorious?
I like easy, unexcited conviviality. For the sober man, really, though
for my part I naturally love a cheerful glass, I will not prescribe my
nature as the law to other natures. So don't abuse the sober man.
Conviviality is one good thing, and sobriety is another good thing.
So don't be one-sided."

"Well, if I am one-sided, it is the wine. Indeed, indeed, I have indulged too genially. My excitement upon slight provocation shows
it. But yours is a stronger head; drink you. By the way, talking of geniality, it is much on the increase in these days, ain't it?"

"It is, and I hail the fact. Nothing better attests the advance of
the humanitarian spirit. In former and less humanitarian ages—the
ages of amphitheatres and gladiators—geniality was mostly confined to the fireside and table. But in our age—the age of joint-
stock companies and free-and-easies[8]—it is with this precious
quality as with precious gold in old Peru, which Pizarro[9] found
making up the scullion's sauce-pot as the Inca's crown. Yes, we
golden boys, the moderns, have geniality everywhere—a bounty
broadcast like noonlight."

"True, true; my sentiments again. Geniality has invaded each department and profession. We have genial senators, genial authors,
genial lecturers, genial doctors, genial clergymen, genial surgeons,
and the next thing we shall have genial hangmen."

"As to the last-named sort of person," said the cosmopolitan, "I

8. Music halls or brothels as well as taverns. That is, in the modern world geniality does
not have to manifest itself only at home but in the cheerful larger world of magnanimous, confident joint business ventures, and convivial intercourse in welcoming taverns.
9. Francisco Pizarro (1478?–1541), Spanish conqueror of the Incans. He captured the Incan king Atahualipa in 1532 and, after extorting an enormous ransom, treacherously had
him killed in 1533. Americans had been fascinated by the telling of the story in William
Hickling Prescott's *History of the Conquest of Peru* (1847).

trust that the advancing spirit of geniality will at last enable us to dispense with him. No murderers—no hangmen. And surely, when the whole world shall have been genialized, it will be as out of place to talk of murderers, as in a Christianized world to talk of sinners."

"To pursue the thought," said the other, "every blessing is attended with some evil, and—"

"Stay," said the cosmopolitan, "that may be better let pass for a loose saying, than for hopeful doctrine."

"Well, assuming the saying's truth, it would apply to the future supremacy of the genial spirit, since then it will fare with the hangman as it did with the weaver when the spinning-jenny whizzed into the ascendant. Thrown out of employment, what could Jack Ketch[1] turn his hand to? Butchering?"

"That he could turn his hand to it seems probable; but that, under the circumstances, it would be appropriate, might in some minds admit of a question. For one, I am inclined to think—and I trust it will not be held fastidiousness—that it would hardly be suitable to the dignity of our nature, that an individual, once employed in attending the last hours of human unfortunates, should, that office being extinct, transfer himself to the business of attending the last hours of unfortunate cattle. I would suggest that the individual turn valet—a vocation to which he would, perhaps, appear not wholly inadapted by his familiar dexterity about the person. In particular, for giving a finishing tie to a gentleman's cravat, I know few who would, in all likelihood, be, from previous occupation, better fitted than the professional person in question."

"Are you in earnest?" regarding the serene speaker with unaffected curiosity; "are you really in earnest?"

"I trust I am never otherwise," was the mildly earnest reply; "but talking of the advance of geniality, I am not without hopes that it will eventually exert its influence even upon so difficult a subject as the misanthrope."

"A genial misanthrope! I thought I had stretched the rope pretty hard in talking of genial hangmen. A genial misanthrope is no more conceivable than a surly philanthropist."

"True," lightly depositing in an unbroken little cylinder the ashes of his cigar, "true, the two you name are well opposed."

"Why, you talk as if there *was* such a being as a surly philanthropist."

"I do. My eccentric friend, whom you call Coonskins, is an example. Does he not, as I explained to you, hide under a surly air a philanthropic heart? Now, the genial misanthrope, when, in the process of eras, he shall turn up, will be the converse of this; under

---

1. Notorious hangman under Charles II, remembered for bungling the beheadings of Lord Russell (1683) and the duke of Monmouth (1685).

an affable air, he will hide a misanthropical heart. In short, the genial misanthrope will be a new kind of monster, but still no small
improvement upon the original one, since, instead of making faces
and throwing stones at people, like that poor old crazy man, Timon,
he will take steps, fiddle in hand, and set the tickled world a' dancing. In a word, as the progress of Christianization mellows those in
manner whom it cannot mend in mind, much the same will it prove
with the progress of genialization. And so, thanks to geniality, the
misanthrope, reclaimed from his boorish address, will take on refinement and softness—to so genial a degree, indeed, that it may
possibly fall out that the misanthrope of the coming century will be
almost as popular as, I am sincerely sorry to say, some philanthropists of the present time would seem not to be, as witness my eccentric friend named before."

"Well," cried the other, a little weary, perhaps, of a speculation so
abstract, "well, however it may be with the century to come, certainly in the century which is, whatever else one may be, he must
be genial or he is nothing. So fill up, fill up, and be genial!"

"I am trying my best," said the cosmopolitan, still calmly companionable. "A moment since, we talked of Pizarro, gold, and Peru;
no doubt, now, you remember that when the Spaniard first entered
Atahalpa's treasure-chamber, and saw such profusion of plate
stacked up, right and left, with the wantonness of old barrels in a
brewer's yard, the needy fellow felt a twinge of misgiving, of want of
confidence, as to the genuineness of an opulence so profuse. He
went about rapping the shining vases with his knuckles. But it was
all gold, pure gold, good gold, sterling gold, which how cheerfully
would have been stamped such at Goldsmiths' Hall.[2] And just so
those needy minds, which, through their own insincerity, having no
confidence in mankind, doubt lest the liberal geniality of this age
be spurious. They are small Pizarros in their way—by the very
princeliness of men's geniality stunned into distrust of it."

"Far be such distrust from you and me, my genial friend," cried
the other fervently; "fill up, fill up!"

"Well, this all along seems a division of labor," smiled the cosmopolitan. "I do about all the drinking, and you do about all—the
genial. But yours is a nature competent to do that to a large population. And now, my friend," with a peculiarly grave air, evidently
foreshadowing something not unimportant, and very likely of close
personal interest; "wine, you know, opens the heart, and—"

"Opens it!" with exultation, "it thaws it right out. Every heart is
ice-bound till wine melt it, and reveal the tender grass and sweet

---

2. Site in London where gold articles were tested for purity and then stamped before receiving governmental authorization to be sold. The word *hallmark* literally means a mark
applied at Goldsmiths' Hall.

herbage budding below, with every dear secret, hidden before like a dropped jewel in a snow-bank, lying there unsuspected through winter till spring."

"And just in that way, my dear Charlie, is one of my little secrets now to be shown forth."

"Ah!" eagerly moving round his chair, "what is it?"

"Be not so impetuous, my dear Charlie. Let me explain. You see, naturally, I am a man not overgifted with assurance; in general, I am, if anything, diffidently reserved; so, if I shall presently seem otherwise, the reason is, that you, by the geniality you have evinced in all your talk, and especially the noble way in which, while affirming your good opinion of men, you intimated that you never could prove false to any man, but most by your indignation at a particularly illiberal passage in Polonius' advice—in short, in short," with extreme embarrassment, "how shall I express what I mean, unless I add that by your whole character you impel me to throw myself upon your nobleness; in one word, put confidence in you, a generous confidence?"

"I see, I see," with heightened interest, "something of moment you wish to confide. Now, what is it, Frank? Love affair?"

"No, not that."

"What, then, my *dear* Frank? Speak—depend upon me to the last. Out with it."

"Out it shall come, then," said the cosmopolitan. "I am in want, urgent want, of money."

Chapter 31.

A METAMORPHOSIS MORE SURPRISING THAN ANY IN OVID.[3]

"In want of money!" pushing back his chair as from a suddenly-disclosed man-trap or crater.

"Yes," naïvely assented the cosmopolitan, "and you are going to loan me fifty dollars. I could almost wish I was in need of more, only for your sake. Yes, my dear Charlie, for your sake; that you might the better prove your noble kindliness, my dear Charlie."

"None of your dear Charlies," cried the other, springing to his feet, and buttoning up his coat, as if hastily to depart upon a long journey.

"Why, why, why?" painfully looking up.

"None of your why, why, whys!" tossing out a foot, "go to the devil, sir! Beggar, impostor!—never so deceived in a man in my life."

---

3. The *Metamorphoses* by the Roman poet Ovid, or Publius Ovidius Naso (43 B.C.E.–17 C.E.), contains many stories of magical transformations such as Philomel's becoming a nightingale, referred to in chapter 10. Melville was seeing *The Confidence-Man* as his own *Metamorphoses*, although some of the shape changing he depicts is less a matter of exterior form than in Ovid.

Chapter 32.

SHOWING THAT THE AGE OF MAGIC AND MAGICIANS IS NOT YET OVER.

While speaking or rather hissing those words, the boon companion underwent much such a change as one reads of in fairy-books. Out of old materials sprang a new creature. Cadmus glided into the snake.[4]

The cosmopolitan rose, the traces of previous feeling vanished; looked steadfastly at his transformed friend a moment, then, taking ten half-eagles from his pocket, stooped down, and laid them, one by one, in a circle round him; and, retiring a pace, waved his long tasseled pipe with the air of a necromancer, an air heightened by his costume, accompanying each wave with a solemn murmur of cabalistical words.

Meantime, he within the magic-ring stood suddenly rapt, exhibiting every symptom of a successful charm—a turned cheek, a fixed attitude, a frozen eye; spellbound, not more by the waving wand than by the ten invincible talismans on the floor.

"Reappear, reappear, reappear, oh, my former friend! Replace this hideous apparition with thy blest shape, and be the token of thy return the words, 'My dear Frank.' "

"My dear Frank," now cried the restored friend, cordially stepping out of the ring, with regained self-possession regaining lost identity, "My dear Frank, what a funny man you are; full of fun as an egg of meat. How could you tell me that absurd story of your being in need? But I relish a good joke too well to spoil it by letting on. Of course, I humored the thing; and, on my side, put on all the cruel airs you would have me. Come, this little episode of fictitious estrangement will but enhance the delightful reality. Let us sit down again, and finish our bottle."

"With all my heart," said the cosmopolitan, dropping the necromancer with the same facility with which he had assumed it. "Yes," he added, soberly picking up the gold pieces, and returning them with a chink to his pocket, "yes, I am something of a funny man

4. In Greek myth as retold in Ovid's *Metamorphoses* Cadmus killed a giant snake that had killed his men and stared at it until Athena warned him that one day he would become a snake himself. Throughout a long and seemingly blessed life he forgot the prophecy, but in the end he was turned into a snake. The word *glided* connects Melville's imagery for classical metamorphoses (and shape changing in more recent secular and religious literature) to his recurrent and perhaps highly idiosyncratic imagery for thought processes and the phenomenon of dissolving and merging scenes and identities, which is obvious in his works since *Omoo* (1847). Soon after his intense engagement with Shakespeare's plays in 1849, Melville seized on Prospero's imagery in his famous repudiation of his powers to describe this peculiar phenomenon he had long recognized in himself, a tendency to perceive one real or imaginary figure merging into another and perhaps reforming into the original shape—very much like the modern idea of morphing (see Parker 2.12–15).

now and then; while for you, Charlie," eying him in tenderness, "what you say about your humoring the thing is true enough; never did man second a joke better than you did just now. You played your part better than I did mine; you played it, Charlie, to the life."

"You see, I once belonged to an amateur play company; that accounts for it. But come, fill up, and let's talk of something else."

"Well," acquiesced the cosmopolitan, seating himself, and quietly brimming his glass, "what shall we talk about?"

"Oh, anything you please," a sort of nervously accommodating.

"Well, suppose we talk about Charlemont?"

"Charlemont? What's Charlemont? Who's Charlemont?"

"You shall hear, my dear Charlie," answered the cosmopolitan. "I will tell you the story of Charlemont, the gentleman-madman."

Chapter 33.

WHICH MAY PASS FOR WHATEVER IT MAY PROVE TO BE WORTH.

But ere be given the rather grave story of Charlemont, a reply must in civility be made to a certain voice which methinks I hear, that, in view of past chapters, and more particularly the last, where certain antics appear, exclaims: How unreal all this is! Who did ever dress or act like your cosmopolitan? And who, it might be returned, did ever dress or act like harlequin?

Strange, that in a work of amusement, this severe fidelity to real life should be exacted by any one, who, by taking up such a work, sufficiently shows that he is not unwilling to drop real life, and turn, for a time, to something different. Yes, it is, indeed, strange that any one should clamor for the thing he is weary of; that any one, who, for any cause, finds real life dull, should yet demand of him who is to divert his attention from it, that he should be true to that dullness.

There is another class, and with this class we side, who sit down to a work of amusement tolerantly as they sit at a play, and with much the same expectations and feelings. They look that fancy shall evoke scenes different from those of the same old crowd round the custom-house counter, and same old dishes on the boarding-house table, with characters unlike those of the same old acquaintances they meet in the same old way every day in the same old street. And as, in real life, the proprieties will not allow people to act out themselves with that unreserve permitted to the stage; so, in books of fiction, they look not only for more entertainment, but, at bottom, even for more reality, than real life itself can show. Thus, though they want novelty, they want nature, too; but nature unfettered, exhilarated, in effect transformed. In this way of thinking, the people in a fiction, like the people in a play, must dress as nobody exactly dresses, talk as nobody exactly talks, act as nobody exactly acts. It is with fiction as with religion: it should present another world, and yet one to which we feel the tie.

If, then, something is to be pardoned to well-meant endeavor, surely a little is to be allowed to that writer who, in all his scenes, does but seek to minister to what, as he understands it, is the implied wish of the more indulgent lovers of entertainment, before whom harlequin can never appear in a coat too parti-colored, or cut capers too fantastic.

One word more. Though every one knows how bootless it is to be in all cases vindicating one's self, never mind how convinced one may be that he is never in the wrong; yet, so precious to man is the approbation of his kind, that to rest, though but under an imaginary censure applied to but a work of imagination, is no easy thing. The mention of this weakness will explain why all such readers as may think they perceive something inharmonious between the boisterous hilarity of the cosmopolitan with the bristling cynic, and his restrained good-nature with the boon-companion, are now referred to that chapter[5] where some similar apparent inconsistency in another character is, on general principles, modestly endeavored to be apologized for.

Chapter 34.

IN WHICH THE COSMOPOLITAN TELLS THE STORY OF THE GENTLEMAN-MADMAN.

"Charlemont was a young merchant of French descent, living in St. Louis—a man not deficient in mind, and possessed of that sterling and captivating kindliness, seldom in perfection seen but in youthful bachelors, united at times to a remarkable sort of gracefully devil-may-care and witty good-humor. Of course, he was admired by everybody, and loved, as only mankind can love, by not a few. But in his twenty-ninth year a change came over him. Like one whose hair turns gray in a night, so in a day Charlemont turned from affable to morose. His acquaintances were passed without greeting; while, as for his confidential friends, them he pointedly, unscrupulously, and with a kind of fierceness, cut dead.

"One, provoked by such conduct, would fain have resented it with words as disdainful; while another, shocked by the change, and, in concern for a friend, magnanimously overlooking affronts, implored to know what sudden, secret grief had distempered him. But from resentment and from tenderness Charlemont alike turned away.

5. I.e., chapter 14.

"Ere long, to the general surprise, the merchant Charlemont was gazetted,[6] and the same day it was reported that he had withdrawn from town, but not before placing his entire property in the hands of responsible assignees for the benefit of creditors.

"Whither he had vanished, none could guess. At length, nothing being heard, it was surmised that he must have made away with himself—a surmise, doubtless, originating in the remembrance of the change some months previous to his bankruptcy—a change of a sort only to be ascribed to a mind suddenly thrown from its balance.

"Years passed. It was spring-time, and lo, one bright morning, Charlemont lounged into the St. Louis coffee-houses—gay, polite, humane, companionable, and dressed in the height of costly elegance. Not only was he alive, but he was himself again. Upon meeting with old acquaintances, he made the first advances, and in such a manner that it was impossible not to meet him half-way. Upon other old friends, whom he did not chance casually to meet, he either personally called, or left his card and compliments for them; and to several, sent presents of game or hampers of wine.

"They say the world is sometimes harshly unforgiving, but it was not so to Charlemont. The world feels a return of love for one who returns to it as he did. Expressive of its renewed interest was a whisper, an inquiring whisper, how now, exactly, so long after his bankruptcy, it fared with Charlemont's purse. Rumor, seldom at a loss for answers, replied that he had spent nine years in Marseilles in France, and there acquiring a second fortune, had returned with it, a man devoted henceforth to genial friendships.

"Added years went by, and the restored wanderer still the same; or rather, by his noble qualities, grew up like golden maize in the encouraging sun of good opinions. But still the latent wonder was, what had caused that change in him at a period when, pretty much as now, he was, to all appearance, in the possession of the same fortune, the same friends, the same popularity. But nobody thought it would be the thing to question him here.

"At last, at a dinner at his house, when all the guests but one had successively departed; this remaining guest, an old acquaintance, being just enough under the influence of wine to set aside the fear of touching upon a delicate point, ventured, in a way which perhaps spoke more favorably for his heart than his tact, to beg of his host to explain the one enigma of his life. Deep melancholy overspread the before cheery face of Charlemont; he sat for some moments tremulously silent; then pushing a full decanter towards the guest, in a choked voice, said: 'No, no! when by art, and care, and

---

6. Listed in newspaper notices of bankruptcies.

time, flowers are made to bloom over a grave, who would seek to dig all up again only to know the mystery?—The wine.' When both glasses were filled, Charlemont took his, and lifting it, added lowly: 'If ever, in days to come, you shall see ruin at hand, and, thinking you understand mankind, shall tremble for your friendships, and tremble for your pride; and, partly through love for the one and fear for the other, shall resolve to be beforehand with the world, and save it from a sin by prospectively taking that sin to yourself, then will you do as one I now dream of once did, and like him will you suffer; but how fortunate and how grateful should you be, if like him, after all that had happened, you could be a little happy again.'

"When the guest went away, it was with the persuasion, that though outwardly restored in mind as in fortune, yet, some taint of Charlemont's old malady survived, and that it was not well for friends to touch one dangerous string."

Chapter 35.

IN WHICH THE COSMOPOLITAN STRIKINGLY EVINCES THE ARTLESSNESS OF HIS NATURE.

"Well, what do you think of the story of Charlemont?" mildly asked he who had told it.

"A very strange one," answered the auditor, who had been such not with perfect ease, "but is it true?"

"Of course not; it is a story which I told with the purpose of every story-teller—to amuse. Hence, if it seem strange to you, that strangeness is the romance; it is what contrasts it with real life; it is the invention, in brief, the fiction as opposed to the fact. For do but ask yourself, my dear Charlie," lovingly leaning over towards him, "I rest it with your own heart now, whether such a forereaching motive as Charlemont hinted he had acted on in his change—whether such a motive, I say, were a sort of one at all justified by the nature of human society? Would you, for one, turn the cold shoulder to a friend—a convivial one, say, whose pennilessness should be suddenly revealed to you?"

"How can you ask me, my dear Frank? You know I would scorn such meanness." But rising somewhat disconcerted—"really, early as it is, I think I must retire; my head," putting up his hand to it, "feels unpleasantly; this confounded elixir of logwood,[7] little as I drank of it, has played the deuce with me."

"Little as you drank of this elixir of logwood? Why, Charlie, you

---

7. A decoction for bellyache was made from chips of the Mexican or West Indian tree logwood, with cinnamon added to make it palatable. Logwood was also used to color adulterated red wine.

are losing your mind. To talk so of the genuine, mellow old port. Yes, I think that by all means you had better away, and sleep it off. There—don't apologize—don't explain—go, go—I understand you exactly. I will see you to-morrow."

Chapter 36.

IN WHICH THE COSMOPOLITAN IS ACCOSTED BY A MYSTIC, WHEREUPON ENSUES PRETTY MUCH SUCH TALK AS MIGHT BE EXPECTED.

As, not without some haste, the boon companion withdrew, a stranger advanced, and touching the cosmopolitan, said: "I think I heard you say you would see that man again. Be warned; don't you do so."

He turned, surveying the speaker; a blue-eyed man, sandy-haired, and Saxon-looking; perhaps five and forty; tall, and, but for a certain angularity, well made; little touch of the drawing-room about him, but a look of plain propriety of a Puritan sort, with a kind of farmer dignity.[8] His age seemed betokened more by his brow, placidly thoughtful, than by his general aspect, which had that look of youthfulness in maturity, peculiar sometimes to habitual health of body, the original gift of nature, or in part the effect or reward of steady temperance of the passions, kept so, perhaps, by constitution as much as morality. A neat, comely, almost ruddy cheek, coolly fresh, like a red clover-blossom at coolish dawn—the color of warmth preserved by the virtue of chill. Toning the whole man, was one-knows-not-what of shrewdness and mythiness,[9] strangely jumbled; in that way, he seemed a kind of cross between a Yankee peddler and a Tartar priest,[1] though it seemed as if, at a

8. Egbert S. Oliver (1946) first argued in detail that Mark Winsome is modeled physically and philosophically on Ralph Waldo Emerson (1803–1882), failed Unitarian minister, successful lecturer and essayist. The effectiveness of the portrait depends on its being one sided; as he marked his copy of Emerson's essays, Melville alternatively disdained Emerson for his obliviousness to human suffering and admired him for his persistent challenging of received opinion. For Melville, in his blindness to human suffering Emerson was still very much a New England Unitarian (Parker 2.66–67).

9. Watson G. Branch's conjecture that "mythiness" is an error for "mysticness" is possible. *Mistiness* is a less powerful word, but *mist* is used in *A Fable for Critics* (see n. 1, below). Melville had learned much of Emerson and Thoreau from his friend Evert A. Duyckinck and would have seen this comment, very likely by Duyckinck, in the New York *Literary World* for October 16, 1847: "Ingenuity and Yankee shrewdness is the forte of Mr. Emerson, obscured or enlightened as the case may be, by his Platonic and Transcendental doctrine or modes of expression." In a letter from Boston to Duyckinck (March 3, 1849) Melville said that he had expected to find Emerson, as a lecturer, "full of transcendentalisms, myths, & oracular gibberish" but had been pleasantly surprised to find him "quite intelligible." He found one gaping flaw: "the insinuation, that had he lived in those days when the world was made, he might have offered some valuable suggestions." In his characterization of Emerson as a "Plato who talks thro' his nose" Melville was acknowledging the combination of Greek idealism and Yankee shrewdness even while calling attention to Emerson's Yankee accent.

1. Emerson the embodier of contradictions was a commonplace already, as in James Russell Lowell's popular satiric poem, *A Fable for Critics* (1848), where Emerson is said to

pinch, the first would not in all probability play second fiddle to the last.

"Sir," said the cosmopolitan, rising and bowing with slow dignity, "if I cannot with unmixed satisfaction hail a hint pointed at one who has just been clinking the social glass with me, on the other hand, I am not disposed to underrate the motive which, in the present case, could alone have prompted such an intimation. My friend, whose seat is still warm, has retired for the night, leaving more or less in his bottle here. Pray, sit down in his seat, and partake with me; and then, if you choose to hint aught further unfavorable to the man, the genial warmth of whose person in part passes into yours, and whose genial hospitality meanders through you—be it so."

"Quite beautiful conceits," said the stranger, now scholastically and artistically eying the picturesque speaker, as if he were a statue in the Pitti Palace;[2] "very beautiful:" then with the gravest interest, "yours, sir, if I mistake not, must be a beautiful soul—one full of all love and truth; for where beauty is, there must those be."

"A pleasing belief," rejoined the cosmopolitan, beginning with an even air, "and to confess, long ago it pleased me. Yes, with you and Schiller,[3] I am pleased to believe that beauty is at bottom incompatible with ill, and therefore am so eccentric as to have confidence in the latent benignity of that beautiful creature, the rattle-snake, whose lithe neck and burnished maze of tawny gold, as he sleekly curls aloft in the sun, who on the prairie can behold without wonder?"

As he breathed these words, he seemed so to enter into their spirit—as some earnest descriptive speakers will—as unconsciously to wreathe his form and sidelong crest his head, till he all but seemed the creature described. Meantime, the stranger regarded him with little surprise, apparently, though with much contemplativeness of a mystical sort, and presently said: "When charmed by the beauty of that viper, did it never occur to you to change personalities with him? to feel what it was to be a snake? to glide unsuspected in grass? to sting, to kill at a touch; your whole beautiful

---

have "A Greek head on right Yankee shoulders, whose range / Has Olympus for one pole, for t'other the Exchange" (i.e., the stock market). Furthermore, he is "A Plotinus-Montaigne, where the Egyptian's gold mist / And the Gascon's shrewd wit cheek-by-jowl co-exist" (Plotinus the ancient Egyptian mystic, Montaigne being from Gascony, in France.) Lowell included Duyckinck (unadmiringly) in this survey of American literature and its promoters, but not Melville, although he knew Melville's first book, *Typee*, (1846).

2. In Florence, Italy, which houses a large collection of sixteenth- and seventeenth-century works of art, principally by Italian masters such as Michelangelo and Raphael. Melville visited the Pitti Palace in March 1857, after completing *The Confidence-Man*.

3. Johann Christoph Friedrich von Schiller (1759–1805), German dramatist, poet, historian, and aesthetic theorist. His essay "On the Sublime" is often read as if he equated the beautiful with the good, as English Neo-Platonists did in the seventeenth century.

body one iridescent scabbard of death? In short, did the wish never occur to you to feel yourself exempt from knowledge, and conscience, and revel for a while in the care-free, joyous life of a perfectly instinctive, unscrupulous, and irresponsible creature?"

"Such a wish," replied the other, not perceptibly disturbed, "I must confess, never consciously was mine. Such a wish, indeed, could hardly occur to ordinary imaginations, and mine I cannot think much above the average."

"But now that the idea is suggested," said the stranger, with infantile intellectuality, "does it not raise the desire?"

"Hardly. For though I do not think I have any uncharitable prejudice against the rattle-snake, still, I should not like to be one. If I were a rattle-snake now, there would be no such thing as being genial with men—men would be afraid of me, and then I should be a very lonesome and miserable rattle-snake."

"True, men would be afraid of you. And why? Because of your rattle, your hollow rattle—a sound, as I have been told, like the shaking together of small, dry skulls in a tune of the Waltz of Death.[4] And here we have another beautiful truth. When any creature is by its make inimical to other creatures, nature in effect labels that creature, much as an apothecary does a poison. So that whoever is destroyed by a rattle-snake, or other harmful agent, it is his own fault. He should have respected the label. Hence that significant passage in Scripture, 'Who will pity the charmer that is bitten with a serpent?' "[5]

"*I* would pity him," said the cosmopolitan, a little bluntly, perhaps.

"But don't you think," rejoined the other, still maintaining his passionless air, "don't you think, that for a man to pity where nature is pitiless, is a little presuming?"

"Let casuists decide the casuistry, but the compassion the heart decides for itself. But, sir," deepening in seriousness, "as I now for the first realize, you but a moment since introduced the word irresponsible in a way I am not used to. Now, sir, though, out of a tolerant spirit, as I hope, I try my best never to be frightened at any speculation, so long as it is pursued in honesty, yet, for once, I must acknowledge that you do really, in the point cited, cause me uneasiness; because a proper view of the universe, that view which is suited to breed a proper confidence, teaches, if I err not, that since all things are justly presided over, not very many living agents but must be some way accountable."

---

4. One "Waltz of Death" was included in London performances of "The Phantom Dancers; or, The Wili's Bride," beginning in 1846.
5. In the Apocrypha, Ecclesiasticus 12.13: "Who will pity a charmer that is bitten with a serpent, or any such as come nigh wild beasts?"

"Is a rattle-snake accountable?" asked the stranger with such a preternaturally cold, gemmy glance out of his pellucid blue eye, that he seemed more a metaphysical merman than a feeling man; "is a rattle-snake accountable?"

"If I will not affirm that it is," returned the other, with the caution of no inexperienced thinker, "neither will I deny it. But if we suppose it so, I need not say that such accountability is neither to you, nor me, nor the Court of Common Pleas, but to something superior."[6]

He was proceeding, when the stranger would have interrupted him; but as reading his argument in his eye, the cosmopolitan, without waiting for it to be put into words, at once spoke to it: "You object to my supposition, for but such it is, that the rattle-snake's accountability is not by nature manifest; but might not much the same thing be urged against man's? A *reductio ad absurdum*, proving the objection vain. But if now," he continued, "you consider what capacity for mischief there is in a rattle-snake (observe, I do not charge it with being mischievous, I but say it has the capacity), could you well avoid admitting that that would be no symmetrical view of the universe which should maintain that, while to man it is forbidden to kill, without judicial cause, his fellow, yet the rattle-snake has an implied permit of unaccountability to murder any creature it takes capricious umbrage at—man included?—But," with a wearied air, "this is no genial talk; at least it is not so to me. Zeal at unawares embarked me in it. I regret it. Pray, sit down, and take some of this wine."

"Your suggestions are new to me," said the other, with a kind of condescending appreciativeness, as of one who, out of devotion to knowledge, disdains not to appropriate the least crumb of it, even from a pauper's board; "and, as I am a very Athenian in hailing a new thought,[7] I cannot consent to let it drop so abruptly. Now, the rattle-snake—"

"Nothing more about rattle-snakes, I beseech," in distress; "I must positively decline to reënter upon that subject. Sit down, sir, I beg, and take some of this wine."

"To invite me to sit down with you is hospitable," collaterally acquiescing now in the change of topics; "and hospitality being fabled to be of oriental origin, and forming, as it does, the subject of a pleasing Arabian romance, as well as being a very romantic thing in itself—hence I always hear the expressions of hospitality with

6. Something superior is either worldly, like a supreme court, or in this book suffused with references to the Book of Revelation, an otherworldly court, the "Last Assizes" (Melville in *Billy Budd*) or the Last Judgment (see also n. 3, p. 55, and n. 7, p. 152).

7. As open minded as an ideally liberal resident of Athens at the height of classical Greek civilization.

pleasure.[8] But, as for the wine, my regard for that beverage is so extreme, and I am so fearful of letting it sate me, that I keep my love for it in the lasting condition of an untried abstraction. Briefly, I quaff immense draughts of wine from the page of Hafiz,[9] but wine from a cup I seldom as much as sip."

The cosmopolitan turned a mild glance upon the speaker, who, now occupying the chair opposite him, sat there purely and coldly radiant as a prism. It seemed as if one could almost hear him vitreously chime and ring. That moment a waiter passed, whom, arresting with a sign, the cosmopolitan bid go bring a goblet of ice-water.[1] "Ice it well, waiter," said he; "and now," turning to the stranger, "will you, if you please, give me your reason for the warning words you first addressed to me?"

"I hope they were not such warnings as most warnings are," said the stranger; "warnings which do not forewarn, but in mockery come after the fact. And yet something in you bids me think now, that whatever latent design your impostor friend might have had upon you, it as yet remains unaccomplished. You read his label."

"And what did it say? 'This is a genial soul.' So you see you must either give up your doctrine of labels, or else your prejudice against my friend. But tell me," with renewed earnestness, "what do you take him for? What is he?"

"What are you? What am I? Nobody knows who anybody is. The data which life furnishes, towards forming a true estimate of any being, are as insufficient to that end as in geometry one side given would be to determine the triangle."

"But is not this doctrine of triangles someway inconsistent with your doctrine of labels?"

"Yes; but what of that? I seldom care to be consistent.[2] In a philosophical view, consistency is a certain level at all times, maintained in all the thoughts of one's mind. But, since nature is nearly all hill

8. In *The Arabian Nights* and other literature, as in life, Arabs were known for their elaborate, formal hospitality.
9. Fourteenth-century Persian poet, known for his lyrics celebrating love and wine. Melville knew some of Hafiz's poems in translation as early as 1850.
1. In "The Poet" (1844) Emerson does not condemn drugs but on the contrary makes clear that he understands "why bards love wine, mead, narcotics, coffee, tea, opium, the fumes of sandalwood and tobacco" and all other "coarser or finer *quasi*-mechanical substitutes for the true nectar, which is the ravishment of the intellect by coming nearer to the fact." Yet such appealing substitutes are delusive, he holds, because no one can ever take any advantage of Nature "by a trick." Emerson concludes that "the poet's habit of living should be set on a key so low that the common influences should delight him. His cheerfulness should be the gift of the sunlight; the air should suffice for his inspiration, and he should be tipsy with water." (*Inspiration* carries the sense of the fumes or smells the poet breathes in.)
2. An allusion to an already famous and later a notoriously misunderstood passage in Emerson's "Self-Reliance" (1841): "A foolish consistency is the hobgoblin of little minds, adored by little statesmen and philosophers and divines. With consistency a great soul has simply nothing to do" ("divines": ministers). When quoted, the crucial word *foolish* is often omitted.

and dale, how can one keep naturally advancing in knowledge without submitting to the natural inequalities in the progress? Advance
into knowledge is just like advance upon the grand Erie canal,
where, from the character of the country, change of level is inevitable; you are locked up and locked down[3] with perpetual inconsistencies, and yet all the time you get on; while the dullest part of
the whole route is what the boatmen call the 'long level'—a consis-
tently-flat surface of sixty miles through stagnant swamps."

"In one particular," rejoined the cosmopolitan, "your simile is,
perhaps, unfortunate. For, after all these weary lockings-up and
lockings-down, upon how much of a higher plain do you finally
stand? Enough to make it an object? Having from youth been
taught reverence for knowledge, you must pardon me if, on but this
one account, I reject your analogy. But really you someway bewitch
me with your tempting discourse, so that I keep straying from my
point unawares. You tell me you cannot certainly know who or what
my friend is; pray, what do you conjecture him to be?"

"I conjecture him to be what, among the ancient Egyptians, was
called a ——" using some unknown word.[4]

"A ——! And what is that?"

"A —— is what Proclus,[5] in a little note to his third book on the
theology of Plato, defines as —— ——" coming out with a sentence
of Greek.

Holding up his glass, and steadily looking through its transparency, the cosmopolitan rejoined: "That, in so defining the thing,
Proclus set it to modern understandings in the most crystal light it
was susceptible of, I will not rashly deny; still, if you could put the
definition in words suited to perceptions like mine, I should take it
for a favor."

"A favor!" slightly lifting his cool eyebrows; "a bridal favor I un-

---

3. Authorized by the New York State legislature in 1817, the Erie Canal opened in 1825,
   stretching from Albany on the navigable Hudson River to Buffalo, linking the Great
   Lakes (and later the upper Midwest) to New York City and the Atlantic. Because of elevation differences, boats had to move from one level to another through eighty-three
   locks, stopping in "lock chambers" until they were floated to the level of each new lock
   or canal segment. (Melville unsuccessfully tried to gain employment on the canal as a
   surveyor in 1839.)
4. A standard jibe by journalists for secular papers was that the Transcendentalists were
   unintelligible; but religious conservatives raised the more serious allegation that they
   were heretical. Parsons Cooke (1800–1864), the rigorously Calvinistic minister of the
   Lynn, Massachusetts, First Congregational Church, had denounced Unitarianism as
   early as 1829 and was a vigorous opponent of Transcendentalism (as an offshoot of Unitarianism). In 1857, as editor of the Boston *Puritan Recorder*, Cooke described the lecture system as attempting to substitute itself for the preaching of the Gospel. An acute
   comment on this controversy can be found in the Boston *Christian Freeman and Family
   Visiter* [sic] for April 24, 1857.
5. The last major classical Greek philosopher, in what was by then Byzantium, Proclus
   (412?–485 C.E.) wrote treatises on the theological ideas of Plato (427?–347 B.C.E.), the
   great Greek philosopher and aesthetician. Emersonian Transcendentalism includes aspects of Platonic idealism.

derstand, a knot of white ribands, a very beautiful type of the purity of true marriage; but of other favors I am yet to learn; and still, in a vague way, the word, as you employ it, strikes me as unpleasingly significant in general of some poor, unheroic submission to being done good to."

Here the goblet of iced-water was brought, and, in compliance with a sign from the cosmopolitan, was placed before the stranger, who, not before expressing acknowledgments, took a draught, apparently refreshing—its very coldness, as with some is the case, proving not entirely uncongenial.

At last, setting down the goblet, and gently wiping from his lips the beads of water freshly clinging there as to the valve of a coral-shell upon a reef, he turned upon the cosmopolitan, and, in a manner the most cool, self-possessed, and matter-of-fact possible, said: "I hold to the metempsychosis; and whoever I may be now, I feel that I was once the stoic Arrian,[6] and have inklings of having been equally puzzled by a word in the current language of that former time, very probably answering to your word *favor*."

"Would you favor me by explaining?" said the cosmopolitan, blandly.

"Sir," responded the stranger, with a very slight degree of severity, "I like lucidity, of all things, and am afraid I shall hardly be able to converse satisfactorily with you, unless you bear it in mind."

The cosmopolitan ruminatingly eyed him awhile, then said: "The best way, as I have heard, to get out of a labyrinth, is to retrace one's steps. I will accordingly retrace mine, and beg you will accompany me. In short, once again to return to the point: for what reason did you warn me against my friend?"

"Briefly, then, and clearly, because, as before said, I conjecture him to be what, among the ancient Egyptians—"

"Pray, now," earnestly deprecated the cosmopolitan, "pray, now, why disturb the repose of those ancient Egyptians? What to us are their words or their thoughts? Are we pauper Arabs, without a house of our own, that, with the mummies, we must turn squatters among the dust of the Catacombs?"[7]

"Pharaoh's poorest brick-maker[8] lies proudlier in his rags than the Emperor of all the Russias in his hollands," oracularly said the

---

6. Born in Bithynia in what is now northwest Turkey (95?–180), published his student notes on the lectures of the stoic Epictetus and later became a military historian.
7. Underground cemeteries used in ancient times throughout the Mediterranean world. In Egypt there are catacombs near Alexandria and Cairo.
8. The humblest Hebrew in Egypt, as described in Exodus 1.14: "And they [the Egyptian taskmasters, or overseers] made their lives bitter with hard bondage, in morter, and in brick, and in all manner of service in the field: all their service, wherein they made them serve, was with rigour." When Pharaoh became angered, he stopped providing the Hebrews with straw necessary to make bricks. They were forced to gather the straw themselves, yet produce the same number of bricks as before (Exodus 5.6–18).

stranger; "for death, though in a worm, is majestic; while life, though in a king, is contemptible. So talk not against mummies. It is a part of my mission to teach mankind a due reverence for mummies."

Fortunately, to arrest these incoherencies, or rather, to vary them, a haggard, inspired-looking man now approached—a crazy beggar, asking alms under the form of peddling a rhapsodical tract, composed by himself, and setting forth his claims to some rhapsodical apostleship.[9] Though ragged and dirty, there was about him no touch of vulgarity; for, by nature, his manner was not unrefined, his frame slender, and appeared the more so from the broad, untanned frontlet of his brow, tangled over with a disheveled mass of raven curls, throwing a still deeper tinge upon a complexion like that of a shriveled berry. Nothing could exceed his look of picturesque Italian ruin and dethronement, heightened by what seemed just one glimmering peep of reason, insufficient to do him any lasting good, but enough, perhaps, to suggest a torment of latent doubts at times, whether his addled dream of glory were true.

Accepting the tract offered him, the cosmopolitan glanced over it, and, seeming to see just what it was, closed it, put it in his pocket, eyed the man a moment, then, leaning over and presenting him with a shilling, said to him, in tones kind and considerate: "I am sorry, my friend, that I happen to be engaged just now; but, having purchased your work, I promise myself much satisfaction in its perusal at my earliest leisure."

In his tattered, single-breasted frock-coat, buttoned meagerly up to his chin, the shatter-brain made him a bow, which, for courtesy, would not have misbecome a viscount, then turned with silent appeal to the stranger. But the stranger sat more like a cold prism than ever, while an expression of keen Yankee cuteness,[1] now replacing his former mystical one, lent added icicles to his aspect. His whole air said: "Nothing from me." The repulsed petitioner threw a look full of resentful pride and cracked disdain upon him, and went his way.

"Come, now," said the cosmopolitan, a little reproachfully, "you ought to have sympathized with that man, tell me, did you feel no fellow-feeling? Look at his tract here, quite in the transcendental vein."

"Excuse me," said the stranger, declining the tract, "I never patronize scoundrels."

"Scoundrels?"

9. Harrison Hayford (1959) assembled evidence that this crazy beggar was suggested by Edgar Allan Poe, whom Melville probably glimpsed around lower Manhattan in the years just after his return from whaling in the Pacific (see in *Melville's Prisoners*, 2003, in Selected Bibliography).
1. I.e., acuteness; sharpness, shrewdness.

"I detected in him, sir, a damning peep of sense—damning, I say; for sense in a seeming madman is scoundrelism. I take him for a cunning vagabond, who picks up a vagabond living by adroitly playing the madman.[2] Did you not remark how he flinched under my eye?"

"Really," drawing a long, astonished breath, "I could hardly have divined in you a temper so subtly distrustful. Flinched? to be sure he did, poor fellow; you received him with so lame a welcome. As for his adroitly playing the madman, invidious critics might object the same to some one or two strolling magi of these days. But that is a matter I know nothing about. But, once more, and for the last time, to return to the point: why sir, did you warn me against my friend? I shall rejoice, if, as I think it will prove, your want of confidence in my friend rests upon a basis equally slender with your distrust of the lunatic. Come, why did you warn me? Put it, I beseech, in few words, and those English."

"I warned you against him because he is suspected for what on these boats is known—so they tell me—as a Mississippi operator."

"An operator,[3] ah? he operates, does he? My friend, then, is something like what the Indians call a Great Medicine, is he? He operates, he purges, he drains off the repletions."

"I perceive, sir," said the stranger, constitutionally obtuse to the pleasant drollery, "that your notion, of what is called a Great Medicine, needs correction. The Great Medicine among the Indians is less a bolus than a man in grave esteem for his politic sagacity."

"And is not my friend politic? Is not my friend sagacious? By your own definition, is not my friend a Great Medicine?"

"No, he is an operator, a Mississippi operator; an equivocal character. That he is such, I little doubt, having had him pointed out to me as such by one desirous of initiating me into any little novelty of this western region, where I never before traveled. And, sir, if I am not mistaken, you also are a stranger here (but, indeed, where in this strange universe is not one a stranger?) and that is a reason why I felt moved to warn you against a companion who could not be otherwise than perilous to one of a free and trustful disposition. But I repeat the hope, that, thus far at least, he has not succeeded with you, and trust that, for the future, he will not."

"Thank you for your concern; but hardly can I equally thank you for so steadily maintaining the hypothesis of my friend's objectionableness. True, I but made his acquaintance for the first to-day, and know little of his antecedents; but that would seem no just reason

2. A jibe at Emerson's success on the American lecture circuit, which Melville had witnessed in 1849.
3. Swindler. The butt of this long joke is the Transcendental refusal to acknowledge evil, a sticking point whenever Melville tried to enjoy reading Emerson. Winsome can unmask the ordinary Mississippi con man Charlie Noble but unwittingly talks at length with the supreme Confidence Man.

why a nature like his should not of itself inspire confidence. And since your own knowledge of the gentleman is not, by your account, so exact as it might be, you will pardon me if I decline to welcome any further suggestions unflattering to him. Indeed, sir," with friendly decision, "let us change the subject."

Chapter 37.

THE MYSTICAL MASTER INTRODUCES THE PRACTICAL DISCIPLE.

"Both, the subject and the interlocutor,"[4] replied the stranger rising, and waiting the return towards him of a promenader, that moment turning at the further end of his walk.

"Egbert!" said he, calling.

Egbert, a well-dressed, commercial-looking gentleman of about thirty, responded in a way strikingly deferential, and in a moment stood near, in the attitude less an equal companion apparently than a confidential follower.

"This," said the stranger, taking Egbert[5] by the hand and leading him to the cosmopolitan, "this is Egbert, a disciple. I wish you to know Egbert. Egbert was the first among mankind to reduce to practice the principles of Mark Winsome—principles previously accounted as less adapted to life than the closet. Egbert," turning to the disciple, who, with seeming modesty, a little shrank under these compliments, "Egbert, this," with a salute towards the cosmopolitan, "is, like all of us, a stranger. I wish you, Egbert, to know this brother stranger; be communicative with him. Particularly if, by anything hitherto dropped, his curiosity has been roused as to the precise nature of my philosophy, I trust you will not leave such curiosity ungratified. You, Egbert, by simply setting forth your practice, can do more to enlighten one as to my theory, than I myself can by mere speech. Indeed, it is by you that I myself best understand myself. For to every philosophy are certain rear parts, very important parts, and these, like the rear of one's head, are best seen by reflection. Now, as in a glass, you, Egbert, in your life, reflect to me the more important part of my system. He, who approves you, approves the philosophy of Mark Winsome."

Though portions of this harangue may, perhaps, in the phraseology seem self-complaisant, yet no trace of self-complacency was perceptible in the speaker's manner, which throughout was plain,

4. The person being conversed with, but in the particular sense of the man in the middle of a blackface line of minstrel performers who engages the others in comical chat. Throughout the chapter the disciple never gets to speak a word.
5. Egbert S. Oliver (1946) first assembled evidence that Egbert is modeled on Thoreau, known in the 1840s and 1850s for his application of Emerson's principles. Melville may also have known that Thoreau sometimes lectured and may have assumed, wrongly, this follower of Emerson was very popular with audiences.

unassuming, dignified, and manly; the teacher and prophet seemed to lurk more in the idea, so to speak, than in the mere bearing of him who was the vehicle of it.

"Sir," said the cosmopolitan, who seemed not a little interested in this new aspect of matters, "you speak of a certain philosophy, and a more or less occult one it may be, and hint of its bearing upon practical life; pray, tell me, if the study of this philosophy tends to the same formation of character with the experiences of the world?"

"It does; and that is the test of its truth; for any philosophy that, being in operation contradictory to the ways of the world, tends to produce a character at odds with it, such a philosophy must necessarily be but a cheat and a dream."

"You a little surprise me," answered the cosmopolitan; "for, from an occasional profundity in you, and also from your allusions to a profound work on the theology of Plato, it would seem but natural to surmise that, if you are the originator of any philosophy, it must needs so partake of the abstruse, as to exalt it above the comparatively vile uses of life."

"No uncommon mistake with regard to me," rejoined the other. Then meekly standing like a Raphael: "If still in golden accents old Memnon[6] murmurs his riddle, none the less does the balance-sheet of every man's ledger unriddle the profit or loss of life. Sir," with calm energy, "man came into this world, not to sit down and muse, not to befog himself with vain subtleties, but to gird up his loins and to work. Mystery is in the morning, and mystery in the night, and the beauty of mystery is everywhere; but still the plain truth remains, that mouth and purse must be filled. If, hitherto, you have supposed me a visionary, be undeceived. I am no one-ideaed one, either; no more than the seers before me. Was not Seneca[7] a usurer? Bacon[8] a courtier? and Swedenborg,[9] though with one eye on the in-

---

6. In Greek mythology, a young hero who was slain by Achilles in the Trojan War. A statue near Thebes, in Egypt, actually in honor of Amenhotep III, began emitting a musical sound at sunrise after it was cracked in an earthquake, and Greek visitors associated it with Memnon, whom they fancied to be calling each morning to his mother, Aurora, the goddess of the dawn. In book 7, chapter 6 of *Pierre* (1852) Melville's hero names a menacing stone in an American landscape for the Memnon statue, and Melville makes much of the legend, finding in it "the Hamletism of three thousand years ago: 'The flower of virtue cropped by a too rare mischance.' " As depicted by John Milton in *Paradise Lost*, book 5, Raphael is chosen to go down to Eden to warn Adam that Satan has escaped from hell and is plotting against Adam. In the following books the "affable Arch-angel" (7.41; *affable*: easy to speak to) patiently answers Adam's questions about God's expelling Satan and his angels from heaven and creating a new world, the one Adam inhabits. Melville marked *Paradise Lost* 5.277–85 in his copy, where Raphael's beauty is described, and underlined part of line 283 ("And colours dipp'd in heaven") in the description of Raphael's middle pair of wings that "Girt like a starry zone his waist, and round / Skirted his loins and thighs with downy gold / And colours dipp'd in heaven."
7. See n. 7, p. 57.
8. See n. 9, p. 58, and n. 8, p. 140.
9. Emmanuel Swedenborg (1688–1772), Swedish mystic who conversed with "invisible" angels, was a brilliant engineer highly prized by King Charles XII of Sweden, for whom

visible, did he not keep the other on the main chance? Along with whatever else it may be given me to be, I am a man of serviceable knowledge, and a man of the world. Know me for such. And as for my disciple here," turning towards him, "if you look to find any soft Utopianisms and last year's sunsets in him, I smile to think how he will set you right. The doctrines I have taught him will, I trust, lead him neither to the mad-house nor the poor-house, as so many other doctrines have served credulous sticklers. Furthermore," glancing upon him paternally, "Egbert is both my disciple and my poet. For poetry is not a thing of ink and rhyme, but of thought and act, and, in the latter way, is by any one to be found anywhere, when in useful action sought. In a word, my disciple here is a thriving young merchant, a practical poet in the West India trade.[1] There," presenting Egbert's hand to the cosmopolitan, "I join you, and leave you." With which words, and without bowing, the master withdrew.

Chapter 38.

THE DISCIPLE UNBENDS, AND CONSENTS TO ACT A SOCIAL PART.

In the master's presence the disciple had stood as one not ignorant of his place; modesty was in his expression, with a sort of reverential depression. But the presence of the superior withdrawn, he seemed lithely to shoot up erect from beneath it, like one of those wire men from a toy snuff-box.

He was, as before said, a young man of about thirty. His countenance of that neuter sort, which, in repose, is neither prepossessing nor disagreeable; so that it seemed quite uncertain how he would turn out. His dress was neat, with just enough of the mode to save it from the reproach of originality; in which general respect, though with a readjustment of details, his costume seemed modeled upon his master's. But, upon the whole, he was, to all appearances, the last person in the world that one would take for the disciple of any transcendental philosophy; though, indeed, something about his sharp nose and shaved chin seemed to hint that if mysticism, as a lesson, ever came in his way, he might, with the characteristic knack of a true New-Englander, turn even so profitless a thing to some profitable account.

"Well," said he, now familiarly seating himself in the vacated chair, "what do you think of Mark? Sublime fellow, ain't he?"

"That each member of the human guild is worthy respect, my

he designed innovative dry docks, canals, and other structures. From Emerson's "The Over-Soul" (1841) and elsewhere Melville knew of the Transcendentalists' interest in Swedenborg's "illuminations."

1. A recollection of Thoreau's comment on "the West Indian provinces of the fancy and imagination" in *Walden*, chapter 1, paragraph 8.

friend," rejoined the cosmopolitan, "is a fact which no admirer of that guild will question; but that, in view of higher natures, the word sublime, so frequently applied to them, can, without confusion, be also applied to man, is a point which man will decide for himself; though, indeed, if he decide it in the affirmative, it is not for me to object. But I am curious to know more of that philosophy of which, at present, I have but inklings. You, its first disciple among men, it seems, are peculiarly qualified to expound it. Have you any objections to begin now?"

"None at all," squaring himself to the table. "Where shall I begin? At first principles?"

"You remember that it was in a practical way that you were represented as being fitted for the clear exposition. Now, what you call first principles, I have, in some things, found to be more or less vague. Permit me, then, in a plain way, to suppose some common case in real life, and that done, I would like you to tell me how you, the practical disciple of the philosophy I wish to know about, would, in that case, conduct."

"A business-like view. Propose the case."

"Not only the case, but the persons. The case is this: There are two friends, friends from childhood, bosom-friends; one of whom, for the first time, being in need, for the first time seeks a loan from the other, who, so far as fortune goes, is more than competent to grant it. And the persons are to be you and I: you, the friend from whom the loan is sought—I, the friend who seeks it; you, the disciple of the philosophy in question—I, a common man, with no more philosophy than to know that when I am comfortably warm I don't feel cold, and when I have the ague I shake. Mind, now, you must work up your imagination, and, as much as possible, talk and behave just as if the case supposed were a fact. For brevity, you shall call me Frank, and I will call you Charlie. Are you agreed?"

"Perfectly. You begin."

The cosmopolitan paused a moment, then, assuming a serious and care-worn air, suitable to the part to be enacted, addressed his hypothesized friend.

Chapter 39.

THE HYPOTHETICAL FRIENDS.

"Charlie, I am going to put confidence in you."

"You always have, and with reason. What is it, Frank?"

"Charlie, I am in want—urgent want of money."

"That's not well."

"But it *will* be well, Charlie, if you loan me a hundred dollars. I would not ask this of you, only my need is sore, and you and I have so long shared hearts and minds together, however unequally on my side, that nothing remains to prove our friendship than, with the same inequality on my side, to share purses. You will do me the favor, won't you?"

"Favor? What do you mean, by asking me to do you a favor?"

"Why, Charlie, you never used to talk so."

"Because, Frank, you on your side, never used to talk so."

"But won't you loan me the money?"

"No, Frank."

"Why?"

"Because my rule forbids. I give away money, but never loan it; and of course the man who calls himself my friend is above receiving alms. The negotiation of a loan is a business transaction. And I will transact no business with a friend. What a friend is, he is socially and intellectually; and I rate social and intellectual friendship too high to degrade it on either side into a pecuniary make-shift. To be sure there are, and I have, what is called business friends; that is, commercial acquaintances, very convenient persons. But I draw a red-ink line between them and my friends in the true sense—my friends social and intellectual. In brief, a true friend has nothing to do with loans; he should have a soul above loans. Loans are such unfriendly accommodations as are to be had from the soulless corporation[2] of a bank, by giving the regular security and paying the regular discount."

"An *unfriendly* accommodation? Do those words go together handsomely?"

"Like the poor farmer's team, of an old man and a cow—not handsomely, but to the purpose. Look, Frank, a loan of money on interest is a sale of money on credit. To sell a thing on credit may be an accommodation, but where is the friendliness? Few men in their senses, except operators, borrow money on interest, except upon a necessity akin to starvation. Well, now, where is the friendliness of my letting a starving man have, say, the money's worth of a barrel of flour upon the condition that, on a given day, he shall let me have the money's worth of a barrel and a half of flour; especially if I add this further proviso, that if he fail so to do, I shall then, to secure to myself the money's worth of my barrel and his half barrel, put his heart up at public auction, and, as it is cruel to part families, throw in his wife's and children's?"

"I understand," with a pathetic shudder; "but even did it come to that, such a step on the creditor's part, let us, for the honor of human nature, hope, were less the intention than the contingency."

2. The English jurist Edward Coke (1552–1634) in the case of "Sutton's Hospital" (1612) ruled that corporations had "no souls"—and therefore no moral responsibility.

"But, Frank, a contingency not unprovided for in the taking beforehand of due securities."

"Still, Charlie, was not the loan in the first place a friend's act?"

"And the auction in the last place an enemy's act. Don't you see? The enmity lies couched in the friendship, just as the ruin in the relief."

"I must be very stupid to-day, Charlie, but really, I can't understand this. Excuse me, my dear friend, but it strikes me that in going into the philosophy of the subject, you go somewhat out of your depth."

"So said the incautious wader-out to the ocean; but the ocean replied: 'It is just the other way, my wet friend,' and drowned him."

"That, Charlie, is a fable about as unjust to the ocean, as some of Æsop's are to the animals.[3] The ocean is a magnanimous element, and would scorn to assassinate a poor fellow, let alone taunting him in the act. But I don't understand what you say about enmity couched in friendship, and ruin in relief."

"I will illustrate, Frank. The needy man is a train slipped off the rail. He who loans him money on interest is the one who, by way of accommodation, helps get the train back where it belongs; but then, by way of making all square, and a little more, telegraphs to an agent, thirty miles a-head by a precipice, to throw just there, on his account, a beam across the track. Your needy man's principal-and-interest friend is, I say again, a friend with an enmity in reserve. No, no, my dear friend, no interest for me. I scorn interest."

"Well, Charlie, none need you charge. Loan me without interest."

"That would be alms again."

"Alms, if the sum borrowed is returned?"

"Yes: an alms, not of the principal, but the interest."

"Well, I am in sore need, so I will not decline the alms. Seeing that it is you, Charlie, gratefully will I accept the alms of the interest. No humiliation between friends."

"Now, how in the refined view of friendship[4] can you suffer your-

---

3. Aesop (sixth century B.C.E.) is the supposed author of a collection of Greek fables. The characters in the fables are animals, but the tales illustrate morals applicable to human beings. The mention of Aesop links to references elsewhere in this book to human beings (like Philomela, p. 61 herein) who turn into animals and superhuman beings who take animal shapes (like Satan appearing as a black dog, n. 6, p. 224 herein). In 1862 Melville read William Hazlitt's comment on Aesop in his lecture "On Wit and Humour," the introduction to *Lectures on the English Comic Writers* (New York, 1859): "He saw in man a talking, absurd, obstinate, proud, angry animal; and clothed these abstractions with wings, or a beak, or tail, or claws, or long ears, as they appeared embodied in these hieroglyphics in the brute creation." Melville underlined the words *He saw* through *angry animal* then showed his own thinking about Aesop by noting, "one more adjective wanting—cruel." ("Wanting": lacking.)

4. Melville is satirizing rarefied Transcendental (and Unitarian) notions about friendship. One or more of these was in his mind: a section of "Wednesday" in Thoreau's *A Week on the Concord and Merrimack Rivers* ("Nothing is so difficult as to help a Friend in matters

self to talk so, my dear Frank? It pains me. For though I am not of the sour mind of Solomon, that, in the hour of need, a stranger is better than a brother; yet, I entirely agree with my sublime master, who, in his Essay on Friendship, says so nobly, that if he want[5] a terrestrial convenience, not to his friend celestial (or friend social and intellectual) would he go; no: for his terrestrial convenience, to his friend terrestrial (or humbler business-friend) he goes. Very lucidly he adds the reason: Because, for the superior nature, which on no account can ever descend to do good, to be annoyed with requests to do it, when the inferior one, which by no instruction can ever rise above that capacity, stands always inclined to it—this is unsuitable."

"Then I will not consider you as my friend celestial, but as the other."

"It racks me to come to that; but, to oblige you, I'll do it. We are business friends; business is business. You want to negotiate a loan. Very good. On what paper? Will you pay three per cent. a month? Where is your security?"

"Surely, you will not exact those formalities from your old schoolmate—him with whom you have so often sauntered down the groves of Academe, discoursing of the beauty of virtue, and the grace that is in kindliness—and all for so paltry a sum. Security? Our being fellow-academics, and friends from childhood up, is security."

"Pardon me, my dear Frank, our being fellow-academics is the worst of securities; while, our having been friends from childhood up is just no security at all. You forget we are now business friends."

"And you, on your side, forget, Charlie, that as your business friend I can give you no security; my need being so sore that I cannot get an indorser."

"No indorser, then, no business loan."

"Since then, Charlie, neither as the one nor the other sort of friend you have defined, can I prevail with you; how if, combining the two, I sue as both?"

---

which do not require the aid of Friendship, but only a cheap and useful service"); or of "Visitors" in *Walden* ("Objects of charity are not guests"); or Emerson's essay on "Friendship," which is pointedly alluded to just below (see p. 205 herein). Melville may well have related Transcendental coldness to the character Tigillius in Horace's *Satire* 1.2, who would not give any money to a cold and starving friend lest he be thought extravagant.

5. Lack, is in need of. Cf. Proverbs 18.24: "there is a friend that sticketh closer than a brother" and 27.10: "Thine own friend, and thy father's friend, forsake not; neither go into thy brother's house in the day of thy calamity: for better is a neighbour that is near than a brother far off." In the copy of *The Whale* (the English edition of *Moby-Dick*) that he gave his brother-in-law John C. Hoadley on January 6, 1854, Melville wrote: "John C. Hoadley from his friend Herman Melville"; he then footnoted *friend* this way: "If my good brother John take exception to the use of the word *friend* here, thinking there is a *nearer* word; I beg him to remember that saying in the Good Book, which hints there is a *friend* that sticketh CLOSER than a *brother*."

"Are you a centaur?"

"When all is said then, what good have I of your friendship, regarded in what light you will?"

"The good which is in the philosophy of Mark Winsome, as reduced to practice by a practical disciple."

"And why don't you add, much good may the philosophy of Mark Winsome do me? Ah," turning invokingly, "what is friendship, if it be not the helping hand and the feeling heart, the good Samaritan pouring out at need the purse as the vial!"[6]

"Now, my dear Frank, don't be childish. Through tears never did man see his way in the dark. I should hold you unworthy that sincere friendship I bear you, could I think that friendship in the ideal is too lofty for you to conceive. And let me tell you, my dear Frank, that you would seriously shake the foundations of our love, if ever again you should repeat the present scene. The philosophy, which is mine in the strongest way, teaches plain-dealing. Let me, then, now, as at the most suitable time, candidly disclose certain circumstances you seem in ignorance of. Though our friendship began in boyhood, think not that, on my side at least, it began injudiciously. Boys are little men, it is said. You, I juvenilely picked out for my friend, for your favorable points at the time; not the least of which were your good manners, handsome dress, and your parents' rank and repute of wealth. In short, like any grown man, boy though I was, I went into the market and chose me my mutton, not for its leanness, but its fatness. In other words, there seemed in you, the schoolboy who always had silver in his pocket, a reasonable probability that you would never stand in lean need of fat succor; and if my early impression has not been verified by the event, it is only because of the caprice of fortune producing a fallibility of human expectations, however discreet."

"Oh, that I should listen to this cold-blooded disclosure!"

"A little cold blood in your ardent veins, my dear Frank, wouldn't do you any harm, let me tell you. Cold-blooded? You say that, because my disclosure seems to involve a vile prudence on my side. But not so. My reason for choosing you in part for the points I have mentioned, was solely with a view of preserving inviolate the delicacy of the connection. For—do but think of it—what more distressing to delicate friendship, formed early, than your friend's eventually, in manhood, dropping in of a rainy night for his little loan of five dollars or so? Can delicate friendship stand that? And, on the other side, would delicate friendship, so long as it retained its delicacy, do that? Would you not instinctively say of your drip-

---

6. See n. 7, p. 82. The Samaritan gives immediate aid to the man who fell among thieves, "pouring in oil and wine" on his wounds, then puts him "on his own beast" and takes him to an inn for further care (Luke 10.34).

ping friend in the entry, 'I have been deceived, fraudulently deceived, in this man; he is no true friend that, in platonic love to demand love-rites?' "

"And rites, doubly rights, they are, cruel Charlie!"

"Take it how you will, heed well how, by too importunately claiming those rights, as you call them, you shake those foundations I hinted of. For though, as it turns out, I, in my early friendship, built me a fair house on a poor site; yet such pains and cost have I lavished on that house, that, after all, it is dear to me. No, I would not lose the sweet boon of your friendship, Frank. But beware."

"And of what? Of being in need? Oh, Charlie! you talk not to a god, a being who in himself holds his own estate, but to a man who, being a man, is the sport of fate's wind and wave, and who mounts towards heaven or sinks towards hell, as the billows roll him in trough or on crest."

"Tut! Frank. Man is no such poor devil as that comes to—no poor drifting sea-weed of the universe. Man has a soul; which, if he will, puts him beyond fortune's finger and the future's spite. Don't whine like fortune's whipped dog, Frank, or by the heart of a true friend, I will cut ye."

"Cut me you have already, cruel Charlie, and to the quick. Call to mind the days we went nutting, the times we walked in the woods, arms wreathed about each other, showing trunks invined like the trees:—oh, Charlie!"

"Pish! we were boys."

"Then lucky the fate of the first-born of Egypt,[7] cold in the grave ere maturity struck them with a sharper frost.—Charlie?"

"Fie! you're a girl."

"Help, help, Charlie, I want help!"

"Help? to say nothing of the friend, there is something wrong about the man who wants help. There is somewhere a defect, a want, in brief, a need, a crying need, somewhere about that man."

"So there is, Charlie.—Help, Help!"

"How foolish a cry, when to implore help, is itself the proof of undesert of it."

"Oh, this, all along, is not you, Charlie, but some ventriloquist who usurps your larynx. It is Mark Winsome that speaks, not Charlie."

"If so, thank heaven, the voice of Mark Winsome is not alien but congenial to my larynx. If the philosophy of that illustrious teacher find little response among mankind at large, it is less that they do

7. "And it came to pass, that at midnight the Lord smote all the firstborn in the land of Egypt, from the firstborn of Pharaoh that sat on his throne unto the firstborn of the captive that was in the dungeon; and all the firstborn of cattle" (Exodus 12.29).

not possess teachable tempers, than because they are so unfortunate as not to have natures predisposed to accord with him."

"Welcome, that compliment to humanity," exclaimed Frank with energy, "the truer because unintended. And long in this respect may humanity remain what you affirm it. And long it will; since humanity, inwardly feeling how subject it is to straits, and hence how precious is help, will, for selfishness' sake, if no other, long postpone ratifying a philosophy that banishes help from the world. But Charlie, Charlie! speak as you used to; tell me you will help me. Were the case reversed, not less freely would I loan you the money than you would ask me to loan it."

"*I* ask? *I* ask a loan? Frank, by this hand, under no circumstances would I accept a loan, though without asking pressed on me. The experience of China Aster might warn me."

"And what was that?"

"Not very unlike the experience of the man that built himself a palace of moon-beams, and when the moon set was surprised that his palace vanished with it. I will tell you about China Aster. I wish I could do so in my own words, but unhappily the original storyteller here has so tyrannized over me, that it is quite impossible for me to repeat his incidents without sliding into his style. I forewarn you of this, that you may not think me so maudlin as, in some parts, the story would seem to make its narrator. It is too bad that any intellect, especially in so small a matter, should have such power to impose itself upon another, against its best exerted will, too. However, it is satisfaction to know that the main moral, to which all tends, I fully approve. But, to begin."

Chapter 40.

IN WHICH THE STORY OF CHINA ASTER[8] IS AT SECOND-HAND TOLD BY
ONE WHO, WHILE NOT DISAPPROVING THE MORAL, DISCLAIMS THE
SPIRIT OF THE STYLE.

"China Aster was a young candle-maker of Marietta, at the mouth of the Muskingum—one whose trade would seem a kind of subordinate branch of that parent craft and mystery of the hosts of heaven, to be the means, effectively or otherwise, of shedding some light through the darkness of a planet benighted. But he made little

8. See Parker's "Damned by Dollars" (p. 329 herein) and "The Root of All Was a Friendly Loan" (p. 340 herein). On the subject of Melville's finances the biography by Parker in grim detail supersedes all earlier accounts. Below: "Marietta, the first permanent settlement on the Ohio, was . . . made up entirely of renowed men of the Revolution: officers and soldiers, who . . . found themselves turned loose upon the world, their private fortunes ruined. . . . Such men projected cities, opened farms, and laid wide and strong the foundation of future empire" (T. B. Thorpe, "Remembrances of the Mississippi," 1855).

money by the business. Much ado had poor China Aster and his family to live; he could, if he chose, light up from his stores a whole street, but not so easily could he light up with prosperity the hearts of his household.

"Now, China Aster, it so happened, had a friend, Orchis, a shoe-maker; one whose calling it is to defend the understandings[9] of men from naked contact with the substance of things: a very useful vocation, and which, spite of all the wiseacres may prophesy, will hardly go out of fashion so long as rocks are hard and flints will gall. All at once, by a capital prize in a lottery, this useful shoe-maker was raised from a bench to a sofa. A small nabob was the shoemaker now, and the understandings of men, let them shift for themselves. Not that Orchis was, by prosperity, elated into heart-lessness. Not at all. Because, in his fine apparel, strolling one morning into the candlery, and gayly switching about at the candle-boxes with his gold-headed cane—while poor China Aster, with his greasy paper cap and leather apron, was selling one candle for one penny to a poor orange-woman, who, with the patronizing coolness of a liberal customer, required it to be carefully rolled up and tied in a half sheet of paper—lively Orchis, the woman being gone, dis-continued his gay switchings and said: 'This is poor business for you, friend China Aster; your capital is too small. You must drop this vile tallow and hold up pure spermaceti to the world. I tell you what it is, you shall have one thousand dollars to extend with. In fact, you must make money, China Aster. I don't like to see your lit-tle boy paddling about without shoes, as he does.'

" 'Heaven bless your goodness, friend Orchis,' replied the candle-maker, 'but don't take it illy if I call to mind the word of my uncle, the blacksmith, who, when a loan was offered him, declined it, say-ing: "To ply my own hammer, light though it be, I think best, rather than piece it out heavier by welding to it a bit off a neighbor's ham-mer, though that may have some weight to spare; otherwise, were the borrowed bit suddenly wanted again, it might not split off at the welding, but too much to one side or the other." '

" 'Nonsense, friend China Aster, don't be so honest; your boy is barefoot. Besides, a rich man lose by a poor man? Or a friend be the worse by a friend? China Aster, I am afraid that, in leaning over into your vats here, this morning, you have spilled out your wis-dom. Hush! I won't hear any more. Where's your desk? Oh, here.' With that, Orchis dashed off a check on his bank, and off-handedly presenting it, said: 'There, friend China Aster, is your one thousand dollars; when you make it ten thousand, as you soon enough will (for experience, the only true knowledge, teaches me that, for every

9. The punning on "understandings" recalls the cobbler's puns (e.g., on mending soles) in the first scene of Shakespeare's *Julius Caesar*.

one, good luck is in store), then, China Aster, why, then you can return me the money or not, just as you please. But, in any event,
give yourself no concern, for I shall never demand payment.'

"Now, as kind heaven will so have it that to a hungry man bread
is a great temptation, and, therefore, he is not too harshly to be
blamed, if, when freely offered, he take it, even though it be uncertain whether he shall ever be able to reciprocate; so, to a poor man,
proffered money is equally enticing, and the worst that can be said
of him, if he accept it, is just what can be said in the other case of
the hungry man. In short, the poor candle-maker's scrupulous
morality succumbed to his unscrupulous necessity, as is now and
then apt to be the case. He took the check, and was about carefully
putting it away for the present, when Orchis, switching about again
with his gold-headed cane, said: 'By-the-way, China Aster, it don't
mean anything, but suppose you make a little memorandum of this;
won't do any harm, you know.' So China Aster gave Orchis his note
for one thousand dollars on demand. Orchis took it, and looked at
it a moment, 'Pooh, I told you, friend China Aster, I wasn't going
ever to make any *demand*.' Then tearing up the note, and switching
away again at the candle-boxes, said, carelessly; 'Put it at four
years.' So China Aster gave Orchis his note for one thousand dollars at four years. 'You see I'll never trouble you about this,' said Orchis, slipping it in his pocket-book, 'give yourself no further
thought, friend China Aster, than how best to invest your money.
And don't forget my hint about spermaceti. Go into that, and I'll
buy all my light of you,' with which encouraging words, he, with
wonted, rattling kindness, took leave.[1]

"China Aster remained standing just where Orchis had left him;
when, suddenly, two elderly friends, having nothing better to do,
dropped in for a chat. The chat over, China Aster, in greasy cap and
apron, ran after Orchis, and said: 'Friend Orchis, heaven will reward you for your good intentions, but here is your check, and now
give me my note.'

" 'Your honesty is a bore, China Aster,' said Orchis, not without
displeasure. 'I won't take the check from you.'

" 'Then you must take it from the pavement, Orchis,' said China
Aster; and, picking up a stone, he placed the check under it on the
walk.

" 'China Aster,' said Orchis, inquisitively eying him, 'after my

---

1. Melville had made Benjamin Franklin a featured character in his *Israel Potter* (serialized
1854–55; published in book form in 1855). According to *The Autobiography*, Franklin's
father had been "a Tallow Chandler and Soap-Boiler," a maker of candles and soap.
Later, the elaborate tombstone may also echo Franklin. With Franklin already in mind,
Melville may have been recalling Franklin's description of the consequences of his having listened to the blandishments of Governor Keith and the fearfulness of his "daily apprehensions of being called upon by Vernon" for repayment of money.

leaving the candlery just now, what asses dropped in there to advise with you, that now you hurry after me, and act so like a fool? Shouldn't wonder if it was those two old asses that the boys nick-name Old Plain Talk and Old Prudence.'[2]

" 'Yes, it was those two, Orchis, but don't call them names.'

" 'A brace of spavined old croakers. Old Plain Talk had a shrew for a wife, and that's made him shrewish; and Old Prudence, when a boy, broke down in an apple-stall, and that discouraged him for life. No better sport for a knowing spark like me than to hear Old Plain Talk wheeze out his sour old saws, while Old Prudence stands by, leaning on his staff, wagging his frosty old pow,[3] and chiming in at every clause.'

" 'How can you speak so, friend Orchis, of those who were my fa-ther's friends?'

" 'Save me from my friends, if those old croakers were Old Hon-esty's friends. I call your father so, for every one used to. Why did they let him go in his old age on the town? Why, China Aster, I've often heard from my mother, the chronicler, that those two old fel-lows, with Old Conscience—as the boys called the crabbed old quaker, that's dead now—they three used to go to the poor-house when your father was there, and get round his bed, and talk to him for all the world as Eliphaz, Bildad, and Zophar did to poor old pau-per Job.[4] Yes, Job's comforters were Old Plain Talk, and Old Pru-dence, and Old Conscience, to your poor old father. Friends? I should like to know who you call foes? With their everlasting croak-ing and reproaching they tormented poor Old Honesty, your father, to death.'

"At these words, recalling the sad end of his worthy parent, China Aster could not restrain some tears. Upon which Orchis said: 'Why, China Aster, you are the dolefulest creature. Why don't you, China Aster, take a bright view of life? You will never get on in your business or anything else, if you don't take the bright view of

2. Old Plain Talk and Old Prudence, like the advisers mentioned later, have names that re-call the bluntly allegorical characters in John Bunyan's *Pilgrim's Progress*, those whose names identify what the lawyer in "Bartleby" would call their "grand points."
3. Head (from *poll*, as in "poll tax").
4. Job's great sufferings began when Satan came among the sons of God, after walking to and fro in the earth, only to have God boast that Job was "a perfect and an upright man," beyond Satan's power to tempt. When Satan accepts this challenge, God allows Satan full power over Job's property and people, requiring only that Satan not take Job's life. Job's consequent suffering and his behavior in his suffering make this book of the Bible controversial. When Job's three friends hear of the "evil that was come upon him," they come "every one from his own place; Eliphaz the Temanite, and Bildad the Shuhite, and Zophar the Naamathite: for they had made an appointment together to come to mourn with him and to comfort him" (Job 2.11). Eliphaz, Bildad, and Zophar, like many would-be comforters, first mourn with Job then rigorously lecture him on what they see as Job's probable faults rather than commiserate with him on his truly undeserved sufferings. They stay on the scene, comforting their friend, from Job 2.11 to 25.6. (Melville used the name Bildad in *Moby-Dick* as one of the owners of the *Pequod*.)

life. It's the ruination of a man to take the dismal one.' Then, gayly poking at him with his gold-headed cane, 'Why don't you, then? Why don't you be bright and hopeful, like me? Why don't you have confidence, China Aster?'

" 'I'm sure I don't know, friend Orchis,' soberly replied China Aster, 'but may be my not having drawn a lottery-prize, like you, may make some difference.'

" 'Nonsense! before I knew anything about the prize I was gay as a lark, just as gay as I am now. In fact, it has always been a principle with me to hold to the bright view.'

"Upon this, China Aster looked a little hard at Orchis, because the truth was, that until the lucky prize came to him, Orchis had gone under the nickname of Doleful Dumps, he having been beforetimes of a hypochondriac turn, so much so as to save up and put by a few dollars of his scanty earnings against that rainy day he used to groan so much about.

" 'I tell you what it is, now, friend China Aster,' said Orchis, pointing down to the check under the stone, and then slapping his pocket, 'the check shall lie there if you say so, but your note shan't keep it company. In fact, China Aster, I am too sincerely your friend to take advantage of a passing fit of the blues in you. You *shall* reap the benefit of my friendship.' With which, buttoning up his coat in a jiffy, away he ran, leaving the check behind.

"At first, China Aster was going to tear it up, but thinking that this ought not to be done except in the presence of the drawer of the check, he mused a while, and picking it up, trudged back to the candlery, fully resolved to call upon Orchis soon as his day's work was over, and destroy the check before his eyes. But it so happened that when China Aster called, Orchis was out, and, having waited for him a weary time in vain, China Aster went home, still with the check, but still resolved not to keep it another day. Bright and early next morning he would a second time go after Orchis, and would, no doubt, make a sure thing of it, by finding him in his bed; for since the lottery-prize came to him, Orchis, besides becoming more cheery, had also grown a little lazy. But as destiny would have it, that same night China Aster had a dream, in which a being in the guise of a smiling angel, and holding a kind of cornucopia in her hand, hovered over him, pouring down showers of small gold dollars, thick as kernels of corn. 'I am Bright Future, friend China Aster,' said the angel, 'and if you do what friend Orchis would have you do, just see what will come of it.' With which Bright Future, with another swing of her cornucopia, poured such another shower of small gold dollars upon him, that it seemed to bank him up all round, and he waded about in it like a maltster in malt.

"Now, dreams are wonderful things, as everybody knows—so

wonderful, indeed, that some people stop not short of ascribing them directly to heaven; and China Aster, who was of a proper turn of mind in everything, thought that in consideration of the dream, it would be but well to wait a little, ere seeking Orchis again. During the day, China Aster's mind dwelling continually upon the dream, he was so full of it, that when Old Plain Talk dropped in to see him, just before dinner-time, as he often did, out of the interest he took in Old Honesty's son, China Aster told all about his vision, adding that he could not think that so radiant an angel could deceive; and, indeed, talked at such a rate that one would have thought he believed the angel some beautiful human philanthropist. Something in this sort Old Plain Talk understood him, and, accordingly, in his plain way, said: 'China Aster, you tell me that an angel appeared to you in a dream. Now, what does that amount to but this, that you dreamed an angel appeared to you? Go right away, China Aster, and return the check, as I advised you before. If friend Prudence were here, he would say just the same thing.' With which words Old Plain Talk went off to find friend Prudence, but not succeeding, was returning to the candlery himself, when, at distance mistaking him for a dun who had long annoyed him, China Aster in a panic barred all his doors, and ran to the back part of the candlery, where no knock could be heard.

"By this sad mistake, being left with no friend to argue the other side of the question, China Aster was so worked upon at last, by musing over his dream, that nothing would do but he must get the check cashed, and lay out the money the very same day in buying a good lot of spermaceti to make into candles, by which operation he counted upon turning a better penny than he ever had before in his life;[5] in fact, this he believed would prove the foundation of that famous fortune which the angel had promised him.

"Now, in using the money, China Aster was resolved punctually to pay the interest every six months till the principal should be returned, howbeit not a word about such a thing had been breathed by Orchis; though, indeed, according to custom, as well as law, in such matters, interest would legitimately accrue on the loan, nothing to the contrary having been put in the bond. Whether Orchis at the time had this in mind or not, there is no sure telling; but, to all appearance, he never so much as cared to think about the matter, one way or other.

"Though the spermaceti venture rather disappointed China Aster's sanguine expectations, yet he made out to pay the first six months' interest, and though his next venture turned out still less

5. See Parker's "The Root of All Was a Friendly Loan" and "Damned by Dollars" for indications that this is an allusion to Melville's own history, his having undertaken a very ambitious and exceedingly risky venture in spermaceti, the book *Moby-Dick*.

prosperously, yet by pinching his family in the matter of fresh meat, and, what pained him still more, his boys' schooling, he contrived to pay the second six months' interest, sincerely grieved that integrity, as well as its opposite, though not in an equal degree, costs something, sometimes.

"Meanwhile, Orchis had gone on a trip to Europe by advice of a physician; it so happening that, since the lottery-prize came to him, it had been discovered to Orchis that his health was not very firm, though he had never complained of anything before but a slight ailing of the spleen, scarce worth talking about at the time. So Orchis, being abroad, could not help China Aster's paying his interest as he did, however much he might have been opposed to it; for China Aster paid it to Orchis's agent, who was of too business-like a turn to decline interest regularly paid in on a loan.

"But overmuch to trouble the agent on that score was not again to be the fate of China Aster; for, not being of that skeptical spirit which refuses to trust customers, his third venture resulted, through bad debts, in almost a total loss—a bad blow for the candle-maker. Neither did Old Plain Talk and Old Prudence neglect the opportunity to read him an uncheerful enough lesson upon the consequences of his disregarding their advice in the matter of having nothing to do with borrowed money. 'It's all just as I predicted,' said Old Plain Talk, blowing his old nose with his old bandana. 'Yea, indeed is it,' chimed in Old Prudence, rapping his staff on the floor, and then leaning upon it, looking with solemn forebodings upon China Aster. Low-spirited enough felt the poor candle-maker; till all at once who should come with a bright face to him but his bright friend, the angel, in another dream. Again the cornucopia poured out its treasure, and promised still more. Revived by the vision, he resolved not to be down-hearted, but up and at it once more—contrary to the advice of Old Plain Talk, backed as usual by his crony, which was to the effect, that, under present circumstances, the best thing China Aster could do, would be to wind up his business, settle, if he could, all his liabilities, and then go to work as a journeyman, by which he could earn good wages, and give up, from that time henceforth, all thoughts of rising above being a paid subordinate to men more able than himself, for China Aster's career thus far plainly proved him the legitimate son of Old Honesty, who, as every one knew, had never shown much business-talent, so little, in fact, that many said of him that he had no business to be in business. And just this plain saying Plain Talk now plainly applied to China Aster, and Old Prudence never disagreed with him. But the angel in the dream did, and, maugre[6] Plain Talk, put quite other notions into the candle-maker.

6. Despite.

"He considered what he should do towards reëstablishing himself. Doubtless, had Orchis been in the country, he would have aided him in this strait. As it was, he applied to others; and as in the world, much as some may hint to the contrary, an honest man in misfortune still can find friends to stay by him and help him, even so it proved with China Aster, who at last succeeded in borrowing from a rich old farmer the sum of six hundred dollars, at the usual interest of money-lenders, upon the security of a secret bond signed by China Aster's wife and himself, to the effect that all such right and title to any property that should be left her by a well-to-do childless uncle, an invalid tanner, such property should, in the event of China Aster's failing to return the borrowed sum on the given day, be the lawful possession of the money-lender. True, it was just as much as China Aster could possibly do to induce his wife, a careful woman, to sign this bond; because she had always regarded her promised share in her uncle's estate as an anchor well to windward of the hard times in which China Aster had always been more or less involved, and from which, in her bosom, she never had seen much chance of his freeing himself. Some notion may be had of China Aster's standing in the heart and head of his wife, by a short sentence commonly used in reply to such persons as happened to sound her on the point. 'China Aster,' she would say, 'is a good husband, but a bad business man!' Indeed, she was a connection on the maternal side of Old Plain Talk's. But had not China Aster taken good care not to let Old Plain Talk and Old Prudence hear of his dealings with the old farmer, ten to one they would, in some way, have interfered with his success in that quarter.

"It has been hinted that the honesty of China Aster was what mainly induced the money-lender to befriend him in his misfortune, and this must be apparent; for, had China Aster been a different man, the money-lender might have dreaded lest, in the event of his failing to meet his note, he might some way prove slippery—more especially as, in the hour of distress, worked upon by remorse for so jeopardizing his wife's money, his heart might prove a traitor to his bond, not to hint that it was more than doubtful how such a secret security and claim, as in the last resort would be the old farmer's, would stand in a court of law. But though one inference from all this may be, that had China Aster been something else than what he was, he would not have been trusted, and, therefore, he would have been effectually shut out from running his own and wife's head into the usurer's noose; yet those who, when everything at last came out, maintained that, in this view and to this extent, the honesty of the candle-maker was no advantage to him, in so saying, such persons said what every good heart must deplore, and no prudent tongue will admit.

"It may be mentioned, that the old farmer made China Aster take part of his loan in three old dried-up cows and one lame horse, not improved by the glanders.[7] These were thrown in at a pretty high figure, the old money-lender having a singular prejudice in regard to the high value of any sort of stock raised on his farm. With a great deal of difficulty, and at more loss, China Aster disposed of his cattle at public auction, no private purchaser being found who could be prevailed upon to invest. And now, raking and scraping in every way, and working early and late, China Aster at last started afresh, nor without again largely and confidently extending himself. However, he did not try his hand at the spermaceti again, but, admonished by experience, returned to tallow. But, having bought a good lot of it, by the time he got it into candles, tallow fell so low, and candles with it, that his candles per pound barely sold for what he had paid for the tallow. Meantime, a year's unpaid interest had accrued on Orchis' loan, but China Aster gave himself not so much concern about that as about the interest now due to the old farmer. But he was glad that the principal there had yet some time to run. However, the skinny old fellow gave him some trouble by coming after him every day or two on a scraggy old white horse,[8] furnished with a musty old saddle, and goaded into his shambling old paces with a withered old raw hide. All the neighbors said that surely Death himself on the pale horse was after poor China Aster now. And something so it proved; for, ere long, China Aster found himself involved in troubles mortal enough.

"At this juncture Orchis was heard of. Orchis, it seemed, had returned from his travels, and clandestinely married, and, in a kind of queer way, was living in Pennsylvania among his wife's relations, who, among other things, had induced him to join a church, or rather semi-religious school, of Come-Outers;[9] and what was still

7. A highly contagious disease caused by a bacterium and marked by such horrific symptoms as enlargement and hardening of the glands beneath and within the lower jaw.
8. Revelation 6.8: "And I looked, and beheld a pale horse: and his name that sat on him was Death, and Hell followed with him."
9. The name Come-Outers derives from Paul, 2 Corinthians 6.17, an injunction not to be unequally yoked together with unbelievers: "Wherefore come out from among them, and be ye separate, saith the Lord, and touch not the unclean thing; and I will receive you." Melville puns on the term, making it apply to those who reveal far too much, who let too much "hang out." The term gained currency during the presidential campaign of 1848 when in central and western New York a small minority of antislavery Christians separated themselves from different Protestant denominations and formed temporary churches where they could freely express their abolitionist convictions. Dr. Thomas Low Nichols, who decisively influenced Melville's career (Parker 1.377–78), in *Forty Years of American Life* summed up the Come-Outers: "They were for coming out of the old and entering into the new in everything. They were opposed to government and refused to pay taxes, do military duty, or serve on juries: [they were opposed] to the Sabbath, churches, and religious ceremonials of all kinds: to marriage, the family, and all the arbitrary and conventional institutions of society. . . . Some went so far in their fight with civilization as not only to renounce property, and the use of money, but, in the warm season, to go without clothes, which they declared to be a social bondage unworthy of freemen and philosophers."

more, Orchis, without coming to the spot himself, had sent word to his agent to dispose of some of his property in Marietta, and remit him the proceeds. Within a year after, China Aster received a letter from Orchis, commending him for his punctuality in paying the first year's interest, and regretting the necessity that he (Orchis) was now under of using all his dividends; so he relied upon China Aster's paying the next six months' interest, and of course with the back interest. Not more surprised than alarmed, China Aster thought of taking steamboat to go and see Orchis, but he was saved that expense by the unexpected arrival in Marietta of Orchis in person, suddenly called there by that strange kind of capriciousness lately characterizing him. No sooner did China Aster hear of his old friend's arrival than he hurried to call upon him. He found him curiously rusty in dress, sallow in cheek, and decidedly less gay and cordial in manner, which the more surprised China Aster, because, in former days, he had more than once heard Orchis, in his light rattling way, declare that all he (Orchis) wanted to make him a perfectly happy, hilarious, and benignant man, was a voyage to Europe and a wife, with a free development of his inmost nature.

"Upon China Aster's stating his case, his rusted friend was silent for a time; then, in an odd way, said that he would not crowd China Aster, but still his (Orchis') necessities were urgent. Could not China Aster mortgage the candlery? He was honest, and must have moneyed friends; and could he not press his sales of candles? Could not the market be forced a little in that particular? The profits on candles must be very great. Seeing, now, that Orchis had the notion that the candle-making business was a very profitable one, and knowing sorely enough what an error was here, China Aster tried to undeceive him. But he could not drive the truth into Orchis—Orchis being very obtuse here, and, at the same time, strange to say, very melancholy. Finally, Orchis glanced off from so unpleasing a subject into the most unexpected reflections, taken from a religious point of view, upon the unstableness and deceitfulness of the human heart. But having, as he thought, experienced something of that sort of thing, China Aster did not take exception to his friend's observations, but still refrained from so doing, almost as much for the sake of sympathetic sociality as anything else. Presently, Orchis, without much ceremony, rose, and saying he must write a letter to his wife, bade his friend good-bye, but without warmly shaking him by the hand as of old.

"In much concern at the change, China Aster made earnest inquiries in suitable quarters, as to what things, as yet unheard of, had befallen Orchis, to bring about such a revolution; and learned at last that, besides traveling, and getting married, and joining the sect of Come-Outers, Orchis had somehow got a bad dyspepsia, and lost considerable property through a breach of trust on the part of a factor in New York. Telling these things to Old Plain Talk, that man of some knowledge of the world shook his old head, and told China Aster that, though he hoped it might prove otherwise, yet it seemed to him that all he had communicated about Orchis worked together for bad omens as to his future forbearance—especially, he added with a grim sort of smile, in view of his joining the sect of Come-Outers; for, if some men knew what was their inmost natures, instead of coming out with it, they would try their best to keep it in, which, indeed, was the way with the prudent sort. In all which sour notions Old Prudence, as usual, chimed in.

"When interest-day came again, China Aster, by the utmost exertions, could only pay Orchis' agent a small part of what was due, and a part of that was made up by his children's gift money (bright tenpenny pieces and new quarters, kept in their little money-boxes), and pawning his best clothes, with those of his wife and children, so that all were subjected to the hardship of staying away from church. And the old usurer, too, now beginning to be obstreperous, China Aster paid him his interest and some other pressing debts with money got by, at last, mortgaging the candlery.

"When next interest-day came round for Orchis, not a penny could be raised. With much grief of heart, China Aster so informed Orchis' agent. Meantime, the note to the old usurer fell due, and nothing from China Aster was ready to meet it; yet, as heaven sends its rain on the just and unjust alike, by a coincidence not unfavorable to the old farmer, the well-to-do uncle, the tanner, having died, the usurer entered upon possession of such part of his property left by will to the wife of China Aster. When still the next interest-day for Orchis came round, it found China Aster worse off than ever; for, besides his other troubles, he was now weak with sickness. Feebly dragging himself to Orchis' agent, he met him in the street, told him just how it was; upon which the agent, with a grave enough face, said that he had instructions from his employer not to crowd him about the interest at present, but to say to him that about the time the note would mature, Orchis would have heavy liabilities to meet, and therefore the note must at that time be certainly paid, and, of course, the back interest with it; and not only so, but, as Orchis had had to allow the interest for good part of the time, he hoped that, for the back interest, China Aster would, in reciprocation, have no objections to allowing interest on the interest annually. To be sure, this was not the law; but, between friends who accommodate each other, it was the custom.

"Just then, Old Plain Talk with Old Prudence turned the corner, coming plump upon China Aster as the agent left him; and whether it was a sun-stroke, or whether they accidentally ran against him, or whether it was his being so weak, or whether it was everything together, or how it was exactly, there is no telling, but poor China Aster fell to the earth, and, striking his head sharply, was picked up senseless. It was a day in July; such a light and heat as only the midsummer banks of the inland Ohio know. China Aster was taken home on a door; lingered a few days with a wandering mind, and kept wandering on, till at last, at dead of night, when nobody was aware, his spirit wandered away into the other world.

"Old Plain Talk and Old Prudence, neither of whom ever omitted attending any funeral, which, indeed, was their chief exercise— these two were among the sincerest mourners who followed the remains of the son of their ancient friend to the grave.

"It is needless to tell of the executions that followed; how that the candlery was sold by the mortgagee; how Orchis never got a penny for his loan; and how, in the case of the poor widow, chastisement was tempered with mercy; for, though she was left penniless, she was not left childless. Yet, unmindful of the alleviation, a spirit of complaint, at what she impatiently called the bitterness of her lot and the hardness of the world, so preyed upon her, as ere long to hurry her from the obscurity of indigence to the deeper shades of the tomb.

"But though the straits in which China Aster had left his family had, besides apparently dimming the world's regard, likewise seemed to dim its sense of the probity of its deceased head, and though this, as some thought, did not speak well for the world, yet it happened in this case, as in others, that, though the world may for a time seem insensible to that merit which lies under a cloud, yet, sooner or later, it always renders honor where honor is due; for, upon the death of the widow, the freemen of Marietta, as a tribute of respect for China Aster, and an expression of their conviction of his high moral worth, passed a resolution, that, until they attained maturity, his children should be considered the town's guests. No mere verbal compliment, like those of some public bodies; for, on the same day, the orphans were officially installed in that hospitable edifice where their worthy grandfather, the town's guest before them, had breathed his last breath.

"But sometimes honor may be paid to the memory of an honest man, and still his mound remain without a monument. Not so, however, with the candle-maker. At an early day, Plain Talk had procured a plain stone, and was digesting in his mind what pithy word or two to place upon it, when there was discovered, in China Aster's otherwise empty wallet, an epitaph, written, probably, in one of those disconsolate hours, attended with more or less mental aberration, perhaps, so frequent with him for some months prior to his end. A memorandum on the back expressed the wish that it might be placed over his grave. Though with the sentiment of the epitaph Plain Talk did not disagree, he himself being at times of a hypochondriac turn—at least, so many said—yet the language struck him as too much drawn out; so, after consultation with Old Prudence, he decided upon making use of the epitaph, yet not without verbal retrenchments. And though, when these were made, the thing still appeared wordy to him, nevertheless, thinking that, since a dead man was to be spoken about, it was but just to let him speak for himself, especially when he spoke sincerely, and when, by so doing, the more salutary lesson would be given, he had the re-trenched inscription chiseled as follows upon the stone:

'HERE LIE

THE REMAINS OF

CHINA ASTER THE CANDLE-MAKER,

WHOSE CAREER

WAS AN EXAMPLE OF THE TRUTH OF SCRIPTURE, AS FOUND

IN THE

SOBER PHILOSOPHY

OF

SOLOMON THE WISE;

FOR HE WAS RUINED BY ALLOWING HIMSELF TO BE PERSUADED,

AGAINST HIS BETTER SENSE,

INTO THE FREE INDULGENCE OF CONFIDENCE,

AND

AN ARDENTLY BRIGHT VIEW OF LIFE,

TO THE EXCLUSION

OF

THAT COUNSEL WHICH COMES BY HEEDING

THE

OPPOSITE VIEW.'

"This inscription raised some talk in the town, and was rather severely criticised by the capitalist—one of a very cheerful turn—who had secured his loan to China Aster by the mortgage; and though it also proved obnoxious to the man who, in town-meeting, had first moved for the compliment to China Aster's memory, and, indeed, was deemed by him a sort of slur upon the candle-maker, to that degree that he refused to believe that the candle-maker himself had composed it, charging Old Plain Talk with the authorship, alleging that the internal evidence showed that none but that veteran old croaker could have penned such a jeremiade—yet, for all this, the stone stood. In everything, of course, Old Plain Talk was seconded by Old Prudence; who, one day going to the grave-yard, in great-coat and over-shoes—for, though it was a sunshiny morning, he thought that, owing to heavy dews, dampness might lurk in the ground—long stood before the stone, sharply leaning over on his staff, spectacles on nose, spelling out the epitaph word by word; and, afterwards meeting Old Plain Talk in the street, gave a great rap with his stick, and said: 'Friend Plain Talk, that epitaph will do very well. Nevertheless, one short sentence is wanting.' Upon which, Plain Talk said it was too late, the chiseled words being so arranged, after the usual manner of such inscriptions, that nothing could be interlined. 'Then,' said Old Prudence, 'I will put it in the shape of a postscript.' Accordingly, with the approbation of Old Plain Talk, he had the following words chiseled at the left-hand corner of the stone, and pretty low down:

'The root of all was a friendly loan.' "[1]

Chapter 41.

ENDING WITH A RUPTURE OF THE HYPOTHESIS.

"With what heart," cried Frank, still in character, "have you told me this story? A story I can no way approve; for its moral, if accepted, would drain me of all reliance upon my last stay, and, therefore, of my last courage in life. For, what was that bright view of China Aster but a cheerful trust that, if he but kept up a brave heart, worked hard, and ever hoped for the best, all at last would go well? If your purpose, Charlie, in telling me this story, was to pain me, and keenly, you have succeeded; but, if it was to destroy my last confidence, I praise God you have not."

"Confidence?" cried Charlie, who, on his side, seemed with his whole heart to enter into the spirit of the thing, "what has confidence to do with the matter? That moral of the story, which I am for commending to you, is this: the folly, on both sides, of a friend's helping a friend. For was not that loan of Orchis to China Aster the first step towards their estrangement? And did it not bring about what in effect was the enmity of Orchis? I tell you, Frank, true friendship, like other precious things, is not rashly to be meddled

---

1. "Root" suggests an ambiguous allusion to 1 Timothy 6.10: "For the love of money is the root of all evil." (For all his attention to the wording of his Bibles, Melville was capable of forgetting that it was not "money" but "the love of money" which Paul said was the root of all evil; see the 2001 Norton Critical Edition *Moby-Dick*, 21.) The topic of borrowing from a friend recalls Melville's mentions of Polonius, who advises his son: "Neither a borrower nor a lender be; / For loan oft loses both itself and friend; / And borrowing dulls the edge of husbandry" (*Hamlet* 1.3.75–77 in Melville's Hilliard, Gray edition).

with. And what more meddlesome between friends than a loan? A
regular marplot.[2] For how can you help that the helper must turn
out a creditor? And creditor and friend, can they ever be one? no,
not in the most lenient case; since, out of lenity to forego one's
claim, is less to be a friendly creditor than to cease to be a creditor
at all. But it will not do to rely upon this lenity, no, not in the best
man; for the best man, as the worst, is subject to all mortal contin-
gencies. He may travel, he may marry, he may join the Come-
Outers, or some equally untoward school or sect, not to speak of
other things that more or less tend to new-cast the character. And
were there nothing else, who shall answer for his digestion, upon
which so much depends?"

"But Charlie, dear Charlie—"

"Nay, wait.—You have hearkened to my story in vain, if you do
not see that, however indulgent and right-minded I may seem to
you now, that is no guarantee for the future. And into the power of
that uncertain personality which, through the mutability of my humanity, I may hereafter become, should not common sense dis-
suade you, my dear Frank, from putting yourself? Consider. Would
you, in your present need, be willing to accept a loan from a friend,
securing him by a mortgage on your homestead, and do so, knowing that you had no reason to feel satisfied that the mortgage might
not eventually be transferred into the hands of a foe? Yet the difference between this man and that man is not so great as the difference between what the same man be to-day and what he may be in
days to come. For there is no bent of heart or turn of thought
which any man holds by virtue of an unalterable nature or will.
Even those feelings and opinions deemed most identical with eternal right and truth, it is not impossible but that, as personal persuasions, they may in reality be but the result of some chance tip of
Fate's elbow in throwing her dice. For, not to go into the first seeds
of things, and passing by the accident of parentage predisposing to
this or that habit of mind, descend below these, and tell me, if you
change this man's experiences or that man's books, will wisdom go
surety for his unchanged convictions? As particular food begets
particular dreams, so particular experiences or books particular
feelings or beliefs. I will hear nothing of that fine babble about development and its laws; there is no development in opinion and
feeling but the developments of time and tide. You may deem all
this talk idle, Frank; but conscience bids me show you how funda-
mental the reasons for treating you as I do."

"But Charlie, dear Charlie, what new notions are these? I
thought that man was no poor drifting weed of the universe, as you

2. A character whose well-intentioned meddling jeopardizes the success of a romance in
   The Busy Body (1709), a play by Susannah Centlivre (1669–1723).

phrased it; that, if so minded, he could have a will, a way, a thought, and a heart of his own. But now you have turned everything upside down again, with an inconsistency that amazes and shocks me."

"Inconsistency? Bah!"

"There speaks the ventriloquist again," sighed Frank, in bitterness.

Illy pleased, it may be, by this repetition of an allusion little flattering to his originality, however much so to his docility, the disciple sought to carry it off by exclaiming: "Yes, I turn over day and night, with indefatigable pains, the sublime pages of my master, and unfortunately for you, my dear friend, I find nothing *there* that leads me to think otherwise than I do. But enough: in this matter the experience of China Aster teaches a moral more to the point than anything Mark Winsome can offer, or I either."

"I cannot think so, Charlie; for neither am I China Aster, nor do I stand in his position. The loan to China Aster was to extend his business with; the loan I seek is to relieve my necessities."

"Your dress, my dear Frank, is respectable; your cheek is not gaunt. Why talk of necessities when nakedness and starvation beget the only real necessities?"

"But I need relief, Charlie; and so sorely, that I now conjure you to forget that I was ever your friend, while I apply to you only as a fellow-being, whom, surely, you will not turn away."

"That I will not. Take off your hat, bow over to the ground, and supplicate an alms of me in the way of London streets, and you shall not be a sturdy beggar in vain. But no man drops pennies into the hat of a friend, let me tell you. If you turn beggar, then, for the honor of noble friendship, I turn stranger."

"Enough," cried the other, rising, and with a toss of his shoulders seeming disdainfully to throw off the character he had assumed. "Enough. I have had my fill of the philosophy of Mark Winsome as put into action. And moonshiny as it in theory may be, yet a very practical philosophy it turns out in effect, as he himself engaged I should find. But, miserable for my race should I be, if I thought he spoke truth when he claimed, for proof of the soundness of his system, that the study of it tended to much the same formation of character with the experiences of the world.—Apt disciple! Why wrinkle the brow, and waste the oil both of life and the lamp, only to turn out a head kept cool by the under ice of the heart? What your illustrious magian[3] has taught you, any poor, old, broken-down, heart-shrunken dandy might have lisped. Pray, leave me, and

3. Wise man (here used ironically). Magi are members of a priestly order from Media or Persia, familiar from the three magi or three wise men who came to see Jesus in Bethlehem (Matthew 2.1–12).

with you take the last dregs of your inhuman philosophy. And here, take this shilling, and at the first wood-landing buy yourself a few chips to warm the frozen natures of you and your philosopher by."

With these words and a grand scorn the cosmopolitan turned on his heel, leaving his companion at a loss to determine where exactly the fictitious character had been dropped, and the real one, if any, resumed. If any, because, with pointed meaning, there occurred to him, as he gazed after the cosmopolitan, these familiar lines:

> "All the world's a stage,
> And all the men and women merely players,
> Who have their exits and their entrances,
> And one man in his time plays many parts."[4]

Chapter 42.

UPON THE HEEL OF THE LAST SCENE THE COSMOPOLITAN ENTERS THE
BARBER'S SHOP,[5] A BENEDICTION ON HIS LIPS.

"Bless you, barber!"

Now, owing to the lateness of the hour, the barber had been all alone until within the ten minutes last passed; when, finding himself rather dullish company to himself, he thought he would have a good time with Souter John and Tam O'Shanter, otherwise called Somnus and Morpheus,[6] two very good fellows, though one was not very bright, and the other an arrant rattle-brain, who, though much listened to by some, no wise man would believe under oath.

In short, with back presented to the glare of his lamps, and so to

---

4. Shakespeare's *As You Like It* 2.7.139–42 is slightly altered from Melville's Hilliard, Gray edition, where the third line begins "They" instead of "Who." A sharp implication enlivens this much-overused passage—that the Confidence Man might have been making many entrances and exits while playing "many parts."

5. Barber stories are a staple in literature, as in *Don Quixote* and *The Arabian Nights*, but Melville may have had in mind a story in P. T. Barnum's recent *The Life of P. T. Barnum Written by Himself* (1855) where the running heads were eye-catching: "UP THE MISSISSIPPI." "THE MYSTIFIED BARBER." "FRIGHTFUL TRANSFORMATION." Melville himself contributed a racy anecdote to the genre, according to an alert lad who grew up to become a famous editor, Ferris Greenslet (Parker 2.890–91).

6. Souter Johnny and Tam o' Shanter are drinking companions in Robert Burns's narrative poem "Tam o' Shanter" (1791). On his drunken way home Tom o' Shanter spies on a scene of devilish erotic revelry in the Kirk (church) of Alloway where the Devil, Old Nick, in "shape of beast, / a towzie tyke, black, grim, and large," plays the bagpipes. ("Towzie tyke": shaggy dog, shaggy like unraveled strands of rope [tow]. In Scots dialect *tyke*, meaning "dog or cur," did not imply small.) Sexually excited by a newly dead "winsome wench" (whose dancing has also excited "even Satan" into glowering passion, Tom reveals himself by calling out his admiration of the wench ("Weel done, Cutty-sark" [short skirt]) and then is chased and almost caught by the "hellish legion." Burns's "deil" (Devil) in the shape of a large black dog recalls the comparison (Chapter 3) of Black Guinea with a large, shaggy black dog, a Newfoundland. In Greco-Roman mythology Somnus was the god of sleep, and Morpheus was the god of dreams who sent human forms to the minds of sleepers. Judging by his needing reassurance that his visitor is just a human being, the barber had been in an alcoholic sleep troubled by the Devil, witches, and the risen dead like those Tam o' Shanter encountered.

the door, the honest barber was taking what are called cat-naps, and dreaming in his chair; so that, upon suddenly hearing the benediction above, pronounced in tones not unangelic, starting up, half awake, he stared before him, but saw nothing, for the stranger stood behind. What with cat-naps, dreams, and bewilderments, therefore, the voice seemed a sort of spiritual manifestation to him; so that, for the moment, he stood all agape, eyes fixed, and one arm in the air.

"Why, barber, are you reaching up to catch birds there with salt?"

"Ah!" turning round disenchanted, "it is only a man, then."

"*Only* a man? As if to be but man were nothing. But don't be too sure what I am. You call me *man*, just as the townsfolk called the angels who, in man's form, came to Lot's house; just as the Jew rustics called the devils who, in man's form, haunted the tombs.[7] You can conclude nothing absolute from the human form, barber."

"But I can conclude something from that sort of talk, with that sort of dress," shrewdly thought the barber, eying him with regained self-possession, and not without some latent touch of apprehension at being alone with him. What was passing in his mind seemed divined by the other, who now, more rationally and gravely, and as if he expected it should be attended to, said: "Whatever else you may conclude upon, it is my desire that you conclude to give me a good shave," at the same time loosening his neck-cloth. "Are you competent to a good shave, barber?"

"No broker more so, sir," answered the barber, whom the business-like proposition instinctively made confine to business-ends his views of the visitor.

"Broker? What has a broker to do with lather? A broker I have always understood to be a worthy dealer in certain papers and metals."

"He, he!" taking him now for some dry sort of joker, whose jokes, he being a customer, it might be as well to appreciate, "he, he! You understand well enough, sir. Take this seat, sir," laying his hand on a great stuffed chair, high-backed and high-armed, crimson-covered, and raised on a sort of dais, and which seemed but to lack a canopy and quarterings, to make it in aspect quite a throne, "take this seat, sir."

---

7. Still more reminders that human-looking shapes may be inhabited by supernatural beings. In Genesis 19.5 the people of Sodom demand to see the two men inside Lot's house, not realizing that they are angels: "And they called unto Lot, and said unto him, Where are the men which came in to thee this night? bring them out unto us, that we may know them." ("Know" in this context may be sexual.) When Jesus came into the country of Gergesenes (Matthew 8.28–33) "there met him two possessed with devils, coming out of the tombs, exceeding fierce, so that no man might pass by that way." Jesus casts out the devils, which then run down into a herd of swine. The whole herd ran "violently down a steep place into the sea, and perished in the waters." The King James wording is ambiguous as to whether the devils drowned or whether the devils and the men they had possessed all drowned.

"Thank you," sitting down; "and now, pray, explain that about the broker. But look, look—what's this?" suddenly rising, and pointing, with his long pipe, towards a gilt notification swinging among colored flypapers from the ceiling, like a tavern sign, " 'No Trust'? No trust means distrust; distrust means no confidence. Barber," turning upon him excitedly, "what fell suspiciousness prompts this scandalous confession? My life!" stamping his foot,[8] "if but to tell a dog that you have no confidence in him be matter for affront to the dog, what an insult to take that way the whole haughty race of man by the beard! By my heart, sir! but at least you are valiant; backing the spleen of Thersites[9] with the pluck of Agamemnon."

"Your sort of talk, sir, is not exactly in my line," said the barber, rather ruefully, being now again hopeless of his customer, and not without return of uneasiness; "not in my line, sir," he emphatically repeated.

"But the taking of mankind by the nose is; a habit, barber, which I sadly fear has insensibly bred in you a disrespect for man. For how, indeed, may respectful conceptions of him coexist with the perpetual habit of taking him by the nose? But, tell me, though I, too, clearly see the import of your notification, I do not, as yet, perceive the object. What is it?"

"Now you speak a little in my line, sir," said the barber, not unrelieved at this return to plain talk; "that notification I find very useful, sparing me much work which would not pay. Yes, I lost a good deal, off and on, before putting that up," gratefully glancing towards it.

"But what is its object? Surely, you don't mean to say, in so many words, that you have no confidence? For instance, now," flinging aside his neck-cloth, throwing back his blouse, and reseating himself on the tonsorial throne, at sight of which proceeding the barber mechanically filled a cup with hot water from a copper vessel over a spirit-lamp, "for instance, now, suppose I say to you, 'Barber, my dear barber, unhappily I have no small change by me to-night, but shave me, and depend upon your money to-morrow'—suppose I should say that now, you would put trust in me, wouldn't you? You would have confidence?"

"Seeing that it is you, sir," with complaisance replied the barber, now mixing the lather, "seeing that it is *you*, sir, I won't answer that question. No need to."

8. Since the Devil in folklore has cloven feet, he may well command attention when stamping for emphasis.
9. Familiar to Melville from Shakespeare's *Troilus and Cressida*. Like Timon and Apemantus, Thersites is one of Shakespeare's embittered, misanthropic characters who rail out unwelcome truths. The cosmopolitan is charging the barber with bringing the power of a heroic Greek king (Agamemnon) to aid a peevish railer against mankind.

"Of course, of course—in that view. But, as a supposition—you would have confidence in me, wouldn't you?"

"Why—yes, yes."

"Then why that sign?"

"Ah, sir, all people ain't like you," was the smooth reply, at the same time, as if smoothly to close the debate, beginning smoothly to apply the lather, which operation, however, was, by a motion, protested against by the subject, but only out of a desire to rejoin, which was done in these words:

"All people ain't like me. Then I must be either better or worse than most people. Worse, you could not mean; no, barber, you could not mean that; hardly that. It remains, then, that you think me better than most people. But that I ain't vain enough to believe; though, from vanity, I confess, I could never yet, by my best wrestlings, entirely free myself; nor, indeed, to be frank, am I at bottom over anxious to—this same vanity, barber, being so harmless, so useful, so comfortable, so pleasingly preposterous a passion."

"Very true, sir; and upon my honor, sir, you talk very well. But the lather is getting a little cold, sir."

"Better cold lather, barber, than a cold heart. Why that cold sign? Ah, I don't wonder you try to shirk the confession. You feel in your soul how ungenerous a hint is there. And yet, barber, now that I look into your eyes—which somehow speak to me of the mother that must have so often looked into them before me—I dare say, though you may not think it, that the spirit of that notification is not one with your nature. For look now, setting business views aside, regarding the thing in an abstract light; in short, supposing a case, barber; supposing, I say, you see a stranger, his face accidentally averted, but his visible part very respectable-looking; what now, barber—I put it to your conscience, to your charity—what would be your impression of that man, in a moral point of view? Being in a signal sense a stranger, would you, for that, signally set him down for a knave?"

"Certainly not, sir; by no means," cried the barber, humanely resentful.

"You would upon the face of him—"

"Hold, sir," said the barber, "nothing about the face; you remember, sir, that is out of sight."

"I forgot that. Well then, you would, upon the *back* of him, conclude him to be, not improbably, some worthy sort of person; in short, an honest man; wouldn't you?"

"Not unlikely I should, sir."

"Well now—don't be so impatient with your brush, barber—suppose that honest man meet you by night in some dark corner of the boat where his face would still remain unseen, asking you to trust him for a shave—how then?"

"Wouldn't trust him, sir."

"But is not an honest man to be trusted?"

"Why—why—yes, sir."

"There! don't you see, now?"

"See what?" asked the disconcerted barber, rather vexedly.

"Why, you stand self-contradicted, barber; don't you?"

"No," doggedly.

"Barber," gravely, and after a pause of concern, "the enemies of our race have a saying that insincerity is the most universal and inveterate vice of man—the lasting bar to real amelioration, whether of individuals or of the world. Don't you now, barber, by your stubbornness on this occasion, give color to such a calumny?"

"Hity-tity!" cried the barber, losing patience, and with it respect; "stubbornness?" Then clattering round the brush in the cup, "Will you be shaved, or won't you?"

"Barber, I will be shaved, and with pleasure; but, pray, don't raise your voice that way. Why, now, if you go through life gritting your teeth in that fashion, what a comfortless time you will have."

"I take as much comfort in this world as you or any other man," cried the barber, whom the other's sweetness of temper seemed rather to exasperate than soothe.

"To resent the imputation of anything like unhappiness I have often observed to be peculiar to certain orders of men," said the other pensively, and half to himself, "just as to be indifferent to that imputation, from holding happiness but for a secondary good and inferior grace, I have observed to be equally peculiar to other kinds of men. Pray, barber," innocently looking up, "which think you is the superior creature?"

"All this sort of talk," cried the barber, still unmollified, "is, as I told you once before, not in my line. In a few minutes I shall shut up this shop. Will you be shaved?"

"Shave away, barber. What hinders?" turning up his face like a flower.

The shaving began, and proceeded in silence, till at length it became necessary to prepare to relather a little—affording an opportunity for resuming the subject, which, on one side, was not let slip.

"Barber," with a kind of cautious kindliness, feeling his way, "barber, now have a little patience with me; do; trust me, I wish not to offend. I have been thinking over that supposed case of the man with the averted face, and I cannot rid my mind of the impression that, by your opposite replies to my questions at the time, you showed yourself much of a piece with a good many other men—

that is, you have confidence, and then again, you have none. Now, what I would ask is, do you think it sensible standing for a sensible man, one foot on confidence and the other on suspicion? Don't you think, barber, that you ought to elect? Don't you think consistency requires that you should either say 'I have confidence in all men,' and take down your notification; or else say, 'I suspect all men,' and keep it up?"

This dispassionate, if not deferential, way of putting the case, did not fail to impress the barber, and proportionately conciliate him. Likewise, from its pointedness, it served to make him thoughtful; for, instead of going to the copper vessel for more water, as he had purposed, he halted half-way towards it, and, after a pause, cup in hand, said: "Sir, I hope you would not do me injustice. I don't say, and can't say, and wouldn't say, that I suspect all men; but I *do* say that strangers are not to be trusted, and so," pointing up to the sign, "no trust."

"But look, now, I beg, barber," rejoined the other deprecatingly, not presuming too much upon the barber's changed temper; "look, now; to say that strangers are not to be trusted, does not that imply something like saying that mankind is not to be trusted; for the mass of mankind, are they not necessarily strangers to each individual man? Come, come, my friend," winningly, "you are no Timon to hold the mass of mankind untrustworthy. Take down your notification; it is misanthropical; much the same sign that Timon traced with charcoal on the forehead of a skull stuck over his cave.[1] Take it down, barber; take it down to-night. Trust men. Just try the experiment of trusting men for this one little trip. Come now, I'm a philanthropist, and will insure you against losing a cent."

The barber shook his head dryly, and answered, "Sir, you must excuse me. I have a family."[2]

---

1. In Melville's edition of Shakespeare's *Timon of Athens* this seemingly corrupt passage is emended to make a soldier find this line written in Timon's cave (not on his tomb): "Timon is dead, who hath outstretched his span." Then in Melville's copy the soldier concludes that "Some beast reared this; there does not live a man" (5.4.3–4). The soldier cannot read the words incised on the actual tomb, so he takes a wax impression of them. The first folio says: "Some Beast reade this; There do's not live a Man." Why Melville thought Timon had drawn words on a skull with charcoal (a word that does not occur in Shakespeare) has not been explained. Melville does not seem to be characterizing the Cosmopolitan by making him misrepresent the play. One possibility is that Melville was echoing the stage direction he had seen in an edition of Shakespeare; another is that he had seen an illustrated edition with such a sign on a skull.
2. The barber, felicitously named William Cream, a nominal Christian, implicitly rejects Jesus' words to the disciples after the rich young man has gone away: "And every one that hath forsaken houses, or brethren, or sisters, or father, or mother, or wife, or children, or lands, for my name's sake, shall receive an hundredfold, and shall inherit everlasting life" (Matthew 19.29; see also Mark 10.29–30).

Chapter 43.

VERY CHARMING.

"So you are a philanthropist, sir," added the barber with an illu-minated look; "that accounts, then, for all. Very odd sort of man the philanthropist. You are the second one, sir, I have seen. Very odd sort of man, indeed, the philanthropist. Ah, sir," again meditatively stirring in the shaving-cup, "I sadly fear, lest you philanthropists know better what goodness is, than what men are." Then, eying him as if he were some strange creature behind cage-bars, "So you are a philanthropist, sir."

"I am Philanthropos,[3] and love mankind. And, what is more than you do, barber, I trust them."

Here the barber, casually recalled to his business, would have re-plenished his shaving-cup, but finding now that on his last visit to the water-vessel he had not replaced it over the lamp, he did so now; and, while waiting for it to heat again, became almost as so-ciable as if the heating water were meant for whisky-punch; and al-most as pleasantly garrulous as the pleasant barbers in romances.

"Sir," said he, taking a throne beside his customer (for in a row there were three thrones on the dais, as for the three kings of Cologne, those patron saints of the barber),[4] "sir, you say you trust men. Well, I suppose I might share some of your trust, were it not for this trade, that I follow, too much letting me in behind the scenes."

"I think I understand," with a saddened look; "and much the same thing I have heard from persons in pursuits different from yours—from the lawyer, from the congressman, from the editor, not to mention others, each, with a strange kind of melancholy vanity, claiming for his vocation the distinction of affording the surest in-lets to the conviction that man is no better than he should be. All of which testimony, if reliable, would, by mutual corroboration, justify some disturbance in a good man's mind. But no, no; it is a mis-take—all a mistake."

"True, sir, very true," assented the barber.

"Glad to hear that," brightening up.

"Not so fast, sir," said the barber; "I agree with you in thinking that the lawyer, and the congressman, and the editor, are in error,

---

3. "I am Philanthropos" (the lover of mankind) plays off against "I am *misanthropos*, and hate mankind" in *Timon of Athens* 4.3.54 (quoted from Melville's Hillard, Gray edition).

4. The supposed relics of the three magi (the wise men from the east who sought "The King of the Jews" in Matthew 2) were taken to the Cologne Cathedral in Germany in the twelfth century. They are sometimes cited as patron saints of travelers (as is Saint Christopher), but (in a pun worthy of his brother Allan) Melville makes the wise men the patrons of barbers, who are heavy users of cologne.

but only in so far as each claims peculiar facilities for the sort of knowledge in question; because, you see, sir, the truth is, that every trade or pursuit which brings one into contact with the facts, sir, such trade or pursuit is equally an avenue to those facts."

"*How* exactly is that?"

"Why, sir, in my opinion—and for the last twenty years I have, at odd times, turned the matter over some in my mind—he who comes to know man, will not remain in ignorance of man. I think I am not rash in saying that; am I, sir?"

"Barber, you talk like an oracle—obscurely, barber, obscurely."

"Well, sir," with some self-complacency, "the barber has always been held an oracle, but as for the obscurity, that I don't admit."

"But pray, now, by your account, what precisely may be this mysterious knowledge gained in your trade? I grant you, indeed, as before hinted, that your trade, imposing on you the necessity of functionally tweaking the noses of mankind, is, in that respect, unfortunate, very much so; nevertheless, a well-regulated imagination should be proof even to such a provocation to improper conceits. But what I want to learn from you, barber, is, how does the mere handling of the outside of men's heads lead you to distrust the inside of their hearts?"

"What, sir, to say nothing more, can one be forever dealing in macassar oil, hair dyes, cosmetics, false moustaches, wigs, and toupees, and still believe that men are wholly what they look to be? What think you, sir, are a thoughtful barber's reflections, when, behind a careful curtain, he shaves the thin, dead stubble off a head, and then dismisses it to the world, radiant in curling auburn? To contrast the shamefaced air behind the curtain, the fearful looking forward to being possibly discovered there by a prying acquaintance, with the cheerful assurance and challenging pride with which the same man steps forth again, a gay deception,[5] into the street, while some honest, shock-headed fellow humbly gives him the wall. Ah, sir, they may talk of the courage of truth, but my trade teaches me that truth sometimes is sheepish. Lies, lies, sir, brave lies are the lions!"

"You twist the moral, barber; you sadly twist it. Look, now; take it this way: A modest man thrust out naked into the street, would he not be abashed? Take him in and clothe him; would not his confidence be restored? And in either case, is any reproach involved? Now, what is true of the whole, holds proportionably true of the

5. A *gay deceiver* then meant a Lothario, a libertine; much later it successively acquired various homosexual implications. The sense of "gay deceivers" as breast enlargers for women or artificial enhancements for men such as "false moustaches, wigs, and toupees" would fit the context here; if Melville intended such a play on the usual meaning, his usage is very early.

part. The bald head is a nakedness which the wig is a coat to. To feel uneasy at the possibility of the exposure of one's nakedness at top, and to feel comforted by the consciousness of having it clothed—these feelings, instead of being dishonorable to a bald man, do, in fact, but attest a proper respect for himself and his fellows. And as for the deception, you may as well call the fine roof of a fine chateau a deception, since, like a fine wig, it also is an artificial cover to the head, and equally, in the common eye, decorates the wearer.—I have confuted you, my dear barber; I have confounded you."

"Pardon," said the barber, "but I do not see that you have. His coat and his roof no man pretends to palm off as a part of himself, but the bald man palms off hair, not his, for his own."

"Not *his*, barber? If he have fairly purchased his hair, the law will protect him in its ownership, even against the claims of the head on which it grew. But it cannot be that you believe what you say, barber; you talk merely for the humor. I could not think so of you as to suppose that you would contentedly deal in the impostures you condemn."

"Ah, sir, I must live."

"And can't you do that without sinning against your conscience, as you believe? Take up some other calling."

"Wouldn't mend the matter much, sir."

"Do you think, then, barber, that, in a certain point, all the trades and callings of men are much on a par? Fatal, indeed," raising his hand, "inexpressibly dreadful, the trade of the barber, if to such conclusions it necessarily leads. Barber," eying him not without emotion, "you appear to me not so much a misbeliever, as a man misled. Now, let me set you on the right track; let me restore you to trust in human nature, and by no other means than the very trade that has brought you to suspect it."

"You mean, sir, you would have me try the experiment of taking down that notification," again pointing to it with his brush; "but, dear me, while I sit chatting here, the water boils over."

With which words, and such a well-pleased, sly, snug, expression, as they say some men have when they think their little stratagem has succeeded, he hurried to the copper vessel, and soon had his cup foaming up with white bubbles, as if it were a mug of new ale.

Meantime, the other would have fain gone on with the discourse; but the cunning barber lathered him with so generous a brush, so piled up the foam on him, that his face looked like the yeasty crest of a billow, and vain to think of talking under it, as for a drowning priest in the sea to exhort his fellow-sinners on a raft. Nothing would do, but he must keep his mouth shut. Doubtless, the interval was not, in a meditative way, unimproved; for, upon the traces of the operation being at last removed, the cosmopolitan rose, and, for added refreshment, washed his face and hands; and having generally readjusted himself, began, at last, addressing the barber in a manner different, singularly so, from his previous one. Hard to say exactly what the manner was, any more than to hint it was a sort of magical; in a benign way, not wholly unlike the manner, fabled or otherwise, of certain creatures in nature, which have the power of persuasive fascination—the power of holding another creature by the button of the eye, as it were, despite the serious disinclination, and, indeed, earnest protest, of the victim. With this manner the conclusion of the matter was not out of keeping; for, in the end, all argument and expostulation proved vain, the barber being irresistibly persuaded to agree to try, for the remainder of the present trip, the experiment of trusting men, as both phrased it. True, to save his credit as a free agent, he was loud in averring that it was only for the novelty of the thing that he so agreed, and he required the other, as before volunteered, to go security to him against any loss that might ensue; but still the fact remained, that he engaged to trust men, a thing he had before said he would not do, at least not unreservedly. Still the more to save his credit, he now insisted upon it, as a last point, that the agreement should be put in black and white, especially the security part. The other made no demur; pen, ink, and paper were provided, and grave as any notary the cosmopolitan sat down, but, ere taking the pen, glanced up at the notification, and said: "First down with that sign, barber—Timon's sign, there; down with it."

This, being in the agreement, was done—though a little reluctantly—with an eye to the future, the sign being carefully put away in a drawer.

"Now, then, for the writing," said the cosmopolitan, squaring himself. "Ah," with a sigh, "I shall make a poor lawyer, I fear. Ain't used, you see, barber, to a business which, ignoring the principle of honor, holds no nail fast till clinched. Strange, barber," taking up the blank paper, "that such flimsy stuff as this should make such strong hawsers; vile hawsers, too. Barber," starting up, "I won't put it in black and white. It were a reflection upon our joint honor. I will take your word, and you shall take mine."

"But your memory may be none of the best, sir. Well for you, on your side, to have it in black and white, just for a memorandum like, you know."

"That, indeed! Yes, and it would help *your* memory, too, wouldn't it, barber? Yours, on your side, being a little weak, too, I dare say. Ah, barber! how ingenious we human beings are; and how kindly we reciprocate each other's little delicacies, don't we? What better proof, now, that we are kind, considerate fellows, with responsive fellow-feelings—eh, barber? But to business. Let me see. What's your name, barber?"

"William Cream, sir."

Pondering a moment, he began to write; and, after some corrections, leaned back, and read aloud the following:

"AGREEMENT

"Between

"FRANK GOODMAN, Philanthropist, and Citizen of the World,

"and

"WILLIAM CREAM, Barber of the Mississippi steamer, Fidèle.

"The first hereby agrees to make good to the last any loss that may come from his trusting mankind, in the way of his vocation, for the residue of the present trip; PROVIDED that William Cream keep out of sight, for the given term, his notification of 'No TRUST,' and by no other mode convey any, the least hint or intimation, tending to discourage men from soliciting trust from him, in the way of his vocation, for the time above specified; but, on the contrary, he do, by all proper and reasonable words, gestures, manners, and looks, evince a perfect confidence in all men, especially strangers; otherwise, this agreement to be void.

"Done, in good faith, this 1st day of April, 18—, at a quarter to twelve o'clock, P.M., in the shop of said William Cream, on board the said boat, Fidèle."

"There, barber; will that do?"

"That will do," said the barber, "only now put down your name."

Both signatures being affixed, the question was started by the barber, who should have custody of the instrument; which point, however, he settled for himself, by proposing that both should go together to the captain, and give the document into his hands—the barber hinting that this would be a safe proceeding, because the captain was necessarily a party disinterested, and, what was more, could not, from the nature of the present case, make anything by a breach of trust. All of which was listened to with some surprise and concern.

"Why, barber," said the cosmopolitan, "this don't show the right spirit; for me, I have confidence in the captain purely because he is a man; but he shall have nothing to do with our affair; for if you have no confidence in me, barber, I have in you. There, keep the paper yourself," handing it magnanimously.

"Very good," said the barber, "and now nothing remains but for me to receive the cash."

Though the mention of that word, or any of its singularly numerous equivalents, in serious neighborhood to a requisition upon one's purse, is attended with a more or less noteworthy effect upon the human countenance, producing in many an abrupt fall of it—in others, a writhing and screwing up of the features to a point not undistressing to behold, in some, attended with a blank pallor and fatal consternation—yet no trace of any of these symptoms was visible upon the countenance of the cosmopolitan, notwithstanding nothing could be more sudden and unexpected than the barber's demand.

"You speak of cash, barber; pray in what connection?"

"In a nearer one, sir," answered the barber, less blandly, "than I thought the man with the sweet voice stood, who wanted me to trust him once for a shave, on the score of being a sort of thirteenth cousin."

"Indeed, and what did you say to him?"

"I said, 'Thank you, sir, but I don't see the connection.' "

"How could you so unsweetly answer one with a sweet voice?"

"Because, I recalled what the son of Sirach says in the True Book: 'An enemy speaketh sweetly with his lips;' and so I did what the son of Sirach advises in such cases: 'I believed not his many words.' "[6]

"What, barber, do you say that such cynical sort of things are in the True Book, by which, of course, you mean the Bible?"

"Yes, and plenty more to the same effect. Read the Book of Proverbs."

"That's strange, now, barber; for I never happen to have met with those passages you cite. Before I go to bed this night, I'll inspect the Bible I saw on the cabin-table, to-day. But mind, you mustn't quote the True Book that way to people coming in here; it would be impliedly a violation of the contract. But you don't know how glad I feel that you have for one while signed off all that sort of thing."

"No, sir; not unless you down with the cash."

"Cash again! What do you mean?"

"Why, in this paper here, you engage, sir, to insure me against a certain loss, and—"

"Certain? Is it so *certain* you are going to lose?"

"Why, that way of taking the word may not be amiss, but I didn't mean it so. I meant a *certain* loss; you understand, a CERTAIN loss, that is to say, a certain loss. Now then, sir, what use your mere writing and saying you will insure me, unless beforehand you place in my hands a money-pledge, sufficient to that end?"

6. "An enemy speaketh sweetly with his lips, but in his heart he imagineth how to throw thee into a pit: he will weep with his eyes, but if he find opportunity, he will not be satisfied with blood" (Ecclesiasticus 12.16). "Affect not to be made equal unto him in talk, and believe not his many words: for with much communication will he tempt thee, and smiling upon thee will get out thy secrets" (Ecclesiasticus 13.11). The alternate title of the apocryphal Book of the Ecclesiasticus is "The Wisdom of Jesus the Son of Sirach." Because the book's author, Jesus, shares the same name with Christ, there may be an intended ambiguity on Melville's part.

"I see; the material pledge."

"Yes, and I will put it low; say fifty dollars."

"Now what sort of a beginning is this? You, barber, for a given time engage to trust man, to put confidence in men, and, for your first step, make a demand implying no confidence in the very man you engage with. But fifty dollars is nothing, and I would let you have it cheerfully, only I unfortunately happen to have but little change with me just now."

"But you have money in your trunk, though?"

"To be sure. But you see—in fact, barber, you must be consistent. No, I won't let you have the money now; I won't let you violate the inmost spirit of our contract, that way. So good-night, and I will see you again."

"Stay, sir"—humming and hawing—"you have forgotten something."

"Handkerchief?—gloves? No, forgotten nothing. Good-night."

"Stay, sir—the—the shaving."

"Ah, I *did* forget that. But now that it strikes me, I shan't pay you at present. Look at your agreement; you must trust. Tut! against loss you hold the guarantee. Good-night, my dear barber."

With which words he sauntered off, leaving the barber in a maze, staring after.

But it holding true in fascination as in natural philosophy, that nothing can act where it is not, so the barber was not long now in being restored to his self-possession and senses; the first evidence of which perhaps was, that, drawing forth his notification from the drawer, he put it back where it belonged; while, as for the agreement, that he tore up; which he felt the more free to do from the impression that in all human probability he would never again see the person who had drawn it. Whether that impression proved well-founded or not, does not appear. But in after days, telling the night's adventure to his friends, the worthy barber always spoke of his queer customer as the man-charmer—as certain East Indians are called snake-charmers—and all his friends united in thinking him QUITE AN ORIGINAL.

Chapter 44.

IN WHICH THE LAST THREE WORDS OF THE LAST CHAPTER ARE MADE
THE TEXT OF DISCOURSE, WHICH WILL BE SURE OF RECEIVING MORE
OR LESS ATTENTION FROM THOSE READERS WHO DO NOT SKIP IT.

"QUITE AN ORIGINAL:" A phrase, we fancy, rather oftener used by the young, or the unlearned, or the untraveled, than by the old, or the well-read, or the man who has made the grand tour. Certainly, the sense of originality exists at its highest in an infant, and probably at its lowest in him who has completed the circle of the sciences.

As for original characters in fiction, a grateful reader will, on meeting with one, keep the anniversary of that day. True, we sometimes hear of an author who, at one creation, produces some two or three score such characters; it may be possible. But they can hardly be original in the sense that Hamlet is, or Don Quixote, or Milton's Satan.[7] That is to say, they are not, in a thorough sense, original at all. They are novel, or singular, or striking, or captivating, or all four at once.[8]

More likely, they are what are called odd characters; but for that, are no more original, than what is called an odd genius, in his way, is. But, if original, whence came they? Or where did the novelist pick them up?

Where does any novelist pick up any character? For the most part, in town, to be sure. Every great town is a kind of man-show, where the novelist goes for his stock, just as the agriculturist goes to the cattle-show for his. But in the one fair, new species of quadrupeds are hardly more rare, than in the other are new species of characters—that is, original ones. Their rarity may still the more appear from this, that, while characters, merely singular, imply but singular forms so to speak, original ones, truly so, imply original instincts.

In short, a due conception of what is to be held for this sort of personage in fiction would make him almost as much of a prodigy there, as in real history is a new law-giver, a revolutionizing philosopher, or the founder of a new religion.

In nearly all the original characters, loosely accounted such in works of invention, there is discernible something prevailingly local, or of the age; which circumstance, of itself, would seem to invalidate the claim, judged by the principles here suggested.

Furthermore, if we consider, what is popularly held to entitle characters in fiction to being deemed original, is but something personal—confined to itself. The character sheds not its character-

7. The original characters Hamlet, Don Quixote, and Milton's Satan, all played high roles in Melville's intellectual, emotional, and aesthetic life, although direct evidence is skimpy for Don Quixote. See *Pierre* book 7, chapter 6 on "Hamletism," defined as "The flower of virtue cropped by a too rare mischance"; and book 9, chapter 2 on "the hopeless gloom" of the "interior meanings" of the play. See *Moby-Dick* chapter 26 for Melville's association of John Bunyan (the author of *Pilgrim's Progress*), Miguel de Cervantes Saavedra (the author of *Don Quixote*), and President Andrew Jackson as "selectest champions" chosen from among the "kingly commons." For Melville's markings regarding Satan in *Paradise Lost* see Grey and Robillard (Selected Bibliography). When the Melvilles left Arrowhead for New York City in 1863 they left behind in the dining room John Martin's 1820s mezzotint of *Paradise Lost* 2.5 ("Satan exalted sat").

8. Melville is expressing skepticism toward the achievement of the most popular novelist of the era, Charles Dickens, widely hailed for creating many original characters (see Thomas Quirk on pp. 265–66 herein).

istic on its surroundings, whereas, the original character, essentially such, is like a revolving Drummond light,[9] raying away from itself all round it—everything is lit by it, everything starts up to it (mark how it is with Hamlet), so that, in certain minds, there follows upon the adequate conception of such a character, an effect, in its way, akin to that which in Genesis attends upon the beginning of things.

For much the same reason that there is but one planet to one orbit, so can there be but one such original character to one work of invention. Two would conflict to chaos. In this view, to say that there are more than one to a book, is good presumption there is none at all. But for new, singular, striking, odd, eccentric, and all sorts of entertaining and instructive characters, a good fiction may be full of them. To produce such characters, an author, beside other things, must have seen much, and seen through much: to produce but one original character, he must have had much luck.

There would seem but one point in common between this sort of phenomenon in fiction and all other sorts: it cannot be born in the author's imagination—it being as true in literature as in zoology, that all life is from the egg.

In the endeavor to show, if possible, the impropriety of the phrase, *Quite an Original*, as applied by the barber's friends, we have, at unawares, been led into a dissertation bordering upon the prosy, perhaps upon the smoky. If so, the best use the smoke can be turned to, will be, by retiring under cover of it, in good trim as may be, to the story.

Chapter 45.

THE COSMOPOLITAN INCREASES IN SERIOUSNESS.

In the middle of the gentlemen's cabin burned a solar lamp,[1] swung from the ceiling, and whose shade of ground glass was all round fancifully variegated, in transparency, with the image of a horned altar, from which flames rose, alternate with the figure of a robed man, his head encircled by a halo. The light of this lamp, af-

9. Another memory of the showman P. T. Barnum in the 1840s. "Powerful Drummond lights were placed at the top of the [American] Museum, which, in the darkest night, threw a flood of light up and down Broadway, from the Battery to Niblo's, that would enable one to read a newspaper in the street. These were the first Drummond lights ever seen in New York, and they made people talk, and so advertised my Museum" (Barnum, *Struggles and Triumphs: or Forty Years' Recollections*, 1883, 61). Niblo's Garden, a fashionable theater, was far up Broadway at Prince (north of Broome, just south of Houston).
1. Introduced in Philadelphia around 1840, this light has an oil container just under the burner, to reduce shadows, and a metal ring that encircles the flame and stretches it higher. Tall glass cylinders (chimneys) were sometimes inserted inside round globes, some of cut and etched glass, either abstract or figural. The best oil was whale oil; kerosene became the fuel of choice after the Pennsylvania oil fields were developed after

ter dazzlingly striking on marble, snow-white and round—the slab
of a centre-table beneath—on all sides went rippling off with ever-
diminishing distinctness, till, like circles from a stone dropped in
water, the rays died dimly away in the furthest nook of the place.

Here and there, true to their place, but not to their function,
swung other lamps, barren planets, which had either gone out from
exhaustion, or been extinguished by such occupants of berths as
the light annoyed, or who wanted to sleep, not see.

By a perverse man, in a berth not remote, the remaining lamp
would have been extinguished as well, had not a steward forbade,
saying that the commands of the captain required it to be kept
burning till the natural light of day should come to relieve it. This
steward, who, like many in his vocation, was apt to be a little free-
spoken at times, had been provoked by the man's pertinacity to remind him, not only of the sad consequences which might, upon
occasion, ensue from the cabin being left in darkness, but, also, of
the circumstance that, in a place full of strangers, to show one's
self anxious to produce darkness there, such an anxiety was, to say
the least, not becoming. So the lamp—last survivor of many—
burned on, inwardly blessed by those in some berths, and inwardly
execrated by those in others.

Keeping his lone vigils beneath his lone lamp, which lighted his
book on the table, sat a clean, comely, old man, his head snowy as
the marble, and a countenance like that which imagination as-
cribes to good Simeon, when, having at last beheld the Master of
Faith, he blessed him and departed in peace.[2] From his hale look of
greenness in winter, and his hands ingrained with the tan, less, apparently, of the present summer, than of accumulated ones past,
the old man seemed a well-to-do farmer, happily dismissed, after a
thrifty life of activity, from the fields to the fireside—one of those
who, at three-score-and-ten, are fresh-hearted as at fifteen; to
whom seclusion gives a boon more blessed than knowledge, and at
last sends them to heaven untainted by the world, because ignorant

---

the Civil War. Foster explains the symbolism this way: "the light of the Old and New Testaments, to judge from its two transparencies, the horned altar and the robed man with
a halo. On Mount Sinai the Lord gave Moses directions for making the altar, with 'the
horns of it upon the four corners thereof' (Exodus 27.2)"; the haloed man would be Jesus. In Revelation 9.13 the disciple John hears details about the coming of the apocalypse from an angel speaking in "a voice from the four horns of the golden altar which is
before God."

2. "And, behold, there was a man in Jerusalem, whose name was Simeon; and the same
   man was just and devout, waiting for the consolation of Israel: and the Holy Ghost was
   upon him. And it was revealed unto him by the Holy Ghost, that he should not see
   death, before he had seen the Lord's Christ. And he came by the Spirit into the temple:
   and when the parents brought in the child Jesus, to do for him after the custom of the
   law, Then took he him up in his arms, and blessed God, and said, Lord, now lettest thou
   thy servant depart in peace, according to thy word: For mine eyes have seen thy salvation, Which thou hast prepared before the face of all people; A light to lighten the Gentiles, and the glory of thy people Israel" (Luke 2.25–32).

of it; just as a countryman putting up at a London inn, and never stirring out of it as a sight-seer, will leave London at last without once being lost in its fog, or soiled by its mud.

Redolent from the barber's shop, as any bridegroom tripping to the bridal chamber might come,[3] and by his look of cheeriness seeming to dispense a sort of morning through the night, in came the cosmopolitan; but marking the old man, and how he was occupied, he toned himself down, and trod softly, and took a seat on the other side of the table, and said nothing. Still, there was a kind of waiting expression about him.

"Sir," said the old man, after looking up puzzled at him a moment, "sir," said he, "one would think this was a coffee-house, and it was war-time, and I had a newspaper here with great news, and the only copy to be had, you sit there looking at me so eager."

"And so you *have* good news there, sir—the very best of good news."[4]

"Too good to be true," here came from one of the curtained berths.

"Hark!" said the cosmopolitan. "Some one talks in his sleep."

"Yes," said the old man, "and you—*you* seem to be talking in a dream. Why speak you, sir, of news, and all that, when you must see this is a book I have here—the Bible, not a newspaper?"

"I know that; and when you are through with it—but not a moment sooner—I will thank you for it. It belongs to the boat, I believe—a present from a society."

"Oh, take it, take it!"

"Nay, sir, I did not mean to touch you at all. I simply stated the fact in explanation of my waiting here—nothing more. Read on, sir, or you will distress me."

This courtesy was not without effect. Removing his spectacles, and saying he had about finished his chapter, the old man kindly presented the volume, which was received with thanks equally kind. After reading for some minutes, until his expression merged from attentiveness into seriousness, and from that into a kind of pain, the cosmopolitan slowly laid down the book, and turning to the old man, who thus far had been watching him with benign curiosity, said: "Can you, my aged friend, resolve me a doubt—a disturbing doubt?"

"There are doubts, sir," replied the old man, with a changed

---

3. Jesus is more than once called the bridegroom (see Matthew 9.15 and the parable of the virgins in Matthew 25.1–13). The book begins with the conflict between the words of the New Testament on the slate of the mute and the words "NO TRUST" written on a sign. The book draws to a close with a repetition of that opposition.
4. The old man puns (apparently unconsciously) on the Anglo-Saxon roots of Gospel, "good news."

countenance, "there are doubts, sir, which, if man have them, it is not man that can solve them."

"True; but look, now, what my doubt is. I am one who thinks well of man. I love man. I have confidence in man. But what was told me not a half-hour since? I was told that I would find it written— 'Believe not his many words—an enemy speaketh sweetly with his lips'—and also I was told that I would find a good deal more to the same effect, and all in this book. I could not think it; and, coming here to look for myself, what do I read? Not only just what was quoted, but also, as was engaged, more to the same purpose, such as this: 'With much communication he will tempt thee; he will smile upon thee, and speak thee fair, and say What wantest thou? If thou be for his profit he will use thee; he will make thee bare, and will not be sorry for it. Observe and take good heed. When thou hearest these things, awake in thy sleep.' "[5]

"Who's that describing the confidence-man?" here came from the berth again.

"Awake in his sleep, sure enough, ain't he?" said the cosmopolitan, again looking off in surprise. "Same voice as before, ain't it? Strange sort of dreamy man, that. Which is his berth, pray?"

"Never mind *him*, sir," said the old man anxiously, "but tell me truly, did you, indeed, read from the book just now?"

"I did," with changed air, "and gall and wormwood it is to me, a truster in man; to me, a philanthropist."

"Why," moved, "you don't mean to say, that what you repeated is really down there? Man and boy, I have read the good book this seventy years, and don't remember seeing anything like that. Let me see it," rising earnestly, and going round to him.

"There it is; and there—and there"—turning over the leaves, and pointing to the sentences one by one; "there—all down in the 'Wisdom of Jesus, the Son of Sirach.' "

"Ah!" cried the old man, brightening up, "now I know. Look," turning the leaves forward and back, till all the Old Testament lay flat on one side, and all the New Testament flat on the other, while in his fingers he supported vertically the portion between, "look, sir, all this to the right is certain truth, and all this to the left is certain truth, but all I hold in my hand here is apocrypha."

"Apocrypha?"[6]

---

5. In Ecclesiasticus 13 these passages occur in verses 11, 6, 4, 5, and 13. The first American edition's error of "bear" for "bare" (in "he will make thee bare"), noted by Foster, probably arose from Melville's bad handwriting rather than his rewriting of the text.

6. The Apocrypha (from the Greek meaning "hidden") are certain books of the Old Testament of doubtful authority or "uncertain credit," as the old man says. Though not always incorporated into Protestant editions of the Bible, in the nineteenth century these books were frequently included between the Old and New Testaments.

"Yes; and there's the word in black and white," pointing to it. "And what says the word? It says as much as 'not warranted;' for what do college men say of anything of that sort? They say it is apocryphal. The word itself, I've heard from the pulpit, implies something of uncertain credit. So if your disturbance be raised from aught in this apocrypha," again taking up the pages, "in that case, think no more of it, for it's apocrypha."

"What's that about the Apocalypse?"[7] here, a third time, came from the berth.

"He's seeing visions now, ain't he?" said the cosmopolitan, once more looking in the direction of the interruption. "But, sir," resuming, "I cannot tell you how thankful I am for your reminding me about the apocrypha here. For the moment, its being such escaped me. Fact is, when all is bound up together, it's sometimes confusing. The uncanonical part should be bound distinct. And, now that I think of it, how well did those learned doctors who rejected for us this whole book of Sirach. I never read anything so calculated to destroy man's confidence in man. This son of Sirach even says—I saw it but just now: 'Take heed of thy friends;'[8] not, observe, thy seeming friends, thy hypocritical friends, thy false friends, but thy *friends*, thy real friends—that is to say, not the truest friend in the world is to be implicitly trusted. Can Rochefoucault equal that?[9] I should not wonder if his view of human nature, like Machiavelli's,[1] was taken from this Son of Sirach. And to call it wisdom—the Wisdom of the Son of Sirach! Wisdom, indeed! What an ugly thing wisdom must be! Give me the folly that dimples the cheek, say I, rather than the wisdom that curdles the blood. But no, no; it ain't wisdom; it's apocrypha, as you say, sir. For how can that be trustworthy that teaches distrust?"

"I tell you what it is," here cried the same voice as before, only now in less of mockery, "if you two don't know enough to sleep, don't be keeping wiser men awake. And if you want to know what wisdom is, go find it under your blankets."

"Wisdom?" cried another voice with a brogue; "arrah, and is't wisdom the two geese are gabbling about all this while? To bed with ye, ye divils, and don't be after burning your fingers with the likes of wisdom."

"We must talk lower," said the old man; "I fear we have annoyed these good people."

7. An Apocalypse is any prophetic writing that reveals the future, especially one that predicts a cosmic cataclysm. The Book of Revelation is also called by its Greek name, "The Apocalypse," the book that reveals the future.
8. "Separate thyself from thine enemies, and take heed of thy friends" (Ecclesiasticus 6.13; see n. 6, p. 235).
9. I.e., could Rochefoucauld equal that in worldliness and cynicism (see n. 7, p. 167).
1. Machiavelli's *The Prince* could be read as advocating that a ruler trust no one and betray everyone (see n. 7, p. 36, and n. 6, p. 135).

"I should be sorry if wisdom annoyed any one," said the other; "but we will lower our voices, as you say. To resume: taking the thing as I did, can you be surprised at my uneasiness in reading passages so charged with the spirit of distrust?"

"No, sir, I am not surprised," said the old man; then added: "from what you say, I see you are something of my way of thinking—you think that to distrust the creature, is a kind of distrusting of the Creator. Well, my young friend, what is it? This is rather late for you to be about. What do you want of me?"

These questions were put to a boy in the fragment of an old linen coat, bedraggled and yellow, who, coming in from the deck bare-footed on the soft carpet, had been unheard. All pointed and flut-tering, the rags of the little fellow's red-flannel shirt, mixed with those of his yellow coat, flamed about him like the painted flames in the robes of a victim in *auto-da-fe*.[2] His face, too, wore such a polish of seasoned grime, that his sloe-eyes sparkled from out it like lustrous sparks in fresh coal. He was a juvenile peddler, or *marchand*, as the polite French might have called him, of travelers' conveniences; and, having no allotted sleeping-place, had, in his wanderings about the boat, spied, through glass doors, the two in the cabin; and, late though it was, thought it might never be too much so for turning a penny.

Among other things, he carried a curious affair—a miniature ma-hogany door, hinged to its frame, and suitably furnished in all re-spects but one, which will shortly appear. This little door he now meaningly held before the old man, who, after staring at it a while, said: "Go thy ways with thy toys, child."

"Now, may I never get so old and wise as that comes to," laughed the boy through his grime; and, by so doing, disclosing leopard-like teeth, like those of Murillo's[3] wild beggar-boy's.

"The divils are laughing now, are they?" here came the brogue from the berth. "What do the divils find to laugh about in wisdom, begorrah? To bed with ye, ye divils, and no more of ye."

2. Act of faith (literally); a heretic bound at the stake and being burned alive in the Span-ish Inquisition. In thinking to dedicate the book to victims of auto-da-fe, Melville was seeing himself as a writer who had been burned at the stake by low church religious re-viewers. In his sermon "On Beggary" (New York *New World* December 5, 1840) Orville Dewey declared that beggary "is pregnant with meaning. Its tattered garments are stamped with more, and alas! far other, than heraldic insignia. Idleness, improvidence, and ruin are written upon every fluttering shred of its 'looped and windowed ragged-ness.' The victim at the *auto da fé* did not more certainly wear the garment of doom." (Dewey's quotation is from Shakespeare's *King Lear*, 3.4.31.)

3. Bartolome Murillo (1617–1682), Spanish painter famous in his own time for exalted biblical scenes but in the 1850s for moodily romanticized street urchins, often depicted as begging, eating, and playing with dogs. Later Melville owned the art book *The Works of the Eminent Masters*, which reproduced a painting called "The Beggar Boy." Melville's main period of collecting prints (he could not afford to collect oil paintings) came later, after he had a job at the New York Custom House, but already in the 1850s he had bought at least some prints, including the John Martin depiction of Satan.

"You see, child, you have disturbed that person," said the old man; "you mustn't laugh any more."

"Ah, now," said the cosmopolitan, "don't, pray, say that; don't let him think that poor Laughter is persecuted for a fool in this world."

"Well," said the old man to the boy, "you must, at any rate, speak very low."

"Yes, that wouldn't be amiss, perhaps," said the cosmopolitan; "but, my fine fellow, you were about saying something to my aged friend here; what was it?"

"Oh," with a lowered voice, coolly opening and shutting his little door, "only this: when I kept a toy-stand at the fair in Cincinnati last month, I sold more than one old man a child's rattle."

"No doubt of it," said the old man. "I myself often buy such things for my little grandchildren."

"But these old men I talk of were old bachelors."

The old man stared at him a moment; then, whispering to the cosmopolitan: "Strange boy, this; sort of simple, ain't he? Don't know much, hey?"

"Not much," said the boy, "or I wouldn't be so ragged."

"Why, child, what sharp ears you have!" exclaimed the old man.

"If they were duller, I would hear less ill of myself," said the boy.

"You seem pretty wise, my lad," said the cosmopolitan; "why don't you sell your wisdom, and buy a coat?"

"Faith," said the boy, "that's what I did to-day, and this is the coat that the price of my wisdom bought. But won't you trade? See, now, it is not the door I want to sell; I only carry the door round for a specimen, like. Look now, sir," standing the thing up on the table, "supposing this little door is your state-room door; well," opening it, "you go in for the night; you close your door behind you—thus. Now, is all safe?"

"I suppose so, child," said the old man.

"Of course it is, my fine fellow," said the cosmopolitan.

"All safe. Well. Now, about two o'clock in the morning, say, a soft-handed gentleman comes softly and tries the knob here—thus; in creeps my soft-handed gentleman; and hey, presto! how comes on the soft cash?"

"I see, I see, child," said the old man; "your fine gentleman is a fine thief, and there's no lock to your little door to keep him out;" with which words he peered at it more closely than before.

"Well, now," again showing his white teeth, "well, now, some of you old folks are knowing 'uns, sure enough; but now comes the great invention," producing a small steel contrivance, very simple but ingenious, and which, being clapped on the inside of the little door, secured it as with a bolt. "There now," admiringly holding it off at arm's-length, "there now, let that soft-handed gentleman come now a' softly trying this little knob here, and let him keep a' trying till he finds his head as soft as his hand. Buy the traveler's patent lock, sir, only twenty-five cents."

"Dear me," cried the old man, "this beats printing. Yes, child, I will have one, and use it this very night."

With the phlegm of an old banker pouching the change, the boy now turned to the other: "Sell you one, sir?"

"Excuse me, my fine fellow, but I never use such blacksmiths' things."

"Those who give the blacksmith most work seldom do," said the boy, tipping him a wink expressive of a degree of indefinite know-ingness, not uninteresting to consider in one of his years. But the wink was not marked by the old man, nor, to all appearances, by him for whom it was intended.

"Now then," said the boy, again addressing the old man. "With your traveler's lock on your door to-night, you will think yourself all safe, won't you?"

"I think I will, child."

"But how about the window?"

"Dear me, the window, child. I never thought of that. I must see to that."

"Never you mind about the window," said the boy, "nor, to be honor bright,[4] about the traveler's lock either, (though I ain't sorry for selling one), do you just buy one of these little jokers," produc-ing a number of suspender-like objects, which he dangled before the old man; "money-belts, sir; only fifty cents."

"Money-belt? never heard of such a thing."

"A sort of pocket-book," said the boy, "only a safer sort. Very good for travelers."

"Oh, a pocket-book. Queer looking pocket-books though, seems to me, Ain't they rather long and narrow for pocket-books?"

"They go round the waist, sir, inside," said the boy; "door open or locked, wide awake on your feet or fast asleep in your chair, impos-sible to be robbed with a money-belt."

"I see, I see. It *would* be hard to rob one's money-belt. And I was told to-day the Mississippi is a bad river for pick-pockets. How much are they?"

"Only fifty cents, sir."

"I'll take one. There!"

"Thank-ee. And now there's a present for ye," with which, draw-

---

4. As at 106.9, colloquial assurance of truth, like "scout's honor." On May 1, 1881, and March 8, 1882, Melville responded to autograph seekers by writing "Honor bright—"

ing from his breast a batch of little papers, he threw one before the old man, who, looking at it, read "*Counterfeit Detector*."[5]

"Very good thing," said the boy, "I give it to all my customers who trade seventy-five cents' worth; best present can be made them. Sell you a money-belt, sir?" turning to the cosmopolitan.

"Excuse me, my fine fellow, but I never use that sort of thing; my money I carry loose."

"Loose bait ain't bad," said the boy, "look a lie and find the truth; don't care about a Counterfeit Detector, do ye? or is the wind East, d'ye think?"

"Child," said the old man in some concern, "you mustn't sit up any longer, it affects your mind; there, go away, go to bed."

"If I had some people's brains to lie on, I would," said the boy, "but planks is hard, you know."

"Go, child—go, go!"

"Yes, child,—yes, yes," said the boy, with which roguish parody, by way of congé, he scraped back his hard foot on the woven flowers of the carpet, much as a mischievous steer in May scrapes back his horny hoof in the pasture; and then with a flourish of his hat—which, like the rest of his tatters, was, thanks to hard times, a belonging beyond his years, though not beyond his experience, being a grown man's cast-off beaver—turned, and with the air of a young Caffre, quitted the place.

"That's a strange boy," said the old man, looking after him. "I wonder who's his mother; and whether she knows what late hours he keeps?"

"The probability is," observed the other, "that his mother does not know. But if you remember, sir, you were saying something, when the boy interrupted you with his door."

"So I was.—Let me see," unmindful of his purchases for the moment, "what, now, was it? What was that I was saying? Do *you* remember?"

"Not perfectly, sir; but, if I am not mistaken, it was something like this: you hoped you did not distrust the creature; for that would imply distrust of the Creator."

"Yes, that was something like it," mechanically and unintelligently letting his eye fall now on his purchases.

"Pray, will you put your money in your belt to-night?"

"It's best, ain't it?" with a slight start. "Never too late to be cautious. 'Beware of pick-pockets' is all over the boat."

5. Among the most common of these books were ones by John. S. Dye, including *Dye's Counterfeit Detector and Universal Bank Note Gazetteer* (1850) and *Dye's Bank Mirror and Illustrated Counterfeit Detector* (1852). They were needed because banks issued their own bank notes, there being no U.S. national currency until the start of the Civil War, in 1861, when the North issued a five-dollar bill.

"Yes, and it must have been the Son of Sirach, or some other morbid cynic, who put them there. But that's not to the purpose. Since you are minded to it, pray, sir, let me help you about the belt. I think that, between us, we can make a secure thing of it."

"Oh no, no, no!" said the old man, not unperturbed, "no, no, I wouldn't trouble you for the world," then, nervously folding up the belt, "and I won't be so impolite as to do it for myself, before you, either. But, now that I think of it," after a pause, carefully taking a little wad from a remote corner of his vest pocket, "here are two bills they gave me at St. Louis, yesterday. No doubt they are all right; but just to pass time, I'll compare them with the Detector here. Blessed boy to make me such a present. Public benefactor, that little boy!"

Laying the Detector square before him on the table, he then, with something of the air of an officer bringing by the collar a brace of culprits to the bar, placed the two bills opposite the Detector, upon which, the examination began, lasting some time, prosecuted with no small research and vigilance, the forefinger of the right hand proving of lawyer-like efficacy in tracing out and pointing the evidence, whichever way it might go.

After watching him a while, the cosmopolitan said in a formal voice, "Well, what say you, Mr. Foreman; guilty, or not guilty?—Not guilty, ain't it?"

"I don't know, I don't know," returned the old man, perplexed, "there's so many marks of all sorts to go by, it makes it a kind of uncertain. Here, now, is this bill," touching one, "it looks to be a three dollar bill on the Vicksburgh Trust and Insurance Banking Company. Well, the Detector says—"

"But why, in this case, care what it says? Trust and Insurance! What more would you have?"

"No; but the Detector says, among fifty other things, that, if a good bill, it must have, thickened here and there into the substance of the paper, little wavy spots of red; and it says they must have a kind of silky feel, being made by the lint of a red silk handkerchief stirred up in the paper-maker's vat—the paper being made to order for the company."

"Well, and is—"

"Stay. But then it adds, that sign is not always to be relied on; for some good bills get so worn, the red marks get rubbed out. And that's the case with my bill here—see how old it is—or else it's a counterfeit, or else—I don't see right—or else—dear, dear me—I don't know what else to think."

"What a peck of trouble that Detector makes for you now; believe me, the bill is good; don't be so distrustful. Proves what I've always thought, that much of the want of confidence, in these days, is owing to these Counterfeit Detectors you see on every desk and counter. Puts people up to suspecting good bills. Throw it away, I beg, if only because of the trouble it breeds you."

"No; it's troublesome, but I think I'll keep it.—Stay, now, here's another sign. It says that, if the bill is good, it must have in one corner, mixed in with the vignette, the figure of a goose, very small, indeed, all but microscopic; and, for added precaution, like the figure of Napoleon outlined by the tree, not observable, even if magnified, unless the attention is directed to it.[6] Now, pore over it as I will, I can't see this goose."

"Can't see the goose? why, I can; and a famous goose it is. There" (reaching over and pointing to a spot in the vignette).

"I don't see it—dear me—I don't see the goose. Is it a real goose?"

"A perfect goose; beautiful goose."

"Dear, dear, I don't see it."

"Then throw that Detector away, I say again; it only makes you purblind; don't you see what a wild-goose chase it has led you? The bill is good. Throw the Detector away."

"No; it ain't so satisfactory as I thought for, but I must examine this other bill."

"As you please, but I can't in conscience assist you any more; pray, then, excuse me."

So, while the old man with much painstakings resumed his work, the cosmopolitan, to allow him every facility, resumed his reading. At length, seeing that he had given up his undertaking as hopeless, and was at leisure again, the cosmopolitan addressed some gravely interesting remarks to him about the book before him, and, presently, becoming more and more grave, said, as he turned the large volume slowly over on the table, and with much difficulty traced the faded remains of the gilt inscription giving the name of the society who had presented it to the boat, "Ah, sir, though every one must be pleased at the thought of the presence in public places of such a book, yet there is something that abates the satisfaction. Look at this volume; on the outside, battered as any old valise in the baggage-room; and inside, white and virgin as the hearts of lilies in bud."

"So it is, so it is," said the old man sadly, his attention for the first directed to the circumstance.

"Nor is this the only time," continued the other, "that I have ob-

6. The allusion is to a then-popular engraving published in London in 1830, "The Shade of Napoleon Visiting His Tomb" (in St. Helena in the South Atlantic). ("Shade": ghost.) In this example of "hidden art," most viewers at first see two conspicuous trees near the gravestone then only later perceive the ghost of Napoleon in military regalia caught in full outline between the trees, brooding over his own tomb.

served these public Bibles in boats and hotels. All much like this—old without, and new within. True, this aptly typifies that internal freshness, the best mark of truth, however ancient; but then, it speaks not so well as could be wished for the good book's esteem in the minds of the traveling public. I may err, but it seems to me that if more confidence was put in it by the traveling public, it would hardly be so."

With an expression very unlike that with which he had bent over the Detector, the old man sat meditating upon his companion's remarks a while; and, at last, with a rapt look, said: "And yet, of all people, the traveling public most need to put trust in that guardianship which is made known in this book."

"True, true," thoughtfully assented the other.

"And one would think they would want to, and be glad to," continued the old man kindling; "for, in all our wanderings through this vale, how pleasant, not less than obligatory, to feel that we need start at no wild alarms, provide for no wild perils; trusting in that Power which is alike able and willing to protect us when we cannot ourselves."

His manner produced something answering to it in the cosmopolitan, who, leaning over towards him, said sadly: "Though this is a theme on which travelers seldom talk to each other, yet, to you, sir, I will say, that I share something of your sense of security. I have moved much about the world, and still keep at it; nevertheless, though in this land, and especially in these parts of it, some stories are told about steamboats and railroads fitted to make one a little apprehensive, yet, I may say that, neither by land nor by water, am I ever seriously disquieted, however, at times, transiently uneasy; since, with you, sir, I believe in a Committee of Safety,[7] holding silent sessions over all, in an invisible patrol, most alert when we soundest sleep, and whose beat lies as much through forests as towns, along rivers as streets. In short, I never forget that passage of Scripture which says, 'Jehovah shall be thy confidence.'[8] The traveler who has not this trust, what miserable misgivings must be his; or, what vain, short-sighted care must he take of himself."

7. Travel by railroads and steamships was in fact extremely hazardous, a point of Hawthorne's satire in his 1843 "The Celestial Railroad" (p. 429 herein). In July 1852 Hawthorne's sister Louise was among the 80 passengers who died just north of Manhattan when the steamship Henry Clay crashed into the east bank of the Hudson after racing with the steamship *Armenia*. The narrator in the first paragraph of Melville's "Cock-A-Doodle-Doo!" (1853) laments the many recent "dreadful casualties, by locomotive and steamer." In the French Revolution, the Committees of Safety were at first moderate in their attempt to safeguard the nation during a period of instability but became instruments of terror. Melville alludes to God's guardian angels—like the Recording Angel, figures derived from the Bible but colored by their assimilation into popular culture, where individuals are sometimes thought to be accompanied by a personal guardian angel.

8. "For the Lord shall be thy confidence, and shall keep thy foot from being taken" (Proverbs 3.26).

"Even so," said the old man, lowly.

"There is a chapter," continued the other, again taking the book, "which, as not amiss, I must read you. But this lamp, solar-lamp as it is, begins to burn dimly."

"So it does, so it does," said the old man with changed air, "dear me, it must be very late. I must to bed, to bed! Let me see," rising and looking wistfully all round, first on the stools and settees, and then on the carpet, "let me see, let me see;—is there anything I have forgot,—forgot? Something I a sort of dimly remember. Something, my son—careful man—told me at starting this morning, this very morning. Something about seeing to—something before I got into my berth. What could it be? Something for safety. Oh, my poor old memory!"

"Let me give a little guess, sir. Life-preserver?"

"So it was. He told me not to omit seeing I had a life-preserver in my state-room; said the boat supplied them, too. But where are they? I don't see any. What are they like?"

"They are something like this, sir, I believe," lifting a brown stool with a curved tin compartment underneath; "yes, this, I think, is a life-preserver, sir; and a very good one, I should say, though I don't pretend to know much about such things, never using them myself."[9]

"Why, indeed, now! Who would have thought it? *that* a life-preserver? That's the very stool I was sitting on, ain't it?"

"It is. And that shows that one's life is looked out for, when he ain't looking out for it himself. In fact, any of these stools here will float you, sir, should the boat hit a snag, and go down in the dark. But, since you want one in your room, pray take this one," handing it to him. "I think I can recommend this one; the tin part," rapping it with his knuckles, "seems so perfect—sounds so very hollow."

"Sure it's *quite* perfect, though?" Then, anxiously putting on his spectacles, he scrutinized it pretty closely—"well soldered? quite tight?"

"I should say so, sir; though, indeed, as I said, I never use this sort of thing, myself. Still, I think that in case of a wreck, barring sharp-pointed timbers, you could have confidence in that stool for a special providence."

"Then, good-night, good-night; and Providence have both of us in its good keeping."

"Be sure it will," eying the old man with sympathy, as for the mo-

---

9. Jeffrey Auerbach in a book on the Crystal Palace, *The Great Exhibition of 1851: A Nation on Display* (1999), cites an innovation on display, a "patent portable water-closet," which could convert into a floating life-preserver. As William Braswell (1943) explained, in this ship of fools the best life preserver one can expect is a stool that conceals a chamberpot under the seat. The Cosmopolitan may never use such things because he is not really a human being.

ment he stood, money-belt in hand, and life-preserver under arm, "be sure it will, sir, since in Providence, as in man, you and I equally put trust. But, bless me, we are being left in the dark here. Pah! what a smell, too."

"Ah, my way now," cried the old man, peering before him, "where lies my way to my state-room?"

"I have indifferent eyes, and will show you; but, first, for the good of all lungs, let me extinguish this lamp."

The next moment, the waning light expired, and with it the waning flames of the horned altar, and the waning halo round the robed man's brow;[1] while in the darkness which ensued, the cosmopolitan kindly led the old man away. Something further may follow of this Masquerade.

---

1. This ambiguous ending strikes many readers as suggesting, if not promising, that a sequel will follow. The biographical evidence is against that reading, but in the next months, especially while traveling in the Mediterranean, Melville encountered situations that reminded him of his book. In Venice on April 5, 1857, he noted in his journal that his guide Antonio was a "good character for Con. Man" and added a note in that entry: "(For Con. Man)."

A Note on the Text

The existence of the Northwestern-Newberry (NN) Edition of *The Confidence-Man* in *The Writings of Herman Melville* means that this Norton Critical Edition (NCE) does not have to contain an elaborate textual apparatus, especially because the textual situation simple. Parker's work on the text for the 1971 NCE went directly into the 1984 NN Edition. Because Parker now makes some new emendations for the first time, the present text does not reprint the NN edition but can be defined simply as a new edition conservatively emended from the American edition of 1857. This NCE is a slightly corrected reprint from *The Confidence-Man: His Masquerade* (New York: Dix, Edwards & Co., 1857), the edition set from the manuscript primarily or wholly in the hand of Melville's sister Augusta. As in 1971, a record is printed of emendations. Anyone interested in the full publication history and bibliographical descriptions of the nineteenth-century editions will go to the NN edition.

The NN edition of *The Confidence-Man* remains essential for photographic reproductions and transcriptions of "The River" and several surviving fragments from draft pages of chapter 14 and the contents pages (found in the attic at Arrowhead, Melville's Berkshire farmhouse, by his nieces early in the twentieth century). Most significant are the drafts of one of the three chapters on aesthetic issues, chapter 14, "Worth the Consideration of Those to Whom It May Prove Worth Considering." (In this NCE, Elizabeth Foster and Harrison Hayford analyze the effects of Melville's elaborate revisions of that chapter.)

The English edition (London: Longman, Brown, Green, Longmans, & Roberts, 1857) was set from proofs of the American edition. The only two variants of any length between the American and the English editions are both footnotes apparently inserted in the English edition to define Yankeeisms: a footnote on "weed" ("Crape on his hat"; p. 21) and another on "sophomore" ("A student in his second year"; p. 33) The full list of variants printed in the NN Edition is of little significance, because it reveals no revisions or corrections by Melville and no expurgations by the English publisher. About the only deliberate revisions in the English edition, aside from the two added footnotes, seem to be someone's attempt to change occurrences of "nigh" into "near" and of "illy" into "ill." Almost all of the variant English readings, in short, are routine memorial substitutions or routine "improvements" of the American proofs. Because the English corrections have no special authority we do not attribute any of the emendations below to the English edition.

In this NCE we silently correct several errors due merely to shifting or damaged type that occurred in printing the American edition (such as "abox" for "a box"). We silently correct several blunders caused by the inaccurate breaking of words at the end of a line (e.g., "snap-/ing") except when some ambiguity results (e.g., "in / deed"). We silently correct upside down type (as in "uufortunate" for "unfortunate") and correct "ihat" (meaning "that"). We also silently correct obvious mistakes, such as "in the the" for "in the" or "freind" for "friend." All such items are included in the NN lists unless they are correct in the surviving proofs at the Houghton Library.

Not even his sister Augusta was able to copy Melville's handwriting infallibly, and a good many wrong words got into the American text. They stayed on in the English text because they were not merely wrong forms of words but totally wrong words, and the English reader, or compositor, although competent, found none of these errors. Our more significant emendations of words (such as "number" for the first edition's "murder") are footnoted in the text of this NCE. A few wrong words may well remain in the text, still undetected despite the scrutiny of Foster and all subsequent editors.

5.22	evidently not	evidently
6.11	magic	music
15.17	Corcovado	Cocovarde
19.27	men,	men
21.32	clergyman	clergymen
26.7	ACQUAINTANCE	ACQUANTANCE
27.2	Virginia	Pennsylvania
27.21	"don't	don't
29.26	strangers, I	strangers. I
36.11	fraternal	paternal
40.5	scoffer?	scoffer,
40.7	falsehood?	falsehood.
40.26	negro?	negro.
41.15	one-legged	one-eyed
44.1	exempted him	exempted
44.20	prejudice	prejudices

44.37	thereby	there by
50.1	World's	world's
50.1	Charity	charity
51.3	World's	world's
51.3	Charity	charity
51.10	World's	world's
51.10	Charity	Charity
53.39	hesitate?	hesitate.
55.28	company?	company.
56.6	added,	added
57.17	stand 'way	stand-way
59.22	Arimanius	Ariamius
63.23	*Rapids*	*Rapias*
63.43	pray?	pray,
72.14	permissible	not permissible
73.16	law!	law?
74.17	brightening.	brightening."
74.19-20	brightening. Seriously	brightening seriously
75.25	caterpillar	butterfly
75.26	butterfly	caterpillar
75.31	life. As	life as
75.31	elsewhere, experience	elsewhere. Experience
80.4	wish	wish,
80.4	friend	friend,
83.3	saying,	saying
85.5	'Medea	"Medea
85.6	Æson?'	Æson?"
86.25	incurable.	incurable?
90.4	Iapis	Japus
91.7	"ladies	ladies
91.33	bead	lead
97.42	all together	altogether
98.7	"since	since
100.4	story?	story.
105.19	hoist-posts	horse-posts
106.15	money."	money.
108.26	"His	His
109.21	him, all	him. All
112.8	'Ah	"Ah
112.10	Green.'	Green.
115.8	trust?	trust.
118.14	Girardeau	Giradeau
118.19	Girardeau	Giradeau
119.13	Girardeau	Giradeau
121.30	'possums,	'possums,'

125.19	have	has
127.15	sir,'	sir,
127.16	'has	has
127.44	set?	set.
128.2	ones?	ones.
129.7	butterfly' "	butterfly."
129.32	you,	you
130.14	suppose?"	suppose.
132.5	boys,	boys'
139.30	cured?'	cured?
140.33	men?	men.
142.29	mean	mean;
142.29	it;	it
143.2	confinement?"	confinement?
145.4	short	stout
145.4	stout	short
152.5	burke	burk
152.10	indeed	in/deed
153.6	is	it
158.40	marauding	maurauding
159.32	number	murder
166.9	Brinvillierses	Brinvilliarses
168.37	'Politics,'	"Politics,"
173.15	grave!"	grave!
176.7	principle	principal
179.24	humane	human
180.25	Charlie	Frank
180.27	drink	drink,
180.27	it,	it
181.32	everywhere	everwhere
184.24	cosmopolitan.	cosmopolitan
184.27	SURPRISING	SUPRISING
195.29	favor."	favor.
198.4	eye?"	eye?'
198.18	then,	then
201.14	you.	you,
201.38	respect,	respect
202.39	it,	it
203.6	you	you,
203.6	mean,	mean
204.23	principal-and-interest	principle-and-interest
204.30	principal	principle
205.1	Frank?	Frank.
205.6	terrestrial	terrestial
207.36	it."	it.

207.39	Charlie."	Charlie.
208.2	him."	him.
208.11	it."	it.
209.14	heartlessness.	heartlessness
214.19	Talk	Talk,
216.26	"At	At
217.13	him.	him
220.13	stone:	stone.
221.7	Friend	Friend,
223.2	own.	own?
226.4	" 'No	"No
226.4	Trust'?	Trust?"
226.5	No	"No
229.7	up?	up.
231.21	hearts?"	hearts?
232.4	bald	bold
241.13	bare	bear
242.1	white,"	white,'
242.34	now	more
242.36	wisdom."	wisdom
245.24	"nor	nor
245.34	boy;	boy

The River†

A source for Melville's "The River" (first titled "The Mississippi") is Timothy Flint's *A Condensed Geography and History of the Western States; or, The Mississippi Valley* (1828), in one edition or another or perhaps as repeated in a pamphlet on John Banvard's panorama of the Mississippi. In the NN Edition of *The Confidence-Man* Harrison Hayford traces the comical range of known possibilities where Melville could have encountered this material and also shows that Melville did *not* demonstrably use Flint's better known *Recollections of the Last Ten Years in the Valley of the Mississippi* (1826). Melville would have seen a good many analogs, if not actual sources, in set pieces on the Mississippi published in many newspapers, magazines, and books, such as a good example of the genre, "The Mississippi," found online by Scott Norsworthy in the *Missouri* Republican for July 10, 1845, and forwarded to the editors. An overt theme or sometimes a subtext in the examples yet discovered is exuberant nationalism, a celebration of the majestic features in President Thomas Jefferson's Louisiana Purchase as a setting befitting the heroic expansion of white settlers into the west. By early training and character Melville liked the challenge of writing his own version of popular theme topics, such as the Dead Letter Office. Once he decided to write a book set on the Mississippi, a warming-up exercise would be to try his hand at something many others had done well at. After writing such a fine celebratory piece he would have seen that it had no place in a book in which many things are questioned rather than championed and in which few characters behave with unambiguous heroism. And the more he looked at realistic reminiscences of the Mississippi such as T. B. Thorpe published in 1855 (see Selected Bibliography), the more he would have seen that his own aims were different. He dropped "The River."

As the word Abraham means the father of a great multitude of men so the word Missippii means the father of a great multitude of waters. His tribes stream in from east & west, exceeding fruitful the lands they enrich. In this granary of a continent this basin of the Missippii must not the nations be greatly multiplied & blest?

† This text of Melville's manuscript "The River" is based on Harrison Hayford's genetic transcription in the NN Edition (1984), 497 and 499 (facing photographic reproductions of the manuscript pages), and is used by permission of the Northwestern University Press and the Houghton Library, Harvard University. We follow Melville in several slips and misspellings, conspicuously of "Mississippi" and "ie" words like "field." Hayford acknowledges the transcriptions by Jay Leyda in *The Melville Log* (1951), Elizabeth S. Foster in her 1954 Hendricks House Edition, H. Bruce Franklin in his Bobbs-Merrill Edition (1967), and Robert R. Allan in the 1971 NCE, then proffers eight new readings of his own. A near-miraculous recovery is the name "Timon" in the first inscription of the last sentence, "the Timon snows from his solitudes," where later Melville marked "Timon" out. On this name, as Hayford humorously says, "all previous editors threw in the towel."

258

Above the Falls of St: Anthony for the most part he winds evenly on between banks of flags or through tracts of pine over marble sands in waters so clear that the deepest fish have the visable flight of the bird. Undisturbed as the lowly life in its bosom feeds the lordly life on its shores, the coronetted elk & the deer, while in the walrus form of some couched rock in the channel, furred over with moss, the furred bear on the marge seems to eye his amphibious brother. Wood and wave wed, man is remote. The Unsung Time, the Golden Age of the billow.

By his Fall, though he rise not again, the unhumbled river ennobles himself now deepens now proudly expands, now first forms his character & begins that career whose majestic amenity if not overborne by feirce onsets of torrents shall end only with ocean.

Like a larger Susquehannah like a long-drawn bison herd he browses on through the prairie, here & there expanding into archipelagoes cycladean in beauty, while fissured & verdant, a long China Wall, the bluffs sweep bluely away. Glad & content the sacred river glides on.

But at St: Louis the course of this dream is run. Down on it like a Pawnee from ambush foams the yellow-painted Missouri. The calmness is gone, the grouped isles disappear, the shores are jagged & rent, the hue of the water is clayed, the before moderate current is rapid & vexed. The peace of the Upper River seems broken in the Lower, nor is it ever renewed.

The Missouri seems rather a hostile element than a filial flood. Longer, stronger than the father of waters like Jupiter he dethrones his sire & reigns in his stead. Under the benign name Mississippi it is in truth the Missouri that now rolls to the Gulf, the Missouri that with the snows from his solitudes freezes the warmth of the genial zones, the Missouri that by open assault or artful sap sweeps away forest & feild grave-yard & town, the Missouri that not a tributary but an invader enters the sea, long disdaining to yeild his white wave to the blue.

Melville's Sources for Chapters 14 and 44 and His Revisions

ELIZABETH S. FOSTER

[The "Shock of Wit" in Melville's Revisions of Chapter 14]†

Any reader who observes the changes that Melville made from verson to version will see some of the reasons why the novel is obscure. It is immediately apparent that Melville's fear of wounding religious sensibilities was a real one and strong enough to account for his having buried his religious allegory pretty effectively in his novel. For example, Melville liked the following sentence well enough to carry it over intact (except for a shift to the subjunctive) * * * but he deleted it before publication: "So that the worst that can be said of any author in this particular, is that he shares a fault, if fault it be, with the author of authors." He gradually softened the following sentence until the first part was gone altogether and the second reduced to the word "contrasts": "And it is with man as with his maker: what makes him hard to comprehend is his inconsistency." Also, he finally stuck out every phrase or sentence which makes a clear assertion of his agnosticism, e.g.: "And possibly it may be in the one case as the other [human nature and the divine nature], that the expression of ignorance is wisdom . . ." He deleted a ringing sentence which says that sooner or later Nature "puts out every one who anyway pretends to be acquainted with the whole of her, which is indispensable to fitly comprehending any part of her." (Melville capitalizes "Nature" throughout, but not "author of authors.")
Furthermore, the style that Melville invented or evolved for the

---

† From Elizabeth S. Foster, ed., Appendix to *The Confidence-Man* (New York: Hendricks House, 1954), 375–77. Foster's physical analysis of the fragments has been superseded by the Northwestern-Newberry "Manuscript Fragments" (with photofacsimiles), 401–99. Anyone wanting to work with the manuscripts will go to the NN Edition, and after that to the Houghton Library, so we have omitted Foster's potentially confusing labels of versions as "B" and "D." The fuller NN analysis does not supersede Foster's elegant tracing out of the direction and purpose of Melville's revisions.

expository parts of this novel desiderates understatement, under-emphasis, litotes, and complexity that looks like simplicity. As we see him in his revisions moving always in these directions, and away from the loose structure, open clarity, and directness of his earliest versions of passages, we watch many ideas growing less and less obvious. Let us look in a general way at these revisions.

If any testimony were needed that artistry, taste, and genius presided at the composition of this novel, it could be found in the consistency with which Melville's tireless revision pushed towards one wished-for, clearly defined, and hitherto uncreated style, the style proper to the mood and matter of his unique novel.

In revision Melville tended to expand first, and later to contract. He expanded by pausing to emphasize or clarify a point * * *; by adding new material or allowing the old to ramify; and by adding qualifying words and phrases which almost invariably softened or weakened the meaning (e.g., "still be" becomes "still run the risk of being," and "fate . . . as" becomes "fare . . . something as"). He shortened in two ways: he cut out whole sentences and passages, almost every one of which would have been considered sacrilegious or infidel by many of his contemporaries; and with unsparing hand he pruned away superfluous words and predications.

Some of Melville's revisions of diction show him groping for the exact word. A very great many of them show him carefully convert-ing statement to understatement: "proof sufficient" becomes "proof presumptive" and finally "some presumption"; "is" becomes "may prove"; "prove otherwise" becomes "prove not so much so"; "al-ways" becomes "mainly"; "many characters" becomes "no few char-acters"; "is" becomes "would seem"; "it would" becomes "it ought to"; "a fatal objection" becomes "an adequate objection"; "always varies" becomes "subject to variation"; "are bound to" becomes "may." Only once or twice does Melville make his language stronger in revision: "different" becomes "conflicting"; "excluded" becomes "excluded with contempt."

In keeping with this hushing of the voice, this meticulous mod-eration of thought, this elegant avoidance of vulgar emphasis in language, is the toning down of color, of metaphor and simile: the sequestered youth is described first as "pine green," and then merely as "at fault" upon entering real life; a comparison of incon-sistent characters with some of the beasts in Revelation is deleted. Only those comparisons are finally retained which are, not fanciful or decorative, but as functional as an axle.

The same consistency of purpose is seen in Melville's syntactical revisions. By combining sentences, shrinking predication, subordi-nating, he not only achieves a classical economy and purity but also diminishes the emphasis that some of his thoughts enjoyed while

they stood alone. * * * His favorite method of achieving understatement by subordination, an achievement which may be seen in
the sentence just mentioned, is to set main thoughts on relative
grounds by tucking them into the terms of a comparison and then
to put the whole upon even more minor and tentative grounds by
introducing it with "Upon the whole, it might rather be thought,
that . . .," or "Which may appear the less improbable if it be considered that. . . ." Thus the very syntax abets the hinting and whispering which are the language of this novel.

The other object or end of Melville's syntactical revisions was
tension, tautness, strength in sentence structure. He increased par-
allelism regularly and periodic structure frequently from revision to
revision as he combined and reduced sentences. He reversed the
terms of comparisons, sometimes to make them conform better to
the logic of the context, but often to gain suspense and climax,
as in the next-to-last paragraph. The sentences, particularly the
balanced and periodic ones, uncoil like springs, with a lithe, inex-
orable, cool precision. But this relentless movement of the sentence is half hidden beneath the mild language, the hesitating
modifications, and emerges at the period with the shock of wit. In
his revisions we may see Melville with infinite pains achieving in
his sentences that fine ironic contrast and tension between mild-
mannered, leisurely surface and stern dialectic beneath, which is
the mode of his novel.

HARRISON HAYFORD

[Melville's "Smoky" Revisions of Chapter 14]†

Altogether, Melville's changes in wording subsequent to the last
surviving manuscript version demonstrate that although the basic
sentence-by-sentence layout of the chapter (except for sentence 29)
was by now set, the wording of individual sentences was still fluid.
The last half of the chapter (sentences 17–28) underwent substantial changes, gaining, in addition to sentence 29, an extra clause
(19) and a transitional phrase (26A). Throughout, by numerous
deletions and substitutions, Melville pruned away unnecessary
words and eliminated awkward repetitions. In sentence 10, for example, "the characters of no few people he is in living contact with"
becomes "living character," and "of it" is deleted because the refer-

† From "Manuscript Fragments" in the "Editorial Appendix" of *The Confidence-Man*
(Evanston and Chicago: Northwestern University Press and the Newberry Library,
1984), 462. Reprinted by permission of Northwestern University Press.

ence of "phantoms" is clear without the prepositional phrase. When "mere" is added to sentence 10, it is deleted from sentence 25. Likewise "of human nature" disappears from the end of sentence 26 when "professing to portray human nature" appears in the first part of the sentence. Often there is no reason apparent for Melville's simple substitution of one word or phrase for another. One striking tendency, however, does emerge: his diction becomes more qualified, more noncommittal, in the narrator's words in Chapter 44, more "smoky": "we have, unawares, been led into a dissertation bordering upon the prosy, perhaps upon the smoky. If so the best use the smoke can be turned to, will be, by retiring under cover of it, in good trim as may be, to the story." Thus "otherwise" is changed to "not so much so" (sentence 6), "the universal" to "a pretty general and pretty thorough" (25), and "fatal" to "adequate" (27). Many of these changes occur in verbs: "is" to "bears" and "was" to "seemed" (20), "is" to "may prove" (24), "be" to "run risk of being" (26A), and "would" to "ought to" (26B). Categorical words are deleted: "essentially" (7A), "absolutely" (14), and "invariably" (24); while qualifying ones are added: "someway" and "in certain cases" (17), and "something" (26B). Even when a couple of more definite words are added or substituted, as in "with contempt" (24) and "conflicting" (25), they occur in statements already undermined by noncommittal diction, leaving their force obscured by a haze of "smoke."

TOM QUIRK

[Sources for Chapters 14 and 44 in *The Confidence-Man*]†

The three interpolated chapters on literature (14, 33, and 44) in *The Confidence-Man* serve, superficially at least, as apologies to the reader for certain shortcomings he may find in the representation of some of the characters in the novel. Chapters 14 and 44, however, appear to have been prompted less by the imagined complaints of readers than by the author's personal reactions to writers as unlike as Montaigne and a contemporary reviewer for *Putnam's Magazine*.

Chapter 14 describes the contradictory expectations of readers of fiction—that a fictional character be consistent but also that "fiction based on fact should never be contradictory to it." Melville continues:

---

† Retitled from Tom Quirk, "Two Sources in *The Confidence-Man*," *Melville Society Extracts* 39 (September 1979), 12–13, and reprinted by permission of the author.

and is it not a fact, that, in real life, a consistent character is a
rara avis? Which being so, the distaste of readers to the contrary sort in books, can hardly arise from any sense of their untrueness. It may rather be from perplexity as to understanding
them. But if the acutest sage be often at his wits' ends to understand living character, shall those who are not sages expect
to run and read character in those mere phantoms which flit
along a page, like shadows along a wall? That fiction, where
every character can, by reason of its consistency, be comprehended at a glance, either exhibits but sections of character,
making them appear for wholes, or else is very untrue to reality;
while, on the other hand, that author who draws a character,
even though to common view incongruous in its parts, as the
flying-squirrel, and, at different periods, as much at variance
with itself as the caterpillar is with the butterfly into which it
changes, may yet, in so doing, be not false but faithful to facts.

Melville's statement of this problem, which provides occasion for
the "comedy of thought" of Chapter 14, echoes the sentiments and
to some extent the reasoning of Montaigne as he had expressed
them in "Of the Inconsistency of Our Actions." There, the Gascon
philosopher wrote:

There seems indeed some possibility of forming a judgment of
a man from the habitual features of his life, but, considering
the natural instability of our manners and opinions, I have often thought even the best authors a little mistaken in so obsti-
nately endeavouring to mould us into any consistent and solid
contexture. They choose some general air, and according to
that arrange and interpret all the actions of a man, of which, if
some be so stiff and stubborn that they cannot bend or turn
them to any uniformity to the rest, they then, without further
ceremony, impute them to dissimulation.[1]

Melville owned a copy of Montaigne's *Essays*, and at some time
wrote an amusing and affectionate poem about the man entitled
"Montaigne and His Kitten." His mention of the "acutest sage" in
the passage quoted above is probably in reference to the humane
skeptic whom Melville personally admired. Moreover, while the author may have shared Montaigne's misgivings about the consistency
of human character, like Montaigne he harbored some hope that
man's true nature might eventually be discovered. For both men
conclude their speculations on the same note: Montaigne arguing
that we must "penetrate the very soul, and there discover by what

---

1. Melville purchased a copy of Montaigne on January 18, 1848 (Sealts, *Melville's Reading*,
   entry 366). The edition has not been identified, but it is likely that he acquired a copy of
   the Hazlitt edition of the Cotton translation published by J. Templeman of London, the
   source of my quotations.

springs the motion is guided"; and Melville suggesting [in chapter 14] that "the more earnest psychologists may, in the face of previous failures, still cherish expectations with regard to some mode of infallibly discovering the heart of man." The business of Montaigne's essay, however, is to make an observation about human nature. Melville's concern is less with life than literature. Nevertheless, this chapter appears to be an extension and amplification of the bare suggestions about literary creation Melville found in Montaigne.

The second response and perhaps the more interesting one, because it is a reaction against rather than an extension of literary opinion, is found in Melville's discussion of original characters in Chapter 44. "As for original characters in fiction," he writes,

> a grateful reader will, on meeting with one, keep the anniversary of that day. True, we sometimes hear of an author who, at one creation, produces some two or three score such characters; it may be possible. But they can hardly be original in the sense that Hamlet is, or Don Quixote, or Milton's Satan. That is to say, they are not, in a thorough sense, original at all. They are novel, or singular, or striking, or captivating, or all four at once.

Melville's "hearing" of an author who supposedly produced a score of originals in a single work may well have reference to a review of *Bleak House* which appeared in the November 1853 issue of *Putnam's*.

Melville kept most of his back issues of this magazine, and when he contracted with Dix and Edwards for an edition of his *Putnam's* stories in January 1856, he wrote the publishers that he would read proof from those copies and requested they send the issues he had misplaced. Melville's writing of "The Piazza" as a preface and his preparation of the stories for the edition obviously interrupted his composition of *The Confidence-Man*; but it may also have turned his attention to an essay about a writer who, it was claimed, had no concept of plot but whose genius lay in the production of original characters. On the page following the conclusion of the first part of "Bartleby the Scrivener," published in the November 1853 issue of *Putnam's*, there appears an essay entitled "Characters in Bleak House." In it the reviewer claimed Dickens' real talent lay in character creation:

> But, such has been the prodigal affluence of his genius in scattering his characters, that we take up a new number of one of his stories and feel ourselves wronged if we do not find half a dozen or more of new people, whose names and characteristics we can no more forget, than we can those of our own schoolfellows, or the members of our own household. Yet there

is nothing so rare in literature as the creation of a new character; from the time of Shakespeare to Fielding there were not
half a dozen added to the realm of fiction. . . Fielding made a
very considerable addition to the populousness of the world of
fiction, and since his time there have been many more added;
but the creations of Dickens are more numerous than those of
all the authors that preceded him, from the days of Fielding
and Smollet, put together.[2]

Melville is skeptical of such extravagant claims. A novel may contain "all sorts of entertaining and instructive characters," he writes,
but truly original characters are extremely rare; moreover, he adds
that there can "be but one such original character to one work of
invention. Two would conflict to chaos" [chapter 44].

That Melville would balk at the suggestion that a novel might
contain a number of new or original characters is to his credit. For
in *The Confidence-Man* he had produced such memorable figures
as the Titan, the Missouri bachelor, Charlie Noble, Black Guinea,
and the like. But he apparently could not believe they possessed
anything more than a certain "striking" quality any more than he
could believe Dickens could fill his pages with true originals. Nor
could he claim originality for the most interesting character in the
book, Frank Goodman, the cosmopolitan. The supposed purpose of
Chapter 44 is to show that that character is not deserving of the title "quite an original."

Melville generally hides behind the veil of his "smoky" prose in
this novel, but in the three interpolated chapters on character creation he enters into his narrative and speaks directly to the reader.
And each chapter offers an unusual and undisguised glimpse of the
author's own literary opinions. But it was not Melville's habit to
reason from abstract principles to concrete examples; rather, he
was more inclined to elaborate upon the particulars of his personal
experience or his reading. It is interesting to note, therefore, that in
at least two of these chapters (suggesting the possibility of a source
for Chapter 33 as well) Melville's discursive remarks were not dis-
embodied commentary but personal responses to his reading—one
as the amplification of the thoughts of a classic writer whom he
personally admired and the other as the reaction against the literary
opinions of a contemporary reviewer.[3]

2. *Putnam's Monthly Magazine of American Literature, Science, and Art* (November 1853),
   558–562.
3. Evidence is overwhelming that no one in the Melville household from the early 1840s
   through much of the 1850s could escape knowing the latest novel by Charles Dickens
   (1812–1870). Sometimes the newest work was read aloud at night, in the family semicircle in front of the hearth, as serial instalments arrived, before book publication (see
   Dickens in the indexes of Parker's two volumes). To some extent Melville defined his
   own fiction against the methods of Dickens, who was almost universally acknowledged
   as the greatest literary genius of his time [Editors' note].

CONTEMPORARY
REVIEWS

The summary and analysis of contemporary reviews of *The Confidence-Man* in the NN Edition, section 6 (316–30), stands up well, despite Richard E. Winslow III's several subsequent discoveries in New England papers and Parker's few 1997 finds in the Colindale Branch of the British Library. The then-known reviews of *The Confidence-Man* are printed in *Herman Melville: The Contemporary Reviews* (1995), edited by Brian Higgins and Hershel Parker. The reviews of some of Melville's earlier books are significant because they thwarted his career or pushed him into new directions. Notably, while enraged and terrified at the looming loss of his career, Melville wrote responses to some of the reviews of *Moby-Dick* into the text of *Pierre* after he had already accepted a very bad contract from his publishers, the Harper Brothers. Nothing like that happened with the reviews of *The Confidence-Man*, which were published, it seems likely, after Melville had already determined to give up writing fiction for the foreseeable future. The reviews that Melville saw in London (during his days there at the end of April 1857) and in the United States only confirmed his decision. Few American reviews were much more than negligible either in themselves or in their effect on Melville.

The sample of reviews offered here emphasizes the English reception, for the London reviewers paid, at best, scrupulous attention and came very close to penetrating Melville's allegory. Furthermore, the London reviews have more historical significance than the American ones. Fresh evidence about the way *Moby-Dick*—usually in the English version, *The Whale*—was passed lovingly from one British literary person to another is still emerging in the twenty-first century. There were parallel lines of transmission with some leaping of lines: a Pre-Raphaelites' line, a Working Men's Movement line, a sort of early sexologist line, a Leicester line, a nautical authors and Children of the Empire line, a yet-unexplored Anglo-Irish line, a Bloomsbury line. A marvelous book may yet be written on that topic, a sketch of which is given in section 8 of the NN Edition's "Historical Note" to *Moby-Dick*. Some of these London reviews of *The Confidence-Man*, long, intelligent, and in major reviewing organs, must have played some yet undetermined part in keeping alive Melville's underground British reputation.

ANONYMOUS

[A Sketchy Affair]†

A sketchy affair, like other tales by the same author. Sly humor peeps out occasionally, though buried under quite too many words, and you read on and on, expecting something more than you ever find, to be choked off at the end of the book like the audience of a Turkish story teller, without getting the end of the story.[1]

† Philadelphia *North American and United States Gazette* (April 4, 1857).
1. A session of Turkish storytelling even in modern times can go on for ten hours or more and can accommodate swift shifts of scene and subject [Editors' note].

ANONYMOUS

[A "Ubiquitous" Rogue]†

One of the indigenous characters who has figured long in our journals, courts, and cities, is 'the Confidence Man'; his doings form one of the staples of villainy, and an element in the romance of roguery. Countless are the dodges attributed to this ubiquitous personage, and his adventures would equal those of Jonathan Wild.[1] It is not to wondered at, therefore, that the subject caught the fancy of Herman Melville—an author who deals equally well in the material description and the metaphysical insight of human life. He has added by his 'Confidence Man' to the number of original subjects—an achievement for the modern *raconteur*, who has to glean in a field so often harvested. The plan and treatment are alike Melvillish; and the story more popularly elaborated than is usual with the author. *The Confidence Man—His Masquerade*—is a taking title. Dix, Edwards & Co. have brought it out in their best style.

ANONYMOUS

[A Morality Enacted by Masqued Players]‡

The Confidence Man is a morality enacted by masqued players. The credulous and the sceptical appear upon the stage in various quaint costumes, and discourse sententiously on the art of human life, as developed by those who believe and those who suspect. We leave the inference to be traced by Mr. Melville's readers,—some of whom, possibly, may wait for a promised sequel to the book before deciding as to the lucidity or opaqueness of the author's final meaning. There is a stage, with a set of elaborate scenery, but there is strictly no drama, the incidents being those of a masquerade, while the theatre is a steampalace on the Mississippi. Here 'the Confidence-Man' encounters his antagonists and disciples,—and their dialogues occupy the chief part of the volume. Mr. Melville is lavish in aphorism, epigram, and metaphor. When he is not didactic, he is luxuriously picturesque; and, although his style is one,

---

† Boston *Evening Transcript* (April 10, 1857).
1. Wild (1682?–1725), an English super-criminal until his execution, was the subject of Henry Fielding's dark political satire *The History of the Life of the Late Mr. Jonathan Wild the Great* (1743) [Editors' note].
‡ London *Athenæum* 1537 (April 11, 1857), 462–463.

from its peculiarities, difficult to manage, he has now obtained a mastery over it, and pours his colours over the narration with discretion as well as prodigality. All his interlocutors have studied the lore of old philosophy: they have all their wise sayings, of satire or speculation, to enrich the colloquy; so that, while the mighty riverboat, Fidèle, steams up the Mississippi, between low, vine-tangled banks, flat as tow-paths, a voyage of twelve hundred miles, 'from apple to orange, from clime to clime,' we grow so familiar with the passengers that they seem at last to form a little world of persons mutually interested, generally eccentric, but in no case dull. Mr. Melville has a strange fashion of inaugurating his moral miracle-play,—the synopsis of which, in the Table of Contents, is like a reflection of 'The Ancient Mariner,' interspersed with some touches vaguely derived from the dialecticians of the eighteenth century. One sentence, leading into the first chapter, immediately fixes the attention:—

"At sunrise on a first of April, there appeared, suddenly as Manco Capac at the lake Titicaca, a man in cream colours, at the waterside, in the city of St. Louis."

This is a mute. The other personages are fantastically attired, or rather, by an adroit use of language, common things are suggested under uncommon aspects. The cosmopolitan himself is an oracle of confidence; and, finally, bargains with a barber whose motto has been "No trust," to indemnify him against any loss that may ensue from the obliteration of that motto for a certain term, during which the barber shall not only shave mankind for ready money, but grant credit. The agreement is signed.—

" 'Very good,' said the barber . . . 'I will see you again' " [chapter 43, paragraphs 35–55].

Such is the spirit of the book. These are the masqueraders among whom moves the cosmopolitan philanthropist, honeying their hearts with words of benignity and social faith.—

"Natives of all sorts, and foreigners . . . grinning negroes, and Sioux chiefs solemn as high-priests" [chapter 2, paragraph 28].

A "limping, gimlet-eyed, sour-faced" discharged customhouse officer,—a crippled Nigritian beggar,—a blue-eyed episcopalian,—a prime and palmy gentleman with gold sleeve-buttons,—a young Byronic student,—a plump and pleasant lady,—a rich man,—a business man,—"a man with a travelling-cap,"—a soldier of fortune,—a man with no memory, come under the influence of the philanthropist's experimental doctrine, with varying results, and much cordial philosophy is extracted from their talk, fragant with poetry or bitter with cynicism. The "Confidence-Man" confides even in wine that has a truthful tinge. "He who could mistrust poison in this wine would mistrust consumption in Hebe's cheek." And then is pronounced the eulogy of the Press,—not that which rolls, and groans, and rattles by night in printing-offices, but that which gushes with bright juice on the Rhine, in Madeira and Mitylene, on the Douro and the Moselle, golden or pale tinted, or red as roses in the bud. Passing this, we select one example of Mr. Melville's picture-making.—

"In the middle of the gentleman's cabin . . . the rays died dimly away in the furthest nook of the place" [chapter 45, paragraph 1].

Full of thought, conceit, and fancy, of affectation and originality, this book is not unexceptionably meritorious, but it is invariably graphic, fresh, and entertaining.

ANONYMOUS

[Philosophy Brought "Into the Living World"]†

In this book, also, philosophy is brought out of its cloisters into the living world; but the issue raised is more simple:—whether men are to be trusted or suspected? Mr. Melville has a manner wholly different from that of the anonymous writer who has produced "The Metaphysicians."[1] He is less scholastic, and more sentimental; his style is not so severe; on the contrary, festoons of exuberant fancy decorate the discussion of abstract problems; the controversialists pause ever and anon while a vivid, natural Mississippi landscape is rapidly painted before the mind; the narrative is almost rhythmic, the talk is cordial, bright American touches are scattered over the perspective—the great steamboat deck, the river coasts, the groups belonging to various gradations of New-World life. In his Pacific stories Mr. Melville wrote as with an Indian pencil, steeping the entire relation in colours almost too brilliant for reality; his books were all stars, twinkles, flashes, vistas of green and crimson, diamond and crystal;[2] he has now tempered himself, and studied the effect of neutral tints. He has also added satire to his repertory, and, as he uses it scrupulously, he uses it well. His fault is a disposition to discourse upon too large a scale, and to keep his typical characters too long in one attitude upon the stage. Lest we should seem to imply that the masquerade is dramatic in form, it is as well

† London *Leader* 8 (April 11, 1857), 356.
1. *The Metaphysicians*, an anonymous novel, was being reviewed in the same lot of books [Editors' note].
2. Gorgeous meticulously detailed scenes produced in the Mughal empire of India (1526–1857) were much on display in London, for in 1857 the British were conquering the last of the Mughal rulers. This was a high compliment to Melville, because these pictures dazzled the beholder with reds, vermilions, golds, browns, and greens [Editors' note].

to describe its construction. It is a strangely diversified narration of events taking place during the voyage of a Mississippi river boat, a cosmopolitan philanthropist, the apostle of a doctrine, being the centre and inspiration of the whole. The charm of the book is owing to its originality and to its constant flow of description, character-stretching and dialogue, deeply toned and skillfully contrasted.

ANONYMOUS

[Melville as "A Mediaeval Jester"]†

We notice this book at length for much the same reason as Dr. Livingston[1] describes his travels in Monomotapa, holding that its perusal has constituted a feat which few will attempt, and fewer still accomplish. Those who, remembering the nature of the author's former performances, take it up in the expectation of encountering a wild and stirring fiction, will be tolerably sure to lay it down ere long with an uncomfortable sensation of dizziness in the head, and yet some such introduction under false pretences seems to afford it its only chance of being taken up at all. For who will meddle with a book professing to inculcate philosophical truths through the medium of nonsensical people talking nonsense—the best definition of its scope and character that a somewhat prolonged consideration has enabled us to suggest. A novel it is not, unless a novel means forty-five conversations held on board a steamer, conducted by personages who might pass for the errata of creation, and so far resembling the Dialogues of Plato as to be undoubted Greek to ordinary men. Looking at the substance of these colloquies, they cannot be pronounced altogether valueless; looking only at the form, they might well be esteemed the compositions of a March hare[2] with a literary turn of mind. It is not till a lengthened perusal—a perusal more lengthened than many readers will be willing to accord—has familiarized us with the quaintness of the style, and until long domestication with the incomprehensible interlocutors has infected us with something of their own eccentricity, that our faculties, like the eyes of prisoners accustomed to the dark, become sufficiently acute to discern the golden grains which the author has made it his business to hide away from us.

---

† London *Literary Gazette* 2099 (April 11, 1857): 348–49. All notes are the editors'.
1. David Livingston (1813–1873), the missionary-doctor, back in England after being thought dead (not for the last time), was known to be engaged in writing his *Missionary Travels* (1858), in which he explains that *Monomotapa* means "chief"—a man, not a place.
2. A hare in breeding season (March) is wild and excitable; the male may, for instance, perform startlingly sudden and high vertical leaps beside or over the female.

It is due to Mr. Melville to say, that he is by no means unconscious of his own absurdities, which, in one of his comparatively lu-
cid intervals, he attempts to justify and defend:—

"But ere be given . . . cut capers too fantastic" [chapter 33, paragraphs 1–4].

This is ingenious, but it begs the question. We do, as Mr.
Melville says, desire to see nature "unfettered, exhilarated," in fiction we do *not* want to see her "transformed." We are glad to see
the novelist create imaginary scenes and persons, nay, even characters whose type is not to be found in nature. But we demand that,
in so doing, he should observe certain ill-defined but sufficiently
understood rules of probability. His fictitious creatures must be
such as Nature might herself have made, supposing their being to
have entered into her design. We must have fitness of organs, sym-
metry of proportions, no impossibilities, no monstrosities. As to
harlequin, we think it very possible indeed that his coat may be too
parti-coloured, and his capers too fantastic, and conceive, moreover, that Mr. Melville's present production supplies an unanswer-
able proof of the truth of both positions. We should be sorry, in
saying this, to be confounded with the cold unimaginative critics,
who could see nothing but extravagance in some of our author's
earlier fictions—in the first volume of 'Mardi,' that archipelago of
lovely descriptions is led in glittering reaches of vivid nautical narrative—the conception of 'The Whale,' ghostly and grand as the
great grey sweep of the ridged and rolling sea. But these wild beauties were introduced to us with a congruity of outward accompani-
ment lacking here. The isles of 'Mardi' were in Polynesia, not off
the United States. Captain Ahab did not chase Moby Dick in a
Mississippi steamboat. If the language was extraordinary, the speakers were extraordinary too. If we had extravaganzas like the following outpouring on the subject of port wine, at least they were not
put into the mouths of Yankee cabin passengers:—

"A shade passed over the cosmopolitan . . . in perfidious and
murderous drugs!" [chapter 29, paragraph 14–16].

The best of it is, that this belauded beverage is all the time what
one of the speakers afterwards calls "elixir of logwood."

This is not much better than Tilburina in white satin,[3] yet such
passages form the staple of the book. It is, of course, very possible
that there may be method in all this madness, and that the author
may have a plan, which must needs be a very deep one indeed. Certainly we can obtain no inkling of it. It may be that he has chosen to
act the part of a mediaeval jester, conveying weighty truths under a

3. Richard Sheridan in his satirical comedy *The Critic* (1779) makes fun of conventional
   treatments of insane heroines in the theater by his stage direction: "Enter Tilburina,
   stark mad in white satin."

semblance antic and ludicrous; if so, we can only recommend him for the future not to jingle his bells so loud. There is no catching the accents of wisdom amid all this clattering exuberance of folly. Those who wish to teach should not begin by assuming a mask so grotesque as to keep listeners on the laugh, or frighten them away. Whether Mr. Melville really does mean to teach anything is, we are aware, a matter of considerable uncertainty. To describe his book, one had need to be a Höllen-Breughel;[4] to understand its purport, one should be something of a Sphinx. It may be a *bonâ fide* eulogy on the blessedness of reposing "confidence"—but we are not at all confident of this. Perhaps it is a hoax on the public—an emulation of Barnum.[5] Perhaps the mild man in mourning, who goes about requesting everybody to put confidence in him, is an emblem of Mr. Melville himself, imploring toleration for three hundred and fifty-three pages of rambling, on the speculation of there being something to the purpose in the three hundred and fifty-fourth; which, by the way, there is not, unless the oracular announcement that "something further may follow of this masquerade," is to be regarded in that light. We are not denying that this tangled web of obscurity is shot with many a gleam of shrewd and subtle thought—that this caldron, so thick and slab with nonsense, often bursts into the bright, brief bubbles of fancy and wit. The greater the pity to see these good things so thrown away. The following scene, in the first chapter, for example, seems to us sufficiently graphic to raise expectations very indifferently justified by the sequel:—

"Pausing at this spot . . . but also deaf" [chapter 1, paragraph 5–12].

It will be seen that Mr. Melville can still write powerfully when it pleases him. Even when most wayward, he yet gives evidence of much latent genius, which, however, like latent heat is of little use either to him or to us. We should wish to meet him again in his legitimate department, as the prose-poet of the ocean; if, however, he will persist in indoctrinating us with his views concerning the *vrai*, we trust he will at least condescend to pay, for the future, some slight attention to the *vraisemblable*.[6] He has ruined this book, as he did 'Pierre,' by a strained effort after excessive originality. When will he discover that—

> "Standing on the head makes not
> Either for ease or dignity?"[7]

4. The Dutch painter Pieter Breughel the Younger (1564–1638) was so called because of his fiery (hellish) scenes thronged with demons.
5. Phineas Taylor Barnum (1810–1891), the American showman, repeatedly alluded to in *The Confidence-Man*.
6. Lifelike. "*Vrai*": true.
7. From "The Angel in the House" (1854), Canto 7.2, by the English poet Coventry Patmore (1823–1896).

276

ANONYMOUS

[Hardly "A Genuine Sketch of American Society"]†

The precise design of Mr. Herman Melville in *The Confidence Man, his Masquerade*, is not very clear. Satire on many American smartnesses, and on the gullibility of mankind which enables those smartnesses to succeed, is indeed an evident object of the author. He stops short of any continuous pungent effect; because his plan is not distinctly felt, and the framework is very inartistical; also because the execution is upon the whole flat, at least to an English reader, who does not appreciate what appear to be local allusions.

A Mississippi steam-boat is the scene of the piece; and the passengers are the actors, or rather the talkers. There is a misanthropist, looking like a dismissed official soured against the government and humanity, whose pleasure it is to regard the dark side of things and to infuse distrust into the compassionate mind. There is the President and Transfer Agent of the "Black Rapids Coal Company," who does a little business on board, by dint of some secret accomplices and his own pleasant plausibility and affected reluctance. A herb-doctor is a prominent person, who gets rid of his medicine by immutable patience and his dexterity in playing upon the fears and hopes of the sick. The "Confidence-Man" is the character most continually before the reader. He is collecting subscriptions for a "Widow and Orphan Asylum recently founded among the Seminoles," and he succeeds greatly in fleecing the passengers by his quiet impudence and his insinuating fluency; the persons who effectually resist being middle-aged or elderly well-to-do gentlemen, who cut short his advances: "You—pish! why will the captain suffer these begging fellows to come on board?" There are various other persons who bear a part in the discourses: one or two tell stories; and the author himself sometimes directly appears in a chapter of disquisition.

Besides the defective plan and the general flatness of execution, there seems too great a success on the part of the rogues, from the great gullibility of the gulls. If implicit reliance could be placed on the fiction as a genuine sketch of American society, it might be said that poverty there as elsewhere goes to the wall, and that the freedom of the constitution does not extend to social intercourse unless where the arms and physical strength of some border man compel the fears of the genteel to grudgingly overcome their reluctance for the time. This reliance we cannot give. The spirit of the satire seems drawn from the European writers of the seventeenth and

† London *Spectator* 30 (April 11, 1857): 398–99.

eighteenth centuries, with some of Mr. Melville's own Old World observations superadded. It sometimes becomes a question how much belongs to the New World, how much to the Old, and how much to exaggerated representation, impressing a received truth in the form of fiction. The power of wealth, connexion, and respectability, to overbear right, while poor and friendless innocence suffers, may be illustrated in the following story of a begging cripple, told to the herb-doctor; or it may instance the unscrupulous invention of vagrant impostors; but it can scarcely be taken as a true picture of justice towards the poor at New York.

"'Well, I was born in New York . . . and I hobbled off'" [chapter 19, paragraphs 27–53].

ANONYMOUS

[Ineffably Meaningless and Trashy]†

This is a volume of 394 pages, and XLV. chapters. We have turned and examined several pages, and find the work ineffably meaningless and trashy. We quote the best portion of one chapter [chapter 2]. . . . There is only one set of mortals who we think can see anything but trash in the above, and that set is the compositors who put it in type at so many cents per 1000 ems.[1] It may be that the fanciers of the author of "Typee" may be pleased with this publication; and we, of course, advise all such to procure the volume, and judge for themselves.

ANONYMOUS

[Hard Reading]‡

The admirers of the author of Omoo and Typee will hardly have their expectations realized by this, his latest work. It is a masquerade, acted on board a Mississippi steamboat, and the characters, an odd company, seem all engaged in the game of imposition and credulity. We have found it hard reading. The author says "Something further may follow of this Masquerade." Let us hope it will be better. For sale by Sanborn & Carter.

† Boston *Daily Times* (April 11, 1857).
1. An "em" is a printer's term meaning about a sixth of an inch, from the length a square-cut letter *M* took up on a line [Editors' note].
‡ Portland, Maine, *Transcript* (April 11, 1857).

ANONYMOUS

[The Hardest Nut to Crack]†

Herman Melville, hitherto known to us as one of the brightest and most poetical word-painters of places, here adventures into quite a new field, and treats us, under the form of a fiction, to an analytical inquiry into a few social shams.

The machinery of the story, or drama, as it may perhaps be more accurately called, is simple enough; it is in the filling-up that the skill and ability are apparent. The steamer Fidèle is churning its way over the waters of the Mississippi, from St. Louis to New Orleans, laden with its many-headed changing freight of human beings. Among these moves a philosopher, whose theory, or (to use an Americanism) notion, it is that there is not enough *confidence* in the world—not enough, that is to say, of the real sterling metals but, on the contrary, a great deal of paint and varnish and gilding, which looks so like it as to deceive the foolish and unwary. Accordingly he devotes his time during that voyage in sustaining a series of disguises, under the cover of which he enacts a variety of scenes, and holds long disquisitions with various interlocutors, all which have for their object the impression of his principle, that confidence, and not distrust, is the foundation of happy human intercourse.

All this seems simple enough in the telling, and very likely to be prosy. Not at all. That prosiness is the last crime of which Herman Melville can be accused, will be admitted by all who are familiar with "Omoo," "Typee," "Mardi," "White Jacket," and "Moby Dick." On the contrary, there is a vividness and an intensity about his style which is almost painful for the constant strain upon the attention; and *The Confidence Man* is that of all his works which readers will find the hardest nut to crack.

We are not quite sure whether we have cracked it ourselves—whether there is not another meaning hidden in the depths of the subject other than that which lies near the surface. There is a dry vein of sarcastic humour running throughout which makes us suspect this. And besides, is there not a contradiction apparent in the principles of *The Confidence Man* himself, when he seeks to build his theory of Catholic charity upon a foundation of suspicion? Moreover, there are some parts of the story in which we feel half inclined to doubt whether this apostle of geniality is not, after all, an arch-imposter of the deepest dye; as for example, when he takes

---

† London *Critic* 16 (April 15, 1857), 174–75.

the twenty dollars from the miser upon a promise to treble them for him. Does the miser ever see the colour of his money again? Certainly the reader of the book never does. And then, under what strange and trying disguises does *The Confidence Man* offer his ministrations. Who would ever think of putting confidence in a vendor of nostrums, even though he should talk such excellent wisdom as this?

> The herb-doctor took . . . neither has the other [chapter 16, paragraphs 20–34].

Better still is his reasoning with the grim cynic whom experience had brought to the sweeping conclusion that "all boys are rascals." This time the Confidence Man is the agent for the Domestic Servant Agency Office.

> You deny that a youth . . . a St. Augustine for an ostler" [chapter 22, paragraphs 86–104, condensed].

The contingency of having a St. Augustine for an ostler may be rather remote, but there is something in this which those Pharisees who frown mercilessly upon the follies of youth may profit by. Taking another aspect of this book, who does not perceive a touch of the finest humour in the application of the touchstone whereby the Confidence Man proves the hollowness of his genial friend "the Mississippi Operator."

> "How shall I express . . . Cadmus glided into the snake" [chapter 30, paragraph 79 to chapter 32, paragraph 1].

Our readers will by this time perceive that this is not a common book.

ANONYMOUS

[A Connected Series of Dialogues]†

Mr. Herman Melville, a clever American author, whose Marquesas Island story no reader can have forgotten, has published a fanciful work which he calls a "Masquerade," entitled the *Confidence Man*, consisting not so much of a single narrative as of a connected series of dialogues, quaintly playing upon the character of that confidence of man in man which is or ought to be the basis of all dealing. It is not altogether what it ought to be, hints Mr. Melville by his satire. We are only ready with a blind trust in the man who has

† London *Examiner* (April 18, 1857).

raised mists of self-interest before our eyes. We have not much
confidence in any man who wants to borrow money with his honour as security.

ANONYMOUS

[Melville's "Reckless Perversion of High Abilities"]†

Great unreserve is permitted to the stage, and still greater to a
masquerade; and in this way of thinking, the people in a fiction,
like the people in a play, must dress as nobody exactly dresses; talk
as nobody exactly talks; act as nobody exactly acts,—thus presenting another world, and yet one to which we feel the tie. But it *is*
possible for Harlequin to appear in a coat too parti-colored, and
possible for him to cut too fantastic capers. It is this sin of which
Mr. Melville, in "The Confidence Man," has been wilfully, and
"with malice aforethought," guilty. With the memory of Omoo and
Typee to prove of what, in his earlier and better moods, he was capable and has achieved, we cannot but deplore the reckless perver-
sion of high abilities, apparent in Pierre, or the Ambiguities, and
still more conspicuous in this masquerade.

ANONYMOUS

[A Mass of Writing Undigested and Indigestible]‡

We can make nothing of this masquerade, which, indeed, sav-
ours very much of a mystification. We began the book at the beginning, and, after reading ten or twelve chapters, some of which
contained scenes of admirable dramatic power, while others presented pages of the most vivid description, found, in spite of all
this, that we had not yet obtained the slightest clue to the meaning
(in case there should happen to be any) of the work before us. This
novel, comedy, collection of dialogues, repertory of anecdotes, or
whatever it is, opens (and opens brilliantly, too) on the deck of a
Mississippi steamer. It appeared an excellent idea to lay the opening of a fiction (for the work is a fiction, at all events) on the deck
of a Mississippi steamer. The advantage of selecting a steamer, and
above all a Mississippi steamer, for such a purpose, is evident: you

† Boston *Daily Traveller* (April 20, 1857).
‡ London *Illustrated Times* 4 (April 25, 1857), 266. All notes are the editors'.

can have all your characters present in the vessel, and several of your scenes taking place in different parts of the vessel, if necessary, at the same time; by which means you exhibit a certain variety in your otherwise tedious uniformity. For an opening, the Mississippi steamer is excellent; and we had read at least eight chapters of the work, which opens so excellently, before we were at all struck with the desirability of going ashore. But after the tenth chapter, the steamer began to be rather too much for us; and with the twelfth we experienced symptoms of a feeling slightly resembling nausea. Besides this, we were really getting anxious to know whether there was a story to the book; and, if the contrary should be the case, whether the characters were intended—as seemed probable—not for actual living beings, but for philosophical abstractions, such as might be introduced with more propriety, or with less impropriety, floating about in the atmosphere of the planet Sirius, than on the deck and in the cabin of a Mississippi steamer, drinking, smoking, gambling, and talking about "confidence." Having turned to the last chapter, after the manner of the professed students of novels from the circulating library, we convinced ourselves that, if there was almost no beginning to the story, there was altogether no end to it. Indeed, if the negative of "all's well that ends well" be true, the "Confidence-man" is certainly a very bad book.

After reading the work forwards for twelve chapters and backwards for five, we attacked it in the middle, gnawing at it like Rabelais's dog at the bone,[1] in the hope of extracting something from it at last. But the book is without form and void. We cannot continue the chaotic comparison and say, that "darkness is on the face thereof;" for, although a sad jumble, the book is nevertheless the jumble of a very clever man, and of one who proves himself to be such even in the jumble of which we are speaking.

As a last resource, we read the work from beginning to end; and the result was that we liked it even less than before—for we had at all events not suffered from it. Such a book might have been called "Imaginary Conversations," and the scene should be laid in Tartarus, Hades, Tophet, Purgatory, or at all events some place of which the manners, customs, and mode of speech are unknown to the living.

Perhaps, as we cannot make the reader acquainted with the whole plot or scheme of the work before us, he may expect us to

1. The French writer François Rabelais (1494–1553) in the prologue to *Gargantua* (1532) compares the reader to a dog that has been thrown a fresh bone. The good reader will not treat the book as a light comedy but instead will chew the bone, break it, and suck out all the marrow.

tell him at least why it is called the "Confidence-Man." It is called
the "Confidence-Man" because the principal character, type, spec-
tre, or *ombre-chinoise*[2] of the book, is always talking about confidence to the lesser characters, types, &c., with whom he is brought
into contact. Sometimes the "Confidence-Man" succeeds in begging or borrowing money from his collocutors; at other times he ig-
nominiously fails. But it is not always very evident why he fails, nor
in the other cases is it an atom clearer why he succeeds. For the
rest, no one can say whence the "Confidence-Man" comes, nor
whither he is going.

The principal characters in the book are—

1. The "Confidence-Man" himself, whom, if we mistake not, is a
melancholy individual attired in mourning, who distributes "Odes
on Confidence" about the steamer, and talks on his favourite subject and with his favourite motive to everyone on board; but we
dare not affirm positively that the "Confidence-Man" is identical
with the man in mourning, and with the one who distributes "Odes
on Confidence," or indeed with either—the character generally being deficient in substance and indistinct in outline.

2. A lame black man (we are sure there is a lame black man).

3. A misanthropic, unconfidential white man with a wooden leg,
who denies with ferocity that the lame black man is lame.

4. A student who reads Tacitus, and takes shares in a coal company.

5. The President and Transfer Agent of the Rapids Coal Company, who declares his determination to transact no business
aboard the steamer, and who transacts it accordingly.

6. A realist barber—who is moreover real—indeed almost the
only real human being in the book, if we except, perhaps, the lame
black man (for we still maintain he was lame in spite of the assertions of the white man with the wooden leg).

The description of the barber opening his shop on the deck of
the steamer, hoisting his pole, and putting forth his label bearing
the inscription "No trust!" is one of the best in the volume; and the
scene in which he declines the suggestion of the "Confidence-
Man" to the effect that he should shave on credit, one of the best
scenes.

We should also mention an interesting conversation over a bottle
of wine, in which one man receiving earnest assurances of friendship from another, ventures on the strength of it to apply for a loan,
which is refused with insult—not a very novel situation, but in this

2. Usually plural, *ombres-chinoises*, Chinese shadows (literal translation); a stage presenta-
   tion where shadows of puppets or people in dramatic action are cast, enlarged, on a
   transparency for viewing by the audience.

case well written up to, and altogether excellently treated. Some of the stories introduced in the course of the work are interesting enough (that of Colonel John Murdock [sic], the Indian-hater, for instance), and all are well told. The anecdotes, too, are highly amusing, especially the one narrated by the misanthrope regarding the "confidence-husband," as Mr. Melville might call him. A certain Frenchman from New Orleans being at the theatre, was so charmed with the character of a faithful wife, that he determined forthwith to get married. Accordingly, he married a beautiful girl from Tennessee, "who had at first attracted his attention by her liberal mould, and who was subsequently recommended to him, through her kin, for her equally liberal education and disposition. Though large, the praise proved not too much; for ere long rumour more than corroborated it—whispering that the lady was liberal to a fault. But though various circumstances, which by most persons would have been deemed all but conclusive, were duly recited to the old Frenchman by his friends, yet such was his confidence that not a syllable would he credit, till, chancing one night to return unexpectedly from a journey, upon entering his apartment, a stranger burst from the alcove. 'Begar!' cried he; 'now I *begin* to suspect.' "

In conclusion, the "Confidence-Man" contains a mass of anecdotes, stories, scenes, and sketches undigested, and, in our opinion, indigestible. The more voracious reader may, of course, find them acceptable; but we confess that we have not "stomach for them all." We said that the book belonged to no particular class, but we are almost justified in affirming that its *génre*[3] [sic] is the *génre ennuyeux*. The author in his last line promises "something more of this masquerade." All we can say, in reply to the brilliant author of "Omoo" and "Typee" is, "the less the merrier."

ANONYMOUS

[Melville as Excellent Master of the Ceremonies]†

For the scene of a masquerade a Mississippi steamer on its trip from St. Louis to New Orleans is not ill-chosen; and Mr. Herman Melville makes an excellent master of the ceremonies, rushing hither and thither among the motley crowd, with no ostensible object saving that of making himself agreeable to everybody, and turn-

---

3. The odd accent mark is retained here; the writer means the genre or class of literature called "infinitely tedious" or "boring beyond belief."
† London *John Bull and Britannia* (May 9, 1857).

ing everybody to account for his own jaunty purpose. As for a
thread of a story to tie together the pen-and-ink sketches of American life with which the volume is crowded, he that should look for
it, would assuredly look in vain. Yet there is a vein of philosophy
that runs through the whole; and the conflict between the feeling
of trust, enjoined by every nobler sentiment and higher principle,
and the feeling of distrust engendered by the experience of life, of
which every human breast is, however unconsciously, the perpetual
battle-field, has not often been so forcibly as well as amusingly illustrated as it is in the incoherent ramblings of "the confidence-
man."

ANONYMOUS

[No Prospect of Any Good]†

Herman Melville, author of "Typee," is the writer, and Dix, Edwards & Co. are the publishers, of a volume entitled "The Confidence Man: His Masquerade." We became acquainted with Mr.
Melville some ten years ago, by means of the book "Typee,"—in
which he represents himself, autobiographically, as one of the vilest
of those runaway sailors who escape from work, and from the disagreeable things of civilization, and give themselves to the indul-
gences of a brutish life among the savage inhabitants of the islands
in the Pacific. A worse book than that, in its moral tone and tendency, has rarely been published.[1] We have desired, since then, no
farther acquaintance with the author. Of this new work we have
read enough to show us that though Mr. Herman Melville may
have learned some decency since the time of his experiments in living on the Marquesas Islands, there is no prospect of any good to
be got by reading farther.

---

† New York *Independent* 9 (May 14, 1857), 8.
1. The *Independent* was the stern Congregationist paper that had declared that Melville
was in danger of hell fire for writing *Moby-Dick* and the Harper brothers for publishing
it [Editors' note].

ANONYMOUS

[A Writer "Not in Love or Sympathy with His Kind"]†

The Confidence Man: His Masquerade, gives title to a new work from the pen of Herman Melville—the oddest, most unique, and the most ingenious thing he has yet done. Under various disguises he introduces the same character who, in some form or other, is engaged evermore in cheating. The book is very interesting, and very well written, but it seems to us like the work of one not in love or sympathy with his kind. Under his masquerade, human nature—the author's nature—gets badly "cut up."

ANONYMOUS

[A Strange Book]‡

A strange book, the object of which is difficult to detect, unless it be to prove this wicked world still more full of wickedness than even the most gloomy philosophers have supposed.

The scene is entirely laid on board a Mississippi steamer, where, amidst the crowds assembled on deck, appears a man who acts in such a manner that he is supposed to be deaf and dumb. Falling asleep, and being at last forgotten, the next person brought before our notice is a crippled Negro begging for alms. The deaf and dumb man had commenced teaching "confidence" as a principle, by writing on a slate, and holding up for public teaching the scriptural account of charity as found in St. Paul's Epistles, "Charity thinketh no evil," &c., &c., and on his disappearance the crippled Negro preaches on the same text, as it were, entreating "confidence" in his being a true man, and no impostor on the benevolent principles of a kind and Christian trust, his object, however, being to obtain money for himself. To him succeeds "a man with a weed," i.e. a crape, who enters into discourse with many passengers, and on the same ground of "charity" and "confidence," obtains money for himself and certain institutions with which he is connected. And to the man with the weed succeed other characters, among whom we find an admirable quack doctor and herb seller, each and all professing to be engaged in some work of benevolence for the human race,

† Springfield, Massachusetts, *Republican* (May 16, 1857).
‡ London *Era* (May 17, 1857).

which combines the practical benefit of putting money into the proposer's pocket.

It is evident, after a time, to the reader, that each and all of these characters from the mute who wrote "charity" on the slate, to the cosmopolitan whom we leave at the end leading to his bed the old man with his money belt, are the masquerades of one man—the "Confidence Man," in fact; the villain who, with the Scripture in his mouth, has mammon in his heart, and a fiendish principle of deceiving all men influencing his every word. In the course of the various scenes of the book one or two call him imposter, and scorn him, but as he turns up immediately after in a fresh character, no result follows these detections. What would Mr. Melville have us learn and believe from his book? That no one lives who acts up to Christian principle? that to profess to act from good feeling is a sign that we are acting solely with the base view of our own interest?

That such is often the case we fear there is no doubt. And that vice conceals itself most cleverly, under the guise of virtue, is but too true. But surely the reverse of this is not so uncommon as "The Confidence Man" might induce us to suppose.

The book is thoroughly original in its plot, and is written in that brilliant and masterly style which the author has already exhibited so well in "Omoo" and "Typee." The pictures, if dark in satire, are full of wit and cleverness, and the "Confidence Man" will become a cant[1] phrase for an impostor who, under the garb of benevolence, is sucking his victim to his own advantage.

ANONYMOUS

[A "Picture of American Society"]†

There are some books which it is almost impossible to review seriously or in a very critical spirit. They occupy among books the same position as Autolycus, or Falstaff, or Flibbertigibbet[1] do among men. Of course they are quite wrong—there are other people in the world besides those who cheat and those who are cheated—all pleasant folks are not rogues, and all good men are not dull and disagreeable. On the contrary, the truth is for the most part, we are thankful to say, the exact opposite of this, and there-

---

1. Criminal slang [Editors' note].
† London *Saturday Review* 3 (May 23, 1857), 484.
1. Normally a chattering person, especially female, but in Shakespeare's *King Lear* 3.4.113 used by Edgar as the name of a foul fiend. Autolycus is a rogue and cheat in Shakespeare's *The Winter's Tale*. Falstaff, a much more complexly brilliant and lovable coward and thief, is the companion of Prince Hal in Shakespeare's two parts of *Henry IV*. He also figures in *The Merry Wives of Windsor* and has an off-stage role in *Henry V* [Editors' note].

fore Mr. Melville's view of life, were it gravely intended, should no
doubt be gravely condemned. But that he has no such intention we
quote his own words to show. He says.—

> There is another class, and with this class we side, who sit
> down to a work of amusement tolerably as they sit at a play,
> and with much the same expectations and feeling. . . . before
> whom harlequin can never appear in a coat too parti-coloured,
> or cut capers too fantastic [chapter 33, paragraphs 3–4, con-
> densed].

Whether this is a very high aim, is another question. All we can
say is that it has been fully attained in the volume before us; and
we lay our frowns aside, and give ourselves up to watch the eccentric transformations of the Confidence-Man, in much the same
spirit as we listen to the first verse of the song of Autolycus.[2]
The scene of this comedy is one of the large American steamers
on the Mississippi—the time of its action, one day—and its hero a
clever impostor, who, under the successive disguises of a deaf
mute, a crippled negro, a disconsolate widower, a charitable collector, a transfer agent, a herb doctor, a servant of the "Philosophical
Intelligence Office," and a cosmopolitan traveller, contrives to take
in almost every one with whom he comes in contact, and to make a
good deal of money by these transactions. The characters are all
wonderfully well sustained and linked together; and the scene of
his exploits gives unlimited scope for the introduction of as many
others as Mr. Melville's satirical pencil likes to sketch, from the
good simple country merchant to the wretched miser, or the wild
Missourian who had been worried into misanthropy by the pranks
of thirty-five boys—and no wonder, poor man, if they were all like
the one whose portrait we subjoin.—
"I say, this thirtieth boy . . . all are rascals" [chapter 22, paragraphs 35–37].
We likewise recommend to those readers who like tales of terror
the story of Colonel John Moredock, the Indian hater. It opens up
a dark page in American history, and throws some light on the feelings with which the backwoodsmen and red men mutually regard
each other, and apparently with very good reason. Let those who
are fond of borrowing money study the fate of the unlucky China
Aster, and take warning by it. The portrait of the mystic philosopher, who "seemed a kind of cross between a Yankee pedler and
a Tartar priest," is good in its way; and so is the practical commentary on his philosophy, contained in the following chapters, which
attack severely, and with considerable power, the pretended philan-

2. In *The Winter's Tale* 4.2 the innocent sounding "When daffodils begin to peer" celebrates the singer's appetite for alcohol and sex [Editors' note].

thropical, but really hard and selfish optimist school, whose opinions seemed not long ago likely to gain many disciples.

There is one point on which we must speak a serious word to Mr.
Melville before parting with him. He is too clever a man to be a
profane one; and yet his occasionally irreverent use of Scriptural
phrases in such a book as the one before us, gives a disagreeable
impression. We hope he will not in future mar his wit and blunt he
edge of his satire by such instances of bad taste. He has, doubtless,
in the present case fallen into them inadvertently, for they are
blemishes belonging generally to a far lower order of mind than
his; and we trust that when the sequel of the masquerade of the
Confidence-Man appears, as he gives us reason to hope that it soon
will, we shall enjoy the pleasure of his society without this draw-
back.

Of the picture of American society which is here shown us, we
cannot say much that is favourable. The money-getting spirit which
appears to pervade every class of men in the States, almost like a
monomania, is vividly portrayed in this satire; together with the
want of trust and honour, and the innumerable "operations" or
"dodges" which it is certain to engender. We wish that our own
country was free from this vice, but some late commercial transactions prove us to be little, if at all, behind our Transatlantic cousins
in this respect, and we gladly hail the assistance of so powerful a
satirist as Mr. Melville in attacking the most dangerous and the
most debasing tendency of the age.

ANONYMOUS

[Melville as Keen and Bitter Observer]†

We are not among those who have had faith in Herman Melville's South Pacific travels so much as in his strength of imagination. The "Confidence-Man" shows him in a new character—that
of satirist, and a very keen, somewhat bitter, observer. His hero, like
Mr. Melville in his earlier works, asks confidence of everybody under different masks of mendicancy, and is, on the whole, pretty successful. The scene is on board an American steamboat—that
epitome of the American world—and a variety of characters are
hustled on the stage to bring out the Confidence-Man's peculiarities: it is, in fact, a puppet-show; and, much as Punch is bothered
by the Beadle, and calmly gets the better of all his enemies, his wife

† London *Westminster and Foreign Quarterly Review* (July 12, 1857), 310–11.

in the bargain,[1] the Confidence-Man succeeds in baffling the one-legged man, whose suspicions and snappish incredulity constantly waylay him, and in counting a series of victims. Money is of course the great test of confidence, or credit in its place. Money and credit follow the Confidence-Man through all his transformations—misers find it impossible to resist him. It required close knowledge of the world, and of the Yankee world, to write such a book and make the satire acute and telling, and the scenes not too improbable for the faith given to fiction. Perhaps the moral is the gullibility of the great Republic, when taken on its own tack. At all events, it is a wide enough moral to have numerous applications, and sends minor shafts to right and left. Several capital anecdotes are told, and well told; but we are conscious of a certain hardness in the book, from the absence of humour, where so much humanity is shuffled into close neighbourhood. And with the absence of humour, too, there is an absence of kindliness. The view of human nature is severe and sombre—at least, that is the impression left on our mind. It wants relief, and is written too much in the spirit of Timon; who, indeed, saw life as it is, but first wasted his money, and then shut his heart, so that for him there was nothing save naked rock, without moss and flower. A moneyless man and a heartless man are not good exponents of our state. Mr. Melville has delineated with passable correctness, but he has forgotten to infuse the colours that exist in nature. The fault may lie in the uniqueness of the construction. Spread over a larger canvas, and taking in more of the innumerable sides of humanity, the picture might have been as accurate, the satire as sharp, and the author would not have laid himself open to the charge of harshness. Few Americans write so powerfully as Mr. Melville, or in better English, and we shall look forward with pleasure to his promised continuation of the masquerade. The first part is a remarkable work, and will add to his reputation.

1. In "Punch and Judy" puppet shows, played for adult audiences, the male figure, Punch, successively took arms against his troubles, whacking one source of misery after another; the beadle, who summons people to court, gets beaten as a representative of all petty officialdom. The shows were not seen as sadistic but as celebrating the determination of Everyman to resist his troubles, even to the point of fighting and killing the Devil at the end.

ANONYMOUS

[A Dull and Dismally Monotonous Book]†

Mr. Herman Melville has been well known for a dozen years past, both in this country and Europe, as the author of a number of tales, the most popular and best of which are stories of the sea, such as "Typee," Omoo," and "Moby Dick." Of late years, Mr. M. has turned his attention to another species of composition more akin to the modern novel. "Pierre, or the Ambiguities," is an example of this; highly extravagant and unnatural, but original and interesting in its construction and characters. His last production, "The Confidence Man," is one of the dullest and most dismally monotonous books we remember to have read, and it has been our unavoidable misfortune to peruse, in the fulfillment of journalistic duty, a number of volumes through, which nothing but a sense of obligation would have sustained us. "Typee," one of, if not the first of his works, is the best, and "The Confidence Man" the last, decidedly the worst. So Mr. M.'s authorship is toward the nadir rather than the zenith, and he has been progressing in the form of an inverted climax.

† Cincinnati *Enquirer* (February 3, 1858).

BIOGRAPHICAL
OVERVIEWS

HERSHEL PARKER

The Confidence Man's Masquerade†

An early definition of a Melville-lover was offered in 1851 by the reviewer of *The Whale* (the English title of *Moby-Dick*) in the London *News of the World*: "There are people who delight in mulligatawny. They love curry at its warmest point. Ginger cannot be too hot in the mouth for them. Such people, we should think, constitute the admirers of Herman Melville." At the end of the nineteenth century a Canadian enthusiast gave another flattering description of those who should read the neglected *Moby-Dick*: "To the class of gentleman-adventurer, to those who love both books and free life under the wide and open sky, it must always appeal." The second definition slights Melville's female enthusiasts, who range from Sophia Hawthorne to Virginia Woolf and beyond. Both definitions slight an aspect of Melville central in most of *Moby-Dick* and crucial in every page of *The Confidence-Man*. For all the power of *Moby-Dick*, another touchstone for identifying a Melvillean is *The Confidence-Man: His Masquerade*. The true Melvillean loves *metaphysical* mulligatawny. He, or she, likes satirical curry hot in the mouth, savors the ginger of blasphemy in diabolical ragouts, relishes punning with ideas perhaps more than punning with words. The Melvillean validates Saint Paul's "mystery of inquity" in freaks of intimation and makes a well-thumbed textbook of Saint Augustine on Original Sin, the firmest article of faith being that human nature, like the divine nature, is "past finding out." In unepic moods, the Melvillean likes *The Confidence-Man* almost as much as *Moby-Dick*.

What happens on the Mississippi steamboat *Fidèle* is relentless chicanery, both quotidian and cosmic. A mysterious mute in cream colors has his "advent" at the water side in St. Louis on the morning of an April Fool's Day. Garbed to suggest Jesus, and traversing the deck with mottoes from I Corinthians 13 placarded on his slate, he is the Devil (or *is* he?), playfully sauntering to and fro on the deck of the American ship of faith, the way Satan goes to and fro on the earth in the book of Job. He assumes eight disguises that are linked by a series of double entendres (the second, a Negro cripple, insists that the "others" know him "as well as dis poor old darkie knows hisself") and by serpent imagery and biblical allusions that project the most trivial conversations into a metaphysical realm. Except for his role as the unfortunate man with the weed (the emblem of mourning), in which he sets up a victim for later

† This essay appears for the first time in this Norton Critical Edition.

plying, the Confidence Man comes preaching faith in man, nature, the universe, and God, confident that the most tranquilized are the most vulnerable. In a series of conversations, some pungently collo- quial, some abstractly formal, he explores among the passengers va- rieties of gulls, skeptics, and even lower-case confidence men (such as the Alabama crook Charles Arnold Noble or the philosophical swindler Mark Winsome). Not only is his object to procure a little money and to enter a few souls in his satanic transfer-book, it is to demonstrate in fair play that Christianity is not alive in America. Only two of the passengers are at all worthy to oppose his bland- ishments—the "invalid Titan," who exhausts his energy in a single physical attack on the Confidence Man in his guise as the herb- doctor, and Pitch, the Missouri bachelor, who except for one soft-headed moment *sticks* (like pitch, or tar) to his theological convictions despite the analogical arguments of the Confidence Man as representative of an employment agency. True Christians may just possibly exist, however; Charlie Noble tells of "the Indian- hater *par excellence*," a soul peeping out but once in an age, and John Moredock stands as an Indian-hater (or Devil-hater) *manqué*. At the end, in his guise as the cosmopolitan, the Confidence Man extinguishes a lamp that symbolizes the Old and the New Testa- ments, relegating Christianity to the row of religions that once burned but now swing in darkness. Midnight being past, the play- fulness is over, and the cosmopolitan ominously leads an old man out of the gentlemen's cabin into the darkness of the deck.

In the "Memorandum of Agreement" for the American edition signed by Melville's lawyer-brother Allan, the title was "The Confi- dence-Man his Masquerade," where "His Masquerade" is plainly not a subtitle but an essential part of the main title. Having mistak- enly concluded that the sound "s" in possessives was a contraction of "his," English printers in the Renaissance put "his" into texts in wholly unhistorical ways, importing this false genitive into titles of books such as one by Samuel Purchas that pleased Melville, the 1625 *Purchas His Pilgrimes*, which would have been spoken as "Purchases Pilgrims" (and written today as "Purchas's Pilgrims"). Melville wrote the title to be pronounced *The Confidence-Man's Masquerade*, and meant the *"His"* to indicate, from the start, along with some chapter titles reminiscent of those in eighteenth-century English novels, that this was in some ways a quaintly bookish book—the product of a learned antiquarian thinker, not merely a whaleman turned writer of adventures.

The Confidence-Man, set on a "ship of fools" like Sebastian Brant's 1494 *Narrenschiff* or Alexander Barclay's 1509 translation (as *Ship of Fools*), was published patly on April Fool's Day, 1857. It was the tenth book Melville published in his eleven-year career as a prose writer. The seventh book he wrote, *The Isle of the Cross*, finished in May 1853, was rejected by his publishers, Harper & Brothers, and (we assume) later destroyed; he wrote eleven books in those eleven years. After *The Confidence-Man* Melville lived thirty-four years. About 1858, he began making himself into a poet, and he wrote five books of poetry. One volume was completed and rejected (twice) in 1860. Its contents are only to be guessed at, but some of the poems in it are probably among those still in his desk when he died in 1891. In 1866 he published a volume of Civil War poems, *Battle-Pieces, and Aspects of the War*, in 1876 a two-volume, eighteen-thousand-line centennial poem, *Clarel; a Poem and a Pilgrimage in the Holy Land*; in 1888 he printed privately *John Marr and Other Sailors*, and in 1891, the year of his death, printed *Timoleon and Other Ventures in Minor Verse* the same way. *The Confidence-Man* marked the end of his losing battle to meet two contradictory compulsions—to be as popular as he needed to be and as profound as he thought he could be.

Typee (1846) and *Omoo* (1847) were highly embroidered autobiographical accounts, one of captivity among South Sea cannibals, the other of Polynesian beachcombing. The writing created few tensions for him, since each was as good as he could write at the time and each was a popular success. The tensions came after publication, when reviewers from the evangelical denominations, particularly the missionary-minded Presbyterians, denounced him as traducing the Protestant missionaries who were industriously civilizing and Christianizing the Polynesian natives—and thereby destroying the cultures while enslaving and enfeebling the people, according to Melville, an eyewitness. The inner conflict began as he wrote *Mardi* (1849), his massive grab bag (recalling François Rabelais's *Pantagruel* and *Gargantua* and Robert Burton's *Anatomy of Melancholy*)—realistic South Sea adventure mixed with satirical encounters in an imaginary archipelago and an allegorical travelog through American and European politics. (Early in the last full year of his work on the book, 1848, the American war with Mexico ended; then revolutions broke out in Europe, branding it in Melville's memory as the "Red Year.") *Mardi* was Melville's declaration of the literary independence he was to win later, in *Moby-Dick*, but most reviewers wanted another racy tale from the hearty sailor-writer, not a literateur's portable symposium on religion, philosophy, art, and politics. To compensate for *Mardi*, Melville wrote the realistic *Redburn* (1849) and *White-Jacket* (1850)—both in a four-month stretch in the heat of the New York summer of 1849. He regarded them as "two *jobs*" which he had "done for money—being forced to it, as other men are to sawing wood." From London in mid-December 1849 Melville lamented to Evert Duyckinck how critics had treated him when he attempted to write a great book, *Mardi*: "What a madness & anguish it is, that an author can never—under no conceivable circumstances—be at all frank with his readers.—Could I, for one, be frank with them—how would they cease their railing—those at least who have railed." In October 1850, part way through his next book, he moved his family to a farm south of Pittsfield, Massachusetts. There in early May while finishing *Moby-Dick* (1851), he wrote to Nathaniel Hawthorne: "What I feel most moved to write, that is banned,—it will not pay. Yet, altogether, write the *other* way I cannot. So the product is a final hash, and all my books are botches." In *Pierre* (1852), Melville undertook his most strenuous challenge yet, to write a profound psychological study in the form of a story the book-buying audience could accept as "a regular romance, with a mysterious plot to it, & stirring passions at work." Simultaneously, the book was to pursue a psychological analysis more profound than any he had grappled with in *Moby-Dick*. He had written Hawthorne: "Leviathan is not the biggest fish;—I have heard of Krakens." He finished the book at the end of 1851 (only six weeks after *Moby-Dick* was published) and took it to the Harpers in New York City. Armored with the news that *Moby-Dick* was not selling well, the Harper brothers offered him an impossible contract—20 cents on the dollar where 50 cents on the dollar had not kept him solvent. After a few days, Melville reconciled himself to the contract but kept the manuscript and, abruptly declaring that his young hero had been a juvenile author, wrote into it what became a profound but reckless, near-suicidal account of his own thwarted literary career. Even before it was published, the Harpers began dropping the word in literary circles that Melville was a little crazy, specifying "a little" so as not to deter anyone from buying *Typee* and the other adventure books. The New York literary clique gossiped that *Pierre* showed that Melville had written himself out. Soon a New York paper printed a sober news item: "Herman Melville Crazy," and other reviewers denounced the book as insane.

During a few months in which he endured the reviews of *Pierre*, Melville tried to interest Hawthorne in writing a story he had heard about a woman named Agatha Hatch who had rescued and married a sailor, only to be deserted, and to find much later that he had formed a new bigamous marriage. The story, he thought, was in Hawthorne's vein. Understanding at last that Hawthorne (having written the campaign biography of his friend Franklin Pierce), was focused only on becoming the new American consul at Liverpool, Melville wrote the story of the long-suffering woman himself, from late December 1852 until on or about May 22, 1853, calling it *The Isle of the Cross* (a title I discovered only in 1987). When the

Harpers refused it, he settled down to writing short stories and serials for *Putnam's Monthly* and *Harper's New Monthly Magazine*—published anonymously, according to magazine policy. A few of the stories between *Pierre* and *The Confidence-Man* are of almost pathological secrecy, innocuous enough to be palmed off on his genteel publishers but concealing outrageous religious, sexual, and mock-autobiographical allegories. Literature offered Melville a means of expressing his true feelings by elaborately convoluted aesthetic dodges. *The Confidence-Man* is tightly linked to these tales. The story of Charlemont, the gentleman-madman (chapter 34), reads like a companion piece to the tale "Jimmy Rose" (*Harper's*, November 1855). Like "Bartleby" and others of the stories, *The Confidence-Man* was inspired by newspaper accounts—this time of the arrest in Albany in April 1855, of "Samuel Willis," whose felonious exploits under another alias had inspired a New York journalist to coin the term "confidence man" six years earlier, during the summer Melville wrote *Redburn* and *White-Jacket*. Like some of the stories, also, it manifests a love of allegory as inveterate as Hawthorne's own and is written in a shifty, deceptive style appropriate to a once popular adventure writer who, not permitted to write frankly, had perforce become a literary sleight-of-hand man.

Just before he began *Moby-Dick* Melville referred to himself in a travel diary as a "a pondering man." With the failure of his career and his health, he began re-examining from his rural vantage point not only his own life but also the short life of his country. It *was* a short life. His grandfathers had helped create the new nation—Thomas Melvill, a hero of the Boston Tea Party of 1773, and Peter Gansevoort, the defender of Fort Stanwix who kept British troops marching down from Canada from joining up with forces marching from New York City. As he brooded, now deeply in debt and subject to debilitating bouts of physical pain, Melville lost his early exuberant sense of American destiny and began meditating instead on what was happening to the national character. What Melville saw uniting "Samuel Willis," P. T. Barnum, and Ralph Waldo Emerson—along with many other "representative men" (Emerson's phrase) of his own time—was an appeal for confidence. For that matter, in 1850 a man calling himself "Herman Melville" had traveled about "remote parts of Georgia and North Carolina" so successfully that "persons near the scene of his exploits" had written skeptically to the Harpers "for the purpose of getting reliable information on the subject of this stranger's claims to the authorship of Mr. Melville's books." The New York *Journal*, in reporting on the doings of this impostor, reminded its readers that some early English reviewers had decided that the name attached to books about adventures in Polynesia was only an "assumed name," whereas in fact "Herman Melville" was "the real name of the writer of those works." When the term "confidence man" was coined in New York in 1849 the emphasis had been on *confidence*, the special ploy of a swindler who took a watch or money from a victim specifically as a token of confidence in him. He was "the *confidence* man," and only later, as the term proved infinitely adaptable (for instance, to "confidence girls in Brooklyn"), did people begin to use *confidence man* loosely as a synonym for any crook or swindler.

Melville saw in politics, in society, in religion, in philosophy, and in personal relationships the blithe fatuity of a new country that had sold itself on the notion of a divinely manifest destiny. Cheery Americans were confident in being good nominal Christians in a nominally Christian country, bedeviled, to be sure, by true believers who might travel to Utah Territory to establish a new theocracy, for example, but, most days, secure from being embarrassed by witnessing fanatics in the process of selling all they owned and abandoning their families to follow Jesus. Americans were confident in the probity of Wall Street and ready to apply its methods to social problems. Americans could succumb to confidence in sweeping social reforms based on appeals to man's rational altruism. American practitioners of the late-Gothic psychological novel could be confident of financial and critical success if only they would "challenge astonishment at the tangled web of some character, and then raise admiration still greater at their satisfactory unraveling of it." Readers could cherish their confidence in the intellectual and aesthetic value of soporifically tidy fiction, in which characters are ultimately consistent and plot strings are ruthlessly pulled tight at the end. Anxious Americans were placing confidence in pseudo-sciences like phrenology and psychology, which had "for their end the revelation of human nature on fixed principles." Hopeful Americans were putting confidence in the curative powers of Nature, or, as a fair substitute, in patent panaceas guaranteed to cure all ailments, physical or psychic. Triumphant Americans were confident in the justness of all American wars, including undeclared ones like Polk's late Mexican incursion (an "Executive's War"), which Melville had attacked in *Mardi*. Americans were imbued with confidence that the American press was dedicated to the disinterested pursuit of truth. American Transcendentalists were putting confidence in idealistic doctrines (on friendship, say) that required no application to daily life, and the philosophical parents of Transcendentalism, the Unitarians, were promoting confidence in the belief that reports of poverty in the United States were exaggerated and, in any case, that what seemed like poverty was due to the laziness of the complainant. Jesus might have said that you would always have the poor with you, but New York Unitarians were confident that city streets would be far more pleasant with all beggars removed from them. In the middle of the abolitionist crusade—during the horrors of "Bleeding Kansas"—many Americans were still confident in the "happy results" attending the formation of the federal union; after all, in 1850 most Americans had celebrated the passage of the Compromise, which provided for the return of captured runaway slaves to their masters. Many would-be Christians even retained confidence that, despite all evidence to the contrary, a loving Providence still dispatched his guardian angels to preserve his servants. *The Confidence-Man* was a dazzlingly comprehensive indictment of American confidence on a national scale, but for a century no reader saw its profound coherence.

In 1857 Melville's mention of journalistic commonplaces such as accounts of Mississippi steamboat diddlers, American outlaws, spirit-rapping, hard-shell Baptists, Charity organizers, Fourierites and other Utopian reformers, western land frauds, Barnum's freaks and frauds, hydrotherapeutic treatments, herbal cure-alls, prowling Jesuits (the subject of the anti-Catholic paranoia of Know-Nothing America-Firsters), aggrieved Mexican War veterans, prison reformers, abolitionism, and Come-Outers—all such references worked to mislead most readers into thinking they had in hand only an unusually talky series of contemporary riverboat sketches. Deluded by the surface of the book, none of the first readers put on known record their realization that Melville had worked real people into the book. John Moredock was a veritable Indian-hater of early Illinois, whose story Melville had lifted from James Hall, an author Evert A. Duyckinck had included in the same Wiley & Putnam series in which *Typee* was published. Melville infused Hall's factual account with religious imagery that transformed the frontier history into a metaphysical allegory, where his attitude toward real American Indians was altogether irrelevant. Both in physique and philosophy, Mark Winsome is based on Ralph Waldo Emerson, whom Melville had heard lecture and whose essays he had read. The ragged peddler who silently appeals to Winsome may contain some of Melville's memories of a wraith from his first years in New York City, Edgar Allan Poe, when Duyckinck was editing both the poet-tale writer and the South Sea adventurer. Winsome's disciple Egbert is a portrait of Henry David Thoreau, whose first book, *A Week on the Concord and Merrimack Rivers*, Melville had borrowed from Duyckinck. (In 1851, Thoreau's former neighbor Hawthorne had joked about the title of that book with Melville.) The readers in 1857 who knew that Calvin Edson was the "Living Skeleton" in P. T. Barnum's American Museum did not realize that Emerson was aboard the *Fidèle*. Modern readers, alerted that Emerson is aboard, may unknowingly pass by clusters of contemporary allusions that any American would have caught in 1857. The denseness of contemporary references creates stumbling blocks, as do the thickly strewn echoes of eighteenth-century and early-nineteenth-century literary and philosophical topics. (More than most nineteenth-century books, this one now cries out for explanatory footnotes.)

Another stumbling block in 1857, especially for readers who still thought of Melville as the author of Polynesian romances, is that the book is a satirical allegory. Reviewers had regarded the Americanized Gothic romance, *Pierre*, as an insane aberration, and some in 1857 had no notion that Melville had been writing for magazines anonymously in the years since *Pierre*, much less that some of those tales had been infused with allegorical meanings. The books published after *Pierre*, *Israel Potter*, the story of a Revolutionary soldier stranded for decades in England (1855), and *The Piazza Tales* (1856), a gathering of some of the *Putnam's* stories, reassured the public that Melville was at last back on his good behavior, shunning anything weighty, but neither book made him much money. With the barest of help readers ought to have understood some of the allegory, for in *The Confidence-Man*, instead of using private references as in some of the stories, Melville was using conventional devices familiar through the Bible as well as secular literature such as Hawthorne's stories, conspicuously "The Celestial Railroad," an updating of John Bunyan's *Pilgrim's Progress* in which nominal Christians want to take the fast and easy way to heaven. Modern literary critics who know of Melville's interest in Spenser, Milton, and Hawthorne, and know that he was steeped in the Bible, can see the pattern of imagery that links together serpent, Indian, and Devil throughout the book, most clearly in "The Metaphysics of Indian-hating," an updating of his earlier satiric exposition of the same tragic perceptions about nominal Christians and the impracticability of true Christianity, Plotinus Plinlimmon's pamphlet in *Pierre*.

Still another stumbling block is the thickness of classical and biblical allusions and values. No contemporary reviewer suspected that the writer of these steamboat sketches was living imaginatively in the ancient world as he knew it from translations of the Greek and Roman writers, all intermixed with the Bible. No review saw a pattern in the use of Athens, in particular, which is evoked in *The Confidence*-Man by characters from Greek myth; by names of real people of classical times, ranging from historians to philosophers; by the settings of two of Shakespeare's plays, *A Midsummer Night's Dream* and *Timon of Athens*. The first readers of Melville's earlier books were steeped enough in the Bible to catch, and resent, his covert playing with sacred texts. Quite aside from their ferocious attacks on Melville for exposing the misdeeds of missionaries in the South Seas (and the actions of wives of Hawaiian missionaries, who harnessed natives to carts and whipped them down the roads), the religious reviewers had attacked Melville for use of scriptural language in secular contexts and for blasphemous application of biblical texts, as in Ishmael's elaborately justifying his decision to worship Yojo with Queequeg, in *Moby-Dick*. More than any other group, the religious reviewers, including those not writing for specifically religious papers and magazines, had destroyed Melville's career, so that by the time he was writing *Moby-Dick* he thought of himself very seriously as the victim of religious persecution, to the point of identifying with people burned at the stake during witchcraft frenzies. He toyed with the daring idea of dedicating *The Confidence-Man* to "victims of Auto da Fe," victims of the Spanish Inquisition, the Catholic equivalent of his persecution by American Protestants of the "lower" and more missionary-minded churches such as Presbyterians, Congregationalists, and Methodists. The shift in genre from South Sea romance to Mississippi steamboat conversations misled reviewers, none of whom accused *The Confidence-Man* of being a critique of American Christianity. (In London only the reviewer in the *Saturday Review*, printed in this volume, recognized Melville's pervasive irreverence; in the United States only the New York *Churchman* complained about Melville's characteristic defect, "a disposition to metaphysical speculation.")

Modern critics have identified most of the biblical fragments which inform many of the conversations on the *Fidèle*, and can see, for instance, the cosmic irony in the tricking of the old miser, who in a death-bed confidence cries, "I confide, I confide; help, friend my distrust!" They face another hazard—the inability to accept for the course of the book the Christian absolutism against which Melville judges the things of this world. Critics have praised the Methodist clergyman, though Melville meant his militancy to stand as a violation of the Sermon on the Mount. Some have rejoiced that the Indian-hating Moredock was humane enough to lay aside his rifle at times and dwell with his family in loving domesticity, not realizing that Melville sees Moredock as a worthy Christian Devil-hater during his dedicated Indian-hunting and sees him as a back-slider from his absolute vow during his hearth-side moments. Some have lauded the barber as a good family man as well as a good businessman, yet Melville sees him as the kind of nominal Christian who would never be so foolish as to forsake "houses, or brethren, or sisters, or father, or mother, or wife, or children, or lands," for Jesus's sake. Explicit or implicit in almost every conversation is the distinction between otherworldly morality (represented by the Sermon on the Mount) and the morality of this world (represented by the barber's "No Trust" sign and embodied in such characters as Winsome and Egbert as well as such literary and historical personages as Polonius and Lord Chesterfield). A dozen times the phrase *this world* is used in *The Confidence-Man*, by the narrator and by characters; each occurrence summons or almost summons to mind the other world of the Bible where other standards of behavior and possibilities for behavior may prevail. The reader is reminded particularly of the contrast between "this world" and the world "which is to come" (as in the subtitle of Bunyan's *The Pilgrim's Progress*). Modern readers may need to make an intellectual and emotional leap to understand Melville's attraction to Jesus' criteria for what his followers must do and to share the heartsickness that underlies Melville's satirical analyses of the impracticability of Christianity "in this world."

Most of all, Melville's new style baffled his reviewers and can still frustrate readers until they surrender to his new way of communicating richly, a way far removed from the ebullient exuberance of *Moby-Dick*. The "narrative" at first seems slowed—if not actually retarded—by multiple examples of litotes, where constructions such as "not unlikely," "not wholly without self-reproach," "less unrefined," and "not unsusceptible" almost (but not quite) turn double negatives into positives. The style relies on elaborately qualified "assertions," which may be hedgingly offered and ambiguously retracted. In this sentence from chapter 13 the narrator's prose reflects the calm refusal of John Truman (the Confidence Man as the man with the book) to admit that misfortune, much less evil, exists in the universe:

> When the merchant, strange to say, opposed views so calm and impartial, and again, with some warmth, deplored the case of the unfortunate man, his companion, not without seriousness, checked him, saying, that this would never do; that, though but in the most exceptional case, to admit the existence of unmerited misery, more particularly if alleged to have been brought about by unhindered arts of the wicked, such an admission was, to say the least, not prudent; since, with some, it might unfavorably bias their most important persuasions.

Blandly denying that a conviction of the existence of a Providence should be "in any way made dependent upon such variabilities as everyday events," lest that conviction be in thinking minds "subject to fluctuations akin to those of the stock-exchange during a long and uncertain war," Truman innocently glances at his transfer book, where he keeps the accounts begun during that "dubious battle on the plains of heaven" described in Milton (*Paradise Lost*, 1.104). Melville's first metaphysical joke lies in having the Confidence Man (the Devil himself) so thoughtfully deny the existence of evil. Funnier still, this conversation caps a cumulative joke based on the fact that the merchant has encountered the Confidence Man in more than one of his disguises. The merchant learns the story of the vicious wife from the "unfortunate man" with the weed (mourning band) on his hat, then hears the story confirmed and filled out by the man in gray. Then Roberts tells the story to his old interlocutor in his new disguise as the man with the book, who firmly refuses to believe it ever happened—as of course it had not. The astonished reader who pursues the meaning comma past comma to the end is rewarded by the perception of Melville's superbly controlled combination of metaphysical satire and low comedy.

The wayfaring reader who keeps faith despite the snare guns and pitfalls of *The Confidence-Man* receives the literary equivalent of Christian's reward in *Pilgrim's Progress*. Despite his lamentation about "madness & anguish," Melville still tried to be "frank" with his best readers, unlike his smooth Cosmopolitan, who gives his name as Francis or Frank Goodman. The reader shares Melville's personal triumph in emerging from introverted private writing yet paradoxically managing to pass off on his publisher a metaphysical American satire in the guise of Western rogue fiction. The reader delights in the verve with which Melville works out his intricate philosophical dialectics within the framework of a low comic yet cosmic joke, and experiences pleasure and awe in perceiving the complex coherency of Melville's mordant vision of his times. The reader rejoices in watching the functioning of a unique style forged in private agonies but used to communicate, not to conceal. The reader exults in his or her own acumen in unmasking the very Devil, it seems, while any sophomorean vainglory at that literary detecting is lost in the new profundity of the conviction that mankind is indeed fearfully and wonderfully made. The Melvillean's ultimate reward is exhilaration—intellectual and aesthetic— of a sustained intensity almost unmatched in English and American literature, comparable to almost nothing except some early works by Jonathan Swift (such as *A Tale of a Tub*) and some late works by Vladimir Nabokov (such as *Pale Fire*). In some moods, to rephrase an earlier statement, the Melvillean relishes *The Confidence-Man* as much, or almost as much, as *Moby-Dick*.

JOHANNES DIETRICH BERGMANN

From The Original Confidence Man†

When Evert Duyckinck received a copy of Herman Melville's *The Confidence-Man: His Masquerade* in late March 1857, he wrote to his brother George that the book had "a grand subject for a satirist like Voltaire or Swift—and being a kind of original American idea might be made to evolve a picture of our life and manners."[1] There is no record of what Melville's friend thought after he read the novel, but most of his contemporaries seem to have concluded that *The Confidence-Man* made very little of the satiric subject which Duyckinck recognized. The novel, Melville's last, was a critical and popular failure until the middle of the present century, when many readers began to appreciate the satirical complexities of the book and of its central character, the Confidence-Man.

The Confidence-Man is based in major part upon a popular contemporary confidence man figure. In fact, Melville's character has his origins in a particular real life criminal so well known in the 1850s that many readers of *The Confidence-Man* could not have helped but connect him with the novel as they read it. They may even, like Evert Duyckinck, have recognized the "original American idea" from the title of the book alone. It is my purpose to tell the story of the "Original Confidence Man," as the criminal was called, and demonstrate that his crimes and the contemporary reactions to

---

† Reprinted from *American Quarterly* 21 (Autumn 1969), 560–577. Copyright © The American Studies Association. Reprinted with permission of The Johns Hopkins University Press. All notes are Bergmann's unless otherwise noted. After his 1951 *The Melville Log* was published Jay Leyda had discovered a secondhand report (in the Springfield *Republican*) of the rearrest of the Original Confidence Man in 1855 and, as Bergmann says, sent the item to Elizabeth S. Foster, who cited it in her 1954 edition (299). Bergmann not only went back to the source of the item in the *Republican*, the Albany *Evening Journal*, but went back beyond the 1855 papers and discovered the earlier arrest of this criminal in 1849, when a New York City journalist coined the term *the confidence man* to identify the crook's distinctive ploy. In the summer of 1849 Melville was in New York City writing two longish books, *Redburn* and *White-Jacket*, but surely able to take some notice of the local sensation, in which his friend Evert A. Duyckinck was a commentator. In 1855 Melville was in Pittsfield, Massachusetts, where the nearest big in-state newspaper was the Springfield *Republican*, which often printed items about him and other Berkshire worthies, and in a mood to reflect on how badly he had been served by his own overconfidence, however justifiable it had seemed in May 1851, when the most important thing in his life was to make his whaling book as good as it could be (see Parker, "Damned by Dollars," p. 329 herein) In part of this full study omitted here, Bergmann demonstrates that the term *the confidence man* made its way immediately and permanently into the American language. Anyone who works with American newspapers in the 1850s can supplement Bergmann's items, for journalists took genuine pleasure in using the new term [Editors' note].

1. 31 March 1857, from Jay Leyda, *The Melville Log*, 563. (Evert also wrote to George on November 18, 1856, that the title *The Confidence-Man* announced by Dix & Edwards was "a fine playful subject for a humorist & philosopher" [*Log*, 531], with a slight correction, the added ampersand [Editors' addition]).

them provided an important source for Melville to draw upon when he created his Confidence-Man.

On July 7, 1849 a swindler was arrested in New York City on the complaint of Mr. Thomas McDonald, who claimed that he had been tricked out of his expensive gold watch. The arrest made a minor sensation in the daily press because of the swindler's rather remarkable methods. The New York *Herald* of July 8 describes the arrest in this way:

> *Arrest of the Confidence Man.*—For the last few months a man has been travelling about the city, known as the "Confidence Man;" that is, he would go up to a perfect stranger in the street, and being a man of genteel appearance, would easily command an interview. Upon this interview he would say, after some little conversation, "have you confidence in me to trust me with your watch until to-morrow;" the stranger, at this novel request, supposing him to be some old acquaintance, not at the moment recollected, allows him to take the watch, thus placing "confidence" in the honesty of the stranger, who walks off laughing, and the other, supposing it to be a joke, allows him so to do. In this way many have been duped, and the last that we recollect was a Mr. Thomas McDonald, of No. 276 Madison street, who, on the 12th of May last, was met by this "Confidence Man" in William street, who in the manner as above described, took from him a gold lever watch valued at $110; and yesterday, singularly enough, Mr. McDonald was passing along Liberty street, when who should he meet but the "Confidence-Man" who had stolen his watch. Officer Swayse, of the Third ward, being near at hand, took the accused into custody on the charge made by Mr. McDonald. . . . On the prisoner being taken before Justice McGrath, he was recognized as an old offender, by the name of Wm. Thompson, and is said to be a graduate of the college at Sing Sing. The magistrate committed him to the prison for a further hearing. It will be well for all those persons who have been defrauded by the "Confidence Man," to call at the police court, Tombs, and take a view of him.

The swindler Thompson (other possible names appear later) used an extremely concentrated version of the age-old confidence game. The confidence man makes the victim assume that he can have confidence in him, and then asks that the confiding man demonstrate that confidence in some way. In Thompson's game, the confidence was obtained apparently because the victim assumed Thompson was an old acquaintance (whose name, embarrassingly, was not remembered) and assumed this because of the very confident way the "Confidence Man" presented himself. What is noteworthy about Thompson's swindle is not just his rather astonishing ability to condense all the steps of the usual confidence game into a brief exchange but also that his game provides a strikingly clear illustration of just what a confidence game is.

Thompson certainly was not the first swindler to allow his victim to place confidence in him, but he was the first such swindler to whom the particular title *confidence man* was applied. The reason is evident: he used the word *confidence* in his swindle.[2]

Three days after its account of the arrest of the "Confidence Man" the *Herald* kept the new word and the subject before the public by publishing, on July 11, an article entitled " 'The Confidence Man' on a large Scale." It is a fascinating piece which enlivens the account of the arrest and finds in it the possibility of a satiric theme. I quote it in full:

> During the last week or ten days, the public have been entertained by the police reporters with several amusing descriptions of the transactions of a certain financial genius, who rejoices in the *soubriquet* of the "Confidence Man." It appears that the personage who has earned this euphonious and winning designation, has been in the habit of exercising his powers of moral suasion to an extent almost equal to that attained by Father Mathew himself.[3] Accosting a well-dressed gentleman in the street, the "Confidence Man," in a familiar manner, and with an easy *nonchalance*, worthy of Chesterfield, would playfully put the inquiry—"Are you really disposed to put any confidence in me?" This interrogatory, thus put, generally met an affirmative answer. After all, there is a great deal of "the milk of human kindness" even in the inhabitants of great cities, and he must be a very obdurate sinner who can resist a really scientific appeal to his vanity. "Well, then," continues the "Confidence Man," "just lend me your watch till tomorrow!" The victim, already in the snare of the fowler, complies, with a grin; and, jokingly receiving one of Tobias' best,[4] the "Confidence Man" disappears around the next corner. To-morrow comes, but not with it the watch, or the charmer; and Mr. "Done Brown" finally awakes to a sense of his folly, when he tells his sad story, amid the suppressed titterings of hard-hearted policemen, in the office of Mr. Justice McGrath, at the Tombs.[5] Fate, how-

---

2. The citations for "confidence man" in the OED, the *Dictionary of Americanisms on Historical Principles*, the *Dictionary of American English*, and Eric Partridge's *Dictionary of the Underworld* are all of later dates than July 8, 1849. The contemporary commentaries on Thompson's arrest all assert that the term is original with him, and if he was not the "Original Confidence Man," he was certainly thought to be in 1849.
3. Father Mathew was an English Temperance preacher in New York in July 1849.
4. M. I. Tobias & Company of Liverpool were makers of fine watches.
5. The New York City jail, as in *The Confidence-Man*, chapter 19 [Editors' note]. Below, "malicious joy" is from the English poet John Dryden (1631–1700) in his translation of Horace's *Odes*, Book 3, Ode 29, stanza 9, where Fortune oppresses men "with malicious joy" [Editors' note].

ever, is hard. It may be true that fortune favors the brave; but sometimes, "with malicious joy," she puts the bravest in limbo. The "Confidence Man," at present, occupies a very small apartment in a famous building in Centre street.

But while lamenting the sudden withdrawal of this distinguished "operator" from the active business of "the street," we cannot exclaim with the Moor—"Othello's occupation's gone!"[6] As you saunter through some of those fashionable streets and squares which ornament the upper part of this magnificent city, you cannot fail to be struck by the splendor of some of the *palazzos* which meet the eye in all directions. Lordly dwellings are they, of marble and granite—with imposing porticoes—and great windows of stained glass—and extensive conservatories filled with rarest exotics—and massive doors and stairways of costly wood—and curiously carved with gilded balustrades—and lofty ceilings, painted in the highest style of modern ornamental art—and superb chandeliers—and grand *dressoirs*, loaded with vessels of gold and silver,—and luxurious couches covered with the richest velvet—and tapestried carpets yielding like a mossy bank beneath the foot—and beds of softest down, decked like that of "the strange woman" in the Proverbs,[7] with coverings of tapestry, with carved works, with fine linen of Egypt, and perfumed with myrrh, aloes and cinnamon! Splendid equipages, with coachmen and footmen, and valets and attendants of all sorts, arrayed in livery, very flaming and very *outré* to be sure, are waiting in front of those places for their precious freight, composed of the snub-nosed matrons and daughters of those aristocratic houses. Over the whole scene there is an air of that ostentatious expenditure, and that vulgar display in which the possessors of suddenly acquired wealth are so prone to gratify their low and selfish feelings. But still there are all the evidences of a lavish and almost profligate expenditure. Our curiosity is excited. We exclaim:—

> "The things we see are vastly rich and rare,
> We wonder how the devil they got there!"[8]

After all, the mystery may be readily solved. Those *palazzos*, with all their costly furniture, and all their splendid equipages,

6. Shakespeare's *Othello* 3.3.357, the Moor's lament as he begins to believe Iago's lies about his wife, Desdemona, and his lieutenant, Cassio [Editors' note].
7. Proverbs 2.16, 5.3, 5.20, 6.24, 7.5, 20.16, 22.14, 23.27, 23.33, and 27.13. Perhaps the most often quoted is 5.3: "For the lips of a strange woman drop as an honeycomb, and her mouth is smoother than oil" [Editors' note].
8. A deliberately twisted adaptation of Alexander Pope's "Epistle to Dr. Arbuthnot; or, Prologue to the Satires," lines 171–72, where the idea is that we know the base things that are perserved in amber (like the emendations preserved in Shakespeare's or Milton's texts) are "neither rich nor rare" but are bothersome enough to make us "wonder how the devil they got there" [Editors' note].

have been the product of the same genius in their proprietors, which has made the "Confidence Man" immortal and a prisoner at "the Tombs." His genius has been employed on a small scale in Broadway. Theirs has been employed in Wall street. That's all the difference. He has obtained half a dozen watches. They have pocketed millions of dollars. He is a swindler. They are exemplars of honesty. He is a rogue. They are financiers. He is collared by the police. They are cherished by society. He eats the fare of a prison. They enjoy the luxuries of a palace. He is a mean, beggarly, timid, narrow-minded wretch, who has not a sou above a chronometer. They are respectable, princely, bold, high-soaring "operators," who are to be satisfied only with the plunder of a whole community.

How is it done? What is the secret? What is the machinery? How does it happen that the "Confidence Man," with his genius, address, tact, and skill, sleeps at "the Tombs," instead of reposing on softest down in the fashionable *faubourgs*[9] of the metropolis of the union? Listen. He struck too low! Miserable wretch! He should have gone to Albany and obtained a charter for a new railroad company. He should have issued a flaming prospectus of another grand scheme of international improvement. He should have entered his own name as a stockholder, to the amount of one hundred thousand dollars. He should have called to his aid a few chosen associates. He should have quietly got rid of his stock; but on the faith of it got a controlling share in the management of the concern. He should have got all the contracts on his own terms. He should have involved the company in debt, by a corrupt and profligate expenditure of the capital subscribed in good faith by poor men and men of moderate means. He should have negotiated a loan, and taken it himself, at his own rates. He should have secured himself by the capital of the concern. He should have run the company into all sorts of difficulty. He should have depreciated the stock by every means in his power. He should have brought the stockholders into bankruptcy. He should have sold out the whole concern, and got all into his own hands, in payment of his "bonds." He should have drawn, during all the time occupied by this process of "confidence," a munificent salary; and, choosing the proper, appropriate, exact nick of time, he should have retired to a life of virtuous ease, the possessor of a clear conscience, and one million of dollars!

All this the "Confidence Man" did not do. Afflicted with obstinate blindness, his steps would not take hold[1] on the paths that lead to Wall street and a palace. Let him rot, then, in "the

9. A district in a city (formerly, an area outside the city walls) [Editors' note].
1. In Proverbs 5.5 the feet of a "strange" woman "go down to death; her steps take hold on hell."

Tombs," while the "Confidence Man on a large scale" fattens, in his palace, on the blood and sweat of the green ones of the land! Let him eat the mouldy crust and drink the turbid water of the prison; while the real "Confidence Man" lazily mumbles the choicest dainties and quaffs the regal wine of Burgundy! Let his ears ring with the harsh discords of "the Tombs;" while the true "Confidence Man" is wooed to delicious repose by siren voices, and strains, soft and melting as those of the harp of Æolus![2] Let him rot in "the Tombs," we say again, while the genuine "Confidence Man" stands one of the Corinthian[3] columns of society—heads the lists of benevolent institutions —sits in the grandest pew of the grandest temple—spreads new snares for new victims—and heaps up fresh fuel for the day of wrath, which will one day follow the mandate of the God of Justice and the poor man! Success, then, to the real "Confidence Man." Long life to the real "Confidence Man!"— the "Confidence Man" of Wall street—the "Confidence Man" of the palace uptown—the "Confidence Man" who battens and fattens on the plunder coming from the poor man and the man of moderate means! As for the "Confidence Man" of the Tombs," he is a cheat, a humbug, a delusion, a sham, a mockery! Let him rot!

Only four days after the arrest of the criminal who had inspired the term, the *Herald* found that there were literary possibilities in the idea of a "Confidence Man." The angry satire exposes to its readers a confidence man in operation in New York far more dangerous than the paltry Thompson. The Wall street manipulator, using the same techniques as the small-time swindler, manages to defraud much larger numbers of people on a much larger scale. The satire points out not only the complete absence of humanity and responsibility in the large-scale confidence man, but also the absence of humanity and responsibility in the society which does not see the financier for what he is. The society is condemned for its assumption that wealth is to be admired and respected. But more specifically the *Herald* satire uses the "Confidence Man" theme to attack the established financial society of New York by suggesting that the principles of business on Wall street differ not at all from the principles of the criminal Thompson. Significantly, in Thompson's swindle the confidence-asking method is amusing for its very audacity and ingenuity; in the Wall street manipulator's swindle, however, the method is vicious and evil. It is more than a difference in degree; if Thompson succeeds in getting confidence,

2. In Greek myth, the god of the winds. The popular instrument called an Aeolean harp was so strung that it could vibrate and make sounds in a breeze; Melville had one on the porch of his New York City house in his last years [Editors' note].
3. The most elaborate order of columns in Greek architecture [Editors' note].

he is victimizing very few; if the financier succeeds in getting confidence, he is thought to be a "good businessman" for his success, and then the society as a whole is seen to be corrupt, divided into fools and knaves.

The facts of the "Confidence Man's" arrest and the content of the *Herald* satire were well known in the most important literary circles of New York. Lewis Gaylord Clark, editor of the *Knickerbocker*, commented on the satire in his "Editor's Table" column for September 1849:[4]

> One of the good effects resulting from the arrest of the 'Confidence-Man' was an article in the '*Herald*' daily journal, from the pen, we suspect, of Dr. Houston, the accomplished congressional reporter, upon '*The Confidence-Man of Society.*' It was a masterly, trenchant satire, as true as it was keen; and but for its length, and for the fact that it has been widely circulated, we should have transferred it entire to these pages.

The note is significant because it indicates that Clark was well aware of the "Confidence Man" and the *Herald* satire and because it suggests an author for the satire. George Houston was a close associate of James Gordon Bennett from the founding of the *Herald* until Houston's death in 1849, some time after the satire was published.

On August 18, 1849, another commentary on the arrest of the "Confidence Man" was carried by the *Literary World* of Evert and George Duyckinck:

> The Confidence Man, the new species of the Jeremy Diddler recently a subject of police fingering, and still later impressed into the service of Burton's comicalities in Chambers street, is excellently handled by a clever pen in the *Merchants' Ledger*, which we are glad to see has a column for the credit as well as for the debtor side of humanity. It is not the worst thing that may be said of a country that it gives birth to a confidence man:—
>
> "Who is there that does not recollect in the circle of his acquaintance, a smart gentleman who, with his coat buttoned to the throat and hair pushed back, extends his arms at public meetings in a wordy harangue? This is the young confidence man of politics. In private life you remember perfectly the middle-aged gentleman with well-developed person and white waistcoat, who lays down the law in reference to the state of trade, sub-treasury and the tariff—and who subscribes steadily

---

4. *Knickerbocker*, 34 (September 1849), 279. The title given for the satire is incorrect, but Clark could not be alluding to any other *Herald* piece. The satire was "widely circulated" by its reprinting in at least *Weekly Herald, Edition for Europe*, July 11, 1849, p. 212; *Weekly Herald*, July 14, 1849, p. 220; and the New Orleans *Picayune*, July 21, 1849.

to Hunt's excellent magazine (which he never reads). This is
the confidence man of merchandise. . . .

"That one poor swindler, like the one under arrest, should
have been able to drive so considerable a trade on an appeal to
so simple a quality as the confidence of man in man, shows
that all virtue and humanity of nature is not entirely extinct in
the nineteenth century. It is a good thing, and speaks well for
human nature, that, at this late day, in spite of all the hardening of civilization, and all the warning of newspapers, men *can
be swindled*.

"The man who is *always* on his guard, *always* proof against
appeal, who cannot be beguiled into the weakness of pity by
any story—is far gone, in our opinion, toward being himself a
hardened villain. He may steer clear of petty larceny and open
swindling—but mark that man well in his intercourse with his
fellows—they have no confidence in him, as he has none in
them. He lives coldly among his people—he walks an iceberg
in the marts of trade and social life—and when he dies, may
Heaven have that confidence in him which he had not in his
fellow mortals."[5]

That a paper called the *Merchants' Ledger* finds a meaning in the
arrest of the "Confidence Man" which is quite different from that
found by the *Herald* is perhaps understandable. In fact, the paragraphs seem almost the business community's reply to the "warning
of newspapers." In any case, the rebuttal indicates the wealth of
complexity and ambiguity and contradiction possible in what was
becoming the theme of the "Confidence Man."

* * *

Evidence that Melville was aware of—and even using incidents
from the career of—Thompson is provided by the reappearance of
that confidence man in 1855 in Albany. Melville was at that time
living on his farm, Arrowhead, near Pittsfield, Massachusetts. It is
thought that he began and worked on *The Confidence-Man* some
time between April 1855 and May 1856, finishing it in late spring
or early summer 1856, after *The Piazza Tales* went to press.[6] The
reappearance of the first confidence man in Albany in April and
May 1855 certainly provided him with material for his novel.

The Albany *Evening Journal* of April 28, 1855 printed an article
entitled "The Original Confidence Man in Town.—A Short Chapter
on Misplaced Confidence." The article describes the activities of
"Samuel Willis" in a jewelry store in Albany:

5. As Bergmann indicates, Paul Smith had pointed this item out in "*The Confidence-Man*
and the Literary World of New York," *Nineteenth-Century Fiction*, 16 (March 1962),
329–37 [Editors' note].
6. This dating is pretty much what Parker arrives at in *Herman Melville*, volume 2 [Editors'
note].

He called into a jewelry store on Broadway and said to the proprietor: "How do you do, Mr. Myers?" Receiving no reply, he added "Don't you know me?" to which Mr. M. replied that he did not. "My name is Samuel Willis. You are mistaken, for I have met you three or four times." He then said he had something of a private nature to communicate to Mr. Myers, and that he wished to see him alone. The two then walked to the end of the counter, when Willis said to Myers, "I guess you are a Mason,"—to which Myers replied that he was—when Willis asked him if he would not give a brother a shilling if he needed it. By some shrewd management. Myers was induced to give him six or seven dollars.

The Springfield *Daily Republican* reprinted this Albany *Evening Journal* article on May 5, and Melville, living in nearby Pittsfield, could easily have seen either newspaper. In any case, in Chapter IV of *The Confidence-Man*, "Renewal of Old Acquaintance," the "man with the weed" approaches a merchant the same way "Willis" approached the jewelry store owner in Albany, asserting an old acquaintance unremembered by the victim, and finally using exactly the same trick and, in part, exactly the same words which "Willis" did. The "man with the weed" says:

> "If I remember, you are a mason, Mr. Roberts?"
> "Yes, yes."
> Averting himself a moment, as to recover from a return of agitation, the stranger grasped the other's hand; "and would you not loan a brother a shilling if he needed it?"
>   (*The Confidence-Man*, p. 22)

Surely Melville must have seen the account in either the Albany or the Springfield paper. If he read the account in the Albany *Evening Journal*, he would also have seen on the same day a separate article, not reprinted by the Springfield *Daily Republican*, entitled "Brief History of the Confidence Man." This piece specifically connects the "Willis" arrested in Albany to the Thompson arrested in New York City in 1849. The writer of the article explains that he has searched the files of the *National Police Gazette* and discovered the facts about the man who was the "Original Confidence Man."

*   *   *

DENNIS C. MARNON

Old Major Melvill and "this Worlds Goods"†[1]

> But whoso hath this world's goods, and seeth his brother have
> need, and shutteth up his bowels of *compassion* from him, how
> dwelleth the love of God in him?
>
> —1 John 3.17

> ¿What kind of man is that, who full of opulence, in whose hands
> abundance overflows, can look on virtue in distress . . . without af-
> ford to the suffereds some relief?
>
> —T. M. Acosta, letter to General Henry A. S. Dearborn, Febru-
> ary 1, 1820[2]

> Nor is there any danger that charitable efforts will impoverish us
> as a people.
>
> —David Dudley Field, ed. *A History of the County of Berkshire,
> Massachusetts*. Pittsfield: S. W. Bush, 1829

> The danger is not very imminent.
>
> —Herman Melville's annotation in his copy of Field[3]

In 1811, Major Thomas Melvill, responding to a letter from the
Reverend David Swan, a relative from Leven, near Edinburgh, reflected on his life in Boston since his extended visit to Scotland in
the early 1770s: "With respect to myself since I left that country I
have experienced several changes of Fortune, but am now, although
not among those who are called rich in this Worlds Goods, *am* in
easy and comfortable circumstances, holding a respectable Office
under the Government."[4] It is true that his private interests as a

† Permission to cite original manuscript material kindly granted by Massachusetts Histor-
ical Society, Houghton Library, Harvard University, Berkshire Athenaeum, Pittsfield,
Massachusetts, American Antiquarian Society, Massachusetts Supreme Judicial Court,
Archives and Records Preservation, New England Historic Genealogical Society, and
New York Public Library, Manuscripts Division.

1. General biographical information about Thomas Melvill Sr. (TM,Sr) (1751–1832),
Thomas Melvill Jr (TM Jr) (1776–1845), and Allan Melvill (AM) (1782–1832) used in
this article is found in Hershel Parker, *Herman Melville: A Biography, Volume 1,
1819–1851* (Baltimore: Johns Hopkins Univ. Press, 1996) (cited as HP V1), and Jay
Leyda, *The Melville Log: A Documentary Life of Herman Melville, 1819–1891*, 2nd ed.,
with a supplement (New York: Gordian Press, 1969) (cited as *Log*). Manuscript and mi-
crofilm collections consulted include those of Houghton Library of the Harvard College
Library (HCL), Massachusetts Historical Society (MHS), American Antiquarian Society
(AAS), New York Public Library, Manuscripts Division, Gansevoort-Lansing Collection
(NYPL-GL), Berkshire Athenaeum (BeA), National Archives and Record Administration
(NARA), and Massachusetts State Archives (MSA).
2. Acosta, "A Rascally Impostor" who tried to con Old Major Melvill, in a begging letter to
Dearborn (MHS, Ms. S-252).
3. *Log*, p. 378.
4. TM,Sr to the Reverend David Swan, May 6, 1811: BeA, Melville-Morewood Collection,
VIII-1, Genealogical Papers (with copies at MHS, Shaw Papers, and NYPL-GL, Melville
Family Papers).

merchant had suffered[5] during the devastating Siege of Boston and during his service in Crafts's artillery regiment during the Revolution. And it is also true that later his private business interests outside his appointments with the federal government, first as surveyor (1789) and then as naval officer (1811) of the Port of Boston, had fluctuated along with those of other New England investors in the early decades of the new nation. Yet some of the greatest threats to Major Melvill's ease and comfort over the years before and after 1811 came, not from general economic or political conditions but rather from within his family, first in his business dealings with his oldest son, Thomas, and then in his substantial, outstanding loans over many years to his son Allan.

Thomas Junior's financial collapse as a businessman in Paris at the beginning of the nineteenth century embroiled Major Melvill, and to a lesser extent Allan, in multiple lawsuits[6] brought by Boston creditors in the Court of Common Pleas seeking payments totaling nearly $100,000. To his European creditors in 1803, Thomas Junior was in debt an additional £35,000.[7] Allan's frantic letters[8] from Boston to his brother in France in 1802–03 show how Thomas Junior's reckless behavior and soaring debt came close to destroying his father's finances. But the father pulled through and, at least financially, pulled back. At a distance of nearly a decade, Major Melvill explained to the Reverend Swan that, in obvious contrast to his own current position of security, ease and comfort, ". . . my eldest son Thomas has been absent in France many years; he was very unfortunate in business and is not pleasantly situated." If the father was cool in his account of Thomas at the time, he was warm and confident in recommending to his relative his second son, Allan, then traveling in England, as a "discreet well informed amiable young man"[9] of character and promise.

In the same year as the major's letter to Swan, Thomas Junior, still in debt abroad and at home, returned to Boston and lived with his young family in his father's well-appointed home on Green Street until he received a commission in the War of 1812. As commissary for prisoners, with the rank of major, he served in Pittsfield, Massachusetts, near the New York border. Through various supplies contracts during the war, Thomas Junior was able to make

---

5. "Thomas Melvill (Melville)," in Richard A. Harrison, *Princetonians, 1769–1775: A Biographical Dictionary*, (Princeton: Princeton Univ. Press, 1980), vol. 2, p. 35.
6. MHS, Shaw Papers, March–April 1803 (plaintiffs included Thomas Amory, the estate of James Tisdale, John and George Washington Appleton).
7. TM,Jr to TM,Sr, September 14, 1803: HCL, bMS Am 1233 (12).
8. Most notably, AM to TM,Jr, January 10, 1803 and January 29, 1803. NYPL-GL, Melville Family Papers, box 307, AM's private letter book, 1802–1818.
9. TM,Sr to the Reverend David Swan, May 6, 1811: BeA, Melville-Morewood Collection, VIII-1 Genealogical Papers.

large profits and repay $14,000[1] of the $15,000 he still owed his father from a decade earlier. After the war, Thomas Junior stayed in Pittsfield and worked the large farm his father purchased from Elkanah Watson in 1816. Long-term prosperity, however, eluded the Old Major's firstborn. Not only had Thomas Junior failed to repay the rest of his American creditors from his Paris days but he soon became mired in additional personal debt after the war. Thomas Junior's motives in repaying almost all his debts to his father while ignoring his other creditors—old and new—resulted in widely noticed charges of collusion that threatened the Old Major's reappointment to his respectable position of naval officer of the Port of Boston and Charlestown. Daniel Webster and Lemuel Shaw were able to defend the Thomases Senior and Junior successfully against the charges of hiding the latter's assets from creditors; but one creditor in particular, Charles Jarvis, pressed successfully for Thomas Junior's imprisonment for debt. From 1816 through the early 1830s, Thomas Junior repeatedly fell into debt and ended up in prison. In addition to embarrassing the comfortable, prominent Boston Melvills by these regular imprisonments for debt, Thomas Junior more than once in the 1820s exasperated the Old Major by failing to realize enough income from the farm to cover basic expenses and taxes and then turning to his father for more money.[2]

In the meantime, Allan, after some early success in Boston as an importer of French goods, moved his family and business in 1818 to New York City, where he was unable to sustain his success. New debt was added to old, both within the family and within his business circle. In time he stopped paying even the interest on substantial loans from his father.[3] In 1830, with his affairs tangled and his reputation tarnished, he retreated to Albany, home of his wife's distinguished and wealthy family, the Gansevoorts. Bankrupt and broken, he contracted a fever and died, delirious, in January 1832, leaving a widow and eight children, including twelve-year-old Herman, the third child and second son. As Thomas Junior and, later, Allan moved from one unpleasant situation to another in their business lives, both made considerable and frequent demands on the resources of their father, until he took specific steps in his will of February 1829, to protect his estate and the interests of his other children. The Old Major, conscious of his own successes and those

1. MHS, Shaw Papers: draft document of TM,Sr (in Lemuel Shaw's hand), dated November 3, 1815, containing an account of the charges of collusion, the outcome of the inquiry, and details of TM,Jr's subsequent imprisonment for debt.
2. TM,Sr to TM,Jr, February 20, 1824: HCL, bMS Am 1233 (8).
3. Massachusetts Supreme Judicial Court, Archives and Records Preservation, Suffolk County Probate Court Records, Docket 30003: "Thomas Melville, Will," "Schedule of Notes, &c. belonging to said deceased Estate . . . incapable of exact valuation." For copies of the original will and related papers and for her expert advice, I am grateful to Elizabeth C. Bouvier, Head of Archives, Massachusetts Supreme Judicial Court.

of his merchant father before him, must have wondered if his first two sons, overly confident and overly committed to speculation, had any business being in business.

But in 1811, some of his sons' business failures had been weathered and others, many others, were still far off. In writing to his kinsman in Scotland, the Old Major could pronounce his life good. Indeed, at that particular moment he had reason to look forward with confidence to increased ease and comfort in life, for the Reverend Swan's letter[4] had contained information that convinced Old Major Melvill he was the heir-at-law of the vast estates of General Robert Melville, of Scotland, who had died in 1809.

However self-effacing he may have been about his share of worldly goods in a letter to his humble Scottish relative, when it came time to press his claims on the general's estates, said to be worth "not less than £100,000,"[5] the Old Major helped his sons Thomas and Allan compile a family genealogy[6] that established a blood and legal tie to the general and made particular note of some of Thomas Melvill's early advantages in life, despite having been left an orphan in 1761 at the age of ten. Placed in the care of his maternal grandmother, Mary Cargill, "a most respectable, and intelligent Lady," young Thomas, an only child, "inherited a handsome Fortune from his father," a Boston merchant who had immigrated to New England in 1748. Probate records[7] show that young Thomas Melvill inherited almost £3,000 or approximately $15,000 at 1761 exchange rates[8] (and as much as $360,000 in 2005 buying power). After graduating from Boston Latin and from the College of New Jersey (Princeton), where he trained for the ministry, Melvill visited Scotland and England. When he returned to Boston,[9] he abandoned the ministry and took up business and radical politics, joining the Long Room Club, supporting the Sons of Liberty, and forming close friendships with Samuel Adams, John Hancock, and Paul Revere—serving with the last in Crafts's artillery regiment. He was one of the "Aboriginals" who participated in the Boston Tea Party in December 1773 as part of his commitment to the "holy cause of his country."[1] The following summer, he

4. The Reverend David Swan to TM,Sr, January 7, 1811: HCL, bMS Am 188.6 (39).
5. TM,Sr to AM, May 6, 1811: BeA, Melville-Morewood Collection, VIII-1, Genealogical Papers. Nothing came of these claims.
6. New England Historic Genealogical Society (NEHGS), "Paternal Line of the Melvill Family, of Boston, (Massachusetts.)," Mss C 257.
7. Suffolk County Probate Court, Docket 12563, microfilm series, box 2, and Record Books, vol. 63, pp. 65–78, microfilm series, box 56.
8. John J. McCusker, *How Much Is That in Real Money? A Historical Commodity Price Index*, 2nd ed., revised and enlarged (Worcester: AAS, 2001), pp. 41–70; see also the online site of Economic History Resources, *What Is Its Relative Value in US dollars?* (http://eh.net/hmit/compare).
9. Harrison, pp. 33–34.
1. NEHGS, Mss C 257.

married Priscilla Scollay, daughter of a wealthy Boston merchant and political leader. From his share of ownership of the privateer *Speedwell* in the Revolutionary War,[2] to his lucrative state and federal government posts,[3] to his numerous investments in businesses and mortgages in Federal-era Boston, Thomas Melvill minded the main chance for six decades with more success than most, despite several reversals and despite having two sons deeply in debt to him.

Whatever changes in fortune he experienced earlier in life, the Old Major amassed a considerable estate in his final three decades. When he wrote his will in 1829 the Old Major could look with satisfaction on the fruits of his life-long prudence, a virtue and strategy he had urged on Thomas Junior repeatedly during the latter's years in business in Paris.[4] At the time of his death, in his eighty-second year, in September 1832, the Old Major had the resources to provide for each of his seven children or their families "a handsome Fortune" almost identical in value to the one his father had left him. In probate documents,[5] the Old Major's real estate holdings—the family homestead in Boston, the Watson farm of 260 acres and some smaller properties in Pittsfield, and the former Billings house and land in Hadley—were valued at $27,670. His personal estate (furniture, household belongings, personal effects, farm equipment) was valued at just over $2,000. His holdings of cash, stocks, debt certificates, mortgages, church pews and shares, and personal notes came to just over $75,000. The surviving executors of his estate—the Old Major's son-in-law, John D'Wolf, and Lemuel Shaw, a close friend of both the Old Major and Allan, a long-time legal adviser to the family, and Herman Melville's future father-in-law—set the aggregate value of the estate as $104,699.50, not including Allan Melvill's notes of more than $17,000 (with unpaid interest, the debt amounted to more than $22,000 in the reckoning of the executors), and the notes of several others, including Henry A. S. Dearborn, totaling more than $1,300. The purchasing power today of $105,000 in 1832 money is approximately $2,200,000.[6] The Old Major's widow, Priscilla Scollay

2. Harrison, pp. 34–35, and Gardner Weld Allen, *Massachusetts Privateers of the Revolution* (Boston: MHS, 1927), p. 282.

3. In the 1828 issue of *A Register of Officers and Agents, Civil, Military, and Naval, in the Service of the United States . . .* (Washington City: Peter Force, 1828), p. 33, TM,Sr's annual salary is listed as $3,000. For sake of comparison, the salary for Henry A. S. Dearborn, the collector for the Port of Boston, is listed as $4,000, and those for the vice president of the United States and for the chief justice of the Supreme Court, $5,000.

4. TM,Sr to TM,Jr, February 3, 1798, February 28, 1798, and May 9, 1798: HCL, bMS Am 1233 (7). The letter of May 9 is representative: "I shall only say, that I have no doubt that you will in all your transactions be guided by that prudence & caution that the times *most certainly* require."

5. Massachusetts Supreme Judicial Court, Archives and Records Preservation, Suffolk County Probate Court Records, Docket 30003: "Thomas Melville. Will," "An Inventory of the estate of Thomas Melvill . . . appraised . . ."

6. McCusker, pp. 41–70.

Melvill, a nominal executor of her husband's will, was of course the beneficiary of his estate during her life time, specific legacies excepted (and one of those specific legacies stipulated in 1829 was $120 to Allan's wife, Maria Gansevoort Melville). After Priscilla's death, the Old Major's will called for the estate to be divided among the seven children or their families and heirs. Mrs. Melvill died in April 1833, and five of the children received as their inheritance equal shares of cash, personal effects, and other assets. But as their share of the estate, Thomas Junior and his family were given the use and income of the Pittsfield properties, which were to be held in trust by the executors. The relatively small debts Thomas Junior owed his father at the time of the latter's death were canceled by the terms of the will, as were the small debts the other children had incurred to their father. Unforgiven were Allan's seven outstanding loans, totaling more than $17,000, plus another $5,000 in interest. These debts were noted in the will and were declared payable to the father's estate, at Allan's specific request to his father. The debts owed to the estate by Allan, also named an executor of the estate when his father's will was written, exceeded what would have been his share of the general inheritance, and his family got nothing in the division of assets among the children in 1833. Because Allan's debts to his father were impossible to collect, they were listed by the surviving executors as assets without specific value. Allan died eight months before his father, and in the end, Allan's widow Maria received only that specific legacy of $120 from the Old Major paid immediately after his death. After joining with Maria and her children in court to keep Allan's creditors from attaching their parent's estate, the Boston Melvills sued Maria and her children to protect their own inheritances and offered no substantial assistance to Allan's desperate family. In a letter of June 1833 to Shaw, then chief justice of Massachusetts, Maria bemoaned the inexplicable "apparent utter desertion" of her family by the Boston Melvills, long known for their "Charities to Friends & Strangers to their Blood."[7]

The Old Major's investments[8] late in life were conservative and liquid: short-term certificates of deposit and bank shares spread cautiously over several institutions, shares in several insurance companies, term certificates from the city of Boston, and mortgages to family members and friends. Taking advantage of resolves passed by the Massachusetts legislature allowing the state to borrow from private individuals, the Old Major lent substantial sums of money—from $7,000 to $10,000—to the state on short-term notes[9] at 5 percent during the years he served in the legislature, after his removal from the naval officer's position in 1829 by the incoming Jackson administration. In 1830 and 1831, the Old Major made additional loans to Allan totaling more than $5,500, the last in a series of loans that began in 1818 with a note of $6,500 from the Old Major when Allan was setting up business in New York City. Writing at that time to his brother-in-law, Peter Gansevoort, Allan described his father as someone "on whom I can rely with confidence in any absolute emergency."[1] But by 1829 there were limits that prudence placed on the father's confidence, and his will reflected that simple fact. Though by 1830 Allan was heading inexorably toward ruin and was in constant need of funds to provide necessities for his large young family, the patriarch still had three unmarried daughters living at home, as well as three other married children for whom he was determined to provide. Absolute emergency or not, he made no changes to the terms of his will before or after Allan died bankrupt in January 1832.

The inventory of the estate of Thomas Melvill, Esquire, submitted for probate shows just how much ease and comfort (and how many worldly goods) the Old Major had garnered in life and was able to share with his immediate family and visiting grandchildren.[2] His home at 20 Green Street had a library of 260 books and "sundry pamphlets," even after a gift of 21 volumes[3] and 50 pamphlets in 1824 to the newly founded Columbian Society in Marblehead. Much of the reading matter in the home was religious in nature, including "much used" collections of sermons; and the Old Major continued to add to his collection of books in his final months. But the home also had card tables; cupboards full of silver services; "Brussels carpets" on the floors; upholstered furniture everywhere; and dozens of cider, wine, and champagne bottles in the cellar. Merchant receipts[4] from the 1820s and early 1830s in his estate papers show the Old Major to have been a well-fed, well-dressed (his knee breeches of "sup^r fine" material were newly made, even if old-fashioned in style), well-coiffed-and-powdered gentleman of a certain age, the "last of the cocked hats" seen regularly on

9. *Documents Printed by Order of the House of Representatives of the Commonwealth of Massachusetts, during the Session of the General Court* . . . (Boston: Dutton & Wentworth, 1831–32), 1831, no. 3, pp. 11–12, 27, no. 9, p. 29; 1832, no. 1, p. 28.

1. AM to Peter Gansevoort, December 11, 1818: Michael Paul Rogin, *Subversive Genealogy: The Politics and Art of Herman Melville* (Berkeley: Univ. of California Press, 1983), p. 250.

2. Massachusetts Supreme Judicial Court, Archives and Records Preservation, Suffolk County Probate Court Records, Docket 30003: "Thomas Melville. Will," "An Inventory of the estate of Thomas Melvill . . . appraised . . ."

3. Wm. B. Adams to TM, Sr, June 20, 1824, MHS, Shaw Papers.

4. MHS, Shaw Papers (receipts from grocers, vintners, clothiers, stationers, barbers, and livery services).

Boston's crooked streets. In his "green old age,"[5] to use Allan's phrase, Thomas Senior was still a productive, engaged leader in his community and unquestionably a much more substantial citizen than the desiccated figure in colonial dress made famous in Oliver Wendell Holmes's poem, "The Last Leaf" (1831).[6] To the end, the Old Major looked both to his civic and familial duties and to his comforts, cultivating a knowledgeable palate and a willingness, if not a determination, to irrigate the aridity of dry duty and parental concern "with a fertilizing decoction of strong waters."[7]

More telling of the pleasant circumstances of the Boston Melvills than the probate documents is a "Memorandum"[8] sent by Thomas Junior to the executors of his father's estate in May 1833, following the death of his mother. In it, Thomas Junior outlines his claims as firstborn to many family heirlooms not listed in the estate inventory or asks about the intended disposition of others. His claims and questions convey a good sense of the warmth, taste, and comfort of the "mansion house," which the young Herman Melville visited for extended stays in 1827 and 1829. Thomas Junior describes a variety of family portraits displayed throughout his parents' home—his own portrait (sent to Boston from Paris), a miniature of his first wife, whom he met and married in France; large oil portraits of his parents by Francis Alexander; profiles of his deceased sister, Nancy, and his deceased brother John; and a portrait of his recently deceased brother Allan. He also lists other works of art in the house, like a colored Gainsborough engraving, a small oil painting of the Virgin and Child, an engraving of Dr. Samuel Cooper (who married his parents and christened him at the Brattle Street Church), an engraving of Lord Melvill, and a copy of Jefferson's first inaugural address printed on satin. Unmentioned is the small monochromatic portrait of Sam Adams, a copy by another hand after the large striking Copley original (Thomas Junior's and Allan's sister Priscilla later left the copy to Harvard, where it now hangs in Houghton Library; the Copley original is in the Museum of Fine Arts, Boston).[9] Other amenities noted but not claimed in the memorandum are the family piano, a number of pieces of silver, porcelain tea sets, and jewelry. Thomas also asks for family treasures that no doubt had more appeal to young visiting grandsons than delicate porcelain vases and imposing mahogany furniture

---

5. AM to Martin Van Buren, as secretary of state, March 19, 1829: NARA. "Letters of Application and Recommendation During the Administration of Andrew Jackson, 1829–1837" (M0639, RG59), Film 0639, Roll 16.

6. HP VI, pp. 54–55.

7. *Billy Budd, Sailor (An Inside Narrative)*, Reading text and genetic text, ed. from the manuscript with introduction and notes by Harrison Hayford and Merton M. Sealts Jr. (Chicago: Univ. of Chicago Press, 1962), p. 46.

8. Dated May 21, 1833: MHS, Shaw Papers.

9. HP VI, p. 82.

with a Cargill provenance: the bottle of tea preserved as a relic of the Old Major's participation in the Boston Tea Party as one of the "Mohawks," documents relating to the American Revolution, the Old Major's muskets, his fire bucket, and the bludgeon with which he was attacked during the unrest stirred in Boston by Jefferson's embargo. Though neither the probate inventory nor Thomas's memorandum mentions it, we already know that the glittering glass ship, fully rigged, once on display on his grandfather's desk was unforgettable to a young son-of-a-gentleman. For the young and old of the Melvill family, 20 Green Street was a home of ease and comfort, thanks to the handsome fortune the Old Major inherited, cautiously cultivated, and protected, when necessary, with prudence.

To Maria Gansevoort Melville, the "apparent utter desertion" by the Boston Melvills of Allan's family after his death was "singular" and "inexplicable," especially since the family's "Charities to Friends & Strangers to their Blood" were widely known. While Maria pointedly included her children's Boston aunts in her complaint,[1] she had Allan's recently deceased father foremost in mind while pouring out her grievances to Shaw, Allan's friend and an executor of the Old Major's estate. The patriarch of the family had indeed set a fine example of public service and charity. After resigning his commission in Crafts's artillery regiment in 1778 because he was unable to support his family on the uncertain pay from military service, he was, for the rest of the Revolutionary War, a member of the Boston Committee of Correspondence, Inspection, and Safety, an organization responsible for governing the military and security affairs for the town.[2] Before the war Melvill had been elected clerk of the market and a justice of the peace, and from 1779 to 1825, he served forty-seven years as a fire warden and twenty-five years as chairman of the board of wardens. Over the years, he was appointed manager of a lottery to build a glass-blowing factory in Boston, a member of the Board of Visitors for the state prison in 1810,[3] and a Boston delegate to the 1820 Massachusetts Constitutional Convention. He was one of the original incorporators of Massachusetts General Hospital[4] and was appointed at various times by the state legislature as a director of the State Bank. After

1. *Log*, p. 59.
2. Harrison, pp. 34–35, and "Thomas Melvill," in Clifford K. Shipton, *Biographical Sketches of Those Who Attended Harvard College in the Classes 1768–1771*, (Sibley's Harvard Graduates, Vol. XVII), pp. 184–186. TM,Sr was given a Harvard honorary M.A. in 1773 (having earned but not received that degree at Princeton) and was placed in the class of 1769.
3. HCL, bMS Am 1233 (88).
4. N. I. Bowditch, *A History of the Massachusetts General Hospital* (Boston: John Wilson, 1851), p. 401.

his removal as naval officer of the Port of Boston and Charlestown by the Jackson administration in 1829, he was elected as a representative of Boston to the state legislature from 1830 until his death in 1832. His estate papers document that he was also an active supporter of many local institutions, including the Massachusetts Horticultural Society, the Boston Library, the Boston Marine Society, and the Massachusetts Lodge of Freemasons.

In addition to assuming various civic duties, Thomas Senior contributed to the larger community through numerous charitable activities. From 1786 on, he was a member, like his father before him, of the Scots Charitable Society; and in 1799 he served as its president. He had a long association with the Massachusetts Humane Society; and at the time of his death, he was president of the Massachusetts Charitable Society.[5] He contributed regularly to the Brattle Street Association for Aiding Religious Charities and, at a time when Maria was struggling in Albany to provide basic necessities for her children after Allan's death, to the Boston Asylum for Indigent Boys.[6]

Looking at this record of public service and community charity, Maria Gansevoort Melville protested the apparent lack of private compassion for her children shown by the Old Major after Allan's death and before his own. Looking at his obligations to his other adult children; at the amount of Allan's indebtedness; and perhaps at Maria's prominent, wealthy family in Albany, Thomas Senior may well have felt that he had done already all that he could in conscience do for Allan and his family.

Well-off and well-known in public charitable causes, Old Major Melvill attracted, perhaps inevitably, the attention of an individual interested in partaking in his share of this world's goods. On April 6, 1822, Levi Lincoln Jr. wrote to Melvill to describe a series of recent "impositions" on some of Worcester's "most distinguished Citizens" by "a Stranger calling himself *Arguilles* and representing himself to be a South American & from the Republic of Peru." The Stranger "had in an eminent degree the manners of a Gentleman. . . . His personal appearance and address were exceedingly prepossessing . . . and his dress fashionable." He had "sufficient of a foreign accent to designate him as a Spaniard or a Frenchman." Lincoln, son of the former governor of Massachusetts, was in 1822 a member of the state house of representatives and would go on to serve as governor, then as a congressman, and finally as mayor of Worcester. That he was among the distinguished went without saying; that he was one of those imposed upon by the Stranger was conveyed in all but

5. Shipton, pp. 184–186, and Harrison, pp. 34–35.
6. MHS, Shaw Papers, scattered within folders covering the period 1829–33.

words. Lincoln informed the Old Major that Arguilles "claimed the honor of being known to you" and was lodging with his family "in your neighborhood." Lincoln provided a detailed account of the Stranger in case the Old Major knew Arguilles "or any Foreigner by *any name*, answering my discription, as I have reason to believe that he is not particular about his name or occupation." The matter had some urgency for Lincoln since on "Tuesday last he [Arguilles] *literally* absconded under circumstances of peculiar mortification to those who were so unfortunate as to have noticed him." Lincoln concluded that "the public should be cautioned against suffering from further impositions" at the hand of the Stranger.[7]

In his reply to Lincoln on April 11, 1822,[8] the Old Major confirmed that he had in fact been approached by such a person, although in a different guise, and shrewdly judged that "from the discription you give of a Stranger, calling himself *Arguilles*, and from the account he gave of himself, there can be *no doubt* that he is the same person who was in [Boston] . . . in the year 1820 for several months." Confirming Lincoln's belief that the Stranger shifted names and professions as circumstances warranted, Melvill continued, misremembering the name slightly, "He then went by the Name of *Acostás*. While here he wrote begging letters to many of the Gentlemen in this Town, say, both Genl. Dearborns, Mr Thorndike, myself & others. He became so troublesome in this way that steps were taken to find out who he was . . . but without success. . . . . I inclose Young Genl Dearbornes oppinion of him, in which oppinion myself and many others coincide." The enclosure is no longer with Melvill's letter (in the Lincoln Papers at the American Antiquarian Society), but on one of T. M. Acosta's "begging letters" to Henry A. S. Dearborn in 1820 (at the Massachusetts Historical Society), the young general wrote as a docket note[9] a decidedly firm opinion of him, updated with the latest information: "T. M. Acosta[.] A Rascally Impostor who got money from me & my friends, as an object of charity. August 1822. This villain has again appeared in Dorchester under the name of Mareno. & deceived Parson [Thaddeus Mason] Harris & others?"

7. Levi Lincoln Jr. to TM,Sr, April 6, 1822: MHS, Shaw Papers.
8. TM,Sr to Levi Lincoln, April 11, 1822: AAS, Lincoln Family Papers, Mss. Dept., Mss. boxes "L."
9. T. M. Acosta to Henry A. S. Dearborn, February 7, 1820: MHS, Ms. S-252. The MHS catalog gives the name as "Manero." Though there are some striking parallels in phrasing and tactics between scenes in *The Confidence-Man* and the contents of the letters of Acosta, Dearborn, Levi Lincoln, and TM,Sr—parallels that are easy to highlight by careful selection—I do not take the events in Boston in 1820–22 to be a "source" for Melville's dark comedy. There is, so far as I know, no hard evidence that Melville knew what had gone on. But the Acosta/Arguilles/Mareno episode does provide a tantalizing analogue of a con man's timeless, diverse methods (an "endless variety of rascality," to borrow Melville's phrase, p. 122) and reminds us, if reminder we need, just how vividly the novelist captured the type more than thirty years later.

Seven letters from Acosta to the Dearborns,[1] from the initial begging letter of January 30, 1820, to his final letter of May 24 of the same year, protesting but agreeing to respect Henry A. S. Dearborn's wish to end all communication, are preserved at the Massachusetts Historical Society. The letters show, step by step, just how the Stranger won the trust, confidence, and purses of charitable Bostonians and how he then kept turning the screw until suspicions were aroused. Though more verbosely than the Stranger in the opening chapter of *The Confidence-Man*, the Stranger in Boston fashioned his opening letter to the Dearborns around the very same scriptural text used by the man with flaxen hair and a white fur cap. Acosta's begging takes the form of a meditation on charity, rich in biblical paraphrase and constructed with an artfully simulated foreign grasp of English grammar and syntax:

Sir

One of the principal characteristic of a Christian is *love:* therefore, though we must have affection one towards another, it is our most solemn duty to dispense our particular benevolence and due attention to those who are in real *want*, and *merit* our consideration: endeavouring to do to them as we would wishes others should do for us. In doing such acts, the precepts of the Lord ought to directs our hands.

What a delight is to a true Christian to feel the woes and miseries of others with a genuine and proper sympathy of soul! Compassion is of heavenly birth, and distinguished our race from the rest of earthly creation, as the Apostle says in Corinth. 1. Chap. XIII.

I am a foreigner, without a friend here; entirely out of money or resources. . . .

What follows in this letter and later ones is a vague account of misfortunes—involving political exile and a shipwreck—that befell him, his wife, and children, leaving them "at the eve of perish by hunger, could, and despondency of mind." The Stranger acknowledges that he has written to another potential benefactor in Boston, but, echoing 1 John 3.17, he laments that this particular Bostonian's "bosom was locked against compassion!!" Acosta asks Dearborn to visit him at his "furnished room in Second Street," at the house of his cross-purposely named landlady, Mrs. Prudent. Young General Dearborn did visit Acosta the next morning and, in return for his "real sympathy, and genuine nobleness," received additional *"Confidential"* letters from Acosta asking first for clothes and shoes and then for steadily increasing but never large sums of

---

1. MHS, Ms. S-252. For the complex relations between the Dearborns and the Melvills, see Parker, Volume One, and *Log*, passim.

cash for physician's bills, rent, and an overdue fare for the packet trip from New York to Boston. Each benefaction from Dearborn (clothes, books, and money) drew forth additional details of the Stranger's past, details that seem calculated to appeal to now-prosperous veterans of the Revolutionary War and their families: a political refugee from Santiago, Chile, Acosta expected support any day from friends abroad who would help him "to proceed to South America, to my dear country, to my own home, to the bosom of my friends, and to fulfill my duties there against tyranny and hypocrisy of our impotent and ingrateful Spaniars." A "Doctor of Laws," he was at the moment composing several works for the press. More lucratively, he was also composing more begging letters to other wealthy Bostonians. In time, the recipients of these letters compared notes among themselves, and, as Major Melvill's reply to Levi Lincoln makes clear, aggressively sought out confirmation of Acosta's story. As federal customs officers and political appointees, both Henry A. S. Dearborn, collector of customs for the Port of Boston and the Old Major's immediate superior, and Melvill had many contacts in international trade and diplomacy. Once the questions began, an unmasking was inevitable. Melvill reported the dénouement to Levi Lincoln Jr. "As soon as he discovered that attempts were making [i.e., were being made] to find out who he was he immediately decamped. . . . [He] was thought to be a gambler & something worse."[2]

Well connected often means well informed and well protected, and so it was for Old Major Melvill in his brief encounter with this prepossessing, cosmopolitan, identity-shifting adult exemplar of the "natural state of rascality."[3] By the time Acosta turned his attention to the Old Major—after Dearborn's dismissal of him and before learning of the close personal and professional ties among Melvill, the Dearborns, and Boston's "most distinguished Citizens"—the alarm against the Impostor's "deception and deviltry"[4] had been raised. Perhaps rushed by circumstances of pending exposure, Acosta's begging letter to Melvill lacked the expansive reflections and scriptural flourishes of his correspondence with the Dearborns, but his litany of woes and his distinctive prose remained largely unchanged:

Respected Sir

Without entering in hard and tedious details about misfortunes, permit me to impart to you: that I am today entirely out of money, bread, meat and friends, or resources at present. . . . Destituted

2. AAS, Lincoln Family Papers, Mss. Dept., Mss. boxes "L."
3. *The Confidence-Man*, p. 122.
4. *The Confidence-Man*, p. 41.

now of means, of society, or humane being to comfort me, I now supplicate you . . . to visit us today, or to favored me with a line to enable me to assist my wife and children at this cruel moments.

June 19, 1820[5]

Since first contacting the Dearborns, Acosta had moved to other lodgings in the same neighborhood and was now the tenant of a Mr. Keen. The discerning Old Major, who knew that more than the streets of Boston may be very crooked, did not need the hint offered by a landlord's or landlady's cautionary name. He made immediate, blunt inquiries, and Acosta found it necessary to follow his begging letter to Melvill ("Promise not to pay now, but to be grateful.") with a note the next day asking for the return of his begging letter and expressing his dismay "that Mr. M. would pay attention to aspersion or prejudices against this unofender foreigner, entirely unknown here."[6] For the Old Major, the danger of misplaced charity in this instance was never very imminent, and, as he indicated in his response to Levi Lincoln, he suffered no peculiar mortifications at the hands of the Stranger whose masquerade in the Boston area lasted from 1820 to 1822. Though others in his circle of friends had later encounters with Acosta in different guises, it seems that the last word the Old Major received on the Rascally Impostor (or something worse) was Levi Lincoln's news that he had absconded on Tuesday, April 2, 1822, apparently after a busy and successful Monday.

STEPHEN D. HOY

Melville's Bubbles†

In Melville's era, bursts of financial optimism precipitated into national panics in 1819, 1837, and 1857. Analysts of these panics frequently compared them to two archetypal bubbles that burst in 1720, the Mississippi scheme and the South Sea Bubble. These financial crises had an important impact on Melville's perspective.

The mismanagement of a Paris bank by Scots economist John Law led to the Mississippi bubble. Law convinced French king Louis XV that banks could safely issue an unlimited quantity of notes without regard to the bank's specie reserve. Under royal authority, he gained exclusive trading rights in the Mississippi valley. With essentially unrestricted credit and unbounded demand for

---

5. Acosta to TM,Sr, June 19, 1820: HCL, bMS Am 1233 (17).
6. Acosta to TM,Sr, June 20, 1820: MHS, Shaw Papers.
† This essay appears for the first time in this Norton Critical Edition.

goods and services, prices dramatically inflated. The scheme collapsed when the king withdrew support for the bank's notes.

The South Sea Company was a British joint stock company that held a monopoly on trade in the Pacific. Agents crowded Exchange Alley, and values of shares rose under sustained speculative pressure from optimistic investors. When news of the Paris crisis reached London, the stock-jobbing mania was at its peak, but the speculative bubble would soon burst. The impending decline was widely foreseen. Caricatures of stock-jobbers were published as exotic characters selling shares in fanciful ventures, a vision of "The World in Masquerade."[1] When the French and British schemes collapsed, the resulting economic devastation affected international commerce for years.

In the era of free banking that preceded the Civil War, the United States did not have a uniform national currency. Each bank issued its own notes to supplement hard currency like US coins and Spanish reals. Banks backed their notes with a promise of redemption in gold or silver. State banks in the northeast maintained a capital reserve under prudent supervision, but banks in western states like Michigan, Illinois, and Indiana were unregulated. Unscrupulous capitalists opened wildcat banks in remote communities of the West where the promise of redemption was impossible to fulfill. In addition to a confusing proliferation of legitimate and worthless notes, the risk of encountering bogus currency was high. Melville satirizes this situation by portraying a cautious old man checking the validity of currency with a cumbersome Counterfeit Detector (*The Confidence-Man*, Ch 45).

Even in a healthy business climate, the cycle of confidence and panic operates on a personal scale. A major risk for a businessman in his reliance on speculative ventures that might burst into business failure and bankruptcy. Melville relates the tale of Charlemont (*CM*, Ch 34–35), a genial bachelor who inexplicably turns away from his associates as he reaches the brink of bankruptcy. In several aspects, Charlemont resembles Melville's father, Allan Melvill, a dry-goods importer who operated a wholesale trade in New York. Allan relied heavily on notes drawn against his inheritance, bit by bit draining his assets to the brink of disaster. His business optimism held firm until a scheme failed in 1830. The details of this scheme remain cloudy, but it seems Allan relied heavily on confidential relations with unscrupulous business partners. To escape creditors he could not re-pay, Allan Melvill fled with his family up-

1. "Century of Caricatures," from the *Spectator*, reprinted in *Littell's Living Age* 19 (October 21, 1848), 126. A review of Thomas Wright's *England under the House of Hanover; its History and Condition during the Reigns of the Three Georges, illustrated from the caricatures and Satires of the Day* (1848).

river to his wife's family home in Albany, disappearing from the city one night in much the same way Charlemont disappeared from his friends. Unlike Charlemont, Allan never experienced a triumphant return, dying in a fever in 1832.

Melville's life was deeply affected by a lack of employment opportunities during the severe economic depression that extended from 1837 through 1843. Young Herman competed for opportunities in a job market with an unemployment rate that peaked at ninety percent in some urban areas. In 1837 he worked on his uncle's farm near Pittsfield, Massachusetts, and taught at a rural school near there. At times he probably worked as a day laborer. Late in 1838 he tried to improve his prospects by training as a surveyor at Lansingburgh Academy, hoping his uncle Peter Gansevoort's political connections would help him land a job on the largest construction project of the era, the Erie Canal. After an entry-level position failed to materialize, he signed on a merchant ship in June 1839 for a round trip to Liverpool. Late that year, he took a teaching job across the Hudson from Albany. In early 1840 he was teaching near Lansingburgh. Finally, in June 1840 he left with a friend, Eli Fly, to visit his uncle in Galena, the largest city in Illinois, hoping to find work there. His uncle had lost his own job a few months earlier when he was caught stealing from his employer. The young men returned home, perhaps boarding a paddle wheeler down the Mississippi to Cairo. Melville got another job teaching somewhere near Lansingburgh, but by autumn both he and Fly were in New York where his brother Gansevoort practiced law. Fly landed a job as a scrivener, but Herman lacked a vital skill—a fair hand. In fact, his handwriting was hieroglyphic in its illegibility.

In recognition that "the plain truth remains, that mouth and purse must be filled," (CM, Ch 36) Gansevoort helped his brother find a berth on a whaler out of New Bedford. Herman needed a way to support himself and avoid burdening his family, but his sailing early in January 1841 was a desperate act. Few hands who shipped on a whaler returned on the same vessel, and many never returned at all. By the time his ship entered the harbor at Nukuheva in the Marquesas in early 1842, the able seaman was ready to jump. The alluring beauties who swarmed the deck in the customary Polynesian welcome may have helped set aside any doubts about his decision. For a few weeks, Melville and a shipmate lived in captive splendor among a reclusive tribe only slightly marked by contact with white men. The tribe's anti-Victorian mores provided him with enticing material for spinning yarns on his next two whaling ships and during an extended stay in Hawaii in 1843. At sea and ashore, and especially while voyaging in the Pacific as a sailor on the *United States*, the man-of-war in which he returned around

Cape Horn in 1844, he perfected a teasing style that piously eschewed sexual bragging but all the while encouraged the listener to speculate about the likelihood that he had been happily licentious. Once he got home, Melville was sure he could make a book of his peep at Polynesian life. Full of confidence, he believed that if his first book succeeded he could earn a living as an author.

Buoyed upward by the unprecedented popularity of his South Sea narratives *Typee* and *Omoo*, Melville ventured greater literary risks. But the bubble burst when his inspired metaphysical romances, *Mardi, Moby-Dick*, and *Pierre*, failed to return worldly profits sufficient to meet his financial commitments. With *The Confidence-Man*, Melville displaces his personal experiences with misplaced self-confidence into a satirical social masquerade of a revived Mississippi scheme.

HERSHEL PARKER

From Damned by Dollars†

In the summer of 1847, after a year-long engagement, Herman Melville, already the author of *Typee* (1846) and *Omoo* (1847), did not have enough money to marry Elizabeth Shaw, the daughter of Lemuel Shaw, the Chief Justice of the Supreme Court of Massachusetts. At their marriage, Shaw set Melville up in New York City, advancing him $2,000, a thousand of which went as down payment on a twenty-one year indenture of lease on a house on Fourth Avenue priced at $6,000. There Melville finished *Mardi* at the end of 1848 and when it failed with reviewers wrote two books the next summer, *Redburn* in June and July, *White-Jacket* in August and September. In October 1849 he sailed for England, hoping to sell *White-Jacket* on good terms, and then to make a Grand Tour of Europe and the Mediterranean region to gather material for future books.

* * *

Starting in February, 1850, after his return from England, Melville worked hard on his whaling book, probably writing at first without much reference to source books. His visit to Pittsfield, Massachusetts in July 1850 began merely as a vacation at his late

† This essay, Copyright 2001 by Hershel Parker, was written as the Samuel D. Rusitzky Lecture at the Old Dartmouth Historical Society New Bedford Whaling Museum on Johnny Cake Hill (across from the Seamen's Bethel), June 26, 1997, and first printed in the 2001 NCE of *Moby-Dick*, edited by Hershel Parker and Harrison Hayford. Here it is revised and much condensed, but, as background for *The Confidence-Man*, four new paragraphs are inserted dealing with the crisis of April–June 1856.

uncle's farm, but he brought the whaling manuscript with him, and for at least a few days in the second half of August he worked on it there. The widow and children had sold the great old house, in need of repairs—moldering, but a mansion—and the land (250 acres) for $6,500; the purchasers, the Morewoods, would not take possession for several months. Melville had not known the farm was for sale. Once he found that he had just missed the chance to buy the farm (which one of his cousins in 1848 had called his "first love"), he was filled with an absolutely irrational jealousy. Then once he had made friends with Nathaniel Hawthorne, who for several months had been living outside nearby Lenox, Melville knew that if he were to do justice to his book he had to live in the Berkshires, starting immediately. The most important thing in his life was that he make the whole book as great as the part he had written.

Melville was persuasive. His father-in-law, after already advancing him the $2,000 in 1847, advanced him $3,000 more toward the purchase of Dr. John Brewster's farm adjoining the old Melvill property. For a total of $6,500—exactly the price of the Melvill farm—he bought a much smaller farm (160 acres) and a decrepit old farmhouse—a house that had never been grand, as his uncle's had been and would be again. This might seem barely rational of Shaw. But for his money Shaw got the assurance that as long as he paid his annual September visit to hold court in Lenox he could see his daughter and her family in Pittsfield, and during the rest of the year she would be only a direct ride away on the new railroad that ran right across Massachusetts.

In mid-September 1850 Melville probably turned over to Brewster the $3,000 that Shaw had just advanced him. He arranged at the same time that Brewster would hold a mortgage of $1,500 on the property. That leaves a discrepancy of $2,000. The best I can figure it, Brewster agreed, orally, to wait a while for the $2,000, say a month or two, until the indenture of lease on the highly desirable Fourth Avenue house could be sold at a tidy profit and Melville could turn over $2,000 of the proceeds to him. When Melville returned to New York, T. D. Stewart (a friend from Lansingburgh) offered to loan him whatever he needed to tide him over, but Melville refused: he would not need the loan. In October 1850 Melville and his wife along with his mother and three of his sisters moved to the farm, which he promptly named Arrowhead. The discomforts and inadequacies of the farmhouse became more apparent all the time, and by the end of February 1851 it was clear that the cooking facilities were too primitive for the cook (they always had a cook or else were actively recruiting one), the outdoor well was inconvenient, they needed an inside kitchen pump, the parlor walls were soiled, some of the upholstered furniture looked worse after the move, certain rooms needed painting, and the barn in particular required painting. In the dead of winter, Melville hired men to start the renovations—maybe before the first of March. The first order of business was grotesquely impractical—digging foundations in the still-frozen ground, and not just for a kitchen and a wood house but also for a narrow piazza on the cold north side of the house. This piazza, too small for a whole family to use, would be Herman's vantage point for viewing Greylock from the first floor, just below his small window in his writing room for viewing it before starting his day's task.

In March the lease on the house in town was sold at last, the buyer paying $7,000, of which $5,000 went to the mortgage, which had remained at that figure. That left $2,000 for Melville, minus any rents or other fees that he may have owed. If he were behind in payments on the mortgage, then that amount would have come out of the $2,000. In any case, as he admitted five years later, the sum received had fallen "short of the amount expected to have been realized." Instead of having $2,000 to turn over to Dr. Brewster, six months late, perhaps with no interest being charged on it, he had somewhat less than $2,000, and he had workmen to pay as well as Dr. Brewster. He would need more money, just to pay Dr. Brewster the remainder of the purchase money, not counting the $1,500 mortgage. In March Melville began thinking of taking Mr. Stewart up on his generous offer to help a friend in need, but as a last resort. First, on April 25, Melville wrote to Fletcher Harper asking for an advance on his whaling manuscript. A clerk at the Harpers brought Melville's account up to date on April 29, and on April 30 the Harpers sent their refusal, citing their "extensive and expensive addition" to their plant and pointing out that Melville was already in debt to them for "nearly seven hundred dollars."

At once, on May 1, Melville borrowed $2,050 from Stewart, for five years, at 9 percent interest. Some of the money, maybe a good deal of it, went to make up the $2,000 Melville had to pay Dr. Brewster, and some of it went for the workmen at Arrowhead. Some of it was earmarked to pay a compositor in New York City, for in his anger at the Harpers Melville decided to pay for the setting and plating of the book himself in the hope of selling the plates to another publisher for a better deal than the Harpers would give him. In early May, not later, as we had thought, Melville carried the bulk of the manuscript to town, and left it with Robert Craighead, the man who had stereotyped *Typee* for Wiley & Putnam. *Moby-Dick* had to be a great financial success, and there was some hope that it would be. Richard Bentley, Melville's British publisher, gave Melville a note for £150 (about $700, after Melville took a penalty for cashing the note early). Melville had the money to make the $90 annual mortgage payment to Dr. Brewster in September and to pay Stewart his semi-annual interest of $92.50 on November 1, 1851, more than a month after the three-volume *The Whale* was published in London, a week after the Melvilles' second child, Stanwix, was born, and two weeks before the publication of the Harper *Moby-Dick*. (The American title, a last minute substitution, reached London too late to be given to the book there.)

Normally, many British reviews of Melville's books had been reprinted in the United States. This time, for crucial weeks, the only reviews of the three-volume *The Whale* known in the United States were two hostile ones published in London on the same day, October 25, in the *Athenæum* and the *Spectator*. They were hostile largely because (due to some blunder at the printing house, where the etymology and extracts were pushed into the back of the third volume) there was no epilogue in the English edition to explain just how Ishmael survived. The loss of the epilogue tainted the whole British reception, freeing hostile reviewers to write scathingly of Melville, and forcing friendly reviewers to find ways of praising the book despite such an obvious flaw. The fact that only the *Athenæum* and the *Spectator* reviews were reprinted in the United States was worse than bad luck—it was disastrous for Melville.

On November 20, 1851, the reviewer in the Boston *Post* saved himself work by constructing his long review mainly from the *Athenæum*, which had declared that the style of Melville's tale was "in places disfigured by mad (rather than bad) English; and its ca-tastrophe is hastily, weakly, and obscurely managed." As it hap-pened, the *Athenæum* did not spell out just what was wrong with the "catastrophe" it condemned. The reviewer in the *Post* confessed not to have read quite halfway through the book, and so had no no-tion of what the ending was like. Any Bostonian might have laid aside the *Post* knowing that the London paper had been contemp-tuous of *Moby-Dick* but having no idea why the reviewer thought the catastrophe was so bad. In case anyone in Boston had missed the review in the *Post*, the sister paper the *Statesman* reprinted it in full, long quotations from the *Athenæum* intact, two days later, on November 22. The *Spectator* review was reprinted in the New York *International Magazine* for December, and not reprinted again, as far as is known. The *Spectator* gave a clearer indication what was wrong with the ending of the London edition, saying that the *Pe-quod* "sinks with all on board into the depths of the illimitable ocean," narrator presumably included, but the complaint was muf-fled by the different charge that Melville continually violated an-other rule, "by beginning in the autobiographical form and changing ad libitum into the narrative"—something that any reader halfway into the book might have agreed with.

Long before he saw a set of *The Whale*, Melville saw at least what the *Post* reprinted from the *Athenæum*, but unless he saw the *International Magazine* he did not know for sure that the epilogue had been omitted from *The Whale*. He made no protest to Bentley, it is clear, and no American reviewer read the *International Magazine* and seized the chance to challenge the Londoners: "Aren't these Brits odd? They are saying Ishmael does not survive, but right here in my copy Ishmael is rescued by the *Rachel*." Later Melville saw a handful of some of the short quotations from a few reviews besides those in the *Athenæum* and the *Spectator*, including the ones in *John Bull* and the *Leader*, but he never, in all the rest of his life, ever had any idea that despite the loss of the epilogue many British reviewers had showered honor on him as a great prose stylist.

In the United States there was strong praise from some reviewers, but it did not last long, and it was submerged by the ferocious religious reviews, such as the one in the New York *Independent* on November 20: "The Judgment day will hold him [Melville] liable for not turning his talents to better account, when, too, both authors and publishers of injurious books will be conjointly answerable for the influence of those books upon the wide circle of immortal minds on which they have written their mark. The bookmaker and the book-publisher had better do their work with a view to the trial it must undergo at the bar of God." The low church religious press would have leapt on Melville anyhow, but Duyckinck lent intellectual and literary respectability to such pious denunciations.

In the first two weeks after publication the Harpers sold 1,535 copies of *Moby-Dick*, but in the next two months or so they sold only 471 more, and after that sales dwindled rapidly. Meanwhile, Melville was writing a new book, a psychological novel based on what he had learned about his own mind in the last years and in which he played off Dutch Calvinist Christianity against Bostonian—and British—feel-good Unitarianism. Self-analysis had begun in earnest two and a half years earlier, after Melville had written *Redburn* as a fast, easy book because much of it was autobiographical. In early June of 1849, as he wrote that story, Melville had done a reckless thing, to use his later words: he had dipped an angle into the well of childhood, gone fishing in his own memory, where who knew what monstrous creatures might be brought up. The intense psychological unfolding that began in the act of writing *Redburn* (or the aftermath of having written it) had allowed Melville to write *Moby-Dick* and *Pierre*—the first version of *Pierre*.

Melville took the manuscript to New York about the first day of

1852, just as some extremely hostile religious reviews of *Moby-Dick* were appearing. The Harpers read the manuscript and offered him an impossible contract: not the usual fifty cents on the dollar after costs but twenty cents on the dollar after costs. *Moby-Dick* was not going to be as popular as *Typee*, not even as popular as *Redburn*, sales figures already showed. What was he to do? What he did, after a few days, was reckless to the point of being suicidal. He began enlarging the manuscript with pages about Pierre as a juvenile author (a wholly new turn in an already completed manuscript), then with pages about Pierre's immaturely attempting a great book. In some of these pages he maligned Pierre's publishers. The Harpers honored their contract to publish *Pierre*, on such ruinous terms to the author, but by the next summer, perhaps even before the ferocious reviews of *Pierre* began to appear, they quietly began letting literary people know that they thought Melville was crazy—"a little crazy," to be exact—not too crazy to keep people from buying *Redburn* and *White-Jacket*. *Pierre* lost Melville his English publisher, who figured if he continued to sell copies of the books he had in print he would eventually lose only £350 ($1,650) or thereabouts by publishing Melville, somewhat short of $50,000 in present purchasing power. Bentley would have printed *Pierre*, expurgated (as he had silently expurgated *The Whale*, without consulting Melville at all), if Melville had taken his generous offer to publish it without an advance and to divide any profits it made.

                                    *   *   *

During most of 1851 Melville had felt little guilt about his secretly borrowing $2,050 from Stewart: after all, the whaling book was so good that it had to succeed, and he could pay Stewart back before his wife and father-in-law found out about the loan. After January 1852, when he knew the Harper contract was disastrous, he may have hoped against hope for three or four months that all would work out, that Bentley would like *Pierre* and offer a handsome advance, or even that against all odds *Pierre* might sell so well in the United States that he would make money—even at twenty cents for every dollar the Harpers took in (after recouping their expenses) rather than fifty cents. Melville may have denied in January 1852 and denied again in April and May 1852 that his career was over, however long he might try to postpone the death gasps.

When *Pierre* was published in the summer of 1852 it was savaged as no significant American book had ever been savaged. "Herman Melville Crazy," read a headline I discovered decades ago. Reviewers already had called Melville crazy for writing *Moby-Dick*, and accusations that he was insane recurred, still more strongly, in the reviews of *Pierre*, confirming in the minds of his mother-in-law and his wife's brother and two half-brothers that Melville was insane as well as a failure. That fall Melville tried to interest Hawthorne in writing a story he had heard that summer about a woman on the coast of Massachusetts who had nursed a shipwrecked sailor and married him, only to have him desert her. From mid-December 1852 or so, Melville wrote the story himself, finishing it on or around May 22, 1853, the day his first daughter, Elizabeth, was born. The fate of *Moby-Dick* and *Pierre*, and his new labors on the book about the abandoned woman, *The Isle of the Cross*, had taken their toll on his health. As a sailor, Melville had been an athlete, and late in 1849, on the voyage to England, could still climb "up to the mast-head, by way of gymnastics." That vigor disappeared. In a memorandum made after his death Melville's widow recalled: "We all felt anxious about the strain on his health in Spring of 1853"— perhaps as early as April, when his mother was so concerned that she wrote her brother Peter Gansevoort hoping he could persuade his political friends to gain Herman a foreign consulship from the new president, Hawthorne's college friend Franklin Pierce: "The constant in-door confinement with little intermission to which Hermans occupation as author compels him, does not agree with him. This constant working of the brain, & excitement of the imagination, is wearing Herman out." The year before, on May 1, 1852, Melville had defaulted on the semi-annual interest payment of $92.50 that he owed his friend Stewart, and he had defaulted on it that November. His mother's letter was written a week before he defaulted for the third time on his interest payments to Stewart. Elizabeth Shaw Melville may have recalled this period in early spring as the time when the family was most concerned about Melville, but the worst came at the end of spring, in June, when he carried *The Isle of the Cross* to New York City only to have the Harpers refuse to publish it, just at the time when it was quite clear that he had no hope of gaining a foreign consulship.

Melville was thoroughly whipped, but bravely he started writing short stories within weeks or even days of returning home with the manuscript of *The Isle of the Cross*, which he retained for some months, at least, and probably some years, before presumably destroying it. When a single letter of his has sold for much more than $100,000, the value of that manuscript, if it emerged today, might rival that of the most expensive paintings in the world. But in September 1853, with the manuscript in his possession still, Melville defaulted on the payment of $90 due to Dr. Brewster. The money went for preparations for the wedding of his sister Kate to John C. Hoadley. Several weeks later, he defaulted, as he did every six months now, on the interest he owed Stewart.

Melville wrote to the Harpers late in November 1853 that he had "in hand, and pretty well towards completion," a book, "partly of nautical adventure"; then he qualified himself: "or rather, chiefly, of Tortoise Hunting Adventure." At that time he promised it for "some time in the coming January," and asked for and received the advance—a dollar for each of the three hundred estimated pages. He had specified that he was expecting "the old basis—half profits"— not the punitive terms he had accepted for *Pierre*. Now he paid Dr. Brewster the $90 he should have paid in September. This slight relief was followed by catastrophe. On December 10, 1853, much of the Harper stock of printed books and sheets was destroyed by fire, and the brothers charged Melville all over again for their costs before giving him royalties on his books—in effect, hanging on to the next $1,000 or so he earned. That is, to emphasize the unconscionable nature of their behavior, the Harpers recouped their losses in the fire by charging their expenses against him not once but twice. For his part, Melville decided to get more money from another publisher for the tortoise story, or for *part* of the tortoise material—or at least for material also dealing with tortoises. The batch of pages Melville sent to George Putnam on February 6, 1854, seems to be what was published in the March *Putnam's* as the first four sketches of *The Encantadas*, the second of which was "Two Sides to a Tortoise."

In mid-February 1854 Melville endured a "horrid week" of pain in his eyes (words Allan Melville quoted back to their sister Augusta on March 1). Melville had been crowding Augusta with pages to copy for him, overworking her and overworking himself. He was suffering from public shame brought on him by *Pierre*, private shame at having been late with a payment to Brewster, and shame at his continually defaulting on the interest he owed Stewart, compounded by shame at doing something with the tortoise material that looks less than honorable, no matter that the Harpers were themselves behaving abominably. No wonder he was sick.

In the next two years Melville wrote a full-length book, *Israel Potter*; several stories; and "Benito Cereno," which proved long enough to be serialized in three installments at the end of 1855. Early that year, with "Benito Cereno" far along, if not quite finished, he collapsed. In her memoir his widow recorded: "In Feb 1855 he had his first attack of severe rheumatism in his back—so that he was helpless." How long he was helpless is not clear. The timing of the attack suggests the possibility of couvade, because his wife gave birth to her fourth child, Frances, on March 2, 1855. This pregnancy had proceeded in pace with the monthly installments of *Israel Potter*, the last of which appeared in March, before book publication. Melville knew that his sister Kate Hoadley was also pregnant (she bore her daughter on May 30, 1855). In "Tartarus of Maids" Melville made the narrator say: "But what made the thing I saw so specially terrible to me was the metallic necessity, the unbudging fatality which governed it." The unbudging fatality of the gestation process was a reminder to him, during each of the last two of his wife's pregnancies, of the passing of months, including the Mays and Novembers in which he missed interest payments to Stewart and the September in which he had missed a payment to Brewster. (He missed the September 1855 payment, too.) The day of reckoning was approaching remorselessly—May 1, 1856—and Melville was progressively less able even to hope to avert the disaster. Malcolm's life had begun in triumph; Stanwix's life had begun in distress—with Lizzie's horribly painful breast infection and the doctor-enforced early weaning of the baby, while Melville was reading reviews of *Moby-Dick* and writing *Pierre*. Melville's daughters' lives began when his state was even more miserable. After Bessie's birth Melville had failed to get *The Isle of the Cross* into print and had failed to obtain a consulship; before Frances's birth he had become helpless from rheumatism.

According to his widow, Melville's first attack of severe rheumatism in February 1855 was followed in June by an attack of sciatica, which lasted through August, according to some comments made in September 1855. Nevertheless, later that year Melville began a satire on American optimism, *The Confidence-Man*, and continued to work on it during the early months of 1856; during all this time, apparently, T. D. Stewart was threatening to seize the farm—the same property already mortgaged to Dr. Brewster. Melville wrote his plight into the manuscript in the story of China Aster. In April 1856, just before the entire loan of $2,050 and back interest (and probably interest on the interest) became due, after living with the literally crippling secret of his debt since the first of May 1851, Melville began advertising half of the farm for sale in the Pittsfield *Sun*.

Melville had probably consulted his lawyer-brother Allan before inserting the advertisement, but in early May 1856 he went to Allan and Sophia's on 26th Street in New York City. The brothers decided on a course of action, here told from what Melville wrote to his father-in-law on May 12. Having advertised the main wooded area of his farm in the local paper, Melville put the entire farm and farmhouse in "the hands of a broker" in New York City, hoping to profit on the new vogue among wealthy New Yorkers for acquiring or building summer houses. The way the brothers figured it, by the sale of the whole farm Herman might realize "through its enhanced value" a sum "sufficient to pay off Dr Brewster's mortgage," to pay off a mortgage (to be drawn up) to his father-in-law, Lemuel Shaw, for the amount he had advanced toward the purchase of the farm ($3,000), and also enough to repay what Melville owed Stewart (what he would do if there was not money to repay *all* of what he owed Stewart is not clear: ask Shaw for the balance?). What were they going to do, postdate the mortgage to Shaw, the Chief Justice of the Supreme Court of Massachusetts, as a transparent stratagem for protecting the property? It is doubtful that either of the brothers thought of actually *paying* anything back to Shaw. At some point in these weeks, presumably before he advertised half of the farm for sale, Melville had to confess to his wife what he had done in 1851. On May 12, confessing it all to Judge Shaw, Melville explained that the money from Stewart had been "expended in building the new kitchen, wood-house, piazza, making alterations, painting,—and, in short, all those improvements made upon these premises during the first year of occupancy; and likewise a part went towards making up the deficiency in the sum received from the sale of the New York house, which sum fell short of the amount expected to have been realized and paid over to Dr. Brewster as part of the purchase-money for the farm; and the residue went for current expenses"— which had included paying for the plating of *The Whale*, as it was then called. He went on to state his hopes for what he might achieve by "the sale of the wooded part (reserving two or three acres of wood)": "to obtain such a sum as that Mr Stewart can, in whole or in part, be paid out of it, and yet leave a balance, which, added to the value of the remaining portion of the farm, will nearly equal the original price of the whole." Astoundingly, this turned out not to be merely wishful thinking.

By far the trickiest legal fancy work which Allan undertook was helping Herman try, all belatedly, to protect Lizzie's "dowry." By now the husband and wife had faced the consequences of Melville's indebtedness, as Melville wrote on May 12: "Lizzie & I have concluded that it may be best for us to remove into some suitable house in the village, that is, if the whole farm can be advantageously sold." He accompanied the letter with the mortgage Allan had drawn up: "To the extent of the amount you advanced towards the purchase of this farm, I have always considered the farm to that extent, but nominally mine, (my real ownership at present being in its enhanced value), and my notes, given you at the time, as representing, less an ordinary debt, than a sort of trust, or both together. Agreeably to this, my view of the matter from the beginning, I have executed to you a mortgage for the sum." The after-the-fact mortgage, like a post-dated deed, was pretty clearly improper if not illegal, an expedient, Stewart would have argued, had the matter come to trial, to defraud him of his just prior claims against Melville's assets. Herman's letter came as a shock to Shaw, and of course he refused to participate in anything so dubious as the mortgage ploy. Just the month before Richard Henry Dana, Jr., had written in his journal: "The truth is, Judge Shaw is a man of intense & doating bi-asses, in religious, political & social matters. Unitarianism, Harvard College, the social and political respectabilities of Boston are his idola specus & fori." Neither "intense" and "doating" biasses such as Dana detailed nor intense scrupulosity in financial and legal matters prevented Shaw from being also a generous and loving father, hardly more so to his own three sons than to Herman.

Rather than reproaching Herman in his reply on May 14, Shaw gave him at least general "assurances" but warned him not to put the mortgage "on record &c." and advised against telling Stewart of its existence. Perhaps dreading what he might find, and withhold-ing comment until he knew the worst, he asked Herman for a de-tailed statement of his debts and his assets. On May 22, Bessie's third birthday, Melville toted up his debts: "Omitting Mr Stewart's claim there is nothing payable by me except $90 being last year's interest on the $1500 mortgage [held by Brewster], and perhaps $50 on inconsiderable bills. I know not whether I ought to include (as a present indebtedness) a balance of some $400 against me in the last Acct: from the Harpers; a balance which would not have been against me but for my loss of about $1000 in their fire, and the extra charges against me, consequent upon the fire, in making new impressions, ahead of the immediate demand, of the books. The acct: will gradually be squared (as the original balance has al-ready been lessened) by sales. Before the fire, the books (not in-cluding any new publication) were a nominal resource to me of some two or three hundred dollars a year; though less was realised, owing to my obtaining, from time to time, considerable advances, upon which interest had to be paid." (This bears emphasizing again: the all but unbelievably mercenary Harpers had charged Melville twice for printing and binding, and were charging him in-terest on their advances to him.)

In this letter of May 22 Melville listed his meager assets: "After the present acct: is squared, the books will very likely be a mod-erate resource to me again. I have certain books in hand [*The Confidence-Man*, perhaps *The Isle of the Cross*, perhaps parts of *The Tortoise Hunters*] which may or may not fetch in money. My immediate resources are what I can get for articles sent to maga-zines." In a postscript he wrote: "I should have mentioned above a book to be published this week [*The Piazza Tales*], from which some returns will ere long be had. Likewise some further returns, not much, may be looked for from a book [*Israel Potter*] published about a year ago by Mr Putnam.—The articles in Harpers Magazine are paid for without respect to my book acct: with them." In re-sponse to Shaw's inquiries about the house they might rent in the village, Melville informed him: "I have learned (without more special inquiry) that a suitable house might be had for about $150 a year." He was not quite throwing himself, Lizzie, and the four children upon Shaw's tender mercies; he was, after all, trying, however tardily, to protect Shaw's advances of money on Lizzie's behalf and he was taking active measures to sell part or all of the farm in order to meet his most pressing obligations. And now he was being cautious about what he could expect from his "books" in hand.

For once, luck favored Melville, and he managed to sell off half the farm swiftly, in June. Yet the sale was not simple (as Lion G. Miles recently discovered): the buyer paid for the property in three annual installments, nothing up front. Shaw must have advanced the money himself to pay off Stewart then recouped it out of the buyer's 1857 and 1858 payments. Loving and magnanimous still, Shaw recognized how ill Herman was and advanced him still more money for a trip abroad in hopes of restoring his health. Before he sailed, Melville had completed *The Confidence-Man*, which on its publication in 1857 earned him not a penny, so he was out for the paper and ink in which he wrote it, and the paper and ink with which his sister Augusta copied it, and Augusta had copied it for nothing. At least she could hold it in print, unlike *The Isle of the Cross*, which she had also copied.

HERSHEL PARKER

"The Root of All Was a Friendly Loan"†

Probably in early 1856, about the time he put half his farm up for sale, Melville composed one of the strangest sections of *The Confidence-Man*, "The Story of China Aster," an experiment in maudlinity in the spirit of woeful tales of gamblers and drunkards, familiar to Melville readers from the center section of chapter 112 of *Moby-Dick*, "The Blacksmith." The teller of this story about a friendly loan is Egbert, the imitator of Mark Winsome, the Emerson figure. For the fictional master and disciple, as for Emerson and Thoreau, friendship could be kept at an ideal level: you never have to assist a friend because no true friend would ever betray friendship by asking for help. While Egbert is play-acting the role of another character (a Mississippi swindler who takes the name Charlie Noble) he warns the Cosmopolitan (the Devil, whom he

---

† This piece is condensed and adapted from " 'The Story of China Aster': A Tentative Explication," in the 1971 NCE *The Confidence-Man*. Melville's letters to his father-in-law Lemuel Shaw in May 1856 were first published by Patricia Barber in 1977 and are quoted more fully in "Damned by Dollars" (pp. 337–40 herein) and reprinted in volume 14 of the NN Edition, *Correspondence*.

does not recognize) that he cannot repeat China Aster's story without "sliding" into the style of "the original story-teller": "I forewarn you of this, that you may not think me so maudlin as, in some parts, the story would seem to make its narrator."

Although orphaned from the outset, the story seems plainly enough an allegory of the artist as light giver, parallel to the allegory of seedsman as writer in "The Tartarus of Maids." China Aster, the candle maker from Marietta, Ohio, is a man in the business of enlightening the world, much as an author is. His candles sell slowly, yet he has stores enough of them to light up a whole street. Melville's Pierre had bought cigars by selling his sonnets then had lighted his cigars by the flames of printed copies of those sonnets. Melville could have outdone Pierre—could have lighted Broadway brighter than Barnum with copies of *Moby-Dick* and *Pierre*, before the fire of 1853, or with the manuscript of *The Isle of the Cross* and other rejected and unpublished writings such as "The Two Temples."

Seeing himself as, like China Aster, a lightgiver in poverty, Melville worked into the story oblique, distorted, and some might think perversely hilarious versions of incidents from his own life. China Aster's father, like Melville's own father, had died deep in debt, and "had no business to be in business." Like Orchis, Judge Shaw left for Europe in 1853, just when Melville might most have benefited from a trip himself, after *Pierre* had been savaged in 1852 and just after the Harpers had rejected *The Isle of the Cross*. When China Aster wants to reestablish himself, he borrows $600 from a rich old farmer, at the cost of inducing his wife to sign a bond surrendering a prospective inheritance if he failed. In 1971 I observed: "One could suspect some oblique allusion to the T. D. S. who loaned Melville $2050 in 1851, or perhaps to the Harpers, who made him advances against his books."[1] China Aster's friend Orchis, the shoemaker, whom we now must think of as a caricature of Melville's former friend Tertullus D. Stewart, is in the business of keeping men from contact with reality. The real Stewart, as far as we know, did nothing worse than to volunteer, around October 1850, to loan Melville "any sum" he might need to get settled into Arrowhead (Melville to Lemuel Shaw, May 12, 1856).

In Shakespearean puns we are told that Orchis has a calling "to defend the understandings of men from naked contact with the substance of things." Presumably one should think by contrast of China Aster's own light-giving vocation: his function is to *reveal* reality, not to protect men from it. Orchis urges China Aster to change his business tactics: "You must drop this vile tallow and

---

1. For how much we have learned about T. D. S. and the Harpers, see "Damned by Dollars," pp. 329–40 herein.

hold up pure spermaceti to the world." The "vile tallow" could refer to the short stories that Melville had begun to write in the fifties, for, ambitious as a few of them are, stories like "The Happy Failure," "The Fiddler," and "The 'Gees" are products of an energy obviously less than that apparent in *Moby-Dick*. The injunction to hold up pure spermaceti may well be a suggestion (made by many reviewers) that Melville turn again to ambitious sea fiction, or even specifically to write another whaling story like *Moby-Dick*. If the vats into which China Aster's wisdom may have been spilled are allegorical, they would presumably stand for Melville's inkwells. Later the comment that China Aster's "candles per pound barely sold for what he had paid for the tallow" would be an oblique admission that Melville's stories, although well enough paid for, were not enough to get him out of debt. Just as China Aster might have been able to settle his accounts and earn money as a journeyman, "a paid subordinate to men more able than himself," Melville might have been more successful doing what he steadfastly refused to do in his more ambitious days—become a hack writer of reviews on demand from Duyckinck or another editor.

Having seduced poor China Aster into expanding his business with the help of a loan, Orchis dashes off a check on his bank, and off-handedly presenting it, says: "There, friend China Aster, is your one thousand dollars; when you make it ten thousand, as you soon enough will (for experience, the only true knowledge, teaches me that, for every one, good luck is in store), then, China Aster, why, then you can return me the money or not, just as you please. But, in any event, give yourself no concern, for I shall never demand payment." For all his offhandedness, Orchis does, subsequently, casually suggest that China Aster make a little memorandum of the loan, "at four years." Orchis's agent collects both interest and, in due course, principal, even to the point of seizing an inheritance of China Aster's wife. Having become a workaday American version of Job in his miserable sufferings, China Aster dies; then his impoverished widow dies, and their children go to the poor house. China Aster had left his epitaph, and his Job's comforters, Plain Talk and Old Prudence, arrange to have it chiseled upon his tombstone. China Aster had been ruined "by allowing himself to be persuaded, against his better sense, into the free indulgence of confidence, and an ardently bright view of life." Later the comforters decide something else has to be added "at the left-hand corner of the stone, and pretty low down": "The root of all was a friendly loan."

Just as Mr. Myers "was induced" to give Samuel Willis, the Original Confidence Man, six or seven dollars, Melville had been (in his own word) "induced" to accept the loan from Stewart. Melville must have thought he had disguised any autobiographical element, and what we see, even after knowing about "T. D. S.," is shadowy and smoky. It looks as if, full of pain, writing, very probably, before he knew that his father-in-law would save him from disaster and that a buyer would appear for half the farm, Melville, for the time being, could only see himself as the passive victim of a former friend who had lured him into debt with cheery blandishments.

HERSHEL PARKER

A Note on Melville's Fascination with Criminals, Punishment, and Execution†

In a book named for a criminal who gave the language the term *confidence man* it is fitting that Melville show, in the first chapter, familiarity with the bandits Measan, Murrel, and the Harpes. In fact Melville was fascinated by criminal types, beginning with Satan, the first to lead a revolt against God, and with Cain, the first human murderer. He was also fascinated by methods of punishment, particularly public executions, crucifixions, autos da fe, or modern British and American hangings.[1] In the navy Melville was forced to witness some 150 floggings of sailors with the cat-o'-nine-tails, and by criticizing the practice in *White-Jacket* (written 1849, published 1850) he became a hero to the anti-flogging movement of 1850. In London in November 1849 he, in a crowd of many thousands (thirty to fifty thousand) that also included Charles Dickens, witnessed the rooftop hanging of a notorious criminal couple, Frederick and Maria Manning, who had murdered her lover out of greed. As a present for his father-in-law, Lemuel Shaw, the chief justice of the supreme court of Massachusetts, Melville bought a broadside describing the hangings. (In June 1856 a London crowd about as large watched the hanging of the poisoner William Palmer, mentioned in *The Confidence-Man*, chapter 26.) Lemuel Shaw was the judge who on April 1, 1850, early in Melville's writing of *Moby-Dick*, pronounced sentence in the notorious Harvard Murder case, declaring that John Webster, a professor of chemistry, should be hanged by the neck until dead for the murder of Dr. George Parkman in November 1849. Melville was abroad at the time of the murder but home for the public revilement of Judge Shaw and his assault by vicious and shockingly obscene letters, signed and unsigned. The public execution of

---

† This essay appears for the first time in this Norton Critical Edition.
1. See "Who Is Happier" (p. 368 herein), from chapter 17 of *Typee*, where Melville refers knowingly to gibbeting and to the last man to be drawn and quartered in England.

Webster took place in Leverett Square, Boston, on August 30, 1850.

In "Bartleby" (where the hero dies in the Tombs, the Manhattan jail) Melville showed his knowledge of a notorious murder that had taken place when he was at sea. John C. Colt, brother of the Samuel Colt who patented the Colt's revolver, in 1841 murdered Samuel Adams in Colt's office on the second floor of a building at Broadway and Chambers (near where Melville's brothers Gansevoort and Allan had an office), then packed the body for shipment to New Orleans. The next year Colt managed to get a knife in jail and stabbed himself to death just before he was to be hanged. The Egyptian-looking Tombs appealed to Melville's love of antique architecture, but for him it was peopled by remarkable criminals. Tom Hyer, a Manhattan butcher and bareknuckles brawler, one of the first inmates of the Tombs (in 1838), beat the jailer unconscious (Parker 2.226–27). Melville remembered him and memorialized him in *Israel Potter* (chapter 22, serialized in *Putnam's Monthly* in February 1855). Melville admired heroic rowdydom, judging from his naming Hyer after so long, and from his fascination with Luther Fox, the original of Steelkilt in *Moby-Dick*, who killed the mate of his ship (Parker 1.252–53) simply because he did not know how a man could back away from a very bad situation without losing face.

In the light of Melville's secret agonies over the debt he incurred to his friend T. D. Stewart on May 1, 1851, is it significant that some of William Palmer's victims were creditors of his, and that John C. Colt and Professor John Webster each murdered a man who had made him a friendly loan?

JONATHAN A. COOK

Melville, the Classics, and *The Confidence-Man*†

Herman Melville was a life-long student of the Greek and Roman classics, as demonstrated by the many allusions to classical mythology, philosophy, history, literature, art, and architecture that permeate his writings, early and late. Melville's acquaintance with the classics, the textual foundations of Western culture, was largely the fruit of self-instruction by means of translations, since he had only limited training in Latin and probably none in Greek during his brief secondary education. As a schoolboy in New York and Albany, Melville was exposed to Greek and Roman history and biography, but he was not given the well-rounded classical education of

† This essay appears for the first time in this Norton Critical Edition.

his older brother Gansevoort; indeed, his full-time schooling ended at the age of twelve in 1831. Little is known of his program of study at the Albany Classical School in the spring of 1835; more assuredly, he enrolled in a program exclusively devoted to Latin from September 1836 to March 1837 at the Albany Academy, but had to stop because of the decline in his family's financial situation. Further stimulus to his intellectual development during the later 1830s was provided by his memberships in the Albany Young Men's Association for Mutual Improvement, the Ciceronian Debating Society, and the Philo Logos Society, all of which exposed him to the formal arts of debate and public speaking, with their basis in classical rhetoric, especially the writings of Cicero.[1]

Little is known of the course of Melville's reading during his years at sea in the early 1840s, but by the time of publication of his first book, *Typee* (1846), he was already well embarked on the intense intellectual growth that he described in a letter to Hawthorne as dating from his twenty-fifth year, when he returned home from the Pacific in 1844. Beginning with his third novel, *Mardi* (1849), Melville developed a distinctive form of philosophical fiction that combined engaging story-telling with erudite allusiveness. In this and subsequent works Melville accordingly showed himself well acquainted with most of the principal schools of ancient philosophy (Platonism, Aristotelianism, Cynicism, Epicureanism, Stoicism, Skepticism, Neoplatonism) as well as with the main outlines of Greek and Roman mythology, history, literature, and art. (The figure of Socrates in Plato's dialogues made a particularly strong impression upon him, as evident in the characterization of the philosopher Babbalanja in *Mardi*.) Such erudition could only have come from Melville's remarkably wide habits of reading, aided at this time (1847–50) by a membership in the New York Society Library and the extensive private library of his close friend, the editor and critic Evert Duyckinck. Soon after completing *Mardi*, Melville saw fit to equip himself with a complete *Classical Library*, a thirty-seven-volume series produced by his publisher, the Harper Brothers, containing histories by Herodotus, Thucydides, Xenophon, Livy, Sallust, and Caesar; orations by Demosthenes and Cicero (together with some of the latter's rhetorical and philosophical treatises); drama by Aeschylus, Sophocles, and Euripides; epics by Homer and Virgil; poetry by Pindar, Anacreon, Horace, and Ovid; satires by Juvenal and Persius; and fables by Phaedrus. It is not known how many of these works Melville actually read (or reread),

1. On Melville's educational career as a youth, see William H. Gilman, *Melville's Early Life and "Redburn"* (New York: New York University Press, 1951), chapters 1–3; David K. Titus, "Herman Melville at the Albany Academy," *Melville Society Extracts* 42 (1980), 1, 4–10; and Hershel Parker, *Herman Melville: A Biography; Vol. 1, 1819–1851* (Baltimore: Johns Hopkins University Press, 1996), chapters 2–6.

but the acquisition was symptomatic of his rapidly expanding intellectual horizons in the later 1840s. In addition to the aforemen-
tioned authors, he apparently familiarized himself at this time with
philosophical works of Plato, Aristotle, Lucretius, Epictetus, and
Marcus Aurelius; histories of Tacitus, Suetonius, Arrian, and Pro-
copius; moral essays of Seneca and Plutarch; antiquarian compila-
tions of Gellius and Athenaeus; natural history of Pliny the Elder;
epigrams of Martial; and satire of Lucian. He also gained knowledge of classical literature and civilization from some of his favorite
sixteenth- and seventeenth-century writers like Montaigne, Shakespeare, Robert Burton, and Sir Thomas Browne, as well as from
such extensive scholarly resources as Pierre Bayle's *Historical and
Critical Dictionary* (1710), *The Penny Cyclopaedia of the Society for
the Diffusion of Useful Knowledge* (1833–43), and Charles Anthon's
Classical Dictionary (1841), the work of America's leading early
nineteenth-century classicist.[2]

The classical influences present in *The Confidence-Man* go to
the very heart of Melville's narrative structure and content; for the
novel can be read as a modern exemplar of the classically based
literary genre known as Menippean satire, named after a third-
century B.C.E. Greek Cynic philosopher who wrote free-wheeling
seriocomic harangues on moral subjects in prose interspersed with
verse. (The "Cynics," named for their allegedly "dog-like" habits,
advocated austere living, self-sufficiency, and adherence to the laws

2. A comprehensive listing of Melville's reference to classical subjects in his writings is
available in Gail Coffler, *Melville's Classical Allusions* (Westport, CT: Greenwood Press,
1985). For the documentary evidence on Melville's reading, see Merton M. Sealts Jr.,
Melville's Reading, rev. ed. (Columbia: University of South Carolina Press, 1988);
Melville's copy of the Harper's *Classical Library* is item no. 147. On Melville's knowledge
of classical philosophy, see Sealts, "Herman Melville's Reading in Ancient Philosophy"
(diss., Yale University, 1942); "Melville's Neoplatonic Originals," *Modern Language Notes*
67 (1952), 80–86; and "Melville and the Platonic Tradition," in *Pursuing Melville
1940–1980* (Madison: University of Wisconsin Press, 1982), 278–336. Other studies of
classical influences in Melville's writings include William Braswell, "Melville's Use of
Seneca," *American Literature* (1940), 98–104; R. W. B. Lewis, "Melville on Homer,"
American Literature (1950), 166–76; T. R. Drake, "Melville and Aristotle: The Conclu-
sion of *Moby-Dick* as Classical Tragedy," *Boston University Studies in English* 3 (1957),
45–50; H. Bruce Franklin, *The Wake of the Gods: Melville's Mythology* (Stanford, CA:
Stanford University Press, 1963); Mario D'Avanzo, "Ahab, the Grecian Pantheon and
Shelley's *Prometheus Bound*," *Books at Brown* 24 (1971), 19–44; Gerard M. Sweeney,
Melville's Use of Classical Mythology (Amsterdam: Rodopi, 1975); Robert D. Richardson,
Myth and Literature in the American Renaissance (Bloomington: Indiana University
Press, 1978), chapter 7; Michael E. Levin, "Ahab as Socratic Philosopher: The Myth of
the Cave Inverted," *ATQ: American Transcendental Quarterly* 41 (1979), 61–73; Shirley
M. Dettlaff, "Ionian Form and Esau's Waste: Melville's View of Art in *Clarel*," *American
Literature* 54 (1982); 212–28; Gail Coffler, "Classicism in Melville's Style," *Essays in
Arts and Sciences* 16 (1987), 73–84; Coffler, "Classical Iconography in the Aesthetics of
Billy Budd, Sailor," in Christopher Sten, ed., *Savage Eye: Melville and the Visual Arts*
(Kent, OH: Kent State University Press, 1991), 257–76; Michele Ronnik, "Melville's
Classical Library," *Melville Society Extracts* 94 (1993), 6–11; Sanford E. Marovitz and
A.C. Christodoulou, eds., *Melville "Among the Nations": Proceedings of an International
Conference, Volos, Greece, July 2–6, 1997* (Kent, OH: Kent State University Press,
2001); and Jonathan A. Cook, "*Moby-Dick*, Myth, and Classical Moralism: Bulkington
as Hercules," *Leviathan* 5 (March 2003), 15–28.

of nature.) One of Menippus's most influential followers was the second-century writer Lucian, author of several volumes of richly imaginative satirical dialogues, discourses, moral fables, and narratives; in some of these Menippus himself appears as a character unmasking pretense among both gods and humanity. (Melville read Lucian in a two-volume 1820 translation by William Tooke, as cited in the "Extracts" section of *Moby-Dick*.) Menippean satire, for which the literary critic Northrop Frye has proposed the less cumbersome term "anatomy," is characterized by witty philosophical dialogues and discourses, often with an encyclopedic range of reference. As developed by such disparate later writers as Erasmus, Rabelais, Burton, Swift, Fielding, Voltaire, Thomas Love Peacock, Aldous Huxley, Vladimir Nabokov, and Thomas Pynchon, modern Menippean satires consist of open-ended intellectual inquiries structured around a loose narrative thread. Written with the intent to hold ideas, attitudes, and ideologies up to critical scrutiny, such works show little attention to plot and character development found in the main traditions of the novel. Instead, these narrative or discursive satires incorporate a variety of subgenres such as allegory and dream vision, catalogue and list, debate and dialogue, diatribe and invective, fable and parable, imaginary voyage and tall tale, mock encomium and lecture, pamphlet and epistle, picaresque and romance, symposium and banquet, treatise and compendium. As in other forms of satire, there may be an infusion of topical subject matter, while the whole work is leavened with wit, irony, parody, and burlesque, all in the interest of attacking the traditional moral targets of the satirical mode, vice and folly.[3]

With its loquacious but mysterious protagonist, and its constant focus on the issues of "charity" (altruism) and "confidence" (faith), *The Confidence-Man* mirrors the discursive world of Menippean satire or anatomy. Along with its encyclopedic examination of contemporary American ideas and institutions, as found in the confidence man's encounters with a variety of national character types,

3. For a more extensive discussion of the form of *The Confidence-Man*, see Jonathan A. Cook, *Satirical Apocalypse: An Anatomy of Melville's The Confidence-Man* (Westport, CT: Greenwood Press, 1996), chapter 2. For Northrop Frye's use of the term *anatomy* as a substitute for Menippean satire, see *Anatomy of Criticism* (Princeton, NJ: Princeton University Press, 1957), 308–12; see also Philip Stevick, "Novel and Anatomy: Notes toward an Amplification of Frye," *Criticism* 10 (1968), 153–65. For an informative recent survey of satire as a literary mode, see Dustin Griffin, *Satire: A Critical Reintroduction* (Lexington: University Press of Kentucky, 1994). For a convenient reference guide to Menippean satire and criticism of the genre, see Eugene P. Kirk, *Menippean Satire: An Annotated Catalogue of Texts and Criticism* (New York: Garland, 1980). On the development of classical Menippean satire, see Joel C. Relihan, *Ancient Menippean Satire* (Baltimore: Johns Hopkins University Press, 1993). On Lucian and his extensive influence, see Christopher Robinson, *Lucian and His Influence in Europe* (Chapel Hill: University of North Carolina Press, 1979). Melville read Lucian in the edition published as *Lucian of Samosata from the Greek with the Comments and Illustrations of Wieland and Others*, trans. William Tooke, 2 vols. (London: Longman, Hurst, Rees, Orme, & Brown, 1830).

we find references to a number of classical philosophers (Aristotle, Cicero, Diogenes, Epictetus, Heraclitus, Plato, Proclus, Seneca, Socrates) and authors (Aeschylus, Aesop, Anacreon, Arrian, Horace, Juvenal, Lucian, Ovid, Tacitus, Thucydides, Virgil); also included are allusions to various figures from classical mythology (Apollo, Astrea, Cadmus, Endymion, Hebe, Hercules, Orpheus, Venus), history (Alexander, Augustus Caesar, Hannibal, Julian the Apostate, Phalaris, Pontius Pilate, Thrasea Paetus), and literature (Aeneas, Agamemnon, Cassandra, Medea, Memnon, Thersites, Timon).[4]

A noteworthy indication of the Menippean form of *The Confidence-Man* is the centrally placed symposium or drinking party in chapters 25–35 involving the genial cosmopolitan and the professional con artist Charlie Noble, with its broad range of conversational topics; such free-ranging dialogues over food and drink were part of the tradition, beginning with the parvenu millionaire Trimalchio's feast in Petronius's first-century *Satyricon*, and later continuing with Rabelais' giant eaters and drinkers.

Some of *The Confidence-Man*'s allusions to classical authors and thinkers are also potential reminders of the novel's Menippean form. The title of chapter 22, "In the polite spirit of the Tusculan disputations," refers to one of Cicero's late philosophical treatises in which tenets of the chief contemporary schools of philosophy— Academic (Platonic), Peripatetic (Aristotelian), Stoic, and Epicurean —are reviewed in a discussion of the proper means for overcoming adversity (pain, distress, fear of death), and finding happiness in virtue. The allusion tells us little about the contents of Chapter 22, but it does prepare us for the formal debate, more Socratic than Ciceronian, conducted by the confidence man in his guise as the representative of the "Philosophical Intelligence Office" with the sturdy backwoodsman Pitch. The P.I.O. man is attempting to convince Pitch, not about attaining the "good life" through virtue, as in the *Tusculan Disputations*, but rather about taking on a supposedly "good" boy as his farm assistant. On the other hand, Pitch's subsequent debate with the cosmopolitan, the next guise of the confidence man, hinges on the backwoodsman's climactic attempt to identify his interlocutor as a type of misanthropic Diogenes, alluding to the fourth-century B.C.E. Cynic philosopher famous for living in a tub in the Athenian market, conducting a fruitless search for an honest man, and telling Alexander the Great to get out of his sunlight when the emperor was talking to him. (Much of the information on Diogenes the Cynic was contained in Diogenes Laertius's third-century *Lives and Opinions of Eminent Philosophers*, a

---

4. See Coffler, *Melville's Classical Allusions*, 30–31, 57–58.

copy of which Melville owned in an 1853 London edition.) Diogenes characterized himself using the original Greek term *cosmopolites*, or "citizen of the world"; hence Pitch's association of the cosmopolitan with Diogenes is in one sense accurate enough, even though the cosmopolitan indignantly denies the connection. The allusion to the famous Cynic is, in any case, appropriate for a literary work grounded in the discursive world of Menippean satire.

Allusions to classical authors also contribute to the thematic development of *The Confidence-Man*, particularly in relation to its depiction of the beguiling ambiguities—or undoubted iniquities—of both human and the divine nature. In chapter 5 of the novel, for example, the confidence man in the guise of the man with the weed (a token of mourning) chides the college sophomore for his reading of Tacitus. Picking a passage at random in the sophomore's volume, the man with the weed reads aloud, "In general a black and shameful period lies before me." The confidence man is in fact reading from a translation of Tacitus's *Annals* first published in London as part of a six-volume edition of the writer's works, translated by Arthur Murphy.[5] The quoted passage introduces the historian's description of Tiberius's reign of terror beginning in 29 C.E. after the death of his mother Augusta, and conducted from the island of Capri. Reacting to the obvious grimness of the passage, the man with the weed makes a rhetorical assault on Tacitus's allegedly dark view of human nature (to which the tongue-tied sophomore is unable to reply), going on to note:

> "I have long been of opinion that these classics are the bane of colleges; for—not to hint of the immorality of Ovid, Horace, Anacreon, and the rest, and the dangerous theology of Eschylus and others—where will one find views so injurious to human nature as in Thucydides, Juvenal, Lucian, but more particularly Tacitus? When I consider that, ever since the revival of learning, these classics have been the favorites of successive generations of students and studious men, I tremble to think of that mass of unsuspected heresy on every vital topic which for centuries must have simmered unsurmised in the heart of Christendom."

Given the ironic indirections of the narrative, we can assume the confidence man is bluffing about the allegedly baleful effects of reading Tacitus, whom the semi-autobiographical narrator of *Redburn* a few years earlier had praised as "unmatchable Tacitus" for

---

5. The identification of the sophomore's edition of Tacitus was made in Helen P. Trimpi, "Harlequin Confidence-Man: The Satirical Tradition of Commedia Dell'Arte and Pantomime in Melville's *The Confidence-Man*," *Texas Studies in Literature and Language* 16 (1974), 184. The first American printing of the Arthur Murphy translation was in Philadelphia in 1813, with a new one-volume edition appearing there in 1836.

his scathing portrait of the "diabolical" Tiberius (chapter 55). Moreover, many of the classical authors cited by the confidence man here
were those found in the *Classical Library* that Melville himself purchased in 1849. Hence we can be sure that the man with the weed,
who attacks these authors as a strategy to gain the sophomore's confidence, is ironically inverting Melville's admiration for them, since
he too had relatively dark views of human nature, and frequently
heretical ideas about Christian dogma. Indeed, by the time he came
to write *The Confidence-Man*, Melville was more aware than ever of
the worldly corruptions of contemporary Christianity, compared to
which the philosophical systems of the ancient world provided a
compelling alternative. So, too, the shallow optimism of the expanding American nation of the mid-1850s made such sober recorders of
human folly and iniquity as Thucydides, Seneca, Tacitus, Suetonius,
Juvenal, and Plutarch a potential intellectual refuge for a mind increasingly alienated from his contemporaries.

In a number of important aspects of both its form and content,
then, *The Confidence-Man* is grounded in the Greek and Roman
classics. In form, the novel drew on a long tradition of satirical critique and philosophical debate with classical origins, while themat-
ically its allusions to classical authors provided a benchmark for the
acknowledgment of evil and injustice in the universe that Melville
believed was lacking in his own era.

Melville's respect for the achievements of classical civilization is
nowhere more succinctly expressed than in the remarks he made to
two visiting Williams College students in 1859, two years after *The
Confidence-Man* was published. One of the students left a revealing
portrait of the author:

> Though it was apparent that he possessed a mind of an as-
> piring, ambitious order, full of elastic energy and illuminated
> with the rich colors of a poetic fancy, he was evidently a disap-
> pointed man, soured by criticism and disgusted with the civi-
> lized world and with our Christendom in general and in
> particular. The ancient dignity of Homeric times afforded the
> only state of humanity, individual or social, to which he could
> turn with any complacency. What little there was of meaning
> in the religions of the present day had come down from Plato.
> All our philosophy and all our art and poetry was either derived
> or imitated from the ancient Greeks.[6]

With his career as a professional writer of fiction behind him for
lack of an audience, Melville was understandably disillusioned with

---

6. Jay Leyda, *The Melville Log: A Documentary Life of Herman Melville 1819–1891*, 2 vols.
(New York: Gordian Press, 1969), 2.605; see also Hershel Parker, *Herman Melville: A
Biography; Vol. 2, 1851–1891* (Baltimore: Johns Hopkins University Press, 2002),
398–99.

the contemporary "civilized" world and its dominant system of belief, both of which he had trenchantly critiqued in his fiction. In such a condition, his knowledge of classical culture—here typified by that culture's greatest poet and philosopher—remained an intellectual haven that would help him make the transition from philosophical novelist to philosophical poet for the second half of his writing career.

HERMAN MELVILLE (AS RECORDED BY EVERT A. DUYCKINCK)

[Melville's After-Table Talk, October 1, 1856]†

Herman Melville passed the evening with me—fresh from his mountain charged to the muzzle with his sailor metaphysics and jargon of things unknowable. But a good stirring evening—ploughing deep and bringing to the surface some rich fruits of thought and experience—Melville instanced Rt Burton as atheistical—in the exquisite irony of his passages on some sacred matters; cited a

---

† The October 1, 1856, entry in Evert Duyckinck's diary (in the Duyckinck Collection of the New York Public Library), reprinted by permission of the Duyckinck Family Papers, Manuscripts and Archives Division, The New York Public Library; Astor, Lenox and Tilden Foundations. The entry records some topics that were on Melville's mind as he finished *The Confidence-Man*. The mountain referred to is Mount Greylock, north of Pittsfield, Massachusetts, which Duyckinck and his brother had ascended in 1851 with members of Melville's family and his neighbor, Sarah Morewood. Melville after the early 1850s is often portrayed as a silent man, but also as a great talker when the mood was on him, as it was on this night, when he was looking forward to sailing for Scotland en route to the Mediterranean, but also was full of American anecdotes. In this quotation the hard to read "Rt" (Robert) may be "old"; Duyckinck did like to refer to Robert Burton as "Old Burton." All the topics Duyckinck recorded touch on themes of *The Confidence-Man*—covert atheism in literature, the conniving of an unfaithful young wife, secret blasphemy among the lower social orders, and the bitter contrast between a life destined for disaster and one destined for triumph.

Melville might have found any number of passages in Burton to be secretly atheistical. The story of how Lydia and Pyrrhus deceived her jealous husband Nicostratus by convincing him that a pear tree was enchanted is from the Seventh Day, the Ninth Novel, of the *Decameron*, composed 1349–51 by the Italian writer Giovanni Boccaccio (1313–1375). Melville may have known Judge John Worth Edmonds (1799–1874), a New York City lawyer and later a justice of the New York supreme court, since his brother Allan was a New York lawyer and his father-in-law was chief justice of the supreme court of Massachusetts. Edmonds had been prison inspector at Sing Sing, north of New York City, and since 1853 had been the most prominent convert to Spiritualism, the cause of his resignation from the state supreme court. Many of his spirit messages came from two men important to *The Confidence-Man*, Francis Bacon (see n. 9, p. 58 herein) and Emanuel Swedenborg (see n. 9, p. 200 herein). Taylor was experiencing the height of his celebrity (see n. 2, p. 137 herein), and Melville had every right to feel jealous of him.

The travel journal Melville kept during the next months of his European and Near Eastern tour provides detailed evidence of his states of mind in response to his sometimes overwhelming experiences (such as his visit to the Pyramids), but this little entry of Duyckinck's is the best evidence for the sort of topics that were on his mind immediately after finishing *The Confidence-Man*.

good story from the Decameron the *Enchantment* of the husband in the tree; a story from judge Edmonds of a prayer meeting of female convicts at Sing Sing which the Judge was invited to witness and agreed to, provided he was introduced where he could not be seen. It was an orgie of indecency and blasphemy. Said of Bayard Taylor that as some augur predicted the misfortunes of Charles I from the infelicity of his countenance so Taylor's prosperity 'borne up by the Gods' was written in his face.

NATHANIEL HAWTHORNE

[With Melville on Terms of Sociability and Confidence]†

November 20th, Thursday. A week ago last Monday, Herman Melville came to see me at the Consulate,[1] looking much as he used to do (a little paler, and perhaps a little sadder), in a rough outside coat, and with his characteristic gravity and reserve of manner. He had crossed from New York to Glasgow in a screw steamer, about a fortnight before, and had since been seeing Edinburgh and other interesting places. I felt rather awkward at first; because this is the first time I have met him since my ineffectual attempt to get him a consular appointment from General Pierce. However, I failed only from real lack of power to serve him; so there was no reason to be ashamed, and we soon found ourselves on pretty much our former terms of sociability and confidence. Melville has not been well, of late; he has been affected with neuralgic complaints in his head and limbs, and no doubt has suffered from too constant literary occupation, pursued without much success, latterly; and his writings, for a long while past,[2] have indicated a morbid state of mind. So he left his place at Pittsfield, and has established his wife and family, I believe, with his father-in law in Boston, and is thus far on his way to Constantinople. I do not wonder that he found it necessary to take an airing through the world, after so many years of toilsome pen-labor and domestic life, following upon so wild and adventurous a youth as his was. I invited him to come and stay with us at

† From *The English Notebooks of Nathaniel Hawthorne*, edited by Randall Stewart (New York: MLA, 1941), 423–24. Reprinted by permission. All notes are the editors'.
1. In 1853 after his inauguration as president his college friend Franklin Pierce had appointed Hawthorne as consul to Liverpool, the most lucrative political plum at his disposal.
2. Hawthorne praised *Moby-Dick*, which was dedicated to him, we know from Melville's response. Hawthorne can only mean *Pierre* (1852) and some of the stories that had reached him in *Harper's New Monthly Magazine* and *Putnam's Monthly.*

Southport,[3] as long as he might remain in this vicinity; and, accordingly, he did come, the next day, taking with him, by way of baggage, the least little bit of a bundle, which, he told me, contained a night shirt and a tooth-brush. He is a person of very gentlemanly instincts in every respect, save that he is a little heterodox in the matter of clean linen.

He stayed with us from Tuesday till Thursday; and, on the intervening day, we took a pretty long walk together, and sat down in a hollow among the sand hills (sheltering ourselves from the high, cool wind) and smoked a cigar. Melville, as he always does, began to reason of Providence and futurity, and of everything that lies beyond human ken, and informed me that he had "pretty much made up his mind to be annihilated";[4] but still he does not seem to rest in that anticipation; and, I think, will never rest until he gets hold of a definite belief. It is strange how he persists—and has persisted ever since I knew him, and probably long before—in wandering to-and fro over these deserts, as dismal and monotonous as the sand hills amid which we were sitting. He can neither believe, nor be comfortable in his unbelief; and he is too honest and courageous not to try to do one or the other. If he were a religious man, he would be one of the most truly religious and reverential; he has a very high and noble nature, and better worth immortality than most of us.

HERSHEL PARKER

Melville as a Student of Aesthetics†

When he wrote *The Confidence-Man* Melville had already made himself into one of the greatest writers in the world, but the field of aesthetics was a blank to him except for what he had picked up through his yet-unsystematic reading on the subject and through self-observation during his growth as a writer. Melville thought well for a time of his friend Hawthorne's attempt at dramatizing aesthetic issues in "The Artist of the Beautiful," where the destruction of a unique work of art, the achievement of a lifetime, is not important to the artist: "When the artist rose high enough to achieve the

3. A vacation town on the Irish Sea north of Liverpool.
4. Steeped in Milton as both men were, Hawthorne would have heard Melville's words as an echo of Satan's boast in book 6 of *Paradise Lost* that he cannot be killed piecemeal, an organ at a time, but only by total annihilation (being reduced to nothingness). The passage was a favorite of Melville's older brother Gansevoort, and in his own copy of the poem Herman Melville underlined "Cannot but by annihilating die" and drew a vertical line at the left (see Grey and Robillard in the Selected Bibliography).
† Adapted from passages in Hershel Parker's *Herman Melville: A Biography, 1851–1891.* Copyright © 1996 Hershel Parker. Reprinted by permission of the author and The Johns Hopkins University Press.

Beautiful, the symbol by which he made it perceptible to mortal senses became of little value in his eyes, while his spirit possessed itself in the enjoyment of the Reality." This would be as if writing *Moby-Dick* and then destroying the manuscript should have satisfied Melville. More precisely, it would be as if Melville's destruction of his *The Isle of the Cross* (completed in 1853 and rejected by the Harpers) cost him not a pang. Melville could not for long content himself with a theory of art for artist's sake.

Melville's greatest textbooks for the study of aesthetics proved to be the eight volumes in his set of *Modern British Essayists*, in his library since early 1849, especially the volume containing Francis Jeffrey's essays from *The Edinburgh Review*. In his preface Jeffrey explained carefully that "The Edinburgh Review . . . aimed high from the beginning:—And, refusing to confine itself to the humble task of pronouncing on the mere literary merits of the works that came before it, professed to go deeply into *the Principles* on which its judgments were to be rested; as well as to take large and original views of all the important questions to which those works might relate." In twenty-first-century terminology, the great quarterly magazine, from the first, aspired to address theoretical issues, issues involving aesthetics.

In *The Confidence-Man* Melville tested his new interest in three chapters on aesthetics (14, 33, and 44). As Tom Quirk has shown, Melville's immediate provocations for these chapters included an essay by Michel de .Montaigne and a magazine comment on Charles Dickens. In Europe and the Near East during late 1856 and early 1857 Melville pondered on ancient and Renaissance artistic treasures, and received a memorable lecture from at least one great artist, the sculptor Hiram Powers, in Florence. He had begun a lifelong study of aesthetics, but, as he acknowledged at the start of his lecture on "Statues in Rome" late in 1857, he was still "neither critic nor connoisseur." Fumbling early stages of his pursuit are evident in this first lecture, where he enunciated a rudimentary democratic theory of art appreciation: "the creations of Art" may be appreciated "by those ignorant of its critical science, or indifferent to it." (See Parker 2.357–362.) He reflected further on aesthetic issues as he made himself into a poet during 1858 and 1859, then during a voyage to San Francisco in 1860 he thought carefully about the national significances of epic poems and what it would take to write one himself.

More sophisticated stages in Melville's study of aesthetics emerged in a remarkable course of reading while living for many weeks in a rented house in New York City early in 1862. Many books survive from that period, some with lavish marginalia (Parker 2.482–505). (Melville had no income: the money for bookbuying was from his wife's inheritance after her father's death in 1861.) In March 1862 or soon afterwards, Melville copied out some advice about good writing from Lord Jeffrey's essay on the Italian playwright Victor Alfieri, perhaps from the reprinting of the essay in the Jeffrey *Modern British Essayists* volume. However, Melville made his notes not in Jeffrey (perhaps he was using a borrowed copy) but in a book he had just bought, William Hazlitt's *Lectures on the English Comic Writers*. Opposite the introductory lecture ("On Wit and Humour") Melville summarized, within quotation marks, some of Jeffrey's arguments about literary style:

> "Worked throughout with a fine and careful hand.—Figures of mere ostentation.—Show-pieces of fine writing.—Nature is not confined to conciseness, but at times amplifies.—Too sententious & strained a diction.—The solidity of the structure is apt to prove oppressive to the *ordinary* reader. Too great uniformity.["] "Wanting flow & sweetness.—Strives to give a fictitious force & energy by condensation & emphasis & inversion.—Chastened gravity.—Temperance and propriety of delineation of the passions." [In the middle of the page Melville wrote these words off to the right side to identify his source: "Jeffrey on Alfieri."]

In the next weeks Melville made increasingly systematic purchases of volumes of recent and contemporary poetry, including works by second-rank or not-yet-established poets, along with some works which discussed aesthetic ideas and one classic multi-volume art history. Melville was reading what he was buying, and reading purposefully. The man who had invented Ahab's search for the White Whale had embarked on what soon became an obsessive search for a personal aesthetic credo.

On April 6, 1862, Melville made one of the most important of his 1862 purchases, Matthew Arnold's *Poems* (Boston, 1856). The preface, which had first appeared in the 1853 edition, was an aesthetic document being taken seriously by Arnold's and Melville's contemporaries, and within a generation treated as on a theoretical level with some of Dryden's and Wordsworth's aesthetic arguments. Among Victorian aesthetic documents, it was almost on a par with the third volume of John Ruskin's *Modern Painters*. Whatever Melville thought of Arnold's poems, he recognized the Arnold of the "Preface" as a thinker worth grappling with. Although at moments Melville found in Arnold an ameliorative spirit too near to Ralph Waldo Emerson's, he found some of the ideas provocatively expressed. Melville underlined "the all-importance of the choice of a subject," scored what Arnold said about "one moral impression left by a great action treated as a whole," marked the qualities Arnold praised in classical works ("their intense significance, their noble simplicity, and their calm pathos"), marked the warning against "the jargon of modern criticism," and heavily marked this sentence: "If they are endeavoring to practise any art, they remember the plain and simple proceedings of the old artists, who attained their grand results by penetrating themselves with some noble and significant action, not by inflating themselves with a belief in the preëminent importance and greatness of their own times." He also marked a passage quoting Goethe on two kinds of *dilettanti* in poetry: "he who neglects the indispensable mechanical part, and thinks he has done enough if he show spirituality and feeling; and he who seeks to arrive at poetry merely by mechanism . . . without soul and matter."

Melville took Arnold as a friendly interpreter of Greek theories of tragedy, paying attention to what Arnold said about greater actions and nobler personages, as in this passage: "For what reason was the Greek tragic poet confined to so limited a range of subjects? Because there are so few actions which unite in themselves, in the highest degree, the conditions of excellence. . . . A few actions, therefore, eminently adapted for tragedy, maintained almost exclusive possession of the Greek tragic stage." Arnold quoted from Aristotle, "All depends upon the subject." Throughout the essay Melville also focused upon Arnold's allusions to "expression"—"a certain baldness of expression in Greek tragedy"; Shakespeare's "wonderful gift of expression," particularly in a summation of three things for a modern writer to learn from the ancients: "the all-importance of the choice of a subject; the necessity of accurate construction; and the subordinate character of expression." Melville responded profoundly to the peroration in which Arnold discounted modern chauvinism and argued that serious poets, steeped in the past, will not "talk of their mission, nor of interpreting their age, nor of the coming Poet."

At last Melville had found a contemporary whom he could respect (on the whole) as a soulmate, or at least, in the political idiom of his youth, a good-enough Morgan of a soulmate. Reading Arnold's "Preface" concluded Melville's prolonged phase of gathering and testing ideas on aesthetics. Now, however odd it was to have Arnold as his liberator, Melville began to distill what he had been learning for months and to integrate it with his own long-held convictions about his own experience as a reader and writer. If he had been working on a manuscript, he could have written his new ideas into it. Instead, he put aside the all-important copy of Arnold and took up a work he had bought in March, Giorgio Vasari's *Lives of the Most Eminent Painters, Sculptors, and Architects*, the great history of Renaissance Italian art. Wanting to make his record in a set he intended to be consulting over and over again, he started his notes on the recto of the front flyleaf of the first volume. "Attain the highest result.—" he wrote, echoing what Arnold had said about the old artists in his peroration. Next Melville wrote: "A quality of Grasp.—" Melville was thinking of Robert Browning's Andrea del Sarto, the artist who knew that the great artist's reach should exceed his grasp. For decades Melville scholars often minimized the significance of Wordsworth to him because no one had seen his copy of Wordsworth; we now wrongly minimize the significance of Browning to him simply because no one has seen his copy or copies of Browning, whom he had read at least since 1849, when the English forger Thomas Powell introduced "My Last Duchess" (under another title) to readers of the *Literary World*. Here in the Vasari (which Melville knew was Browning's source for "Andrea del Sarto") Melville alternated between Arnold and Browning, reverting next to Arnold for the ideas that clustered about the single word "Expression." What Melville jotted down was "The habitual choice of noble subjects.—/ The Expression.—"

The idea that aesthetic finish was fullness and not polish had been one of Melville's own for many years (witness in chapter 32 of *Moby-Dick* his tribute to the builders of the Cathedral of Cologne). After "The Expression.—" he continued:

> Get in as much as you can.—
>   Finish is completeness, fullness,
> not polish.—

Then he continued with lines on greatness:

> Greatness is a matter of scale,—
>   Clearness & firmness.—
> The greatest number of the greatest ideas.—

At that point he stopped listing and began to elaborate:

> Greatness is determined for a man at his birth. There is no making oneself great, in any act or art. But there is such a thing as the development of greatness—prolonged, painful, and painstaking.

Earlier in 1862 he had marked in Disraeli's *Calumnies and Quarrels* that learning made no man wiser: "wit and wisdom are born with a man." Greatness was determined at birth. But Melville had also, for months now, been marking and using the term painstaking as he tried to weigh the significance of hard application in the production of art. He had marked what Lord Byron's biographer Thomas Moore said of himself, that he had been "a far more slow and pains-taking workman than ever would be guessed" from the result, and Melville had himself defended the English banker and poet Samuel Rogers (in his argumentative marginalia in William Hazlitt's *Lectures*) as "a painstaking man of talent." Now, at last, Melville was summing up the disparate injunctions and admonitions he had been absorbing (and had been testing against his own experience), and was able to jot down, in a place where he could keep it, an integrated aesthetic credo.

With his notes from Lord Jeffrey in his Hazlitt and his notes from Matthew Arnold and others in his Vasari, Melville's aesthetic investigations of the previous months came to a satisfying conclusion. He had done his winter's research and reflection, and was ready to go home to Arrowhead. In a poem he said that Claude Lorraine found no gain "Wavering in theory's wildering maze." This winter Melville was not wavering in theory's wildering maze: he had distilled practical advice from people who had thought seriously about aesthetic issues, and at the end of his quest he had defined his own aesthetic credo.

BACKGROUNDS,
SOURCES, AND
CRITICISM

Utopias, Sects, Cults, and Cure-Alls

HERSHEL PARKER

Delusions of a "Terrestrial Paradise"†

A profoundly and instinctively religious man, Melville knew better than any other American writer of his time the self-righteous cruelty of religious persecution. His first two books, *Typee* (1846) and *Omoo* (1847), which exposed the mistreatment of Polynesians by missionaries and their wives, had been viciously condemned by Presbyterian, Congregational, and Methodist reviewers, spokesmen for what now would be called the "Religious Right." After being forced to expurgate the criticisms of missionaries out of his first book, Melville came to feel he was waging an ongoing struggle against being silenced. At the time he was finishing *Moby-Dick* he identified with Europeans tortured to death by witch-hunters in the seventeenth century. Then or later he began identifying with "heretics" (Jews, Protestants, disobedient Catholics, East Indians, and American Indians) who had been tortured by Torquemada and other Inquisitors. In 1856, Melville thought of dedicating *The Confidence-Man* to all the victims of Auto da Fe, those tortured to death by the Spanish Inquisition.

The Confidence-Man is full of religious allusions. Most of them, some explicit, some more subtle, are allusions to the Hebrew and Christian scriptures. The book may be said to be *overfull* of biblical allusions since Melville worked in references not only to the Old and the New Testaments but also to the Apocrypha, which he knew in the translation made for the King James Version.[1] Melville was not only enthralled by the Bible, he was intensely curious about rival manifestations of the divine such as Greek and Persian myths and, indeed, all the world's gods, from the Polynesian gods he had

---

† This essay appears for the first time in this Norton Critical Edition.
1. All biblical allusions yet identified are footnoted in this NCE printing.

touched with his own hands and other Eastern deities to the Incan gods. In the 1840s and 1850s, the heyday of American sectarian secession and schism, Melville became an alert and knowledgeable witness to contemporary manifestations of religious revelation, and through his cyclopaedias and other books he became something of a self-taught expert on religions throughout recorded history. There is a vivid anecdote dateable to a summer in the early 1850s, 1852 or possibly 1854, recorded by the diplomat Maunsell B. Field in *Memories of Many Men* (1874). Field and the American artist Felix Darley had visited Melville (the "most silent" man of Field's acquaintance) and then taken him with them across the road to visit Oliver Wendell Holmes. At Holmes's grand house, Holmesdale, "somehow, the conversation drifted to East India religions and mythologies, and soon there arose a discussion between Holmes and Melville, which was conducted with the most amazing skill and brilliancy on both sides. It lasted for hours, and Darley and I had nothing to do but listen. I never chanced to hear better talking in my life. It was so absorbing that we took no note of time, and the Doctor lost his dinner, as we lost ours." References in *The Confidence-Man* to many of the world's religions and to specifically American sects, such as hard-shell Baptists and the Come-Outers, are shrewdly telling, not casual.

From childhood Melville knew colonies of American Shakers, the offshoot of the Society of Friends, or Quakers, who believed that Mother Ann was the reincarnation of Jesus, and who practiced celibacy. The Niskayuna colony was in Watervliet, New York, adjacent to West Troy, across the Hudson from Melville's mother's home from 1838 to 1847 in Lansingburgh, north of Albany. ("Gabriel" in *Moby-Dick*, chapter 71, is described as formerly a "great prophet" at "Neskyeuna," where he descended from heaven by means of a trapdoor during their "cracked, secret meetings.") Another Shaker colony was in Hancock Village, near Pittsfield. In 1850 Melville supplemented his first-hand knowledge by purchasing a recent book, *A Summary View of the Millenial Church, or United Society of Believers, Commonly Called Shakers*. While living in Pittsfield, Melville treated the establishment in Hancock Village as a tourist attraction, taking his New York friends to see the Shakers "at their spasms." No one seemed to think that gawking at religious worshipers was in any way peculiar. In these years the Melvilles bought small baskets and other craft items from the Shakers but showed no inkling that the minimalist style of furniture making would outlast the celibates. In 1851 Melville drove Hawthorne and his son Julian to Lebanon—an all male outing, the Hawthorne males comprising the oldest and the youngest. Aghast at the Shaker males for having to make their attempts at personal hygiene in full view of at least one other man, Hawthorne consoled himself that by adhering to celibacy the sect would soon become extinct—the sooner the better. Having lived in forecastles, Melville experienced no such instinctive horror.

The American Republic was so young as to be considered no more than a great experiment by many, but, oddly enough, other people were convinced that the Last Day, the end of the world, was at hand. Melville came home from the Pacific to Lansingburgh, New York, the cold week in October 1844 when a millenarian sect, coincidentally called Millerites, followers of Williams Miller (1782–1849), were camped out waiting for Jesus' return. Miller had calculated that the world would end exactly six thousand years after Creation, and after some mathematical fumbles, he had recalculated, fixing the date as October 22, 1844. Once the tumult over Herman's arrival home had faded, anyone who wanted to could go outside and look up in the sky. Members of the Millerite sect, who had proselytized across the Hudson River in Waterford, were expecting the return of Jesus, not to the Holy Land but to the United States, and many of them had been waiting all night in encampments, thinly clad, so as to be awake when He descended. (Children died from exposure in such a camp in Pennsylvania.) On October 13, before Herman's discharge from the navy, in Boston, Jesus had left the Mercy Seat, they said, and, traveling at suitably divine but not magical speed, was due to appear in the heavens on this day, the twenty-second. Herman's homecoming had been overshadowed by the return to the Empire State of his brother, Gansevoort Melville, the "orator of the human race," but it could have been overshadowed by the Second Coming of Jesus. After the "Great Disappointment" of October 1844, the Millerites divided. Some, rejecting the doctrine of the Trinity, became Unitarians; some devised new dietary laws, updating those Jehovah gave the Hebrews in Leviticus; some, assuming that Miller had simply miscalculated the end of the world again, became forerunners of the modern Seventh Day Adventists.

For years Melville pondered the news about the violent persecution which accompanied the westward push of the quintessentially American homemade religion promulgated by a fellow Upstate New Yorker, Joseph Smith. Early in 1850 Melville thought that his intensely personal and ambitious third book, *Mardi*, had been driven into wild mystic exile in the wilderness just as the Mormons had been driven across the Great Plains to Utah Territory. Besides, like other Americans he was intrigued by the adoption of polygamy by the Mormons in 1843—he more than most, perhaps, since he had stayed briefly in the Marquesas Islands with a society where one might have multiple sexual partners and had described the sexual practices of that society in *Typee* (1846). Mormons were often thought of as millennarians, like the Millerites, as the "Latter Day" in their full name could be interpreted: "The Church of Jesus Christ of Latter Day Saints."

During Melville's early career a great number of social experiments were tested on American soil. British prison reformers were honored by name in *The Confidence-Man*, but Melville had nothing but horror at the innovation in penology in Pennsylvania, where some prisoners in Moyamensing[2] were condemned to "perpetual solitude in the very heart of our population" (as he said in *Typee*). He was horrified that Coronation Hospital on Blackwell's Island[3] could become a dumping ground for cripples. Many more sweeping reforms, not of institutions but of the whole society, were being proposed and actually tested, most of them communistic, or communal, and many of them alluring in descriptions—"soft Utopianisms," Melville called them in *The Confidence-Man*. Horace Greeley used his New York *Tribune* to proselyte for some of these Utopias, thereby stirring up wrath and anxiety in religious and social conservatives. The most notable theorists were the French communist Charles Fourier, who inspirited the experimenters at Brook Farm, outside Boston, and Robert Owen, known as the father of English socialism, who founded the communistic colony at New Harmony, Indiana. Noncommunal American social reformers, themselves splintered into myriad beliefs, nevertheless mustered something like general disapproval of some of the experiments. For example, there were no prominent defenders of Theophilus Gates's Free Love Valley in Chester County, Pennsylvania, just south of Philadelphia, which was broken in 1844 by successful persecution on charges of adultery, or the Free Love experiment in Berlin Heights, Ohio, to which Melville alluded in his second lecture (1858), the year after *The Confidence-Man* was published.

Several of the sects, cults, and fads Melville mentions in *The Confidence-Man* were interrelated, followers of one often moving on to another, as Patricia Cline Cohen shows in "A Confident Tide of Reformers."[4] In *The Confidence-Man* Fourier is referred to as "the projector of an impossible dream," and former residents of the Fourieristic Brook Farm had gone on to diverse lives, notably in journalism. Walter Channing, a Unitarian, determined by a sort of world's charity to achieve the "Prevention of Pauperism." Later he moved into a kind of primitive Christianity and abolitionism. Adin Ballou (1803–1890), a Universalist then Unitarian minister who

2. See n. 3, p. 151 herein.
3. See n. 1, p. 102 herein.
4. See p. 398 herein.

founded the utopian community of Hopedale, Massachusetts, became a Temperance advocate, an abolitionist, and a pacifist before promoting "Practical Christianity," an attempt to act in accordance with Jesus's teachings. In November 1845, after Robert Owen visited Hopedale, Ballou published this account:

> Mr. Owen has vast schemes to develop, and vast hopes of speedy success in establishing a great model of the new social state; which will quite instantaneously, as he thinks, bring the human race into a terrestrial Paradise. He insists on obtaining a million of dollars to be expended in lands, buildings, machinery, conveniences and beautifications, for his model Community; all to be finished and in perfect order, before he introduces to their new home the well-selected population who are to inhabit it. He flatters himself he shall be able, by some means, to induce capitalists, or perhaps Congress, to furnish the capital for this object. We were obliged to shake an incredulous head and tell him frankly how groundless, in our judgment, all such splendid anticipations must prove. He took it in good part, and declared his confidence unshaken, and his hopes undiscouragable by any man's unbelief." (Quoted by John Humphrey Noyes, *History of American Socialisms* [Philadelphia: J. B. Lippincott, 1870], p. 89.)

Ironically, within a few years of the Millerite Great Disappointment, sisters in Upstate New York—that hotbed of cultists—caused thousands of Americans to sit at tables in darkened rooms waiting for rappings to put them in contact with the spirits of the dead—looking backwards, it seemed, instead of toward the end of the world. Yet spiritualists could be millenarians. After Robert Owen converted to Spiritualism in 1852 he began receiving messages from world leaders long dead, and called for another "World's Convention" to announce the millennium's arrival in 1855. By that time he felt that Modern Spiritualism had to accommodate the practice of free love, which he advocated in the journal *The Social Revolutionist*. Come-Outers (who figure in "The Story of China Aster") notoriously went from year-round abolitionism to seasonal nudism.

Many of the Spirit-rappers and mediums of the Spiritualism movement, Owen among them, were influenced by the views of the Swedish mystic Emanuel Swedenborg on the unnaturalness of marriage and the necessity of free love. Melville knew that Swedenborg's conversations with angels and his denial of the existence of Satan had influenced the former Unitarian minister Ralph Waldo Emerson, whose "The Over-Soul," was not mystical at all but a genuinely American essay, comical, if you thought about it: a rigorously practical Yankee guide to varieties of mystical religious experiences. (Melville knew Transcendentalism itself as a cold New England off-shoot from a cold British and Bostonian Unitarianism and, ulti-mately, Deism.) The water-curists Dr. and Mrs. Thomas L. Nichols both advocated Free Love based on the idea of "Individual Sover-eignty" and "Modern Spiritualism"; also, they were advocates of vegetarianism and Mrs. Nichols linked Free Love to women's rights. Dr. Nichols, a friend of two of Melville's brothers, had fig-ured momentously in Melville's career in 1845 when he read the sailor's manuscript in his brothers' law office on Wall Street and urged that Gansevoort carry it to England, where he was to become secretary of the American Legation. Melville had surely in some ways influenced Nichols, who was privileged to read, prepublica-tion, an account of a sexual orgy on shipboard and an account of the practice of polyandry ashore (see Parker 1.377–378). In the United States even people with anomalously formed bodies found themselves the subject of intense sexual speculation. Not even the Mormons with their plural marriages could challenge and unsettle quiet American imaginations more than the news, year by year, of births to the sisters who had married Chang and Eng, the con-joined "Siamese" twins, mentioned in *The Confidence-Man*. Six years after *The Confidence-Man*, in 1863, for a time Mormon mar-riages and Chang and Eng seemed less intriguing than the marriage of the dwarf displayed by P. T. Barnum as "Tom Thumb" (really, Charles Stratton, 1838–1883, forty inches or so tall), to Lavinia Warren (1841–1918), some three feet tall.

Melville had declared in *Typee* (chapter 26) that the penalty of the Fall of Man pressed "very lightly upon the valley of Typee." What Melville saw in the sects, cults, and cure-alls that ran so ri-otously in the years before the Civil War was a general national re-jection of Genesis 3.19 ("In the sweat of thy face shalt thou eat bread"). For Melville, who recognized a psychological truth in Calvinism, any "terrestrial Paradise" in Indiana, or Massachusetts or Utah, was a chimera. For Utopian schemers, healthful agricul-tural labor was to become one zestful part of a daily routine that in-cluded private reading and high-minded conversation. God meant labor as punishment, but hydropathy, or the water-cure, where pa-tients were soaked in water or doused with water, un-Calvinistically claimed to be relieving people of pain. Nature was also Fallen, Calvinists held, so herbs were suspect, and might well turn out to be poisonous rather than beneficial, while herb-doctoring might be seen as a sacrilegious profession conducted in contempt of the scriptures. Named in *The Confidence-Man* along with psychology were palmistry, physiognomy, phrenology—all of which claimed to reveal human nature on fixed biological principles. The phrenologists, for example, those who read people's character by the bumps on their skulls, were impudently invading what Melville in *Clarel* called the "allusive chambers" of the human psyche—and evading the theological reality of what the apostle Paul called the "mystery of iniquity." Medical experiments and advances, even including the experiments with anesthesia in the 1840s, could all be seen by a Calvinist as defying God's plan for mankind to work, suffer, and atone—in short, as evading the penalty of the Fall imposed on mankind in the Garden of Eden. Yet in 1842 Melville in the Marquesan islands had come close to glimpsing a real society mystically and magically close to a terrestrial Paradise, better than any Owen envisioned. Late in life, in the poem "To Ned," he recalled the islands as "Authentic Edens in a Pagan sea," before they were overrun in the next decades by "Pelf and Trade"—and by Christian evangelists whose well-meaning efforts ended in destruction of culture and disease or death of the natives. The marvel would be, he decided, if any mortal twice could "touch a Paradise," once in a still edenic South Pacific, then again in a Christian heaven.

HERMAN MELVILLE

[Who Is Happier: Polynesian Savage or Self-Complacent European?]†

As I extended my wanderings in the valley and grew more familiar with the habits of its inmates, I was fain to confess that, despite the disadvantages of his condition, the Polynesian savage, surrounded by all the luxurious provisions of nature, enjoyed an infinitely happier, though certainly a less intellectual existence, than the self-complacent European.

The naked wretch who shivers beneath the bleak skies, and starves among the inhospitable wilds of Terra-del-Fuego,[1] might indeed be made happier by civilization, for it would alleviate his physical wants. But the voluptuous Indian,[2] with every desire supplied, whom Providence has bountifully provided with all the sources of

---

† From chapter 17 of *Narrative of a Four Months' Residence among the Natives of a Valley of the Marquesas Islands; or, A Peep at Polynesian Life* (London: John Murray, 1846). Murray added Melville's preferred main title, *Typee*, in 1847 and retained it through 1893. This passage was also printed in the first American edition (New York: Wiley & Putnam; 1846), but Melville was forced to remove it after a few months. For the rest of his life the text of *Typee* for sale in the United States lacked this passage and other criticisms of the missionaries. This passage is missing from some online texts in the twenty-first century. All notes are the editors'.

1. Desolate region at the southern tip of South America.
2. Here, any native of the Asian subcontinent or islands nearby.

pure and natural enjoyment, and from whom are removed so many of the ills and pains of life—what has he to desire at the hands of Civilization? She may "cultivate his mind,"—may "elevate his thoughts,"—these I believe are the established phrases—but will he be the happier? Let the once smiling and populous Hawiian islands, with their now diseased, starving, and dying natives, answer the question. The missionaries may seek to disguise the matter as they will, but the facts are incontrovertible; and the devoutest Christian who visits that group with an unbiased mind, must go away mournfully asking—"Are these, alas! the fruits of twenty-five years of enlightening?"

In a primitive state of society, the enjoyments of life, though few and simple, are spread over a great extent, and are unalloyed; but Civilization, for every advantage she imparts, holds a hundred evils in reserve;—the heart burnings, the jealousies, the social rivalries, the family dissensions, and the thousand self-inflicted discomforts of refined life, which make up in units the swelling aggregate of human misery, are unknown among these unsophisticated people.

But it will be urged that these shocking unprincipled wretches are cannibals. Very true; and a rather bad trait in their character it must be allowed. But they are such only when they seek to gratify the passion of revenge upon their enemies; and I ask whether the mere eating of human flesh so very far exceeds in barbarity that custom[3] which only a few years since was practiced in enlightened England:—a convicted traitor, perhaps a man found guilty of honesty, patriotism, and suchlike heinous crimes, had his head lopped off with a huge axe, his bowels dragged out and thrown into a fire; while his body, carved into four quarters, was with his head exposed upon pikes, and permitted to rot and fester among the public haunts of men!

The fiend-like skill we display in the invention of all manner of death-dealing engines, the vindictiveness with which we carry on our wars, and the misery and desolation that follow in their train, are enough of themselves to distinguish the white civilized man as the most ferocious animal on the face of the earth.

His remorseless cruelty is seen in many of the institutions of our own favored land. There is one in particular lately adopted in one of the States of the Union,[4] which purports to have been dictated by the most merciful considerations. To destroy our malefactors piece-meal, drying up in their veins, drop by drop, the blood we are too chicken-hearted to shed by a single blow which would at once

---

3. Gibbeting, hanging on a gallows in chains, not just to kill but to keep for a time on public display. Some forty-three years earlier Colonel Edward Despard (1755–1803) had suffered this extreme from of gibbeting for treason (conspiring with Irish patriots).
4. I.e., Pennsylvania (see chapter 26 of *The Confidence-Man*).

put a period to their sufferings, is deemed to be infinitely preferable to the old-fashioned punishment of gibbeting—much less annoying to the victim, and more in accordance with the refined spirit of the age; and yet how feeble is all language to describe the horrors we inflict upon these wretches, whom we mason up in the cells of our prisons, and condemn to perpetual solitude in the very heart of our population.

But it is needless to multiply the examples of civilized barbarity; they far exceed in the amount of misery they cause the crimes which we regard with such abhorrence in our less enlightened fellow-creatures.

The term "Savage" is, I conceive, often misapplied, and indeed when I consider the vices, cruelties, and enormities of every kind that spring up in the tainted atmosphere of a feverish civilization, I am inclined to think that so far as the relative wickedness of the parties is concerned, four or five Marquesan Islanders sent to the United States as Missionaries might be quite as useful as an equal number of Americans despatched to the Islands in a similar capacity.

I once heard it given as an instance of the frightful depravity of a certain tribe in the Pacific, that they had no word in their language to express the idea of virtue. The assertion was unfounded; but were it otherwise, it might be met by stating that their language is almost entirely destitute of terms to express the delightful ideas conveyed by our endless catalogue of civilized crimes.

HERMAN MELVILLE

[Must Christianizing the Heathen Destroy the Heathen?]†

The penalty of the Fall[1] presses very lightly upon the valley of Typee; for, with the one solitary exception of striking a light, I

---

† *From* chapter 26 of *Narrative of a Four Months' Residence among the Natives of a Valley of the Marquesas Islands; or, A Peep at Polynesian Life* (London: John Murray, 1846). Draft pages of the *Typee* manuscript discovered in 1983 show that this passage was a late addition. It was reprinted in the first American edition but censored out of the "Revised Edition" later in 1846 and for the rest of Melville's life was missing from copies of *Typee* sold in the United States. The original uncensored version, the Murray text, throughout Melville's lifetime went all over the British Empire paired with his second book, *Omoo* (1847) in the prestigious "Home and Colonial Library." Like a passage from chapter 17 (see p. 367 herein) this passage is also missing from some online texts in the twenty-first century. All notes are the editors'.

1. In Genesis 3, God's curse of Adam for his and Eve's sin. Thenceforth, according to the curse, men must earn their living by the sweat of their face, gaining food from an earth that is also cursed, and after eating in sorrow all the days of their lives must suffer death. Woman's curse is the pain of childbirth and (apparently) subservience to men (who will "rule over" them).

scarcely saw any piece of work performed there which caused the sweat to stand upon a single brow. As for digging and delving for a livelihood, the thing is altogether unknown. Nature has planted the bread-fruit and the banana, and in her own good time she brings them to maturity, when the idle savage stretches forth his hand, and satisfies his appetite.

Ill-fated people! I shudder when I think of the change a few years will produce in their paradisaical abode; and probably when the most destructive vices, and the worst attendances on civilization, shall have driven all peace and happiness from the valley, the magnanimous French[2] will proclaim to the world that the Marquesas Islands have been converted to Christianity! and this the Catholic world will doubtless consider as a glorious event. Heaven help the "Isles of the Sea!"—The sympathy which Christendom feels for them has, alas! in too many instances proved their bane.

How little do some of these poor islanders comprehend when they look around them, that no inconsiderable part of their disasters originate in certain tea-party excitements,[3] under the influence of which benevolent-looking gentlemen in white cravats solicit alms, and old ladies in spectacles, and young ladies in sober russet low gowns, contribute sixpences towards the creation of a fund, the object of which is to ameliorate the spiritual condition of the Polynesians, but whose end has almost invariably been to accomplish their temporal destruction!

Let the savages be civilized, but civilize them with benefits, and not with evils; and let heathenism be destroyed, but not by destroying the heathen. The Anglo-Saxon hive[4] have extirpated Paganism from the greater part of the North American continent; but with it they have likewise extirpated the greater portion of the Red race. Civilization is gradually sweeping from the earth the lingering vestiges of Paganism, and at the same time the shrinking forms of its unhappy worshippers.

Among the islands of Polynesia, no sooner are the images overturned, the temples demolished, and the idolaters converted into *nominal* Christians, than disease, vice, and premature death make their appearance. The depopulated land is then recruited from the rapacious hordes of enlightened individuals who settle themselves

2. In June 1842 when Melville arrived on a whaler in the Nukuheva Bay in the Marquesas Islands, he saw in the bay the French flagship *La Reine Blanche* (the white queen) and a squadron of men-of-war, Rear Admiral Du Petit-Thouars having just declared the islands to be the property of France. Later Melville saw the same fleet as it took possession of Tahiti. The irony of "magnanimous" is informed by his memory of the French exercise of naked power.
3. Genteel meetings in the United States at which those attending were expected to contribute funds to send missionaries to the heathen.
4. This sweeping and loose construction includes the British in Canada as well as descendants of British settlers in the United States.

within its borders, and clamorously announce the progress of the Truth. Neat villas, trim gardens, shaven lawns, spires, and cupolas arise, while the poor savage soon finds himself an interloper in the country of his fathers, and that too on the very site of the hut where he was born. The spontaneous fruits of the earth, which God in his wisdom had ordained for the support of the indolent natives, remorselessly seized upon and appropriated by the stranger, are devoured before the eyes of the starving inhabitants, or sent on board the numerous vessels which now touch at their shores.

When the famished wretches are cut off in this manner from their natural supplies, they are told by their benefactors to work and earn their support by the sweat of their brows! But to no fine gentleman born to hereditary opulence does manual labor come more unkindly than to the luxurious Indian[5] when thus robbed of the bounty of Heaven. Habituated to a life of indolence, he cannot and will not exert himself; and want, disease, and vice, all evils of foreign growth, soon terminate his miserable existence.

But what matters all this? Behold the glorious result!—The abominations of Paganism have given way to the pure rites of the Christian worship,—the ignorant savage has been supplanted by the refined European! Look at Honolulu, the metropolis of the Sandwich Islands![6]—A community of disinterested merchants, and devoted self-exiled heralds of the Cross, located on the very spot that twenty years ago was defiled by the presence of idolatry. What a subject for an eloquent Bible-meeting orator! Nor has such an opportunity for a display of missionary rhetoric been allowed to pass by unimproved!—But when these philanthropists send us such glowing accounts of one half of their labors, why does their modesty restrain them from publishing the other half of the good they have wrought?—Not until I visited Honolulu was I aware of the fact that the small remnant of the natives had been civilized into draught horses,[7] and evangelized into beasts of burden. But so it is. They have been literally broken into the traces, and are harnessed to the vehicles of their spiritual instructors like so many dumb brutes!

Among a multitude of similar exhibitions that I saw, I shall never forget a robust, red-faced, and very lady-like personage, a missionary's spouse, who day after day for months together took her regular airings in a little go-cart drawn by two of the islanders, one an old grey-headed man, and the other a rogueish stripling, both being, with the exception of the fig-leaf, as naked as when they were born. Over a level piece of ground this pair of *draught* bipeds would

---

5. Not an American Indian but an inhabitant of the warm areas of the Asian subcontinent or islands close to it, or by extension inhabitant of Polynesia.
6. The then-current name for the Hawaiian Islands.
7. Horses trained to "draw" (pull) wagons or carts.

go with a shambling, unsightly trot, the youngster hanging back all the time like a knowing horse, while the old hack plodded on and did all the work.

Rattling along through the streets of the town in this stylish equipage, the lady looks about her as magnificently as any queen driven in state to her coronation. A sudden elevation, and a sandy road, however, soon disturb her serenity. The small wheels become imbedded in the loose soil,—the old stager stands tugging and sweating, while the young one frisks about and does nothing; not an inch does the chariot budge. Will the tender-hearted lady, who has left friends and home for the good of the souls of the poor heathen, will she think a little about their bodies and get out, and ease the wretched old man until the ascent is mounted? Not she; she could not dream of it. To be sure, she used to think nothing of driving the cows to pasture on the old farm in New England; but times have changed since then. So she retains her seat and bawls out, "Hookee! hookee!" (pull, pull.) The old gentleman, frightened at the sound, labors away harder than ever; and the younger one makes a great show of straining himself, but takes care to keep one eye on his mistress, in order to know when to dodge out of harm's way. At last the good lady loses all patience; "Hookee! hookee!" and rap goes the heavy handle of her huge fan over the naked skull of the old savage; while the young one shies to one side and keeps beyond its range. "Hookee! hookee!" again she cries—"Hookee tata kannaka!" (pull strong, men,)—but all in vain, and she is obliged in the end to dismount and, sad necessity! actually to walk to the top of the hill.

At the town where this paragon of humility resides, is a spacious and elegant American chapel,[8] where divine service is regularly performed. Twice every Sabbath towards the close of the exercises may be seen a score or two of little waggons ranged along the railing in front of the edifice, with two squalid native footmen in the livery of nakedness standing by each, and waiting for the dismission of the congregation to draw their superiors home.

Lest the slightest misconception should arise from anything thrown out in this chapter, or indeed in any other part of the volume, let me here observe, that against the cause of missions in the abstract no Christian can possibly be opposed: it is in truth a just and holy cause. But if the great end proposed by it be spiritual, the agency employed to accomplish that end is purely earthly; and, although the object in view be the achievement of much good, that agency may nevertheless be productive of evil. In short, missionary undertaking, however it may be blessed of Heaven, is in itself but human; and subject, like everything else, to errors and abuses. And

8. See Parker's biography 1.248–49 for a description of this seamen's chapel in Honolulu.

have not errors and abuses crept into the most sacred places, and may there not be unworthy or incapable missionaries abroad, as well as ecclesiastics of a similar character at home? May not the unworthiness or incapacity of those who assume apostolic functions upon the remote islands of the sea more easily escape detection by the world at large than if it were displayed in the heart of a city? An unwarranted confidence in the sanctity of its apostles—a proneness to regard them as incapable of guile—and an impatience of the least suspicion as to their rectitude as men or Christians, have ever been prevailing faults in the Church. Nor is this to be wondered at: for subject as Christianity is to the assaults of unprincipled foes, we are naturally disposed to regard everything like an exposure of ecclesiastical misconduct as the offspring of malevolence or irreligious feeling. Not even this last consideration, however, shall deter me from the honest expression of my sentiments.

There is something decidedly wrong in the practical operations of the Sandwich Islands Mission. Those who from pure religious motives contribute to the support of this enterprise, should take care to ascertain that their donations, flowing through many devious channels, at last effect their legitimate object, the conversion of the Hawiians. I urge this not because I doubt the moral probity of those who disburse these funds, but because I know that they are not rightly applied. To read pathetic accounts of missionary hardships, and glowing descriptions of conversions, and baptisms taking place beneath palm-trees, is one thing; and to go to the Sandwich Islands and see the missionaries dwelling in picturesque and prettily-furnished coral-rock villas, whilst the miserable natives are committing all sorts of immoralities around them, is quite another.

In justice to the missionaries, however, I will willingly admit, that whatever evils may have resulted from their collective mismanagement of the business of the mission, and from the want of vital piety evinced by some of their number, still the present deplorable condition of the Sandwich Islands is by no means wholly chargeable against them. The demoralising influence of a dissolute foreign population, and the frequent visits of all descriptions of vessels, have tended not a little to increase the evils alluded to. In a word, here, as in every case where Civilization has in any way been introduced among those whom we call savages, she has scattered her vices, and withheld her blessings.

As wise a man as Shakspeare has said, that the bearer of evil tidings hath but a losing office;[9] and so I suppose will it prove with me, in communicating to the trusting friends of the Hawiian Mis-

<hr>

9. 2 *Henry IV* 1.1.103, where Northumberland fears the worst when Morton arrives from the battle at Shrewsbury—fears that his son Harry Percy, known as Hotspur, has been killed. Before he allows Morton to deliver the news, Northumberland says (in the text

sion what has been disclosed in various portions of this narrative. I am persuaded, however, that as these disclosures will by their very nature attract attention, so they will lead to something which will not be without ultimate benefit to the cause of Christianity in the Sandwich Islands.

I have but one thing more to add in connection with this subject—those things which I have stated as facts will remain facts, in spite of whatever the bigoted or incredulous may say or write against them. My reflections, however, on those facts may not be free from error. If such be the case, I claim no further indulgence than should be conceded to every man whose object is to do good.

HERMAN MELVILLE

From They Discourse of Alma†

Babbalanja mildly observed, "Mohi: without seeking to accuse you of uttering falsehoods; since what you relate rests not upon testimony of your own; permit me, to question the fidelity of your account of Alma. The prophet came to dissipate errors, you say; but superadded to many that have survived the past, ten thousand others have originated in various constructions of the principles of Alma himself. The prophet came to do away all gods but one; but since the days of Alma, the idols of Maramma have more than quadrupled. The prophet came to make us Mardians more virtuous and happy; but along with all previous good, the same wars, crimes,

---

Melville bought later, in 1849) "the first bringer of unwelcome news / Hath but a losing office; and his tongue / Sounds ever after as a sullen bell, / Remembered knolling a departing friend."

† From *Mardi: And a Voyage Thither* (New York: Harper & Brothers, 1849), volume 2, chapter 9, "They Discourse of Alma" (chapter 113 in one-volume editions). Melville's third book, *Mardi*, begins as Polynesian adventure in an open boat and becomes a sort of island-hopping symposium. In chapter 105, the travelers view the island of Maramma, which resembles both the Holy Land and Vatican City. The central peak, Ofo, is called "inaccessible to man," though many pilgrims try to reach it. The philosophical Babbalanja allows for the possibility that some seekers have indeed attained the summit. Having landed at Maramma, they witness the efforts of one boy to shake off the control of Pani, the blind guide, and to seek the peak in his own way, following "the divine instinct" in him (chapter 106). After the boy is seized and borne away (presumably to be burned alive), Babbalanja reveals that his "own sire was burnt for his temerity; and in this very isle" (chapter 113). In the preceding passage, Mohi, the historian of the group, takes the ecumenical line that Alma (Latin for soul), the divine prophet and teacher, had appeared in the world at long intervals "under the different titles of Brami, Manko, and Alma"— references to Brahma (the "supreme soul" of the Hindus), Manco Capac (the Peruvian god mentioned at the start of *The Confidence-Man*), and Jesus. Mohi takes the divine manifestation in the shape of Alma as the "last revelation" (see the last paragraph of *The Confidence-Man*). The passage printed here contains Babblanja's reflections on a persistent theme in Melville, the failure of Christians to be Christian, as well as an early reference to what became a preoccupation of Melville's, victims of auto-da-fe, heretics burned at the stake.

and miseries, which existed in Alma's day, under various modifications are yet extant. Nay: take from your chronicles, Mohi, the history of those horrors, one way or other, resulting from the doings of
Alma's nominal followers, and your chronicles would not so frequently make mention of blood. The prophet came to guarantee
our eternal felicity; but according to what is held in Maramma, that
felicity rests on so hard a proviso, that to a thinking mind, but very
few of our sinful race may secure it. For one, then, I wholly reject
your Alma; not so much, because of all that is hard to be understood in his histories; as because of obvious and undeniable things
all round us; which, to me, seem at war with an unreserved faith
in his doctrines as promulgated here in Maramma. Besides; every
thing in this isle strengthens my incredulity; I never was so thorough a disbeliever as now."

"Let the winds be laid," cried Mohi, "while your rash confession
is being made in this sacred lake."

Said Media, "Philosopher; remember the boy, and they that
seized him."

"Ah! I do indeed remember him. Poor youth! in his agony, how
my heart yearned toward his. But that very prudence which you
deny me, my lord, prevented me from saying aught in his behalf.
Have you not observed, that until now, when we are completely by
ourselves, I have refrained from freely discoursing of what we have
seen in this island? Trust me, my lord, there is no man, that bears
more in mind the necessity of being either a believer or a hypocrite
in Maramma, and the imminent peril of being honest here, than I,
Babbalanja. And have I not reason to be wary, when in my boyhood,
my own sire was burnt for his temerity; and in this very isle? Just
Oro! it was done in the name of Alma,—what wonder then, that, at
times, I almost hate that sound. And from those flames, they de-
voutly swore he went to others,—horrible fable!"

DR. JOHN WAKEFIELD FRANCIS

[The Bostonian Heresy Invades Manhattan]†

If my memory fails me not, in the month of May, 1819, arrived in this city William Ellery Channing[1] with a coadjutor, both distinguished preachers of the Unitarian persuasion, of Boston. They were solicitous to procure a suitable place of worship. They made application at churches of different denominations of religious belief, to be accommodated at the intermediate hours between the morning and afternoon service, but in vain. They next urged their request at several of the public charities where convenient apartments might be found, but with the same result. * * * [The College of Physicians and Surgeons, in Barclay Street, of which Dr. Francis was registrar, agreed to let Channing "perform divine service" in the hall of the college.]

On the following Sabbath, Dr. Channing entered the professional desk of the larger lecture-room, and delivered, in his mellowed accents, a discourse to a crowded audience, among whom were his associate brother preacher, and several professors of the college. But two or three days had transpired, from the occurrence of this first preaching of Unitarianism, before it was loudly spoken of, and in terms of disapprobation not the mildest. The censure on such a pernicious toleration came strongest from the Presbyterian order of clergy. I heard but one prominent Episcopalian condemn

---

† From *Old New York: or, Reminiscences of the Past Sixty Years*, originally published in 1858, reprinted with an introduction by Henry T. Tuckerman (New York, 1866), 151–157, the source of the present text. Dr. Francis (1789–1861) was a great public figure in New York City for many years, a brilliant obstetrician and an encourager of science, the arts, and literature. In the 1866 *Old New York*, Tuckerman (1813–1871) quoted a letter from a New York correspondent of a New Orleans newspaper that celebrated Dr. Francis's public achievements and his hospitality in his great house on Bond Street. Among the notable guests mentioned was "M—— (when in town) taciturn, but genial, and when warmed up capitally racy and pungent." Tuckerman dated the newspaper article as 1850. In 2004 Scott Norsworthy discovered a January 24, 1855, New York *Times* reprinting of the article from the New Orleans *Commercial Bulletin*, and Parker then retrieved the December 5, 1854, article from his photocopies of letters from New York in the *Commercial Bulletin*. "Melville" is spelled out in the New Orleans paper, removing any doubt that Melville was referred to, and set as "MELVILLE" in the *Times*; Tuckerman had in hand both printings, variants show, so he knew the writer if he did not write the article himself. Norsworthy's discovery removes the strongest testimony that Melville as early as 1850 could strike an observer as "taciturn." Melville had been, it is now clear, a remarkably outgoing, ebullient man in social groups until after the disastrous reception of *Pierre* in 1852 and his failure to get *The Isle of the Cross* into print in 1853. See Parker 1.571–572 and 2.933 for Melville at Dr. Francis's house, and 2.481, 484–491, and 555 for Melville's enduring friendship with Tuckerman, a poet, literary critic, and the United States' most zealous champion of the liberation and unification of Italy. All notes are the editors'.

1. Channing (1780–1842), leading Boston Unitarian minister and (in his 1830 "Remarks on American Literature") a literary propagandist. In "The Moral Argument against Calvinism" (1820) he argued that human nature is not "fallen" or naturally depraved.

the whole affair, but that condemnation was in emphatic phraseology. * * * Some three days after that memorable Sunday, I accidentally met the great theological thunderbolt of the times, Dr.
John M. Mason, in the bookstore[2] of that intelligent publisher and
learned bibliopole, James Eastburn. Mason soon approached me,
and in earnestness exclaimed, "You doctors have been engaged in a
wrongful work; you have permitted heresy to come in among us,
and have countenanced its approach. You have furnished accommodations for the devil's disciples." * * * Such was the beginning
of Unitarian public worship in this city.

* * * Unitarianism had indeed its advocates among us long before the pilgrimage of Channing in 1819. Everybody at all versed in
the progress of religious creeds in this country will, I believe, assign
to Dr. James Freeman[3] the distinction of having been the first Unitarian minister of the first Unitarian church in New England. He
promulgated his faith from the pulpit of King's Chapel in Boston,
which church however, had been vacant for some time owing to political circumstances growing out of the American Revolution. He
thus became the means of converting the first Episcopal church of
the New England States into the first Unitarian church. Having
been refused ordination by Bishop Seabury,[4] of Connecticut, Freeman received a law ordination by his society alone, as their rector
and minister, in 1787. The distinguished Channing, who had been
a rigid Calvinist, was converted by Freeman into a Unitarian. John
Kirkland,[5] so long the admired President of Harvard University, impressed with like theological doctrines, was sedulous in his calling, and earnest in making known the "Light of Nature," a work of
curious metaphysical research from the acute mind of Abraham
Tucker,[6] published under the assumed name of Edward Search.

That our Boston friends had favored us with disciples of that faith
in this city before that time is most certain, else a society of that or-

2. The Literary Rooms at Broadway and Pine. John Mitchell Mason (1770–1829) was a
Presbyterian minister.
3. Freeman (1759–1835), who took the pulpit of the previously Anglican King's Chapel in
1785, defined Unitarianism in the United States when his congregation voted to retain
the Book of Common Prayer but to delete from it all references to the Trinity (God the
Father, the Son, and the Holy Spirit). Dr. Francis uses "Episcopal" as the new name for
American Anglicans after the Revolution.
4. Samuel Seabury became an Episcopal bishop in 1784, having been consecrated by Scottish bishops at Aberdeen after English bishops refused to consecrate him. Although a
member of a "high" and already somewhat liberal church, Seabury did not regard James
Freeman as a Christian because he did not believe in the Trinity.
5. John Thornton Kirkland (1770–1840), Unitarian president of Harvard 1810–28.
6. Tucker (1705–1774), English philosopher, whose very lengthy The Light of Nature Pursued' (1768–78) became a source book for emerging English Unitarianism. Melville read
carefully an abridgment of Tucker made by William Hazlitt before giving it to his brother
Allan's brother-in-law Richard Lathers in 1853. In Pierre he made brilliant use of it in
characterizing the unbenevolent philosopher, Plotinus Plinlimmon, who leaves a handsome edition of Tucker at his door, not needing to read it because he has already attained to a sufficiently selfish state of being. See Tucker on benevolence (p. 378 herein).

der of believers could not have been so rapidly formed as appears by their organization in Chambers street in 1821, when the Rev. Edward Everett delivered the dedication sermon, with suitable exercises by the Rev. Henry Ware, Jun.;[7] again, at the installation of their new building, corner of Prince and Mercer streets, in 1826, when Dr. Channing preached the dedication sermon, and the Rev. Dr. Walker offered the final prayer. Still further, we find the Church of the Messiah, in Broadway, consecrated and the installation sermon delivered by Dr. Walker, and the pastoral duties assigned to Dr. Dewey; but, for some years past, these have been discharged by Dr. Osgood.[8] And again, we find the organization of the Church of the Divine Unity completed in 1845, the pastoral duties devolving on Dr. Bellows; and again, the last-named church being disposed of to the Universalist Society, we witness the magnificent edifice for Unitarian worship, called All Souls' Church, situated on the Fourth Avenue, consecrated December 25, 1855, the Rev. Dr. Bellows,[9] pastor.

ABRAHAM TUCKER

From Benevolence†

* * * Lastly, under justice the philosopher must include benevolence, and charity; but nobody else would esteem that person a

7. Ware (1794–1843) was pastor of the Second Church in Boston (Unitarian) until he relinquished the post to young Ralph Waldo Emerson in 1828, who resigned in 1831 after preaching a sermon on his principled inability to administer communion (called the "Lord's Supper" by some Protestants). Ware became professor of pulpit eloquence at Harvard Divinity School (1829–42), where he had the great displeasure of hearing Emerson's indictment, the "Divinity School Address" of 1838. Everett (1794–1865), Unitarian, American orator, governor of Massachusetts (1836–40), and president of Harvard (1846–49), who is remembered for delivering the two-hour principal address at Gettysburg on November 19, 1863, when Abraham Lincoln also spoke but for only two or three minutes.

8. Dr. Samuel Osgood (1812–1880), the longtime minister of the Unitarian Church of the Messiah in Manhattan, conducted the funeral services for the Melvilles' son Malcolm at All Souls Church in 1867 during the absence abroad of Dr. Bellows (see n. 9 below). Dr. James Walker, Unitarian minister at Charlestown (adjoining Cambridge), president of Harvard (1853–60). Orville Dewey (1812–1880) preached the funeral sermon of Melville's wife's father, Judge Lemuel Shaw, in 1861, and baptized the three younger Melville children in 1863.

9. Henry W. Bellows (1814–1882), longtime minister of All Souls (usually spelled with no apostrophe). Located at Fourth Avenue and Twentieth Street, the church was popularly known, from its striations, as the Church of the Holy Zebra. Bellows baptized Malcolm Melville at the Melville home in September 1849. After the Melvilles returned to New York City in 1863, Elizabeth Shaw Melville rented a pew at All Souls for many years (giving it up only in years of extreme financial hardship) and relied on Bellows for pastoral advice on her difficulties with her husband. See Bellows on American Indians (p. 463 herein).

† From Abraham Tucker, *An Abridgement [by William Hazlitt] of The Light of Nature Pursued* (London: Johnson, 1807). Melville gave his copy to his brother Allan's brother-in-law, Richard Lathers, in August 1853. Lathers prized it, and (now in private hands) it is one of the few books known to survive from Lathers's great library.

friend or good neighbour who should do no more to serve another than he was in *strict justice* bound to do.

2. For this reason I have made a distinct article of benevolence, and indeed I do not see why it may not as well be reckoned the root of justice as a branch of it, for we seldom think of behaving dishonestly to our friends; and if we had a proper regard for all mankind, this would be sufficient of itself to prevent us from ever dealing unjustly with any body. Justice (at least in the common conceptions of mankind) only restrains from doing wrong: good nature prompts us to do all the service in our power. A debt and a favour seem essentially distinct, so that the one cannot be the other; a man is bound to render to every one his due, but in doing a kindness he must be free from all obligation, or it ceases to be a kindness. When a man pays you what he owes, you do not thank him for it, he only escapes the censure to which he would otherwise have been liable; but if he does you a service you had no right to expect, he then deserves your acknowledgements. I think benevolence may be defined a diffused love to the whole species; and whoever has this desire habitually, will feel a satisfaction in acts of kindness proportionable to the good to result from them, which will urge him to perform them for his own sake whenever they fall in his way.

3. Persons deficient in this quality endeavour to run it down, and justify their own narrow views, by alleging that it is only selfishness in a particular form: for if the benevolent man does a goodnatured thing, it is because he likes it, so that he acts to please himself, and self is still at the bottom. Where then, say they, is his merit? What is he better than we? He follows his own inclination, and so do we: the only difference between us is a difference of tastes. To this we might answer, grant it, but this difference of taste makes all the difference; one man's taste leads him to do me all the good he can, and your's to do me all the mischief in your power. Now this is all that I am concerned with. You would not surely have me feel and act in the same manner towards you that I do towards him? For though you may both equally please yourselves, you cannot expect equally to please me. In the next place, I shall deny that acts of real kindness, how much soever they may proceed from inclination, have any thing selfish in them. Men are led into this mistake by laying too much stress on etymology, for selfishness being derived from self, they learnedly infer that whatever is done to please oneself must fall under that appellation. Wearing woollen clothes, or eating mutton, does not make a man sheepish, nor does his looking into a book now and then render him bookish; so neither is every thing selfish, that relates to oneself. If somebody should tell you, that such a one was a very selfish person, and for proof of it give a

long account of his being once caught on horseback in a shower of rain, that he took shelter under a tree, alighted, put on his great coat, and was wholly busied in muffling himself up, without having a single thought all the while about his wife or children, his friends, or his country; would you not take it for banter, or should you think the person or his behaviour could be called selfish in any propriety of speech? Or what if a man agreeable and obliging in company should desire another lump of sugar in his tea to please his own palate, would you pronounce him a whit the more selfish on that account? So that selfishness is not having a regard for oneself, but having no regard for any thing else.

4. We have shewn above, that the desire of satisfaction is the spring of all our actions, so that if that rendered them selfish, there would be no use for the term, nor any distinction between selfish and disinterested: for the wise and foolish, the good and the wicked, the thoughtful and the giddy, all follow the impulse of present satisfaction. The following of inclination, therefore, does not constitute selfishness, for in this respect all men are alike; the difference results from what they severally fix their inclinations upon; for it is the object of desire, the ultimate point in prospect, that denominates an action one thing or another. Neither need we seek for any greater refinement or purity of motives than this pleasure of pleasing others; we may lawfully follow our pleasure, provided it be directed to so laudable an object. The good old rule holds in this as in other cases, of doing and standing affected to others as we would have them disposed towards us: now what more can we desire of others than that they should take delight in pleasing us? Could your family, your neighbours, your acquaintance, come and say with perfect sincerity, Sir, please to let us know in what we can serve you, for we shall take the greatest pleasure in doing it, what would you require of them more? Would you answer them, look ye, good folks, while you take delight in serving me, you do it to please yourselves, so I do not thank you for it: but if you would lay a real obligation upon me, you must first hate me with all your might, and then the services you may do me will be purely disinterested. Surely he that could make this reply must have a very whimsical turn of thought and a strong tincture of envy, since he cannot be content to receive a kindness, unless the person conferring it puts himself to uneasiness in doing it.

5. As an action takes its quality not from the thing done, but from the thing intended, benevolence to be genuine must be free and voluntary; for what we are drawn or over-persuaded to do, does not proceed from inclination, and is rather an act of compulsion than choice. There is a softness and milkiness of temper that cannot say nay to any thing; but he that can never refuse a favour, can

hardly be said to grant one, for it is wrested from him, not given; he does it to rid himself of an importunity and save the trouble of a denial, in which case it is a weakness rather than a virtue. Hence goodnature is often called, and sometimes really proceeds from, folly, which gets no thanks even where it proves most serviceable to us. * * *

HERMAN MELVILLE

From Chronometricals and Horologicals†

"But why then does God now and then send a heavenly chronometer (as a meteoric stone) into the world, uselessly as it would seem, to give the lie to all the world's time-keepers? Because he is unwilling to leave man without some occasional testimony to this:—that though man's Chinese notions of things may answer well enough here, they are by no means universally applicable, and that the central Greenwich in which He dwells goes by a somewhat different method from this world. And yet it follows not from this, that God's truth is one thing and man's truth another; but—as above hinted, and as will be further elucidated in subsequent lectures—by their very contradictions they are made to correspond.

"By inference it follows, also, that he who finding in himself a chronometrical soul, seeks practically to force that heavenly time upon the earth; in such an attempt he can never succeed, with an absolute and essential success. And as for himself, if he seek to regulate his own daily conduct by it, he will but array all men's earthly time-keepers against him, and thereby work himself woe and death. Both these things are plainly evinced in the character and fate of Christ, and the past and present condition of the religion he taught. But here one thing is to be especially observed. Though Christ encountered woe in both the precept and the practice of his

---

† From Herman Melville, *Pierre, or, The Ambiguities* (New York: Harper & Brothers, 1851), *pp. 43*, *the concluding portions of what is commonly referred to as "the Plinlimmon Pamphlet,"* the full title of which is "EI, / by / Plotinus Plinlimmon, / (In Three Hundred and Thirty-three Lectures.) / Lecture First. / Chronometricals and Horologicals, / (*Being not so much the Portal, as part of the temporary Scaffold to the Portal of this new Philosophy.*) "Ei" is Greek for "If." See the passage in *Moby-Dick* (chapter 114) on the endlessly circling stages of thought and life in which there is a temporary rest in "manhood's pondering repose of If." Plotinus (204–270), the Egypt-born Roman philosopher, wrote interpretations and elaborations of Plato six centuries after the death of the Greek philosopher. Melville uses his name to suggest abstruse philosophy. Plinlimmon is a mountain in Wales. Melville knew the 1757 poem "The Bard" by the English poet Thomas Gray (1716–1771), which questions whether Modred's magic song "Made huge Plinlimmon bow his cloud-topp'd head" (1.3.33–34). In the preface to *Pierre* Melville similarly asks if Mount Greylock might (if properly worshiped) "benignantly incline his hoary crown or no." All notes are the editors'.

chronometricals, yet did he remain throughout entirely without folly or sin. Whereas, almost invariably, with inferior beings, the absolute effort to live in this world according to the strict letter of the chronometricals is, somehow, apt to involve those inferior beings eventually in strange, *unique* follies and sins, unimagined before. It is the story of the Ephesian matron, allegorized.[1]

"To any earnest man of insight, a faithful contemplation of these ideas concerning Chronometricals and Horologicals, will serve to render provisionally far less dark some few of the otherwise obscurest things which have hitherto tormented the honest-thinking men of all ages. What man who carries a heavenly soul in him, has not groaned to perceive, that unless he committed a sort of suicide as to the practical things of this world, he never can hope to regulate his earthly conduct by that same heavenly soul? And yet by an infallible instinct he knows, that that monitor can not be wrong in itself.

"And where is the earnest and righteous philosopher, gentlemen, who looking right and left, and up and down, through all the ages of the world, the present included; where is there such an one who has not a thousand times been struck with a sort of infidel idea, that whatever other worlds God may be Lord of, he is not the Lord of this; for else this world would seem to give the lie to Him; so utterly repugnant seem its ways to the instinctively known ways of Heaven. But it is not, and can not be so; nor will he who regards this chronometrical conceit aright, ever more be conscious of that horrible idea. For he will then see, or seem to see, that this world's seeming incompatibility with God, absolutely results from its meridianal correspondence with him.

*   *   *

"This chronometrical conceit does by no means involve the justification of all the acts which wicked men may perform. For in their wickedness downright wicked men sin as much against their own horologes, as against the heavenly chronometer. That this is so,

---

1. In *The Satiricon* (chapters 111 and 112) by the Roman writer Petronius Arbiter (27–66) is the story of a chaste widow who accompanies her husband's body into the burial vault where in an excess of grief she refuses all food, determined to die. In her weakened condition she is seduced by a sentinel assigned to bodies hanging outside. When one of the bodies is stolen, she offers to substitute her husband's body so as to save the sentinel from punishment with death. The point is that extreme idealism may lead to extreme sins. Melville may have known the story from Jeremy Taylor's *The Rules and Exercises of Holy Dying* (chapter 5, section 8), where Taylor expands the details of the story to show how immoderate grief can consume itself thereby making the body vulnerable to other and improper feelings. A modern telling is in Christopher Fry's long one-act play, *A Phoenix Too Frequent* (1946). The actions of the Ephesian matron may be compared with what happens to a diluted Indian hater in chapter 26 of *The Confidence-Man*: after enduring prolonged loneliness in dedication to his vow he may be "suddenly seized with a sort of calenture" and hurry openly toward the first smoke and throw himself on the mercy of an Indian. A truly dedicated Indian hater, says Melville's Judge Hall, an "Indian-hater *par excellence*," if he exists at all, is a soul "peeping out but once an age."

their spontaneous liability to remorse does plainly evince. No, this conceit merely goes to show, that for the mass of men, the highest abstract heavenly righteousness is not only impossible, but would be entirely out of place, and positively wrong in a world like this. To turn the left cheek if the right be smitten,[2] is chronometrical; hence, no average son of man ever did such a thing. To give *all* that thou hast to the poor,[3] this too is chronometrical; hence no average son of man ever did such a thing. Nevertheless, if a man gives with a certain self-considerate generosity to the poor; abstains from doing downright ill to any man; does his convenient best in a general way to do good to his whole race; takes watchful loving care of his wife and children, relatives, and friends; is perfectly tolerant to all other men's opinions, whatever they may be; is an honest dealer, an honest citizen, and all that; and more especially if he believe that there is a God for infidels, as well as for believers, and acts upon that belief; then, though such a man falls infinitely short of the chronometrical standard, though all his actions are entirely horo-logic;—yet such a man need never lastingly despond, because he is sometimes guilty of some minor offense:—hasty words, impulsively returning a blow, fits of domestic petulance, selfish enjoyment of a glass of wine while he knows there are those around him who lack a loaf of bread. I say he need never lastingly despond on account of his perpetual liability to these things; because *not* to do them, and

2. From Jesus' Sermon on the Mount, Matthew 5.39: "But I say unto you, That ye resist not evil: but whosoever shall smite thee on thy right cheek, turn to him the other also."
3. Matthew 19.21, what Jesus says to the rich young man who wanted to become one of his followers: "If thou wilt be perfect, go and sell that thou hast, and give to the poor, and thou shalt have treasure in heaven: and come and follow me." This is too hard a condition, according to Matthew 19.22: "when the young man heard that saying, he went away sorrowful: for he had great possessions." Melville had long nursed a grievance against English Utilitarians, judging them by Jesus' standards for what one had to do to become one of his followers. He had taken an extract in *Moby-Dick* from *Natural Theology* (1802) by William Paley, the man who systematized the arguments of the early Utilitarian Abraham Tucker. (Sound-alike theological and philosophical sects *were* alike: all the prominent British Unitarians of Melville's time were Utilitarians or had been highly influenced by Utilitarians.) Years later, in 1862, a passage in *Germany*, by Madame de Stael-Holstein, caught his eye: "A man, regarded in a religious light, is as much as the entire human race." Melville marked that and commented: "This was an early and innate conviction of mine, suggested by my revulsion from the counting-room philosophy of Paley." Early and innate was his revulsion against the Utilitarians. In writing *Pierre* he had at hand William Hazlitt's lengthy condensation of the diffuse, redundant work by Tucker, in the 1807 edition titled *An Abridgement of "The Light of Nature Pursued."* The five sections—"Of the Human Mind," "Principles of Human Conduct," "Natural Religion," "Established Doctrines," and "Miscellaneous Subjects"—made up a coolly rational textbook on human psychology, including the psychology of social behavior and the psychology of religion. The section on "Benevolence" offered him a hint for his characterization of Plotinus Plinlimmon in *Pierre*. (In book 21 Plinlimmon rejects, unopened, a gift of books, among which is a fine edition of Abraham Tucker: he has nothing to learn from Tucker.) Melville does not disagree with the Utilitarians who see that biblical Christianity is impracticable; the difference is the way he feels about that conclusion. To them religious absolutism is irrational, inconvenient, and of course unworkable because it is against human nature; to Melville the impracticability of Christianity is infinitely tragic.

their like, would be to be an angel, a chronometer; whereas, he is a man and a horologe.

"Yet does the horologe itself teach, that all liabilities to these things should be checked as much as possible, though it is certain they can never be utterly eradicated. They are only to be checked, then, because, if entirely unrestrained, they would finally run into utter selfishness and human demonism, which, as before hinted, are not by any means justified by the horologe.

"In short, this Chronometrical and Horological conceit, in sum, seems to teach this:—That in things terrestrial (horological) a man must not be governed by ideas celestial (chronometrical); that certain minor self-renunciations in this life his own mere instinct for his own every-day general well-being will teach him to make, but he must by no means make a complete unconditional sacrifice of himself in behalf of any other being, or any cause, or any conceit. (For, does aught else completely and unconditionally sacrifice itself for him? God's own sun does not abate one title of its heat in July, however you swoon with that heat in the sun. And if it *did* abate its heat on your behalf, then the wheat and the rye would not ripen; and so, for the incidental benefit of one, a whole population would suffer.)

"A virtuous expediency, then, seems the highest desirable or attainable earthly excellence for the mass of men, and is the only earthly excellence that their Creator intended for them. When they go to heaven, it will be quite another thing. There, they can freely turn the left cheek, because there the right cheek will never be smitten. There they can freely give all to the poor, for *there* there will be no poor to give to. A due appreciation of this matter will do good to man. For, hitherto, being authoritatively taught by his dogmatical teachers that he must, while on earth, aim at heaven, and attain it, too, in all his earthly acts, on pain of eternal wrath; and finding by experience that this is utterly impossible; in his despair, he is too apt to run clean away into all manner of moral abandonment, self-deceit, and hypocrisy (cloaked, however, mostly under an aspect of the most respectable devotion); or else he openly runs, like a mad dog, into atheism. Whereas, let men be taught those Chronometricals and Horologicals, and while still retaining every common-sense incentive to whatever of virtue be practicable and desirable, and having these incentives strengthened, too, by the consciousness of powers to attain their mark; then there would be an end to that fatal despair of becoming at all good, which has too often proved the vice-producing result in many minds of the undiluted chronometrical doctrines hitherto taught to mankind. But if any man say, that such a doctrine as this I lay down is false, is impious; I would charitably refer that man to the history of Christendom for the last 1800 years; and ask him, whether, in spite of all the maxims of Christ, that history is not just as full of blood, violence, wrong, and iniquity of every kind, as any previous portion of the world's story? Therefore, it follows, that so far as practical results are concerned—regarded in a purely earthly light—the only great original moral doctrine of Christianity (*i. e.* the chronometrical gratuitous return of good for evil, as distinguished from the horological forgiveness of injuries taught by some of the Pagan philosophers), has been found (horologically) a false one; because after 1800 years' inculcation from tens of thousands of pulpits, it has proved entirely impracticable.

"I but lay down, then, what the best mortal men do daily practice; and what all really wicked men are very far removed from. I present consolation to the earnest man, who, among all his human frailties, is still agonizingly conscious of the beauty of chronometrical excellence. I hold up a practicable virtue to the vicious; and interfere not with the eternal truth, that, sooner or later, in all cases, downright vice is down-right woe.

"Moreover: if——"

But here the pamphlet was torn, and came to a most untidy termination.

ORVILLE DEWEY

[The Minister's Burden: Being Expected to Sympathize with the Afflicted]†

Another thing I will be so frank as to say on leaving New York, and that is, that it was a great moral relief to me to lay down the burden of the parochial charge. I regretted to leave New York; I could have wished to live and die among the friends I had there; I should make it my plan now to spend my winters there, if I could afford it: but that particular relation to society,—no man, it seems to me, can heartily enter into it without feeling it to weight heavily upon him. Sympathy with affliction is the trial-point of the clergyman's office. In the natural and ordinary relations of life every man has enough of it. But to take into one's heart, more or less, the personal and domestic sorrows of two or three hundred families, is a burden which no man who has not borne it can conceive of. I sometimes doubt whether it was ever meant that any man, or at least any profession of men, should bear it; whether the general

† From *Autobiography and Letters of Orville Dewey, D. D.*, ed. Mary E. Dewey (Boston: Roberts Brothers, 1883), 104–06.

ministrations of the pulpit to affliction should not suffice, leaving
the application to the hearer in this case as in other cases; whether
the clergyman's relations to distress and suffering should not be
like every other man's,—general with his acquaintance, intimate
with his friends; whether, if there were nothing conventional or
customary about this matter, most families would not prefer to be
left to themselves, without a professional call from their minister.
Suppose that there were no rule with regard to it; that the clergyman, like every other man, went where his feelings carried him, or
his relations warranted; that it was no more expected of him, as a
matter of course, to call upon a bereaved family, than of any other
of their acquaintance,—would not that be a better state of things? I
am sure I should prefer it, if I were a parishioner. When, indeed,
the minister of religion wishes to turn to wise account the suffering
of sickness or of bereavement, let him choose the proper time: reflection best comes after; it is not in the midst of groans and agonies, of sobs and lamentations, that deep religious impressions are
usually made.

I have a suspicion withal, that there is something semi-barbaric
in these immediate and urgent ministrations to affliction,—something of the Indian[1] or Oriental fashion,—or something derived
from the elder time, when the priest was wise and the people rude.
For ignorant people, who have no resources nor reflections of their
own, such ministrations may be proper and needful now. I may be
in the wrong about all this. Perhaps I ought to suspect it. There is
more that is hereditary in us all, I suppose, than we know. My father never could bear the sight of sickness or distress: it made him
faint. There is a firmness, doubtless, that is better than this; but I
have it not. Very likely I am wrong. My friend Putnam[2] lately tried
to convince me of it, in a conversation we had; maintaining that the
parochial relation ought not to be, and need not be, that burden
upon the mind which I found it. And I really feel bound on such a
point, rather than myself, to trust him, one of the most finely balanced natures I ever knew. Why, then, do I say all these things? Because, in giving an account of myself, I suppose I ought to say and
confess what a jumble of *pros* and *cons* I am. Heaven knows I have
tried hard to keep right; and if I am not as full as I can hold of one-
sided and erratic opinions, I think it some praise. . . .[3] I do strive to
keep in my mind a whole rounded circle of truth and opinion. It
would be pleasant to let every mental tendency run its length; but I
could not do so. It may be pride or narrowness; but I *must* keep on
some terms with *myself*. I cannot find my understanding falling into

---

1. As in India (not a reference to American Indians) [Editors' note].
2. "Rev. George Putnam, D. D., of Roxbury, Mass" [Mary E. Dewey's note].
3. Ellipses in the original [Editors' note].

contradiction with the judgments it formed last month or last year, without suspecting not only that there was something wrong then, but that there is something wrong now, to be resisted. That "there is a mean in things" is held, I believe, to be but a mean apothegm now-a-days; but I do not hold it to be such. All my life I have endeavored to hold a balance against the swayings of my mind to the one side and the other of every question. I suppose this appears in my course, such as it has been, in religion, in politics, on the subject of slavery, of peace, of temperance, etc. It may appear to be dulness or tameness or time-serving or cowardice or folly, but I simply do not believe it to be either.

HERMAN MELVILLE

[Why Sensitive People Should Not Let Themselves Feel Pity]†

Rolled away under his desk, I found a blanket; under the empty grate, a blacking box and brush; on a chair, a tin basin, with soap and a ragged towel; in a newspaper a few crumbs of ginger-nuts and a morsel of cheese. Yes, thought I, it is evident enough that Bartleby has been making his home here, keeping bachelor's hall all by himself. Immediately then the thought came sweeping across me, What miserable friendlessness and loneliness are here revealed! His poverty is great; but his solitude, how horrible! Think of it. Of a Sunday, Wall-street is deserted as Petra;[1] and every night of every day it is an emptiness. This building too, which of week-days hums with industry and life, at nightfall echoes with sheer vacancy, and all through Sunday is forlorn. And here Bartleby makes his home; sole spectator of a solitude which he has seen all populous—a sort of innocent and transformed Marius brooding among the ruins of Carthage![2]

† From the first instalment of "Bartleby, the Scrivener. A Story of Wall-Street," *Putnam's New Monthly Magazine*, 2 (November 1853), 554–56. At the outset, the narrator, a rather elderly lawyer, describes himself as a man "who, from his youth upwards, has been filled with a profound conviction that the easiest way of life is the best," an "eminently *safe* man" whose first grand point is "prudence" and whose second is "method." Here he discovers that his strange employee has been living in the office. All notes are the editors'.
1. In Melville's youth John Lloyd Stephens printed line drawings of the newly discovered ancient city of Petra in *Incidents of Travel in Egypt, Arabia Petraea, and the Holy Land* (1837). The 1989 film *Indiana Jones and the Last Crusade* contains some gorgeously photographed scenes of Petra (in present-day Jordan). Photographs are readily available on the Internet.
2. Melville was familiar from childhood with the name and work of the painter John Vanderlyn (1775–1852), for there was at least one Vanderlyn painting in the Melvill family, a chalk portrait of Melville's Uncle Thomas (information from Dennis Marnon). The 1807 painting *Gaius Marius amid the Ruins of Carthage* depicts the former Roman Consul in temporary exile preparing for a final bloody return to power.

For the first time in my life a feeling of overpowering stinging melancholy seized me. Before, I had never experienced aught but a not-unpleasing sadness. The bond of a common humanity now drew me irresistibly to gloom. A fraternal melancholy! For both I and Bartleby were sons of Adam.[3] I remembered the bright silks and sparkling faces I had seen that day in gala trim, swan-like sailing down the Mississippi of Broadway; and I contrasted them with the pallid copyist, and thought to myself, Ah, happiness courts the light, so we deem the world is gay; but misery hides aloof, so we deem that misery there is none. These sad fancyings—chimeras, doubtless, of a sick and silly brain—led on to other and more special thoughts, concerning the eccentricities of Bartleby. Presentiments of strange discoveries hovered round me. The scrivener's pale form appeared to me laid out, among uncaring strangers, in its shivering winding sheet.

Suddenly I was attracted by Bartleby's closed desk, the key in open sight left in the lock.

I mean no mischief, seek the gratification of no heartless curiosity, thought I; besides, the desk is mine and its contents too, so I will make bold to look within.

*   *   *

Revolving all these things, and coupling them with the recently discovered fact that he made my office his constant abiding place and home, and not forgetful of his morbid moodiness; revolving all these things, a prudential feeling began to steal over me. My first emotions had been those of pure melancholy and sincerest pity; but just in proportion as the forlornness of Bartleby grew and grew to my imagination, did that same melancholy merge into fear, that pity into repulsion. So true it is, and so terrible too, that up to a certain point the thought or sight of misery enlists our best affections; but, in certain special cases, beyond that point it does not. They err who would assert that invariably this is owing to the inherent selfishness of the human heart. It rather proceeds from a certain hopelessness of remedying excessive and organic ill. To a sensitive being, pity is not seldom pain. And when at last it is perceived that such pity cannot lead to effectual succor, common sense bids the soul be rid of it. What I saw that morning persuaded me that the scrivener was the victim of innate and incurable disorder. I might give alms to his body; but his body did not pain him; it was his soul that suffered, and his soul I could not reach.

I did not accomplish the purpose of going to Trinity Church that morning. Somehow, the things I had seen disqualified me for the time from church-going.

3. Doomed to sorrow and death, as Adam was when God cursed the ground because of Adam's disobedience, then decreed that henceforth men would earn their living by the sweat of their faces. God then exiled Adam and Eve from Eden (Genesis 3).

ORVILLE DEWEY

[Poverty Not a Common Lot]†

It must not be denied that poverty, abject and desperate poverty, is a great evil; but this is not a common lot, and it still more rarely occurs in this country, without faults or vices, which should forbid all complaint. Neither shall it here be urged, on the other hand, that riches are acquired with many labours and kept with many cares and anxieties; for so also it may be said, and truly said, has poverty its toils and anxieties. The true answer to all difficulties on this subject, seems to be, that a "man's life consisteth not in the abundance of things which he possesseth." The answer, in short, may be reduced to a plain matter of fact. There is about as much cheerfulness among the poor as among the rich. And I suspect, about as much contentment too. For we might add, that a man's life, if it consist at all in his possessions, does not consist in what he possesses, but in what he *thinks* himself to possess. Wealth is a comparative term. The desire of property grows, and at the same time the estimate of it lessens, with its accumulation. And thus it may come to pass, that he who possesses thousands may less feel himself to be rich, and to all substantial purposes, may actually be less rich, than he who enjoys a sufficiency.

But not to urge this point, we say, that a man's life does not consist in these things. Happiness, enjoyment, the buoyant spirits of life, the joys of humanity, do not consist in them. They do not depend on this distinction, of being poor or rich. * * *

[T]he shower which heaven sends, falls upon the rich and the poor, upon the high and the low alike; and with still more impartial favour, descends upon the good and the evil, upon the just and the unjust.

This impartiality will be still more manifest, if we reflect, in the third place, that far the greatest and most numerous of the divine favours are granted to all, without any discrimination.

Look, in the first place, at the natural gifts of Providence. The beauty of the earth, the glories of the sky; the vision of the sun and the stars; the beneficent laws of universal being; the frame of society and of government; protecting justice and Almighty providence; whose are these? What power of appropriation can say of any one of these, "this is mine and not another's?" And what one of these

† From *Discourses on Human Nature, Human Life, and the Nature of Religion*, Orville Dewey (New York: C. S. Francis, 1852), 1.189–92, "On Inequality in the Lot of Life." On the title page Dewey is identified as "Pastor of the Church of the Messiah, in New York."

would you part with for the wealth of the Indies, or all the splendors of rank or office? Again, your eye-sight—that regal glance that commands in one act, the outspread and all-surrounding beauty of the fair universe—would you exchange it for a sceptre, or a crown? And the ear—that gathers unto its hidden chambers all music and gladness—would you give it for a kingdom? And that wonderful gift, speech—that breathes its mysterious accents into the listening soul of thy friend; that sends forth its viewless messages through the still air, and imprints them at once upon the ears of thousands; would you barter that gift for the renown of Plato or of Milton?

No, there are unappropriated blessings, blessings which none can appropriate, in every element of nature, in every region of existence, in every inspiration of life, which are infinitely better than all that can be hoarded in treasure, or borne on the breath of fame. All, of which any human being can say, "it is mine," is a toy, is a trifle, compared with what God has provided for the great family of his children! Is *he* poor to whom the great store-house of nature is opened, or does he think himself poor because it is God who has made him rich? Does *he* complain that he cannot have a magnificent palace to dwell in, who dwells in this splendid theatre of the universe; that he cannot behold swelling domes and painted walls, who beholds the "dread magnificence of heaven," and the pictured earth and sky? Do you regret the want of attendants, of a train of servants, to anticipate every wish and bring every comfort at your bidding? Yet how small a thing is it to be waited on, compared with the privilege of being yourself active; compared with the vigour of health and the free use of your limbs and senses? Is it a hardship that your table does not groan with luxuries? But how much better than all luxury, is simple appetite!

ORVILLE DEWEY

[What Distresses the Poor: Artificial Wants]†

* * * What is it that distresses the poor man, and makes poverty in the ordinary condition of it, the burden that it is? It is not, in this country,—it is not usually, hunger, nor cold, nor nakedness. It is

---

† From *Discourses on Human Nature, Human Life, and the Nature of Religion* (New York: C. S. Francis, 1852) 1.395, "Spiritual Interests, Real and Supreme." "Artificial wants": familiar in Melville's time from Benjamin Franklin's "The Way to Wealth," the term means any desire in a person that does not spring from real needs for such "necessaries" as food, liquid, and shelter but is created by perceiving that someone else has something more desirable than what you have. The Franklinian view of all but the most strictly informative advertising would be that it is devoted to creating artificial wants, desire for things that "look pretty" but are not at all necessary.

some artificial want, created by the wrong state of society. It is something nearer yet to us, and yet more unnecessary. It is mortification, discontent, peevish complaining, or envy of a better condition; and all these are evils of the mind. Again, what is it that troubles the rich man, or the man who is successfully striving to be rich? It is not poverty, certainly, nor is it exactly possession. It is occasional disappointment, it is continual anxiety, it is the extravagant desire of property, or worse than all, the vicious abuse of it; and all these too are evils of the mind. * * *

HERMAN MELVILLE

[Why the Poor in the United States Suffer More Than the Poor Elsewhere]†

The native American poor never lose their delicacy or pride; hence, though unreduced to the physical degradation of the European pauper, they yet suffer more in mind than the poor of any other people in the world. Those peculiar social sensibilities nourished by our own peculiar political principles, while they enhance the true dignity of a prosperous American, do but minister to the added wretchedness of the unfortunate; first, by prohibiting their acceptance of what little random relief charity may offer; and, second, by furnishing them with the keenest appreciation of the smarting distinction between their ideal of universal equality and their grind-stone experience of the practical misery and infamy of

† From "Poor Man's Pudding and Rich Man's Crumbs," *Harper's New Monthly Magazine*, 9 (June 1854), 98, toward the end of the first part, "Poor Man's Pudding." The narrator makes these reflections after being received hospitably in the miserable house of the impoverished couple, Dame Coulter and her husband, William. Melville's title alludes to a book by Catharine Sedgwick, the sister of Judge Lemuel Shaw's court clerk at Lenox, Charles Sedgwick. Melville knew the views of the Berkshire novelist Catharine Sedgwick on the issues of the day. Sedgwick, a daughter of Federalism, protected by her inheritances and by the prosperity of her brothers, never had to do battle in the literary marketplace. Her career owed much to her religion, for her first novel, *A New-England Tale* (1822), began as a Unitarian tract. Sedgwick as a Unitarian was not required to make any embarrassing profession of personal salvation. Repelled by the emphasis on eternal damnation in the frontier Calvinism of the lower classes, disgusted by the vulgarity of camp meetings during periods of revivalism in the Berkshires, she distanced herself from reform movements, preferring to address the aspirations and insecurities of the rising middle class in such best-selling didactic books as *Home: Scenes and Character Illustrating Christian Truth* (1835) and *The Poor Rich Man, and the Rich Poor Man* (1836), in which she suggested that despite some legitimate complaints about "the low rates of women's wages," most women were "paid according to their capacity." She was certain that in New England, and even in New York City, poverty was almost always the result of vice or disease. A woman competent as a seamstress could always support herself and live decently, if frugally. Knowing just how wrong Catharine Sedgwick was about how easy it was to earn a living, in *Pierre* Melville introduced his forlorn Isabel with a needle in her hand, sewing.

poverty—a misery and infamy which is, ever has been, and ever will be, precisely the same in India, England, and America.

ORVILLE DEWEY

[Joseph Curtis *vs.* Horace Greeley]†

For more than twenty years he [Joseph Curtis][1] spent half of his time in the schools, walking among them with such intelligent and gentle oversight as to win universal confidence and affection, so that he was commonly called, by teachers and pupils, "Father Curtis."

At the same time, his hand and heart were open to every call of charity. I remember once making him umpire between me and Horace Greeley,[2] the only time that I ever met the latter in company.

---

† From *Autobiography and Letters of Orville Dewey, D. D.*, ed. Mary E. Dewey (Boston: Roberts Brothers, 1883), 90–91. All notes are the editors'.
1. Curtis (1782–1856), first superintendent of the Society for the Reformation of Juvenile Delinquents, which created the House of Refuge for juvenile offenders in 1825. He attended the Church of the Messiah as long as Orville Dewey was pastor, then worshiped at Henry W. Bellows's All Souls Church. Bellows preached his funeral sermon. Orville Dewey helped his Berkshire neighbor Catharine Sedgwick with her *Memoir of Joseph Curtis: A Model Man* (1858) by supplying her a version of this encounter between Curtis and Horace Greeley. In her *Memoir*, quoting Dewey, Sedgwick does not name Greeley:

> Certainly no man ever had less the air about him of professional philanthropy, or less of a too common extravagance and one-sidedness. I remember meeting him one morning in company, and of the party was a gentleman professing something of this character, perhaps, and who made the observation that the most of the distress of the poor and suffering classes was owing to the injustice and neglect of those above them. I said in reply, "Here is Mr. Joseph Curtis, who has walked the streets of New York on errands—well, he will not let me say on *good* errands—for twenty years before ever you or I stepped upon them:—let us hear what *he* says." It was amid considerable philanthropic impatience on the other side that I contrived by a series of questions to extract from Mr. Curtis the opinions, successively, "That the distress of the poor was *not* owing to the rich—that is was owing *mainly* to themselves; that forty-nine fiftieths of all the poor distressed families in the city might, with due exertion and care on the part of all their members, have been free from debt and want, and might always be so."

Sedgwick quotes Dewey as commenting on misguided charity: "What these *annual* rushes of charity for the relief of the poor are doing to wear away the very foundations of character in the lower *strata* of society deserves to be more carefully considered than it has been."
2. Greeley (1811–1872), founder and long-time editor of the New York *Tribune;* a Whig when the Democrats supported slavery, then the Democratic candidate for president against U. S. Grant in 1872. Greeley shared a stage with Melville's brother Gansevoort in 1843 in the cause of Repeal (repeal of the union of Ireland and England) but as a Whig mocked Gansevoort's speeches, which advocated the annexation of Texas, in the election of 1844. In 1847 he published in the *Tribune* his own personal ambivalent review of both *Typee* and *Omoo* in which he puzzled over what was insidiously bad in the books—a subtle luring of the reader into the admiration of sensuality. In 1850 Melville bought Greeley's *Hints on Reform* in which the editor (by no means a Calvinist) put himself on record against the Fourierites who preached the doctrine of the "principle of Progress in Man—a constant improvement founded in the very laws of his being." In

He was saying, after his fashion in the "Tribune,"—he was from nature and training a Democrat, and had no natural right ever to be in the Whig party,—he was saying that the miseries of the poor in New York were all owing to the rich; when I said, "Mr. Greeley, here sits Mr. Joseph Curtis, who has walked the streets of New York for more years than you and I have been here, and I propose that we listen to him." He could not refuse to make the appeal, and so I put a series of questions upon the point to Mr. Curtis. The answers did not please Mr. Greeley. He broke in once or twice, saying, "Am not I to have a chance to speak?" But I persisted and said, "Nay, but we have agreed to listen to Mr. Curtis." The upshot was, that, in his opinion, the miseries of the poor in New York were not owing to the rich, but mainly to themselves; that there was ordinarily remunerative labor enough for them; and that, but in exceptional cases of sickness and especial misfortune, those who fell into utter destitution and beggary came to that pass through their idleness, their recklessness, or their vices. That was always my opinion. They besieged our door from morning till night, and I was obliged to help them, to look after them, to go to their houses; my family was worn out with these offices. But I looked upon beggary as, in all ordinary cases, *prima facie*[3] evidence that there was something wrong behind it.

The great evil and mischief lay in indiscriminate charity. * * *

ORVILLE DEWEY

[Robert Minturn's Scheme to Thwart Dishonest Beggars]†

One day, in the winter I think of 1837, I heard of an association of gentlemen formed to investigate this terrible subject of mendicity in our city, and to find some way of methodizing our charities and protecting them from abuse. I went down immediately to Robert Minturn,[1] who, I was told, took a leading part in this movement, and told him that I had come post-haste to inquire what he and his friends were doing, for that nothing in our city life pressed upon my

---

chapter 23, "Beggars and Borrowers," in *The Autobiography of Horace Greeley, or Recollections of a Busy Life* (1872), Greeley made a careful distinction: "The beggars of New York comprise but a small portion of its sufferers from want; yet they are at once very numerous and remarkably impudent" (193).

3. Evidence compelling at first glance, on the face of it.
† From *Autobiography and Letters of Orville Dewey, D. D.*, ed. Mary E. Dewey (Boston: Roberts Brothers, 1883), 92–94.
1. A wealthy merchant (1805–1866) remembered as a New Yorker who in the early 1850s envisioned Central Park [Editors' note].

mind like this. I used, indeed, to feel at times—and Bellows[2] had the same feeling—as if I would fain fling up my regular professional duties, and plunge into this great sea of city pauperism and misery.

Mr. Minturn told me that he, with four or five others, had taken up this subject. * * * Their plan, when matured, was this: to district the city; to appoint one person in each district to receive all applications for aid; to sell tickets of various values, which we could buy and give the applicant at our doors, to be taken to the agent, who would render the needed help, according to his judgment. Of course the beggars did not like it. I found that, half the time, they would not take the tickets. It would give them some trouble, but the special trouble, doubtless, with the reckless and dishonest among them, was that it would prevent them from availing themselves of the aid of twenty families, all acting in ignorance of what each was doing.

SCOTT NORSWORTHY

The New York *Tribune* on Begging and Charity†

In the 1840s, Horace Greeley's New York *Tribune* devoted numerous columns to the related and controversial subjects of poverty or "pauperism," beggary, and charity. Recognizing "the annoyance of multiplied beggars," the *Tribune* on July 29, 1842, blamed their plight on low wages and chronic unemployment ("City Reform— Street Nuisances, Begging, Alms, Workhouses, &c."). Greeley and other social critics frequently debated the relative merits of public and private relief. Generally dismissive of private charity as "capricious and unreliable" (July 29, 1842), Greeley favored systemic reform of public agencies. He lobbied for a communal "House of Industry" (November 30 and December 1, 1843) to replace the city almshouse, where too many idle paupers (Greeley feared) indulged in "the genteel vices of tippling and smoking" (June 17, 1844).

Critics opposed government assistance. Free-trade advocate J. K. Fisher assured the *Tribune* editor, in a letter published on July 18, 1843, "that paupers, lazzaroni and loafers vanish before a good government as swine vanish from a city where no garbage is thrown to them." Trusting that "[b]enefit societies and private charity will not fail to assist the really deserving," Fisher wanted to ban "all public provision for the poor." A New York *Express* editorial, ex-

---

2. Henry W. Bellows (1814–1882), Unitarian minister at All Souls Church in Manhattan (who in 1849 baptized the first Melville child and became Mrs. Herman Melville's spiritual adviser) [Editors' note].

† This essay appears for the first time in this Norton Critical Edition.

cerpted in the *Tribune* on December 5, 1845 ("St. Anthony Preaching to the Fish"), blasted all schemes "to establish a socie[t]y where there shall be no poor." Taking poverty as evidence of divinely mandated disparities of intelligence and ability, the *Express* regarded reformers as lunatics and worse:

> Now "the philosopher" who steps in, and attempts to invert these ordinances of his Creator, is not only a madman, but, so far forth as he attempts to array the less against the more gifted, of God's creatures, a criminal disturber of the peace, and an enemy of his race. What is he but the serpent that steps into the Paradise of the world . . . ?

The *Tribune* answered that "sickness, paralysis, loss of limbs and organs, will always supply subjects of benevolence in abundance" but refused to accept "that an athletic, willing, skillful man or woman ought to be a pauper" (December 5, 1845).

The issue of public vs. private charity resurfaced in 1846–47 when Greeley was defending socialist principles of "Association" in a series of newspaper debates with rival editor Henry J. Raymond (republished by Harper and Brothers in the 1847 pamphlet *Association Discussed.—A controversy between the New-York Tribune and the Courier and Enquirer*). Greeley lampooned Christian almsgiving with images of impoverished mothers and starving children, to whom evangelists brought tracts but no bread (January 13, 1847). Always troubled by overly spiritual charity, Greeley in *Hints toward Reforms, in Lectures, Addresses, and other Writings* (New York: Harper and Brothers, 1850) admonished the Church to render *material* aid, "something more than an opiate for the consciences of her wealthier devotees" (388). The collectivist economy that Greeley envisioned would do a better job than private philanthropy of taking from charitable New Yorkers and materially giving to the poor: "There is benevolence enough in our City to relieve all the destitution it contains, were it but unimpeded and rightly directed" (January 13, 1847). In rebuttal, Raymond called attention to the vagueness of Greeley's proposals and held up church "sewing societies" as better models of practical benevolence. Raymond comprehensively attributed "all the relief which poverty gets" either to Christianity or "the spirit of Charity which it has infused into every department of social life" (here quoted from the *Tribune*, January 29, 1847).

Bound now to admit the "laudable and vitally necessary" role of privately funded charities, Greeley cited his own "earnest" support of the Association for Improving the Condition of the Poor (January 29, 1847). Founded in 1843 by well-known philanthropists such as banker James Brown (president) and businessman Robert

B. Minturn (treasurer), the association adopted a notably prudent strategy for "the relief of the entire poor of this city," as the *Tribune* announced on February 22, 1844. Instead of cash handouts, beggars would get "printed tickets" referring them to their neighborhood "visitor," the district official empowered to weed out undeserving applicants:

> Street begging will thus be prevented; for there will be no excuse for it, and no reward extended to it. Vagrancy of all kinds will be suppressed, and while we shall be saved from being the dupes of knaves, we shall have the consolation of knowing that no needy person is without aid.

The problem of detecting cheats seemed increasingly important. A progress report published in the *Tribune* on November 19, 1845, stated that the "primary object" of the Association was "to discountenance indiscriminate almsgiving, and put an end to street begging and vagrancy." By observing established procedures, "every benevolent individual may follow the impulses of his own heart, and contribute to the comforts of his suffering fellow beings without the hazard of encouraging imposture or vagrancy." A subsequent *Tribune* article commended the Association for promoting "a wise discrimination between the virtuous poor and mere lazzaroni who live only by fraud and imposture" (February 6, 1846). The *Tribune* elaborated:

> It is not always easy to determine whether a person who asks alms in the street is a worthy object of charity, and men of warm sympathies often give money to such from a fear that, by refusing to do so, they may plant thorns in the hearts of the poor and needy. A member of this Association need not be subjected to any embarrassment on this account. He has only to carry with him a copy of the Society's Directory, find out the residence of the person applying for assistance, and direct him to the Visitor for his District and Section, whose duty it will be to investigate the case and administer relief if necessary. If the solicitor is unwilling to name his residence, you may be pretty certain that he is an imposter.

Shortly after the Association released its two-year report, the *Journal of Commerce* warned readers of bogus appeals on behalf of a "sick lady" who actually lived on Broadway "in good health and comfortable circumstances." The *Tribune* reprinted the cautionary tale but rejected the policy of distrust that the business-oriented *Journal* had implicitly recommended:

> Pauperism (next to Sin) is the ruling Social disease of our time, of which the obvious symptom is Beggary. Probably

three-fourths of all the money given with charitable intent is squandered on idleness and vice. Yet how can a man refuse a dollar when he can spare one, and is told that it will help lift an unfortunate family out of hunger and misery? We must have a very different state of things around us before we can venture to tell men not to give. (November 26, 1845)

Greeley's *Tribune* thus framed the question that Melville's "man in gray" asks even more provocatively in chapter 7 of the *Confidence-Man*: "who will refuse, what Turk or Dyak even, his own little dollar for sweet charity's sake?"

HERMAN MELVILLE

[New-Fangled Notions of the Social State]†

Then * * * there are some reformers who, despairing of civilizing Europe or America according to their rule, have projected establishments in the Pacific where they hope to find a fitting place for the good time coming. Shortly after the publication of "Typee," I myself was waited upon by a pale young man with poetic look, dulcet voice, and Armenian beard—a disciple of Fourier.[1] He asked for information as to the prospects of a select party of seventy or eighty Fourierites emigrating to some of the South Sea islands, more particularly to the valley of Typee in the Marquesas. I replied that my old friends the Typees are undoubtedly good fellows, with strong points for admiration, and that their king is as faithful to his friend as to his bottle. These people have kind hearts and natural urbanity, and are gentlemen by nature; but they have their eccentricities, are quick to anger, and are eminently conservative—they would never tolerate any new-fangled notions of the social state. Sometimes they do not hesitate to put a human being out of the way without the benefit of a trial by jury. The kind way in which they treated my comrade and myself, I concluded, furnished little indication of how they would treat others, and hardly warranted the success of a larger expedition, who might be taken as invaders and possibly eaten.

A company of Free Lovers in Ohio[2] has also proposed to go to the

---

† From Melville's second lecture, "The South Seas" (1858–59), as reconstructed by Merton M. Sealts, Jr. and the Northwestern-Newberry editors for *The Piazza Tales and Other Prose Pieces 1839–1860* (Evanston and Chicago: Northwestern University Press and the Newberry Library, 1987), 416–17. Reprinted by permission of Northwestern University Press. All notes are the editors'.

1. This anecdote about the idealistic youth with a lavish, untrimmed beard, not otherwise documented, has more than a touch of a tall tale about it.

2. In the mid-1840s groups of Free Lovers were founded in the United States, with their own magazine, *Social Revolutionist*. Followers of the French socialist Charles Fourier (1772–1837) had been open to the possibility that members of their communities might

South Seas, and the Mormons of Salt Lake have likewise thought of
these secluded islands upon which to increase and multiply—or this
has been recommended to them, showing the drifting of imagination in that direction. So an acquaintance met in Italy, who had exhausted Jerusalem and Baalbec, and, like the man in the play,[3]
looked into Vesuvius and found "nothing in it," after an hour or two
in conversation with me about the South Seas, started for an Italian
port to sail for Rio en route to the Pacific; I hope that he has steered
clear of the cannibals! The islands are admittedly good asylums—
provided the natives do not object. But I can imagine the peril that
a few ship-loads of Free Lovers would be in, on touching the Polynesian Isles. As for the plan suggested not long since, of making a
home for the Mormons on some large island in Polynesia, where
they could rear their pest houses and be at peace with their "institutions," the natives will resist their encroachments as did the Staten
Islanders that of Quarantine.[4] If sensible men wish to appropriate to
themselves an uninhabited isle, that is all right, but I do not know of
a populated island in the hundred millions of square miles embraced in the South Seas where these "fillibusterers"[5] would not be
imperatively and indignantly expelled by the natives.

PATRICIA CLINE COHEN

A Confident Tide of Reformers†

Melville's microcosm of Americans, the crowds of passengers filling the decks of awe-inspiring steamboats, likely included zealous

---

find greater amorous freedom than regular members of society, and the British utopian
Robert Owen (1771–1858) late in life advocated "Modern Spiritualism," a polite cover
for Free Love. Melville specifically refers to a notorious Free Love colony at Berlin
Heights, Ohio.

3. In *Used Up*, adapted by Dion Boucicault and performed in New York City in 1847, John
Lester Wallack (1820–1888) played Sir Charles Coldstream, the always bored fellow
who dawdles through life. Coldstream's ennui is such that when he looks into the crater
of Vesuvius he professes to be disappointed that it is empty.

4. Staten Islanders had long protested against the port of New York's placing its Quarantine
Station (where transatlantic ships were boarded and checked for contagious diseases) at
the Narrows, off Staten Island, because they feared that ship fever (typhus), smallpox,
cholera, and other diseases might be brought ashore. They were particularly outraged
that invalids from abroad were put ashore not in Manhattan but on Staten Island. On
September 1, 1858, just before Melville started his lecture season, a mob of Staten Islanders had set fire to the Quarantine Hospital in Tompkinsville.

5. A fillibusterer (spelled variously, one or two, one final *er* or two) was not a senator who
delays a vote by talking but a buccaneer or freebooter, especially one who leads a military invasion into a country with which his own nation is at peace. In the news was
William Walker (1824–1860), a Tennesseean who invaded Nicaragua in 1854 and who
proclaimed himself president of Nicaragua in 1856. He surrendered to the U.S. Navy in
1857.

† This essay appears for the first time in this Norton Critical Edition.

reformers of one persuasion or another. Reformers were a breed distinguished by their worry over particular social problems coupled with a confidence that solutions were at hand needing political will or perhaps personal willpower to make them happen. The impulse to reform American society gathered steam from the 1830s to the 1850s, drawing its energy from multiple sources. Evangelical Christianity with its new emphasis on the perfectibility of man spurred many to tackle daunting social problems, and so regions where the Second Great Awakening hit big—New York, New England, Ohio—were also hotbeds of reform. Another large set of progressive-minded reformers drew inspiration from European thinkers who critiqued capitalism and favored model utopian communities that would foster less exploitative social and economic arrangements. Some reformers identified huge systemic problems in need of correction, like slavery in the South, or poverty and wage slavery in the North, while others aimed to reform personal sins, such as alcohol consumption and sexual immorality, which when aggregated over a large population, they argued, presented social problems of serious dimensions. In general reformers shared the conviction that modern life with its urban growth, technological development, and fast-paced economic change created new problems, and they also shared the faith that something ought to be done about these new problems.

An effervescent—contagious even—impulse to reform spread swiftly in antebellum culture. Reformers banded together in organizations that held formal meetings, debated plans of action, and carried messages of reform to a wider public via specialized newspapers, pamphlets, and the lecture circuit. Traveling lecturers—paid agents of various reform groups—spread the news and persuaded listeners to join their cause. Ordinary townsfolk might show up out of curiosity to hear a lecture and get enthused enough in the process to found local auxiliaries of the parent organization. By this means, some thousand village-level antislavery societies dotted the map of northern states. A like number of Female Moral Reform groups, dedicated to rooting out male sexual licentiousness, blossomed by 1040, inspired by the monthly periodical *The Advocate of Moral Reform* published by a group of evangelical women in New York City. And by 1850, women lecturers were on the stump galvanizing audiences in favor of woman's rights. Agents of reform did not always encounter enthusiasm: Abolitionist and woman's rights lecturers often faced hostile crowds and even violent mobs. Lecturers on sexual sin—the few that there were—also faced ridicule and threat, and sometimes obscenity charges.

While it is useful to categorize reforms, as many scholars have done, distinguishing among those that targeted societywide ills like slavery from those that targeted individuals and even the self (as in dietary reform groups praising vegetarianism, or the fads for phrenology, mesmerism, and the water cure), it was often the case that reformers themselves took up an array of causes that mixed and matched fads and reforms. Annual meetings of various groups were nearly always held in big cities over the course of May, so that people could attend several conventions in a row. The "May anniversaries" brought business to hotels as hundreds showed up for meetings on abolition, moral reform, temperance, woman's rights, peace, and health reform. Small wonder, then, that these various movements borrowed strategies from each other and made connections in their messages. One man who lived at Modern Times, a small anarchical village on Long Island founded in 1851 under the banners of "Individual Sovereignty" and "cost the limit of price," later reflected that his fellow villagers embraced "every kind of reform from Abolition of Chattel Slavery, Woman's Rights, Vegetarianism, Hydropathy (and all the pathies), Peace, Anti-Tobacco, Total Abstinence, to the Bloomer Costume. . . . Every new and strange proposition was welcomed by a respectful hearing—debated and considered—and the latest 'Anti' was often thought the truer as being the result of latest experience or riper knowledge."[1]

The strange careers of Mary Gove and Thomas Low Nichols offer two examples of the fluidity of reform. Gove's was the more unusual, in her early challenge to a well-established gender norm that frowned on women speaking in public and her challenge to sexual conventions of the day. Self-taught in the healing arts, she launched herself on a public lecturing career in 1838 offering courses on women's "anatomy and physiology." Gove lectured from Maine to Maryland, planting local "ladies physiology societies" in her wake. She spoke only to female audiences—at first—and dared to include two lectures on sexuality (given separately to single and then married women). Her message, that married women had a right to refuse intimacies with their husbands, gained her bad press but solidarity with the female moral reformers who welcomed her at their conventions. Gove took up diet reform as well, embracing vegetarianism and anti-tobacco and anti-alcohol programs.

Within a few years she proved an early convert to "Associationism," under the banner of the French philosopher Charles Fourier, whose eager disciples in America founded scores of utopian communes where "Attractive Industry" and cooperative living replaced the drudgery of isolated labor. Gove's associationism phase coin-

---

1. Charles A. Codman, "A Brief History of 'The City of Modern Times' Long Island, N.Y.— and a Glorification of some of Its Saints" (ca. 1905), quoted in Roger Wunderlich, *Low Living and High Thinking at Modern Times, New York* (Syracuse: Syracuse University Press, 1992), 4.

cided with her interest in the new water-cure therapy, in which pa-
tients were wrapped in wet sheets or subjected to water falling from
great height on them. Between soaking patients and lecturing on
"Attractive Industry," Gove found time to read the Swedish mystic
cleric Emanuel Swedenborg, whose writings on "conjugial love"
and spiritual marriage were popular among reformers. By the
1850s, Gove had moved into Spiritualism and mediumship, and
then topped everything by publicly advocating "Free Love," a privi-
leging of sexual relationships based on loving union and not lust.

"Free Love," to Gove and her new husband, Thomas Nichols,
meant freedom to follow one's heart in love and sex. Marriage enslaved women, they said; but it also enslaved men. Unloving mari-
tal sex was as bad as the lust of prostitution, they argued; "Free
Love" would purify sexual relationships across America. Not surprisingly, they attracted several thousand followers for their new
creed; and also, not surprisingly, they were strongly denounced as
immoral fanatics.

Thomas Nichols's journey through the thickets of reform began
with his launch into phrenology, which held that the bumps and
contours of a person's head revealed his inner character. Nichols
easily picked up mesmerism as well, and at age nineteen he appeared on stages in Boston to demonstrate his hypnotic skills. He
adopted dietary reform, inspired by health-advocate Sylvester Gra-
ham, and abstained from alcohol. During his decade-long career in
New York journalism he read the manuscript of Herman Melville's
first book, *Typee*, and met the young author. Nichols recommended
he seek publication first in England, as a way of making the book
more attractive to American publishers. It proved to be a good strategy for Melville.

Nichols's period of reform activity blossomed once he met and
married Mary Gove, in a Swedenborgian ceremony. He became a
water-cure doctor and opened a hydropathic school, officiated in
the American Vegetarian Society, and wrote books on woman's
rights and on sex. He helped transition Gove from her earlier line
that women have a right to say *no* to sex—to a right to say *yes* as
well, and to choose their partners. The two reformers moved to
Modern Times on Long Island, whose motto of "Individual sover-
eignty" suited their championship of free choice. Next Nichols
founded the Progressive Union, a Free Love group that looked to
start new utopian communities in the Midwest. Their own attempt
was "Memnonia" in Ohio, a water-cure/spiritualist school for progressive philosophy that rattled the neighbors and created a storm.

Nichols and Gove were fringe reformers, famous for controversy
and for backing reforms that did not become mainstream. We more
often celebrate the pioneers whose reform goals were successful,

such as William Lloyd Garrison with his uncompromising stand against slavery, and Elizabeth Cady Stanton and her devotion to equal rights for women. But Garrison and Stanton lived amid and worked with reformers who thought it possible to hear knocks and thumps from the spirit world and preferred being wrapped in wet sheets to the more aggressive therapies of established medicine of the day. For those unsympathetic to reform, all these new-fangled projects probably seemed strange. Little wonder that when the public encountered them on the decks of steamboats, the confident reformers, assured of their program to change the world, might well have seemed more akin to "confidence men."

SUSAN M. RYAN

From Misgivings: Melville, Race, and the Ambiguities of Benevolence†

[*Identities*]

The charity society publications, advice manuals, juvenile fiction, and cartoons I consider in this essay reveal some of the ways in which antebellum white Americans with access to publication talked about benevolence and its risks. Undeniably, non-whites also used and contested the language of benevolence, often explicitly revealing their racial identities in the process and referring to whites' more voluminous and more widely distributed interventions. African Americans in the urban North, to cite the most prolific of these commentators, at times identified worthy and unworthy supplicants according to the same criteria whites used, but they also offered theoretical and practical critiques of whites' benevolent projects and took free blacks to task for their supposed overreliance on white aid. Native American writers, especially during the Cherokee removal debates of the 1820s and 1830s, attempted to hold Anglo-American leaders to their professions of benevolence, even as they insisted on their people's right to choose their own "friends." And Jewish Americans, who were not generally accorded the privileges of whiteness in the nineteenth century, worked to characterize themselves as a benevolent people who took care of their "own."

† From "Misgivings: Melville, Race, and the Ambiguities of Benevolence," *American Literary History* 12 (Winter 2000), 685–712. Reprinted by permission of the author and Oxford University Press. In this excerpt we use, with the author's permission, two bracketed headings ("Identities" and "Pretenses") that Ryan supplied for the revision of those passages in her *The Grammar of Good Intentions: Race and the Antebellum Culture of Benevolence* (Ithaca, NY: Cornell University Press, 2003).

Anglo-American authors of charity texts, on the other hand, rarely mentioned their own racial identities, though they discussed at length the racial characteristics of "foreigners," slaves, and other outsiders whose social positioning they charted. These authors relied on the fact that most American readers assumed a white standard in public discourse. By exploring their racial identities and the racial constructions inherent in their texts, I undermine the implied universality of antebellum white benevolence and analyze it instead as a raced discourse. The men and women who ran mainstream charity organizations and wrote their reports, who published advice manuals and juvenile literature, and who generally fashioned themselves as charity experts, tended to be Protestant, of Anglo or northern European descent, and relatively well-off economically—though economic security grew increasingly tenuous in the early and mid-nineteenth century (see Sellers 103–201). These authors took various positions on the era's pressing social and political issues, most notably slavery and immigration, but generally agreed that people of means bore some responsibility for alleviating the suffering of others. And they typically wrote for an implied audience much like themselves—sometimes constructed broadly as "concerned and benevolent citizens," sometimes as fellow charity workers and potential donors. When they addressed audiences more distant from themselves—impressionable young people in need of guidance or ideological opponents in need of convincing—they did so with a tone of racial and class solidarity.

To label these speakers *white* is to use an imperfect short-hand. As recent scholarship has shown, the membership and putative character of nineteenth-century whiteness were fluid, contested, and often contradictory constructions, shifting both diachronically and situationally. Antebellum discourses of benevolence were among the many social and linguistic forces working to constitute the category. That is, access to a white racial designation and its attendant privileges depended to some extent on whether one needed help or was in a position to help others. The level of one's participation in benevolent exchange did not single handedly grant the privileges of whiteness or push one unequivocally outside its boundaries. But a group's position, or perceived position, within benevolent hierarchies could affect the degree to which its members were considered "absorbable" into whiteness. That Irish immigrants, for example, were widely believed to constitute a high percentage of urban beggars delayed the group's acceptance into the white mainstream. Building on the logic of such exclusions, one virulently nativist editor went so far as to claim that "professional beggars" were "all of foreign birth," thus implying that the very fact of begging proved an individual's alien status ("Editor's Walk" 11).

More central to my argument, however, is how the language of benevolence informed what it *meant* to be white. Americans of Anglo-Saxon descent—as many whites somewhat erroneously defined themselves (Horsman 4–5)—asserted their natural aggressiveness in commerce and combat, but also insisted on their capacity to care for and improve society's "weaker" members. In their innumerable accounts of these benevolent projects, and particularly in their accounts of deceptions discovered or discouraged, whites arrogated to themselves the rationality and circumspection that they claimed made for successful social uplift. But their representations of such inquiries had contradictory effects, figuring the white benevolent establishment as both exceptionally discerning and essentially trickable—else why the vigilance?

[*Pretences*]

Alongside their deep suspicion of supplicants, antebellum writers who addressed the issue of poor relief expressed a more general conviction that benevolence, if mismanaged, could be hazardous. While a variety of efforts came under attack, benevolent projects attracted the most criticism when they dispensed direct material aid, especially money. Almsgiving was considered dangerous because it afforded the poor at least momentary autonomy, insofar as they could choose whether to purchase necessities or spend the money on alcohol, gambling, or some other vice. Charity experts feared that such autonomy might prove all too seductive, tempting the poor to shun permanently the world of work and consequences. Acknowledging this ambient concern, the Baltimore Association for Improving the Condition of the Poor admitted in 1851 "that the alms of benevolent societies, and of private liberality, are often misapplied, and as often abused by those who receive them." Four pages of caveats followed, all calculated to help charity workers circumvent the designs of the dishonest; chief among these was the injunction "*to withhold all relief from unknown persons*" (17). A supplicant's seemingly honest face, on its own, was not to be trusted. Similarly, the children's story "Benevolence" portrayed a boy who gave alms to an apparently needy man, only to discover later that he was a drunkard who mistreated his "wife and half starved, half clothed children" (36); the boy was horrified to find that his donation had enabled the man to drink himself into a stupor (40). As these texts suggest, the wrong kind of giving, or too much of the right kind, might encourage in the recipient an exaggerated sense of entitlement that could result in "pauperism"—that is, a habit of relying on charity—and related social ills, including vice, indolence, improvidence, and the crime that some commit when "they have become so well-known that begging ceases to be profitable" (Boston Society 15).

Donors, for their part, did not escape scrutiny. The Boston Society for the Prevention of Pauperism went so far as to suggest that what often passes for a benevolent impulse is, in fact, a combination of laziness and squeamishness. "Many are too busy" to make appropriate inquiries regarding beggars, the group's 1859 report asserted, while "others give charity in order to get rid of them; being careless whether the stories which they hear are true or not" (15). Such irresponsible figures resisted the role of the assertive, investigative caregiver, preferring instead the passivity of an isolated, and therefore unmanageable, donation. In other cases, the honesty of benevolent agents—who, as fundraisers, were supplicants as well as donors—was called into question. Stories abounded of charitable collectors who fleeced credulous and well-meaning citizens: the *Colonization Herald* of July 1853, for example, warned Philadelphians of a "heartless man" disguised "in a Friend's garb" who had "been robbing Africa" by pretending to collect donations for the Pennsylvania Colonization Society ("Caution" 147). Those indentified as the objects, or would-be objects, of benevolent efforts had their own doubts about charity agents' sincerity. The Philadelphia-based and white-administered Association for the Care of Coloured Orphans found that "various excuses were urged by coloured people against trusting us with their young dependants [sic], although their real objections evidently arose from a want of confidence in the Association." "It will require time and experience," the report continued, "to remove those fears and apprehensions, which have originated in that system of cruelty and deception, to which the coloured people have been subject for so many generations" (14). These agents saw in their role the potential to undo years of institutionalized racism, even as they found themselves silently accused of it by those they wished to aid.

The suspicion that donors and charity workers faced derived not only from the possibility that they might be lazy, dishonest, or racist, but also from the ever present danger that they might do good incorrectly and thus contribute, however unintentionally, to the moral and social decay of the populace. Thus charity experts worked hard to present themselves as trustworthy donors, largely by elaborating on the widespread notion that the poor could be divided into the worthy and the "vicious," and by outlining their methods for determining where an individual supplicant belonged in that taxonomy. The third edition of *The Young Lady's Guide to the Harmonious Development [sic] of Christian Character* (1841), one of many texts that promoted such divisions, expressed a commonplace sentiment when it warned charity-minded readers that "as a general principle, it is not best to give to *beggars*. . . . The more deserving poor are retiring, and unwilling to make known their wants. It is better to seek out such, as the objects of your charity, than to give indiscriminately to those that ask for it" (Newcomb 215). This approbation of silent sufferers, whose destitution must be discovered by an investigative philanthropy, coexisted with a pervasive suspicion of their designated opposites, those who begged in public and complained audibly of their troubles. The latter group, according to many commentators, lacked appropriate Christian forbearance and sufficient shame in the face of middle-class standards of respectability and were perhaps out to mislead potential donors with invented tales of hardship. The very fact of a public appeal undermined the supplicant's credibility, while qualities of self-assertion and persistence that middle- and upper-class Americans often admired were here considered objectionable.

The central issue in this disapprobation of public begging was the difficulty of verifying the supplicant's claims. Most nineteenth-century Americans perceived urban poverty to be an ever worsening crisis, marked both by an increase in the numbers of people requesting aid and by their greater opportunities for deception. According to David Rothman, colonial Americans' primary concern in determining whom to assist had been jurisdiction rather than the probity of the applicant: they asked, was he or she truly this town's responsibility (3–29)? But by the antebellum period, major cities had grown to the point that beggars could take advantage of their anonymity, moving to different neighborhoods as passersby began to recognize them and thus avoiding the constraints of reputation. Urban deracination, however much it has been cited as a source of loneliness and discontentment, also represented an opportunity to remake oneself.

When begging worked, it did so largely because the beggar elicited the donor's sympathy. But as Glenn Hendler observes in the context of sentimental fiction, sympathy could involve a dangerous selflessness, a too-thorough identification resulting in the loss of oneself (691–92). The processes of identification between beggars and donors that charity workers described were typically less protracted and intense than those experienced by Hendler's sentimental heroines. Nevertheless, individuals who identified too closely with street beggars risked damaging the larger charitable project, in that their resulting selflessness was thought to undermine cautious assessments. Authors of charity texts considered sympathy to be less risky if it were not so vigorously courted, that is, if donors selected the recipients themselves. Under such circumstances charity workers retained the power to identify and investigate the needy, most notably by means of home visits (Boyer 90–94; Ginzberg 61).

By entering the ostensibly needy person's home, the charity agent could take account of his or her environment—the material markers of suffering or comfort and the other human beings who might betray the influence of vice or unmask a deceiver. A hovel full of sick children and sewing projects, after all, signified very differently from one occupied by a drunken spouse and littered with incongruously luxurious goods.

The professional beggars whom these strategies were meant to circumvent engaged in a variety of passing. They faked destitution or illness, pretended to be blind, or borrowed hungry-looking children to make their appeals seem more urgent, all because they preferred such deceptions to working for a living, or so the story goes. As Harryette Mullen has argued, "passing is a kind of theft" within the nineteenth century's cultural logic (73). Those who passed as needy, according to antebellum writers on charity, cheated not only the individual who gave them aid, but also the truly impoverished who went unaided as a result. The professional beggar, according to an 1855 editorial, "tells his sad (made up) story with a broken voice, and a tearful eye—his acting is so natural—his grief so poignant, that the spectator falls into the snare, and is of course robbed on the instant" ("Editor's Walk" 12). Such duplicity, because it called into question the validity of donors' perceptions and judgments, worked to unsettle the hierarchies structuring benevolent exchange. * * * Within the era's benevolent dyads, power was more diffuse than it sometimes appeared. Those who considered themselves arbiters of need had to be circumspect lest they be made into fools. From the donor's perspective, then, the professionalization of beggars—a parody of Americans' investment in occupational expertise—had to be matched by the professionalization of donors (Ginzberg 61–66, 98–132). Charity writers promoted this change by creating an authoritative literature on benevolent practices, by championing rationality over emotion and rule following over impulsiveness, and by publicizing the work of increasingly bureaucratic charity organizations. These efforts accorded with cultural notions of Anglo-Americans' natural and beneficial authority, made possible, they asserted, by their possession of managerial skills that "unruly" immigrants and "shiftless" slaves lacked. While the professionalization of social work would become thoroughly established only after the Civil War, its theoretical foundations and its earliest practical incarnations occurred earlier and owed much to the perception among the "charitable classes" that duplicity represented a pressing, if remediable, threat.

Some, of course, resisted this emphasis on ferreting out trickster-beggars. A number of antebellum authors, especially those who wrote poems and stories aimed at children, represented beggars' uninvestigated claims as entirely credible and urged readers to be generous. A few commentators, such as the prominent Philadelphian Mathew Carey, decried the strict categorization of the poor and argued that, even if poverty were caused by intemperance and vice, one should not "turn a deaf ear or . . . harden the heart to the sufferings of poor fellow mortals. . . . We are all offenders, in a greater or less degree, and have no right to hope for mercy if we extend it not to others" (iv–v). William Logan Fisher, author of *Pauperism and Crime* (1831), proposed that pauperism owed more to structural inequities within the economy than to misguided benevolence. Others made an explicitly religious argument, claiming that God was a more appropriate judge than human beings of who merited assistance, while a small minority, despite the possibility of deception, advocated a studied credulity. South Carolinian Henry L. Pinckney gave voice to this last position when he declared it better "that a little charity should be thrown away, than that the waters should cease to flow. . . . [L]et it fall, like the gentle rain, upon the evil and the good" (15).

Such alternative views illustrate the complexity of the cultural conversation about benevolence and duplicity—but even as these authors presented their arguments against suspicion, they typically acknowledged that suspicion dominated the era's discourses of charity. Donors and potential donors who experienced that mistrust focused much of their attention on reading the body for indications of character and "potential," the potential to attain self-sufficiency as well as the potential to deceive. Because the body offered such unreliable testimony, donors also looked to other means of authentication, from "respectable" references to home visits. The illegible —or worse, the theatrical—supplicant was constantly adapting, shifting tactics, remaking himself/herself in a dialectical relationship with those who attempted to establish rules and safeguards. Dissatisfied with the assurance that, whatever the beggar's true circumstances, their alms met some sort of need, the benevolent sought a guarantee that they were doing well at doing good.

Works Cited

Association for the Care of Coloured Orphans. *First Report of the Association for the Care of Coloured Orphans, Embracing an Account of "the Shelter for Coloured Orphans," Instituted at Philadelphia, in the Year 1822*. Philadelphia: William Brown, 1836.

Baltimore Association for Improving the Condition of the Poor. *Annual Report, Constitution and By-Laws, and Visitor's Manual*. Baltimore: Office of the Association, J. W. Woods, printer, 1851.

Boston Society for the Prevention of Pauperism. *Twenty-Fourth Annual Report of the Boston Society for the Prevention of Pauperism. October, 1859*. Boston: John Wilson and Son, 1859.

Boyer, Paul. *Urban Masses and Moral Order in America, 1820–1920*. Cambridge: Harvard UP, 1978.

Carey, Mathew. Preface. *Essays on the Public Charities of Philadelphia, Intended to Vindicate the Benevolent Societies of the City from the Charge of Encouraging Idleness, and to Place in Strong Relief, Before an Enlightened Public, the Sufferings and Oppression under which the Greater Part of the Females Labour, Who Depend on their Industry for a Support for Themselves and Children. 4th ed. Philadelphia: J. Clarke, 1829.

"The Editor's Walk.—No. I." The Philanthropist, or Sketches of City Life. A Monthly Periodical Jan. 1855: 11–13.

Fisher, William Logan. Pauperism and Crime. Philadelphia: Printed for the Author, 1831.

Ginzberg, Lori D. Women and the Work of Benevolence: Morality, Politics, and Class in the Nineteenth-Century United States. New Haven: Yale UP, 1990.

Hendler, Glenn. "The Limits of Sympathy: Louisa May Alcott and the Sentimental Novel." American Literary History 3 (1991): 685–706.

Horsman, Reginald. Race and Manifest Destiny: The Origins of American Racial Anglo-Saxonism. Cambridge: Harvard UP, 1981.

Mullen, Harryette. "Optic White: Blackness and the Production of Whiteness," diacritics 24.2–3 (1994): 71–89.

Newcomb, Harvey. The Young Lady's Guide to the Harmonious Developement [sic] of Christian Character. 3rd ed., rev. and enl. Boston: James B. Dow, 1841.

Pinckney, Henry L. An Address Delivered Before the Methodist Benevolent Society, at Their Anniversary Meeting, in the Methodist Protestant Church, in Wentworth-Street, on the 1st Monday in July, 1835. Charleston: E. J. Van Brunt, 1835.

Rothman, David. The Discovery of the Asylum: Social Order and Disorder in the New Republic. Boston: Little, Brown, 1971.

Sellers, Charles. The Market Revolution: Jacksonian America, 1815–1846. New York: Oxford UP, 1991.

The Latest Heresy: Melville and the Transcendentalists

HERSHEL PARKER

A Chronology†

Carl Van Vechten was the first on record as understanding that Melville satirized the Transcendentalists in *The Confidence-Man*, but he phrased his discovery ambiguously, calling Melville's book the great Transcendental satire instead of the great satire of Transcendentalism, the phrasing used in the reprinting in this volume. Melville's attitude toward individual Transcendentalists and Transcendentalism in general has been much debated since 1946, when Egbert S. Oliver first laid out evidence for thinking that Melville portrayed Emerson and Thoreau in *The Confidence-Man*. Through his contacts with the New York publishing world, with the Boston social world, and with the Concord writers through Hawthorne, as well through his being published along with Thoreau in *Putnam's*, Melville heard and read much about Emerson and Thoreau. Other selections in this volume show that Melville understood Transcendentalism not as some fresh cult sprung full-grown from Concord but as an outgrowth of Utilitarianism and Unitarianism that carried clear signs of its origins.

1847

CONCORD March 12. *Emerson writes to Evert A. Duyckinck, the editor of Wiley & Putnam's, asking him to consider* "a book of extraordinary merit," *Thoreau's* "An Excursion on the Concord & Merrimack Rivers." See *The Letters of Ralph Waldo Emerson*, ed. Ralph L. Rusk (New York: Columbia University Press, 1939), III, 384.

CONCORD May 28. *Thoreau writes to offer the manuscript to Duyckinck.* See *The Correspondence of Henry David Thoreau*, eds. Walter

---

† This chronology has been cast in the same format as Jay Leyda's *The Melville Log*, from which two items are taken.

Harding and Carl Bode (New York: New York University Press, 1958), p. 181.

CONCORD July 3. *Thoreau sends the "Mss." to Duyckinck by express, asking Duyckinck to acknowledge receiving it. (Correspondence, p. 184.)*

CONCORD July 27. *Thoreau presses Duyckinck for an answer (and gets a negative one):*

It is a little more than three weeks since I returned my mss. sending a letter by mail at the same time for security, so I suppose that you have received it. If Messrs. Wiley & Putnam are not prepared to give their answer now, will you please inform me what further delay if any, is unavoidable, that I may determine whether I had not better carry it elsewhere—for time is of great consequence to me. (*Correspondence*, p. 184.)

NEW YORK July 31. *Melville, a former Wiley & Putnam author and now a friend of the editor, dines in the Astor House with Duyckinck.*

1848

NEW YORK October 31 or later. *In* A Fable for Critics (*New York: G. P. Putnam, 1848), p. 27 and pp. 29–30, James Russell Lowell characterizes Emerson and his imitators in a sensationally popular poem:*

"But, to come back to Emerson, (whom, by the way,
I believe we left waiting,)—his is, we may say,
A Greek head on right Yankee shoulders, whose range
Has Olympus for one pole, for t'other the Exchange;
He seems, to my thinking, (although I'm afraid
The comparison must, long ere this, have been made,)
A Plotinus-Montaigne, where the Egyptian's gold mist
And the Gascon's shrewd wit cheek by-jowl co-exist * * *

"He has imitators in scores, who omit
No part of the man but his wisdom and wit,—
Who go carefully o'er the sky-blue of his brain,
And when he has skimmed it once, skim it again;
If at all they resemble him, you may be sure it is
Because their shoals mirror his mists and obscurities,
As a mud-puddle seems deep as heaven for a minute,
While a cloud that floats o'er is reflected within it.

"There comes [Channing],[1] for instance; to see him's rare sport,
Tread in Emerson's tracks with legs painfully short;
How he jumps, how he strains, and gets red in the face,
To keep step with the mystagogue's natural pace!
He follows as close as a stick to a rocket,
His fingers exploring the prophet's each pocket.
Fie, for shame, brother bard; with good fruit of your own,
Can't you let neighbor Emerson's orchards alone?
Besides, 'tis no use, you'll not find e'en a core,—
[Thoreau] has picked up all the windfalls before.["]

1849

BOSTON February 24. *Melville writes to Evert A. Duyckinck:*[2]
I have heard Emerson since I have been here. Say what they will, he's a great man.

BOSTON March 3. *Melville writes again, defending himself from a comment by the anti-Transcendental Duyckinck:*
Nay, I do not oscillate in Emerson's rainbow,[3] but prefer rather to hang myself in mine own halter than swing in any other man's swing. Yet I think Emerson is more than a brilliant fellow. Be his stuff begged, borrowed, or stolen, or of his own domestic manufacture he is an uncommon man. Swear he is a humbug—then is he no common humbug. Lay it down that had not Sir Thomas Browne lived, Emerson would not have mystified—I will answer, that had not Old Zack's father begot him, Old Zack[4] would never have been the hero of Palo Alto. The truth is that we are all sons, grandsons, or nephews or great-nephews of those who go before us. No one is his own sire.—I was very agreeably disappointed in Mr Emerson. I had heard of him as full of transcendentalisms, myths & oracular

1. Ellery Channing (1818–1901), feckless scion of the Unitarian Channings, poet, editor, and biographer of his friend Thoreau. See 415 herein.
2. Melville's letters, taken from the NN *Correspondence* (1993), used here with permission of the Northwestern University Press, differ slightly from the 1960 Davis-Gilman transcriptions.
3. As Merton M. Sealts Jr. explains in *Pursuing Melville, 1940–1980* (Madison: University of Wisconsin Press, 1982), 252, Melville had seen a cartoon in the New York *Tribune* on February 6, 1849, which portrayed Emerson swinging in an upside down rainbow.
4. Zachary Taylor (1784–1850) was then about to take office as the twelfth president of the United States (1849–50). Melville had satirized him in the series "Authentic Anecdotes of 'Old Zack' " in 1847 (reprinted in the Northwestern-Newberry *Piazza Tales* volume). Writing as a Democrat, Melville was acutely aware that the Democratic president James K. Polk's war against Mexico had set up General Taylor to become the successful Whig candidate for president in 1848. Taylor was victorious at Palo Alto, north of Brownsville, Texas, in the first major battle of the war, May 8, 1846. Taylor's death came in July 1850 just before Melville left New York for his vacation in Pittsfield, during which he met Hawthorne. Sir Thomas Browne (1605–1682), English physician and author of *Religio Medici*, which Melville borrowed from Duyckinck in 1848, and *Vulgar Errors*, which Melville read later.

gibberish; I had only glanced at a book of his once in Putnam's store[5]—that was all I knew of him, till I heard him lecture.—To my surprise, I found him quite intelligible, tho' to say truth, they told me that that night he was unusually plain.—Now, there is a something about every man elevated above mediocrity, which is, for the most part, instinctively perceptible. This I see in Mr Emerson. And frankly, for the sake of the argument, let us call him a fool;—then had I rather be a fool than a wise man.—I love all men who *dive*.[6] Any fish can swim near the surface, but it takes a great whale to go down stairs five miles or more; & if he dont attain the bottom, why, all the lead in Galena[7] can't fashion the plummet that will. I'm not talking of Mr Emerson now—but of the whole corps of thought-divers, that have been diving & coming up again with blood-shot eyes since the world began.

I could readily see in Emerson, notwithstanding his merit, a gaping flaw. It was, the insinuation, that had he lived in those days when the world was made, he might have offered some valuable suggestions. These men are all cracked right across the brow. And never will the pullers-down be able to cope with the builders-up. And this pulling down is easy enough—a keg of powder blew up Brock's Monument—but the man who applied the match, could not, alone, build such a pile to save his soul from the shark-maw of the Devil.[8] But enough of this Plato who talks thro' his nose.[9] To one of your habits of thought, I confess that in my last, I seemed, but only *seemed* irreverent. And do not think, my boy, that because I, impulsively broke forth in jubilations over Shakespeare, that,

---

5. The bookshop of G. P. Putnam at 155 Broadway in New York City.
6. Heyward Ehrlich pointed out that Melville may have been paying a compliment to his friend, because as the New York–Dutch Duyckinck once wrote to his brother, "Duyck-inck means *diving*,—that is to say seeking the hidden pearls of truth—"; see "A Note on Melville's 'Men Who *Dive*,' " *Bulletin of the New York Public Library*, 69 (December 1965), 661–64.
7. In 1840 Melville arrived in Galena, Illinois, named for the lead ore found there, hoping his uncle Thomas could help him find work. His uncle, who had recently been fired for stealing from his employer, was of no help. Melville returned to Lansingburgh, New York, and found a teaching job near home before going to New York City and, after a few weeks, deciding to go to sea on a whaleship.
8. Early in 1840 an Irish-Canadian, Benjamin Lett, blew up the monument erected in Queenston, Ontario, to honor the commander of the British forces who died in battle there, Major General Isaac Brock (1769–1812). Lett fled to northern New York, where he attempted to blow up the *Great Britain* in Oswego harbor. Arrested and convicted, he escaped from a train taking him to the state prison in Auburn and reportedly lived out his life in Illinois and Wisconsin. He was much in the news, suspected of other ter-rorist acts in the months before Melville sailed to the Pacific in January 1841. In *The Confidence-Man* (chapter 27) Melville refers to a shameful episode in American military history, General Hull's surrender of Detroit to Brock. In writing this letter Melville's mind had flashed back to 1840, when he first saw Detroit, then in the midst of the sen-sational innovation in campaigning for the presidency, the Log Cabin campaign.
9. As a New Yorker (never mind that his father was Bostonian) Melville is jibing at the un-pleasing Yankee dialect but also subscribing to James Russell Lowell's characterization of Emerson as both mystical and shrewdly practical.

therefore, I am of the number of the *snobs*[1] who burn their tuns of rancid fat at his shrine. No, I would stand afar off & alone, & burn some pure Palm oil, the product of some overtopping trunk.

—I would to God Shakespeare had lived later, & promenaded in Broadway. Not that I might have had the pleasure of leaving my card for him at the Astor, or made merry with him over a bowl of the fine Duyckinck punch;[2] but that the muzzle which all men wore on their souls in the Elizabethan day, might not have intercepted Shakspere's full articulations. For I hold it a verity, that even Shakspeare, was not a frank man to the uttermost. And, indeed, who in this intolerant Universe is, or can be? But the Declaration of Independence makes a difference.—There, I have driven my horse so hard that I have made my inn before sundown.[3] I was going to say something more—It was this.—You complain that Emerson tho' a denizen of the land of gingerbread, is above munching a plain cake in company of jolly fellows, & swiging off his ale like you & me,[4] Ah, my dear sir, that's his misfortune, not his fault. His belly, sir, is in his chest, & his brains descend down into his neck, & offer an obstacle to a draught of ale or a mouthful of cake. But here I am. Good bye—   H. M.

NEW YORK September 22. *Duyckinck prints a two-page review of* Week *in the* Literary World. *For the most part he is kind to the book he had refused to publish, but he concludes with a complaint:*

The author, we perceive, announces another book, "Walden, or Life in the Woods." We are not so rash or uninformed in the ways of the world as to presume to give counsel to a transcendentalist, so

1. *Snob* has changed meaning drastically. Melville means a fawning, obsequious admirer of a superior; his *snob* has the force of the vulgar modern noun *a suck up*.
2. The Astor Hotel (opened 1836) on Broadway between Vesey and Barclay was the first great hotel in the city. On July 31, 1847, the day before he turned twenty-eight and a few days before his marriage, Melville dined with Evert A. Duyckinck in the great saloon (one hundred by fifty-two feet, Corinthian columns, a colonnade at either end, and a scenic ceiling), then went into the Bartlett and Welford bookstore in the ground floor. Dr. John W. Francis's male-only Sunday evenings in his house on Bond Street were the choicest in New York City, followed by the salon held by Evert A. and George L. Duyckinck in Clinton Place. A New York basement in an upper-class house had windows above ground level. It conventionally held the kitchen (from which food was conveyed upstairs to the dining room), and it could be, as the Duyckinck basement was, elegantly furnished, and comfortable for male guests, because smoking was encouraged there as it might not be upstairs, and sociable drinking was expected.
3. Merrell R. Davis and William H. Gilman, the editors of Melville's *Letters* (1960), explain this "before sundown" passage: "Melville saw that he was approaching the end of the page and in order to make his final comments tightened the spacing."
4. As in *The Confidence-Man* (chapter 30) Melville takes Malvolio in Shakespeare's *Twelfth Night* as a Puritan killjoy, unhappy himself and unwilling that others might take pleasure. Sir Toby, Olivia's kinsman, challenges him (quoted from Melville's Hilliard, Gray edition, 2.3.115): "Dost thou think, because thou art virtuous, there shall be no more cakes and ale?" The Duyckinck circle used this "cakes and ale" passage as a touchstone for defining themselves as good fellows in contrast to uptight Yankees, yet Duyckinck, an Episcopalian, was always uneasy with the freedom of Melville's religious speculations and condemned him sternly in his review of *Moby-Dick*.

we offer no advice; but we may remark as a curious matter of speculation to be solved in the future—the probability or improbability of Mr. Thoreau's ever approaching nearer to the common sense or common wisdom of mankind. He deprecates churches and preachers. Will he allow us to uphold them? or does he belong to the family of Malvolios, whose conceit was so engrossing that it threatened to deprive the world of cakes and ale. "Dost thou think that because thou readest Confucius and art a Confusion there shall be no more steeples and towers? Aye, and bells shall ring too and Bishops shall dine!"

1850

NEW YORK Spring or Summer? *Melville borrows* "Thoreaus Merrimack" *from Duyckinck, and—as Oliver argues—very possibly reads the following passages from* "Wednesday":

If one abates a little the price of his wood, or gives a neighbor his vote at town-meeting, or a barrel of apples, or lends him his wagon frequently, it is esteemed a rare instance of Friendship. . . . Most contemplate only what would be the accidental and trifling advantages of Friendship, as that the Friend can assist in time of need, by his substance, or his influence, or his counsel; but he who foresees such advantages in this relation proves himself blind to its real advantage, or indeed wholly inexperienced in the relation itself. Such services are particular and menial, compared with the perpetual and all-embracing service which it is. * * * We do not wish for Friends to feed and clothe our bodies,—neighbors are kind enough for that,—but to do the like office to our spirits. * * *

Friendship is, at any rate, a relation of perfect equality. It cannot well spare any outward sign of equal obligation and advantage.

Nothing is so difficult as to help a Friend in matters which do not require the aid of Friendship, but only a cheap and trivial service. * * *

NEW YORK July or before. *Melville reads* The Scarlet Letter, *and presumably reads this passage in the introductory* "Custom House" *essay:*

After my fellowship of toil and impracticable schemes, with the dreamy brethren of Brook Farm; after living for three years within the subtile influence of an intellect like Emerson's; after those wild, free days on the Assabeth, indulging fantastic speculations beside our fire of fallen boughs, with Ellery Channing; after talking with Thoreau about pine-trees and Indian relics, in his hermitage at Walden; after growing fastidious by sympathy with the classic refinement of Hillard's culture; after becoming imbued with poetic sentiment at Longfellow's hearth-stone;—it was time, at length, that I should exercise other faculties of my nature, and nourish myself with food for which I had hitherto had little appetite. Even the old Inspector was desirable, as a change of diet, to a man who had known Alcott.

PITTSFIELD Early August. *Melville reads Hawthorne's introduction to* Mosses from an Old Manse (*New York: Wiley and Putnam, 1846*), *in which these passages occur:*

In furtherance of my design, and as if to leave me no pretext for not fulfilling it, there was, in the rear of the house, the most delightful little nook of a study that ever offered its snug seclusion to a scholar. It was here that Emerson wrote "Nature;" for he was then an inhabitant of the Manse, and used to watch the Assyrian dawn and Paphian sunset and moonrise, from the summit of our eastern hill. * * *

The site is identified by the spear and arrow-heads, the chisels, and other implements of war, labor, and the chase, which the plough turns up from the soil. You see a splinter of stone, half hidden between a sod; it looks like nothing worthy of note; but, if you have faith enough to pick it up, behold a relic! Thoreau, who has a strange faculty of finding what the Indians have left behind them, first set me on the search; and I afterwards enriched myself with some very perfect specimens, so rudely wrought that it seemed almost as if chance had fashioned them. * * *

The pond-lily grows abundantly along the margin; that delicious flower which, as Thoreau tells me, opens its virgin bosom to the first sunlight, and perfects its being through the magic of that genial kiss. He has beheld beds of them unfolding in due succession, as the sunrise stole gradually from flower to flower; a sight not to be hoped for, unless when a poet adjusts his inward eye to a proper focus with the outward organ.

PITTSFIELD Late July or early August? *Although he does not mention it in his review of Hawthorne's* Mosses *in* The Literary World (*August 17 and 24, Melville presumably reads "The Celestial Railroad," an allegorical satire on aspects of American optimism and progressivism, including Transcendentalism.*

LENOX September 3–6. *Melville visits the Hawthornes at their cottage by Stockbridge Bowl, after they learn he was the anonymous author of the review in* The Literary World.[5]

He was very careful not to interrupt Mr Hawthorne's mornings—

5. This item, not known in 1951, is printed from the Supplement in Jay Leyda, *The Melville Log* (New York: Gordian Press, 1969), 925, by permission of the publisher.

when he was here. He generally walked off somewhere—& one morning he shut himself into the boudoir & read Mr Emerson's Essays in presence of our beautiful picture. In the afternoon he walked with Mr Hawthorne. He told me he was naturally so silent a man that he was complained of a great deal on this account; but that he found himself talking to Mr Hawthorne to a great extent. He said Mr Hawthorne's great but hospitable silence drew him out— that it was astonishing how *sociable* his silence was. (This Mr Emerson used to feel) He said sometimes they would walk along without talking on either side, but that even then they seemed to be very social.—[Sophia Hawthorne to her sister Elizabeth Peabody; the picture was an engraving of the Transfiguration, a gift from Emerson.]

LENOX September 5 or 6. *In the Hawthornes' "boudoir" Melville reads Emerson's* Essays, *perhaps reacting hostilely to passages like these from "Friendship":*

Friendship may be said to require natures so rare and costly, each so well tempered and so happily adapted, and withal so circumstanced (for even in that particular, a poet says, love demands that the parties be altogether paired), that its satisfaction can very seldom be assured. It cannot subsist in its perfection, say some of those who are learned in this warm lore of the heart, betwixt more than two. I am not quite so strict in my terms, perhaps because I have never known so high a fellowship as others. I please my imagination more with a circle of godlike men and women variously related to each other and between whom subsists a lofty intelligence. But I find this law of *one to one* peremptory for conversation, which is the practice and consummation of friendship. * * *

Let us buy our entrance to this guild by a long probation. Why should we desecrate noble and beautiful souls by intruding on them? Why insist on rash personal relations with your friends? Why go to his house, or know his mother and brother and sisters? Why be visited by him at your own? Are these things material to our covenant? Leave this touching and clawing. Let him be to me a spirit. A message, a thought, a sincerity, a glance from him, I want, but not news, nor pottage. I can get politics and chat and neighborly conveniences from cheaper companions. Should not the society of my friend be to me poetic, pure, universal and great as nature itself?

1851

LENOX and PITTSFIELD October 1850–November 1851. *While they are neighbors, Melville and Hawthorne visit each other several times. They talk metaphysics, but they also gossip. In his old age Melville tells Theodore F. Wolfe an anecdote about Hawthorne's and his daughter Una's several-day (not a week-long) visit to the Melvilles in March, 1851:*

* * * Melville was often at the little red house, where the children knew him as "Mr. Omoo," and less often Hawthorne came to chat with the racy romancer and philosopher by the great chimney. Once he was accompanied by little Una—"Onion" he sometimes called her—and remained a whole week. This visit—certainly unique in the life of the shy Hawthorne—was the topic when, not so long agone, we last looked upon the living face of Melville in his city home. March weather prevented walks abroad, so the pair spent most of the week in smoking and talking metaphysics in the barn,—Hawthorne usually lounging upon a carpenter's bench. When he was leaving, he jocosely declared he would write a report of their psychological discussions for publication in a volume to be called "A Week on a Work-Bench in a Barn," the title being a travesty upon that of Thoreau's then recent book, "A Week on Concord River," etc. (*Literary Shrines*, Philadelphia, 1895, pp. 190–191.)

1852

CONCORD December 2. *On a day when Thoreau was apparently in the village, Melville visits the Hawthornes.*

1854

NEW YORK October. *Thoreau's* Walden *receives a four-page, two-column-per-page review in the issue of* Putnam's Monthly Magazine *which contains Chapter 13 of Melville's* Israel Potter. *The reviewer prints long excerpts from "Economy" and enough of "Solitude" to appall the author of the chapter of* Moby-Dick *called "The Castaway." In the passage quoted, Thoreau declares that he has* "never felt lonesome"; "Why should I feel lonely? Is not our planet in the Milky Way?"

1862[6]

NEW YORK March 22. *M. acquires two volumes by Ralph Waldo Emerson:* Essays. First Series (*Boston, 1847*), & Essays: Second Series (*Boston, 1844*). In the First Series M marks in Essay IV, "Spiritual Laws," p. 126:

[Each man] inclines to do something which is easy to him, and good when it is done, but which no other man can do. He has no ri-

---

6. This item is in Jay Leyda's original 1951 *The Melville Log* but is reprinted here from the 1969 edition, by permission of the publisher. The *x*'s and asterisk are Melville's devices for keying his marginalia to Emerson's text.

val. For the more truly he consults his own powers, the more difference will his work exhibit from the work of any other.

M's comment: True

His ambition is exactly proportioned to his powers.

M's comment: False

& *on p 133:*

The good, compared to the evil which he sees, is as his own good to his own evil. X

M's comment: X A Perfectly good being, therefore, would see no evil.—But what did Christ see?—He saw what made him weep.—However, too, the "Philanthropist"[7] must have been a very bad man—he saw, in jails, so much evil.

M appends additional comment: * To annihilate all this nonsense read the Sermon on the Mount,[8] and consider what it implies.

In Essay VII, "Prudence," M marks on p. 215:

Trust men, and they will be true to you; treat them greatly, and they will show themselves great, though they make an exception in your favor to all their rules of trade. X

M's comment: X God help the poor fellow who squares his life according to this.

& *on p 216:*

The drover, the sailor, buffets it [the storm] all day, and his health renews itself as vigorous a pulse under the sleet, as under the sun of June. X

M's comment: X To one who has weathered Cape Horn as a common sailor what stuff all this is.

In the Second Series (*mistakenly inscribed "March 22, 1861"*) *M marks in Essay I, "The Poet," p. 20:*

Also, we use defects and deformities to a sacred purpose, so expressing our sense that the evils of the world are such only to the evil eye. X

M's comment: X What does the man mean? If Mr Emerson travelling in Egypt should find the plague-spot come out on him—would he consider that an evil sight or not? And if evil, would his eye be evil because it seemed evil to his eye, or rather to his sense using the eye for instrument?

& *on p 24:*

---

7. John Howard (1726–1790), Englishman who used his great inherited fortune to reform prison conditions in the United Kingdom, the Continent, and even Russia, where he died. There were other great English reformers, but to Melville's generation "The Philanthropist" meant one man, John Howard.

8. Beginning with the Beatitudes (the series of declarations of what actions characterize those who are to be blessed) and containing what is known as the Lord's Prayer as well as instructions on renouncing materialism, on forgiveness of others, and on acknowledging one's own sins rather than noticing the sins of others, the Sermon on the Mount (Matthew 5–7) is the fullest and most specific account of the behavior Jesus expected of his followers.

As the limestone of the continent consists of infinite masses of the shells of animalcules, so language is made up of images, or tropes, which now, in their secondary use, have long ceased to remind us of their poetic origin. But the poet names the thing because he sees it, or comes one step nearer to it than any other. X

M's comment: X This is admirable, as many other thoughts of Mr Emerson's are. His gross and astonishing errors & illusions spring from a self-conceit so intensely intellectual and calm that at first one hesitates to call it by its right name. Another species of Mr Emerson's errors, or rather, blindness, proceeds from a defect in the region of the heart.

& *on p 30–31:*

Hence a great number of such as were professionally expressors of Beauty, as painters, poets, musicians, and actors, have been more than others wont to lead a life of pleasure and indulgence; all but the few who received the true nectar; and, as it was an emancipation not into the heavens, but into the freedom of baser places, they were punished for that advantage they won, by a dissipation and deterioration.

M's comment: No, no, no.—Titian—did he deteriorate?—Byron?— Did he.—Mr E. is horribly narrow here. He has his Dardenelles for his every Marmora.—But he keeps nobly on, for all that!

CARL VAN VECHTEN

[The Great Satire of Transcendentalism]†

Let us remember Melville's struggle for faith and the apparent collapse of his career as we approach "The Confidence Man," his last work in prose, save, perhaps, some fugitive magazine pieces

---

† From "The Later Work of Herman Melville," *The Double Dealer: A National Magazine from the South*, 3 (January, 1922), 19. *The Confidence-Man* had been almost forgotten until Van Vechten, then a minor novelist, marveled in the *Double Dealer* that no one had recognized Melville's purpose in writing the book. Declaring that "Emerson's fatuous essay on Friendship is required preparatory reading," Van Vechten pronounced *The Confidence-Man* to be "the great transcendental satire." Later critics sometimes misunderstood the phrase, but the context makes clear that Van Vechten meant that the book was "the great satire of Transcendentalism," the title adopted here. His wistful, wishful concluding question applies to readers of the twenty-first century as well as it did to H. M. Tomlinson (1873–1958), the English novelist who was an eager champion of Melville in what became known as the Melville Revival of the decade after the centennial of Melville's birth, 1919.

The *Double Dealer* (1921–26), an avant-grade New Orleans magazine, published Ernest Hemingway, Sherwood Anderson, and William Faulkner. Van Vechten's essay thus reached a national audience of writers and artists. Van Vechten (1880–1964), a distant cousin of Melville's and wealthy, as the Van Vechtens of Albany were in Melville's own time, is remembered as an early champion of black writers of the Harlem Renaissance, whom he supported with money, with his journalism, and with his celebrity photographs of Harlem luminaries. His friendship with Langston Hughes is documented in *Remember Me to Harlem: The Letters of Langston Hughes and Carl Van Vechten* (2001).

and a privately printed book or two. It is not a novel, nor is it, as Frank Mather Jewett ingenuously suggests, a series of "middle-western sketches." Melville simply carried Brook Farm to the deck of a Mississippi steamboat as in "Mardi" he had carried Europe to the South Seas. Emerson is the confidence man, Emerson who preached being good, not doing good, behaviour rather than service. Why no one has heretofore recognized Melville's purpose in writing this book is a fact I cannot profess to understand. Perhaps some one has, but I can find no record of the discovery. Probably dozens of critics have been influenced by the misleading comments of their forebears into not reading the book at all. At any rate, here Melville has his revenge on those who accused him earlier in his career of transcendental learnings. This is the great transcendental satire. The work assumes the form of a series of dialogues, some-what after the manner of W. H. Mallock's "The New Republic,"[1] ironic dialogues between the representatives of theory and practice, transcendentalism and reality, with the devil's advocate winning the victory. Emerson's fatuous essay on Friendship is required prepara-tory reading for this book. "If a drunkard in a sober fit is the dullest of mortals, an enthusiast in a reason-fit is not the most lively," is a good summing up of Ralph Waldo's "lofty and enthralling circus." Hawthorne may have been secretly pleased with this book, if he un-derstood it, because Emerson confessedly had never been able to finish a book by the good Nathaniel. A recent commentator, H. M. Tomlinson, is content to say of it, in an otherwise glowing account of the genius of its creator, " 'The Confidence Man' is almost un-readable." I wonder if he cannot read the book with eager interest now that I have thrown this light upon it?

BRIAN HIGGINS

Mark Winsome and Egbert: "In the Friendly Spirit"†

Taking Mark Winsome as a portrait of Emerson, Elizabeth S. Foster (1954) declared that the antinomy of "Christian brotherly

---

Outed as a homosexual long before there was a Gay Pride movement, Van Vechten was especially vulnerable when reviled by some as a racist for his *Nigger Heaven* (1926), which Langston Hughes and many others defended. More than thirteen hundred of his photographs, mainly studio portraits of people notable in the arts, including white as well as black celebrities, are in the Library of Congress.

1. The English writer Mallock (1849–1923) satirized Oxford aestheticism and Hellenism in dialogues collected in *The New Republic, or Culture, Faith and Philosophy in an En-glish Country House* (London, 1878), deftly portraying John Ruskin, Matthew Arnold, Walter Pater, and other eminent Victorians.

† First published in the 1971 Norton Critical Edition; reprinted here by permission of the author.

love" and "Emersonian individualism" ("which is, after all, only a rarefied form of enlightened self-interest") is central to, and perhaps primary to, the meaning of *The Confidence-Man* (p. lxxxii). She sees *The Confidence-Man* as "a more sardonic, a more mordant, version of the contrast between chronometrical and horological ethics in *Pierre*." For that part of the Winsome-Egbert episode which treats of the propriety of a friend's helping a friend, Miss Foster's linkage of ideas is especially pertinent, for an awareness of the pervasive Christian references in the episode is essential to an understanding of its satiric intention, while a knowledge of Plinlimmon's Pamphlet in *Pierre* makes all the clearer the nature of Winsome's and Egbert's offenses.

Along with *Pierre*, *The Confidence-Man* is a study of the practicability of biblical Christianity. Throughout the book, beginning with the contrast between the words on the mute's slate and the words on the barber's sign in Chapter 1, Melville constantly uses the teachings of the New Testament as a critical touchstone for the words and actions of his characters. In the course of the Winsome-Egbert chapters the reader sees ever more clearly that, judged by the standards of absolute Christianity, the teachings of Winsome and Egbert are culpably lacking, though by the standards of the world they may be eminently commonsensical. The Christian context is established unobtrusively, but with good comic effect, early in the exposition of the practical side of Winsome's philosophy (Chapter 37, "The mystical master introduces the practical disciple."). Blandly drawing Winsome in, the cosmopolitan asks him if the study of his philosophy "tends to the same formation of character with the experiences of the world." Winsome replies:

> "It does; and that is the test of its truth; for any philosophy that, being in operation contradictory to the ways of the world, tends to produce a character at odds with it, such a philosophy must necessarily be but a cheat and a dream."

His statement may at first sound reasonable, but given Melville's habitual unfavorable contrast of "this world" with another world of more absolute values, it must be recognized as insidious.[1] By implication Winsome is airily dismissing Christianity, along with any other philosophy "in operation contradictory to the ways of the world." Melville clearly enough designed Winsome's teachings to

---

1. It is, moreover, too complacent. Compare Winsome's attitude with that of the "earnest, or enthusiastic youth" in *Pierre* who discovers the disparity between what "good and wise people sincerely say" about the world and what the New Testament says about it: "unless he prove recreant, or unless he prove gullible, or unless he can find the talismanic secret, to reconcile this world with his own soul, then there is no peace for him, no slightest truth for him in this life." Winsome's conclusion that "mouth and purse must be filled" is hardly the talismanic secret Melville had in mind.

oppose those of the New Testament so persistently that biblical passages would be evoked to provide a silent judgment on Winsome's pronouncements. The Winsome *vs.* Christ opposition furnishes a chief source of humor for the episode in the dramatic irony of Winsome's and Egbert's cool sense of the viability of their own views and the reader's consciousness of the unstated but critically operative ethic which damns them.

Winsome's philosophy, as relayed through Egbert, is finally reduced in Chapter 41 to "the folly, on both sides, of a friend's helping a friend."[2] The contrast with the teachings of the New Testament could not be more obvious or specific, for Jesus commands his followers: "Give to him that asketh thee, and from him that would borrow of thee turn not thou away" (Matt. 5:42). Clearly, from this New Testament point of view, where the man that has two coats is told to "impart to him that hath none" (Luke 3:11), arguments about the delicate nature of friendship scarcely justify Egbert's denial of the Christian injunction to give. In fairness to Egbert, he would not completely deny relief to a friend, if that friend renounced the friendship and applied "only as a fellow-being":

> "Take off your hat, bow over to the ground, and supplicate an alms of me in the way of London streets, and you shall not be a sturdy beggar in vain. But no man drops pennies into the hat of a friend, let me tell you. If you turn beggar, then, for the honor of noble friendship, I turn stranger."

The circumstances under which this hypothetical aid is to be given hardly redound to Egbert's credit, and the New Testament again furnishes the relevant criticism: Egbert's hypothetical giving is Pharasaical. Gospel generosity has no prescribed limits, as in the unconditional command in Luke 6:30: "Give to every man that asketh of thee; and of him that taketh away thy goods ask them not again." Furthermore, Egbert's contemptuous alms-giving is opposed to the spirit as well as the letter of the New Testament, violating the passage first suggested by the message of the mute from I Cor. 13:3:

2. While the identification of Winsome with Emerson is demonstrable enough, the justness of Melville's harsh portrait is open to question. There are passages in Emerson's essay on "Friendship" which quite contradict what Egbert says. In contrast to Egbert's celestial relationship, Emerson's friendship can serve terrestrial ends: "It is for aid and comfort through all the relations and passages of life and death." While Egbert speaks of the "delicacy" of friendship, Emerson does "not wish to treat friendship daintily, but with roughest courage." When friends "are real, they are not glass threads, or frostwork, but the solidest thing we know." But there are also in the essay passages assertive of a high sense of self which could easily be interpreted not as a refining to sublimity but as a refining away of friendship. The inconsistencies are not irreconcilable, but without a fairly elaborate defense there is more than sufficient in the essay to create a Winsome from, and one can easily enough see the way in which the essay could represent for Melville that aspect of "non-benevolence" in "Emerson's intense individualism" (Foster, p. lxxvii) and an insidiously paradoxical view of man which exalts him yet treats him without charity.

> And though I bestow all my goods to feed the poor, and
> though I give my body to be burned, and have not charity, it
> profiteth me nothing.

Egbert is oblivious or indifferent to the Christ who is ministered to
when one ministers unto the least of one of his brethren. His refusal to lend even to a friend is a grotesque inversion of Jesus' injunctions to lend to anyone, not merely "to them of whom ye hope
to receive" (Luke 6:34).

A further fault with Winsome's philosophy in the hands of Egbert
is that, in its exaltation of friendship above worldly considerations
such as helping a friend in need, it degenerates into a worldliness
worse than the one it would avoid. In asserting a celestial relationship which can be elevated and sustained above worldly considerations, Egbert is on the surface a counter to Melville's Plinlimmon
who deprecates the introduction of the celestial into terrestrial
situations. In fact, Egbert's views on friendship become so inex-
tricably mixed with mercenary considerations—the avoidance of
relationships likely to prove an embarrassment for pecuniary reasons, the elaborate defense against giving a loan—that Egbert appears ultimately like nothing so much as Plinlimmon's horological
average son-of-man who mixes his Christianity with prudential considerations of worldly practicality. Plinlimmon considers that "the
God at the Heavenly Greenwich" does not "expect common men to
keep Greenwich wisdom in this remote Chinese world of ours; *because such a thing were unprofitable for them here*" (italics added).
He proposes that men be given a horological (or terrestrial) substitute to chronometrical (or celestial) teaching, "while still retaining
every common-sense incentive to whatever of virtue be practicable
and desirable" (from a horological point of view, of course). Plinlimmon's final judgment on the teachings of Christ is this:

> so far as practical results are concerned—regarded in a purely
> earthly light—the only great moral doctrine of Christianity . . .
> has been found (horologically) a false one. . . .

The joke with Plinlimmon is that he introduces worldly considerations as a criticism of a teaching which explicitly denies the validity
of such considerations, a teaching which denies the worth of the
world and counsels men to reject it in favor of something higher.

Egbert is guilty of a similar confusion of the worldly and the
unworldly in his account of the beginning of his friendship with
Frank—a not injudicious beginning, on his part, for he first
weighed Frank's favorable points, not the least of which, he tells
Frank, "were your good manners, handsome dress, and your parents' rank and repute of wealth." He chose his mutton "Not for its

leanness, but its fatness." Egbert's intention was to "preserve inviolate" by these means "the delicacy of the connection":

> "For—do but think of it—what more distressing to delicate
> friendship, formed early, than your friend's eventually, in man-
> hood, dropping in of a rainy night for his little loan of five dol-
> lars or so? Can delicate friendship stand that?"

Apart from the irony of Egbert's strange delicacy, there is the same
confusion of the celestial and terrestrial, the same consideration of
the celestial from a terrestrial point of view that is characteristic of
the Pamphlet. Both here and in his earlier account of loans as "unfriendly accommodations" Egbert demonstrates the misplacing of
reason, prudence, and worldly considerations that marks Plinlimmon's treatment of the Sermon on the Mount.

There are also links between Winsome and the Pamphlet, as in
the mystic's assertion that any philosophy contradictory to the ways
of the world is "a cheat and a dream." Here Winsome denies, in effect, the validity of Christianity for the same reasons given by Plinlimmon:

> Few of us doubt, gentlemen, that human life on this earth is
> but a state of probation; which among other things implies,
> that here below, we mortals have only to do with things provi-
> sional. Accordingly, I hold that all our so-called wisdom is like-
> wise but provisional. . . .

Winsome's words are also similar to Plinlimmon's advice that "in
things terrestrial" a man "must not be governed by ideas celestial."
A particularly specific link between Winsome and Plinlimmon is
the mystic's reference to Francis Bacon: "Was not Seneca a usurer?
Bacon a courtier? and Swedenborg, though with one eye on the invisible, did he not keep the other on the main chance?" In the Pamphlet, which seems indebted to a number of Bacon's essays, Bacon
is a type of worldly practicality. For Melville, Bacon represented
the commonsensical, pragmatic, expedient, nominal Christian—the
same kind of Christian Melville was satirizing through Plinlimmon.
It is obviously appropriate that Bacon be mentioned approvingly by
Winsome, who in his own way shares the same characteristics.[3]
Winsome's insistence on his being "a man of serviceable knowledge" and a "a man of the world" again brings him within the terms
of the Pamphlet and its satirical intention. Likewise the joke
against Egbert that "he might, with the characteristic knack of the
true New-Englander, turn even so profitless a thing [as mysticism]

3. There is further irony in Bacon's thought being by implication balanced against his practical actions as a man of the world, when for Melville Bacon's philosophy represents the
essence of worldliness. It is a neat little joke against Winsome that he should pick on Bacon for an example, at least by implication, of unworldly vision in his writings.

to some profitable account," and the insistence on Egbert as the *practical* disciple, serves to keep before us the Pamphlet's frame of reference and its satire on precisely this practicality and profitableness and serviceability.

While knowledge of Plinlimmon's Pamphlet is not essential to an understanding of the Winsome-Egbert episode, an acquaintance with Melville's satiric intention in that document enables us to see more readily the nature of his satire in the episode and the standpoint from which he is condemning Winsome and Egbert. As a corollary, the episode demonstrates the similarity of the terms in which Melville was thinking in 1852 and four years later when he wrote *The Confidence-Man*.

Melville and the Devil in the Bible and Popular Literature

NATHANIEL HAWTHORNE

[A Satanic Beggar; The Devil in Popular Stories]†

*   *   *

While the merry girl and myself were busy with the show-box,[1] the unceasing rain had driven another wayfarer into the wagon. He seemed pretty nearly of the old show-man's age, but much smaller, leaner, and more withered than he, and less respectably clad in a patched suit of gray; withal, he had a thin, shrewd countenance, and a pair of diminutive gray eyes, which peeped rather too keenly out of their puckered sockets. This old fellow had been joking with the show-man, in a manner which intimated previous acquaintance; but perceiving that the damsel and I had terminated our affairs, he drew forth a folded document and presented it to me. As I had anticipated, it proved to be a circular, written in a very fair and legible hand, and signed by several distinguished gentlemen whom I had never heard of, stating that the bearer had encountered every variety of misfortune, and recommending him to the notice of all charitable people. Previous disbursements had left me no more than a five dollar bill, out of which, however, I offered to make the beggar a donation, provided he would give me change for it. The object of my beneficence looked keenly in my face, and discerned that I had none of that abominable spirit, characteristic though it be, of a full-blooded Yankee, which takes pleasure in detecting every little harmless piece of knavery.

† From "The Seven Vagabonds," in *Twice-Told Tales* (Boston: James Munroe and Company, 1842), 2.174–75, 177–79. Melville knew the story from a copy of this edition given to him by Hawthorne. All notes are the editors'.
1. Most of the story is set in "a huge covered wagon, or, more properly, a small house on wheels," in which the "wandering show man" exhibits "a multitude of little people assembled on a miniature stage." When the proprietor turns the handle of a barrel organ, the figures move according to their occupations, the blacksmith hammering, and so on. The show box referred to is "a neat mahogany box," about two feet square, just brought into the wagon by a young man and girl. The narrator puts his eye to a magnifying window in the box to watch a succession of European scenes displayed by the girl.

'Why, perhaps,' said the ragged old mendicant,[2] 'if the bank is in good standing, I can't say but I may have enough about me to change your bill.'

'It is a bill of the Suffolk Bank,' said I, 'and better than the specie.'

As the beggar had nothing to object, he now produced a small buff leather bag, tied up carefully with a shoe-string. When this was opened, there appeared a very comfortable treasure of silver coins, of all sorts and sizes, and I even fancied that I saw, gleaming among them, the golden plumage of that rare bird in our currency, the American Eagle.[3] In this precious heap was my bank note deposited, the rate of exchange being considerably against me. * * *

* * * Having already satisfied myself as to the several modes in which the four others attained felicity, I next set my mind at work to discover what enjoyments were peculiar to the old "Straggler," as the people of the country would have termed the wandering mendicant and prophet. As he pretended to familiarity with the Devil; so I fancied that he was fitted to pursue and take delight in his way of life, by possessing some of the mental and moral characteristics, the lighter and more comic ones, of the Devil in popular stories. Among them might be reckoned a love of deception for its own sake, a shrewd eye and keen relish for human weakness and ridiculous infirmity, and the talent of petty fraud. Thus to this old man there would be pleasure even in the consciousness so insupportable to some minds, that his whole life was a cheat upon the world, and that so far as he was concerned with the public, his little cunning had the upper hand of its united wisdom. Every day would furnish him with a succession of minute and pungent triumphs; as when, for instance, his importunity wrung a pittance out of the heart of a miser, or when my silly good nature transferred a part of my slender purse to his plump leather bag; or when some ostentatious gentleman should throw a coin to the ragged beggar who was richer than himself; or when, though he would not always be so decidedly diabolical, his pretended wants should make him a sharer in the scanty living of real indigence. And then what an inexhaustible field of enjoyment, both as enabling him to discern so much folly and achieve such quantities of minor mischief, was opened to his sneering spirit by his pretensions to prophetic knowledge.

All this was a sort of happiness which I could conceive of, though I had little sympathy with it. Perhaps had I been then inclined to admit it, I might have found that the roving life was more

2. Beggar.
3. Gold coin worth ten dollars in the 1840s and 1850s.

proper to him than to either of his companions; for Satan, to whom I had compared the poor man, has delighted, ever since the time of Job, in 'wandering up and down upon the earth;' and indeed a crafty disposition, which operates not in deep laid plans, but in disconnected tricks, could not have an adequate scope, unless naturally impelled to a continual change of scene and society. * * *

NATHANIEL HAWTHORNE

The Celestial Railroad†

Not a great while ago, passing through the gate of dreams, I visited that region of the earth in which lies the famous city of Destruction. It interested me much to learn, that, by the public spirit of some of the inhabitants, a railroad has recently been established between this populous and flourishing town, and the Celestial City. Having a little time upon my hands, I resolved to gratify a liberal curiosity by making a trip thither. Accordingly, one fine morning, after paying my bill at the hotel, and directing the porter to stow my luggage behind a coach, I took my seat in the vehicle, and set out for the Station-house. It was my good fortune to enjoy the company of a gentleman—one Mr. Smooth-it-away[1]—who, though he had never actually visited the Celestial City, yet seemed as well acquainted with its laws, customs, policy, and statistics, as with those of the city of Destruction, of which he was a native townsman. Being, moreover, a director of the railroad corporation, and one of its

† First published in the New York *United States Magazine and Democratic Review* (May 1843), the source of the present text. The editors of the Centenary Edition of *Mosses from an Old Manse* (1974) were allowed to compare the manuscript (privately owned) with the first printing; at two points, noted here, the manuscript readings replace errors in the magazine. Like most American Protestants, Hawthorne from childhood had been familiar with *Pilgrim's Progress* (published in two parts, 1678 and 1684), the religious allegory by John Bunyan (1628–1688), a self-taught English tinsmith, soldier, and dissenting minister. The pilgrim of the title is Christian, who makes his way from this sinful world to heaven. The full title summarizes the plot: *The Pilgrim's Progress from This World to That Which Is to Come, Delivered under the Similitude of a Dream wherein Is Discovered the Manner of His Setting Out, His Dangerous Journey, and Safe Arrival at the Desired Country. Progress* here means advancement toward a goal. In Hawthorne's satire, the narrator uses *Pilgrim's Progress* as a reliable map of the topography between the City of Destruction and the Celestial City but is unaware of the moral and psychological significances of the terrain the soul must pass through on its arduous journey to perfection. Mr. Smooth-it-away succeeds insofar as he lulls the narrator into disregarding Bunyan's message that the way to heaven is solitary and arduous, but he finds in the narrator a very modern optimist imbued with the catchphrases of civic boosterism, ready to believe that the smoothest way is the best way. The railroad, in the 1840s the preeminent symbol of progress, for Hawthorne is the perfect symbol for the ultimate modern improvement, a fast easy way to heaven. All notes are the editors'.

1. As his name suggests, he will brush away any doubts about modern improvements that arise in the mind of the narrator, a civic-minded gentleman already disposed to welcome all change as progress.

largest stockholders, he had it in his power to give me all desirable information respecting that praiseworthy enterprise.

Our coach rattled out of the city, and, at a short distance from its outskirts, passed over a bridge, of elegant construction, but somewhat too slight, as I imagined, to sustain any considerable weight. On both sides lay an extensive quagmire, which could not have been more disagreeable either to sight or smell, had all the kennels of the earth emptied their pollution there.

"This," remarked Mr. Smooth-it-away, "is the famous Slough of Despond[2]—a disgrace to all the neighborhood; and the greater, that it might so easily be converted into firm ground."

"I have understood," said I, "that efforts have been made for that purpose, from time immemorial. Bunyan mentions that above twenty thousand cart-loads of wholesome instructions had been thrown in here, without effect."

"Very probably!—and what effect could be anticipated from such unsubstantial stuff?" cried Mr. Smooth-it-away. "You observe this convenient bridge. We obtained a sufficient foundation for it, by throwing into the Slough some editors of books of morality, volumes of French philosophy and German rationalism, tracts, sermons, and essays of modern clergymen, extracts from Plato, Confucius, and various Hindoo sages, together with a few ingenious commentaries upon texts of Scripture—all of which, by some scientific process, have been converted into a mass like granite. The whole bog might be filled up with similar matter."[3]

It really seemed to me, however, that the bridge vibrated and heaved up and down, in a very formidable manner; and, spite of Mr. Smooth-it-away's testimony to the solidity of its foundation, I should be loth to cross it in a crowded omnibus; especially, if each passenger were encumbered with as heavy luggage as that gentleman and myself. Nevertheless, we got over without accident, and

2. In *Pilgrim's Progress* when Christian is mired in the mud of the slough a man "whose name was Help" pulls him out and explains, "This miry slough is such a place as cannot be mended: it is the descent whither the scum and filth that attends conviction for sin doth continually run, and therefore it is called the Slough of Despond; for still, as the sinner is awakened about his lost condition, there arise in his soul many fears and doubts, and discouraging apprehensions, which all of them get together, and settle in this place." According to Bunyan, no quantity of "wholesome instructions" can fill up the Slough of Despond and make it dry ground: despair at sinfulness is part of human inheritance. Travelers on the Celestial Railroad happily shrug off any notion that the soul's progress toward perfection must be long and painful: for such modernists, there is no such thing as Original Sin. To call the slough merely a "quagmire" is to regard it merely as an inconvenience, not a theological crisis any earnest pilgrim must suffer and work through.

3. Repeatedly, the reader will find his or her own equivalents for characters (such as Apollyon, the satanic force modern scientists think they can safely harness) or places (such as Vanity Fair, where at the price of your soul you can buy anything you want, one time). A particular pleasure for each generation of readers of "The Celestial Railroad" is the opportunity to compile the latest modern equivalents of Hawthorne's examples of insubstantial advice.

soon found ourselves at the Station-house. This very neat and spacious edifice is erected on the site of the little Wicket-Gate, which
formerly, as all old pilgrims will recollect, stood directly across the
highway, and, by its inconvenient narrowness, was a great obstruc-
tion to the traveller of liberal mind and expansive stomach. The
reader of John Bunyan will be glad to know, that Christian's old
friend Evangelist, who was accustomed to supply each pilgrim with
a mystic roll,[4] now presides at the ticket-office. Some malicious
persons, it is true, deny the identity of this reputable character with
the Evangelist of old times, and even pretend to bring competent
evidence of an imposture. Without involving myself in the dispute,
I shall merely observe, that, so far as my experience goes, the
square pieces of pasteboard, now delivered to passengers, are much
more convenient and useful along the road, than the antique roll of
parchment. Whether they will be as readily received at the gate of
the Celestial City, I decline giving an opinion.

A large number of passengers were already at the Station-house,
awaiting the departure of the cars. By the aspect and demeanor of
these persons, it was easy to judge that the feelings of the community had undergone a very favorable change, in reference to the celestial pilgrimage. It would have done Bunyan's heart good to see it.
Instead of a lonely and ragged man, with a huge burthen[5] on his
back, plodding along sorrowfully on foot, while the whole city
hooted after him, here were parties of the first gentry and most respectable people in the neighborhood, setting forth towards the Celestial City, as cheerfully as if the pilgrimage were merely a summer
tour. Among the gentlemen were characters of deserved eminence,
magistrates, politicians, and men of wealth, by whose example
religion could not but be greatly recommended to their meaner
brethren. In the ladies' apartment, too, I rejoiced to distinguish
some of those flowers of fashionable society, who are so well fitted
to adorn the most elevated circles of the Celestial City. There was
much pleasant conversation about the news of the day, topics of
business, politics, or the lighter matters of amusement; while religion, though indubitably the main thing at heart, was thrown taste-
fully into the back ground. Even an infidel would have heard little
or nothing to shock his sensibility.

One great convenience of the new method of going on pilgrimage, I must not forget to mention. Our enormous burthens, instead
of being carried on our shoulders, as had been the custom of old,

4. In *Pilgrim's Progress* Evangelist gives Christian a parchment roll in which is written "Fly
   from the wrath to come," Bunyan's paraphrase of John the Baptist as quoted in Matthew 3.7: "O generation of vipers, who hath warned you to flee from the wrath to come?"
5. Burden. The true pilgrim must carry his or her burden of sins, not check them in the
   baggage car.

were all snugly deposited in the baggage-car, and, as I was assured, would be delivered to their respective owners at the journey's end. Another thing likewise, the benevolent reader will be delighted to understand. It may be remembered that there was an ancient feud between Prince Beelzebub[6] and the keeper of the Wicket-Gate, and that the adherents of the former distinguished personage were accustomed to shoot deadly arrows at honest pilgrims, while knocking at the door. This dispute, much to the credit as well of the illustrious potentate above-mentioned, as of the worthy and enlightened Directors of the railroad, has been pacifically arranged, on the principle of mutual compromise. The Prince's subjects are now pretty numerously employed about the Station-house, some in taking care of the baggage, others in collecting fuel, feeding the engines, and such congenial occupations; and I can conscientiously affirm, that persons more attentive to their business, more willing to accommodate, or more generally agreeable to the passengers, are not to be found on any railroad. Every good heart must surely exult at so satisfactory an arrangement of an immemorial difficulty.

"Where is Mr. Great-heart?" inquired I. "Beyond a doubt, the Directors have engaged that famous old champion to be chief conductor on the railroad?"

"Why, no," said Mr. Smooth-it-away, with a dry cough. "He was offered the situation of brake-man; but, to tell you the truth, our friend Great-heart has grown preposterously stiff and narrow, in his old age. He has so often guided pilgrims over the road, on foot, that he considers it a sin to travel in any other fashion. Besides, the old fellow had entered so heartily into the ancient feud with Prince Beelzebub, that he would have been perpetually at blows or ill language with some of the prince's subjects, and thus have embroiled us anew. So, on the whole, we were not sorry when honest Great-heart went off to the Celestial City in a huff, and left us at liberty to choose a more suitable and accommodating man. Yonder comes the conductor of the train. You will probably recognize him at once."

The engine at this moment took its station in advance of the cars, looking, I must confess, much more like a sort of mechanical demon that would hurry us to the infernal regions, than a laudable contrivance for smoothing our way to the Celestial City. On its top sat a personage almost enveloped in smoke and flame, which—not to startle the reader—appeared to gush from his own mouth and stomach, as well as from the engine's brazen abdomen.

"Do my eyes deceive me?" cried I. "What on earth is this! A living creature?—if so, he is own brother to the engine that he rides upon!"

6. The "prince of devils" (Matthew 12.24).

"Poh, poh, you are obtuse!" said Mr. Smooth-it-away, with a hearty laugh. "Don't you know Apollyon, Christian's old enemy, with whom he fought so fierce a battle in the Valley of Humiliation? He was the very fellow to manage the engine; and so we have reconciled him to the custom of going on pilgrimage, and engaged him as chief conductor."

"Bravo, bravo!" exclaimed I, with irrepressible enthusiasm, "this shows the liberality of the age; this proves, if anything can, that all musty prejudices are in a fair way to be obliterated. And how will Christian rejoice to hear of this happy transformation of his old antagonist! I promise myself great pleasure in informing him of it, when we reach the Celestial City."

The passengers being all comfortably seated, we now rattled away merrily, accomplishing a greater distance in ten minutes than Christian probably trudged over in a day. It was laughable while we glanced along, as it were, at the tail of a thunderbolt, to observe two dusty foot-travellers, in the old pilgrim-guise, with cockle-shell[7] and staff, their mystic rolls of parchment in their hands, and their intolerable burthens on their backs. The preposterous obstinacy of these honest people, in persisting to groan and stumble along the difficult pathway, rather than take advantage of modern improvements, excited great mirth among our wiser brotherhood. We greeted the two pilgrims with many pleasant gibes and a roar of laughter; whereupon, they gazed at us with such woeful and absurdly compassionate visages, that our merriment grew tenfold more obstreperous. Apollyon, also, entered heartily into the fun, and contrived to flirt[8] the smoke and flame of the engine, or of his own breath, into their faces, and envelope them in an atmosphere of scalding steam. These little practical jokes amused us mightily, and doubtless afforded the pilgrims the gratification of considering themselves martyrs.

At some distance from the railroad, Mr. Smooth-it-away pointed to a large, antique edifice, which, he observed, was a tavern of long standing, and had formerly been a noted stopping-place for pilgrims. In Bunyan's road book it is mentioned as the Interpreter's House.

"I have long had a curiosity to visit that old mansion," remarked I.

"It is not one of our stations, as you perceive," said my companion. "The keeper was violently opposed to the railroad; and well he might be, as the track left his house of entertainment on one side, and thus was pretty certain to deprive him of all his reputable cus-

---

7. A device worn on pilgrims' hats.
8. Flick.

tomers. But the foot-path still passes his door; and the old gentleman now and then receives a call from some simple traveller, and entertains him with fare as old-fashioned as himself."

Before our talk on this subject came to a conclusion, we were rushing by the place where Christian's burthen fell from his shoulders, at the sight of the Cross. This served as a theme for Mr. Smooth-it-away, Mr. Live-for-the-world, Mr. Hide-sin-in-the-heart, Mr. Scaly-conscience, and a knot of gentlemen from the town of Shun-repentance, to descant[9] upon the inestimable advantages resulting from the safety of our baggage. Myself, and all the passengers indeed, joined with great unanimity in this view of the matter; for our burthens were rich in many things esteemed precious throughout the world; and, especially, we each of us possessed a great variety of favorite Habits, which we trusted would not be out of fashion, even in the polite circles of the Celestial City. It would have been a sad spectacle to see such an assortment of valuable articles tumbling into the sepulchre. Thus pleasantly conversing on the favorable circumstances of our position, as compared with those of past pilgrims, and of narrow-minded ones at the present day, we soon found ourselves at the foot of the Hill Difficulty. Through the very heart of this rocky mountain a tunnel has been constructed, of most admirable architecture, with a lofty arch and a spacious double-track; so that, unless the earth and rocks should chance to crumble down, it will remain an eternal monument of the builder's skill and enterprise. It is a great though incidental advantage, that the materials from the heart of the Hill Difficulty have been employed in filling up the Valley of Humiliation; thus obviating the necessity of descending into that disagreeable and unwholesome hollow.

"This is a wonderful improvement, indeed," said I. "Yet I should have been glad of an opportunity to visit the Palace Beautiful, and be introduced to the charming young ladies—Miss Prudence, Miss Piety, Miss Charity, and the rest—who have the kindness to entertain pilgrims there."

"Young ladies!" cried Mr. Smooth-it-away, as soon as he could speak for laughing. "And charming young ladies! Why, my dear fellow, they are old maids, every soul of them—prim, starched, dry, and angular—and not one of them, I will venture to say, has altered so much as the fashion of her gown, since the days of Christian's pilgrimage."

"Ah, well," said I, much comforted, "then I can very readily dispense with their acquaintance."

The respectable Apollyon was now putting on the steam at a

9. Hold forth, discourse.

prodigious rate; anxious, perhaps, to get rid of the unpleasant reminiscences connected with the spot where he had so disastrously encountered Christian. Consulting Mr. Bunyan's road-book, I perceived that we must now be within a few miles of the Valley of the Shadow of Death; into which doleful region, at our present speed, we should plunge much sooner than seemed at all desirable. In truth, I expected nothing better than to find myself in the ditch on one side, or the quag on the other. But, on communicating my apprehensions to Mr. Smooth-it-away, he assured me that the difficulties of this passage, even in its worst condition, had been vastly exaggerated, and that, in its present state of improvement, I might consider myself as safe as on any railroad in Christendom.

Even while we were speaking, the train shot into the entrance of this dreaded Valley. Though I plead guilty to some foolish palpitations of the heart, during our headlong rush over the causeway here constructed, yet it were unjust to withhold the highest encomiums[1] on the boldness of its original conception, and the ingenuity of those who executed it. It was gratifying, likewise, to observe how much care had been taken to dispel the everlasting bloom, and supply the defect of cheerful sunshine; not a ray of which has ever penetrated among these awful shadows. For this purpose, the inflammable gas, which exudes plentifully from the soil, is collected by means of pipes, and thence communicated to a quadruple row of lamps, along the whole extent of the passage. Thus a radiance has been created, even out of the fiery and sulphurous curse that rests for ever upon the Valley; a radiance hurtful, however, to the eyes, and somewhat bewildering, as I discovered by the changes which it wrought in the visages of my companions. In this respect, as compared with natural daylight, there is the same difference as between truth and falsehood; but if the reader have ever travelled through the dark Valley, he will have learned to be thankful for any light that he could get; if not from the sky above, then from the blasted soil beneath. Such was the red brilliancy of these lamps, that they appeared to build walls of fire on both sides of the track, between which we held our course at lightning speed, while a reverberating thunder filled the Valley with its echoes. Had the engine run off the track—a catastrophe, it is whispered, by no means unprecedented—the bottomless pit, if there be any such place, would undoubtedly have received us. Just as some dismal fooleries of this nature had made my heart quake, there came a tremendous shriek, careering along the Valley as if a thousand devils had burst their lungs to utter it, but which proved to be merely the whistle of the engine, on arriving at a stopping-place.

1. Speeches of praise.

The spot, where we had now paused, is the same that our friend Bunyan—a truthful man, but infected with many fantastic notions—has designated, in terms plainer than I like to repeat, as the mouth of the infernal region. This, however, must be a mistake; inasmuch as Mr. Smooth-it-away, while we remained in the smoky and lurid cavern, took occasion to prove that Tophet[2] has not even a metaphorical existence. The place, he assured us, is no other than the crater of a half-extinct volcano, in which the Directors had caused forges to be set up, for the manufacture of railroad iron. Hence, also, is obtained a plentiful supply of fuel for the use of the engines. Whoever had gazed into the dismal obscurity of the broad cavern-mouth, whence ever and anon darted huge tongues of dusky flame—and had seen the strange, half-shaped monsters, and visions of faces horribly grotesque, into which the smoke seemed to wreathe itself,—and had heard the awful murmurs, and shrieks, and deep shuddering whispers of the blast, sometimes forming itself into words almost articulate,—would have seized upon Mr. Smooth-it-away's comfortable explanation, as greedily as we did. The inhabitants of the cavern, moreover, were unlovely personages, dark, smoke-begrimed, generally deformed, with misshapen feet, and a glow of dusky redness in their eyes; as if their hearts had caught fire, and were blazing out of the upper windows. It struck me as a peculiarity, that the laborers at the forge, and those who brought fuel to the engine, when they began to draw short breath, positively emitted smoke from their mouth and nostrils.

Among the idlers about the train, most of whom were puffing cigars which they had lighted at the flame of the crater, I was perplexed to notice several who, to my certain knowledge, had heretofore set forth by railroad for the Celestial City. They looked dark, wild, and smoky, with a singular resemblance, indeed, to the native inhabitants; like whom, also, they had a disagreeable propensity to ill-natured gibes and sneers, the habit of which had wrought a settled contortion of their visages. Having been on speaking terms with one of these persons—an indolent, good-for-nothing fellow, who went by the name of Take-it-easy—I called to him, and inquired what was his business there.

"Did you not start," said I, "for the Celestial City?"

"That's a fact," said Mr. Take-it-easy, carelessly puffing some smoke into my eyes. "But I heard such bad accounts, that I never took pains to climb the hill, on which the city stands. No business doing—no fun going on—nothing to drink, and no smoking allowed—and a thrumming of church-music from morning till night!

2. Hell.

I would not stay in such a place, if they offered me house-room and living free."

"But, my good Mr. Take-it-easy," cried I, "why take up your residence here, of all places in the world?"

"Oh," said the loafer, with a grin, "it is very warm hereabouts, and I meet with plenty of old acquaintances, and altogether the place suits me. I hope to see you back again, some day soon. A pleasant journey to you!"

While he was speaking, the bell of the engine rang, and we dashed away, after dropping a few passengers, but receiving no new ones. Rattling onward through the Valley, we were dazzled with the fiercely gleaming gas-lamps, as before. But sometimes, in the dark of intense brightness, grim faces, that bore the aspect and expression of individual sins, or evil passions, seemed to thrust themselves through the veil of light, glaring upon us, and stretching forth a great dusky hand, as if to impede our progress. I almost thought, that they were my own sins that appalled me there. These were freaks of imagination—nothing more, certainly,—mere delusions, which I ought to be heartily ashamed of—but, all through the Dark Valley, I was tormented, and pestered, and dolefully bewildered, with the same kind of waking dreams. The mephitic[3] gases of that region intoxicate the brain. As the light of natural day, however, began to struggle with the glow of the lanterns, these vain imaginations lost their vividness, and finally vanished with the first ray of sunshine that greeted our escape from the Valley of the Shadow of Death. Ere we had gone a mile beyond it, I could well nigh have taken my oath, that this whole gloomy passage was a dream.

At the end of the Valley, as John Bunyan mentions, is a cavern, where, in his days, dwelt two cruel giants, Pope and Pagan, who had strewn the ground about their residence with the bones of slaughtered pilgrims. These vile old troglodytes are no longer there; but into their deserted cave another terrible giant has thrust himself, and makes it his business to seize upon honest travellers, and fat them for his table with plentiful meals of smoke, mist, moonshine, raw potatoes, and saw-dust. He is a German by birth, and is called Giant Transcendentalist;[4] but as to his form, his features, his substance, and his nature generally, it is the chief peculiarity of this huge miscreant, that neither he for himself, nor anybody for him, has ever been able to describe

---

3. Foul-smelling.
4. Hawthorne replaces Pope and Pagan, the two giants who threatened Christian in *Pilgrim's Progress*, with Giant Transcendentalist, the modern opponent of old-time Protestantism. The joke depends on the popular perception that Transcendentalists such as Bronson Alcott (notorious for his *Orphic Sayings*) were unintelligible.

them. As we rushed by the cavern's mouth, we caught a hasty glimpse of him, looking somewhat like an ill-proportioned figure, but considerably more like a heap of fog and duskiness. He shouted after us, but in so strange a phraseology, that we knew not what he meant, nor whether to be encouraged or affrighted.

It was late in the day, when the train thundered into the ancient city of Vanity, where Vanity Fair is still at the height of prosperity, and exhibits an epitome of whatever is brilliant, gay, and fascinating, beneath the sun. As I purposed to make a considerable stay here, it gratified me to learn that there is no longer the want of harmony between the townspeople and pilgrims, which impelled the former to such lamentably mistaken measures as the persecution of Christian, and the fiery martyrdom of Faithful. On the contrary, as the new railroad brings with it great trade and a constant influx of strangers, the lord of Vanity Fair is its chief patron, and the capitalists of the city are among the largest stockholders. Many passengers stop to take their pleasure or make their profit in the Fair, instead of going onward to the Celestial City. Indeed, such are the charms of the place, that people often affirm it to be the true and only heaven; stoutly contending that there is no other, that those who seek further are mere dreamers, and that, if the fabled brightness of the Celestial City lay but a bare mile beyond the gates of Vanity, they would not be fools enough to go thither. Without subscribing to these, perhaps, exaggerated encomiums, I can truly say, that my abode in the city was mainly agreeable, and my intercourse with the inhabitants productive of much amusement and instruction.

Being naturally of a serious turn, my attention was directed to the solid advantages derivable from a residence here, rather than to the effervescent pleasures, which are the grand object with too many visitants. The Christian reader, if he have had no accounts of the city later than Bunyan's time, will be surprised to hear that almost every street has its church, and that the reverend clergy are nowhere held in higher respect than at Vanity Fair. And well do they deserve such honorable estimation; for the maxims of wisdom and virtue which fall from their lips, come from as deep a spiritual source, and tend to as lofty a religious aim, as those of the sagest philosophers of old. In justification of this high praise, I need only mention the names of the Rev. Mr. Shallow-deep; the Rev. Mr. Stumble-at-Truth; that fine old clerical character, the Rev. Mr. This-to-day, who expects shortly to resign his pulpit to the Rev. Mr. That-to-morrow; together with the Rev. Mr. Bewilderment; the Rev. Mr. Clog-the-spirit; and, last and greatest, the Rev. Dr. Wind-of-doctrine.[5] The labors of these eminent divines are aided by those

---

5. In Ephesians 4.4 Paul urges new Christians not to be "carried about with every wind of doctrine."

of innumerable lecturers, who diffuse such a various profundity, in all subjects of human or celestial science, that any man may acquire an omnigenous[6] erudition, without the trouble of even learning to read. Thus literature is etherealized by assuming for its medium the human voice; and knowledge, depositing all its heavier particles—except, doubtless, its gold—becomes exhaled into a sound, which forthwith steals into the ever-open ear of the community. These ingenious methods constitute a sort of machinery, by which thought and study are done to every person's hand, without his putting himself to the slightest inconvenience in the matter. There is another species of machine for the wholesale manufacture of individual morality. This excellent result is effected by societies for all manner of virtuous purposes; with which a man has merely to connect himself, throwing, as it were, his quota of virtue into the common stock; and the president and directors will take care that the aggregate amount be well applied. All these, and other wonderful improvements in ethics, religion, and literature, being made plain to my comprehension by the ingenious Mr. Smooth-it-away, inspired me with a vast admiration of Vanity Fair.

It would fill a volume, in an age of pamphlets, were I to record all my observations in this great capital of human business and pleasure. There was an unlimited range of society—the powerful, the wise, the witty, and the famous in every walk of life—princes, presidents, poets, generals, artists, actors, and philantropists, all making their own market at the Fair, and deeming no price too exorbitant for such commodities as hit their fancy. It was well worth one's while, even if he had no idea of buying or selling, to loiter through the bazaars, and observe the various sorts of traffic that were going forward.

Some of the purchasers, I thought, made very foolish bargains. For instance, a young man, having inherited a splendid fortune, laid out a considerable portion of it in the purchase of diseases, and finally spent all the rest for a heavy lot of repentance and a suit of rags. A very pretty girl bartered a heart as clear as crystal, and which seemed her most valuable possession, for another jewel of the same kind, but so worn and defaced as to be utterly worthless. In one shop, there were a great many crowns of laurel and myrtle,[7] which soldiers, authors, statesmen, and various other people, pressed eagerly to buy; some purchased these paltry wreaths with their lives; others by a toilsome servitude of years; and many sacrificed whatever was most valuable, yet finally slunk away without the crown. There was a sort of stock or scrip, called Conscience,

6. All-around, comprehensive.
7. Twigs of laurel or myrtle were wound into wreaths and presented as marks of honor to poets, heroes, and victors of athletic contests in ancient Greece and Rome.

which seemed to be in great demand, and would purchase almost anything. Indeed, few rich commodities were to be obtained without paying a heavy sum in this particular stock, and[8] a man's business was seldom very lucrative, unless he knew precisely when and how to throw his hoard of Conscience into the market. Yet as this stock was the only thing of permanent value, whoever parted with it was sure to find himself a loser, in the long run. Several of the speculations were of a questionable character. Occasionally, a member of congress recruited[9] his pocket by the sale of his constituents; and I was assured that public officers have often sold their country at very moderate prices. Thousands sold their happiness for a whim. Gilded chains were in great demand, and purchased with almost any sacrifice. In truth, those who desired, according to the old adage, to sell anything valuable for a song, might find customers all over the Fair; and there were innumerable messes of pottage, piping hot, for such as chose to buy them with their birth-rights.[1] A few articles, however, could not be found genuine at Vanity Fair. If a customer wished to renew his stock of youth, the dealers offered him a set of false teeth and an auburn wig; if he demanded peace of mind, they recommended opium or a brandy-bottle.

Tracts of land and golden mansions, situate in the Celestial City, were often exchanged, at very disadvantageous rates, for a few years' lease of small, dismal, inconvenient tenements in Vanity Fair. Prince Beelzebub himself took great interest in this sort of traffic, and sometimes condescended to meddle with smaller matters. I once had the pleasure to see him bargaining with a miser for his soul, which, after much ingenious skirmishing on both sides, his Highness succeeded in obtaining at about the value of sixpence. The prince remarked, with a smile, that he was a loser by the bargain.

Day after day, as I walked the streets of Vanity, my manners and deportment became more and more like those of the inhabitants. The place began to seem like home; the idea of pursuing my travels to the Celestial City was almost obliterated from my mind. I was reminded of it, however, by the sight of the same pair of simple pilgrims at whom we had laughed so heartily, when Apollyon puffed smoke and steam into their faces, at the commencement of our journey. There they stood amid the densest bustle of Vanity—the dealers offering them their purple,[2] and fine linen, and jewels; the

8. The manuscript reading replaces the 1843 "as."
9. Replenished, or lined.
1. In Genesis 25.29–34 the older brother, Esau, sells his birthright to Jacob for a mess of pottage (lentils).
2. Color associated with high rank.

men of wit and humor gibing at them; a pair of buxom ladies ogling them askance; while the benevolent Mr. Smooth-it-away whispered some of his wisdom at their elbows, and pointed to a newly-erected temple,—but there were these worthy simpletons, making the scene look wild and monstrous, merely by their sturdy repudiation of all part in its business or pleasures.

One of them—his name was Stick-to-the-right—perceived in my face, I suppose, a species of sympathy and almost admiration, which, to my own great surprise, I could not help feeling for this pragmatic couple. It prompted him to address me.

"Sir," inquired he, with a sad, yet mild and kindly voice, "do you call yourself a pilgrim?"

"Yes," I replied, "my right to that appellation is indubitable. I am merely a sojourner here in Vanity Fair, being bound to the Celestial City by the new railroad."

"Alas, friend," rejoined Mr. Stick-to-the-right, "I do assure you, and beseech you to receive the truth of my words, that that whole concern is a bubble. You may travel on it all your life-time, were you to live thousands of years, and yet never get beyond the limits of Vanity Fair! Yea; though you should deem yourself entering the gates of the Blessed City, it will be nothing but a miserable delusion."

"The Lord of the Celestial City," began the other pilgrim, whose name was Mr. Go-the-old way,[3] "has refused, and will ever refuse, to grant an act of incorporation for this railroad; and unless that be obtained, no passenger can ever hope to enter his dominions. Wherefore, every man who buys a ticket, must lay his account with losing the purchase-money—which is the value of his own soul."

"Poh, nonsense!" said Mr. Smooth-it-away, taking my arm and leading me off, "these fellows ought to be indicted for a libel. If the law stood as it once did in Vanity Fair, we should see them grinning through the iron bars of the prison window."

This incident made a considerable impression on my mind, and contributed with other circumstances to indispose me to a permanent residence in the City of Vanity, although, of course, I was not simple enough to give up my original plan of gliding along easily and commodiously by railroad. Still, I grew anxious to be gone. There was one strange thing that troubled me; amid the occupations or amusements of the fair, nothing was more common than for a person—whether at a feast, theatre, or church, or trafficking for wealth and honors, or whatever he might be doing, and however unseasonable the interruption—suddenly to vanish like a soap-

---

3. Hawthorne replaced the manuscript and magazine reading of "Mr. Foot-it-to-Heaven" with this reading in the 1846 *Mosses from an Old Manse*.

bubble, and be never more seen of his fellows; and so accustomed were the latter to such little accidents, that they went on with their business, as quietly as if nothing had happened. But it was otherwise with me.

Finally, after a pretty long residence at the Fair, I resumed my journey towards the Celestial City, still with Mr. Smooth-it-away at my side. At a short distance beyond the suburbs of Vanity, we passed the ancient silver-mine, of which Demas[4] was the first discoverer, and which is now wrought to great advantage, supplying nearly all the coined currency of the world. A little further onward was the spot where Lot's wife had stood for ages, under the semblance of a pillar of salt.[5] Curious travellers have carried it away piecemeal. Had all regrets been punished as rigorously as this poor dame's were, my yearning for the relinquished delights of Vanity Fair might have produced a similar change in my own corporeal substance, and left me a warning to future pilgrims.

The next remarkable object was a large edifice, constructed of moss-grown stone, but in a modern and airy style of architecture. The engine came to a pause in its vicinity with the usual tremendous shriek.

"This was formerly the castle of the redoubted giant Despair," observed Mr. Smooth-it-away; "but, since his death, Mr. Flimsy-faith has repaired it, and now keeps an excellent house of entertainment here. It is one of our stopping-places."

"It seems but slightly put together," remarked I, looking at the frail, yet ponderous walls. "I do not envy Mr. Flimsy-faith his habitation. Some day it will thunder down upon the heads of the occupants."

"We shall escape, at all events," said Mr. Smooth-it-away; "for Apollyon is putting on the steam again."

The road now plunged into a gorge of the Delectable Mountains, and traversed the field where, in former ages, the blind men[6] wandered and stumbled among the tombs. One of these ancient tomb-stones had been thrust across the track, by some malicious person, and gave the train of cars a terrible jolt. Far up the rugged side of a mountain, I perceived a rusty iron door, half overgrown with bushes and creeping plants, but with smoke issuing from its crevices.

---

4. A worldly man who forsakes St. Paul (2 Timothy 4.10). In *Pilgrim's Progress* the gentleman-like Demas deceptively tries to lure Christian to abandon his journey and enrich himself in a silver mine.
5. In Genesis 19.26 God turns Lot's wife into a pillar of salt because she disobeys His command and looks backward at the destroyed city of Sodom.
6. In *Pilgrim's Progress* they exemplify Proverbs 21.16: "The man that wandereth out of the way of understanding shall remain in the congregation of the dead." Seeing an easier path to heaven they had been seized by Giant Despair; thrown into his dungeons in Doubting Castle; and then blinded and released, hopeless of salvation.

"Is that," inquired I, "the very door in the hill-side, which the shepherds assured Christian was a by-way to Hell?"

"That was a joke on the part of the shepherds," said Mr. Smooth-it-away, with a smile. "It is neither more nor less than the door of a cavern, which they use as a smoke-house for the preparation of mutton hams."

My recollections of the journey are now, for a little space, dim and confused, inasmuch as a singular drowsiness here overcame me, owing to the fact that we were passing over the enchanted ground, the air of which encourages a disposition to sleep. I awoke, however, as soon as we crossed the borders of the pleasant land of Beulah.[7] All the passengers were rubbing their eyes, comparing watches, and congratulating one another on the prospect of arriving so seasonably at the journey's end. The sweet breezes of this happy clime came refreshingly to our nostrils; we beheld the glimmering gush of silver fountains, overhung by trees of beautiful foliage and delicious fruit, which were propagated by grafts from the celestial gardens. Once, as we dashed onward like a hurricane, there was a flutter of wings, and the bright appearance of an angel in the air, speeding forth on some heavenly mission. The engine now announced the close vicinity of the final Station House, by one last and horrible scream, in which there seemed to be distinguishable every kind of wailing and woe, and bitter fierceness of wrath, all mixed up with the wild laughter of a devil or a madman. Throughout our journey, at every stopping-place, Apollyon had exercised his ingenuity in screwing the most abominable sounds out of the whistle of the steam-engine; but, in this closing effort he outdid himself, and created an infernal uproar, which, besides disturbing the peaceful inhabitants of Beulah, must have sent its discord even through the celestial gates.

While the horrid clamor was still ringing in our ears, we heard an exulting strain, as if a thousand instruments of music, with height, and depth, and sweetness in their tones, at once tender and triumphant, were struck in unison, to greet the approach of some illustrious hero, who had fought the good fight and won a glorious victory, and was come to lay aside his battered arms for ever. Looking to ascertain what might be the occasion of this glad harmony, I perceived, on alighting from the cars, that a multitude of shining ones had assembled on the other side of the river, to welcome two poor pilgrims, who were just emerging from its depths. They were the same whom Apollyon and ourselves had persecuted with taunts and gibes, and scalding steam, at the commencement of our jour-

7. Bunyan's land of peace, from Isaiah 62.4: "Thou shalt be called Hephzibah, and thy land Beulah."

ney—the same whose unworldly aspect and impressive words had stirred my conscience, amid the wild revellers of Vanity Fair.

"How amazingly well those men have got on!" cried I to Mr. Smooth-it-away. "I wish we were secure of as good a reception."

"Never fear—never fear!" answered my friend. "Come—make haste; the ferry-boat will be off directly; and in three minutes you will be on the other side of the river. No doubt you will find coaches to carry you up to the city gates."

A steam ferry-boat, the last improvement on this important route, lay at the river side, puffing, snorting, and emitting all those other disagreeable utterances, which betoken the departure to be immediate. I hurried on board with the rest of the passengers, most of whom were in great perturbation; some bawling out for their baggage; some tearing their hair and exclaiming that the boat would explode or sink; some already pale with the heaving of the stream; some gazing affrighted at the ugly aspect of the steersman; and some still dizzy with the slumberous influences of the Enchanted Ground. Looking back to the shore, I was amazed to discern Mr. Smooth-it-away waving his hand in token of farewell!

"Don't you go over to the Celestial City?" exclaimed I.

"Oh, no!" answered he with a queer smile, and that same disagreeable contortion of visage which I had remarked in the inhabitants of the Dark Valley. "Oh, no! I have come thus far only for the sake of your pleasant company. Good bye! We shall meet again."

And then did my excellent friend, Mr. Smooth-it-away, laugh outright; in the midst of which cachinnation, a smoke-wreath issued from his mouth and nostrils, while a twinkle of lurid[8] flame darted out of either eye, proving indubitably that his heart was all of a red blaze. The impudent fiend! To deny the existence of Tophet, when he felt its fiery tortures raging within his breast! I rushed to the side of the boat, intending to fling myself on shore. But the wheels, as they began their revolutions, threw a dash of spray over me, so cold—so deadly cold, with the chill that will never leave those waters, until Death be drowned in his own river—that, with a shiver and a heart-quake, I awoke. Thank heaven, it was a Dream!

---

8. The manuscript reading replaces the 1843 "livid." "Cachinnation": loud, mechanical-sounding laugh.

HERMAN MELVILLE

[The Devil as a Quaker]†

"Yes, Madam, Cain was a godless froward boy, & Reuben (Gen:49) & Absalom" Many pious men have impious children—(Devil as a Quaker)—A formal compact—Imprimis—First—Second.

The aforesaid soul. said soul &c—Duplicates—"How was it about the temptation on the hill?" &c Conversation upon Gabriel, Micheal & Raphel—gentlemanly &c—D begs the hero to form one of a "*Society of D's*"—his name would be weighty &c—Leaves a letter to the D—"My dear D"—"Terra Oblivionis" "Hellites"—At the Astor find him making almxxxx—going to a ball takes a long time making toilette.—The Doctor's coach stops [on?] the way.—"Do you beleive all that stuff? nonsense—the world was never made.—"But Is not this you mentioned *here*—in the scriptures?" Receives visits from the principal d's—"Gentlemen" &c. *Arguments* to persuade—"Would you not rather be below with kings than above with fools?"

HERMAN MELVILLE

[The Devil Is a Curious Chap]‡

"I wonder what the old man wants with this lump of foul lard," said Stubb, not without some disgust at the thought of having to do with so ignoble a leviathan.

"Wants with it?" said Flask, coiling some spare line in the boat's bow, "did you never hear that the ship which but once has a Sperm Whale's head hoisted on her starboard side, and at the same time a Right Whale's on the larboard; did you never hear, Stubb, that that ship can never afterwards capsize?"

"Why not?"

---

† From Melville's notations for a story about the Devil in New York City, written on the verso of the last leaf in volume 7 in his set of the *Dramatic Works of William Shakespeare* (Boston: Hilliard, Gray, 1837). Reprinted by permission of the Houghton Library, Harvard University. This transcription confirms that made by Harrison Hayford and independently verified by several other scholars for "Melville's Notes (1849–51) in a Shakespeare Volume," 955–970 in the Northwestern-Newberry Edition of *Moby-Dick* (1988). The NN Edition was published before Geoffrey Sanborn (see Selected Bibliography) discovered the source of the major set of notations on the persecution of "witches" on the recto of the same leaf. The plays in this volume are *King Lear, Romeo and Juliet, Hamlet,* and *Othello.*

‡ From "Stubb and Flask Kill a Right Whale; and Then have a Talk Over Him," chapter 73, the 1851 Harper edition of *Moby-Dick*, 362–63.

"I don't know, but I heard that gamboge ghost of a Fedallah saying so, and he seems to know all about ships' charms. But I sometimes think he'll charm the ship to no good at last. I don't half like
that chap, Stubb. Did you ever notice how that tusk of his is a sort
of carved into a snake's head, Stubb?"

"Sink him! I never look at him at all; but if ever I get a chance of
a dark night, and he standing hard by the bulwarks, and no one by;
look down there, Flask"—pointing into the sea with a peculiar motion of both hands—"Aye, will I! Flask, I take that Fedallah to be
the devil in disguise. Do you believe that cock and bull story about
his having been stowed away on board ship? He's the devil, I say.
The reason why you don't see his tail, is because he tucks it up out
of sight; he carries it coiled away in his pocket, I guess. Blast him!
now that I think of it, he's always wanting oakum to stuff into the
toes of his boots."

"He sleeps in his boots, don't he? He hasn't got any hammock;
but I've seen him lay of nights in a coil of rigging."

"No doubt, and it's because of his cursed tail; he coils it down, do
ye see, in the eye of the rigging."

"What's the old man have so much to do with him for?"

"Striking up a swap or a bargain, I suppose."

"Bargain?—about what?"

"Why, do ye see, the old man is hard bent after that White
Whale, and the devil there is trying to come round him, and get
him to swap away his silver watch, or his soul, or something of that
sort, and then he'll surrender Moby Dick."

"Pooh! Stubb, you are skylarking; how can Fedallah do that?"

"I don't know, Flask, but the devil is a curious chap, and a wicked
one, I tell ye.[1] Why, they say as how he went a sauntering into the
old flag-ship once, switching his tail about devilish easy and gentle-
manlike, and inquiring if the old governor was at home. Well, he
was at home, and asked the devil what he wanted. The devil,
switching his hoofs, up and says, 'I want John.' 'What for?' says the
old governor. 'What business is that of yours,' says the devil, getting
mad,—'I want to use him.' 'Take him,' says the governor—and by
the Lord, Flask, if the devil didn't give John the Asiatic cholera before he got through with him, I'll eat this whale in one mouthful.
But look sharp—aint you all ready there? Well, then, pull ahead,
and let's get the whale alongside."

"I think I remember some such story as you were telling," said
Flask, when at last the two boats were slowly advancing with their
burden towards the ship, "but I can't remember where."

---

1. What follows is a travesty of the Book of Job [Editors' note].

THOMAS L. McHANEY

The Confidence-Man and Satan's Disguises in *Paradise Lost*†

Arguments about the identity of the deaf-mute who conspicuously boards the steamer *Fidèle* at the beginning of Herman Melville's *The Confidence-Man* (1857) may be resolved by an overlooked passage in Milton's *Paradise Lost* which is an apparent source for much of the description in the novel's opening scene. Henry F. Pommer in *Milton and Melville* (1950), demonstrated Milton's pervasive influence on satanic imagery elsewhere in the book, but he failed to note the allusions in chapter I which play an important part in establishing the terms of the novel and which lead forward suggestively to the final scene, where further allusions, also previously unnoted, occur.[1] Picking up Melville's allusions to Milton in these scenes seems to help answer two questions frequently raised about *The Confidence-Man*: Is the fleecy deaf-mute one of the disguises of the Confidence Man? Is the Confidence Man, in all his guises, always to be identified with the devil? If I am correct, the answer to both questions is Yes. The scheme of the masquerade in the book is much less esoteric than H. Bruce Franklin has argued and much more complete than other commentators have been able to claim; instead of avatars of Vishnu or an unrelated series of authorial afterthoughts, we have in the figure of the Confidence Man nothing less than Satan in disguises traditionally ascribed to him by the Bible, by Milton, and by popular superstition.[2]

Book III of *Paradise Lost* describes the last stages of Satan's flight to earth, where he plans to avenge himself upon God by tempting

† First published in *Nineteenth-Century Fiction*, 30 (September 1975), 200–06, and reprinted by permission of The Regents of the University of California. The notes are the author's unless otherwise noted.
1. Eight years after this article was published, Melville's two-volume set of *The Poetical Works of John Milton* (Boston: Hilliard, Gray, 1836) was discovered. After some dramatic vicissitudes, the set is now at Princeton (see Grey and Robillard in Selected Bibliography). We have changed McHaney's quotations from another edition of *Paradise Lost* to agree with Melville's edition and have identified passages McHaney quotes that Melville marked in his copy, as of course McHaney could not have known. The study by William Pommer that McHaney cites is a tour de force of scholarship, based on the identification of verbal echoes of Milton in Melville without the aid of Melville's marked copy of Milton [Editors' note].
2. Franklin's argument is presented most fully in his *The Wake of the Gods: Melville's Mythology* (Stanford: Stanford Univ. Press, 1963) and briefly in the introduction to his 1967 edition of *The Confidence-Man* for Bobbs-Merrill. Franklin cannot make up his mind about the deaf-mute, writing in his introduction that the reader may see him as "either Christ or Satan masquerading as Christ" (xxv). In his discussion of the Confidence Man's masquerades as avatars of Vishnu, he does identify the deaf-mute as the first avatar.

the special creation, Man. Satan's first stop on the way to earth is the "Paradise of Fools,"[3] a windy limbo into which are blown those who would masquerade as Dominican or Franciscan in order to enter heaven—"eremits and friars / White, black, and grey, with all their trumpery" (III.474–75). From here Satan approaches heaven's gate, and he sees the stairway which leads to the embellished portal:

> The stairs were such as whereon Jacob saw
> Angels ascending and descending, bands
> Of guardians bright, when he from Esau fled
> To Padan-Aram in the field of Luz,
> Dreaming by night under the open sky.
>
> (III.510–14)

He looks down at the world, but he is distracted by the "fleecy star" in the sign of the Ram (III.558 [marked by Melville]) and then drawn to the splendor of the sun, toward which he journeys.

At this point in the story Satan dons his first disguise:

> And now a stripling cherub he appears,
> Not of the prime, yet such as in his face
> Youth smil'd celestial, and to every limb
> Suitable grace diffus'd, so well he feign'd;
> Under a coronet his flowing hair
> In curls on either cheek play'd, wings he wore
> Of many a colour'd plume sprinkled with gold.
>
> (III.636–42)

He approaches the splendid angel of the sun, Uriel, from whom he seeks and receives direction to earth, where he will begin his vengeful gulling of the first family.[4]

A comparison with Melville's novel suggests that this material from Milton was refined into *The Confidence-Man* in a number of places. Amid evocations of the sun-god Manco Capac, the downy-cheeked, flaxen-haired deaf-mute makes his advent upon the ill-fated ship of fools on April Fool's Day, rubbing elbows with the crowd, his strangely presented admonitions of charity ignored by people who have been warned to expect a Confidence Man in masquerade. Rebuffed, he eventually drops his "lamb-like figure" on the deck at the foot of the ladder which leads to the deck above; some of the boatmen of the ship of faith, like the angels in Jacob's

---

3. *Paradise Lost* III.496. Contiguous to the passage quoted is one which has a cruel and pertinent application to Melville: in the "Paradise of fools" "pilgrims roam, that strayed so far to seek / In Golgatha him dead who lives in Heaven" (III.476–77) [Melville marked these two lines.—Editors]. After finishing *The Confidence-Man*, Melville would make his own pilgrimage to the Holy Land and later write about the journey in a similar manner in *Clarel* (1876).

4. Melville annotated the page where these lines appear [Editors' note].

dream, are climbing the ladder "in discharge of their duties."[5] One onlooker suggests that the mute is an escaped convict, a fit description of Milton's Satan, while another describes him as "Jacob dreaming at Luz" (14), a reference to the biblical passage used by Milton.[6] A short while later the fair youth has disappeared, to be followed on board by a succession of highly suspect practitioners of the confidence game who twist their bodies and their language, who fawn and cajole, who deceive and sow doubt. Many of these characters wear appearances which are suggested in the passages from Milton already quoted. The false friars in black, white, and gray of the Paradise of Fools find counterparts in Black Guinea and the man in mourning with his black plumage; the white-clad mute; the gentleman in the gray coat and white tie whom Guinea offers as a reference (21); the white-cravatted Methodist (23); the winsome gentleman in white gloves and white-lined cape (44); and the man in gray, who exclaims about "a white masquerading as a black?" (40). The gold-plumed cherub is suggestive for both the Cosmopolitan in his gaudy coat and the little ragged boy who appears in the novel's final chapters, a true stripling.

In her 1954 edition of *The Confidence-Man*, Elizabeth S. Foster discusses the lamblike man as bearing the "stigmata of the true Christian."[7] Writing that Melville "clearly differentiates" between the mute and the Confidence Man, she does not see him as a devil (Ii–Iii), but in her discussion she does call attention to many passages which identify the Confidence Man, *after* the deaf-mute, with Satan. She notes that Guinea is described as like Satan gulling Eve; she summarizes allusions to Satan pointed out by Pommer; and she cites the reference in chapter 23 of *The Confidence-Man* to the "flunky beast that windeth his way on his belly" (135). She even suggests an identification between Uriel and Pitch, the Missouri bachelor. When Melville's references to Milton's Satan in the first chapter of *The Confidence-Man* are added to this evidence, the identification takes on greater significance. If the deaf-mute can be identified as Satan's first disguise in *The Confidence-Man* and if the child at the end of the novel is both a disguise of Satan and the last Confidence Man, then the other disguises in the novel fall into a logical pattern. They are Satan's other disguises in *Paradise Lost* and elsewhere, and Melville's plan and his artistry are discovered to be, as

5. *The Confidence-Man: His Masquerade*, above, p. 13. Further page references in the text are to the Norton Critical Edition, 2nd ed. The "tossed look" of the mute's clothes and his appearance of having traveled "night and day from some far country" (13) are quite fitting for a character who has been thrown out of heaven and who was known, as in the book of Job, for going to and fro and traveling up and down in the earth.

6. Jacob, with whom the deaf-mute is identified, is himself a confidence man who goes in masquerade to trick his father and who talks his brother out of an inheritance.

7. "Introduction," *The Confidence-Man: His Masquerade* (New York: Hendricks House, 1954), p. 1.

we should have suspected, deliberate and complete.[8] Satan's second disguise in *Paradise Lost* is the cormorant (IV.196), a rapacious bird of dark plumage which has general application to all the birds of prey on the *Fidèle* and specific reference to the man with the weed. Satan's third disguise is the lion and his fourth the tiger (IV.402–3), among the "four-footed kinds" in the garden of Eden; Guinea goes on all fours and behaves like a dog, while the Philosophical Intelligence Officer is fawning and doglike with Pitch, reminding us, as well, of the form first taken by Goethe's Mephistopheles—a black dog.[9] Satan's fifth disguise is a toad and his sixth is the biblical serpent (Book IX). It is as the toad that he tries to gull Eve in a Miltonic passage referred to in Melville's chapter 6 (41). The serpent winds its way symbolically through many passages in *The Confidence-Man*, as Foster and others have pointed out. Going beyond Milton, but in keeping with the context, the man with the book needs no difficult gloss; he is both the Puritan devil, ready to sign up the willing or unsuspecting, and a particularly modern devil, too, who sells stock in the Black Rapids Coal Company. The "yarb doctor" is to be identified with Asclepius, the Greek divinity of medicine and health, who was often represented as a serpent or as holding one in his hand—the Kentucky Titan calls him "Snake!" (94).[1]

Who is to protect the weak and unwary from such a devilish assembly? The old man in chapter 15 cries, "I ought to have a guard*ee*an" (81). But his feeble cry reaches only another guise of the Confidence Man. The guardian angels who might be expected to hover over the ship of faith—the "guardians bright" on the stairway to heaven in Milton's poem—are conspicuous by their absence, as Hershel Parker points out in his note on the "Committee of Safety" in *The Confidence-Man* (249), or as Melville apostrophized in *Pierre*: "Where now are the high beneficences? Whither fled the sweet angels that are alledged guardians to man?"[2] These

---

8. In a review of early criticism of *The Confidence-Man*, "Suggestions on the Future of *The Confidence-Man*," *Papers on English Language and Literature*, 1 (Summer 1965), 241–49, Lawrence Grauman, Jr., writes that it is "unmistakable" that the mute is "emblematic of Christ," but goes on to claim, without any evidence, that he is also the first avatar of the Confidence Man and a devil. The avatars are related to each other, he points out, "by the running motif of black and white, which culminates in the all-color harlequin's garb of the cosmopolitan" (244). To this observation, we can add gray, noting the appropriateness of Melville's color imagery to the passage in Milton.
9. *Faust*, Part I, line 1147 [see n. 9, p. 172 herein.—Editors].
1. At the end of "Solitude" in *Walden*, Thoreau refers to that "old herb-doctor Æsculapius" in the same paragraph that mentions "our great-grandmother Nature's universal, vegetable, botanic medicines," a phrase that seems almost from the lips of Melville's quack. In *Israel Potter*, Melville compared Benjamin Franklin to the biblical Jacob, portrayed him as a kind of confidence man, and called him a herb-doctor. During the serialization of *Israel Potter* in *Putnam's Monthly*, *Walden* was reviewed and "Solitude" quoted extensively, although not the passage on Asclepius (October 1854), pp. 371–78.
2. *Pierre, or The Ambiguities* (Evanston and Chicago: Northwestern Univ. Press, The Newberry Library, 1971), p. 176.

"guardeeans"—who are identified with the crewmen of the *Fidèle* by the Miltonic allusion in chapter 1—offer no help even though they climb the ladder in "discharge of their duties" (13). The one possible exception is the "gruff boatman" who, less obliging than Uriel to Satan, answers Black Guinea's plea for someone to seek his gentlemen friends by saying, "Why don't you go find 'em yourself" (25); this is probably not a crewman of the *Fidèle*, however, but one of the Kentucky boatmen mentioned in the second chapter (16). The angels may be where charity is told to go by the wooden-legged misanthrope—heaven (22).

At the end of *The Confidence-Man* the ragged boy brings us full circle, but with an important difference. In his flamelike red and yellow tatters he is a more devilish version than the mute of Milton's "stripling cherub" in gold-sprinkled, colored plumes. Here is no deaf-mute subtly advocating charity. The gulling is almost over and the last trap is about to be sprung. The victim, the old man in the gentlemen's cabin, has already been distracted from the canonical books of the Bible to the Apocrypha by the Cosmopolitan; now the fast-talking child is able to sell him a devilish assortment of worthless security devices, confirming the old man's loss of faith. The old man has been reading his Bible by a "solar lamp" which bears the image of a "robed man, his head encircled by a halo" (239), a likely representation of Uriel, the angel of the sun in the passage from Milton.[3] Milton found Uriel in Revelation 19.17— "The same whom John saw also in the sun" (III.623 [marked by Melville])—refers to the last book of the Bible several times in the last chapter of his novel. Revelation contains the vision of Satan bound in hell for a thousand years and records the words of Jesus' promise, repeated three times, "I come quickly" (Rev. 19.22). After a thousand years Satan was loosed to "go out to deceive the nations" and was defeated again, but in *The Confidence-Man* Satan is as unbound and free as he was in the journey described by Milton in *Paradise Lost*; he is even welcomed on the *Fidèle* by wise fools like the sophomore who prefers stock in the Black Rapids Coal Company to lots in the New Jerusalem.

"What's that about the Apocalypse?" (242). The words come out of the darkness of the gentlemen's cabin when the Cosmopolitan has distracted the old man from the Canon to the Apocrypha. They provide a kind of rubric to Melville's novel, which is certainly made to dwell on final things. It seems clear that Melville drew on Milton's Satan for the introductory chapter of his book and possibly resorted to the same passage again at the ending in order to bring

---

3. Elizabeth S. Foster identifies the figures on the solar lamp with biblical symbols for the Old and New Testaments. See her notes, p. 363.

together his images and to underline the identification of the Confidence Man with the devil.[4] It is also at least possible that there are more masqueraders—and more devils in the form of Satan's legions—than the chameleon Confidence Man himself: does the scene between the Confidence Man as Cosmopolitan and the equally appropriately named Charles Arnold Noble represent only human chicanery opposed unsuccessfully to the diabolical? And what of William Cream, whose name reminds us of the garb of the mute, whose occupation as barber suggests that he "fleeces," and whose orientalized establishment recalls the sultanic architecture of Milton's hell? He loses his confidence to the Cosmopolitan. Do two devils, one a supreme diabolical being, grapple here? How much of a game Melville is playing is not yet clear. That it is a very deep game, whether we ever get to the bottom of it, is beyond doubt. Chapter 14, its title announces, is "worth the consideration of those to whom it may prove worth considering." We should consider whether, in announcing at the novel's end that "something further may follow of this Masquerade," Melville thought he was announcing either a "Paradise Regained" or a yet darker sequel which could only dramatize God's total abandonment of the world or his supersession by satanic forces.

4. Watson G. Branch, "The Genesis, Composition, and Structure of *The Confidence-Man*," *NCF*, 27 (1973), 424–48, speculates that the deaf-mute and the first chapter of *The Confidence-Man* were late additions to the text. Hershel Parker, in a letter of rejoinder (*NCF*, 28 [1973], 119–24), discusses the evidence for Branch's claims and concludes that there is no firm basis for them. The evidence presented here, that Melville identified his mute with Milton's Satan and used Satan's disguises (from several sources) throughout *The Confidence-Man*, offers support against Branch's position and in favor of Parker's. Like Parker, I believe the deaf-mute is a very good Devil's Joke. The first chapter of *The Confidence-Man* is not an afterthought; it is organic to the whole conception of the novel.

Indian Hating in
The Confidence-Man

Historical Background

The Historical Fact of Indian Hating†

On May 23, 1857, in its review of *The Confidence-Man*, the London *Saturday Review* recommended the story of the Indian hater Colonel John Moredock "to those readers who like tales of terror. It opens up a dark page in American history, and throws some light on the feelings with which the backwoodsmen and red men mutually regard each other, and apparently with very good reason." The London *Reynolds's Newspaper* (June 14, 1857) devoted its review of *The Confidence-Man* to that section:

> This is a book of fragmentary sketches and anecdotes by an American author of celebrity. We do not think it will be found amusing to those who are not thoroughly acquainted with American manners and customs. There is neither plot or story, but simply a collection of trivialities which scarce seem worthy of being published—certainly not of the author. The most interesting sketch is that of Colonel John Moredock, a person who swore never-dying hatred to the American Indians, and who seems to have nourished his vengeance to the last.

Then *Reynolds's* quoted two excerpts, "A Sanguinary Revenge" and "Anecdote of the Colonel." American reviewers of *The Confidence-Man*, being familiar with "Indian hating" as a fact of frontier life, not to say covert national policy, may have taken the Indian-hating section more casually, for in the notices yet discovered no American called special attention to it.

This grim section begins with lines from Joel Barlow's Revolutionary-era epic poem *The Vision of Columbus*, then continues with Melville's direct source for the story of Colonel John Moredock,

† Headnote provided by Hershel Parker.

453

James Hall's account of Indian hating. Next come two of Melville's explicit criticisms of American racism: first, his hostile remarks about Francis Parkman, which he published in an 1849 review of *The Oregon and California Trail* (shortly before Parkman married a second cousin of Melville's); second, some unfashionable comments Melville made in his lecture "The South Seas" on the slaughter of Polynesians by Europeans from their warships. Luckily for anyone who wants a great writer of the past to hold views precisely as enlightened as one's own current views (never *more* enlightened, notice), Melville repeatedly put himself on record against the prevailing racial attitudes of his times. Next we print some comments in 1868 by the Unitarian minister Henry Whitney Bellows, the minister of William Cullen Bryant and many New York City notables, as well as the man who baptized the Melvilles' first child and became the longtime spiritual adviser of Melville's wife. From 1972 comes a grim news report in the New York *Times.* Finally, bringing the topic starkly into the twenty-first century, we print "Indian Hating Today," a chilling personal testimony from the novelist Margaret Coel, written especially for this Norton Critical Edition.

JOEL BARLOW

[Columbus's Questions]†

In Book 2 of Joel Barlow's *The Vision of Columbus* (1787) the title character, the discoverer of America, while jailed in Spain despite his services to the crown, is visited by an angel (named in the 1807 revision, *The Columbiad*, Hesper, the "guardian Genius of the western continent"). Columbus contrasts his encounters with Indians on his first and his second arrivals in the West Indies. From being timid, docile, worshipful, and generous, according to Barlow's Columbus, the islanders became vengeful, bloodthirsty, and treacherous. Columbus asks the angel questions about the inhabitants of the New World, which the angel answers at great length.

In the first lines printed here (2.32–42) Columbus speaks after watching a vision of "the swarthy people" moving in "tribes innumerable." Barlow avails himself frequently of "poetic inversion," so that here it is Columbus's wavering mind that addresses the Power, not the other way around:

> Where'er they turn his eager eyes pursue;
> He saw the same dire visage thro' the whole,
> And mark'd the same fierce savageness of soul:

---

† Headnote provided by Hershel Parker.

In doubt he stood, with anxious thoughts oppress'd,
And thus his wavering mind the Power address'd.
          Say, from what source, O Voice of wisdom, sprung
The countless tribes of this amazing throng?
Where human frames and brutal souls combine,
No force can tame them and no arts refine.
Can these be fashion'd on the social plan?
Or boast a lineage with the race of man?

In a later passage (lines 77–96) modern readers again must allow for old spellings as well as for poetic inversion. The Spaniards tried to make the Indians' views sublime and to display fair virtue's charms. In "our rites prophane" the word *profane* is not an adjective but a verb. Here Columbus complains about the Indians' rejection of Spanish culture and religion:

The arts of civil life we strove to lend,
Their lands to culture and their joys extend,
Sublime their views, fair virtue's charms display,
And point their passage to eternal day.
          Still proud to rove, our offers they disdain,
Insult our friendship and our rites prophane.
In that blest island, still the myriads rest,
Bask in the sunshine, wander with the beast,
Feed on the foe, or from the victor fly,
Rise into life, exhaust their rage, and die.
          Tell then, my Seer, from what dire sons of earth
The brutal people drew their ancient birth?
Whether in realms, the western heavens that close,
A tribe distinct from other nations rose,
Born to subjection; when, in happier time,
A nobler race should hail their fruitful clime.
Or, if a common source all nations claim,
Their lineage, form, and reasoning powers the same,
What sovereign cause, in secret wisdom laid,
This wonderous change in God's own work has made?
Why various powers of soul and tints of face
In different climes diversify the race?[1]

---

1. It would be misleading to call this turgid attempt at a patriotic American epic a popular poem, but it was for some decades widely cited as a model for American poets, especially after the early 1830s, when the pressure rose for American poets to supply a great national literature. The poem embodies racist attitudes in an absolutely pure form, Barlow plainly assuming that all of his readers would hold views precisely like his own. Melville may have had some special reasons for acquainting himself with the poem, because his father's brother had been in contact with Barlow when both were living in post-Revolutionary France [Editors' note].

JAMES HALL

Indian Hating.—Some of the Sources of This Animosity.—Brief Account of Col. Moredock.†

The violent animosity which exists between the people of our frontier and the Indians, has long been a subject of remark. In the early periods of the history of our country, it was easily accounted for, on the ground of mutual aggression. The whites were continually encroaching upon the aborigines, and the latter avenging their wrongs by violent and sudden hostilities. The philanthropist is surprised, however, that such feelings should prevail now, when these atrocious wars have ceased, and when no immediate cause of enmity remains; at least upon our side. Yet the fact is, that the dweller upon the frontier continues to regard the Indian with a degree of terror and hatred, similar to that which he feels towards the rattlesnake or panther, and which can neither be removed by argument, nor appeased by any thing but the destruction of its object.

In order to understand the cause and the operation of these feelings, it is necessary to recollect that the backwoodsmen are a peculiar race. We allude to the pioneers, who, keeping continually in advance of civilization, precede the denser population of our country in its progress westward, and live always upon the frontier. They are the descendants of a people whose habits were identically the same as their own. Their fathers were pioneers. A passion for hunting, and a love for sylvan sports, have induced them to recede continually before the tide of emigration, and have kept them a separate people, whose habits, prejudices, and modes of life have been transmitted from father to son with but little change. From generation to generation they have lived in contact with the Indians. The ancestor met the red men in battle upon the shores of the Atlantic, and his descendants have pursued the footsteps of the retreating tribes, from year to year, throughout a whole century, and from the eastern limits of our great continent to the wide prairies of the west.

America was settled in an age when certain rights, called those of *discovery* and *conquest*, were universally acknowledged; and when the possession of a country was readily conceded to the strongest.

† From *Sketches of History, Life, and Manners, in the West* (Philadelphia: Harrison Hall, 1835), volume 2, chapter 6, 74–82. Hall drew on similar material in his "The Backwoodsman" in *Legends of the West* (1832), in "The Pioneer" in *Tales of the Border* (1835), in "The Indian Hater" in *Legends of the West* in *The Western Souvenir, a Christmas and New Year's Gift for 1829* (1828?), and in *The Wilderness and the War-Path* (1846). This last was in the Library of American Books, edited by Evert A. Duyckinck, the same series in which Melville's *Typee* was published, also in 1846; in advertisements, *Typee* came next after *The Wilderness and the War-Path*.

When more accurate notions of moral right began, with the spread of knowledge, and the dissemination of religious truth, to prevail in public opinion, and regulate the public acts of our government, the pioneers were but slightly affected by the wholesome contagion of such opinions. Novel precepts in morals were not apt to reach men who mingled so little with society in its more refined state, and who shunned the restraints, while they despised the luxuries of social life.

The pioneers, who thus dwelt ever upon the borders of the Indian hunting grounds, forming a barrier between savage and civilized men, have received but few accessions to their numbers by emigration. The great tide of emigration, as it rolls forward, beats upon them and rolls them onward, without either swallowing them up in its mass, or mingling its elements with theirs. They accumulate by natural increase; a few of them return occasionally to the bosom of society, but the great mass moves on.

It is not from a desire of conquest, or thirst of blood, or with any premeditated hostility against the savage, that the pioneer continues to follow him from forest to forest, ever disputing with him the right to the soil, and the privilege of hunting game. It is simply because he shuns a crowded population, delights to rove uncontroled in the woods, and does not believe that an Indian, or any other man has a right to monopolize the hunting grounds, which he considers free to all. When the Indian disputes the propriety of this invasion upon his ancient heritage, the white man feels himself injured, and stands, as the southern folks say, upon his reserved rights.

The history of the borders of England and Scotland, and of all dwellers upon frontiers, who come often into hostile collision, shows, that between such parties an intense hatred is created. It is national antipathy, with the addition of private feud and personal injury. The warfare is carried on by a few individuals, who become known to each other, and a few prominent actors on each side soon become distinguished for their prowess or ferocity. When a stage of public war ostensibly ceases, acts of violence continue to be perpetrated from motives of mere mischief, or for pillage or revenge.

Our pioneers have, as we have said, been born and reared on the frontier, and have, from generation to generation, by successive removals, remained in the same relative situation in respect to the Indians and to our own government. Every child thus reared, learns to hate an Indian, because he always hears him spoken of as an enemy. From the cradle, he listens continually to horrid tales of savage violence, and becomes familiar with narratives of aboriginal cunning and ferocity. Every family can number some of its members or relatives among the victims of a midnight massacre, or can tell of some acquaintance who has suffered a dreadful death at the stake. Traditions of horses stolen, and cattle driven off, and cabins burned, are numberless; are told with great minuteness, and listened to with intense interest. With persons thus reared, hatred towards an Indian becomes a part of their nature, and revenge an instinctive principle. Nor does the evil end here. Although the backwoodsmen, properly so called, retire before that tide of emigration which forms the more stationary population, and eventually fills the country with inhabitants, they usually remain for a time in contact with the first of those who, eventually, succeed them, and impress their own sentiments upon the latter. In the formation of each of the western territories and states, the backwoodsmen have, for a while, formed the majority of the population, and given the tone to public opinion.

If we attempt to reason on this subject, we must reason with a due regard to facts, and to the known principles of human nature. Is it to be wondered at, that a man should fear and detest an Indian, who has been always accustomed to hear him described only as a midnight prowler, watching to murder the mother as she bends over her helpless children, and tearing, with hellish malignity, the babe from the maternal breast? Is it strange, that he whose mother has fallen under the savage tomahawk, or whose father has died a lingering death at the stake, surrounded by yelling fiends in human shape, should indulge the passion of revenge towards the perpetrators of such atrocities? They know the story only as it was told to them. They have only heard one side, and that with all the exaggerations of fear, sorrow, indignation and resentment. They have heard it from the tongue of a father, or from the lips of a mother, or a sister, accompanied with all the particularity which the tale could receive from the vivid impressions of an eye-witness, and with all the eloquence of deeply awakened feeling. They have heard it perhaps at a time when the war-whoop still sounded in the distance, when the rifle still was kept in preparation, and the cabin door was carefully secured with each returning night.

Such are some of the feelings, and of the facts, which operate upon the inhabitants of our frontiers. The impressions which we have described are handed down from generation to generation, and remain in full force long after all danger from the savages has ceased, and all intercourse with them been discontinued.

Besides that general antipathy which pervades the whole community under such circumstances, there have been many instances of individuals who, in consequence of some personal wrong, have vowed eternal hatred to the whole Indian race, and have devoted nearly all of their lives to the fulfilment of a vast scheme of vengeance. A familiar instance is before us in the life of a gentleman, who was known to the writer of this article, and whose history we have often heard repeated by those who were intimately conversant with all the events. We allude to the late Colonel John Moredock, who was a member of the territorial legislature of Illinois, a distinguished militia officer, and a man universally known and respected by the early settlers of that region. We are surprised that the writer of a sketch of the early history of Illinois, which we published some months ago, should have omitted the name of this gentleman, and some others, who were famed for deeds of hardihood, while he has dwelt upon the actions of persons who were comparatively insignificant.

John Moredock was the son of a woman who was married several times, and was as often widowed by the tomahawk of the savage. Her husbands had been pioneers, and with them she had wandered from one territory to another, living always on the frontier. She was at last left a widow, at Vincennes, with a large family of children, and was induced to join a party about to remove to Illinois, to which region a few American families had then recently removed. On the eastern side of Illinois there were no settlements of whites; on the shore of the Mississippi a few spots were occupied by the French; and it was now that our own backwoodsmen began to turn their eyes to this delightful country, and determined to settle in the vicinity of the French villages. Mrs. Moredock and her friends embarked at Vincennes in boats, with the intention of descending the Wabash and Ohio rivers, and ascending the Mississippi. They proceeded in safety until they reached the Grand Tower on the Mississippi, where, owing to the difficulty of the navigation for ascending boats, it became necessary for the boatmen to land, and drag their vessels round a rocky point, which was swept by a violent current. Here a party of Indians, lying in wait, rushed upon them, and murdered the whole party. Mrs. Moredock was among the victims, and *all* her children, except John, who was proceeding with another party.

John Moredock was just entering upon the years of manhood, when he was thus left in a strange land, the sole survivor of his race. He resolved upon executing vengeance, and immediately took measures to discover the actual perpetrators of the massacre. It was ascertained that the outrage was committed by a party of twenty or thirty Indians, belonging to different tribes, who had formed themselves into a lawless predatory band. Moredock watched the motions of this band for more than a year, before an opportunity suitable for his purpose occurred. At length he learned, that they were hunting on the Missouri side of the river, nearly opposite to the recent settlements of the Americans. He raised a party of young men and pursued them; but that time they escaped. Shortly after, he sought them at the head of another party, and had the good fortune to discover them one evening, on an island, whither they had retired to encamp the more securely for the night. Moredock and his friends, about equal in numbers to the Indians, waited until the dead of night, and then landed upon the island, turning adrift their own canoes and those of the enemy, and determined to sacrifice their own lives, or to exterminate the savage band. They were completely successful. Three only of the Indians escaped, by throwing themselves into the river; the rest were slain, while the whites lost not a man.

But Moredock was not satisfied while one of the murderers of his mother remained. He had learned to recognise the names and persons of the three that had escaped, and these he pursued with secret, but untiring diligence, until they all fell by his own hand. Nor was he yet satisfied. He had now become a hunter and a warrior. He was a square-built, muscular man, of remarkable strength and activity. In athletic sports he had few equals; few men would willingly have encountered him in single combat. He was a man of determined courage, and great coolness and steadiness of purpose. He was expert in the use of the rifle and other weapons; and was complete master of those wonderful and numberless expedients by which the woodsman subsists in the forest, pursues the footsteps of an enemy with unerring sagacity, or conceals himself and his design from the discovery of a watchful foe. He had resolved never to spare an Indian, and though he made no boast of this determination, and seldom avowed it, it became the ruling passion of his life. He thought it praiseworthy to kill an Indian; and would roam through the forest silently and alone, for days and weeks, with this single purpose. A solitary red man, who was so unfortunate as to meet him in the woods, was sure to become his victim; if he encountered a party of the enemy, he would either secretly pursue their footsteps until an opportunity for striking a blow occurred, or, if discovered, would elude them by his superior skill. He died about four years ago, an old man, and it is supposed never in his life failed to embrace an opportunity to kill a savage.

The reader must not infer, from this description, that Colonel Moredock was unsocial, ferocious, or by nature cruel. On the contrary, he was a man of warm feelings, and excellent disposition. At home he was like other men, conducting a large farm with industry and success, and gaining the good will of all his neighbours by his popular manners and benevolent deportment. He was cheerful, convivial, and hospitable; and no man in the territory was more generally known, or more universally respected. He was an officer in the ranging service during the war of 1813–14, and acquitted himself with credit; and was afterwards elected to the command of the militia of his country, at a time when such an office was honourable, because it imposed responsibility, and required the exertion of military skill. Colonel Moredock was a member of the legislative council of the territory of Illinois, and at the formation of the state government, was spoken of as a candidate for the office of governor, but refused to permit his name to be used.

There are many cases to be found on the frontier, parallel to that just stated, in which individuals have persevered through life, in the indulgence of a resentment founded either on a personal wrong suffered by the party, or a hatred inherited through successive generations, and perhaps more frequently on a combination of these causes. In a fiction, written by the author, and founded on some of these facts, he has endeavoured to develope and illustrate this feeling through its various details.

HERMAN MELVILLE

All Races: Made in "the Image of God"†

In a brief and appropriate preface Mr Parkman adverts to the representations of the Indian character given by poets and novelists, which he asserts are for the most part mere creations of fancy. He adds that "the Indian is certainly entitled to a high rank among savages, but his good qualities are not those of an Uncas or Outalissi."[1] Now, this is not to be gainsaid. But when in the body of the book we are informed that it is difficult for any white man, after a domestication among the Indians, to hold them much better than brutes; when we are told too, that to such a person, the slaughter of an Indian is indifferent as the slaughter of a buffalo; with all deference, we beg leave to dissent.

It is too often the case, that civilized beings sojourning among savages soon come to regard them with disdain and contempt. But though in many cases this feeling is almost natural, it is not defensible; and it is wholly wrong. Why should we contemn them?—Because we are better than they? Assuredly not; for herein we are rebuked by the story of the Publican and the Pharisee.[2]—Because,

---

† From "Mr Parkman's Tour," Melville's review of Francis Parkman Jr., *The California and Oregon Trail; being Sketches of Prairie and Rocky Mountain Life*, (New York: Putnam, 1849), the New York *Literary World* (March 31, 1849), 291–93. All notes are the editors'.

1. "Good" Indians. Uncas is the title character in James Fenimore Cooper's *The Last of the Mohicans* (1826), the second of the Leather-Stocking Tales. Outalissi, an "Oneyda" warrior, nobly delivers an orphaned white boy to a white settler early in *Gertrude of Wyoming: A Pennsylvania Tale* (1809), by the Scottish poet Thomas Campbell (1777–1844). Wyoming, in northeast Pennsylvania, was scene of a massacre of colonists by the British and their Indian allies in 1778.

2. Jesus' parable in Luke 18.10–13 about the Pharisee (a member of a Jewish priestly sect noted for strict adherance to traditional rules) and the publican (toll taker or tax collector): "Two men went up into the temple to pray; the one a Pharisee, and the other a publican. The Pharisee stood and prayed thus with himself, God, I thank thee, that I am not

then, that in many things we are happier?—But this should be
ground for commiseration, not disdain. Xavier and Eliot despised
not the savages; and had Newton or Milton[3] dwelt among them,
they would not have done so.—When we affect to contemn savages, we should remember that by so doing we asperse our own
progenitors; for they were savages also. Who can swear that among
the naked British barbarians sent to Rome to be stared at more
than 1500 years ago, the ancestor of Bacon[4] might not have been
found?—Why, among the very Thugs of India, or the bloody Dyaks
of Borneo,[5] exists the germ of all that is intellectually elevated and
grand. We are all of us—Anglo-Saxons, Dyaks and Indians—sprung
from one head and made in one image. And if we reject this brotherhood now, we shall be forced to join hands hereafter.—A misfortune is not a fault; and good luck is not meritorious. The savage is
born a savage; and the civilized being but inherits his civilization,
nothing more. Let us not disdain then, but pity. And wherever we
recognize the image of God let us reverence it; though it swing
from the gallows. * * *

HERMAN MELVILLE

[Civilized Atrocities in the South Pacific]†

Why don't the English yachters give up the prosy Mediterranean
and sail out here? Any one who treats the natives fairly is just as

---

as other men are, extortioners, unjust, adulterers, or even as this publican. I fast twice in
the week, I give tithes of all that I possess. And the publican, standing afar off, would
not lift up so much as his eyes unto heaven, but smote upon his breast, saying God be
merciful to me a sinner." The publican, Jesus explained, "went down to his house justified rather than the other," because he had humbled himself instead of exalting himself.

3. Sir Isaac Newton (1642–1727), English scientist, and John Milton (1608–1674), English poet, are named not because of their association with Indians but as the greatest of
their time in their fields. Francis Xavier (1506–1552),Spanish co-founder of the Society
of Jesus (Jesuits), who worked to Christianize India, Ceylon, and Japan. John Eliot
(1604–1690), English-born Massachusetts missionary to local Indians. He learned Al-
gonkian and translated the Bible into that language. One of the original purposes of the
Massachusetts Bay Colony was to convert the natives "to the knowledge and obedience
of the only true God and Savior of mankind."

4. Francis Bacon (1561–1626), English moralist and philosopher who attempted to classify all knowledge; repeatedly mentioned in *The Confidence-Man*. At the end of his life,
in *Billy Budd*, Melville was still fascinated with accounts of golden-haired barbaric Anglo-Saxon prisoners being displayed in Rome in the first several centuries c.e., particularly the reported comment of Pope Gregory around 598 that some beautiful children
were not Angles but angels.

5. A people then notorious as headhunters, proficient in killing by poisoned darts shot
through blowguns. "Thugs": from northern India, worshipers of Kali who strangled their
victims and plundered the corpses; the British suppressed them in Melville's youth.
Melville names both Thugs and Dyaks in *The Confidence-Man*.

† From "The South Seas," Melville's second lecture, for the 1858–59 season, in the Northwestern-Newberry *The Piazza Tales and Other Prose Pieces, 1839–1860*. Reprinted by

safe as if he were on the Nile or Danube. But I am sorry to say we whites have a sad reputation among many of the Polynesians. The natives of these islands are naturally of a kindly and hospitable temper, but there has been implanted among them an almost instinctive hate of the white man. They esteem us, with rare exceptions, such as *some* of the missionaries, the most barbarous, treacherous, irreligious, and devilish creatures on the earth. This may of course be a mere prejudice of these unlettered savages, for have not our traders always treated them with brotherly affection? Who has ever heard of a vessel sustaining the honor of a Christian flag and the spirit of the Christian Gospel by opening its batteries in indiscriminate massacre upon some poor little village on the seaside—splattering the torn bamboo huts with blood and brains of women and children, defenseless and innocent?

HENRY WHITNEY BELLOWS

[Extermination as a Solution]†

We have two Californians aboard, one who just escaped scalping on the Plains this summer, and who thinks extermination the only humane remedy for Indian troubles. He suggests that a milder process might first be tried; designating a tract or reservation, say in Dacotah, and proclaiming to the tribes that all Indians found out of it after a year from date would be dealt with as vermin and shot by any white men falling in with them—abandoning all whites who violated an Indian reservation to any similar fate the Indians might visit upon them. It is astonishing how blood-thirsty a little personal experience of the Indians makes most Americans! I have never known any body crossing the Plains whose humanity survived the passage.

---

permission of Northwestern University Press. There were massacres aplenty through the late eighteenth century and much of the nineteenth century, but the particular massacre Melville alludes to is Lieutenant John Wilkes's attack on a Fijian village on the island of Malolo. Nathaniel Philbrick retells the story in chapter 10 of *Sea of Glory: America's Voyage of Discovery; The U. S. Exploring Expedition, 1838–1842 (2003).*

† From *The Old World in Its New Face* (New York: Harper & Brothers, 1868). Henry Whitney Bellows (1814–1882), longtime pastor of All Souls in Manhattan, was the most prominent Unitarian of his generation and a notable public servant. He served as president of the U.S. Sanitary Commission during the Civil War. His admiring parishioners included many famous New Yorkers such as William Cullen Bryant as well as humbler people such as Elizabeth Shaw Melville, who for a time had to confess that she could not pay her pew rent. In May 1867, on his way to the ship that would take him to Europe, he stopped to advise Elizabeth Melville during a crisis of her marriage to Herman Melville. Bellows sent back reports of his travels to newspapers and magazines then after his return included most of these letters in his two-volume *The Old World in Its New Face.* Bellows wrote the first paragraph printed here (2.82) on a ship in the Mediterranean. The second paragraph is Bellows's comparison of the Druzes ("heretical Mahometans") to American Indians (2.228–29).

* * *

How far love of independence and of certain prescriptive rights influence them, and how far religious fanaticism, none can say. But in the terrible persecution they visited in 1859–1860 upon the Christians of the mountain villages, with whom they had long lived in peace, they manifested a kind of American Indian passion for blood and extinction of their enemies, and pursued them with brand and sword until many scores of towns had been burned and some thousands of lives had been brutally taken. The horror of the Christian world was aroused by their fiend-like murders.

ANONYMOUS

Colombia Trial Reveals Life ("Everyone Kills Indians") on Plains†

VILLAVICENCIO, Colombia, July 6–Out on the llanos, the vast prairies that stretch across Colombia and Venezuela from the Andes to the Orinoco, lawlessness still reigns as it did in the old American West. Swashbuckling cowboys and primitive Indians compete for life and over notions of right with the fast gun and the flashing machete.

Evidence that untamed life on the prairies has changed little since the time of the conquistadores was provided in a courtroom here last week when a half-dozen cowboys charged with murder freely told in horrifying detail how they had lured 16 Indians to their ranch with the promise of a feast and massacred them for fun.

"If I had known that killing Indians was a crime, I would not have wasted all that time walking just so they could lock me up," said 22-year-old Marcelino Jimenez, who hiked for five days to a police outpost after learning the authorities were looking for him.

'Indians Are Animals'

"From childhood, I have been told that everyone kills Indians," said another defendant, who added: "All I did was kill the little Indian girl and finish off two who were more dead than alive anyway." * * *

The accused admitted having lured 18 nomadic Cuiba Indians onto the ranch with the promise of meat, rice, vegetables and fruit set out by two women cooks, and said they had attacked the men,

† From the *New York Times* July 9, 1972.

women and children with guns, machetes and clubs at a pre-arranged signal from the range boss.

Sixteen of the Indians were killed, but two crawled away and reported the incident to a priest, who notified the authorities. After their arrest, the defendants cooperated fully, supplying investigators with every detail of the massacre.

The defense * * * contended that the Government was unfairly trying to apply 20th century laws to ignorant men from a lawless land.

A three-man jury here agreed. After 41 hours of deliberation, they found all eight defendants not guilty on grounds of "invincible ignorance."

MARGARET COEL

Indian Hating Today†

"Nits make lice," stated Colonel John Chivington, exhorting his troops to kill all Indians, including women and children, "little and big." On November 29, 1864, Chivington, in command of the Third Colorado Regiment, attacked the Cheyenne and Arapaho village at Sand Creek in southeastern Colorado, killing 150 Indians in what has become known as the Sand Creek Massacre.

In researching my book *Chief Left Hand*, the biography of one of the leading Arapahos at that time (published by the University of Oklahoma Press), it became obvious that the thirty-year war against the Plains Indians—which the Sand Creek Massacre ignited—was driven by a blatant, outspoken, and socially acceptable hatred of Indian people on the western frontier. Newspapers of the day blared the hatred. "A few months of active extermination against the red devils will bring quiet and nothing else will," said the *Rocky Mountain News*. Speaking to a Denver audience, Major Jacob Downing, who later took part in the Sand Creek Massacre, said, "I think and earnestly believe the Indians to be an obstacle to civilization, and should be exterminated." The historical record does not indicate that anyone in the audience disagreed.

No one would write such articles or give such speeches today. Indian hating is much more subtle than in the nineteenth century when the Plains Indian tribes were struggling against the hordes of gold seekers, homesteaders, and soldiers coming onto their lands. Yet I have been dismayed to find remnants of the hatred that ran through white communities more than a century ago manifesting

† This essay appears for the first time in this Norton Critical Edition.

itself in ways that have convinced me that Indian hating still exists in the modern West.

A few years ago I met another writer, a middle-aged woman from Riverton, Wyoming, which is located on the eastern edge of the Wind River Reservation. The reservation is home to about eight thousand northern Arapahos and Shoshones. Since I have been writing about the Arapaho people in both non-fiction and fiction for almost twenty-five years, I have spent a great deal of time on the reservation, so I was surprised when the woman asked me if I had ever actually gone there.

"Yes, of course," I answered, wondering why she thought that any writer could write about a people and a place without getting to know them.

"I would never go onto the reservation," the woman said. "They're not like us, you know."

I was astounded. Writers, as a group, tend to be blessed with an immense curiosity about everything and everyone. Here was a writer who lived so close to the rich and unique culture of the Indian people on the Wind River Reservation that she could have walked there in fifteen minutes. Yet she chose never to get to know her Indian neighbors because "They're not like us."

If Indians are "not like us," then, it seems to me, it becomes acceptable to hate them, even if it isn't acceptable to admit to hating Indians. In speaking about my books around the West, I've encountered the kind of hostility that can only be the overlay of a deep-seated hatred. The hostility is apparent in the types and tone of the questions from the audience, such as: Why should Indian tribes have the right to all those reservation lands? Why do Indians receive government money for doing nothing? When I try to explain that reservations were lands "reserved" to the tribes by treaty after the rest of their lands had been overrun and that so-called government money is royalty money earned from the lands and dispersed by the government, the audiences often become even more hostile. At one speech, a man dressed like a cowboy snickered out loud that I was nothing more than an Indian lover.

A few years ago, I experienced the hatred toward Indians that still lurks beneath our twenty-first-century veneer. I was attending a conference in Wyoming. As often happens at conferences, several of us decided to go to dinner at a restaurant a few miles away, and one of the men offered to drive us in his van. Just as the van turned into the shopping center where the restaurant was located, a young man with dark skin and black, braided hair, stepped off the sidewalk. "Let's get him," the driver said, swerving toward the man, who stumbled backward, fighting to keep his balance. "Just kidding," the driver said as he jerked the wheel away. Some of the passengers laughed.

I couldn't get the incident out of my mind, and not long afterward, I wrote a similar scene into my novel *The Shadow Dancer*, not because I wanted to make a statement or send a message about prejudice and hatred but because, in my novels, I try to reflect the West that I know, including the prejudice toward Indians that runs beneath the surface of things.

To my shame, I did not have the courage that I gave to my character, Father John O'Malley, who immediately demands that the driver stop. Father John then gets out of the van and walks, despite protests from the driver that it was just a joke. I, on the other hand, endured a silent dinner along with the two other passengers who seemed to be as appalled as I was, before riding back to the conference in the van.

In the novel, Father John knows, just as his creator knows, that eruptions of hatred are no joke. They are a disturbing reminder that, in the West, we have not yet moved out of the shadows of our past.

Political Background

The Politics of Allegorizing Indian Hating†

In the known reviews there is no indication that any of Melville's American readers recognized in "The Metaphysics of Indian Hating" an allusion to a well-known piece of Southwestern Texas adventure called the "Metaphysics of Bear Hunting." Yet, as Scott Norsworthy discovered, the popular sportsman-author Charles Wilkins Webber (1819–1856) had published *his* metaphysics piece in the widely read *American Whig Review* for August 1845 (just as Gansevoort Melville was preparing to sail for London, carrying his young brother Herman's manuscript of his South Sea adventures, *Typee*). Family members of Melville subscribed to this magazine. Vilified in it in 1847 and 1852, he sometimes had to see the magazine more often than he wanted to. Webber reprinted his article in the very popular (and today extremely pricey) *The Hunter-Naturalist. Romance of Sporting or Wild Scenes and Wild Hunters* (1851) and in other editions, including *Romance of Sporting or Wild Scenes and Wild Hunters (The Hunter Naturalist)* (1854). In "Metaphysics of Bear Hunting," professing to have been a "mad and raving skeptic" about religion, Webber claimed that his near-death experience and miraculous salvation in the Texas wilderness

† Headnote provided by Hershel Parker.

had taught him that "GOD IS!" and had left him "the sentient demonstrations, strong as proof of holy writ, of a benevolent and active *Providence*—wielding appreciable laws inscrutably on our behalf." Melville in "Benito Cereno," just before starting *The Confidence-Man*, had delineated the limited psychology of a robust, good-natured New Englander who was confident that there was a benevolent and active Providence above but who did not acknowledge an evil force below. Chances are that Melville had read Webber's exciting article one time or another. With the mighty American Grisly Bears in his mind as symbols of alienation, isolation, and self-devouring introspection (see *Moby-Dick*, chapter 34), Melville seems to have seized an opportunity to play on Webber's title.

As Webber's use indicates, the usual literal meaning of metaphysics in the United States of the mid-nineteenth century was "beyond" or "after" physics, as applied to the portion of the Greek philosopher Aristotle's works not covered by the term *physics*—that is, what Aristotle thought of as the First Philosophy or theology, dealing with the nature of being and the existence of God. Occurrences of the word in reviews of Melville's books help establish the current meaning. On March 24, 1849, the London *Atlas* called Melville's *Mardi* "a compound of 'Robinson Crusoe' and 'Gulliver's Travels,' seasoned throughout with German metaphysics of the most transcendental school," then elaborated: "The great questions of natural religion, necessity, free-will, and so on, which Milton's devils discussed in Pandemonium, are here discussed on a rock in the Pacific Ocean by tatooed and feathered sceptics." On April 21, 1849, the London *John Bull* complained of what it found irreligious aspects of *Mardi*: "To introduce the Saviour of mankind under a fabulous name [Alma], and to talk down the verities of the Christian faith by sophistry, the more than irreverence of which is but flimsily veiled, is a grave offence, not against good taste alone; and we could heartily wish that Mr. Melville had confined himself to the lively and picturesque scenery of which his pencil is master, and, if he be pleased, to such subjects as offer a fair scope for the indulgence of his satirical vein, without introducing crude metaphysics and unsound notions of divinity into a craft of a build far too light for carrying so ponderous a freight." The New York *Evening Mirror* on August 27, 1852, said this of *Pierre:* "The book contains a good deal of fine writing and poetic feeling, but the metaphysics are abominable." The *OED* cites from Melville's acquaintance Oliver Wendell Holmes a newly emerging use of the word *metaphysics* to mean the "theoretical principles" or "higher philosophical rationale" of a branch of knowledge. That meaning fits the context of *The Confidence-Man* well enough, but Melville would have expected his usage to carry also the sense of something like "theological implications" or "religious meanings."

The first scholar to examine *The Confidence-Man* closely, Elizabeth S. Foster (Yale dissertation 1942, Hendricks House edition of *The Confidence-Man*, 1954), discovered that the Moredock section was based on the real Judge James Hall's accounts of the real early settler in Illinois John Moredock, a notable example of a frontier type, the obsessive Indian hater. She understood that Melville was not out merely to retell a tale recently retold by Hall but instead to transform the tale from frontier history to something that contained allegorical significance. Although she all but ignored the word *metaphysics* and slighted the religious terminology associated with Moredock, she dwelt in some detail on how Melville associated the Indians with "the original and irreclaimable villain," the Devil, whom she identified as inhabiting the steamship in the form of the Confidence Man. The next careful reader of the book, John W. Shroeder (1951), pushed Foster's analysis further: "The book supplies, we may say, a running system of Indian-images related to concepts, situations, and persons connected with the theological doctrines of human guilt and damnation. It is interesting to note that the Puritans could account for the Indian only by supposing him to be a descendant of Satan." He also pushed further than Foster in seeing the Indian hater as something like a religious figure: "The Indian-hater has succeeded in locating Evil in its real home; there is no distortion in his vision of spiritual reality."

Ten years later, in 1961, I was a student in Harrison Hayford's Melville seminar at Northwestern University, only two years away from being a telegraph operator at Port Arthur, Texas, with seven years' seniority on the Kansas City Southern Railway. I had brought from the Gulf a familiarity with mid-twentieth-century Southern Baptist doctrine very close to the Dutch Church doctrines Melville had been taught in the first half of the nineteenth century. Foster's Hendricks House edition, published only seven years earlier, was an invaluable vade mecum to the book except, I thought, in matters of religion, for, quite unlike Saint Augustine and John Calvin, she thought of Christianity as one of the "optimistic philosophies which assume that the universe is benevolent and human nature is good" (Foster, lxix). Foster and other critics excepting only Shroeder, I decided, had been too sophisticated to believe in the Fall of Man and too sophisticated, also, to sympathize with the idea of trying to live in absolute obedience to Jesus. To emphasize my theological arguments about this section of *The Confidence-Man*, I borrowed for my seminar paper Melville's chapter title, "The Metaphysics of Indian Hating." At Hayford's invitation, I read the paper before the Melville Society during the December 1961 meeting of the Modern Language Association in Chicago.

Afterward, Professor Roy Male of the University of Oklahoma came up, embarrassed and diffident, to ask how I would talk about Indian hating if I had an Indian in my class. Caught off guard, I answered that I had been born in Comanche, Oklahoma, south of where he taught, and was part Choctaw and Cherokee myself. Like Elizabeth S. Foster, I had not judged Melville for having used race allegorically. "Political correctness" did not have a name in 1961, but neither then nor later did the role of hereditary victimhood and what became known as "identity politics" offer anything attractive to me. If the title and the subject did not bother me, as part Indian, I thought, it should not bother others. After all, I had not been talking about real frontier Indian hating such as Judge James Hall depicted but about how Melville had transformed a grisly frontier phenomenon into a religious allegory scrutinizing the practicability of Christianity. (Like Sherman Alexie and many other American Indians, I refuse to let proponents of political correctness, whatever their color, dictate that I refer to myself as part "Native American.")

I did not say so to Professor Male, but I had grown up knowing about worse wrongs than using race allegorically. From 1942 I remembered one dark impossibly tall ancient kinsman born in Indian Territory the next generation after the Trail of Tears (Indian hating on a sweeping, quasi-genocidal scale), and I bitterly recalled routine twentieth-century job discrimination against half-Indians in the family. Decades later, I know much more about my Cherokee and Choctaw ancestors, thanks to cousins I located through the Internet. I have been astounded to see attached to an e-mail message the 1848 "United States Volunteer Service" Mexican War discharge papers of a great-great grandfather, a black-haired and black-eyed, six-feet five-inch Cherokee-Scot, the father of the kinsman I remembered (rightly, it now seems!) as soaring so high. I have been startled to find that a cousin ranking high in twenty-first-century Choctaw councils possesses photographs, new to me, of my Choctaw-Cherokee grandmother as a girl. But in 1961, in a quintessentially American reversal of fortune, I was being paid to go to school, and my duty as I saw it was to understand Melville, not to intrude my personal history into *The Confidence-Man*.

Perhaps I should have realized some people, less inured to casual racism, would simply think it wrong, always, for any writer to use race allegorically, and that other people would be bothered that Melville had not intuited the possibility that real American Indians might ever be among his readers, Indians who might be offended by his blithely allegorizing the phenomenon of Indian hating.

Granted, Melville was oblivious to the tender feelings of potential Indian readers (and even Indian critics) in his contemporary or future audiences. But think how astounded and bemused *he* would be to know that a two-volume biography of him would be written by anyone at all, particularly by someone with Choctaw and Cherokee blood.

Racial attitudes remain in flux. As late as 1995 I resigned as a panelist for the National Endowment for the Humanities in protest against its well-meaning but nevertheless racist policy that would have required me to identify myself as of one race. Now, in the United States of the twenty-first century, blending of races is more and more a fact of life, and young celebrities in entertainment and sports (flatly refusing to be labeled as of one race) proudly present themselves as dual or multiracial. Reprinting pieces with the words *Indian hating* in the title may still seem, at first glance, provocative or hurtful, as Roy Male feared. Yet righteous political correctness should not obscure that what Melville did with "Indian hating" is religious allegory, after all, a literary device, and, as Emerson said in "The Poet," the "meaner the type by which a law is expressed, the more pungent it is, and the more lasting in the memories of men."

This section includes Foster's ground-breaking discussion of the Indian-hating section as well as the successive refinements by Shroeder and me. Later criticism, while abundant, tends to be colored by a more or less overtly expressed politically correct slant that simply cannot accommodate the idea that Melville himself may actually have meant Indians to be equated with evil, even in a grotesquely ironic religious allegory within a work of fiction. Critics comment on Colonel John Moredock as akin to Melville's Ahab or as a symbol of the American economic system or archetypal guardian of the socially constructed barrier that separates so-called civilization from so-called savagery, or as a confidence man himself, who allows the white community to disapprove of his actions even while enjoying the results of those actions. Other readings see the Indian-hating chapters as implicitly critical of the story's real author, James Hall, or Melville's character Charlie Noble. None of these interpretations, however, presents the Indians themselves as anything but victims, in some cases casting them as representative of all humankind whose role symbolizes the inhumanity of human beings to each other. In this section, as in this Norton Critical Edition as a whole, the focus is on specific historical contexts. Here, as in the historical background section of Indian hating, we focus on where Melville stood on race and religion and how he managed to weigh biblical Christianity against present-day American Christianity by allegorizing the *metaphysics* of the frontier reality of Indian hating. Melville could not have spoken out overtly. Melville could never be wholly frank, as he wrote to Evert A. Duyckinck from London in December 1849, but by use of allegory he could express his convictions about the nominal practice of Christianity and the ultimate impracticability of Christianity.

ELIZABETH S. FOSTER

[Melville's Allegorical Indian as a Type of the Confidence Man]†

As he leaves Pitch, the cosmopolitan is addressed by a stranger, whom some of the passengers suspect to be an "operator," or confidence man. This man has a bilious aspect, and wears clothes which are handsomer and finer than he appears to be. The bilious man, apropos of the misanthropy of Pitch, tells the story of Colonel John Moredock, Indian-hater, as he heard it from his father's friend, Judge James Hall.

* * *

This interpolated account of Indian-hating and Colonel Moredock, which occupies Chapters XXVI and XXVII, is the turning-point of the novel at its symbolical level and the apex of the whole argument; it has been, furthermore, a stumbling-block to several critics. Therefore it will be pertinent here to examine closely Melville's treatment of the material that he borrowed from Judge Hall.

He took his "Metaphysics of Indian-hating" and his story of Moredock largely from Hall's "Indian-hating.—Some of the sources of this animosity.—Brief account of Col. Moredock." Melville says that he is using Hall's language rather closely, as he is; but the reader who compares the two treatments will find that Melville has nevertheless made important changes in style and meaning. He breathes the breath of life and drama into Hall's dry, monotonous style; he varies the tempo; he sharpens and telescopes the narrative in its less important stretches; at the dramatic moment he expands it into a memorable close-up of the hero, " 'chewing the wild news with the wild meat' "; he substitutes the specific, graphic, and connotative for the general and commonplace; he enriches with allusion and enlivens with anecdote. The skilled and experienced story-teller and stylist has transmuted Hall's sketch.

The change that Melville makes in the meaning, though not so obvious, is at least equally important. Both Melville and Hall tell

† From the Introduction to *The Confidence-Man*, ed. Elizabeth S. Foster (New York: Hendricks House, 1954), lxv–lxx.

the following tale: The backwoodsman's persisting hatred of the Indian, after Indian rapine has ceased, is a curious phenomenon. To understand it, one must understand the backwoodsman: from the necessities of a hard, lonely, unassisted life he has become self-reliant and independent; experience is his tutor. From infancy he has heard stories of Indian lying, theft, fraud, perfidy, blood-thirstiness, ferocity; therefore he hates and distrusts all redskins. But the pure Indian-hater is bred when to the tale of Indian atrocities wreaked upon the community is added some unendurable wrong to the backwoodsman's own family. Then he leaves his kin, commits himself to the forest, and as long as his life lasts devotes himself to his implacable vengeance—the murder of Indians. John Moredock, having lost his family in an Indian massacre, sought out the murderers one by one and killed them; after that, though he sometimes returned briefly to the settlements, he spent his life exterminating red men.

Comparison of the two versions will show that Melville keeps Hall's portrait of the Indian-hater substantially the same except for one change. Hall explains that one reason for the backwoodsman's injustice to the Indians was that the pioneers, keeping always beyond the settlements, preserved the antiquated notions of moral right which prevailed when their ancestors entered the woods in the age of conquest and discovery. Melville omits this; he rests the backwoodsman's hatred of Indians squarely upon the harm that he has suffered through Indian perfidy. But Melville's radical change is in the portrait of the Indian: Hall makes him a savage more sinned against than sinning; Melville makes him the original and irreclaimable villain. He carefully omits all of Hall's references to the initial aggressions of the whites; he deletes Hall's extenuating explanations of Indian rapine as revenge for white injustice; and he makes Indian-hating a simple and inevitable consequence of the original and unexplained wickedness of the Indians. Furthermore, through an ironic sentence about the Peace Congress, Melville links Indians with the non-human elements of nature, such as panthers, in a more meaningful way than in the casual coupling in Hall, which merely calls attention to the inimical character of both. There is in Melville's version perhaps a suggestion that the Indian is something not so much sub-human as extra human. Finally, Melville's most conspicuous addition is the idea that the Indian hides his original, implacable malice beneath a mask of virtue and benignity in order to betray men and more easily wreak his hatred upon them: " 'when a tomahawking red man advances the notion of the benignity of the red race, it is but part and parcel with that subtle strategy which he finds so useful in war, in hunting, and the general conduct of life.' " In this Indian of Melville's, readers will have recognized a type of the Confidence Man.

Melville's change in the portrait of the Indian is very significant because it is a real change, not only from its immediate source, as just shown, but also from both Hall's and Melville's customary views on the subject of Indians. Throughout Hall's work, his sympathy for the Indian victims of the determined and heartless aggression of the whites is clear. His attitude is reiterated so often that Melville's change to the antipodal interpretation must have been made with definite purpose. Furthermore, Melville did violence as much to his own views on Indians as to Hall's. So closely similar to Hall's is Melville's usual attitude towards the *acculturation* of savages that readers of *Typee* and *Omoo* might almost think one of Hall's passages (given in the Explanatory Notes) to be an extract from one of those books. In his review of Parkman's *Oregon Trail* in 1849,[1] Melville states concisely his own humanitarian feelings towards Indians and takes exception to Parkman's contempt for savages:

> It is too often the case, that civilized beings sojourning among savages soon come to regard them with disdain and contempt. But though in many cases this feeling is most natural, it is not defensible; and it is wholly wrong. . . . Xavier and Elliott despised not the savages; and had Newton and Milton dwelt among them they would not have done so. . . . We are all of us—Anglo-Saxons, Dyaks, and Indians—sprung from one head, and made in one image. And if we regret this brotherhood now, we shall be forced to join hands hereafter.

By 1856 Melville may have repudiated the religious premise of this position, but there is no reason to believe that he repudiated the humanitarian attitude expressed here and elsewhere. He disclaims personal responsibility for the views in *The Confidence-Man* by putting them in the mouth of the Mississippi operator, who in turn specifically disclaims them and attributes them, quite unjustly, to Judge Hall. They are orphan views. Melville's portrait of the Indian, therefore, was painted, not to represent the American Indian, but to serve as a symbol appropriate to the author's ideas, a symbol, furthermore, which would clarify the argument.

Thus far, the argument of the book has run something like this: Men may choose between two ethical systems, the Christian one of mutual faith and love, announced in I Corinthians 13, and the egoistic, individualistic system epitomized in the barber's sign, "No Trust." The two emblems are the harmless, helpless lamblike man

---

1. First printed in the New York *Literary World* (March 31, 1849); reprinted in volume 9 of the NN Edition of Melville, *The Piazza Tales* &c. [Editors' note].

with his legend, "Charity thinketh no evil," and the barber with his razor. But Christian ethics appear to be ill suited to human nature; those who put their trust in the honesty and good intentions of their fellow men are all duped. Many of the dupes are themselves trustworthy people. But this is equivalent to saying that only fools are honest, and that mankind is divided into fools and knaves. And in this world, as the Missourian Pitch says, the knaves munch up the fools as horses munch up oats. St. Paul's doctrine of charity is at odds with the truth of our world as we know it, since there *is* evil in the universe and in human nature, and since some things are lies. The practice of charity merely stocks a happy hunting-ground for knaves, who take advantage of the doctrine for their selfish purpose. Consequently the doctrine itself, pragmatically viewed, is vicious, since it operates ultimately to undermine and destroy the small quantum of faith and love of which human nature is capable. Not Christianity alone is to blame for this, but all optimistic philosophies which assume that the universe is benevolent and human nature good.

In short, in the story thus far, faith, hope, and charity have been either frauds or snares; one cannot trust God, or nature, or man. Misanthropy, distrust, and a selfish, suspicious individualism have apparently been recommended. Knowledge derived from experience has been exalted and faith decried. Mankind has been divided into fools and knaves.

So simple an analysis of human nature is of course not Herman Melville's final word on "the last complications of that spirit which is affirmed by its Creator to be fearfully and wonderfully made." Some qualification of the cynicism and materialism of the main argument of the story has been made indirectly; the creed: " 'To where it belongs with your charity! To heaven with it! . . . here on earth, true charity dotes, and false charity plots,' " was put in the mouth of a soured misanthrope whose one lone leg may be " 'emblematic of his one-sided view of humanity.' " But this qualification was insufficient (as is obvious from the number of critics who speak of Melville's Timonism and his No-Trust moral in this book). Therefore, before introducing further arguments, Melville gives us an unforgettable picture of a society without faith or charity. Look down the vista of the No-Trust philosophy and see the Indian-hater: individualist, brave, free, kind-hearted, single-minded, self-reliant, experienced, disillusioned, but lost forever to human association with family, friends, and community, and devoted forever to the Indian-hunt, creeping warily through the woods, gun in hand, preying upon his fellow creatures. This is the true philosophy of nature. This is the alternative if we jettison charity—a world of solitary, dehumanized Indian-haters.

JOHN W. SHROEDER

Sources and Symbols for Melville's
Confidence-Man†

Melville criticism seems fated to a slow and uncertain growth. We have come a long way, to be sure, beyond the author who dismissed Melville as one among "several minor writers resident in the city or state of New York." But one chief fault we seem not to have corrected: it is perhaps not over-rash to say that this criticism learns only reluctantly from what it has already accomplished. We know, for instance, that Melville's literary borrowings in such a work as *Moby-Dick* are worth close scrutiny; we also know that the allegory and the symbol lurk everywhere in Melville's pages. But our knowledge is not regularly put to use as a hypothetical principle for the examination of other works. Now I suggest that there is still a good bit to be done with these tools alone, and in this present paper I mean to try to do a part of it. I propose to identify and follow out certain of the sources and symbols which went into one of Melville's least-known works, *The Confidence-Man*.

Nothing in particular happens in this book. The setting is the deck and cabins of a Mississippi steamer, the *Fidèle*, bound on the voyage down-river to New Orleans. On board the vessel, we are introduced to a number of figures: to a negro named Black Guinea, to a Mr. Roberts, a Mr. Ringman, a Mr. Goodman, a Mr. Noble, and various others. We are entertained with several debates and a few interpolated tales. Throughout the book rings the cry of "confidence," taken in both its main senses. Passengers approach other passengers with charitable schemes or demands for charity. There is a deal of talk and a deal of satire.

† "Sources and Symbols for Melville's *Confidence-Man*," PMLA, 66 (June 1951), 364–80. Reprinted by permission of the Modern Language Association of America. Shroeder wrote the first version of this paper before reading Elizabeth S. Foster's 1942 Yale dissertation, "Herman Melville's *The Confidence-Man*: Its Origins and Meaning," and in footnotes in the published paper carefully credited her with anticipating him in several of his findings, large and small, notably her discovery of the diabolic nature of the Confidence Man. He added: "Miss Foster has been most gracious and helpful in discussing with me the question of our independent discoveries." (Three years after Shroeder's article was published, Foster's Hendricks House edition of *The Confidence-Man* was published.) Shroeder also acknowledged the value of Nathalia Wright's *Melville's Use of the* Bible (1949) and he dealt in gingerly fashion with Richard Chase's *Herman Melville: A Critical Study* (1949), calling it a "stimulating interpretation" marred "by a number of factual inaccuracies." (The late Melvillean Howard P. Vincent testified, with mingled horror and admiration, that Chase wrote what became his chapter on *The Confidence-Man* after a hasty, excited reading of the book in a library. See p. xiii herein for the scarcity of this book until the end of the 1940s.) A few of Shroeder's footnoted mentions of now-outdated critical articles are omitted in this reprinting of his own groundbreaking and still valuable essay. Shroeder's demonstration of Melville's debt to Hawthorne's "The Celestial Railroad," in particular, has never been improved [Editors' note].

I think that this description is adequate to the surface of Melville's book. And if we are content to think that the book is nothing more than this surface, we will probably conclude that criticism has done well in letting this work slip out of sight. But we can, I think, set it down as law that Melville is never simply a writer of the surface.

The confidence-man, from whom our book takes its title, is a practiced shape-shifter; his existence is a succession of pious disguises. Among the characters which he assumes is that of collector of funds for the Seminole Widow and Orphan Asylum. The charitable operations of this gentleman are various. He has invented a "Protean easy-chair," designed to ease the torments of both body and conscience. While he was displaying this chair at the London World's Fair, the idea of the "World's Charity" came to him. The Charity, as he explains it (pp. 47–48),

> is to be a society whose members shall comprise deputies from every charity and mission extant, the one object of the society to be the methodization of the world's benevolence; to which end, the present system of voluntary and promiscuous contribution to be done away, and the Society to be empowered by the various governments to levy, annually, one grand benevolence tax upon all mankind; . . . This tax, according to my tables . . . would result in the yearly raising of a fund little short of eight hundred millions; this fund to be annually applied to such objects, and in such modes, as the various charities and missions, in general congress represented, might decree; . . .

The project, he adds, "will frighten none but a retail philanthropist." The passage has a certain independent value as evidence of the confidence-man's character; it relates him to the misled and misleading reformers who figure so largely in Hawthorne's writings. And we need not stop with this suggested parallel. If we go directly to Hawthorne's sketch, "The Celestial Railroad," we can identify something that looks suspiciously like the origin of this scheme: "There is another species of machine for the wholesale manufacture of individual morality. This excellent result is effected by societies for all manner of virtuous purposes, with which a man has merely to connect himself, throwing, as it were, his quota of virtue into the common stock, and the president and directors will take care that the aggregate amount be well applied." This excerpt, it seems to me, is a window which opens between and connects two fictional worlds. Now that our attention has been directed to this source—which sometimes leads us through Hawthorne to *his* source in Bunyan's *Pilgrim's Progress*—a number of interesting parallels become manifest. And these should be of real importance in defining the symbolic setting within which the episodes of *The Confidence-Man* occur.

Hawthorne transferred the protagonist of his sketch from the Celestial Railroad to "a stream ferry boat," with the intention of sending him comfortably on to the Celestial City. And Melville, if my deductions are correct, transmuted this boat into the steamer *Fidèle*, combining his favorite symbol of the boat-as-world with Hawthorne's symbol of the vessel bound for Tophet. Occasional descriptive passages support this identification. Hawthorne's train passed through a dark valley, whose gloom encouraged certain melancholy imaginings in his hero: "As the light of natural day, however, began to struggle with the glow of the lanterns, these vain imaginations lost their vividness, and finally vanished with the first ray of sunshine that greeted our escape from the Valley of the Shadow of Death. Ere we had gone a mile beyond it I could well-nigh have taken my oath that this whole gloomy passage was a dream." Compare the order of events in the above quotation with this passage from Melville: "The sky slides into blue, the bluffs into bloom; the rapid Mississippi expands; runs sparkling and gurgling, all over in eddies; one magnified wake of a seventy-four. The sun comes out, a golden huzzar, from his tent, flashing his helm on the world. All things, warmed in the landscape, leap. Speeds the dædal boat as a dream" (p. 82). And Melville's description of Cairo, where "the old established firm of Fever & Ague is still settling up its unfinished business," is reminiscent of both Hawthorne's Valley of the Shadow and Slough of Despond. There is even one direct verbal echo. "The mephitic gases of that region," says Hawthorne, speaking of the Dark Valley, "intoxicate the brain." At Cairo, Melville's "Don Saturninus Typhus . . . snuffs up the mephitic breeze with zest."

The travellers on the Celestial Railroad stored their luggage and bags away during the trip, Hawthorne's reference, of course, is to the "heavy burden" dropped by the Wall of Salvation by Bunyan's Christian. Both sources may have been in Melville's mind when he wrote of a man in a cream suit (the first figure to appear in his book) that "he had neither trunk, valise, carpet-bag, nor parcel" (p. 9).

There is a gentleman aboard the *Fidèle* who represents the Black Rapids Coal Company. The corporation has a sinister name, certainly; Hawthorne and Bunyan would have appreciated its allegorical possibilities. This particular confidence-man drives a thriving trade. And the precise nature of his goods comes to the surface when he refers to yet another stock for which there is no market:

"You wouldn't like to be concerned in the New Jerusalem, would you?"

"New Jerusalem?"

"Yes, the new and thriving city, so called, in northern Minnesota. . . . Here, here is the map," producing a roll. "There— there, you see, are the public buildings—here the landing—there the park—yonder the botanic gardens—and this, this little dot here, is a perpetual fountain, you understand. You observe there are twenty asterisks. Those are for the lyceums. They have lignum-vitæ rostrums." (pp. 58–59)

Further, the first settlement of this community was by "two fugitives, who had swum over naked from the opposite shore." It is a little difficult to see how criticism has missed the references in this passage. Perhaps it has been a case of misidentification; the settlement sounds vaguely like the Valley of Eden in Dickens' *Martin Chuzzlewit*. From the description, too, it would be not impossible to conclude that this is yet another cony-catching concern. But there are fountains and gardens in Hawthorne which will be potentially helpful here. Speaking of the land of Beulah, Hawthorne said: "The sweet breezes of this happy clime came refreshingly to our nostrils; we beheld the glimmering gush of silver fountains, overhung by trees of beautiful foliage and delicious fruit, which were propagated by grafts from the celestial gardens." And Bunyan will give us a source for our "lignum-vitæ rostrums" and for the agent's "roll." Christian and Hopeful, his two fugitives, were told that in the Celestial City they "shall see the tree of life, and eat of the never-fading fruits thereof." And Christian, when he dropped his burden, was given "a roll with a seal upon it," which he later presented at the gate of the City. It is hard, certainly, to see why criticism has not made more of all this. Richard Chase (p. 190) describes the Black Rapids Coal Company as "a dubious or nonexistent corporation." I suggest, however, that the company, to Melville's mind, was very palpably extant, just as was the New Jerusalem. The parallels to Bunyan and Hawthorne—and more are still to come—make of these concerns the polar opposites of the *Fidèle's* universe.

The agent of the Seminole asylum, it will be recalled, first struck on his plan for the World's Charity while at the London Fair. "I will see," he claims to have said to himself, "if this occasion of vanity cannot supply a hint toward a better profit than was designed" (p. 47). The close association of the words "vanity" and "fair" is evocative, especially when we remember the episode of the Fair in Hawthorne's sketch. The motif occurs elsewhere; the deck of the *Fidèle*, indeed, is like some "Constantinople arcade or bazaar." There is a young fellow on the boat who once kept a "toy-stand at the fair in Cincinnati"; he sold "more than one old man a child's rattle" (p. 244). And a certain cosmopolitan, the most striking of Melville's voyagers, capitalizes the word for us during a discussion with another passenger:

> "Hands off!" cried the bachelor, involuntarily covering dejection with moroseness.
> "Hands off? [the cosmopolitan is speaking] that sort of label won't do in our Fair. Whoever in our Fair has fine feelings loves to feel the nap of fine cloth, especially when a fine fellow wears it." (p. 136)

Other parallels will occur to Melville's reader. The list of the "pilgrims" on the *Fidèle*—"Natives of all sorts, and foreigners; men of business and men of pleasure; parlor men and backwoodsmen; farm-hunters and fame-hunters; . . . English, Irish, German, Scotch, Danes; . . . hard-shell Baptists and clay-eaters; grinning negroes, and Sioux chiefs solemn as high-priests" (p. 16)—may very well owe its accumulation of nouns to Bunyan's example: "And moreover, at this fair there is at all times to be seen jugglings, cheats, games, plays, fools, apes, knaves, and rogues, and that of every kind." "Here is the Britain-row, the French-row, the Italian-row, the Spanish-row, the German-row, where several sorts of vanities are to be sold." Or take the name of Melville's steamer, the *Fidèle*. Faithful was executed by the people of Bunyan's Fair.

At least one character, too, seems to cross from an earlier Fair to Melville's. At Hawthorne's: "Prince Beelzebub himself took great interest in this sort of traffic, and sometimes condescended to meddle with smaller matters. I once had the pleasure to see him bargaining with a miser for his soul, which, after much ingenious skirmishing on both sides, his highness succeeded in obtaining at about the value of sixpence." There is a miser given to precisely this same ingenious skirmishing on Melville's steamer. He purchases a box of herbs from a travelling doctor (whose relation to Prince Beelzebub will be treated subsequently):

> "Say a dollar-and-half. Ugh!"
> "Can't. Am pledged to the one-price system, only honorable one."
> "Take off a shilling—ugh, ugh!"
> "Can't."
> "Ugh, ugh, ugh—I'll take it.—There."
> Grudgingly he handed eight silver coins, but while still in his hand, his cough took him, and they were shaken upon the deck.
> One by one, the herb-doctor picked them up, and, examining them, said: "These are not quarters, these are pistareens; and clipped, and sweated, at that." (p. 110)

Even the distracting fashion in which Melville's actors suddenly disappear from sight may have been suggested by a passage from Hawthorne's dream-vision: "Amid the occupations or amusements of the Fair, nothing was more common than for a person—whether at feast, theatre, or church, or trafficking for wealth and honors, or whatever he might be doing, to vanish like a soap bubble, and be never more seen of his fellows; . . ."

The value of these literary cross references is, I think, extreme. They act to locate the events of *The Confidence-Man* geographically and spiritually. The world of this book is a great Vanity Fair, situated on an allegorical steamboat which, presumably sailing for New Orleans (on the symbolic level, for the New Jerusalem of nineteenth-century optimism and liberal theology), is inclining its course dangerously toward the pits of the Black Rapids Coal Company. Aboard the vessel we have pilgrimaging mankind. And among these pilgrims, the confidence-man is inordinately active; the character and actions of this ambiguous figure must now claim our attention.

The confidence-man, as I have noted before, is a shape-shifter; it is never easy to pin him down and identify him. Let us seize upon the handy figure of Black Guinea as a medium of introduction to our confidence-man. Black Guinea is a negro, presumably crippled, who begs about the deck (p. 17): "In the forward part of the boat, not the least attractive object, for a time, was a grotesque negro cripple, in tow-cloth attire and an old coal-sifter of a tamborine in his hand, who, owing to something wrong about his legs, was, in effect, cut down to the stature of a Newfoundland dog; . . ." When we recall the black-white world of *Benito Cereno*—and when we note that Guinea's tamborine is a "coal-sifter"—we are apt to suspect a certain ominous quality in this negro; he may be an inhabitant of the fiery pit. Whatever he is, however—and the clues to his identity are not many—he is somehow related to the confidence-man we are to meet. Asked whether he can produce any witnesses who will certify his infirmity as real, he replies (p. 21): "Oh yes, oh yes, dar is aboard here a werry nice, good ge'mman wid a weed, and a ge'mman in a gray coat and white tie, what knows all about me; and a ge'mman wid a big book, too; and a yarb doctor; and a ge'mman in a yaller west; and a ge'mman wid a brass plate; and a ge'mman in a wiolet robe; and a ge'mman as is a sodjer; . . ." This is a reasonably complete listing of the confidence-man's masks. Several of these gentlemen appear, invoking confidence and fleecing the public. The man with the weed exchanges a tale of personal misfortune for a friendly loan from a merchant. The man in the gray coat (the Charity Agent) successfully solicits funds for the Seminole

Asylum. The "ge'mman wid a big book" proves to be the agent of the Coal Company. The herb-doctor drives a good trade with the sick. The man with the brass plate is the agent of a Philosophical Intelligence Office; he breaks through the mistrust of a Missouri bachelor and receives, as fee, money to provide the bachelor with a new hired boy. The identification of the other gentlemen on Guinea's list is more difficult. Two pretended soldiers appear, but neither seems qualified to give Guinea a recommendation. We are later introduced, too, to one Charlie Noble (who has a violet vest) and to the cosmopolitan, Francis Goodman, whose costume has something of the robelike in it. I suspect, for reasons which I shall subsequently present, that Noble is akin to the Charity agent, the Black Rapids agent, and the man with the plate, and that Goodman is the confidence-man raised to the highest power (though if this is the case, the long conversation which they hold together is rather difficult to explain). We cannot, it would seem, depend absolutely on Guinea's list; other evidence must be brought to bear in the task of unmasking the confidence-man.

The man with the weed is known as Ringman; the man with the book is Truman; the herb-doctor calls himself "the Happy Man"; the cosmopolitan, as we have noted, is named Francis Goodman. These fellows are apparently of the same allegorical family; Spenser's Sansfoy, Sansjoy, and Sansloy come immediately to mind as a kindred group. And this same surname-element of "man" occurs again in a highly significant passage. The cosmopolitan, late at night, startles the *Fidèle's* barber. The barber, however, quickly recovers from his fright:

> "Ah!" turning round disenchanted, "it is only a man, then."
> "*Only* a man? As if to be but man were nothing. But don't be too sure what I am. You call me *man*, just as the townsfolk called the angels who, in man's form, came to Lot's house; just as the Jew rustics called the devils who, in man's form, haunted the tombs. You can conclude nothing absolute from the human form, barber." (p. 225)

The hint is a good one; the confidence-man is pretty certainly not "only a man." Angel or devil, then, remain as the leading possibilities. And Melville, if we attend to him closely, will resolve the problem for us. Of the disguises voluntarily assumed by the confidence-man—of the masks of his masquerade—we have spoken. And the confidence-man is subject to yet another change—an involuntary metamorphosis—of which we must now speak.

While the man with the weed importuned the merchant for a loan, "a writhing expression stole over him" (p. 29). Later, while accosting yet another traveller, he is described as "sliding nearer," as "quivering down and looking up." The traveller seems under the man's spell; indeed, says Melville, the man "fascinated him" (p. 36). There is only one creature which writhes, quivers, looks up from below while speaking, and fascinates. And he is subsequently named. Later in the book (p. 94), an "invalid Titan" fells the herb-doctor with a blow, and cries at him: "Profane fiddler on heart-strings! Snake!"

Satan and his legions, according to Milton, are doomed to assume at certain periods the form of the reptile. The transformation was a favorite of Hawthorne's. And Melville pushes it to its limits. After the man with the plate has departed with the Missouri bachelor's money, the gulled Missourian finds time to wonder what species of being he has been dealing with: "Analogically, he couples the slanting cut of the equivocator's coat-tails with the sinister cast in his eye; he weighs slyboot's sleek speech in the light imparted by the oblique import of the smooth slope of his worn boot-heels; the insinuator's undulating flunkyisms dovetail into those of the flunky beast that windeth his way on his belly" (p. 135). Both Charlie Noble and Frank Goodman are subject to this reptilian change. Charlie, when asked by Frank for a loan, like "Cadmus glided into the snake" (p. 185). And Frank, later, while praising the "latent benignity" of the rattlesnake, is seen "to wreathe his form and sidelong erect his head, till he all but seemed the creature described" (p. 191). In the barber's shop, Goodman enchants that person by his "persuasive fascination—the power of holding another creature by the button of the eye" (p. 233). When we are told that a clergyman catches, in the expression of the Seminole Asylum agent, "something" (p. 42) which causes him uneasiness,[1] we do not have to exercise much speculative energy in order to discover what that something is. The legions of Satan, patently, are loose about the deck of the *Fidèle*.

Several traits act to set our cosmopolitan apart from the other confidence-men. His philosophical discourse, while basically like that of such fellows as Ringman and Truman in its refusal to recognize the dark side of the universe, is conceived in a freer spirit than is that of his underlings. He has powers of sorcery beyond those exercised by his fellows; he charms Charlie Noble with a tasselled pipe and a magic ring of ten half-eagles (p. 185). Finally, Melville permits him to talk at length with Noble, whose snakemetamorphosis I have already cited as evidence of demonism.

This cosmopolitan, I suggest, is related to that Prince Beelzebub (proverbially a much-travelled gentleman) who personally "took great interest" in the trade of Hawthorne's Vanity Fair. And certain

1. Miss Foster has noted many of these events; her discussion of their import is admirable.

of his comments are alarming; he protests a great love for humanity: "Served up à la Pole, or à la Moor, à la Ladrone, or à la Yankee,
that good dish, man, still delights me; or rather is man a wine I
never weary of comparing and sipping; wherefore am I . . . a sort of
London-Dock-Vault connoisseur, . . . a taster of races; . . . smacking
my lips over this racy creature, man, continually" (p. 138). He declares to Charlie Noble that he has inspected the heart of the Missouri bachelor and "found it an inviting oyster in a forbidding
shell." And Charlie himself pleads, in extenuation of his not smoking, that he "ate of a diabolical ragout at dinner" (p. 174). We need
not go to the Fathers of the Church for this reference. Modern
writers from Poe to C. S. Lewis have noted the Devil's fondness for
the human soul as a dish. While we have Charlie Noble's dinner
before us, it is helpful to remember that Poe's Pierre Bon-Bon offered his soul to the Devil as being particularly qualified for, among
other things, a ragout. These implications, however, while amusing
in themselves, do no more than aid in the identification of our symbolic personages. The question is not what the devil will do with
the human soul when he gets it but how he gets it in the first place.
How, we must inquire, does the confidence-man function in
Melville's Fair?

The man with the brass plate represents himself to the Missouri
bachelor as the agent of a Philosophical Intelligence Office. His
Office, as he explains, engages, in a "small, quiet way," in the "careful analytical study of man, conducted, too, on a quiet theory, and
with an unobtrusive aim wholly our own" (p. 125). The theory, he
continues, he will not trouble to set forth at large. We must set it
forth for him.

The most obvious point to be observed in all our various confidence-men is their continual invocation of confidence; they take
money from their victims only on condition that the victims confide
in them; the payment of cash, we might say, is only the visible symbol of the payment of confidence. And it is obviously a payment
with a dark significance. The name Black Guinea—combining the
Devil's color with a monetary unit—is interesting here; there is apparently a coinage which is especially prized by Prince Beelzebub.
The Missouri bachelor (who has had such bitter experiences with
hired boys that he has resolved to get a machine to do his work),
his distrust lessened by the arguments of the man with the plate,
agrees to admit "some faint, conditional degree of confidence" in
the hired-boy the agent is to send him. He presents the agent with
three dollars. Later, ruminating on his experience after the agent
has gone ashore at a place called "the Devil's Joke," he finds that
there is a sharp discrepancy between the guile exercised and the re-

ward for it. "He revolves, but cannot comprehend, the operation, still less the operator. Was the man a trickster, it must be more for the love than the lucre" (p. 135). We are in a better position than was the bachelor; we are aware that it is not the transfer of money but the transfer of confidence which gives point to the Devil's joke. The analytical study of the Intelligence Office has been well adapted to the accomplishment of its "unobtrusive aim."

In Hawthorne's Fair, there was "a sort of stock or scrip, called Conscience, which seemed to be in great demand, and would purchase almost anything." In Melville's Fair the scrip is confidence; the demand is just as great and the penalty for its payment is, as in the other Fair, damnation. The scrip demanded by the confidence-man is confidence that the world has no dark side; that the boat is unerringly and necessarily bound for the Celestial City; that all the conscience requires is a Protean easy-chair or the medications of the herb-doctor.

The Missouri bachelor is the hardest nut that the confidence-man has to crack. The bachelor is theologically sound; the dark side of the universe is a part of his permanent vision. And we can profitably attend to certain of his views. The bachelor was continually pestered by the confidence-man. Before meeting the man with the plate, he found himself in the company of the herb-doctor. The doctor represents himself as having confidence in nature; he is, indeed, one of her "regularly authorized agents." This is not the sort of recommendation apt to pass with the bachelor, who earlier observed to the sick miser:

> "Natur is good Queen Bess; but who's responsible for the cholera?"
> "But yarbs, yarbs; yarbs are good?"
> "What's deadly-nightshade? Yarb, ain't it?" (p. 111)

There is nothing, says the bachelor, of which he is more suspicious than of nature. Nature carried away his ten thousand dollar plantation; Nature did her best to blind him. "Look you, nature!" he cries (p. 114), "I don't deny but your clover is sweet, and your dandelions don't roar, but whose hailstones smashed my windows?" In brief, the Missourian is very well aware that nature is cursed for man's sake; that the natural evil of the universe—an evil which the confidence-man attempts to conceal—represents to man a perpetual emblem of his fall and consequent perilous spiritual state.

The Bachelor's view on boys partakes of a related theological concept. "Augustine on original sin," says he, "is my text book." He has had hired-boys of every nation and description. "No sir," he tells the man with the plate (p. 122), "No sir, . . . Don't try to oil me; the herb-doctor tried that. My experience, carried now through a course . . . of five and thirty boys, proves to me that boyhood is a natural state of rascality."

The arguments of the man with the plate, as we have seen, ultimately prevail with the bachelor. The agent persuades him that he can safely be confident; even a corrupt boy will in time become a sober, noble man. Goodness is latent in the corrupt boy just as the beard is latent in the boy's face: "supposing, respected sir, that worthy gentleman, Adam, to have been dropped overnight in Eden, . . . could even the learned serpent himself have foreknown that such a downy-chinned little innocent would eventually rival the goat in a beard? Sir, wise as the serpent was, that eventuality would have been entirely hidden from his wisdom." The confidence-man's mention of his master revives the bachelor's suspicions for a moment: "I don't know about that. The devil is very sagacious. To judge by the event, he appears to have understood man better even than the Being who made him" (pp. 126–27). The Devil *is* very sagacious: the success of his agent is excellent witness to the power of his understanding. Our bachelor, like the other dupes at the Fair, finally pays over his confidence—renounces his vision of those qualities in man and the world which should perpetually recall his spiritual danger—and presumably finds himself damned. There is a certain hungry expectation in the cosmopolitan's discovery that this man's soul is an "inviting oyster."

The cosmopolitan engages only twice in the cony-catching which goes on aboard the *Fidèle*. In one instance, he persuades the barber to take down his "No Trust" sign; he then leaves the shop without paying for his shave. The other instance is a more crucial one. It provides the book's last chapter, whose title, "The Cosmopolitan Increases in Seriousness," is enough to alert us. The prince is about to take a hand in the business of his Fair.

"In the middle of the gentlemen's cabin," the chapter begins (p. 238), "burned a solar lamp, swung from the ceiling, and whose shade of ground glass was all round fancifully variegated, in transparency, with the image of a horned altar, from which flames rose, alternate with the figure of a robed man, his head encircled by a halo." The cosmopolitan, "Redolent from the barber's shop, as any bridegroom tripping to the bridal chamber might come, and by his look . . . seeming to dispense a sort of morning through the night," enters the cabin. He finds there "a clean, comely, old man," his head snowy as marble; this old gentleman is seated below the lamp and is studying the Bible.

The atmosphere, plainly, is highly charged with symbolism. I do not intend, indeed, to try to bring all of its symbols out. Richard Chase and Miss Nathalia Wright have written very well concerning some of the threads of meaning woven into this scene; I shall confine my own attention to a series of Biblical references which seem to have gone unnoticed. We must have one more hint before we settle down to them. Beyond the reaches of the lamp's rays, travellers sleep uneasily in their bunks. The conversation of the cosmopolitan and the old man occasionally disturbs one of them. When the cosmopolitan reads aloud the words of the Son of Sirach—"If thou be for his profit he will use thee; he will make thee bear, and will not be sorry for it. Observe and take good heed. When thou hearest these things, awake in thy sleep" (p. 241)—the sleeper, apparently obeying the admonition, inquires, "Who's that describing the confidence man?" And when the old gentleman explains to the cosmopolitan that the words of the Son of Sirach are apocrypha, the sleeper makes an important word-play (p. 242): "What's that about the Apocalypse?" And the Revelation of St. John will, I think, give us many of the hints we want. Here, for example, is a passage of possible relevance to the lamp and the old man (1.12–14):

> And I turned to see the voice that spake with me. And being turned, I saw seven golden candlesticks;
> And in the midst of the seven candlesticks, one like unto the Son of man, clothed with a garment down to the foot, and girt about the paps with a golden girdle.
> And his head and his hairs were white like wool, as white as snow; and his eyes were as a flame of fire.

There is continual mention in the book of St. John the Divine, too, of the lamp, the robes, and the altar. And one altar (which has, of course, its counterparts elsewhere in the Bible) is particularly interesting: "And the sixth angel sounded, and I heard a voice from the four horns of the golden altar which is before God" (9.13). And the cosmopolitan, that strange combination of bridegroom and morning radiance, must owe something to this passage (22.16–17): "I Jesus have sent mine angel to testify unto you these things in the churches. I am the root and the offspring of David, and the bright and morning star. And the Spirit and the bride say, Come." We should now be ready to recross the bridge between the Revelation of St. John and the cabin of the *Fidèle*. We must be careful in utilizing the evidence we have picked up. That the old gentleman is to be identified with the "Son of Man" is not likely. And earlier portions of the book act to negate any suspicion that the cosmopolitan has become Jesus. It is well to remember, in this connection, that Satan also was one of the sons of the morning; the coming of this present bridegroom portends a very different marriage from that of Christ and the Church. The primary function of Melville's references is to locate and define the action about to take place. The world, let us say, is now centered in the *Fidèle's* cabin, and Melville's own version of the Apocalypse is about to unfold before us. Again, as elsewhere in the book, the Devil works by the manipulation of confidence. A young boy enters the cabin; he is the fellow who kept a booth at the Cincinnati fair. Melville's description (p. 243) must be quoted: "All pointed and fluttering, the rags of the little fellow's red-flannel shirt, mixed with those of his yellow coat, flamed about him like the painted flames in the robe of a victim in *auto-da-fé*. His face, too, wore such a polish of seasoned grime, that his sloe-eyes sparked from out it like lustrous sparks in fresh coal." Richard Chase likes this young fellow; he sees in him "the youthful, fiery Prometheus [who] tries to warn the Old God [the white-haired old man] that all is not well." To Chase, the boy is the antagonist of the False Prometheus, who is represented by the cosmopolitan. There are several things wrong with Chase's symbolic identifications. The only persuasion exercised by the boy has as its object the instilling in the old man of confidence in several suspect objects of trade. He sells him a lock for his door; then he points out how a thief might evade the lock and sells him a money belt. He throws in, finally, a *Counterfeit Detector* which does not work. The lad seems to be in league with the cosmopolitan. He tries to sell that gentleman a lock (p. 245):

> "Excuse me, my fine fellow, but I never use such blacksmiths' things."
> "Those who give the blacksmith most work seldom do," said the boy, tipping him a wink. . . . But the wink was not marked by the old man, nor, to all appearances, by him for whom it was intended.

That "to all appearances" is a weasel-phrase; it is possible that the cosmopolitan did not catch the wink, but the very fact that there was a wink is enough to alert us. The description of this flaming lad, indeed—and we may add to it that his laugh disclosed "leopard-like teeth"—is pretty reasonable evidence that he is from the pit, called up by the cosmopolitan to aid in his project against the old man.[2]

The cosmopolitan first induces distrust in the old man and then quiets it. The ground, it appears, must be plowed before it can be planted. The old gentleman was instructed by his son, a careful man, to be certain that he has a life-preserver in his state-room. The confidence-man presents him with a chamber-stool. "In case

2. Again, the "sleeper" is helpful. When the lad laughs, the man in the bunk mutters: "The divils are laughing now, are they? . . . To bed, with ye, ye divils, and no more of ye" (p. 243). Miss Foster notes fully the significance of the many references to the Devil in the book.

of a wreck," he tells the old fellow, "barring sharp-pointed timbers, you could have confidence in that stool for a special providence." "Then," says the old man, "good-night, good-night; and Providence have both of us in its good keeping." Good-night, indeed. The old man, in the gloom of the cabin, inquires where his state-room may be; the cosmopolitan replies:

> "I have indifferent eyes, and will show you; but, first, for the good of all lungs, let me extinguish this lamp."
> The next moment, the waning light expired, and with it the waning flames of the horned altar, and the waning halo round the robed man's brow; while in the darkness which ensued, the cosmopolitan kindly led the old man away. (p. 251)

I cannot resist the temptation to find in the Revelation of St. John a possible origin for this last scene. In the City of God, writes John: "there shall be no night there; and they need no candle, neither light of the sun; For the Lord God giveth them light" (22.5). The point, of course, is that the old gentleman needs the candle and the sun above all other things. In the confidence-man's kingdom, the only light he is apt to find is the Miltonic "darkness visible."

Melville's book of the Apocalypse, it would seem, is more closely allied to the vision of Pope's *Dunciad* than to that of John's Revelation. The confidence-man has triumphed; he leads mankind, through an extinct universe, to his lightless kingdom. Or, to introduce a different set of symbols, the steamboat, filled with those who have confidence in herbs and easy-chairs, nature and boys, coal companies and Indian charities, counterfeit detectors and chamber-stools, has taken a direct course for the pit. Vanity Fair is sold out.

The *Confidence-Man*, manifestly, is a dark book. It ends, like *Pierre* and *Mardi*, in wreck. But it differs from these works in that its wreck symbolizes not Melville's inability to see but the result of his seeing perfectly well. *Moby-Dick*, too, ends in wreck, but there is something beyond; Ahab's destruction is objectified and balanced by the opposition to it of Ishmael's salvation. And in the same way, the triumph of the confidence-man is opposed and objectified, though apparently not negated, by an adversary of heroic proportions.

In the longest of the stories interpolated into the texture of our book, we are introduced to one Colonel John Moredock, an Indian fighter. The Colonel, we hear (p. 146), "hated Indians like snakes." Now hatred of the snake amounts to positive virtue in the cosmos of the *Fidèle*. And the Indian, I suggest, is coupled with the serpent in no accidental fashion. Let us follow the Indian for a little space.

The confidence-man, we recall, made an early appearance as the agent of the Seminole Widow and Orphan Asylum. If the Asylum has, as it must, affinities to the Coal Company, the doctor's herbs (the doctor calls himself a "true Indian doctor"), and the Intelligence office, the advantages of bestowing charity on the Red Man become very dubious indeed. We are later told the tale of Goneril, a strange woman given to eating clay, gifted with the "evil-touch," and possessed by a "calm, clayey, cakey devil." Goneril's figure is "Indian"; her health is "like a squaw's (pp. 68, 67)." Whatever else is to be said of this woman, the savage element in her nature is arresting.

We are to meet more of this imagery. At a houseless landing, two transient figures come aboard the *Fidèle*. One is an "invalid Titan in homespun"; the other, "a puny girl, walking in moccasins, not improbably his child, but evidently of alien maternity, perhaps Creole, or even Camanche." The child is clad in an Indian blanket. Melville, at one point, describes the invalid father as bowing over with pain "like a mainmast yielding to the gale, or Adam to the thunder" (p. 92). Let us take this last hint as a workable theory. The couple might very well be Adam and Eve, cast out of Paradise. Eve may properly be considered as being both Adam's daughter and a child of "alien maternity." And her apple will turn up later in the book. The cosmopolitan and Charlie Noble drink and smoke together for several chapters. When they call for wine, it is brought to them in "a little bark basket, braided with porcupine quills, gayly tinted in the Indian fashion" (p. 165). And when they call for cigars, they come in "a pretty little bit of western pottery, representing some kind of Indian utensil": "Accompanying it were two accessories, also bits of pottery, but smaller, both globes; one in guise of an apple flushed with red and gold to the life; and, through a cleft at top, you saw it was hollow. This was for the ashes" (p. 173). Eve's fruit has become one of Sodom's apples.

The book supplies, we may say, a running system of Indian-images related to concepts, situations, and persons connected with the theological doctrines of human guilt and damnation. It is interesting to note that the Puritans could account for the Indian only by supposing him to be a descendant of Satan. And another link in this long chain is useful. In one of the several chapters which deal with Moredock, Melville tells the story of the Wrights and the Weavers, a little band of frontiersmen from Virginia. After a long and bloody period of hostility with the Indians, the survivors of the group contrived a treaty with Mocmohoc, the enemy chief. Their pact stipulated that the whites would never be expected to enter the chief's lodge together: "Nevertheless, Mocmohoc did, upon a time, with such fine art and pleasing carriage win their confidence, that he brought them all together to a feast of bear's meat, and there, by stratagem, ended them. Years after, over their calcined bones and those of all their families, the chief, reproached for this treachery by a proud hunter whom he had made captive, jeered out, "Treachery? pale face! 'Twas they who broke their covenant first, in coming all together; they that broke it first, in trusting Mocmohoc" (p. 154). This chief certainly is the confidence-man in one of his more open disguises; those critics who incline to think that the confidence-man is Christ—doing good by stealth to man's spirit—should profit by this passage. Mocmohoc's words will stand very well as the motto of Ringman, Truman, Goodman, and the rest.

The ill-fated feast of bear's meat has its symbolic implications. The agent of the Black Rapids Coal Company confesses that his stock has recently undergone a slight devaluation. This depression of the stock he assigns to "the growling, the hypocritical growling, of the bears." "Why," he says, "the most monstrous of all hypocrites are these bears" (p. 56). They are "hypocrites in the simulation of things dark"; they thrive on depression; they are, indeed, experts in the wicked art of creating depression: "scoundrelly bears!" When we make the proper allowance for the speaker, it becomes evident that the bear is the distrustful man; the man who has no confidence in the false, bright side of things; the only man in Melville's universe who has a sporting chance against snakes, Indians, and confidence-men.

The Missouri bachelor was "somewhat ursine in aspect"; he sported "a shaggy spencer of the cloth called bear's-skin" (p. 111). He growled at the man with the plate like "Bruin in a hollow trunk" (p. 126). The confidence-man, as we know, finally took in this bear, just as he took in the Wrights and the Weavers. But there is a mythic figure of whom the bachelor is but a weakened type. He is the dedicated "Indian-hater." The confidence-man cannot trap him. Charlie Noble, who tells the tale of Colonel Moredock to the cosmopolitan,[3] says that he once, having come to a house where the Colonel was sleeping, slipped up into the loft to catch a sight of the hero; the Colonel, however, vanished at his approach.

The Indian-hater is a rarity. Such souls, says Melville, quoting Pope, peep out but once an age. His dedication is a religious one; his is "the solemnity of the Spaniard turned monk." His salvation is a completely individual matter: "The backwoodsman is a lonely man. He is a thoughtful man. He is a man strong and unsophisticated. Impulsive, he is what some might call unprincipled. At any

3. "Hate Indians?" exclaims the cosmopolitan. "Why should he or anybody else hate Indians? *I* admire Indians" (p. 146).

rate, he is self-willed; being one who less hearkens to what others may say about things, than looks for himself, to see what are things themselves. If in straits, there are few to help; he must depend upon himself; he must continually look to himself. Hence self-reliance, to the degree of standing by his own judgment, though it stand alone" (p. 149). The value of individualism and isolation for the achievement of spiritual vision is one of the most interesting things to emerge from this book. The Prince is well aware that they provide a way out of his Fair. Goodman, conversing with the Missouri bachelor, praises the graces of sociability; only remorse, he says, can drive man to "that awful sin of shunning society." The bachelor answers that remorse does nothing of the kind. Cain founded the first city; the pickpocket especially enjoys having his fellows about him.

The Indian-hater is the world's only remedy against the confidence-man; a severe disease calls for a strong purge. Like Ahab, the Indian-hater is an isolated hunter; like Ahab, he is little given to kneeling; like Ahab, he is grave, "as is not unusual with men of his complexion, a sultry and tragical brown." But unlike Ahab, the Indian-hater has succeeded in locating Evil in its real home; there is no distortion in his vision of spiritual reality.

"Something further," wrote Melville at the conclusion of his book, "may follow of this Masquerade." This may or may not represent both spiritual prophecy and a statement of future creative intent. Whatever the case, The Confidence-Man is complete within the limits which it proposes to itself. It is, certainly, complete in the same sense that Pilgrim's Progress and "The Celestial Railroad" are complete. And if we are determined to classify it as to kind, it is by reference to these two allegorical visions of the state of man's soul that we must make our classification.

The reader who knows his Melville will be aware that I have ignored certain crucial problems connected with his book. I have not attempted to identify the man in cream colors—the deaf-mute—with whom the novel begins. I have not offered any explanation as to why Noble and Goodman, if both are from the pit, should unknown to one another carry on their long conversation. I have not attempted to unriddle the tales of Goneril, Charlemont, and China Aster. For these problems I have no answers. But this is not to say that there are no answers, nor is it to say that these characters and passages are mere random digressions. No critic has yet satisfactorily explained why Melville, in Moby-Dick, apparently decided to drop the important character Bulkington overboard shortly after introducing him. No critic has satisfactorily accounted for the presence of the cassock chapter in Moby-Dick. Criticism, in these cases, must be content to explain as much as it possibly can and then rest in the faith that it will in time arrive at a level of interpretation which will resolve these questions.

With these reservations in mind, I am ready to suggest that *The Confidence-Man* is one of the most valuable of the works in Melville's canon. It does not, of course, attain to the depth and imaginative energy which distinguishes *Moby-Dick*. But where *Moby-Dick* itself is often uncertain of its direction—where *Moby-Dick* sets out on false trails and perhaps unrelated mental voyages— *The Confidence-Man* establishes a single, though complex, aim and follows that aim through with what is, for Melville, remarkable fidelity. There are many reasons why *Moby-Dick*, imperfect though it sometimes is, should command our critical preference. But among Melville's other writings—among such things as the incoherent *Mardi*, the ranting *Pierre*, the frigid *Billy-Budd*—*The Confidence-Man* stands as a hale and well-proportioned giant.

HERSHEL PARKER

The Metaphysics of Indian Hating†

Even the closest student of *The Confidence-Man* admits that it "still keeps many, or most, of its secrets."[1] A reader can still share the sense of discovery which informed this paragraph by Sedgwick:[2]

> There is interpolated in *The Confidence-Man* a strange story, the point of which, I believe, has escaped notice. I refer to the story of Colonel Moredock, the Indian-hater, followed by a discussion of the genus "Indian-hater" and the metaphysics of Indian-hating. The allegory here is so transparent that it needs no comment. The point to which it leads is important; to my way of thinking it is the most important thing in the book.

But today the critic of the Indian-hater section cannot be as confident as Sedgwick that the point has escaped notice. Both Elizabeth Foster (p. xci) and Nathalia Wright[3] have agreed that the section is the crux of the book, and the "transparent" allegory has evoked a good deal of comment.[4] In this paper I will survey the arguments of

† From *Nineteenth-Century Fiction*, 18 (September 1963), 165–73. Copyright 1963 by The Regents of the University of California. Reprinted by permission of The Regents.
1. *The Confidence-Man* (New York: Hendricks House, 1954), xlvi, edited by Elizabeth S. Foster. Further references to Foster's Introduction and Notes are given in parentheses within the text.
2. William Ellery Sedgwick, *Herman Melville: The Tragedy of Mind* (Cambridge: Harvard University Press, 1944), 190.
3. *Melville's Use of the Bible* (Durham: Duke University Press, 1949), 56.
4. Sedgwick's discussion of the passage does not justify the use of the word "allegory."

the three major critics of the Indian-hater chapters, John W. Shroeder,[5] Roy Harvey Pearce,[6] and Foster, and point out some unresolved difficulties. Then, often working from their findings, I will interpret the story in terms of the opposing elements of the allegory and in relation to a theme recurring in all of Melville's novels. The Indian-hater story, as I read it, is a tragic study of the impracticability of Christianity, and, more obviously, a satiric allegory in which the Indians are Devils and the Indian-haters are dedicated Christians, and in which the satiric target is the nominal practice of Christianity.

If Shroeder has not "let more light into this book than any other critic," as Miss Foster says (p. xlii), certainly his use of literary cross-references "to locate the events of *The Confidence-Man* geographically and spiritually" (p. 481) is the most illuminating criticism besides her own. Briefly as Shroeder treats the Indian-hater chapters, he indicates convincingly the diabolic nature of the Indians and the god-like character of the Indian-hater. Colonel Moredock, says Shroeder, "has succeeded in locating Evil in its real home; there is no distortion in his vision of spiritual reality." But I would quarrel with Shroeder's conclusion that the only hope in this "dark book" is that "the triumph of the confidence-man is opposed and objectified, though apparently not negated, by an adversary of heroic proportions" (p. 489)—that is, by Moredock. And I suggest that Shroeder, while accurately formulating the terms of the allegory, has missed the ironic inversion of accepted values which is the basis of Melville's gigantic satire.

Pearce's article amounts to a general contradiction of Shroeder's conclusions. He denies that the Indians "are symbols of satanism," and argues from Melville's attitude toward real Indians that he does not use the Indian symbolically in *The Confidence-Man*.[7] Pearce submits "that there is nothing but distortion in the Indian-hater's vision of spiritual reality," and denies that Moredock "functions as a kind of hero" (p. 942). The artistic function of Melville's version of the Indian-hater story—a version in which hatred is called a "devout sentiment" and the hater is praised—"is to be too violent a purge, a terrible irony." In Pearce's reading there is hope neither in the blind

---

5. John W. Shroeder, "Sources and Symbols for Melville's *Confidence-Man*," *PMLA*, 66 (June 1951), 363–380. Page numbers in parentheses are to the reprinting in this Norton Critical Edition.

6. Roy Harvey Pearce, "Melville's Indian-hater: A Note on a Meaning of *The Confidence-Man*," *PMLA*, 67 (December 1952), 942–948. Further references are given in parentheses in the text.

7. But Melville also uses race symbolically in "Benito Cereno," written shortly before *The Confidence-Man* was begun and related to the Indian-hater story by verbal echoes (such as "apostatize" and "Senegal") which build into thematic echoes (such as the impossibility that the diabolic nature can change: the "Papist convert" Francesco is a mulatto, and the half-breed in the Indian-hater story threatens, "Indian blood is in me" (p. 154).

confidence of some of the passengers of the Fidèle nor in More-dock's blind hatred: "The blackness is complete" (p. 948).

Although agreeing with Pearce that the Indian-hater is in no sense a hero (p. 340), Miss Foster finds that "in the Indian-hater chapters the Indian embodies allegorically a primitive, or primal, malign, treacherous force in the universe" (p. 314). Unlike Pearce, she distinguishes between Melville's attitude toward real Indians and his use of them as symbols (pp. 339–340.) She takes exception to Pearce's "blackness": "Melville, though a pessimistic moralist in this novel, is not, I take it, a despairing one. Like many another moralist and writer of comedy, he is concerned to point the dangers of both extremes" (pp. 340–341).[8] Reading the section as one of Melville's warning qualifications of "the cynicism and materialism of the main argument" [i.e., "No Trust"] (p. lxix), she concludes that Melville "gives us an unforgettable picture of a society without faith or charity. . . . This is the alternative if we jettison charity—a world of solitary, dehumanized Indian-haters" (p. lxx).

Despite Miss Foster's tactful mediation between Shroeder and Pearce and despite her own interpretation, major problems remain. Neither Pearce nor Miss Foster has adequately explored the implica-tions of Shroeder's evidence that the Indians are diabolic. Nor has enough been made of the likelihood that in an allegory as carefully structured as The Confidence-Man the antagonist of the satanic In-dians might be in some way religious. Then, Pearce's disgust at the praise accorded Moredock (disgust shared by any reader of the In-dian-hating story as a literal narrative) has not been reconciled with Shroeder's claim that Moredock is the heroic adversary of the Con-fidence Man. The solution lies, I suggest, in taking the episode as al-legory, as Shroeder and Miss Foster do, and in carefully identifying the elements of that allegory. Melville's opposition of the Indian-hater and the Indian constitutes, I believe, a consistent allegory in which Christianity is conceived as the dedicated hatred of Evil at the cost of forsaking human ties, and in which most of the human race is represented as wandering in the backwoods of error, giving lip-service to their religion but failing to embody it in their lives. The allegory is a grotesquely satiric study of the theme which Miss Fos-ter calls the most obvious in the novel, "the failure of Christians to be Christian" (p. liii,) and in the vein of Mardi and Pierre it is a study of the practicability of Christianity as Jesus preached it.

Both Shroeder and Miss Foster offer evidence for the identifica-tion of the allegorical significance of the Indians. Demonstrating

---

8. Foster's moderate position is in accord with the last stanza of "The Conflict of Convic-tions" and with Melville's injunction in the second sketch of "The Encantadas": "Enjoy the bright, keep it turned up perpetually if you can, but be honest, and don't deny the black."

that snakes in *The Confidence-Man* are associated with the Devil as in Genesis, *Paradise Lost*, and Hawthorne's works, Shroeder argues cogently that the coupling of the Indian and the snake at the outset of the Indian-hater story is a deliberate guide to the diabolic nature of the Indians (p. 489).[9] Never definitely calling the Indians Devils, Miss Foster observes that in Mocmohoc "readers will have recognized a type of the Confidence Man" (p. lxvii). She also suggests the possibility that "the Indian is something not so much sub-human as extra-human" (p. lxvii), and that by giving Indian containers for their wine bottles and cigars to the cosmopolitan and Charlie (the ordinary Mississippi confidence man who tells the Moredock story), "Melville meant to remind the reader that they are the Indians of the argument" (p. lxxii). The same function, I would add, is served by Melville's having the cosmopolitan ironically call his pipe a "calumet"—a peace pipe (p. 157). Miss Foster agrees that Shroeder "demonstrates beyond question the diabolic and mythic nature" of the Confidence Man (p. xlii,) but she does not pursue the allegorical associations of the Indians with Devils. Yet if the Confidence Man is associated with snakes and *is* the Devil, while Indians are associated with snakes and at least one Indian is "a type of the Confidence Man," then in Melville's allegorical geometry the Indians are Devils also.

Recognizing the Indians as types of the Devil of Christian literary tradition, we should reasonably expect the Devil's antagonist to be an earnest Christian. But Moredock, who dedicates his life to killing, hardly fits the ordinary conception of a follower of Jesus. The cosmopolitan (the last avatar of the Confidence Man) makes the obvious objection in professing himself unable to believe that a man so loving to his family could be so merciless to his enemies (p. 162). Pearce in a similar spirit rejects Shroeder's interpretation of Moredock as the man who has located Evil in its real home. But repugnant as it is, the logic of the opposition demands that we see Moredock as a Devil-hating Christian, though one who does not

9. Melville's knowledge of the Puritan identification of Indians with Devils is adequately attested by his reference in *Moby-Dick* (Ch. 27) to the "superstitions of some of the earlier Puritans" which might almost lead one to half-believe the Indian Tashtego "to be a son of the Prince of the Powers of the Air." For Melville's interest in Cotton Mather's *Magnalia* during the composition of *The Confidence-Man* see "The Apple-Tree Table" in *Putnam's Monthly* for May, 1856. (reprinted in the Northwestern-Newberry *The Piazza Tales &c* volume). In the *Magnalia*, Mather frequently calls Indians both Devils and snakes. He supposed that the Devil had "decoyed" Indians to the Americas in the hope that the gospel of Jesus would never cross the ocean to shake his control over them. The Indian-devil-snake connections were pervasive in Melville's time, as toward the end of Henry Wadsworth Longfellow's 1858 "The Courtship of Miles Standish" where the angry Standish, in the presence of an Indian, equates shooting red squirrels with shooting "red devils." The Indian, deeply affronted, glides out of the room. Bearing a "serpent's skin, and seeming himself like a serpent," he then winds his sinuous way into the forest. The fact that this poem was long an American schoolroom favorite says a good deal about racial attitudes in the United States.

live up to all of Jesus' commands. The outrageous irony that has escaped notice is that it is when Moredock is murdering Indians that he is Christian and when he is enjoying the comforts of domestic life that he is apostatizing.

Before seeing how the dedication to Indian-hating is described in terms of dedication to Christianity, one must dispose of the cosmopolitan's ironic objection that some parts of Charlie's story do not hang together: "If the man of hate, how could John Moredock be also the man of love?" Considering the familiarity with the Bible which he displays elsewhere, the cosmopolitan should be aware that there is ample biblical authority for being both a man of hate and a man of love. In Amos 5.15 the duality is stated baldly: "Hate the evil, and love the good." Psalm 139, from which Melville quotes earlier (p. 76), is also explicit about the duty to hate: "Do not I hate them, O Lord, that hate thee? and am not I grieved with those that rise up against thee? I hate them with perfect hatred; I count them mine enemies." In this tone Melville's Father Mapple cries: "Woe to him whom this world charms from Gospel duty! Woe to him who seeks to pour oil upon the waters when God has brewed them into a gale!" Father Mapple in his peroration is as implacable as Moredock: "Delight is to him, who gives no quarter in the truth, and kills, and burns, and destroys all sin though he pluck it out from under the robes of Senators and Judges." There is a darker side of Christianity, as Melville is careful to remind us by the cry of "church militant!" when the Methodist minister shakes the one-legged man till his timber-toe clatters "on the deck like a nine-pin" (p. 23), by the mention of Torquemada, the Spanish inquisitor general (p. 66), and by the references to Jesuits (p. 98), to Loyola (p. 129), and to "a victim in *auto-da-fé*" (p. 243).

Once we accept Melville's ironic view of Christianity as the practice of Devil-hating, we are ready to follow the similarity of the dedication to Indian-hating to the dedication to Christianity. Keeping in mind the word "Metaphysics" in the title of Chapter xxvi, we can see the significance of the religious references like "guilty race," "monk," and "cloistered" in Melville's description of how the Indian-hater *par excellence* comes to his resolution (p. 155–56):

> An intenser Hannibal, he makes a vow, the hate of which is a vortex from whose suction scarce the remotest chip of the guilty race may reasonably feel secure. Next, he declares himself and settles his temporal affairs. With the solemnity of a Spaniard turned monk, he takes leave of his kin; or rather, these leave-takings have something of the still more impressive finality of death-bed adieus. Last, he commits himself to the forest primeval; there, so long as life shall be his, to act upon a calm, cloistered scheme of strategical, implacable, and lonesome vengeance.

Later in the conversation (p. 176) Charlie's allusion to Matthew 19 (or Mark 10) emphasizes the similarity of the dedication of the Indian-hater to the way Jesus would have one begin a life as His follower. The whole of the passage just quoted from should be read in the light of Jesus' words to the rich young man, and to His disciples after the young man has gone sorrowfully away, especially the command to dispose of worldly possessions and the reward promised to "every one that hath forsaken houses, or brethren, or sisters, or father, or mother, or wife, or children, or lands, for my name's sake." Moreover, there is a parallel to the Christian's being, as Paul says (Romans 6.2), "dead to sin."

Throughout Charlie's story theological terms are employed to describe the "devout sentiment" of Indian-hating. We are told (p. 156) that there is

> a species of diluted Indian-hater, one whose heart proves not so steely as his brain. Soft enticements of domestic life too often draw him from the ascetic trail; a monk who apostatizes to the world at times. . . . It is with him as with the Papist converts in Senegal; fasting and mortification prove hard to bear.

According to Charlie, Judge Hall "would maintain that there was no vocation whose consistent following calls for such self-containing as that of the Indian-hater *par excellence*" (p. 157). Here Melville is using "vocation" in its literal and theological sense of "calling."[1] Where in Melville's source the real James Hall says that Moredock watched the murderers of his mother for more than a year before attacking them, Melville alters the account to stress Moredock's solitude, for "upwards of a year, alone in the wilds" after his dedication (p. 159).[2] Melville has already made the judge declare that the backwoodsman is "worthy to be compared with Moses in the Exodus" (p. 150). Now he emphasizes Moredock's role as religious leader by making him on one occasion seek the murderers "at the head of a party pledged to serve him for forty days." Here Melville has added to Hall's account the biblical number for times of purgation and preparation—forty. It is Melville (or his storyteller Charlie) who gives Moredock a retributive spirit that speaks like God's "voice calling through the garden" (p. 159). In

1. As in Ephesians 4.1, vocation in Melville often carries the Latin sense of "calling." See *The Confidence-Man* pp. 9 and 157, and for more ambiguous uses pp. 182 and 209. Usage was shifting, but to Melville "avocation" (as at the beginning of "Bartleby") is simply another acceptable form for "vocation" (calling, life work), not meaning anything like "hobby."

2. The reader who has been made constantly aware of Paul's epistles by the allusions to 1 Corinthians 13 may well recall Paul's semi-legendary retreat to the Arabian deserts shortly after his conversion. For the meager biblical source, see Galatians 1.17. It should be noted that for "murder" (p. 159) one should read "number." [Emended in most editions since 1963, including this one.—editors.]

Charlie's story Moredock's manner of being benevolent (p. 160), is in accord with Jesus' command in the Sermon on the Mount (Matthew 6.3): "But when thou doest alms, let not thy left hand know what thy right hand doeth." And, apropos of Moredock's refusal to seek high political office, Judge Hall (according to Charlie) says (p. 161) that the Colonel

> was not unaware that to be a consistent Indian-hater involves the renunciation of ambition, with its objects—the pomps and glories of the world; and since religion, pronouncing such things vanities, accounts it merit to renounce them, therefore, so far as this goes, Indian-hating, whatever may be thought of it in other respects, may be regarded as not wholly without the efficacy of a devout sentiment.

Leaving such vanities behind, the dedicated Indian-haters inhabit the moral wilderness which, as Miss Wright says (p. 379), is "the symbolic scene of mature experience throughout Melville." The Indian-hater *par excellence* is nearly fabulous, a soul "peeping out but once an age" (p. 157). The lesser Indian-hater like Moredock either backslides to domestic life or, desperate from the loneliness which his ascetic vow has imposed, "hurries openly towards the first smoke" (p. 157) and embraces the Indian Devil. For as the pamphlet in *Pierre* has it, efforts at the absolute imitation of Christ may often involve the idealist in "strange, *unique* follies and sins."[3] Those still less devoted, the inhabitants of the fringes of the moral wilderness, the backwoods, are "diluted Indian-haters" who give nominal allegiance to the religious ideals realized (if at all) only by the Indian-hater *par excellence*. They teach their children the traditional hatred of the Indian as Eve teaches her children enmity to the serpent (p. 151; for an allusion to the curse in Genesis see p. 135), and they join in community disapproval of the adversary (p. 151) without ever applying the religion of Indian-hating, or Devil-hating, to their ordinary lives. To repeat Sedgwick's phrase, almost without irony, the allegory is transparent.

With the basic allegory of Indian Devils and Devil-hating Christians established, the story can be interpreted coherently.[4] We are

3. See p. 381, herein. In the Northwestern-Newberry edition (1971) see pp. 88, 91, 106 for Pierre's dedication, which is in crucial ways like that of the Indian-haters. See also p. 215: when the "Enthusiast to Duty" despairs at the impossibility of fulfilling his vow, "he is too apt to run clean away into all manner of moral abandonment, self-deceit, and hypocrisy (cloaked, however, mostly under an aspect of the most respectable devotion); or else he openly runs, like a mad dog, into atheism." The consequences of the Indian-haters' vows are strictly comparable.

4. This reading does not solve every formal difficulty. While it relates the meaning of the section to that of a major theme in this book and Melville's other works, it does not account for the function of the story in the plot. It is presumably a well-chosen gambit in Charlie's nefarious strategy for duping the cosmopolitan, whom the appication of the story is designed to flatter. Pitch is (p. 161) "a sort of comprehensive Colonel Moredock,

spared Pearce's revulsion at the literal story and can appreciate the grisly humor in Melville's outrageous distortion of our habitual way of thinking of Christianity. For in a book in which the Devil comes aboard the world-ship to preach Christianity as an April Fool's joke, it is apt that the best haters be the best Christians. The story of the Weavers and the Wrights can be recognized as not simply a piteous tale of frontier betrayal and violence, but as a warning against making a "covenant" with the Devil (p. 154). The "moral indignation" of the Indians who claim to be maligned (p. 152) is wryly comic, especially since the "Supreme Court" to which is left the question of whether Indians should be permitted to testify for themselves is, within the allegory, the Last Judgment.[5] Any reading of the section with the terms of the allegory in mind will reveal other elements in Melville's mordantly comic study of the discrepancy between the Christianity that Jesus preached and that which nominal Christians practice.

It is not surprising that the reviewers of *The Confidence-Man* in 1857 did not understand the allegory. As Foster shows (pp. xviii–xix), Melville in the mid-1850's habitually concealed his darker meanings from a public unwilling or unable to face them. It is more surprising that the point of the story has "escaped notice" among modern readers, for it is altogether characteristic of Melville. The "failure of Christians to be Christian" is satirized in each of his novels from *Typee* to *Billy Budd, Sailor*, and the tragic impracticability of Christianity is dramatized at length in *Mardi* and *Pierre*. Perhaps readers of the Indian-hater chapters have been, in the pamphlet's word, too "horological" to acknowledge biblical authority for single-minded hatred of Evil, or to acknowledge the Christlikeness of forsaking family and property for religion. The final irony may be that for some modern readers able to accept Melville's darkest meanings Christianity is so "diluted" that they have become insensitive to his satire and, more appallingly, have lost his lacerating ambivalence between the emotional allure of ab-

---

who, too much spreading his passion, shallows it." Moredock, the Pitch figure in the story, is a failure in that he is not, according to Hall's distinctions in Charlie's story, an Indian-hater *par excellence*, for while retaining his antipathy to Indians, Moredock retreats from his struggle in order to establish a family. A difficulty is that no one would want to claim that Charlie is aware of the allegorical meaning of his story or of the true identity of his new companion. It is easy to see why Foster (p. lxviii) calls the views in the story "orphan." In view of Melville's cavalier interpolations into his manuscripts, it may well be wrong to look for a New-Critical aptness of story to storyteller or relevance of dramatic situation to plot as a whole [HP, 1971].

5. This instance of Melville's habit of choosing elaborate legal equivalents or opposites for the Last Judgment may be compared with the cosmopolitan's decision (p. 193) to leave the accountability of the rattlesnake not to "the Court of Common Pleas, but to something superior." Other examples are Elijah's "Grand Jury" (*Moby-Dick*, Ch. 21) and Captain Vere's "Last Assizes" in *Billy Budd, Sailor*, eds Harrison Hayford and Merton M. Sealts, Jr. (Chicago: University of Chicago Press, 1962), 111.

solute obedience to Jesus (the only kind of Christianity worth practicing, he thought) and his rational certitude that Christianity is impracticable. Finally, some modern readers may have lost Melville's profound sense that however much unChristlike Christians deserve to be satirized, the impracticability of Christianity remains tragic.

Selected Bibliography

• indicates works included or excerpted in this Norton Critical Edition

The list here does not aim to include all or even a representative selection of the hundreds of critical pieces on *The Confidence-Man*. True to its subtitle, *American Literary Scholarship: An Annual* (Duke University Press) every year starting in 1963 has devoted a chapter to new publications on Melville. In *ALS* each year's essays and chapters in books on *The Confidence-Man* are listed and briefly characterized. An extensive list of early articles is printed in the Northwestern-Newberry Edition of *The Confidence-Man* under "Sources" following the Historical Note. A few items listed here are referred to elsewhere in the volume without full citation or are included because they are in other ways distinctive. Mainly, this very short bibliography is restricted to the most reliable documentary guides to the study of Melville, especially for the period of *The Confidence-Man*. Our list is so stringently selective that it omits even recent works if we have found them to be pervasively misleading, such as a biography that identifies the April First of the story as before the admission of Missouri as a state in 1821 and a reference guide that asseverates that the Confidence Man in his disguise as Pitch, the huckster, tries to sell property in the "New Jerusalem." In approaching interpretive comments of this book from the earliest to the latest, not excluding, we fear, any by the present editors, the reader might well go armed with the motto of William Cream, the Barber, "NO TRUST," then let each argument justify itself before it is given credence. Users of this Norton Critical Edition should be able to find on the Internet at least one searchable text of *The Confidence-Man*, a boon for locating a phrase from the book or seeing just how often Melville repeated certain names or other words.

Barber, Patricia. "Two New Melville Letters." *American Literature* 49 (November 1977): 418–21. The first printing of the May 1856 letters.

Bercaw, Mary K. *Melville's Sources*. Evanston: Northwestern University Press, 1987. Unlike Sealts's *Melville's Reading* (continued by Olsen-Smith, see below), Bercaw lists books Melville must have used as sources whether or not it can be demonstrated that he ever held a copy of the book in his hands.

Bergmann, Hans. [a.k.a. Johannes D. Bergmann] *God in the Street: New York Writing from the Penny Press to Melville*. Philadelphia: Temple University Press, 1995. Argues provocatively and suggestively for seeing Melville's Mississippi book as also a New York City book.

• Bergmann, Johannes D. "The Original Confidence Man," *American Quarterly* 21 (Fall 1969): 560–77.

Cluff, Randall. " 'Thou Man of the *Evangelist*': Henry Cheever's Review of *Typee*."

Leviathan 3 (March 2001): 61–72. First documentation of how the low-church Protestant reviewers began their attacks on Melville.

Cook, Jonathan A. *Satirical Apocalypse: An Anatomy of Melville's "The Confidence-Man."* Westport, CT: Greenwood, 1996.
Chapter 4 is strong on biblical allusions.

Cowen, Walker. *Melville's Marginalia.* 2 vols. New York: Garland, 1987.
A huge photo-reprint of Cowen's 1965 Harvard dissertation, valuable despite the primitive technology available in the early 1960s. (Cowen typed passages Melville annotated and then tried to simulate Melville's markings and comments on them.) The 1987 volumes do not include books from Melville's library discovered since 1965, among which are several relevant to *The Confidence-Man* (including, in order of discovery, Melville's Wordsworth, Milton, and Spenser). Steven Olsen-Smith is at work on an electronic edition of all Melville's known marginalia.

Eberwein, Jane Donahue. "Joel Barlow and *The Confidence-Man.*" *American Transcendental Quarterly* 24 (Fall 1974): 28–29.

Grey, Robin, and Douglas Robillard, in consultation with Hershel Parker. "Melville's Milton: A Transcription of Melville's Marginalia in His Copy of *The Poetical Works of John Milton.*" *Leviathan* 4 (March and October 2002): 117–204. Reprinted in *Melville and Milton: An Edition and Analysis of Melville's Annotations on Milton,* ed. Robin Grey. Pittsburgh: Duquesne University Press, 2004.

Hayford, Harrison. *Melville's Prisoners.* Foreword by Hershel Parker. Evanston, IL: Northwestern University Press, 2003.
Contains "Poe in *The Confidence-Man.*"

Higgins, Brian, and Hershel Parker. *Herman Melville: The Contemporary Reviews.* Cambridge, UK, and New York: Cambridge University Press, 1995.

Lang, Hans-Joachim, and Benjamin Lease, "Melville's Cosmopolitan: Bayard Taylor in *The Confidence-Man.*" *Amerikanstudien* 22 (1977): 286–89.

Leyda, Jay. *The Melville Log: A Documentary Life of Herman Melville, 1819–1891.* 2 vols. New York: Harcourt Brace, 1951. Reprinted with a supplement, New York: Gordian Press, 1969.
The total length of the 1969 *Log* is 966 pages. For an enlargement incorporating, correcting, and vastly expanding the 1951 and 1969 *Log,* Parker has transcribed thousands of new documents (chronologically arranged, from Melville's birth to death) into his computer as *The New Melville Log.* This electronic chronology, running to some 9000 (not 900) pages, constitutes the greatest single Melville archive because it incorporates items from all known manuscript repositories as well as hundreds of newspapers in dozens of libraries, dozens of nineteenth-century magazines, and books containing biographical material (some published in the twentieth and even the twenty-first century). It may be possible to print a three-volume selection and the entire archive may be put on-line, but it is safe to say only that something (besides Parker's biography) may or may not follow from the creation of this enormous electronic archive based on Leyda's *Log.*

Melville, Herman. *The Confidence-Man.* San Francisco: Chandler, 1968. This useful photofacsimile of the 1857 American edition (with an introduction by John Seelye) is out of print but sometimes available through internet booksellers.

Melville, Herman. *The Writings of Herman Melville.* Edited by Harrison Hayford, Hershel Parker, and G. Thomas Tanselle. Evanston and Chicago: Northwestern University Press and the Newberry Library, 1968–.
The Confidence-Man (1984), volume 10, contains a Historical Note by Watson Branch, Hershel Parker, and Harrison Hayford, with Alma A. MacDougall. Volume 9, *The Piazza Tales and Other Prose Pieces, 1839–1860* (1987), contains a Historical Note by Merton M. Sealts Jr. Melville's *Journals,* edited by Howard C. Horsford with Lynn Horth (series editors Harrison Hayford and G. Thomas Tanselle) are in volume 15 (1989); Melville's *Correspondence,* (revised and augmented from *The Letters of Herman Melville,* 1960, edited by Merrell R. Davis and William M. Gilman), is in volume 14 (1993), edited by Lynn Horth (series editor Harrison Hayford).

Oliver, Egbert S. "Melville's Picture of Emerson and Thoreau in *The Confidence-Man.*" *College English* 8 (November 1946): 61–72.
Imperfectly argued, but convincing.

Olsen-Smith, Steven, and Dennis C. Marnon. "Melville's Marginalia in *The Works of Sir William D'Avenant.*" *Leviathan* 6 (March 2004): 79–102.
Olsen-Smith is at work on an electronic updating of Cowen.

Olsen-Smith, Steven, and Merton M. Sealts Jr. "A Cumulative Supplement to *Melville's Reading (1988)*." *Leviathan* 6 (March 2004): 55–77.
   This incorporates items in earlier supplements by Sealts and then by Steven Olsen-Smith, Sealts's successor as recorder of Melville's library.

Parker, Hershel. "Herman Melville." In *American National Biography*. Vol. 15. New York: Oxford University Press, 1998.
   The most reliable "nutshell" account of Melville's life.

Parker, Hershel. *Herman Melville: A Biography, 1819–1851*. Baltimore: Johns Hopkins University Press, 1996, and *Herman Melville: A Biography, 1851–1891*. Baltimore: Johns Hopkins University Press, 2002.

Quirk, Tom. *Melville's Confidence Man: From Knave to Knight*. Columbia: University of Missouri Press, 1982.

• Quirk, Tom. "Two Sources in *The Confidence-Man*." *Melville Society Extracts* 39 (September 1979): 12–13.

Ryan, Susan M. *The Grammar of Good Intentions: Race and the Antebellum Culture of Benevolence*. Ithaca, NY: Cornell University Press, 2003.

• Ryan, Susan M. "Misgivings: Melville, Race, and the Ambiguities of Benevolence." *American Literary History* 12 (Winter 2000), 685–712.

Sanborn, Geoffrey. "The Name of the Devil: Melville's Other 'Extracts' for *Moby-Dick*." *Nineteenth-Century Literature* 47 (September 1992): 212–35.
   Reveals that jottings on witchcraft and satanism in Melville's Shakespeare are his reading notes on "Superstition and Knowledge" in the July 1823 issue of the London *Quarterly Review*.

Sealts, Merton M., Jr. *Melville's Reading: Revised and Enlarged Edition*. Columbia: University of South Carolina Press, 1988.
   See also Olsen-Smith above.

Spark, Clare L. *Hunting Captain Ahab: Psychological Warfare and the Melville Revival*. Kent, OH: Kent State University Press, 2001.
   Valuable for documentary background on the excitement about *The Confidence-Man* in the late 1940s, especially about Richard Chase's use of Melville to push his political agenda.

Thorpe, T. B. "Remembrances of the Mississippi." *Harper's New Monthly Magazine* 12 (December 1855): 25–41.

Trimpi, Helen. *Melville's Confidence Men and American Politics in the 1850s*. Hamden, CT: Shoe String Press, 1987.
   The most rigorous attempt to identify characters in the book with real people.

Wright, Nathalia. *Melville's Use of the Bible*. Durham, NC: Duke University Press, 1949.